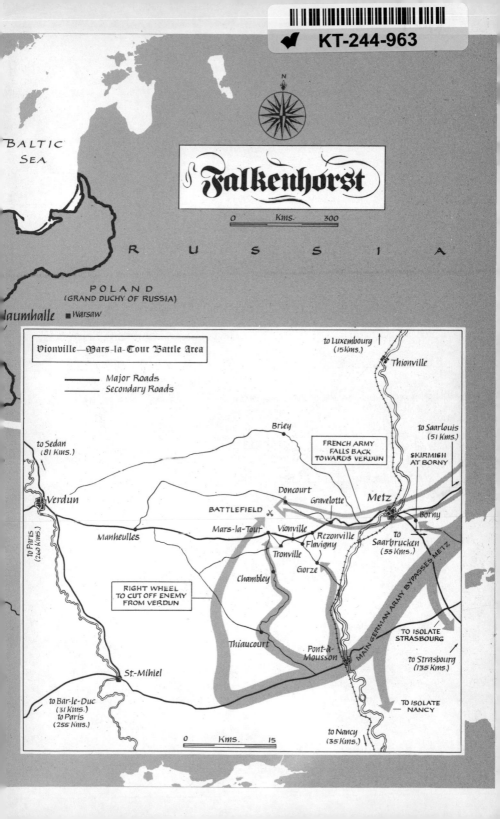

Falkenhorst

Falkenhorst

MARK RASCOVICH

Secker & Warburg
London

First published in England 1974 by
Martin Secker & Warburg Limited
14 Carlisle Street, London W1V 6NN

SBN: 436 40401 X

Printed in Great Britain by
Cox & Wyman Limited
London, Fakenham and Reading

To my wife, Florence

July 1870

The Wedding

✠ ✠

Tessa awoke from an uneasy sleep as the first gray light of dawn began seeping into her room; an icy stab of fear shot through her chest as she caught sight of a faintly luminous white shape standing at the foot of her four-poster bed. The thought which jabbed her mind into full consciousness was that von Karoon had materialized out of his limbo of supernatural legend to haunt her. Then she realized that she was staring in terror at the wedding gown draped over the papier-mâché dummy which the dressmaker had fashioned after her own body.

"You look like a ghost!" she said aloud to it. "A headless ghost of myself. Maybe one night after I'm long dead and gone, I'll wander the halls of Schloss Varn looking exactly like you!" She shuddered and drove the gruesome thought out of her mind. Throwing the warm covers aside, she swung her legs over the edge of the bed, stood up, stretched, and shuffled through the darkness toward the pale square which was the window. There was a patter of raindrops against the glass, and the pine tree outside moaned plaintively as a raw northeast wind tormented its shaggy boughs. Tessa knew that when the old pine moaned, there was a long rainy spell in the offing. "A fine day for a wedding," she exclaimed to herself. "Everybody will get soaked on their way to the church. Father's shako will become frazzled and smelly. Uncle Franz's plumes will wilt and turn him into a wet rooster."

Tessa laughed softly and for a moment wondered why Prussian military nobility leaned toward bearskin headwear while their Austrian counterparts favored those adorned with feathers? There had to be a significance of some kind. Then she thought of Gustaf's helmet with its shiny silver spike which stuck out of the top in perfect alignment with his ramrod backbone, just as if he had been skewered by a medieval lance. Although more practical than either fur or plumes in bad weather, it had a lightning-rod quality which might be fatal in a thunderstorm. On the other hand, no thunderbolt was likely to waste itself on such a modest target as her fiancé, she decided with a shrug.

The little Dresden clock struck five brittle chimes and triggered a sudden panicky feeling that time was running out for her. The civil ceremony in the Guildhall was to be at eleven o'clock. The church at twelve. The wedding feast was to start at two in Schloss Varn's Great Hall. The food, which had been in preparation for a week, would take two hours to eat. The speeches would take two more. Another hour to change into traveling clothes. By seven o'clock she and Gustaf would be rolling through the gates in the coach pulled by Prytzie's four finest dapple grays. A final two hours to Kolberg, then. . . .

Tessa turned away from the window. Quickly moving to the bedtable, she struck a match and lit the lamp, turning up its flame to a full, flickering brightness. Then she went to the big armoire and threw open its doors. There hung her trousseau, heavy brocades and bright taffetas, all new and sewn in Berlin according to the latest Paris modes. But she pushed them aside and fumbled in the back to bring out the riding habit which Lord Bourne had had made for her last year in London. Before laying it out on the bed, she clasped it to her breast for an instant and rubbed her cheek against the smooth twill, breathing in the faint horsey odor which permeated it.

The chambermaids would make their rounds at six-thirty to put pitchers of hot water in each bedroom, but Tessa used the cold dregs in the lavabo to wet her face and dab the sleep from her eyes. She rubbed hard with the washcloth and pinched her cheeks to make them tingle and redden. Tante Lisel had said that the homeliest bride always looked radiant on her wedding day. Poor, well-meaning, tactless Tante Lisel! Tessa peered at herself in the mirror. The lips were thin and colorless, the eyes sunken and glittering with an unnatural light, those cursed freckles horribly prominent, as if a brushful of amber paint had been flicked onto her face. The hair, severely drawn back from her forehead and twisted into a rigidly braided topknot, had a peculiar sheen, resembling tarnished copper. As she peered, she grimaced, then did something she had not done since her breasts had begun ripening. She wriggled out of her woolen nightgown and critically examined her own stark nakedness in the mirror.

"You are ugly!" she told herself. "All bones and angles. No softness. So unfeminine. Ugly." Words and sentences from the discussion with her mother last evening began echoing through her memory. Discussion? No—a *lecture*. An inarticulate, clumsy lecture spoken with deep-rooted revulsions and inhibitions, causing everything her mother said to be either starkly vulgar or veiled in sinister innuendo. The word *animal* had been repeated time and again. Somehow Tessa had found herself thinking back to the summer when she had happened into a pasture where a stallion was taking his mare. The mare had fought him savagely, biting, kicking, and screaming, but he had sunk his teeth into her neck and mounted her, and in the end she had had to submit. *Submit* was another unpleasant word her mother had used last night.

For a moment she desperately wished for the company of her older sister, who had married nearly two years ago and who might talk about intimate matters with less prejudice and inhibition than their mother. But then she reminded herself that Esther was really exactly like their mother—beautiful, nervous, and given to senseless tantrums over trifles while maintaining a dumb calm in any crisis. It was something of a wonder that Esther had become pregnant at last. The pregnancy was a difficult one, requiring her to seclude herself in a darkened bedchamber in her husband's Palatinate castle. No, Esther would have been no use, even if she could have traveled to Schloss Varn for the wedding. The ordeal would have to be faced alone.

Tessa stared at herself until she could bear the sight no longer, then hurriedly dressed in her English sidesaddle riding habit. After she had pulled on her shiny boots and wrapped the voluminous black skirt around her slender waist to conceal the manly breeches encasing her legs, she took another look at herself in the mirror. This time she grinned, made a mock curtsey, and said to the reflection: "Farewell, Right Honorable Anna Marie Theresa von Beckhaus und Varn!" Then she blew out the lamp, opened her bedroom door, and tiptoed into the still-pitch black, second-story hall of the castle. In the utter silence, her spurs made a very faint, very lovely jingle.

The stables were a cheery glow of lanternlight against the shadows of Schloss Varn, which continued to loom as a massive, somber silhouette against the drab dawn. The stable boys had been working all night here, rubbing, scrubbing, and polishing the coaches and tack; now the horses were being led out of their stalls in pairs to be curried by yawning, red-eyed grooms. Master Prytz, the stablemaster, was keeping a sharp eye on the work while momentarily relaxing on a bench and sipping a mug of coffee brewed over the embers of the smithy's forge. He wore his breeches, but instead of boots had on a pair of comfortable slippers; his collarless white shirt was unbuttoned down the front, exposing the coarse gray wool of the underwear he kept on summer and winter. When Tessa walked in through the door he jumped to his feet, so surprised that he forgot to address her formally as the Count Beckhaus und Varn had instructed him to do since she had become an engaged young lady.

"Good heavens, girl! What are you doing here this morning?"

Tessa cracked her crop against the calf of her boot and laughed. "What do you think, Master Prytz? My life doesn't change until eleven this morning. In the meanwhile, Kugel and I will ride as usual, of course."

The grooms stopped their work, respectfully coming to attention, but gaping at her in amazement. Prytz ran stubby fingers through his white mane in a gesture of exasperation. "His Excellency will be furious if I let you ride on the morning of your wedding day. Quite rightly so, too. It's madness. Besides, everybody here has a great deal to do before the festivities begin. And I dare say, so do you, my lady."

"Tessa gave him a steely flash from her green eyes and called out to one of the grooms: "Hans! Saddle up Kugel, if you please. Hurry! I can't waste a minute."

Kanone Kugel heard her voice and also urged Hans to hurry by whinnying excitedly from his stall.

"In weather like this!" Prytz grumbled. "You are already

wet, just from walking down from the castle. It is madness." But he knew her well enough so that, even as he grumbled, he moved to get his boots from the tackroom.

"Don't bother to put on your uniform, Master Prytz," she called after him. "You are too busy here, and I prefer to ride alone anyway."

He spun around. "That is absolutely forbidden, Your Ladyship!" he exclaimed with outright anguish.

Tessa walked up to him and playfully poked him in the chest with her crop. "Very well, then. If you insist on coming along, it will have to be like our old times together. You're Prytzie and I'm Tessa, and we'll have a race to the sea and back. What's more, I bet I can beat you. I bet I'll get clear away and you'll come straggling back alone, all grumpy and sheepish."

The grooms chuckled and winked slyly at each other, but the stablemaster stiffened and jutted out his jaw, which was covered by a white stubble. "My lady is taking unfair advantage of me. But come what may, it is my duty to serve you as best I can."

"That has always been good enough for me, old friend!"

The frown remained on Prytz's face, but his jaw slackened and a faint tremor was to be discerned at the tip of his chin. He stomped into the tackroom and after a few minutes came back wearing boots, a cap, his greatcoat with silver buttons, and a raincape with the von Beckhaus und Varn coat of arms emblazoned on it. For him, the grooms brought out Feldteufel, a four-year-old black stallion; for Tessa, her roan gelding, Kanone Kugel. Feldteufel was in a bad temper and tried to lash out at the other horse. It took two men to hold him, and, after helping Tessa into her sidesaddle, the stablemaster mounted him with an amazing agility for his sixty-four years. To the troublesome animal he growled a threat: "Play the devil with me and I'll burst your black heart!"

They held the horses down to an impatient trot as they rode along the long gravel driveway and out through the main gate. Tessa spurred Kugel into a canter when the sound of hooves could no longer reach the castle. The wind in the pinewoods made the animals more nervous and they champed at their bits, frequently breaking their stride to prance and buck. Feldteufel shied at the shriek of an owl disturbed in its dawn hunt. Master Prytz growled and muttered under his breath while Tessa rode silently, breathing deeply of the humid cold air and letting the fine drizzle wash her face. Although this was the sixteenth of July, the weather was raw. The whole summer had been like this, blustery, wintery, and wet. A "Russian summer" the natives called it, because the wind which brought these storms swept down the Baltic coast from Kurland and Bothnia. It depressed some but exhilarated Tessa and the horses.

Where the road wound out of the woods and across the open fens she gave Kugel his head and cracked his flanks with her crop; with an eager squeal the horse broke into a gallop. When she heard Feldteufel a few yards behind her, she suddenly shouted, "To the sea!" and without warning veered off the road, jumping the shallow ditch to race across the glistening billows of marsh grass. The old stablemaster hesitated only long enough to give her a head start and when he dug his spurs into Feldteufel, the horse almost refused the ditch, coming within a fraction of throwing him. It was a stiff-legged, unbalanced jump which jarred his backbone, and for an awful moment his animal was bolting out of control in a wild rush to catch up. But the gap between the two riders remained a wide one. Kanone Kugel was the swiftest, most surefooted horse of the Schloss Varn stables and Anna Marie Theresa von Beckhaus und Varn the best woman rider in all Prussia. Master Prytz had made her so.

The dunes of the Baltic shore loomed colorless against the yellowish gray of the eastern sky. Between them and the pinewoods, the fens were a rippling green laced by the silver of brackish sloughs which made the ground swampy in between sandy knolls. It was dangerous, hard riding, but both Tessa and Prytz knew every inch of this land and their horses had been foaled on it. She knew several fairly safe ways across which avoided the treacherous soft parts and wider canals, but she was leading the race over the shortest route, galloping along a hard ridge which snaked toward the dunes with swamp on each side. She sailed over a nine-foot wide water barrier formed by a drainage ditch and glanced over her shoulder to see if Prytz would have trouble with it. It looked as if he were faltering, but he actually only reined in slightly and worked his legs to pace Feldteufel for better control. His raincape billowed out like black wings and the big stallion cleared the opposite bank with plenty to spare. "Bravo, Prytzie!" she shouted back. "I can still make you ride!" A terrified marsh hen skittered over the rain-dappled water with hoarse squawks.

When they came up upon the dunes and the ground became spongy sand, Feldteufel began to catch up. They galloped out onto the beach and down to the edge of the sea where Tessa turned sharply and tore along the foaming surge of the surf, throwing up splatters of spray and sand which flew into the old man's face. He had either to veer into deeper water, softer sand, or fall back. Angrily reining in and yanking Feldteufel to an unwilling stop, he bellowed: "Enough!" But Tessa rode on unheeding for another five hundred meters, even urging Kugel into a final burst of speed with her crop and spurs. Then she suddenly whirled him at right angles, driving him right into the sea, and did not stop until the waves surged around his heaving chest. She bent down, scooped up a handful of saltwater and splashed it over her already streaming face.

Master Prytz cantered to the edge of the water and furiously shouted: "Come back here at once, you crazy girl! At once, do you hear!"

Tessa slowly turned Kugel around and walked him ashore, drawing up alongside of the steaming, chastised Feldteufel. She looked into Prytz's livid face and smiled. The smile did not fade as he reprimanded her, gasping for breath: "Have you no sense left at all? Don't you know you'll give both yourself and your horse lung fever? Is this the way you behave after I've worked for years to make a horsewoman out of you? If I were His Excellency, I'd give you a thrashing. If I were your father . . ."

"I wish you were, Prytzie," she quietly injected.

This took him by surprise, and his face reddened even more. For a moment he could say nothing, panting to catch his wind and collect his wits.

"I wish you were, Prytzie," she repeated. "You are the only man I love. The only man who I believe loves me."

He turned his head away, shaking it. "You must not say such things. You are a noblewoman and I am only a servant of your family."

"We are to each other exactly what we feel for each other."

"Come along now. We must walk the horses or they will catch a chill," he told her. After they had moved some distance down the beach without speaking, he clumsily blurted out: "You are marrying a fine young officer. He sits his horse well."

"Thank you," Tessa answered drily.

Master Prytz shut his eyes and seemed to sag in the saddle, his body jerking painfully with the movements of his horse. "I am sorry, my poor Tessa," he said in a low voice. "But what do you expect me to say to you? You begrudge me the customary felicitations. Is it some kind of condolences you want? Or that I urge you to resist the will of your family? If you have any feelings for me at all, then at least allow me the servant's privilege of silence."

"But there has never been silence between us, Prytzie. A lot of laughter, a few tears, and always lots of talk about anything we chose. Never silence."

"You're speaking about when you were the child I was teaching how to ride."

Her voice rose and there was something in it of a frustrated, frightened child. "But I am the same Tessa! I am only eighteen after all! Why must everything suddenly be different even between *us*? Why? Why?"

He leaned toward her and for an instant looked as if he were about to reach out and put his hand on her shoulder; she even leaned toward the expected gesture of affection. But then he stopped himself and stiffened in the saddle. In trying to check his own emotions as well as hers, he unwittingly made his words sound harsh and peremptory: "Because at noon today you must give up many old things and receive into your life many new things. At noon today you will stop being little Tessa, the fairy princess of Schloss Varn, and become Baroness Theresa von Falkenhorst, the wife of a Prussian officer and nobleman."

She violently reined in her horse and this time her shriek was completely that of a child: "But I don't want to!"

"You *must*!" he told her, his voice also rising to a shout.

She stared with shock into the gray eyes which stared back unflinchingly from beneath their thistly white eyebrows. The rain mingled with the tears running down her cheeks, chilling them and washing them away. Her mouth lost its trembling pout and compressed into a hard thin line. When she finally spoke, her voice was low and controlled: "As you say then, Master Prytz, I shall shed all my childish fancies, like asking my father to give you to me as a wedding present. Yes, I was going to ask him that. But now I won't, of course. You don't love me and, come to think of it, you'd remind me too much of him." Kanone Kugel gave a squeal of pain as she cruelly dug her spurs into him and whipped his flank with her crop. His muscles burst into action like released steel springs, propelling him into frantic flight over the dunes toward home.

The old man cried as he tried to follow, and the tears and wind and rain blinded his eyes. He lost control over Feldteufel as the animal wildly rushed a drainage ditch and they fell into the black muddy water with a tremendous splash. The horse struggled up the soggy bank and took off across the fens with his tail sticking straight up, reins and stirrups flying, and reached the stables of Schloss Varn only a few minutes after Tessa had vaulted out of her saddle and run up to the castle. But it was almost an hour later when Master Prytz came staggering in on foot, all bedraggled, mud splattered, and soaked to the skin. The grooms turned their heads aside and snickered loudly among themselves.

Freiherr Albrecht von Falkenhorst was awakened by the sound of rainwater splashing down the spout next to the window. For a sleepy minute he listened to the pleasant sound; then, suddenly realizing its implications for this dawning day of momentous importance to his family, he bounded out of bed and drew aside the curtain. A lake had formed overnight in the courtyard of the inn, the roofs of the village of Varnmunde glistened with rain, and the spire of its church snagged gray wisps out of the scudding clouds as they swept overhead. "Is this kind of weather good or bad luck for a wedding?" he asked himself. "I don't remember which superstition applies. Most marriages contain both good and bad, so it becomes a matter of emphasis." With that trite piece of philosophizing he went to the door to the adjoining room and noisily threw it open. "Get up!" he shouted. "Time has come to prepare the condemned for execution!"

A rumpled mound of quilts and blankets stirred slightly on the bed, and a voice growled testily from beneath them: "Go away!"

Albrecht stepped up to the bed and with a mighty heave ripped off all the covers, revealing his brother's naked body curled up in a fetal position. "Now there's a groom for you! I pity your poor baroness if she will have to face such a sight every morning. Didn't you think of buying yourself a nightshirt?"

Leutnant Baron Gustaf von Falkenhorst uncurled himself, sat up, and held his head in his hands. It ached badly from last night's party, and although he had been unable to sleep at all, he felt he could do so now if left in peace. Glaring at his younger brother with angry, unclear eyes, he snarled: "I warn you, Albrecht! I'm in no mood for your clowning this morning."

"So you're in a temper on this of all days. Or is it simply a bad case of nerves?" Albrecht laughed and ducked as a pillow flew past his head. "Excuse me, Gustaf! I forgot one never mentions nerves to a soldier. Debauchery, yes—nerves, never! All right. Let's say your guts and brain are reacting to being pickled in wine and *kirschwasser*. I prescribe a dose of salts followed by black coffee."

"It's your blathering that's making me sick. Leave me alone."

"But it's my duty to scrub you down, lace you up in your gaudiest uniform, festoon you with all your military knickknacks, then deliver you in good order to meet your appointed fate. Please, just for once, cooperate with your little brother."

"As always you're sticking your nose into matters which don't concern you. You are *not* my best man, thank God!" Gustaf stood up and strode somewhat unsteadily to the lavabo.

Albrecht's laughter turned sardonic. "You don't really expect Rittmeister von Manschott to turn himself into a valet, do you? He's a man of flexible character, but his pomposity would absolutely forbid it." He watched with feigned shock as his brother splashed some drops of water over his face, chest, and armpits, then dabbed himself with a napkin-sized towel. "Come, Gustaf! Isn't a complete bath in order today? Your Baroness might not find the smell of horse and soldier's sweat very romantic. Oh! Forgive me again! I forgot that she herself carries a horsey aroma about her." This time he ducked too late and was drenched from head to toe with the contents of the lavabo. He looked down at the sopping folds of linen plastered against his scrawny frame, but even the chill of cold water could not dampen his caustic good humor. "You shouldn't have done that, dear brother. I was going to lend you this nightshirt for your honeymoon, but now it will never dry out in time." He beat a hasty retreat when Gustaf made a determined move toward his saber hanging over the back of a chair. Slamming the door between their rooms, Albrecht shouted a parting taunt through it: "Your barrack-room manners will never do in a noblewoman's boudoir!"

The younger von Falkenhorst washed very thoroughly and shaved himself without waiting for the maid to bring hot water. His soft whiskers fell easily before the cold razor. He put on clean underwear and then carefully took out of the trunk his Heidelberg fraternity uniform. It was a secondhand outfit which he had been ill able to afford out of his meager student's allowance, but Gustaf had insisted that he not attend the wedding in civilian clothes. The truth was that Gustaf was ashamed of a brother who had dared defy family tradition by refusing to attend a respectable military academy. To him, Heidelberg University, located in the decadent south of Germany, was a hotbed of radical and libertine ideas entirely alien to the Prussian character. There was even talk of treason against the Prussian

Confederation among students, many of them openly favoring France in the current quarrel between Napoleon and Bismarck. Treason in the mind of Gustaf, anyway, who had harangued his brother on the subject only yesterday. "There will be war soon," he had shouted, "and you'll be conscripted as an ordinary soldier! Then we'll knock some sense into you on the drillfield!" He was horrified when Albrecht told him Prussia could conscript nobody out of the Grand Duchy of Baden where Heidelberg was safely located. "You mean you would *hide* there?" Albrecht had shrugged off the question. He was not sure what he would do in case of war and preferred not to think about it.

In picking over his uniform he found several threadbare spots in the green cloth, some frayed strands of gold piping, and a very crucial button dangling loose. Fortunately he had brought along needle and thread. He was just biting off the thread and tying down the button when Rittmeister von Manschott entered without knocking. The commander of Third Squadron of Second Dragoon Guards appeared quite shocked at the work occupying Albrecht's hands and asked in his high-pitched voice: "Is that not something I could have my batman do for you, Freiherr von Falkenhorst?"

"No, thank you," Albrecht cheerfully replied. "I'm quite used to sewing my clothes. I consider I'm actually learning a trade, just in case everything goes to the devil with my illustrious family, you know."

"Perish the thought," von Manschott said, his aquiline features wrinkling into something like a smile. He was wearing a white lounging jacket over the breeches and boots of his best dress uniform, and its embroidered coat of arms covered an excessively large area of the left breast. The lounging jacket failed to lend the slightest casual air to his attire, only making his military bearing seem somewhat foppish. "I took the liberty of ordering breakfast sent up for all of us," he said, glancing into Albrecht's open trunk as if hoping to find something there more suitable for the occasion than the student's uniform. "Is our happy groom awake yet?"

"Yes, indeed! And I would say in dire need of support and guidance from his commanding officer."

Von Manschott's humorless smile became grimly determined. "Leave it to me! This is really a military operation, you know. At least the next six or eight hours of it, anyway. Ha-ha." He stalked up to the door to Gustaf's room, rapped on it, then immediately threw it open, revealing the groom standing in his underwear and urinating into an already half-full chamber pot.

"Good morning, Herr Leutnant Baron von Falkenhorst!"

"Good morning, Herr Rittmeister von Manschott!"

"Yes, it is always best to go into action bone dry. So squeeze out every drop, if you please."

They chuckled at each other, von Manschott because he always laughed at his own jokes, Gustaf because he always found it wise to laugh along with his commander on such occasions. Albrecht spat out a piece of thread and exclaimed: "Ah! The Herr Rittmeister is already a steadying influence. Before long all of his troops will be facing their coming ordeal with cheers and laughter!"

Gustaf scowled at his brother, but von Manschott eagerly nodded his head. "High morale comes from knowing what to expect of a given tactical situation and how to deal with it," he said. "A good commanding officer sees to it his troops are prepared in every way. So what can I do to prepare you better, Herr Leutnant Baron?"

Albrecht stood on the threshold, clutching his secondhand uniform and staring at his elder brother, hoping, indeed praying, he would answer by handing von Manschott the now-brimful chamber pot. But Gustaf carefully put it down under the bed himself and said: "At the moment I wish you had brought our regimental surgeon to do something about my head, Herr Rittmeister."

"No wonder you have a headache! It is suffocating in here!" Von Manschott pulled aside the curtains and flung open the window, allowing a puff of damp cold wind to swirl into the room. "Take a dozen deep breaths of fresh air," he ordered Gustaf, dragging him to the sill. "After a hearty breakfast, my batman will shave you and massage the back of your neck. There–there! Breathe deeply—deeply! Makes one feel good, right? Of course. Absolutely invigorating." He himself followed suit as Gustaf unenthusiastically sucked in great gulps of air.

"You will both catch terrible colds," Albrecht warned and retreated into his own room to get out of the chilling draft.

As the two officers stood at the open window, they were suddenly diverted by the clatter of hooves in the courtyard. Turning their gazes downward, they saw a dragoon trooper rein in his mud-splattered mount and swing out of the saddle. From the lance secured in its boot fluttered the pennant of the Second Dragoon Guard's Regimental Staff and around the trooper's neck hung the bright silver gorget of a courier. The horse was steaming and the man soaked after a hard ride through the cold drizzly morning.

"He seems in a terrible hurry," Gustaf said. "Could anything be wrong at the regiment?"

Von Manschott watched as a stableboy rushed out to take the reins of the horse as he pointed out the side entrance to the inn. "Don't worry. Probably only Colonel von Hardel sending felicitations to you and the Baroness-to-be. Perhaps some extra leave as a special wedding gift." He quickly closed the window when the trooper glanced upward and caught a glimpse of one of his officers in almost total dishabille. "Since I am the more-respectably attired, I shall go downstairs to receive the dispatches," he told Gustaf and left.

While Rittmeister von Manschott was gone, Manke, his batman, arrived with two waiters carrying breakfast trays. They set a table in Albrecht's room, loading it with platters of jellied pigs' feet, fried herring, steamed sausage, boiled oatmeal, and stewed fruits; there was a pot of coffee and one of tea, and an iced bottle of schnapps. Both rooms became filled with odors which tantalized Albrecht's appetite but made Gustaf feel slightly nauseated.

"One thing I'm going to get out of this wedding," Albrecht happily observed, "is a full belly for a change!"

Manke gave him a baleful stare, then correctly gauged Gustaf's condition and desire. "May I pour the Leutnant Baron a tot of schnapps?"

"Yes, thank you, Manke."

The batman stood at attention while Gustaf downed the drink in two searing gulps. For a moment it looked as though he were about to vomit, but he only shuddered, shook his head, managing to suppress everything except a tear which trickled to his chin. With a pointed frown at Albrecht, who was greedily hovering around the breakfast table, he hoarsely said: "We shall await the Herr Rittmeister's return before eating." He then allowed Manke to help him into his breeches and boots. His younger brother was left to dress himself, which he did only after snitching a whole herring off the table and stuffing it into his mouth.

It was ten minutes before Rittmeister von Manschott returned, and it was immediately apparent from his grim expression that the dispatches he held in his hand were not of the nature he had expected. But he was a man who, in spite of a deplorable lack of imagination, possessed an acquired sense of drama, so he did not clumsily blurt out their contents as he crossed the threshold. "It seems there have been momentous developments in Berlin and Paris during the past twenty-four hours," he announced in a clipped, matter-of-fact voice which still contained a high-pitched whine. Then he said to his batman: "Manke, pour three glasses. A toast is in order."

Albrecht suspected at once what was behind this piece of theatrics and turned pale. "If war has been declared, then say so, Herr Rittmeister," he begged.

Gustaf merely stared at his squadron commander and held his breath.

But von Manschott would not allow himself to be hurried. He waited silently while Manke filled the glasses and passed them around. Then he said: "We are all soldiers in the service of His Majesty. Manke, you will join us on this occasion."

Manke's hand trembled slightly as he filled a glass for himself. He raised it to the level of his chin, cracking his heels together and coming to stiff attention.

"To victory!" von Manschott exclaimed, and with a quick motion downed the schnapps.

"To victory!" the Leutnant and batman echoed, emptying their glasses a fraction behind their commander. Albrecht spoke the toast as a question: "To victory?" and barely touched the liquid to his lips. "Then it *is* war?"

Von Manschott put down his glass, dabbed his mouth with a napkin, and spread out the dispatches on the table. "I shall read you these special orders just received from Regimental Headquarters," he said, then proceeded to do so with a formal military delivery:

General mobilization has been proclaimed by His Majesty King Wilhelm I, effective 4 P.M. 15 July 1870, and a state of war shall be considered to exist as of this date between the Kingdom of Prussia, her allied Confederation of German States, and the Empire of France. All military leaves are cancelled forthwith. Officers and men of all of His Majesty's Armed Forces are directed to immediately report to their respective units for battle orders. All Landwehr regiments are herewith ordered mustered and placed under the command of designated regular divisions. Signed: Helmuth von Moltke, Chief of the General Staff.

When he paused to let this sink in, Gustaf von Falkenhorst seemed to draw a sigh of relief and exclaimed: "Well, that is that! Orders are orders, and our duty is clear."

Albrecht stared at him with an amazement which quickly turned to anger. "You can't mean it, Gustaf! You can't possibly be thinking of cancelling the wedding. You can't abandon Marie Theresa at the altar because of a stupid war which hasn't even started yet."

"Didn't you understand what was just read to you, you damned fool?" Gustaf shouted at him. "The war started *yesterday!* There may be battles raging at the frontier right now."

"Just a moment, please," von Manschott coolly injected. "There is more," he announced, shuffling the dispatches. "This one is from Colonel von Hardel and applies to our specific situation." The two brothers listened intently as he read:

The officers and men of Third Squadron, Second Dragoon Guards, currently detached by special order 335–7–10–70 to serve as honor guard and participants in wedding ceremony at Schloss Varn, Varnmunde, shall be granted special leave to remain in attendance to the bride and groom until the marriage ceremony is completed, thereafter immediately to return to their unit. This shall not apply to Leutnant Baron Gustaf von Falkenhorst, who is herewith granted a further forty-eight hours' leave before reporting for duty in the field. The Commanding Officer, officers and men of the Second Dragoon Guards take this opportunity to extend their greetings to the distinguished wedding party at Schloss Varn and to extend their felicitations and best wishes for a long and happy life in a victorious Prussia to the Leutnant Baron and Baroness von Falkenhorst. Signed: Kurt von Hardel, Colonel in Chief, Second Dragoon Guards.

Albrecht broke the following silence by acidly exclaiming: "Isn't that damned nice of the dear man!"

"Yes, it really is," von Manschott answered testily. He slapped Gustaf on the shoulder. "There, you see! There will be no interruption of the festivities. If anything, we now have double cause for rejoicing. The consummation of both love and war, the two greatest things in a man's life!" He folded up the dispatches and shoved them into the pocket of his lounging jacket. Sitting down at the breakfast table, he said: "Manke! You may serve us now."

There were forty-one guests lodged at Schloss Varn, mostly members of the house of von Beckhaus, a very large and prosperous family as opposed to that of von Falkenhorst, which was small and rich only in lineage. When Count Frederick Paul von Beckhaus had married off his eldest daughter, Esther, to a prince of the Palatinate, there had been 114 house guests in the castle and 80 more lodged at various manors of the surrounding countryside. The several banquets during the three days of festivities had required him to provide somewhat over three thousand servings of rich food and drink, plus beer and sausage for a full squadron of Hussars which the Prince had brought along for ceremonial purposes. As far as the Count was concerned, he had shot his bolt on weddings with that affair, and Tessa's wedding had to be a modest one for reasons of retribution as well as economy. The retribution being given to a daughter who for nearly sixteen years had thwarted him with a stubborn independence which always bordered upon, yet never quite exceeded, the bounds of obedience and respect. This girl-child, whom he had so desperately hoped would be a boy, had persisted in blooming into a thistle of purely male intransigence. Like this morning, for instance. It had never occurred to him to forbid her to go riding on the morning of her wedding —yet, she had done exactly that, knowing full well it would throw him into a rage if he found out.

Count Frederick usually sought to blame Tessa's erratic behavior on lack of maternal supervision, and thought this morning of storming into his wife's apartment in the opposite wing of the castle to once again remonstrate with her over her failures as a mother. But in view of her high-strung Austrian nature and penchant for fainting at crucial moments of arguments, he decided it would be unwise to put additional strain on his wife's delicate nervous system, especially since there would be enough unforeseen troubles caused by the abominable weather. Glowering out of the window of his sitting room at the rain-soaked panorama of woods and fens which dissolved into a misty blur of the Baltic, he fumed and grumbled loudly to himself: "Damnation! The road to Varnmunde will be a quagmire, plastering the coaches with mud. The coachmen's uniforms will be ruined. We don't have enough unbrellas. I'll have to share mine with Prince Eugene, who's so damnably fat there won't be room for me. I'll get drenched. Damn! Damn! Damn!"

He stalked back into his bedroom where his valet was just laying out his full-dress uniform as a colonel of the Landwehr, a rank which was almost entirely honorary. The Count's only active military service had been during the internal upheavals of 1848; he had been excused from the war with Austria in 1866 because his brother-in-law had commanded an enemy division. This would not have prevented him from attacking that division with patriotic ferocity since he had always been on bad terms with his Austrian relatives, but his efforts would have doubtless been ineffectual and inglorious. Count Frederick Paul von Beckhaus und Varn was definitely not a military man, his haughty temperament making him impervious to discipline, and his uncommonly short stature causing his saber to drag along the ground. At the age of sixty, he now kept only a single dress uniform for weddings, funerals, and the annual parade muster of his Landwehr regiment. As he looked at it now, he saw no reason to wear it out prematurely by subjecting it to the inclement weather. He would look especially ridiculous if it became soaking wet. "I have decided to wear an ordinary frock coat," he announced to his valet. "Frock coat, raincape, and galoshes, by God! Lay them out and I shall dress after having breakfast downstairs."

With an energy sustained by his bad temper, the Count trotted down the hall, nearly upsetting a couple of maids carrying trays to those guests having breakfast in their rooms. On the main staircase he bowled over a gardner putting the finishing touches on flower garlands hung from the bannister. In the French Salon filled with wedding gifts, the billowing folds of his silk robe swept a pink porcelain cherub off a table, but a footman popped out of nowhere and was sweeping up the pieces even as the Count slammed the door behind him. He burst into the smaller family dining room where the table had been set for those guests who chose to arise for their morning meal. So far only Lord Bourne and Bishop Putzkammer had done so.

"*Gut morgen,*" the Englishman exclaimed in his very bad German, made worse because he spoke through a mouthful of fried kidney. "So *der Tag* is upon us, eh! Jolly good."

"God bless us and our noble house on this auspicious day of rejoicing," the Bishop intoned with a funeral solemnity. The prelate was a distant relative by marriage which, in the Count's uncompromising opinion, made him convenient to have around at functions requiring the formal benedictions of the Almighty, but did not entitle him to pretend full membership in the family of von Beckhaus und Varn. Dropping into his chair at the head of the table, Count Frederick Paul nodded curtly to the Englishman, then snapped at the Bishop: "I'd prefer God to bless my daughter with some common sense, if you please. It wouldn't surprise me if she galloped to the church on horseback and marched up the aisle in her boots and spurs!" He glowered at the confused English lord whom he blamed to no small extent for Tessa's passion for riding. A year ago, she had been boarded at his Dorsetshire estate where she became exposed to English fox-hunting as well as to the English language, showing a far greater talent for the former. Why the English chased foxes on horseback with packs of howling dogs instead of simply shooting them as they did in Prussia confounded the Count. "A damned bunch of nonsense!" he exclaimed, waving away a silver platter full of potatoes and sausage.

"You may not curse in the presence of a man of God, Frederick Paul," Bishop Putzkammer admonished him as he had done so many times before. "And I devoutly pray you and

Marie Theresa will pass this final day together in mutual grace. Then you'll be rid of her, after all!"

"Make damned sure of that by executing your duties without the slightest hitch this noon, Herr Reverend Bishop Putzkammer," the Count testily replied, emphasizing the formal address because he resented being called by his Christian name by the son of a common village pastor. The Bishop fondly hoped that one day his noble relative would make representations at court to have a "von" authorized to the name of Putzkammer. The Count knew this and was determined that it would remain exactly what it deserved to be, plain Putzkammer. He accepted from the maid a bowl of sweet porridge and attacked it with rapid strokes of his spoon.

Lord Bourne had not understood their quickly spoken German, but he sensed it had not been entirely pleasant and that his host was in one of his famous tempers. He allowed the silence at the table to continue until he found it too embarrassing and decided to try to clear the atmosphere with some small talk. He had to do this in French, which he spoke a little better than German and which was the only language he had in common with his host. "It seems to be raining a little, doesn't it?"

"It's raining damn hard."

"Well, they say it's good luck to have rain for a wedding."

"As far as I'm concerned, it will be good luck just to get it over with."

There followed a full two minutes of silence disturbed only by Bishop Putzkammer's very loud munching sounds. Lord Bourne tried again: "I was looking out my window this morning and, 'pon my soul, could swear I saw the Lady Tessa come riding in. Must have been a few minutes after seven o'clock."

With a spoon poised half-way between his mouth and plate, Count Frederick leaned forward with one eyebrow cocked into the furrows of his forehead. "Indeed you did, my lord. Which leads me to ask whether you teach all your English young ladies such simpleminded devotion to horses."

Lord Bourne quickly retreated into a polite, chilly British reserve. "Your daughter came to us as an already accomplished horsewoman, sir."

"That is true. We do teach our women to ride in this country, but only to the extent of decorous recreational promenades along bridle paths. We do not turn them loose on the countryside like marauding Cossacks."

"Nor do we, sir," Lord Bourne replied and, dabbing his mouth with his napkin, rose from the table with a dignified haste. "If you will excuse me, Count Frederick Paul, I shall return to my room to dress for your daughter's wedding." As he was passing through the door, he stopped and suddenly shot back: "I'd also like to say, sir, that in our country we do not *shoot* foxes."

The Count chuckled with deliberate malice. "In our country we do, of course, since that pernicious little beast isn't worth more than a thimble of powder at best. We only use horses and hounds for hunting game of the size of stag and wild boar."

"Ah, yes," Lord Bourne exclaimed with equal malice. "Those *we* hunt on foot." Then he left.

Bishop Putzkammer had been listening intently, his fleshy jowls arrested from their mastication, his unsubtle mind straining to catch innuendos and inflections of a language he could not understand. After the Englishman had gone, he asked: "You were speaking French?"

"Yes."

"Ah-ha! I thought so. And there was a certain unpleasantness in the conversation, obviously." When he received no answer to his prying, he said plaintively: "I have never accepted the universality of French among people of our class. For my own part, I have resisted its use and believe Latin a better language for the nobility, whether ordained or secular."

"Like most of your other beliefs, that one is irrational and utterly divorced from facts, my poor Bishop," Count Frederick told him, then cruelly added: "Furthermore, I must point out to you again that it is presumptuous of you to use the first person plural whenever you mention the family of von Beckhaus und Varn, or Prussian nobility in general. Your marriage to a step-daughter of my second cousin does not entitle you to such a privilege. I resent your usurping it for yourself."

The Bishop dropped his knife and fork onto the plate as if he suddenly suspected the food to be poisoned. His face turned an unhealthy purple color. "You are an arrogant godless man, Count Frederick Paul. You are also extremely rude. To quote a saying in your favorite foreign tongue: *Noblesse oblige*; that is one you should give some thought to."

"I have," the Count snapped back, "and found it compromised by boorish pretentions of the bourgeoisie. While I may sometimes be guilty of arrogance, I certainly am not godless since I thank Him daily for having drawn such a clean, clear line between your kind and mine. It makes it so much simpler to keep you in your place."

The Bishop's eyes bulged in their sockets, then squeezed tightly shut as he brought his pudgy fingers together and mumbled through a hasty grace before rising from the table. He moved toward the door with a pathetic effort at outraged dignity. "This time you have gone much too far, Count Frederick

Paul," he said with a shaking voice. "I shall suffer no more of your insults. If I still decide to officiate at this wedding, it will only be out of consideration for your wife and daughter . . . God help them."

"If you give me the slightest trouble, I'll have you defrocked!" the Count shouted after him. When he found himself alone at the table with ten empty chairs and two white-faced maids standing transfixed at their posts by the pantry door, he chuckled gleefully over having demolished the pompous prelate. His mood improved considerably as he sipped his coffee. He had no fear whatever that Bishop Putzkammer would fail to perform the coming ceremony. The presence of a prince, a duchess, five counts, seven barons, and thirty-odd "vons" virtually guaranteed his performance. The only retaliation he might resort to would be the cutting short of his sermon, and that, of course, would only have a salutary effect upon the proceedings. And shortly after the banquet he would leave instead of lingering for several days as a boring, gluttonous guest, as he had after Esther's wedding.

When Count Frederick motioned over one of the maids to refill his cup, he noticed that her hand shook as she poured. "There-there," he soothed her with a smile. "You mustn't be upset because you saw me dress down the Reverend Bishop. He is not God. Only his lackey."

"Yes, Your Excellency," the maid squeaked and shook even more.

"Damn it, girl! You're spilling the coffee!" the Count shouted.

The other maid rushed up to the table in a brave attempt to bolster her companion, who showed signs of collapsing on the spot. "Elsa is only extra help for today's festivities, Your Excellency," she interceded. "Please forgive her clumsiness."

Count Frederick Paul wagged his head and put on a manner which was supposed to be one of magnanimity. "Oh, all right then. I'm not angry. Not with you, anyway." He smacked the trembling girl on her buttocks, causing a puppylike yelp to burst out of the girl. That made him laugh. "There, you see! Now you're initiated into the brigade of maids of Schloss Varn," he shouted after her as she fled in terror. In bursting through the pantry door, she almost knocked down Knabel, the head butler, who was on his way into the dining room.

Knabel was wearing the elaborate green and silver majordomo uniform and white wig which the Countess von Beckhaus und Varn had imported from Vienna for Esther's wedding; since then he had put on weight and his legs seemed to be bursting out of the velvet knee-breeches. "You look like a perambulating Christmas tree," the Count told him. "You're gaudier than His Royal Highness, the Prince Eugene, and that will never do. What do you want?"

"The Freiherr Albrecht von Falkenhorst has arrived and urgently requests a word with Your Excellency," Knabel announced in a lugubrious voice.

"What? At this hour?"

"He said it was extremely important, or else he would not disturb Your Excellency's breakfast," Knabel said, then added with an ominous inflection: "I believe it may have some effect upon the wedding plans, Your Excellency."

The Count gave a start and his face darkened with returning anger. He had had his doubts about the von Falkenhorst family during the long haggling over the dowry and now they all flashed back through his mind. "Effect on the wedding plans?" he exclaimed, jumping to his feet. "If that petty Silesian satrap is about to disgrace us by backing out now, I'll break his damned neck. And I'll start right in on his little brother!"

The remaining maid let out a gasp of horror and slipped out through the pantry door.

Count Frederick Paul left Knabel far behind as he rushed toward the library, his temper rising to a white heat under the fires of his suspicious imagination. By the time he burst through the library door, he was certain that Gustaf von Falkenhorst was either too sick to appear at his own wedding after last night's wild party at the Varnmunde Gasthaus, or had found courage from the orgiastic imbibing with his regimental comrades to take to his heels, rather than face marriage to Prussia's most eccentric young noblewoman. Count Frederick had never met Gustaf's younger brother before but started shouting at him without bothering over any formal introductions:

"I'm not going to tolerate any boorish behavior, I warn you. All the plans are made. All the conditions agreed upon. You Falkenhorsts will rue the day you dare shame us in front of assembled royalty and peers. And *you*, sir, will rue the day you ran a perfidious errand for your brother!"

Albrecht jerked himself out of the respectful bow he had begun and stared in surprise at the livid little man in the white silk robe. For a moment he doubted that this could really be the supposedly formidable Count von Beckhaus und Varn, but the cocksure haughtiness of his rage told him it could be none other. Quickly recovering his wits, his shocked expression turned into a smile: "Calm yourself, Your Excellency. I am quite sure the wedding may proceed."

"Has there ever been the slightest doubt about it?" Frederick Paul yelled at him.

"Yes, possibly some slight doubt." Albrecht's smile broadened, and it was obvious he was daring to enjoy the situation.

"That is in itself an insult to my daughter and family," the Count bellowed, his voice rising to such a force that it must have carried through the closed library doors. "Pray God you've got a damned good explanation for it!"

"I'd not look to God for the explanation for it, Your Excellency," Albrecht wrily answered. "Napoleon III or King Wilhelm I perhaps, but not God." He waited for a moment to relish the confusion which suddenly flashed over the Count's face, then took pity on him and announced: "General mobilization has been ordered by the King. War with France has started."

Count Frederick Paul's anger drained out of him and with it all the color in his face. He stared at Albrecht for several seconds, then turned away and moved over to the fireplace where he stood swaying slightly on his feet, gazing into the flames swirling around the rock-sized chunks of coal. "Mobilization? War? Oh, the damned fools!" he exclaimed to himself in suppressed anguish. "Oh, the damned fools!"

Albrecht's sardonic smile vanished and was replaced by a surprised look. "Well, it's a relief to find one man who does not rejoice over this news," he soberly observed.

"Rejoice over it? Rejoice when we will probably be invaded and ravished by the French for the two-hundredth time in three centuries? Rejoice over a war for no better cause than the succession to the dessicated, corrupt Spanish throne? Only imbeciles would rejoice over such prospects."

Albrecht sighed. "Alas, Your Excellency has just described the best man and groom of this wedding, then."

Count Frederick Paul turned from the fire and for the first time carefully scrutinized the gaunt young man before him. "And what is the peculiar uniform you are wearing, may I ask?"

Albrecht laughed. "It's not military. I am a student at Heidelberg University. I apologize that it does not fit me better. My tailor is in truth nothing but a pawnbroker."

Count Frederick Paul von Beckhaus und Varn reached out and ran his finger down the green folds which hung in unseemly washboard ripples across Albrecht's sunken chest. "Mine does not really fit me either," he said.

There was a staff of twenty-seven household servants at Schloss Varn, and for the occasion of the wedding, ten more had been recruited as reinforcements. In addition, there were personal attendants brought along by a number of the guests, such as Prince Eugene's valet and footman and the Duchess Harnecke-Warenberg's pretty little French maid Celestine. They all worked efficiently and unobtrusively enough when out front, but in the huge kitchen, the pantries, sculleries, laundry and linen rooms, and through the warren of back halls and staircases of the castle, they gave way to the excitement they all felt. There were chatter and jokes interspersed with outbursts of nervous pique over the innumerable small crises which must occur when preparing for a major social function. There was also a considerable amount of gossiping, and thus it happened that rumors of Albrecht von Falkenhorst's mission began passing among them long before reaching the ears of their masters and mistresses. They spread in quick whispers from maids to footmen to valets to cooks to scullery workers, the completely mistaken premise embellished and dramatized in the process. It started with the table maid's repeating the Count's outburst when Knabel informed him of the Freiherr's arrival, then was compounded when a footman overheard shouting in the library, something to the effect that "the Falkenhorsts would rue the day," something about "an insult to my daughter and family." And yes!—hadn't the Reverend Bishop been seen stalking to his room muttering furiously to himself? It was obvious that something terrible had happened. And what could it be except that young Leutnant Baron von Falkenhorst was backing out of the wedding? It had to be true. There would probably be a duel instead of a happy festival. Bleak disgrace instead of honorable rejoicing. Oskar Mayer, the head chef, who had labored all night on the wedding cake, stared at his fifty-kilogram masterpiece and burst into tears. Twenty minutes after Albrecht's arrival, a frantic chambermaid blurted out her version of the story to the appalled Countess von Beckhaus und Varn as she was being laced into her corset, causing her to collapse in a dead faint. Almost simultaneously another maid burst into Tessa's room and sobbed out the news, but here only the seamstress fainted into a jumbled tangle of ribbons and threads as she was making final adjustments to the wedding gown which the bride was already wearing. Tessa herself merely slumped into a chair, a shimmering white tomboy waif enmeshed in billows of embroidered silk; she exclaimed in a voice remarkably remindful of her father's: "Well, actually I don't give a damn!"

The truth took long enough to be revealed to allow considerable mischief. After escorting Albrecht to the dining room, where he eagerly attacked his second breakfast of the morning, Count Frederick Paul hurried up to Prince Eugene's suite in the East Tower. As the Prince held the military rank of general as well as being sixth in succession to the eclipsed throne of Hanover, he should immediately be informed of the declaration of war. The Count found him in the process of being shaved by his valet, the rubbery folds of his jowls hidden under thick layers of lather. When he heard the news, scarcely a tremor went through his huge rotund body as he said: "It is no more than what could be expected." But encased within the placid corpulence of his physique, the prince had a shrewd mind with a Machiavellian turn to it which had enabled him to salvage something out of the inevitable submission of his own royal house to that of the Prussian Hohenzollerns. His next observation concerned the fact that a number of the highborn guests at Schloss Varn held lukewarm loyalty to the Prussian-led North German Confederation of States. Indeed, he pointed out, some of the Count's relatives-in-law from Austria might suddenly become enemies if that country chose to side with France in an attempt to avenge her humiliation at Sadowa four years ago. The whole matter could become highly embarrassing. While they discussed this painful situation at some length, the rumor about the canceled wedding spread through the castle. It was not until the Count decided to go to the rooms of his ranking Austrian guest, General Baron Piednich, his wife's brother, to confront him directly with the dilemma, that he became aware of what was happening. As he passed down the hall he met the Countess's weeping maid who informed him that Her Ladyship had just fainted.

"Already?" he exclaimed irritably. "The walls of this place must have ears and the rafters mouths that whisper. Well, when she revives, tell her to be brave and carry on if she can."

"B-but it is all so horrible, Your Excellency!" the maid wailed. "A beautiful wedding so cruelly canceled!"

"What? Who told you that?"

"W-why . . . everybody knows about it," she blubbered. "Everybody's talking about it. Everybody's so sorry. . . ."

"It's a lie!" he shouted at her, then turned and ran down the hall, repeating over and over: "Oh damn! Oh damn!" He did not run toward his wife's apartment, but toward his daughter's. Along the way he bumped into poor Knabel, grabbed him by his embroidered lapels, and shook him until his wig slipped to the bridge of his nose. "The wedding is *not* canceled!" he shouted at him. "It's war that's been declared, but the wedding goes on even if Napoleon lays siege to my castle! Now spread *that* among your rumormongering chattels!" Rushing on, he burst in on Tessa and found her still slumped in a chair, watching with amusement as her servants splashed cold water in the face of the prostrate seamstress. "So you've heard it too!" he exclaimed in final exasperation. "In the name of heaven and all its pink angels, what have I done to deserve this mess?"

Tessa smiled at him and calmly answered: "I hope you are not suffering on my account, Papa. I'm sorry for all the trouble you've gone to, but otherwise I'm not in the least upset. After all, I've only met Gustaf twice in my life before and both times found him quite dull. I can do without him very nicely, thank you."

"Daughter, you are the victim of a lie spread by ignorant gossiping servants," her father shouted. "The Baron von Falkenhorst is not deserting you. You will become his wife at noon today exactly as I have arranged. Put any other idea out of your head."

Tessa's smile vanished and her lips compressed as she glared at the chambermaid who had brought her the false story. "If I had the time, I'd give you a good thrashing."

"You don't have any time at all," her father snapped, stepping between her and the quavering maid. "The wedding cortege leaves in exactly forty minutes, at which time you and I will be seated in our carriage ready to do our duty." He cocked his head toward the distant sound of an agonized wail which came from the Countess's apartment directly above Tessa's. "Ah, your mother is calling. I suppose I had better go and comfort her with the complete facts of the situation."

Forgetting to give his daughter those complete facts, he stepped over the still-prostrate seamstress and left.

In a small anteroom of the Guildhall of Varnmunde, the groom and his best man awaited the hour of eleven o'clock. Rittmeister von Manschott sat smoking a cigar, watching through the window with a casually critical eye as the guard of honor from his regiment took their posts around the village square in the pouring rain. Water dripped from their helmets and streaked the flanks of their horses; the guidons and regimental colors hung limp and soggy. Some three hundred villagers and freeholders, all dressed in their best Sunday finery, pushed each other out of the way of the dragoons and up against the walls in chattering clusters, the men with their collars turned up, the women with shawls over their heads; there were very few umbrellas. Some small boys marched back and forth through the puddles, playing soldier with sticks as muskets. The excitement over the big castle wedding was augmented by the electrifying news of WAR—but it would all have been more cheerful if there had been a little sunshine. Von Manschott wondered whether the rain pelting down on this day meant bad luck. For the war, not the wedding. The wedding, as far as he was concerned, had become an obtrusive nuisance.

Gustaf had not as much as mentioned the wedding since dispatching his younger brother to Schloss Varn earlier in the morning. He was pacing restlessly back and forth between the window and door of the anteroom, his brightly polished boots giving forth alternate squeaks of taut leather and jangle of silver spurs. He no longer looked at all ill; indeed, he cut a splendid military figure in his full-dress Dragoon Guards uniform, his face flushed, his eyes aglitter as he talked, talked, and talked on about forthcoming battles against the despised French (they had become despised at least for the last few hours). He was being boyishly bellicose, yet in spite of that, the deeply ingrained Napoleonic legend was betraying its influence. Where would *they* strike first? Where could *they* best be stopped? "We must try to meet their attack across the Rhine, then throw them back across it. Perhaps they will make their thrust from Strasbourg to cut us off from Baden and Würtemberg. Or perhaps drive through the Palatinate and march directly on Berlin. My God,

Herr Rittmeister. We can't let the French break through to Berlin again. This time we must keep them out of Prussia."

Von Manschott smiled his thin smile and said: "General von Moltke is certain to have a plan."

"Yes–yes, I suppose so. But he strikes me as a pedantic type, the schoolmaster of our army who might turn out timid in the field. This won't be like fighting Austria. We're up against another Bonaparte and his staff of marshals, don't forget, and an army whose fathers marched into Moscow. Our only chance is audacity. We must strike hard and fast and unexpectedly."

Von Manschott's smile took an ironic twist. "You amaze me, Gustaf. For such a young officer, you certainly have an amazing grasp of the theories of strategy—not to mention firm opinions about our Commander in Chief."

Gustaf stopped in his tracks. "Oh, forgive me, Herr Rittmeister. I know I'm talking too much. But I must confess to an unbearable excitement."

"That is natural under the circumstances."

"So what do you really think about it? Will we have cavalry action, or will it be nothing but a big chess game of the infantry?"

Von Manschott tapped the ash of his cigar on the floor, taking care to miss the mirror perfection of his boots. "That depends," he shrugged. "The mountains of South Germany are not exactly suited for classical cavalry warfare. The flat country of Brandenburg is better, if it comes to that. But in any case, I don't think we'll want for a good fight. Ah . . . looks like some activity starting out there, so stop worrying about the war." His eyes were following a coach being drawn across the square. But it was not part of the main wedding procession, only Bishop Putzkammer being driven to the church to prepare for the religious part of the ceremony. Several villagers stepped out of the shelter of the walls to bow or curtsey respectfully to the prelate, only to be splashed for their trouble.

Gustaf watched the coach turn out of sight, pulled out a handkerchief, daubed his face with it, and said in a lowered voice: "I must also confess to you, Herr Rittmeister, that I'm not a bit happy with this wedding. I should have known war was coming and postponed it."

"Nonsense," von Manschott protested. "The wedding is very important. You are not shirking your duty, but properly executing it. Our distinguished military families must be perpetuated if we are to remain a strong nation. Let me tell you it is a great satisfaction to me as I go to war that my wife has borne me a son. I trust you will have time to beget one for yourself before riding into battle. I do believe that is what Colonel von Hardel had in mind when he granted you special leave." His smile turned into a smirk, which was almost lecherous, as he noticed Gustaf's confused expression; then he pointedly asked, "Have you ever had a woman, Baron Gustaf?"

Gustaf turned crimson, swallowed hard and answered with an abrupt "No, sir."

Von Manschott's smirk remained as he sighed: "Oh, dear. We've neglected some of your military training, it seems. Well, just do what comes naturally during the next forty-eight hours, and do it as often as you can. It's not unpleasant, you know."

"So I have heard," Gustaf gulped and kept his face glued to the window to hide his embarrassment.

The clock in the church steeple chimed eleven. A brass band moved out from under the eaves of the Guildhall and began playing in the rain, the musicians' red uniforms turning oxblood in color. Suddenly Master Prytz rode into the square on Feldteufel, acting as postillion for the leading coach of the wedding cortege, the one containing His Royal Highness, Prince-General Eugene of Hanover and the bride's mother, Countess Theresa Antoinette von Beckhaus und Varn. The crowd stirred with some desultory cheers. There was a flutter of handkerchiefs and the bobbing of doffed hats; the soldier-children scampered alongside the wheels and hooves splashing over the cobblestones until caught and restrained by their elders. Then came more carriages, all containing the bride's family. The groom's mother had been invited, but she was bedridden with a broken hip. Except for Albrecht, there were no other living Falkenhorsts available to attend this most auspicious union of two fine old Prussian families. But, as perhaps the old Baroness dreamed in her sickbed in faraway Silesia, it was being witnessed with satisfaction by ghosts of the clan which included a string of Teutonic knights as well as Gustaf's recently fallen warrior-father.

"Things are running late," Gustaf observed as he peered through the window. "Four minutes behind as of now. I certainly hope the time will be made up somehow."

When Prince Eugene stepped out of his coach, the band struck up *"Preussen Glorias,"* which may or may not have been an insult since Prussia had been at war with Hanover only four years ago. However, the rotund prince, resplendent in his scarlet Hussars uniform, knew how to control his feelings if he had any residual rancor left in him. He quickly ushered the Countess von Beckhaus und Varn inside out of the rain, then waddled back down the steps of the Guildhall and saluted the Dragoon Guards and villagers, raising his sword and shouting: "Long live

Prussia and a united Germany! God punish France!" The polite cheers suddenly became loud and enthusiastic; the tips of the dragoons' sabers glinted in the rain as they returned the salute. The head and shoulders of Count Frederick Paul popped impatiently out of the window of the last coach in line as the whole procession was held up while Prince Eugene acknowledged a spontaneous ovation. His performance also annoyed Gustaf, who irritably muttered: "He's losing us another couple of minutes."

The door to the anteroom opened and the Mayor of Varnmunde, wearing a blue sash over his frock coat, appeared on the threshold, bowing as he announced: "Gentlemen, the bridal party approaches. Your presence is respectfully requested."

"Yes–yes, we are quite ready," Gustaf eagerly agreed. He buckled on his saber, drew on his left gauntlet, folded the other one neatly under his helmet, which he nestled in the crook of his left arm with the spread-eagle insignia facing precisely to the front, the spike exactly perpendicular. Rittmeister von Manschott took the time to carefully extinguish his cigar and place the unsmoked part in a small silver case which he carried in his hip pocket. "So let us proceed," he said as soon as he had himself and his own accouterments properly arranged for their entrance.

The hall was neither large nor opulent, but absolutely spotless with its scrubbed white plaster, varnished cross timbers, and scoured brick floors. The rain-gray light seeping in through its small windows was augmented by candles in wrought iron holders driven into the oak pillars rising to the open-beam ceiling. Birch and pine garlands had been hung from the rafters and filled the whole room with their woodsy fragrance. There were only six chairs, two of which had been placed in front of the plain oak table on which rested the county registry book wreathed with primroses and daisies. Behind this secular altar for the civil ceremony, the Mayor and Chief Magistrate now took their positions, fidgeting with solemn expressions as the High Constable ushered in the guests. The groom and his best man waited just outside the anteroom.

Prince Eugene entered with Countess Beckhaus und Varn on his arm and seated her and himself. Behind them came Albrecht von Falkenhorst, a slightly ludicrous figure in his ill-fitting fraternity uniform as he awkwardly escorted the aged Dowager Baroness Piednich, the bride's maternal grandmother. The old lady hobbled over the brick floor with a rustling of black silk and starched lace, a bright smile of second childhood illuminating her wrinkled face; to her was given the sixth chair. Then followed the other, younger relatives, who had to stand.

Baron Franz Piednich, wearing the white tunic of an Austrian general, with his buxom wife, Clara. The Duchess Harnecke-Warenberg, née Beckhaus, now unhappily self-conscious in her startling and obviously *French* gown, her hand resting on the embroidered sleeve of Colonel Karl Piednich. The bride's cousin, Leutnant Otto von Beckhaus, escorted her maiden aunt, Ilsa, whose robust figure was draped in green and gold brocade and whose florid face wore the expression of an amiable bulldog. There was a moment of confused shuffling as the party arranged itself in a formal semicircle in front of the table. The Count Frederick Paul von Beckhaus und Varn entered the room with his daughter, stopping just inside the door to allow a footman to help her remove the ordinary black raincape which had been thrown over her wedding gown. Everybody turned to watch. The Dowager Baroness let out a gleefully senile cackle of delight.

"Who is that old crone?" Gustaf whispered to von Manschott out of the corner of his mouth.

"One of your new relatives, my good fellow," his best man hissed back. "Austrian branch, I presume. I notice many Austrians. We may be at war with Austria too, you know, and have to arrest them."

Gustaf showed no reaction whatever.

Anna Marie Theresa von Beckhaus und Varn had an unpleasant sinking feeling in her stomach and her mouth had gone completely dry. She was certain she was as pale as the white lace of her veil, through which the glittering little assembly appeared as shadowy, faceless figures all staring at her. She could not see Gustaf and made no effort to spot him; he would step forward at the appointed moment, no doubt. After the footman had taken her cape and her father's silk hat, and she had been allowed a brief moment to smooth out the folds of her gown, a strong grip closed down over her elbow and exerted a forward pressure. She resisted for a second in a futile gesture of defiance before falling into step behind the High Constable, who was leading them toward the registry book on the table. "I'll never forgive you for this, Father," she rasped softly. If the bitter words wafted through the veil and into Count Frederick's ear, he pretended not to have heard them as he strode noiselessly alongside his daughter in his galoshes, a fixed half-smile on his face.

When they drew up to the chairs and stopped, two figures detached themselves from one side of the room and approached with the click of hard leather heels and the clink of steel. Tessa saw them as identical blurred shapes in blue until they drew closer and the one on the right turned into Gustaf. The appointed moment had arrived. Her father's hand pressed her into a chair. As her groom sat down next to her, his saber scraped noisily against the brick floor. The Dowager Baroness Piednich twittered behind her. The Mayor cleared his throat and launched into his address of welcome, one of those long-winded speeches of his which she knew from experience her father would eventually cut short with a series of peremptory hacking coughs. Pray God, he would do so soon.

While the civil ceremony was going on, attended only by immediate family, carriages slowly jostled through the narrow streets and pulled up to the church one after the other, disgorging a steady flow of uniformed or silk-hatted gentlemen and their formally gowned ladies. The houseguests of Schloss Varn were augmented by those invited from neighboring estates, like the von Eldenhowers, the von der Tanns, and the von Hallenbergs. Last, and signaling the approaching commencement of the ceremony, came those who had attended the preliminary formalities at the Guildhall. The Dragoon Guards, who had moved from the square to the church (where they added considerably to the traffic jam), saluted these later arrivals because they were obviously the most important. All the guests were ushered into the flower-bedecked, candlelit sanctuary which had been built by the first Count von Beckhaus when he had switched from Catholicism to the sect of the new reformist, Martin Luther. Everybody was distributed in the pews according to rank, the lowliest having to stand as there was not enough room. There was much rustling and subdued stamping as raindrops were shaken off clothing, then much whispering among acquaintances: "You've heard the news? War!" "Yes. Poor Tessa marrying an officer." "Don't worry. We'll beat them!" "God punish the French!" A few of the more pious kneeled and put this latter sentiment into formal prayer.

Gustaf did not arrive at the church in a carriage, but rode on horseback like a proper cavalryman. When he and von Manschott had stepped into the Mayor's office in the Guildhall for a glass of wine after the civil ceremony, his brother Albrecht had entered with a message from Count Frederick suggesting that a coach be provided him on account of the heavy rain. "Thank His Excellency for his consideration, but tell him this is not the time for Prussian soldiers to show softness. We shall ride as prearranged." Even Rittmeister von Manschott had looked a little upset over this decision, but he could not very well object without compromising his own military ardor. So they put on their greatcoats and helmets, and to the fawning admiration of the Mayor, mounted their horses and allowed themselves to be drenched as they trotted over to the church. This demonstration of austere soldierly virtue found favor with the equally drenched crowd, who raised a lusty cheer as the groom and best man splashed by. Handing over their mounts to Master Prytz after acknowledging the salute of the honor guard, they hurried into the church through a side door where they dampened the temper of the officious sexton by thrusting their wet overcoats into his arms. An admiring murmur passed through the congregation when Leutnant Baron Gustaf von Falkenhorst and Rittmeister Wolf von Manschott took their position to the right of the altar, ramrod stiff, motionless military figures, waiting.

Tessa had been driven by her father from the Guildhall to the parsonage for the intermission between ceremonies. There waited her four twittering bridesmaids, three cousins whom she saw only on formal occasions such as this, and an old schoolfriend from Mme Deveraux's Finishing School from whom she was already beginning to feel estranged. There also waited a still severely shaken seamstress who was supposed to add to the wedding gown an heirloom bridal train for the bridesmaids to carry, four meters of Brabant lace which had been worn by Tessa's sister, mother, grandmother, and great-aunt. Pastor Hess's library had been converted into a temporary boudoir where the seamstress fussed and fiddled while the quietly efficient Frau Hess tried to steady everybody with cups of strong coffee and reassuring smiles. "You look radiant, my dear," she told Tessa.

"The homeliest bride looks radiant on her wedding day," she answered wryly. "Didn't you know that?"

The pastor's wife did not flinch, nor her smile fade. "Your radiance comes of an inner strength which has yet to assert its full power, my Tessa. The pastor and I have often remarked about it." Reaching out and taking a confusion of pins and ribbons from the fumbling fingers of the seamstress, she proceeded to attach the train with brisk dexterity. Before pronouncing Tessa ready, she went to a cupboard beneath the bookshelves and took out a decanter and glass. "Your father is fortifying himself in our parlor, so I see no reason why you should not too. Who needs it more, after all, you or he? *Prosit*, as the men say!"

Because the bridesmaids and the pastor's wife had been added to the bride's party, it now took a pair of carriages to transport them the bare two hundred meters to the church. As before, Tessa and her father rode alone in silence and it seemed to her that their entire eighteen years of misunderstandings and recriminations were compressed into those three minutes it took to cover that short distance. As they pulled up to the church steps, she heard the harsh command which brought the dragoon honor guard to the salute and seemingly from somewhere high up in the weeping gray sky, bells started dinning her ears. The door to her coach flew open and hands which meant to be eagerly helpful clawed at her; once again she saw everything and everyone as a blur through her veil as they pulled her out under the dripping domes of buffeting umbrellas. The bridesmaids let out subdued squeals as they struggled to keep the heavy train from dragging on the wet stones. Her father's hand clamped down on her elbow again. A gust of wind swirled her silks and lace, bringing to her nostrils a tantalizingly brief tang of the sea and fens; then that smell abruptly changed to the sickly sweet odor of candlewax and cut flowers. The bells faded and were replaced by the pulsing organ notes of Bach's "Processional." They were inside the church now, and she could see the altar glittering mistily ahead with its clusters of candles. Suddenly she became aware of quickly whispered words from close beside her, coming in belated answer to her own bitter ones of an hour ago: "I trust you will not be as unforgiving to your Heavenly Father, daughter, and more graciously submit to His will." Again, there was that horrible word, *submit*.

The same two chairs for the bride and groom had hastily been transferred from the Guildhall to the church and placed before the altar steps where they were seated an arm's length apart while Bishop Putzkammer addressed his sermon to them. He was wearing his most-gorgeously embroidered vestments with a golden miter which made him appear much taller than he was (and, Tessa thought, ogrelike); the emblazoned cross and its sacred initials, *IHS*, curved over his portly belly, rippling in rhythmic emphasis with his booming voice. Behind him stood Pastor Hess, somewhat more simply attired, a benign smile on his face, his bald head continuously nodding in approval of the Bishop's words. Tessa recognized passages from the long sermon he had delivered at her sister's wedding, but the delivery was faster and without many of the elaborations and verbal flourishes. He was obviously not going to risk any crude coughing signals from Count Frederick. In less than six minutes he was finished, and the actual marriage sacrament began. Tessa rose before the prelate, her hand was placed in Gustaf's by her father, and she touched him for the first time since their betrothal last winter. When Bishop Putzkammer put the traditional question to her, she turned and peered hard at the man she was marrying, trying to focus through the mesh of her veil, and gave him the first long, searching look since their last meeting during Easter. Their eyes did not meet because he was staring at the altar, his jaw set, the veins in his neck standing out like cords above his collar. The Bishop was about to repeat the question when she answered in a loud and clear voice, which startled herself as well as everybody else in the church. She did not say: "Yes—I do," but "Yes—I *must.*"

A look of surprise came over Bishop Putzkammer's face, and for an instant he floundered before being able to proceed. They exchanged rings, Gustaf shoving the plain gold band over her finger as if it were a bolt. Then followed the blessing, the pronouncement of their being man and wife in the eyes of God and man, and it was over. Or they *thought* it was over.

"I beg the indulgence of these lovely newlyweds for a few moments," Bishop Putzkammer said as they were about to turn and leave the altar. "A momentous event is taking place today which requires our supplication for God's guidance and support. Let us bow our heads in prayer for the victory of our King and country over our enemy. Let us pray for His blessing of our cause in this just war which has started today."

In spite of many peremptory coughs from Count Frederick Paul, the prayer lasted a full fourteen minutes.

Gustaf von Falkenhorst would gladly have ridden his horse all the way back to the reception at Schloss Varn, and his wife would probably not have objected, but, of course, that was out of the question, war or no war. The trip was to last no more than twenty minutes, yet they both faced it with trepidation since it would not only be their first twenty minutes as man and wife, but the longest time they had ever spent alone together. There were the initial diversions of the departure from the church with its confusion of protecting the bride from the continuing rain as she climbed into her carriage, of waving to the stoically cheering folk who had faithfully waited outside, of nodding to the bandmaster who kept his soaked musicians playing their waterlogged instruments, of acknowledging the salute of the honor guard of dragoons. After pulling away and starting down the cobbled street, they had to watch for and return the waves of aged villagers who had had to remain indoors by their windows; they passed a group of children on the schoolhouse step who sang *lieder* in high-pitched, slightly off-key voices as they rolled by. Then the last house of Varnmunde dropped behind them; the rumble of the wheels and clatter of the hooves softened as the stone paving became the muddy road weaving between fields and fens. They continued to look out of the coach windows, each from his own side, but the diversions were finished and now there was only themselves. Gustaf finally spoke: "I think everything went quite well, Theresa."

"Yes, quite well." (Theresa? Only her father called her Theresa—when he was angry with her.)

"It is a pity about everybody getting wet. Did you get rained on much?"

"No, hardly at all."

"I hope not. It is such a pretty dress."

"Thank you."

A long silence followed during which she became conscious of him staring at her as she kept her own eyes on the distant dunes of the shore where she had ridden with Master Prytz early that morning. She could hear the faint clip-clop of Feldteufel's hoofs as the old stablemaster rode ahead of the coach, and she wondered if he were still angry with her, and if they would have a chance to put things right between them before she left. Then she heard her husband say: "I don't think it would be improper for you to remove your veil now, Theresa."

She felt her face flush, and there was a prickly feeling which she knew had to be her freckles catching on fire. But she peeled back her veil and turning, looked straight at him. If he wanted to stare at her, then she might as well get a good look at him, too. He was really very handsome, but this gave her no pleasure at all since it only made her more conscious of her own plainness. His nose was thin and slightly hooked, his cheekbones high, his chin firm, and the lips would be full if they were not so consciously pressed tight. There was a natural curl to his fair hair. The eyes were as blue as his uniform, perhaps a shade lighter, the lids slightly turned down in the corners, suggesting an infusion of Tartar blood in his more-distant antecedents. They seemed hard eyes, yet as she continued to look into them, she became aware of a certain restless unhappiness in them.

Dropping her glance to his gauntleted hands, she noticed how his fingers were nervously stroking the helmet he held in his lap.

"I am sorry, Gustaf," she suddenly blurted out. "I know how unpleasant this is for you."

His expression did not change, but his voice was mildly startled: "Why do you say that? I find you quite pretty."

She knew he meant to be complimentary, but it struck her as so ridiculous that she could not help smiling. "I was referring to the wedding itself, my poor Gustaf. But thank you anyway . . . for not telling me I look radiant." That changed his expression into a mixture of perplexity and injury; her smile quickly faded and she turned her face away to stare once more toward the sea. When the silence became unbearable, she said: "I went riding out there at dawn this morning."

"You did? *This* morning?"

"Yes. *This* morning," she snapped, deciding she might as well shock him now as later. "It put my father in a terrible temper which, I dare say, will last all day. But I don't care. I am very glad I went riding *this* morning." When she gave him a defiant glance, she was surprised to see a smile relaxing the tense pressure of his lips. "Do you think that is funny?"

"I think it . . . unusual." After a long pause, he said: "I have heard you are an excellent horsewoman. After the war we shall often ride together."

That brought up something which had been preying on her mind ever since she had been told about the mobilization that morning. "Will you be going to war . . . right away?"

"I must first submit to my essential duties to you and our families," he answered with a deep sigh. Suddenly realizing the combined effects of the answer and its tone, he belatedly added: "It will naturally be a pleasure, my dear Theresa."

Submit! How that word had been thrown at her ever since her mother had used it last night in her fumbling lecture on one's duties in the conjugal bed. Now, coming from Gustaf's lips, it filled her with renewed revulsion. He was going to stay for *his* pleasure and *she* was going to have to submit to it—that's what he meant.

They traveled the rest of the way in complete silence and she barely managed to smile at the crowd of tenant farmers, grooms, herders, gamekeepers, and servants who were cheering lustily in the rain as their carriage entered the castle gates. As soon as they were through the front door, Tessa broke away from Gustaf and fled up the main staircase toward her rooms, a covey of happily squealing bridesmaids fluttering behind her. Up there, among the trunks packed for her trip to distant

Silesia, she tried to compose herself for the approaching ordeal of the banquet.

ount Frederick Paul von Beckhaus und Varn had to stand by himself in the main foyer of Schloss Varn and greet the stream of guests as they handed their damp coats and cloaks to the attending footmen. His Countess had been unable to stem a steady flow of tears which had started when Bishop Putzkammer blessed the matrimonial knot and launched into his long martial prayer. She had wept all the way home from the church, this to his special annoyance since they had shared their carriage with Prince Eugene who muttered with embarrassment about "tears of joy." When she attempted to remain by her husband's side near the front door, her weeping continued unabated and, finally, unable to stand any more of it, the Count hissed: "It's not the girl's funeral, dammit! Go upstairs and get control of yourself."

His new son-in-law, whom the Count had not seen since last spring, tried to be helpful by standing stiffly next to him and cracking his heels together in pistol-shot salutes to each couple as they presented themselves; unable to abide this for long either, he had pointedly suggested that Gustaf go find himself some refreshment. So he remained there alone, giving and receiving the usual formal platitudes of such occasions, shaking all hands and kissing a few feminine ones he felt deserving of the honor, an enormously confident little man whose smile sometimes radiated a genuine charm, but which, between greetings, passed under a cloud of serious worry. To Lord Bourne he was completely amiable, conscious that he had been somewhat less so earlier in the day, and even made special amends by kissing Lady Bourne's arthritic knuckles. To Bishop Putzkammer he gave an icily formal salutation which let the prelate know that he did not appreciate his having turned Tessa's wedding ceremony into an occasion to beatify King Wilhelm's quarrel with Napoleon III. The Bishop was conscious of the unspoken reprimand, but, secure in his feeling of sanctimonious patriotism, he brushed it off and strode toward the libations being offered in the Grand Salon.

The last to arrive were Pastor Hess, the Mayor, the Chief Magistrate, and their respective wives, all having been squeezed into the coach at the tail end of the cortege, according to the strict protocol of Prussian nobility. However, Count Frederick Paul made no discriminations as a host and received them with only slightly reserved affability. After pointing them toward the salons (where they would undoubtedly be unsubtly snubbed by most of their fellow guests), the Count looked back toward the still-open front door and glimpsed Master Prytz standing just outside, water dripping off his cap, his cape sopping and plastered against his body. Brushing aside the footmen who jumped to pop open umbrellas over him, he stepped out on the stoop next to his old stablemaster. "You look half-drowned," he told him; then taking a deep breath of the damp salty air, he added: "But at least not suffocating like I am."

Prytz straightened his aching back and gave the Count a military salute as he always did. "It's a bit damp, Your Excellency, but nothing to bother about. You mustn't worry about me."

"Why should I worry about a man who takes brides on cross-country gallops a couple of hours before they are to be married?" Prytz stiffened a little but did not answer. The tone had been sarcastic, yet without the slashing anger with which the formidable little Count could shrivel any man in the county. "Since you and my daughter are so inseparable," he continued, "and since her new husband is about to ride into a war where he'll likely get himself killed, I have decided to give you to her. Get yourself some food and drink, then pack up and be ready to leave."

Master Prytz's eyes seemed to glaze over and his Adam's apple began bobbing over the soaked edge of his collar. His lips moved, but no words came out.

"Well, what about it?" Count Frederick prodded him. "If you are worried about Feldteufel, *my* best stallion as well as your favorite mount . . . then I'll make him a present to you. Ride him to Silesia and see if you can improve their stock with a good sire from Schloss Varn's stables. All right? As a widower you can hardly have anything else tying you down here. Not *me*, that's for damned certain."

Master Prytz found his voice and it came out surprisingly steady: "Your Excellency, the Lady Anna Marie Theresa spoke to me about this same matter this morning and made it very clear she did not desire such an arrangement."

Count Frederick looked pensive for a moment, then moved

himself and his stablemaster over the threshold to get away from a wind-driven splatter of rain. Suddenly he reached out and made him bend down to catch his almost furtive whisper: "I am really asking you to do this for my sake rather than hers, Prytzie. I'm not making it a command. It's a favor I'm begging of you."

"I will go with her, Your Excellency," Prytz answered with gruff emotion.

"Then get ready!" the Count ordered in his normal tone of voice, giving him a strong shove down the steps toward the stables. "Change your clothes and have some hot food before you catch a fever. You're no good to me dead." He remained in the doorway, watching the old man run down the gravel drive with slightly unsteady steps, and when he was well out of ear-shot called softly after him: "Be off and go with God, my Prytzie." He was about to turn and walk back into the castle when he heard the sound of approaching hoofbeats, making him pause and wonder whether there was still another carriage full of guests due to arrive. He was surprised to see five horsemen come riding up, four dragoons led by Rittmeister von Manschott.

The Count waited for the officer to dismount, hand the reins of his horse to one of the troopers, and come up the steps to the door. He had changed into his field uniform and wore a pistol as well as a saber on his belt. "Well, what is this all about?" the Count asked. "I thought you and your men were in a hurry to return to your regiment and protect us against the blood-thirsty French."

Von Manschott saluted. "Yes, Your Excellency. I have sent all but these four back." With a sidelong glance at the footmen who were still standing around the entrance, he lowered his voice to a whisper: "Could I have a brief word with Your Excellency, please?"

"Why not? All I have to occupy me for the moment is a wedding party of sixty-four guests." Taking von Manschott by the arm and steering him to a secluded corner of the foyer, he asked: "What is it, Herr Rittmeister."

The dragoon officer kept his voice very low. "As painful as it is, I must come straight to the point, Your Excellency. There are a number of high Austrian guests in your castle, one of them a general with the Imperial Staff. It is possible that Austria may join France in her war against us. In which case these guests will become our enemies."

Count Frederick looked up into his face with a cold glint in his eyes. "Do you have official orders to deal with this danger-ous situation, Herr Rittmeister?"

"I doubt whether my commanding officer is even aware of it, so I am acting under my own initiative in putting myself and my detachment at your disposal in case of a critical dilemma."

"My brother-in-law General Baron Piednich did not bring his army with him, Herr Rittmeister, so the dilemma could hardly become a military one."

"It would if he and his attending officers escaped, Your Excellency."

"Oh, you propose to detain them?"

If von Manschott was aware of the Count's biting tone, he ignored it and bluntly answered: "If it becomes necessary."

Count Frederick wondered whether he should have worn his colonel's uniform after all, but remembered that officers of the regular army looked with contempt upon those of the Land-wehr. Still he refused to be intimidated and resorted to his most sarcastic manner: "If your war should happen to break out un-der my roof, Herr Rittmeister, I don't think you will find us either outnumbered or outranked. Like my Austrian brother-in-law, the Prince Eugene is a general. . . ."

"A Hanoverian," von Manschott pointedly injected.

". . . Who has given his oath of allegiance to our Confedera-tion," the Count forcefully continued. "My wife's cousin is an Austrian colonel, but then I believe I am a Prussian one. Her nephew, who is a leutnant, is matched by my new son-in-law, who holds a similar rank in your own regiment. So you see, we shall be very evenly matched as long as civilized rules of conduct are observed, *which,*" he added with a threatening rise in his voice, "are the only kind I shall tolerate."

Von Manschott nodded but said with dour obstinacy: "I would like to remain at Your Excellency's beck and call."

"You may remain as a guest who respects the codes of hospitality ruling this house."

"I am certain we live by the same codes," von Manschott answered with a chill in his voice. "I am distressed that I have to bring this to Your Excellency's attention."

"What? You claim to live by the same codes as I?" the Count contemptuously asked. "Or the fact that I have Austrian rela-tions here? In either case it does not matter a snap to me, Herr Rittmeister. You may join us in the drawing rooms after you have removed your weapons and wet overthings and continue your function as best man at this wedding—*not* that of some kind of self-appointed military proconsul." Without bothering to tell him that he and Prince Eugene had discussed the Aus-trian problem earlier that morning, he stalked off to join his other guests.

If Count Frederick Paul was being somewhat parsimonious with the wedding of his younger daughter, it was only relatively speaking, and there were no tangible signs of it in the sumptuous feast being served in the Great Hall of Schloss Varn. Of course, the banquet table was not extended to its full capacity of eighty-eight, but sixty-eight settings were laid out in glittering formal precision which matched the splendor of the wealthier guests. Crystal sparkled like the diamonds of the Austrian ladies, gold and silver plate shone like the medals encrusting many male chests. In front of the bride's and groom's places in the center of the table stood a pair of jeweled Byzantine goblets pillaged by some ancestral von Beckhaus warrior. Twelve liveried waiters served the nine-course wedding breakfast under the watchful generalship of Knabel. It was, in fact, a display of unusual opulence, even for high Prussian nobility, and while the Austrian branch of the family attended the gilded von Beckhaus troth with a suitably blasé attitude, some of the lesser Junkers could not help giving vent to ungracious jealousy. Like the one who surreptitiously whispered in his neighbor's ear: "Our dear Frederick Paul has certainly profited handsomely by associating himself with Rothschild rather than von Moltke."

"Yes, indeed. Railroads and horses. Both important to the military, so he claims . . . but just the same, somehow improper for the head of one of our great families."

"Un-Prussian, one might even say. Decadence must inevitably follow."

Conversation was sporadic at first, rippling up and down the long table in stiffly polite exchanges interspersed with ruder noises from those who had not adopted French etiquette in their manner of drinking consommé. Tessa and Gustaf sat next to each other, yet with an invisible wall between them which their strained half-smiles could not breach. Tessa's expression gradually congealed into one of grim forbearance as the Dowager Baroness Piednich repeatedly nodded at them, cackling, "Dear, dear, lovely lovers." As they finished the soup, Count Frederick rose to make the first of the prescribed round of toasts: "I bid all my friends and relations to raise their glasses to the bride, my beloved daughter, and her new husband, Leutnant Baron Gustaf von Falkenhorst, whom I herewith heartily welcome into our family!" He spoke the words formally, but as if he genuinely meant them, and his smile only momentarily clouded over a contrapuntal sob from his wife. The rafters echoed with the rumble of sixty-eight chairs as everyone rose to drink long life and happiness to the newlyweds, the Dowager Baroness Piednich fussing behind the rest as she struggled to her feet. Tessa remained seated, as did Gustaf, staring down at her plate, grateful that her father had entirely omitted the customary long speech.

After this, led by the more garrulous and uninhibited Austrians, the party began losing some of its stiffness. A good Moselle helped loosen tongues over the fish course and the next toast to the bride and groom, given by her Uncle Franz, the Austrian general, was preceded by a gracious and mildly witty speech about the joys of matrimony which, nevertheless, failed to put Tessa at her ease. During the fowl (stuffed partridge), there was general banter about the wedding and the usual good-natured (yet, insidiously cruel) chiding of the newlyweds. However, that subject was soon exhausted and inevitably war talk began to take over the conversation—to Tessa's great relief and her father's intense annoyance. It was Rittmeister von Manschott's duty as best man to propose the next toast, and in spite of the host's warning coughs, he did so with a long preamble which he managed to turn into a paean to the Second Dragoon Guards Regiment. This austere young officer in his field uniform brought a decided turning point in the atmosphere of the party. From then on, the war came first, the wedding a poor second. The Prussians began to dominate the conversation, the groom eagerly joining in, but the father of the bride became taciturn and was barely able to remain polite. Another who did not respond with any degree of enthusiasm was Albrecht von Falkenhorst. Finding himself sandwiched between the Dowager Baroness Piednich and a maiden von Beckhaus aunt, he merely pantomimed sociability while actually devoting most of his attention to the excellent food, the likes of which he fully realized he would not enjoy again for a long, long time. Occasionally his eyes settled on Tessa, and he would pause to study her with guarded interest, but when she noticed his stare, he flashed her a quick excusing smile and resumed eating.

During the meat course (roast venison), Prince Eugene declaimed on the duty of a young Prussian family to King and country, including some oblique references to the duty of Austrian citizens toward the same King and country; he was obviously trying to remove any doubts as to *his* loyalty to the Prussian cause.

Most surprising, and most appreciated by those who could understand English, was a speech by Lord Bourne: "A Napoleon seems to be on the march again," he told the party, "and it is time to remember old friends and brothers-at-arms who defeated the progenitor of that breed in the early years of this century. I know that I speak for the majority of my countrymen and our House of Lords, of which I am a member, when I say that England has no intention of standing idly by while continental Europe is threatened by a new Bonaparte hegemony. French aggression, whether revolutionary or imperialist by nature, must finally, and for all time, be stopped from upsetting the order and tranquility of civilized society. My lords, ladies, and gentlemen, let us drink to His Majesty King William I and the triumph of his forces in their just struggle." He beamed as everybody jumped to his feet and drank the toast with nearly raucous enthusiasm. When his eyes fell on Gustaf and Tessa, he exclaimed a belated addendum to his effort: "Let us also drink to a splendid young Prussian officer and his bride, a couple in which His Majesty will certainly come to take great pride."

No sooner had the company reseated itself when Prince Eugene brought them back to their feet with an answering toast to England and Queen Victoria: ". . . our beloved cousin-monarch! May the friendship between our two countries endure forever!"

Then Bishop Putzkammer gave the longest speech of all, almost a repeat of his long-winded prayer in church, but this time including some bigoted comparisons between Prussian Lutheranism and French Catholicism. "This must by nature become a holy war," he thundered, "in which the simple purity of our faith will be tested against a decadent one repeatedly corrupted by French tyrants." The effect of his exhortation was slightly compromised by an apology from Count Frederick Paul to the Piednichs present at the table, themselves subjects of a Catholic monarchy. Whereupon the Bishop sourly remarked that while the Piednichs represented a small Protestant minority in Austria, he hoped the day would soon come when the whole country threw off the papist yoke.

The food kept coming, platter upon platter; the wine flowed, red, white, and sparkling gold. When the magnificent wedding cake had been cut, it came time for Gustaf to raise his glass to his new bride. Count Frederick cringed before the prospect of another bellicose speech, this one probably the worse for an immature and narrow military intellect, but he was to be surprised by its succinct brevity:

"I wish to thank you all for these honors," Gustaf said, standing stiffly erect, yet not quite at attention. "I thank you on behalf of my father, who fell on the battlefield of Sadowa four years ago. So that these honors may be well deserved, I swear to you, as I have already done to my King and country, that the family of von Falkenhorst will continue true to their duty and tradition. It will be easier for me to make good this promise with the addition to that family of its newest member, the Baroness Marie Theresa von Falkenhorst. To her I now raise my glass— to my radiant bride!"

Tessa stared up at him with an expression which everyone

mistook for stunned adoration, then turned her face downward to the crumbled piece of cake on her plate with what they thought to be comely humility.

"To Baroness Marie Theresa von Falkenhorst, the radiant bride!" they echoed, and the din of their chorused shout and the sound of their laughter was a mocking noise in Tessa's ears. They did not sit down again. The wedding banquet was over.

Tessa returned to her apartment on the second floor of Schloss Varn for a last time, to change into the brown-and-yellow traveling dress she was to wear on her trip to Silesia. Her trunks had been packed by maids and carried downstairs by footmen. Only one suitcase remained with her toiletries and lingerie. The closets were bare, the drawers empty, her dressing table cleared of all her little personal knickknacks. There was already a lonely, forlorn feeling about the room. The window still rattled with raindrops and the wind still made melancholy sounds in the tall pine trees outside.

As she wriggled out of her wedding gown and turned it over to a maid to be folded up for some as yet unborn Beckhaus or Falkenhorst bride to wear next, her mother came in to pay a final visit. "Oh, dear me," she cried, fluttering her inevitable white lace handkerchief, which she seemed to use as a perennial signal of capitulation. "Everything was absolutely prefect. So don't worry, dearest girl. Don't worry at all."

"Then for heaven's sake stop weeping, Mama," Tessa edgily exclaimed.

The thoroughly conditioned maids discreetly vanished from the boudoir into the adjoining sitting room.

Countess von Beckhaus und Varn dabbed at the tears in her bloodshot eyes. "Yes, yes, I must stop crying," she sobbed in her soft Austrian dialect. "I know how silly it is for me to try to bolster your courage when I have none of my own. I have failed you. I have failed your father. I am the weakling in the family. Not him. Not you. Me!" The handkerchief waved in desperation. "But I have tried my best, God be my witness. I have tried to prepare you for this marriage."

Tessa was standing in her petticoat and bodice, staring

down at the pink-ribboned cotton nightgown folded into her open suitcase. "Yes, Mama. When you finally got around to it last night, you prepared me very thoroughly. I remember every word."

Her mother gave a shocked little shriek and hoarsely whispered: "Oh, no, Tessa! I wasn't referring to ... to the *animal* part so much as ... well, marriage as such, you know. I've tried to set you a good example. I've tried. ..."

"Yes–yes, Mama!" Tessa sharply interrupted her. "Yes, you've tried, I know. But there is one more thing you should tell me if I'm to follow yours and Papa's good example in marriage."

"Why certainly, dearest Tessa. Just ask."

"For how long did you have to sleep with him? How long before you were free to move into your own bedroom with a lock on the door."

The Countess von Beckhaus's face went through a confusion of expressions ranging from pique to despair, then settled into one of resigned misery. Her daughter's question had wounded her deeply, but she also sensed the suppressed anguish which it revealed. "You were too young to understand such things," she answered with a frantic flutter of the handkerchief, "but it was Papa who left *me* to sleep in another part of the castle."

Tessa looked surprised, then bluntly asked: "But you were pleased, weren't you, Mama?"

Countess von Beckhaus shook her head so violently that the mouse-gray curls flew around it. "No. I was ashamed and lonely. I still am." She dropped onto the edge of the bed and appeared ready to collapse completely. "God help us, but we haven't really set any kind of example at all, have we? Except perhaps in keeping up pretenses. I beg you to try to love your husband, my poor Tessa. I beg you to try. For a woman without love, life becomes a meaningless drudgery."

Tessa stared at her mother with a perplexed expression, then reached out and patted her moist cheek with a gesture meant to be tender, but which was merely awkward. "Please, Mama dear, don't carry on so. You were pretty but weak, so it can't come out the same ... I mean, well ... I know I'm ugly but strong and won't let it."

"You are *not* ugly!" her mother wailed. "Oh, why, why can't you be like your sister and accept things the way they are?"

"Esther is pretty too, but ..."

"You simply must try not to be hard like your father!" Suddenly she reached out and clasped Tessa tightly, kissed her, and held her for a long moment before letting go. Then she got up and said: "I can't bear to see you leave, my dearest one, so forgive me if I say good-bye to you now. I would only make a fool of myself if I tried to do it downstairs in front of everybody. You know how angry your papa gets when I can't control myself." She hugged her daughter once more before fleeing the room with a last farewell flutter from her soggy handkerchief as she went through the door.

Before calling the maids back to help her dress, Tessa wiped her mother's tears from her face. There were none of her own.

Besides Countess von Beckhaus und Varn, there were a number of others in the wedding party who would not wait to see the bride and groom off on their honeymoon. They were guests who had to heed the mobilization order and report immediately to their regular regiments or Landwehr units—or at least that was their excuse. After saying good-bye to those people, Count Frederick Paul mingled with the remaining crowd in the Grand Salon, noting with irritation that his wife had again abandoned her duties as hostess. There was war talk all around and he quickly sought refuge in the library, impulsively inviting Albrecht von Falkenhorst to join him, and found Prince Eugene, General Baron Piednich, and Lord Bourne sipping brandy in this more-intimate atmosphere. Here, too, the talk was of war and politics—spoken in French for the benefit of the Englishman—but less bombastic and more succinct.

"Napoleon is clearly the aggressor," Prince Eugene was saying, his bemedaled bulk sprawled in the Count's favorite chair. "But I have little doubt Bismarck tricked him into it."

"Too bad Napoleon is that stupid," Count Frederick said. "As to our Bismarck, he has intrigued against our own King to create a *casus belli* out of a Hohenzollern family matter. I don't trust him."

"Now you must trust your General von Moltke," General Piednich drily observed. "As we Austrians have good reason to know, he will not likely let you down."

"Allow me to point out to you, dear brother-in-law," the Count acidly retorted, "that this time von Moltke will be facing French, not Austrian, troops. Even you extracted so many casualties as price of victory at Sadowa that His Majesty burst into tears when he viewed the battlefield afterwards."

Lord Bourne chuckled. "But surely he stopped weeping when so many German states were united under his crown."

"They will fly the Hohenzollern coop quickly enough if we lose this war," the Count answered with a wry glance at Prince Eugene. "Forgive me for mentioning the possibility in spite of your inspiring speech about not permitting us to lose it."

"I suggested rather, sir, that England will not permit Napoleon to win."

Count Frederick Paul regarded the Englishman through narrowed eyes. "It is true that your queen is conscious of her German blood ties. But on the other hand, her son, the Prince of Wales and heir to the throne, has been openly hostile to Prussian interests since our war with Denmark. He is more influenced by his Danish Princess than his Queen Mother, obviously." He impatiently waved off the polite objection which was formulating on Lord Bourne's lips. "The fundamental question, my lord, is simply this: Would England accept *German* domination of Europe if by some stroke of luck we managed to smash France?"

When Lord Bourne pursed his lips and hesitated, Prince Eugene quickly injected: "We have no more intention of smashing France than we did of smashing Austria four years ago. Our main objective must be to remove Napoleon as sovereign and replace him with a legitimate one who's compatible with the royal houses of Europe. A Bourbon, naturally."

"A Bourbon!" Albrecht von Falkenhorst suddenly snorted in open contempt. "The French have a habit of sticking Bourbon heads into guillotines. Bourbons attract revolutions like rot attracts pestilence." Too late did he remember that Prince Eugene's maternal grandmother had been a Bourbon princess, and found himself facing a royal scowl. Lord Bourne and General Baron Piednich also regarded such outspoken opinions from a mere Heidelberg student with disapproval, but Count Frederick had some trouble hiding a smile. Then the door to the library opened and Tessa came in wearing her hat and overcoat.

She hesitated after crossing the threshold, saying: "I am sorry to disturb you. I only came to say good-bye to Papa."

The Prince heaved himself out of his chair with a broad smile: "But of course, Baroness. We were only chatting over a glass of brandy. Turning into downright flippant chatter, I may say. We will gladly leave you and your father for a few minutes alone together. So come along, gentlemen. Let's go prepare a proper send-off for our bride and groom." His smile returned to a haughty scowl as he lumbered past Albrecht, leading the others out of the library. The young von Falkenhorst ignored him, keeping his eyes on his new sister-in-law. Before leaving, he stepped up to her and said with a grin: "I have been terribly outranked and outshone on this festive occasion, my dear Tessa. Anyway, I'm not much good at speeches and formalities. So please allow me to welcome you into our fold in my own simple way." Before she could react, he suddenly brushed a kiss against her cheek, not a quick polite peck, but rather deliberately and tenderly. It was the first time she had ever been kissed by any man outside of her immediate blood relations.

After he left, Count Frederick chuckled. "He has impudence and he has brains. I think I shall like him. You must cultivate his friendship, Tessa."

"Yes, Father," she answered and passed lightly with her gloved hand over the spot where his lips had touched her cheek.

The Count looked at his daughter and the troubled expression returned to his face. His lips moved as if trying to silently rehearse something he wanted to say to her, but only succeeding in drawing out the painful silence between them. They both knew this meeting would be little different from all the rest, no matter how much each of them might want to understand the other. "Do you feel any happiness at all?" he blurted out at last.

"I can't really describe what it is I feel, Papa," she replied, looking him straight in the eyes.

"Are you afraid?"

"No, Papa."

"Good." He turned away from her and began to pace back and forth in front of the hearth, his hands clasped together and working in a nervous washing motion. "You are not like your mother in that respect. More like me. We are sometimes perplexed by events which overtake us, you and I, and sometimes do not cope with them correctly. But we never succumb to fear. In the end we prevail. I am sure this marriage will be a credit to both the von Beckhaus and von Falkenhorst families. Believe me, it was no impetuous or second choice to be rid of a difficult daughter, but the most carefully considered and best alliance I could arrange for you. Yes–yes . . . I know your mother has probably filled you with romantic twaddle about love. I hope you come to realize that love takes other forms of expression besides those made popular by French and English novelists." He suddenly stopped his pacing and wheeled on her. "I love my family, you know. Therefore I love *you*, my Tessa."

"Yes, Papa," she answered in the measured, flat tone which was her only defense against the peculiarly logical approach he always used in a potentially emotional situation. "But what about Mama? Do you love her too?"

"Your mother was the most beautiful woman I have ever known in my life," he answered without hesitation and with an intensity which betrayed long-sublimated passion. "The most charming and gay and frivolous and unreal fairy princess in all Europe. I fell madly in love with her, married her, and—God forgive me—destroyed her." Checking himself, he wagged a finger at Tessa and exclaimed: "That was a damned impertinent question, Theresa. We shall both forget you ever asked it."

"I shall remember the answer," she quietly replied.

"I never gave it to you," he snapped, then, turning from her, went to his desk and drew a sealed envelope from a drawer. "I want you to put this in your purse. It is a draft for five thousand thalers on the Rothschild bank in Frankfurt, made out in your favor and entirely apart from your dowry. As your husband may resent your having money beyond his control, keep it a secret between us. Use it most discreetly if you ever think it becomes absolutely necessary."

She took the envelope, stared at it for a moment before slipping it into her purse, then whispered barely audibly: "Thank you, Papa."

"Very well, daughter. I suppose your Gustaf is waiting impatiently, so we had better not keep him any longer." He took her by the arm but did not lead her toward the door. Instead he held her for a moment, looking into her face with sadness. "Yes, there are many expressions of many kinds of love," he told her. "Of these, there are two I pray you never come to experience, Tessa. Love motivated by senseless passion and that maintained by guilty pity. Let us go."

he foyer of Schloss Varn was crowded with guests who, for the moment, forgot the war and turned their full attention upon the departing honeymooners. The press was increased by a group of grooms, gamekeepers, and tenant farmers who, coming to serenade the pair, had mercifully been brought in out of the rain; their strong merry voices bellowed out "In the Springtime of Our Love" when Tessa appeared on the arm of her father. Gustaf von Falkenhorst had changed into a field uniform and had been waiting alongside of Rittmeister von Manschott; he now stepped forward and, taking his bride by the hand, began edging toward the door. The bridesmaids swirled around them, all a'twitter as they scattered rose petals in their path. Farewells and well-wishes were shouted. Somebody stepped on the Dowager Baroness Piednich's toe, and she let out a raucous shriek. Prince Eugene boomed: "Long live the house of von Falkenhorst!" Bishop Putzkammer admonished the Almighty with a stentorian voice: "God bless them and make them fruitful!" The singers switched to a rousing rendition of *"Preussen Glorias."* Gustaf kept exclaiming "thank you . . . thank you" over and over, shaking as many of the outstretched hands as he could reach.

Tessa tried to smile but had a sudden frantic feeling which she knew really *was* fear. Glancing around the flushed laughing faces, she hoped that her mother had come down after all, yet knew she most certainly was lying on her bed upstairs, weeping. She had a last glimpse of her father, who was not even looking at her, but had pulled von Manschott aside and was speaking to him in a belligerent whisper. Then she was propelled over the threshold and yanked down the steps toward the coach by a suddenly hurried Gustaf, who kept mumbling thank you to the string of footmen passing a protective umbrella over their heads. The drizzly sunset filled the castle yard with an eerie, yellowish light. A moment before being literally shoved into the coach, she had a glimpse of Prytz seated on Feldteufel and holding a saddleless Kanone Kugel by a lead rein. "Prytzie!" she called to him in anguish. "Prytzie, please come! Please!" Her cry was drowned out by the tumult of their send-off, and she did not catch the old stablemaster's reassuring nod.

The coachman's whip cracked over the four snorting grays, and the carriage jerked forward, crunching through the wet gravel. The sound of singing, turning garbled by shouted farewells from the party clustered under the protection of the roof, began to fade away. After they passed through the gate, there was only the splash of hooves and wheels churning through the puddles which filled the ruts of the road between Varnmunde and Kolberg. Tessa did not look back.

After several minutes, Gustaf made exactly the same observation he had on their return from church: "I think everything went quite well, Theresa."

She nodded, keeping her eyes on the misty twilight of the fens. "Yes, but I'm glad it's over."

His hand patted hers, more an admonishing tap than a caress. "Mind you, we have been highly honored by it all."

"I suppose so."

"I am very pleased over the dignity with which you discharged your duties, my dearest."

She swiveled her head around and looked into his face with a flash of amazement. It seemed to disconcert him, and he stammered: "I hope I did as well."

"My father is very pleased with you, I'm sure," she told him.

"He is an extraordinary man," he said in a tone which was more puzzled than admiring.

The next two kilometers were traveled in a silence which oppressed them both. Then, as they reached the crossroad to Kolberg, they heard the swelling sound of hoofbeats. Gustaf peered back through the coach window. "My goodness! It's von Manschott and his detachment of dragoons." He yanked down the window and shouted outside with unconcealed excitement: "What is this? A special escort?"

Tessa saw von Manschott's horse draw alongside, its muscles rippling as it pranced. The dragoon Captain leaned down toward the window, his face unsmiling. "His Excellency released me to rejoin the regiment," he shouted. "If we are not intruding on your privacy, we shall escort you as far as the turnoff to the railway yards at Wolin. There we entrain for the front."

Gustaf nodded and slumped back in his seat, his jaw set, his lips pressed together. As darkness settled over the countryside, his mood became more brooding and withdrawn, and Tessa made no attempt to alleviate it. Her own was scarcely better as she thought of how each turn of the wheels was taking her closer to the inn at Kolberg and the part of the wedding she dreaded most. She felt a momentary pang of relief when they rolled around a sharp curve and she spotted Master Prytz trotting along behind the last dragoon trooper with her beloved Kugel on a lead. So Prytzie was accompanying her after all. Thank God! Yet, what good could he do her tonight? Or tomorrow night? Or ever? The rebellious young girl and the steadying, kindly old man had had their bonds severed on this day. Perhaps it had already been accomplished during that silly spat on the beach that morning, but in any case, it was now final. As a married woman and the Baroness von Falkenhorst she would not be able to confide in him any more, let alone ask his protection in the presence of her husband. He might as well have remained at Schloss Varn where his father and grandfather had served the von Beckhaus family before him. It was *his* home she was tearing him away from—and for what purpose? Tears suddenly brimmed her eyes and she was about to pull down the window and yell to him to go back when Gustaf's hand closed over her arm, this time firmly with a kneading, pulsing grip:

"You are a strong, brave girl, I know, Theresa," he said haltingly with a pained mixture of determination and embarrassment. "I hope you will understand what must take place on this our wedding night."

She stared at him, her eyes wide, her lips reduced to a fleshy trembling. "I think I know what to expect, Gustaf."

"You do?" he asked with a relieved surprise. The grip on her arm turned into a fitful stroking of her sleeve. "Well, thank you for that, my dearest. And forgive me for not having the faith I should have shown my wonderful new wife. I can only plead the urgency of the military obligation of my family as an excuse for my clumsiness. You see, my father had to wait until he was over fifty years old before he could prove himself in battle. But I now have that opportunity at twenty-two. Please, dear Theresa, understand what this means to me as the only soldier left in our family."

She let out a startled gasp, then her head began to nod in agreement, a smile began spreading over her face, the first genuine one all day. "Yes–yes, Gustaf! I understand. Understand completely. It means your duty as a soldier must come before all else."

Before answering her, he leaned out the window and shouted to the coachman an order to stop the carriage. "That is exactly right, Theresa," his hold on her arm shifting to her hands, which he began crushing in his own. "You will be my prize and my booty which I will claim only after acquitting myself with honor. I am calling on your own courage as well as mine. Hard as it is, it must be so!"

Her smile almost turned to laughter, but he could not see that in the very dim interior of the coach. "Yes, Gustaf! Go with your regiment!"

"My mother will greet you at Glaumhalle. You will explain my absence to her."

"Certainly. And don't worry. I will manage the trip very nicely with Master Prytz to help me."

He drew a tremendous sigh of relief. "Splendid, my dearest! I will take your horse. It is a magnificent animal which will remind me of you and bring me luck."

"My horse? My Kanone Kugel?" Tessa exclaimed with a strident note of shock in her voice. Quickly recovering herself, she agreed with considerably dampened enthusiasm. "Very well, then. Take him. But I will miss him."

"Thank you, my Theresa." With an impetuous, boyish action, he yanked her to him and put a hard, dry kiss on the exact spot on her cheek where his brother's lips had touched a couple of hours earlier. Then he threw open the door and jumped down onto the muddy road.

Rittmeister von Manschott had halted his dragoons behind the carriage and now asked with some impatience: "What is the matter, Gustaf?"

"Nothing, except that I am reporting for active duty as of now, Herr Rittmeister," Gustaf told him, then called out to one of the troopers: "You will remove your saddle and reins. Put them on the animal being led by the Baroness's servant. You will ride your own horse bareback to the depot in Wolin."

Von Manschott did not countermand the order, but there was a sarcastic tinge in his high-pitched voice when he asked: "What is the matter with you? Have you had a lover's quarrel already?"

"The Baron and I have agreed he must rejoin his regiment immediately," Tessa interjected, also climbing out of the coach. "He can't be left behind when the rest of you ride off to war."

"Couldn't the war do without him for a couple of days?" von Manschott inquired.

"It is I who cannot do without it," Gustaf firmly replied. He did not spend the few minutes it took to saddle up Kanone Kugel with Tessa, but walked back to where Master Prytz remained stonily seated on Feldteufel. "I charge you with the safety of my wife on her trip to my home in Silesia," he told the stablemaster. "You will proceed to Kolberg where you will spend the night. From there you will return the coach to Schloss Varn and take the first train to Breslau where you will be met and conducted to Glaumhalle. Understood?"

"I have already been charged with the safety of the Baroness and know what to do, Herr Leutnant Baron," Prytz answered with cold politeness. He did not at all approve of what was taking place, but Gustaf was too preoccupied to notice as he handed him a thin, rather frayed leather wallet, saying: "Here is enough money to take care of your meals, tickets, and lodgings along the way. I expect you to handle such things for the Baroness, Herr Stallmeister."

"Of course, Herr Leutnant Baron," Prytz agreed and, giving the wallet an almost contemptuous glance, tucked it away inside his soaked raincape. "The Baroness will want for nothing, you may be sure."

Gustaf swung into Kugel's saddle, and when the horse felt the unfamiliar rider mounting him, he reared and spun. But Gustaf quickly brought him under control with the firm, hard hands and legs of a seasoned cavalryman, then trotted up to Tessa where she stood by the coach. She thought he was going to kiss her again as he leaned down to her with a happy smile, but his mouth was only seeking her ear for a quick parting whisper:

"Remember, you will be my prize and my booty when I return, beloved! For that day I will fight to the last! *Auf Wiedersehen!*"

Tessa reached out, not for him, but for a farewell caress on Kugel's glossy, arching neck. It was a very fleeting touch of her gloved hand before Gustaf spurred out of reach and was cantering off without a backward glance along the road to Wolin. The troopers fell in behind him, giving her curious, puzzled glances as they passed. Rittmeister von Manschott paused for a moment, looking almost angry as he blurted out: "Well, it may be a very short war, Baroness. The last one with Austria lasted exactly six weeks, so this one should be over before winter sets in. Long wars are a thing of the past."

Tessa caught herself from laughing and exclaiming: "Take your time! Make it a good, long one!" Instead she managed a demure "Thank you, Herr Rittmeister, for your concern. I shall be quite all right."

Von Manschott gave a peculiar grunt and a snappy salute, then hurried after his vanishing column of dragoons. Tessa remained standing there staring after them, and just before they were swallowed up in the drizzly twilight, she shouted: "You take good care of my Kugel, you hear! Good care!"

There was no answer except some mournful whistling calls from loons winging low over the marshlands.

Master Prytz walked Feldteufel up alongside the coach and stared down at her, his face contorted with emotion. "Oh, my God, I wish I could comfort you, Baroness Tessa," he exclaimed in a low, anguished voice.

She looked up at him, smiling as the raindrops ran over her freckled face. "You can, Prytzie. Tie poor old Feldteufel to a lead and join me in the coach. Both you and he need a rest after a very hard day. Come on, Prytzie! We are off to Silesia, just you and I alone. You and I alone, just like in the good old days!"

August 1870

Vionville

Prince Eugene of Hanover was among the few generals on either side of the Franco-Prussian War who suspected there would be a great battle on this day. This was in some respects surprising because the Prince was not supposed to be concerned with battles as such, but rather their feeding with human and animal fodder; in another respect it was not so surprising since he possessed a genuine military talent despite his unsoldierly corpulence (which to his dismay had actually increased during the course of a brief three weeks of campaigning and two violent battles). The Prince had what his French enemy called *coup d'oeil* for a tactical situation as well as an astute appreciation of the overall strategic one—a rare combination even among generals. He might have made a fine warrior-king if the Hohenzollerns had left him a kingdom to inherit, or he would have made a shrewd corps commander if his Prussian overlords did not take his royal heritage more seriously than his military one. As it was, they even resented his presence in the van of their armies advancing into Lorraine and suspected his motives in insisting on making his commission more than a symbolic sinecure from Royal Headquarters. King Wilhelm I had been polite to him there, as had Crown Prince Frederick and the Chief of the General Staff, Helmuth von Moltke. But others had found ways of reminding him of their suspicions. Now the Prince was on top of a hill overlooking the open farmlands surrounding the lovely Lorraine village of Vionville—where was bivouacked, as if it were on peacetime maneuvers, an entire French cavalry division.

Prince Eugene was, of course, not alone on this grassy knoll topped by a shading cluster of oaks. He had with him what he jokingly referred to as "my staff," a single adjutant and one orderly, respectively a detached, overaged Landwehr captain and his personal valet whom he had connived into uniform for the duration of hostilities and thus had the state take over his modest salary. Anton, the valet, had initially gone along with the arrangement with a docile enthusiasm, anticipating an easy job that carried with it considerable military prestige within his particular milieu; so had Hauptmann Krindle, who in peacetime filled the dual position of postmaster and surveyor for a small Hanoverian township. Both of these worthies had been shocked to find themselves frequently under enemy fire while serving His Royal Highness and spent much of their time, as they were doing at this moment, making themselves as inconspicuous as possible. In a very different way, so did the Prince who never forced his presence upon the field commanders of the Second Army, making a point of keeping himself somewhat apart from their inner councils—yet close enough to gain a good idea of what was going on. Ten feet from where he was sitting on a thronelike stump stood General von Redern, a thrusting cavalry brigadier, contemplating the French encampment like a wolf contemplating a fold of sheep. By his side was the division commander, General von Rheinbaben, an officer who was more fox than wolf. Ranged behind them was their coterie of staff officers, couriers, and color sergeants. The silver of helmets and breastplates, the blues and whites and reds of uniforms were set splendidly aglow by the sun now bursting through the morning mists hanging over the eastern hills. The enemy pickets, posted less than a mile away, had to be either blind or afflicted by dawn drowsiness not to spot them.

An argument, or something as close to an argument which protocol would allow, was taking place between the division commander and his cavalry brigadier. Von Redern wanted to sweep down the hill with his entire brigade in an attack which would scatter the French division and cut the Verdun road at Vionville; he wanted to do it immediately while the element of surprise was in his favor and while there was a good prospect of overwhelming what he guessed to be the cavalry spearhead of the French Army before it could call up massive reinforcements. Von Redern was willing and eager to gamble on a shrewd estimate of the enemy's weakness, but his division commander was reluctant to make any move without exact knowledge of their strength: "We might not be facing a spearhead at all," von Rheinbaben pointed out, "but a flanking force which will retaliate with an enveloping counterattack. Don't forget we have outrun our own infantry and that's a fact, not a guess, gentlemen."

"The chances are excellent that this is the van of an army retreating to escape complete encirclement, Your Excellency," von Redern impatiently pleaded. "A solid blow struck now may fool them into believing their worst fears are realized."

"That sounds too pat for me, my dear von Redern," the division commander answered, his helmet glinting brightly as he shook his head. "For my own part, I believe Marshal Bazaine's entire army is concentrated within a few kilometers of where we are standing. That will make upward of 200 thousand men against my single division."

"We have two corps not very far to the south of us, Your Excellency. They will march to the sound of our guns and arrive within two hours at the most."

"Yes, but piecemeal. They'll trickle into a sausage grinder prepared by an alerted French butcher."

"That is a stationary machine which can hardly be efficiently operated by a butcher on the run, Your Excellency," von Redern wryly observed.

"The cavalry division down there hardly looks like it is running, Herr General," von Rheinbaben retorted with annoyance creeping into his voice. "Look how beautifully their tents are aligned! How considerately they are foddering their mounts! And bless me, I do believe I hear a bugle calling the troopers to morning mess!"

"If I have any choice when to attack a Frenchman, it will be when he thinks he's about to enjoy a meal," von Redern growled. The staff chuckled, but he did not.

Prince Eugene heard this polite squabbling between two high Prussian officers whose self-control masked so much frustration and uncertainty, but he took no part in it, pretending to be entirely preoccupied in examining the countryside through his telescope. He knew his advice would not be welcomed by either party, although if he had seen fit to give it, he would have allowed both views certain consideration. There was no doubt in the Prince's mind that the French Army of the Rhine was in full retreat toward Verdun and, therefore, psychologically vulnerable to a bold attack such as von Redern was advocating; he also estimated that after their bloody delaying action at Borny and subsequent funneling of their withdrawal through Metz, only their van could have reached as far as Vionville a mere two days later. Yet, as von Rheinbaben was insisting, the main body of the army could not be far away, probably within eyeshot of this observation point. True, there were no rising clouds of dust to suggest marching formations of troops, but then it was still only a little after six in the morning and they had probably not broken bivouac as yet. Ignoring Vionville for the moment, Prince Eugene aimed his telescope at the nearby hamlet of Flavigny, then at Rezonville, a village a few miles east along the Metz–Verdun road. He noticed that there was more smoke rising out of both communities than would be normal for the breakfast fires of their small populace. There was smoke, too, subtly blended into the haze hanging over the wooded slopes to the northeast of rolling open fields. He thought he caught a flash of red among the trees, perhaps the red trousers of French infantry? But he could only spy a single definite figure of a man out there, a lone peasant working in one of those fields, his scythe winking with each stroke as he stolidly cut hay out of the ripe grass. The Prince whimsically focused his attention on him for a moment and muttered: "You're wasting your time, poor little farmer. Run home and hide before you meet the Grim Reaper who will harvest this land today!"

"We shall bring up our four batteries of horse artillery and bombard the enemy at once," General von Rheinbaben announced, ending the bickering with a direct order. "That will shake their nerves and perhaps prod their supporting units into revealing their positions to us!"

"And ours to them," von Redern grumbled sourly, but so low that his protest was not heard. The staff officers hurriedly ran for their horses, and galloped down the reverse slope of the hill to pass on the order for the bombardment to the brigade hidden in the draw behind it. General von Rheinbaben withdrew at a more dignified pace to rejoin his messtrain for a belated breakfast. Only Prince Eugene and von Redern did not move from their exposed positions on the crest, their own adjutants and orderlies waiting impatiently behind them. The Prince sat for a while longer, staring placidly over the beautiful peaceful vista of the fields and hills of Lorraine, his jowls already gleaming with the sweat which another stifling August day was about to steam out of him in pungent streams. Then he heaved himself to his feet and waddled up alongside the brigadier whose eyes were still burning into the French bivouac as he visualized it being shattered and overrun by a thundering charge. His sharp chin trembled with resentment, his thin lips pressed hard over the profane recriminations he wanted to shout.

"The crux of this situation is to get our infantry here in time," the Prince casually observed.

Von Redern turned and scowled at the fat Hanoverian princeling whose dusty, perspiration-stained green uniform seemed to be straining at every seam and button in an effort to hold together his unsoldierly figure. He did not even wear a helmet, but one of those plain garrison caps which was several sizes too small for his pear-shaped head. The brigadier had never been formally presented to the Prince but had heard some of his junior officers disrespectfully refer to him as "the Royal Pudding." He came close to doing this himself in his edgy temper: "Indeed an astute observation, Your Royal . . . Highness. But the time is *now.*"

Prince Eugene was not put off by the sharp, sarcastic tone. "Whether this battle opens with a cavalry charge or a cannonade may make little difference in the long run," he explained pleasantly. "It is said that war is a game of opportunities in which one must create fresh ones out of those lost."

"Indeed, Your Highness," von Redern sourly repeated and to indicate he was in no mood for platitudes out of military academy classrooms, turned away and strode toward his horse.

"If your division commander will not attack without additional infantry support, then we must quickly bring him some to bolster his resolve," Prince Eugene said, neither pursuing the brigadier nor specially raising his voice. "This could be done while the time is still *now.*"

Von Redern took a few more steps toward his mount, then stopped and faced the Prince. "How?" he asked.

"By loading them into commissary wagons whose cargoes are temporarily dumped along the roadside. I have forty such wagons between here and Thiaucourt. Each one could carry between twelve and eighteen infantrymen. A whole battalion could be delivered fresh and ready to fight in a little over one hour."

"Why did Your Highness not make this suggestion to General von Rheinbaben?" von Redern asked.

Prince Eugene fixed his gaze on a lark soaring with ecstatic trills above his head: "I only just thought of it," he blandly replied. "Anyway, it is an idea which would appeal more to you than to him."

"Well, Your Highness is not under my command. My permission for such a scheme is neither necessary nor proper."

"I need a fast-riding, determined young officer to carry the order back and organize its execution without delay," the Prince said, looking him straight in the eyes.

Von Redern stared back with an expression suggesting a change of attitude toward Prince Eugene as well as an awakening interest in his plan. Suddenly he snapped: "Come with me!" and mounted his horse.

The two generals and their attendants rode down the thinly wooded slope toward the scrubby dell where von Redern's brigade had spent the preceding hours of darkness without unsaddling their horses or setting up bivouac. Prince Eugene had dozed with them, propped against a tree trunk with a smelly, damp blanket wrapped around his body and nothing but a leafy bough overhead to protect him from the threatening summer storms prowling the night. Von Redern had rested in the same manner, but without sleeping at all as he listened to distant thunder, aware that it could mask the sound of cannon fire as well as the stealthy approach of a French patrol. They were both dedicated officers, von Redern and Prince Eugene of Hanover, but there the similarity ended. The lean, hard cavalry brigadier, with sideburns bristling like black wire around his bony jaw, was as restless and full of latent energy as his prancing warhorse; to him, war was a fulfillment of all his purpose in life. The almost-grotesquely corpulent Intendantur General, showing the stodgy impassivity of the very fat as he awkwardly posted along on a huge gray mare, believed rather that war was the means to an important end for himself as well as for his nation —the two being in his own mind quite inseparable. He was in his way just as hard a man as the brigadier. He had, for instance, developed some fearful running saddle sores which stubbornly refused to heal and which he as stubbornly ignored; his feet had become so swollen that his boots would have to be cut off in order to salve his feet in the cool Lorraine brooks, a luxury he denied himself because his spare pair were somewhere far in the rear with his baggage. Unlike most obese people, Prince Eugene had a very high tolerance of pain and discomfort and rarely allowed them to disturb his imperturbable demeanor, an excellent military virtue really, but one which in his case unfortunately deceived many into believing him lethargic, self-contented, and a little slow witted. General von Redern, who was hopelessly prejudiced against any physical handicap not connected with battle wounds, nevertheless sensed a shrewd intelligence and initiative in the Royal Pudding and had decided to take advantage of it. As he trotted down the hill slightly ahead of the Prince of Hanover, he was already fully prepared to try out the unorthodox scheme of horse-carting infantry reinforcements into a fluid line of battle. It might make it possible then, within the next few hours, to hammer the French with cannons, cavalry, and infantry, perhaps turning them in confusion back to the fortress-trap of Metz and cutting them off from Paris. It might work—*if* they could be deceived into believing they had run into major German forces—*if* the Prince's commissary wagons could deliver the men quickly enough—*if* General von Rheinbaben did not procrastinate!

As they reached the scrubby dell in the floor of the valley, the four batteries of horse artillery attached to the cavalry brigade were pulling out with a clatter of cannons and caissons, the pounding hooves and wheels throwing clods of dirt into the air as they drove up the hill. Beneath the trees, three regiments of cavalry waited in concealment, mounted and ready to emerge in close order. Von Redern swung onto the narrow lane which was not much more than a path and reined in by the regimental banner of the Second Dragoon Guards, addressing its commanding officer: "Good morning, Kurt! You may dismount your men while the artillerists perform some target practice against the French encampment beyond that hill."

Colonel von Hardel made a wry grimace. "No attack then?"

"Well, don't entirely give up on it," the brigadier told him, and waited for the Prince to come puffing up alongside him before explaining with only a trace of sarcasm: "His Highness the Prince General of Hanover seems quite certain there will be a good battle here today."

"Yes, I do believe it very likely, gentlemen," the Prince confirmed, smiling affably at the Colonel and several junior officers seated on their horses near him. Suddenly he recognized one of them and his smile broadened: "My dear Baron Gustaf!" he exclaimed. "What a pleasant surprise to see you so soon again. And to find you here in France already. I trust you left your new Baroness comfortably settled in Silesia?"

Leutnant Baron Gustaf von Falkenhorst's face registered something close to shock and turned very red as all eyes focused upon him for a moment: "Good morning, Your Royal Highness," he stammered. "Y-yes, I'm sure Marie Theresa is doing well."

"Excellent! Her father, who is presently with His Majesty's Headquarters, will be delighted to hear this news. Are you well yourself?"

"Very well, Your Royal Highness."

"May we please get on with the campaign," von Redern acidly inquired, then turning to the commander of Second Dragoon Guards, he tersely informed him of the Prince's plan to bring up infantry in commissary wagons and his need of a reliable officer to ride to the rear and set the operation in motion. Von Hardel looked skeptical and annoyed, but twisted around

in his saddle to order an adjutant to pick a man for the assignment.

"I have the greatest confidence in Leutnant Baron von Falkenhorst," Prince Eugene pointedly declared.

Von Hardel immediately protested. "The Leutnant Baron
has been put in command of my Third Squadron. I can't easily
spare him if we are expected to go into action."

"Oh, let him have von Falkenhorst, for God's sake," von
Redern snapped. "If you can't spare one leutnant out of your
whole regiment, Kurt, something must be damned wrong with
your chain of command." With that he wheeled his horse and
cantered off.

Prince Eugene led Gustaf aside to a more-secluded spot
and, taking a writing pad out of his saddlebag, braced it against
the pommel to write out his orders. "Well, then, tell me how you
really have been getting along, my boy," he softly said as he
wrote.

"Very well, Your Royal Highness," Gustaf curtly repeated,
keeping his eyes on the artillery deploying along the crest of the
hill above them.

The Prince caught the resentful inflection. "Ah, so you are
enjoying the war, eh?" he said drily. "Yes, it's heady stuff, this.
One of the dangers in it, quite apart from getting one's head
blown off, is of finding oneself enjoying it too much."

"My only enjoyment is doing my assigned duty with my
regiment," Gustaf replied. "I cannot permit myself any other
for the time being, Your Royal Highness."

Aware that Gustaf hated being taken away from his regiment before an impending battle, the Prince tried to word his
orders in such a way as to make the young officer realize he was
to do more than run a mere courier's errand. *Leutnant Baron von
Falkenhorst is authorized by me*, he was scrawling in pencil, *to
requisition and unload all commissary and ammunition wagons presently between Puxieu and Thiaucourt and use them to transport forward
units of infantry urgently needed to support an attack upon the enemy
forces at Vionville. Any delay caused him in executing his mission may
endanger the outcome of an important battle and will be severely dealt
with.* After a moment's hesitation he signed it: *E. von Hanover,
Major General*, instead of with his usual royal flourish.

After allowing Gustaf to read it, he also gave him verbal
instructions: "I expect you to see to it these orders are carried
out, not just delivered. I leave up to your own judgment how
you handle the infantry commanders, but I don't think they'll
argue much when offered to ride their men into battle rather
than to march them all the way at the double. Don't hesitate to

gallop the wagons or even cut them cross-country if this will gain time. We are counting on you, Baron Gustaf."

"I shall do my best, Your Highness," Gustaf said smartly, but still without any great enthusiasm.

"Then be off! *Glück-sein!*"

As soon as the Leutnant had galloped away, the Prince's adjutant, who had sharp ears but a sluggish mind, moved in and whined: "I could have handled the matter for Your Highness without bothering any officer of a line regiment."

Prince Eugene contemplated him through heavy, half-closed eyes and smiled complacently: "Certainly you could, my good Captain Krindle, but I was saving you for an even more important mission. You know that our main line of advance lies south of this position. All our forces should be urged to turn north as soon as possible. Ride back, Krindle, and tell every commander you meet along the way that a battle is shaping up here. Ride all the way back to Pont-à-Mousson where you should find Royal Headquarters established by now. Tell them Bazaine's army is strung out along the Metz–Verdun road like a migration of gypsies."

Krindle, who had observed no such sight from on top of the hill, looked appalled. "Will His Highness please put these orders in writing too?" he asked, wanting to clear himself from any personal responsibility for such a momentous act as diverting the entire Second Army from its prescribed line of advance.

The Prince sighed and quickly scribbled down his last spoken sentence: *Bazaine's army is strung out along the Metz–Verdun road like a migration of gypsies—Eugene H.* His adjutant accepted the sheet of paper and frowned over its message, but before he could object, Prince Eugene's voice spoke to him with an unusual threatening rumble: "Good-bye, Krindle!" And as if to urge him on his way, the cannons on the hill suddenly roared out their first salvo. Krindle flinched, turned his horse, and cantered down the dusty lane, shaking his head.

As soon as he was gone, Prince Eugene drove his long-suffering mare snorting up the slope and back to his former observation point. Heaving himself out of the saddle, he sank down in elephantine comfort among the daisies and bluebells dancing to the concussion of the cannons, there to watch the effects of von Rheinbaben's opening bombardment in the battle of Vionville.

Sub-lieutenant Victor de Bretagne, the youngest and most precocious junior officer of the Twelfth Imperial Cuirassiers, had just been ordered to leave the breakfast table when a shell from the first German salvo exploded squarely inside the regimental officer's mess tent, blowing it into blood-and coffee-soaked tatters of canvas, sausage, and human shreds. The force of the explosion rolled him head over heels along the ground with such violence that he was for a moment completely stunned, his mind stalling foolishly on its last piece of coherent thought before the tremendous shock, his mouth unconsciously screaming out its bare substance: "TREASON! . . . STUPIDITY!"

With the very momentum of his fall he rolled back up on his feet and stood there reeling, with all the buttons ripped off his tunic and his scarlet breeches torn open at both knees. Then he drunkenly stumbled back toward the bloody shards of the tent, wading right into the carnage, and dazedly exclaimed: "I beg your pardon, *mon colonel* . . . but I meant to say . . . I believe deliberate treason before crass stupidity . . . I mean. . . ." He blinked and tried to rub the dirt and gunpowder cinders out of his eyes and, through the fearful ringing in his ears, thought he heard Colonel Bouchard's high-pitched voice yelling back: "He thinks! Who in hell allows this snotnosed sub-lieutenant to ruin my digestion by *thinking!* Throw the insolent young bastard out!"

There followed an awful vacuum of silence and, as his vision cleared, Victor de Bretagne was startled to see that Colonel Bouchard's intestines were the same purplish gray color as those of the hogs he used to watch being slaughtered on his father's Touraine farm. The voice had only been an imaginary echo of the Colonel's last bad-tempered outburst during his final few seconds of life on earth. "I meant to say, sir," Victor whispered with trembling contrition to the squashed remains of his commanding officer, "that it is easier to cope with treason than stupidity."

There was no answer this time, of course, but the stillness gave way to the rising wail of the next approaching salvo, culminating in a cascade of explosions. Dirt and splinters erupted in brown fountains, and bits of tents fluttered skyward among serpentine fragments of their guy ropes. Horses began to scream, but not as yet the men. Regimental Sergeant Major Rodignolle came bounding through the smoke, the red-checkered napkin he wore to protect his cuirass during meals fluttering from his neck, his bald cranium gleaming like ivory above the sunburn line of his lost helmet. He stopped next to Sub-lieutenant de Bretagne, stared down at the bodies lying in the shambles of the breakfast table, and began to call out their names: "Colonel Bouchard! . . . Major Brieux! . . . Captain Caulbert! . . . Captain Allençon! . . . Lieutenant Feraussin! . . ."

Suddenly realizing he was calling the roll of the dead, he turned on the boy at his side and blurted out his name in utter disbelief: "Sub-lieutenant de Bretagne?"

Victor shook himself and began coming out of his dazed condition. "Yes, Sergeant. I'm the only one left. Me, the snot-nosed insolent young bastard of a sub-lieutenant. All right, then! Have the buglers sound the call to arms. The regiment will immediately evacuate the bivouac area and form up in extended attack formation facing south."

Another salvo howled in and crashed into the camp and now the screams of men mingled with those of frantic horses trying to break away from their pickets.

"Quickly, Sergeant Rodignolle!" the young Sub-lieutenant bawled at the veteran trooper. "Quickly, before panic does more damage than a few surprise cannon balls!"

The Sergeant Major rushed off, shouting for the buglers, but Victor de Bretagne momentarily remained where he was standing, now staring up at the smoking hill crest from where the enemy guns were belching fire. He bitterly recalled that less than twenty minutes ago Lieutenant Feraussin had reported to Colonel Bouchard that suspicious activity had been spotted on that hill, only to be told it was probably their own IV Corps deploying along their flank. So they had sat down to breakfast and now all the officers of the Twelfth Cuirassiers were ingloriously dead. All but one sub-lieutenant, saved by his own impudent challenge of the High Command's conduct of the war and his being ordered from the table like an impertinent schoolboy. Well, now he would have to prove his real worth; the military decisions, even if minor tactical ones, were now entirely up to him. He noticed that the slopes leading up to the German artillery positions were open and not too steep. If there were no enemy infantry defending it, it might be possible to charge up the hill and actually capture those guns. If the other two regiments of the division supported him, the possibility was even excellent. He turned and glanced toward the neighboring encampment just in time to see them receive their first salvos. The Germans were raking the whole division piecemeal, which had to mean they did not have many batteries up there, probably only the horse-artillery of a reconnoitering cavalry brigade. Good! He was closest to the enemy and would lead the charge which the rest of the division was bound to follow up. Victor coolly trotted toward his horse through the crowd of running troopers, only to find that along with most of the other officers' mounts, it had broken its tether and bolted. But Colonel Bouchard's black mare was still there, struggling against the picket lines which had entangled her. He quickly calmed and freed the animal, vaulted into the saddle, and, grabbing up the regimental standard in passing, galloped out into the middle of a freshly mowed field beyond the smoking bivouac. There he stopped with the shells whining over his head and waved the banner in a clear signal to rally around him.

Sergeant Major Rodignolle did his job well and the troopers, all seasoned regulars, overcame their initial confusion to heed the bugle calls piercing the din of the bombardment. They began closing up in ragged squadrons behind their surviving officer, the ranks gradually swelling as stragglers managed to catch their scattered mounts and dash into their places. There were fewer casualties than de Bretagne had feared, but at any moment the German gunners might add to their number if they switched their aim from the encampment to the regiment assembling in the open field. Victor realized the danger and trotted down the lines, ordering the sergeants and corporals to spread their men out. He then placed himself at the head of their surging formations and calmly awaited the last of the stragglers. When Rodignolle galloped up with a bugler, he was told by the battered, bareheaded Sub-lieutenant that their objective was to charge up the hill, overrun and capture the enemy cannons.

"But that means charging up nearly two kilometers of open slopes, *mon lieutenant,*" the Sergeant Major protested.

Victor looked back to see if either of the other two regiments had recovered enough from its surprise to come to his support, but troopers were still scurrying among burning tents or chasing after bolted horses. "Their senior officers must have survived," he wryly muttered to himself, then answered Rodignolle: "The closer we get to the enemy, the safer we'll be. They'll have trouble depressing their pieces to shoot downhill. Sound advance at the trot, attack formation by squadrons!"

The bugler blew the call, strong and clear. Four hundred seventy sabers rattled out of their scabbards and flashed in the smoky morning sunlight. Four hundred seventy horses made the yellow stubble field tremble as they broke into a trot. *"Vive l'Empereur! Vive la France!"* a lone boyish voice yelled out. Four hundred seventy throats echoed the battle cry with a roar, and suddenly the Twelfth Cuirassiers were advancing with perfect discipline and high morale toward the thundering German guns on top of the hill. But their heroic charge was stopped by a colonel from General Forton's staff who came galloping obliquely across their line of advance and reined in his horse in front of Victor de Bretagne. "What the devil is going on here?" he demanded.

Victor impatiently explained the obvious to him. "I am

going to stop the German artillery from bothering our division, *mon colonel.*"

"*You* are!"

"Certainly, since Colonel Bouchard has been killed along with all our other officers. But the regiment and I are ready to fight, as you can see."

The Staff Colonel took a deep breath, rolled his eyes back into his head, then said: "I must relieve you as commanding officer of the Twelfth, my boy, and according to General Forton's plan, order their withdrawal north of Vionville. You may wheel your squadrons about-face!"

Victor de Bretagne's face glowed an angry red beneath the smudges of powder. "You mean more retreat? No counter-attack? We're even to give up Vionville?" Even as he spoke, a ranging shot from the hill burst a hundred yards short of the halted regiment, sending a ripple of nervous prancing through the closest squadron.

"Damn it all, you'll get your men shot to pieces out here, little *sous-lieutenant!*" the Colonel shouted.

"Not I—you, sir!" Victor dared to shout back at him. "It is *you* who stopped a charging regiment in its tracks and turned it into a sitting duck!"

The Staff Colonel came close to falling off his horse out of pure shock. But he was sobered by another German shell which exploded so close that it showered his immaculate uniform with dirt. Closing his eyes to shut out the sight of the insubordinate Sub-lieutenant, he screamed at the startled bugler: "Blow the withdrawal call, damn it! At once!"

The quaking bugler raised his instrument to his lips and blew the call. Fittingly, it ended on a terribly sour note.

As Gustaf von Falkenhorst rode back along the winding lane escorted by a single dragoon corporal whom von Manschott had insisted accompany him, he began to realize how exposed and overextended was the position of General von Redern's brigade. After leaving the German troops hidden in the dell behind the hill, they met no others for several kilometers. Except for the receding rumble of the four batteries bombarding the Vionville encampment, it was all quietly peaceful, yet a quietness holding the sullen threat of ambush. There might be a detachment of *chasseurs* waiting to pounce on them out of that shadowed copse; or a lurking *franc-tireur* could be crouching in the tall grass of that sunny ridge, ready to pick them off with his rifle.

Gustaf's irritation at having been singled out by the Royal Pudding, for what had at first seemed a capricious mission, was giving way to a certain excitement with the understanding of the mission's potential perils and importance. If he felt fear, it was not of being overwhelmed in a glorious encounter with a patrol of French regulars, but rather of being ignominiously shot down, *murdered* by a despised civilian guerrilla whose bullet would most likely strike him from behind. Being as yet entirely innocent of the seasoned professional's cynical outlook on such things, he was sickened by the prospect of being found dead in some foreign ditch with the fatal wound located in the posterior part of his body. Without relaxing his vigilance, he diverted his mind with other thoughts. The totally unexpected encounter with Prince Eugene had inevitably kindled memories of the wedding at Schloss Varn—now a dreamlike event out of the distant past, even if it had really happened only one month ago.

Two weeks earlier he had written Marie Theresa exactly twelve lines, entirely inspired by the handsome offers of two Rittmeisters and a Leutnant Colonel to buy Kanone Kugel from him. He had felt sure she would be flattered to know that three high-ranking Prussian officers coveted her splendid horse and that he, in turn, appreciated the animal enough to turn them down. It never occurred to him to tell her his reasons might have something to do with *sentiment*—simply because they did not. He had quickly found out that Kanone Kugel was by far his most valuable weapon in this war, more so than his saber or his pistol. The magnificent roan gelding not only looked fit for a field marshal, but had flashing speed and tremendous endurance, which made him the ideal mount for this grueling warfare of maneuvering. Because he remembered Tessa's affection for Kanone Kugel and had himself developed a kindred feeling for the horse, he had thought this common interest worthy of a few lines. Now, while holding down the splendid animal to a brisk canter in order to conserve its strength for what might become a very long ride, he suddenly found himself irritated with Marie Theresa for not having answered his letter. Had he been wrong about her? Could she be just another ordinary female with deep feelings for no other animals besides cats and lapdogs?

The corporal, a Pomeranian farmer's son named Johan

Kluge, cantered along behind his leutnant with a doglike fidelity and an acceptance of danger—the result of a very phlegmatic philosophy about his part in the war. If an enemy patrol jumped them, he would fight as well as he knew how and with a much better chance of survival than he had faced at the Battle of Froeshwiller where troopers were trampled to death when they fell off their horses. As for those guerrillas so reviled by the officers, he knew all about that breed through his grandfather who had fought as one against the first Napoleon and who, in spite of his bellicose bragging, was only good at strutting with a musket.

These French *francs-tireurs*, also ordinary farmers and villagers, were probably no better. Like hornets, they might make pests of themselves, but one had to be terribly unlucky to be seriously hurt by them. In the meanwhile, the earthy fragrance of the lovely countryside lulled Corporal Kluge into pleasant recollections of his native Pomeranian farmlands. Those did not look the same, of course, Pomerania being flat as a pancake, but he had noticed that all farmlands he had ridden through with the army, from Westphalia to Baden, Alsace to Lorraine, had certain fragrances in common. You could shut your eyes and carry yourself back home with your nose.

Gustaf and his escorting corporal had to ride for nearly a half hour before meeting any German forces and then they were not the infantry units he hoped for, but a Corps Headquarters detachment guarded by a squadron of Uhlans. General Voigt-Rhetz, the Commander of the X Corps, was evidently making a personal reconnaissance sweep, and when he ran into the lone dragoon Leutnant traveling posthaste in the opposite direction, had him stopped for a brief interrogation:

"Where is the enemy?"

"About ten kilometers north, Your Excellency."

"Where is your brigade?"

"About eight kilometers north, Your Excellency."

"And attacking?"

"Only with artillery, Your Excellency."

"Damnation! By whose orders?"

The question confused Gustaf a little, and he had to think for a moment before answering: "I only know my own orders, Your Excellency, which are to summon and expedite infantry reinforcements." He started to pull out Prince Eugene's written order to show to the corps commander, but General Voigt-Rhetz was suddenly extremely eager to press on.

"Thank you, Leutnant, and carry on," he snapped, then bellowed: "Forward! . . . Ga-a-allop!" and tore off so fast that his staff and escort had trouble keeping up with him. Leutnant

Baron Gustaf von Falkenhorst and Corporal Kluge were shoved off the narrow lane into the bordering brambles in order to let them pass. Ten minutes later they entered Chambley, a tiny hamlet which they had briefly occupied the previous afternoon. The single main street with its shuttered houses slept, silent and deserted in the sun. Not an infantryman or commissary wagon was in sight, but they found four Uhlans lounging in front of the plain little brick schoolhouse. Gustaf reined in Kugel and asked a dusty sergeant: "Where the devil is everybody?"

"Who, Herr Leutnant?" the sergeant countered with a grin. "The inhabitants of this rat's nest? Hiding in their holes. The French Army? Still running faster than we can catch'm, I guess. Our boys? Well, a few pushing ahead and a lot more kind of sidling along the south'ard of here."

The road south of Chambley was wider but had taken rain from last night's thundershowers and was full of muddy puddles not yet dried out by the hot morning sun. The horses and riders were splattered with mud as they rode through. They passed a very old, senile-looking peasant carrying a pair of trussed live chickens over a bowed shoulder; he took off his cap with an exaggerated flourish and cackled: *"Bonjour, messieurs les merdeurs!"*

"Guten morgen, Herr Grosspapa!" Kluge answered him with an equally exaggerated salute, thinking that the Herr Leutnant Baron could at least have humored the old fellow with a nod.

A half-kilometer farther on they finally met the first contingent of infantry, a company of Bavarians slogging along at a leisurely route march behind their mounted captain. Gustaf drew up alongside the commander to explain what would be expected of him. "When I send up the wagons, Herr Hauptmann, please load your men into them without delay and proceed north as fast as you can. Do you wish to check my written orders to confirm this?"

"Oh, not at all, Herr Leutnant!" the Bavarian Captain exclaimed affably. "Any empty wagons going our way would instantly be requisitioned by my lads. Couldn't possibly stop'm. Was just thinking myself what a beautiful day for a wagon ride. Lovely weather we're having for a change."

Gustaf gave him a chilly stare, conveying exactly what he thought of frivolous Bavarians; then, without another word, spurred Kugel onward. Just beyond the next rise he met an entire battalion of the Twenty-second Prussian Grenadiers. *Prussians*, thank God! But just to make sure he was taken seriously, he spurred Kugel into a full gallop to make a dramatic approach. A bewhiskered major plodding along at the head of his troops on a comfortable mare contemplated him with a coldly circumspect appraisal. "Produce those wagons, Herr Leutnant," he said, "and then I'll consider whether to use them to advance my battalion far beyond the support of our main forces."

Gustaf did not remain to argue but hurried on in search of Prince Eugene's supply train which he was beginning to fear was located far more than an hour's ride to the rear. Finally, about a kilometer behind the battalion of grenadiers, he came upon part of it—ten wagons pulled off the road while the horses were being watered in a stream. A grizzled Intendantur Sergeant who looked like he might have fought with Blücher at Waterloo was in charge. "I'm too busy with a war to play games with excited leutnants," he objected in a voice sifting like gravel through his moustache.

Corporal Kluge suddenly shed his complacent attitude and reached for his saber: "You dare to be insubordinate to a dragoon officer, you old donkey? I'll skewer your mangy hide!"

Gustaf restrained Kluge sharply and, pulling out Prince Eugene's written order, handed it down to the old man, then waited while he adjusted a pair of dirty spectacles on his nose and carefully traced each word with a gnarled finger. "Who is General E. von Hanover?" he finally asked with a shrug. "Nobody I've ever heard of."

"The Prince General Eugene of Hanover who commands the Second Army, Intendantur," Gustaf informed him, snatching back the sheet of paper. "I will give you exactly ten minutes to unload your wagons, hitch up your horses, and start them north at the gallop."

"The Herr Leutnant will personally have to guarantee that signature," the old Sergeant said, adding with guileless insolence, "I don't have the pleasure of His Royal Highness's aquaintance."

"Ten minutes, Sergeant! Corporal Kluge will see to it you don't dawdle." Gustaf turned away and splashed Kugel into the stream where he allowed the now-lathering horse to slake its thirst with a few draughts of the cool water. He was hot and thirsty himself and would have liked to plunge in to wash off the sticky sweat. But he yanked Kugel's muzzle out of the water and spurred him over to the other bank, then up the grassy slope of a hill. When he reached its crest, he dismounted and began to scan the surrounding countryside.

The view was excellent, with a wide panorama of undulating woodlands and meadows shimmering in the hot rays of a sun which had burned off the morning mist. But Gustaf ignored the pastoral beauty of the scenery. His eyes crinkled against the glare as they searched the yellowish ribbon of the road winding its course southward along the valley to where it joined with another running east-west. The junction was clogged with ant-like columns of infantry, some branching off to the north, others continuing westward toward the distant Meuse hills. Between their crawling formations he could make out slender centipedes of horsedrawn caissons and artillery pieces; between those, strings of beetle shapes—supply wagons! Damn! The closest ones were a good two kilometers away as the crow flies and *west* of the junction. It would take another hour to reach them, unload them, fill them with infantrymen, and get them turned around and rolling north. Peering in the direction of Vionville, he could see a pall of smoke hanging over the last intervening ridge on the horizon and drifting into the cumulus clouds gathering for another afternoon of summer storms; even when he took off his helmet and cocked his ears in that direction, he could no longer hear the faintest rumble of cannon fire. Had the battle fizzled out before it had really developed? Was he now expending his all in a wasted effort toward the culmination of a horrible tactical blunder? Would he henceforth be snickered at as the naïve pawn of the Royal Pudding? "Why me?" he suddenly shouted aloud, furiously kicking a clump of poppies into a flutter of red petals.

Then his sharp young eyes caught both the formation of the Bavarians and the longer, darker one of the Prussian grenadiers, inching their way up the valley toward the distant reddish blob which was the hamlet of Chambley occupied by four Uhlans. The ten wagons he had found so far would accommodate, at the most, two hundred of those six hundred infantrymen. And that dour grenadier Major was highly unlikely to split his command and allow only part of it to be carted ahead. On the other hand, the frivolous Bavarian Captain might well make good his seemingly joking acceptance of the scheme. Suddenly making up his mind, Gustaf quickly remounted Kanone Kugel and drove him back down the hillside, across the stream, and in among the wagons being unloaded by the loudly grumbling detachment of teamsters. Corporal Kluge was keeping hard on the heels of the old Intendantur Sergeant, who was urging his men on with snarls and growls.

"Corporal Kluge! You will take the first three wagons and report to the Captain of the Bavarian company with my compliments. As soon as he has loaded his men into them, you will lead them back to our brigade as fast as you can." Turning to the surly Intendantur Sergeant, Gustaf told him: "You will report with the rest of the wagons to the commander of the Prussian grenadiers who will be with the first infantry unit you will meet along this road. Tell him ten more wagons will be sent to him as quickly as I can round them up, which should be within an hour. Respectfully suggest to the Major that he meanwhile use the seven available wagons. Can you make a respectful suggestion to a major, Sergeant?"

"Never have in my life before," the old soldier growled back.

"Good. You're in for a fresh experience in your dull life. And you'd better carry it off to perfection." Without pausing for his reaction, Gustaf kicked Kugel's flanks and gave him his head in a wild gallop down the road toward the clogged junction he had spied from the top of the hill. "Now you must show me the very best you have, my lovely!" he shouted into the horse's ears which were lying back flat as he pounded along. "Show me the very best and maybe I'll write a letter about you that will move your mistress to send us an answer!"

It was raining in Silesia on this sixteenth day of August 1870. Not a thin drizzle, but a steady downpour which had continued for the past two days. Water cascaded off the roof of Glaumhalle and streamed down its granite walls to form a turbid moat around its foundations. There was no moaning pine growing near any window, nor any rustling ivy to soften the wet nakedness of the stone facade. The wind swept unobstructed from the Polish plains to the east, producing harsh whistling sounds out of the grim square structure standing like a fortress on its barren hilltop. The road leading down the valley from its rough courtyard of eroded topsoil had turned into a stream full of miniature rapids. Early that morning, the postman had splashed his swaybacked nag up this tumbling course and delivered Gustaf's letter which had become limp and soggy after lying in the soaked mail bag for two days while the postman made his rounds of this thinly populated frontier district. And the letter had been a full ten days in transit from France due to delays caused by priority military traffic.

Tessa carefully opened the damp folds of paper and glanced through the few lines of the first written communication she had received from her husband. Then she read them aloud to the Dowager Baroness Hildebrun von Falkenhorst, a shapeless bundle of black widow's weeds slouched as usual in the manor's only comfortable chair next to the sooty fireplace in the sitting room.

My Dear Theresa, Tessa read to her, *I want you to know that Kugel and I are both doing well. We crossed into France two days ago (August 2) and so far the most exciting thing to happen is that a Rittmeister and a Leutnant Colonel each offered to buy your horse for very handsome sums of money. It is difficult to refuse respected superior officers. Even though the von Beckhaus breed of horses is so famous, both you and the stables of Schloss Varn should be highly flattered. There have been several battles which we unfortunately missed but which must have been won (praise God!) since we are still advancing and the enemy retreating. Kindly convey my affectionate regards to my mother, the Baroness Hildebrun von F. Your devoted husband, Gustaf.*

"God's curse on the filthy Frenchmen," the Baroness Hildebrun rasped, her eyes flaring into dull red embers of hatred. "God bless and save my dear boy Gustaf, named, you know, after his noble father who was slain by those pig-suckling Austrians. You know the Austrians, don't you, dearie. Of course. Your mother is one, isn't she."

Tessa sighed and reread the letter to herself by the light of the single lamp illuminating the gloomy little salon. "You don't think he would actually *sell* Kugel?" she worriedly asked her mother-in-law. "Surely he knows he's really *my* horse?"

The twisted leg propped up on a frayed footstool began to twitch. "Your horse? You dare claim the horse my son rides in war as your own? Such brazen selfishness!"

"Kugel was given to me by my father on the very day he was foaled," Tessa explained with steely patience. "I broke him to the saddle myself. Nobody but me ever rode him before Gustaf took him away."

The twitching spread from the leg until the whole black body began to shake in the chair, where it became more coiled than slouched. "He should have taken you too, virgin-strumpet!" the Baroness Hildebrun spat at her. "Damnation! I expected him to present me with his wife, not a spoiled snip of a betrothed maiden. I piss on your maidenly airs, dearie."

How the old woman knew she was still a virgin, Tessa had no idea. But her senseless, profane outbursts no longer shocked her. And she had lately dared some cutting ripostes of her own: "I've overheard language like that among my father's stableboys, Baroness Hildebrun," she quietly said. "It has no effect on me at all."

The black body uncoiled and suddenly a cane lashed out

with a hiss as it cut through empty air. But Tessa had jumped out of the way, having developed experience in this too. For a moment her mother-in-law became all tangled up in the voluminous folds of her widow's weeds and squirmed violently in the chair to free herself, curses pouring out of her which turned from rage to agony as pain shot through her ill-mended broken hip. Gradually the raucous screeching exhausted itself and turned into a visible dribble of venom running down her stubbled chin. The squirming and twitching subsided to a feeble palsy and her rasping voice became a pitiable whimper: "Bring me my medicine, dearie. Oh, please God, stoke the fire. I'm so cold, cold, cold. . . ."

Tessa fetched the bottle of patent elixir, a concoction of syrup, berry juices, and pure alcohol. Pouring a tot into a glass, she approached the chair with a wary eye on the cane, now resting inertly in a limp arthritic claw. The red glow in the eyes had faded to a filmy amber shaded by the transparent parchment of their drooping lids. The scabby slash of a mouth eagerly pursed toward the glass, but Tessa knew better than to be lured too close. She reached out and put the medicine down on the flat part of the chair's armrest, then backed off and busied herself with the fire. "Thank you, dearie," the Dowager Baroness Hildebrun wheezed.

"I am going for a walk," Tessa told her. "A walk. Not a ride, so don't get all upset about it."

"Yes, dearest girl. I only worry about your getting too close to the frontier. Oh God, that damned frontier on our very doorstep. The Poles are pigs! The Russians brutes! The Frenchmen whoremongers!" She spoke with a barely audible whisper, almost as if she were cursing out her last breath. But her right claw firmly clutched the glass of medicine and she slurped the amber liquid with a gurgle.

"The nearest Frenchman is eight hundred kilometers away," Tessa dryly reassured her.

"Never mind the damned French," the Baroness hissed with a resurgent temper which confirmed the potency of her medicine. "Just you worry about getting me to the closet. I've need of you."

"I took you less than fifteen minutes ago, Madame Baroness," Tessa protested.

"Don't argue with me, damn you! Help me up!" The cane began whistling through the air again, first in wild saber slashes toward Tessa, then with jabbing thrusts at the floor as she tried to lever herself out of the chair. But she could not get to her feet without help.

Tessa ignored her wild thrashing and moved well beyond

the dangerous periphery of the cane. During the past two weeks, her principal function in this blighted household had been to help the viciously senile old dowager to the reeking little niche beneath the main staircase which she called "the closet," there to prop her up on its oak seat whose surface was worn to a silken brown patina by generations of von Falkenhorst buttocks. She decided at this very moment that she would do so no more, regardless of the consequences. "I am going for a walk, Madame Baroness. On my way out, I'll ask one of your servants to attend you."

"I'll do it right here in my chair!" her mother-in-law threatened with a shrill screech.

"Good day, Madame," Tessa answered as she fled through the door.

"Good day and God damn you to hell, dearie-virgin-strumpet-maiden!"

Tessa climbed the dark staircase to the small room on the second floor which had been Gustaf's and was now assigned to her. It was a monastically austere stone chamber, furnished with a plain hard bed, a chair, a table, and an armoire, all made of the same wood with the same dull patina as the lid of the closet. On the whitewashed wall hung a single picture, a tinted print depicting Martin Luther nailing his famous theses to the door of the Wittenberg church. Beneath the picture, nestling on spikes driven into the masonry, rested the tarnished saber which had fallen from the hands of Gustaf's mortally wounded father on the battlefield of Sadowa. There should have been a splendid view of the forested hills to the west, but the window was too small and deeply recessed to let but a little dim rain-gray light through its streaming panes. As there was little space in the armoire, which still contained Gustaf's hunting clothes and old cadet uniforms, Tessa was living out of her trunks, which lined the free wall space, their lids open. Her trousseau, muted in drab pastels as it was, provided the only splash of color in the dreary little room. She hated it. But hated it less than any other part of Glaumhalle because here at least she could find some privacy. Not privacy to cry alone. She did not cry, not even out of rage and frustration. But she would sit on the bed with a pained, puzzled frown on her pale, freckled face, staring at the floor— as she did now for several minutes before kicking off her shoes and pulling on the riding boots which were no longer as beautifully polished as they had been at Schloss Varn.

Before leaving the room, she folded Gustaf's letter and tucked it into the purse she kept hidden beneath a layer of petticoats in one of her trunks. As she was doing this, her eye was caught by another envelope in the purse, the one containing the draft on the Rothschild's bank given to her by her father. She stared at it for a long time, then out of the window as if weighing an important decision, then, instead of returning the purse to its hiding place, took it with her.

Tessa went downstairs by the back staircase, which bypassed the sitting room and spiraled down into the dim, stale cave of a kitchen. Anna, the gaunt cook with a mole on the tip-end of her nose, and Lena, the mousy chattel of a maid, were scrubbing turnips in the sink. "The Baroness Hildebrun needs attending," Tessa informed them as she took a raincape off a peg and wrapped it around herself. The only two house servants of Glaumhalle curtseyed properly but with dour silence full of resentment. They knew well what kind of attending the dowager needed. Both of them bore marks of her cane.

Tessa paused on the kitchen stoop, flanked by splashing falls of rainwater streaming off the portico. With eyes closed, she took several deep lungsful of fresh air which was mercifully free of the musty, moulding atmosphere trapped inside Glaumhalle. She imagined a tinge of the sea in the clean, wet wind but knew the Baltic was a full three hundred kilometers away, so that the faintly salty tang had to come from the soaked inland sea of grass which rippled a dull green through drifting palls of rain far to the east. Opening her eyes, she stared hard in that direction. Sometimes one could spot Cossack patrols out there, riding in ragged unmilitary formations on their fleet little horses. But this morning the entire sweeping vista was lifeless and silent beyond the weeping downpour and sobbing wind. Tessa had promised herself that one day, perhaps a day when the forbidden meadowlands beyond the frontier were shrouded in dirty weather like this, she would ford the tumbling river which marked the outer limits of Glaumhalle and Silesia and mighty Prussia herself, to gallop off in a wild, exhilarating foray across those fantastic fields of grass. Let the Cossacks chase her! God in Heaven, if she had Kugel back and was riding him, the legendary Taras Bulba himself could not catch her! A wonderful dream of escape, but a foolish one right now, of course. So she drove it out of her mind and turned, refreshed by the inspiring fantasy, to the practical problem of the moment: how to cope with her mother-in-law and her new life in their dilapidated baronial outpost of the kingdom.

Tessa tucked her purse inside the cape to protect it from the rain, hitched up her skirt, and started across the yard, skipping over its tracery of puddles and rivulets. She headed toward the stable, a slab-sided structure which was Glaumhalle's original keep, built by the founding Falkenhorst knight in the early fourteenth century. The "new" manor, designed and erected by

Gustaf's great-great-grandfather with a royal grant from King Frederick Wilhelm, was really nothing but an enlarged duplicate of the old, equally slab-sided and built of the same unadorned blocks of granite, but with small windows instead of the smaller defensive embrasures. The two buildings did not clash with each other despite their three hundred years' difference in age, which, in a way, was a tribute to the changelessness of Teutonic tradition. Great-great-grandfather von Falkenhorst had renamed his estate Neu Glaumhalle in 1746, but by the time young great-grandfather took it over in 1769, the *Neu* had been dropped.

The old stable-barn complex was referred to as *der Feste* ("the keep"), which was not quite as euphemistic as it sounded. True, it presently sheltered nothing but a few horses in what had once been its Great Hall, and a few menial field hands in chambers where once Teutonic knights of the famous Falkenhorst line had been conceived, born, and if they were unlucky enough to survive glorious death in battle, had died. However, if by some blighted chance the Tartar hordes of the steppes retraced their old paths of conquest, or the volatile and restless neighbors who, sometimes acting as Russians, sometimes as Poles, and sometimes as freebooting brigands, decided to force the frontier and attack Glaumhalle as a hated symbol of Prussian superiority, it could again fulfill its original purpose and offer a formidable resistance from its commanding hilltop.

The inside of the keep was dark and permeated with a smell of horse manure, hay, and leather which was not unpleasant. A very out-of-date coach sagged on its springs, funereal black with purple, tassled curtains drawn over its windows. Three shaggy nags dreamed listlessly at their mangers, barely flicking their ears at the sound of Tessa's footsteps. But Feldteufel occupied one of several deserted stalls and eagerly whinnied when he heard her enter. "Hello, old fellow," she greeted him and took the time to press her cheek against his warm muzzle. "Are you lonely in this gloomy place? Well, so am I. But soon we'll change things to suit us better—you'll see."

Moving on through the tackroom, containing far more musty tack than the stable had horses, she knocked on the door to the windowless cubicle where the displaced stablemaster of Schloss Varn had established himself. On hearing his gruff "*Hinein,*" she threw open the door and unceremoniously entered, causing the old man to shoot to his feet with a shocked expression, throwing down the newspaper he had been reading and fumbling with the buttons of his open shirt. "In heaven's name, my lady," he exclaimed, "why did you not send for me? This place. . . ."

"This place is better than where I live," Tessa interjected, "so make no apologies, Prytzie."

Master Prytz had indeed managed to impart a certain spartan cosiness to his room which was immaculately clean and somehow reflected a scrubbed brightness from the polished brass lantern by whose light he had been reading. The cot was covered with Feldteufel's best blanket, the Beckhaus und Varn escutcheon precisely centered over the pillow. His uniform and cap hung from a low beam, his shirts and underwear were neatly folded on a shelf, with his perfectly polished boots standing at attention against the wall. There was a white cloth and a Bible on the table. Like a fastidious convict resigned to a long sentence, Prytz had made his cell as livable as possible, but there was, of course, nowhere for a visiting lady to be comfortably seated. Tessa perched herself on the very edge of the cot so as not to wrinkle its perfection or dampen it with her wet cape. She motioned him to sit in his chair, but he chose to remain standing, grumbling: "This is quite improper, my lady."

"It's hardly the time or place for proprieties, so why bother about them?" she said, wrinkling her freckled nose with a wry smile. Looking into his face, she noticed the deepening of its lines and the droop of its once-bristling moustache. Those eyes which had remained so youthfully sharp beyond his sixtieth year, were bloodshot and unhappy. "Tell me truthfully, Prytzie. You are homesick, aren't you? Terribly homesick." It was a statement she wanted confirmed rather than a question.

"It would be unnatural of us not to miss a home like Schloss Varn," he told her.

She deliberately ignored the "us" in his reply. "As unnatural as to feel at home in Glaumhalle?"

"One must expect such things to take time."

"More time than perhaps either of us cares to waste."

"We are not given any choice, my lady," he said, trying to sound stern.

"You are, my Prytzie," she answered with a steady gaze into his face. "You are free to go home."

"No, I am not," he flatly contradicted her. "My place is here at your call, my duty to serve you, Your Ladyship."

"I am releasing you from that duty and sending you home," she announced.

The old man flinched and everything about him stiffened, except his chin which began to tremble. "If I left you, I would never be able to face His Excellency, your father, again. Nor ever cross the beloved threshold of Schloss Varn. Nor even behold from afar her blessed fields. I would become truly homeless."

✠

"Don't be silly, Prytzie," Tessa snapped. "It is for your own good. You deserve better than this and I simply can't bear to have you on my conscience. Not on top of everything else that's troubling me. So go home—*please!*"

Master Prytz abruptly sat down. "My lady will have to command me to leave." He took advantage of her moment's hesitation to add: "If you are so burdened with troubles, why not share them with me?"

Tessa thought about their last ride together on the morning of her wedding day when she had cried out to him in childish anguish, only to be rebuffed with stoic platitudes. She loved this old man but was not past subjecting him to petty retributions. "I am burdened by a wish to kill my mother-in-law," she answered with a sardonic gleam in her green eyes which failed to soften the viciousness of what she was saying.

Prytz was so aghast that he forgot to use the formal address: "You must be joking, my Tessa!"

"Perhaps—perhaps not," she laughed. "But I suppose the old witch will likely die on her own soon enough." Her hilarity suddenly turned to bitterness. Jumping up from the cot, she began pacing the floor exactly as her father would when in one of his tempers. "How long will she hang on, that's what troubles me. For how long will I have to listen to her snarling and whining and cackling and crying? Do you know she constantly fouls herself like an infant? That this great noblewoman swears like a harlot? That she rations out firewood and lantern oil from a locked closet in her bedroom, then curses the cold and darkness? That she prays like one possessed but gets God and the Devil all mixed up? That she screams at me when I'm near, then whimpers for me when I'm not? Opens her arms to me, then lashes at me with her stick? And do you know, my poor Prytzie, that *you* are plotting to cut her throat and remove from it the stinking little pouch which contains all her jewelry?"

"I am? . . ." Master Prytz gaped in horror.

"Of course you are, you Pomeranian rascal!" She horrified him even more by switching to a very realistic imitation of the screeching Dowager Baroness Hildebrun. " 'Can't tell me a sensible Prussian count would give away a loyal trusted servant to a snip of a second daughter marrying an impoverished leutnant. Poppycock! He rid himself of a damned malingerer and cut-throat, that's what he did. Palmed him off on us! Satan scorch his slick hide!' "

Master Prytz put his hands over his ears and turned his face to the wall. "Stop, for God's sake, Tessa! I can't listen to such words from your lips. Not even joking. . . ."

She stopped her agitated pacing and with her own voice shouted at him: "I'm not joking now, Prytzie, dammit!"

There followed a long oppressive silence in the cubicle, through which could be heard the faint murmur of rain trickling through some leaking part of the keep. Tessa sank back down on the cot and Prytz turned from the wall, and the two of them stared at each other, the old man with misery, the young girl with grim resignation. "I am giving you a last chance to go home," she said to him, her voice now completely controlled.

He simply shook his head and said: "I knew things were unhappy for you, but I had no idea they were this bad. You must write your husband. Didn't you get a letter from him this morning?"

"It was rather a letter from my horse," Tessa answered with a flash of a smile which immediately turned into a frown. "I'm afraid my lovely Kugel will either get killed in battle or be sold to some soldier flashing a fat purse in my husband's face. But never mind that now. I take it you refuse to go home, then."

"Absolutely."

"So be it," she exclaimed with a sigh which contained a strong measure of relief. "You are staying of your own free will, Prytzie. And I thank you for it. But I have no intention of letting things go on the way they are. Let the old hag in the manor rant and rave all she wants, but I refuse to accept any more this slow rotting of Glaumhalle. The foundations are sound and they stand on a thousand hectares of good land. You and I are going to make this place fit to live in."

A glint of the old light came back into Master Prytz's eyes, but he could not help expressing a doubtful: "We are?"

Tessa opened her purse, took out the envelope given to her by her father, and handed it to Master Prytz. "There is a draft for five thousand thalers. A special wedding present aside from my dowry, so it's my own money given me by my father. I want you to saddle up Feldteufel and ride to Breslau where you will open an account for me with a good bank. Then you will purchase supplies and materials to restore this ruin. Then engage enough workmen and servants—our workmen and servants, mind you—to get the job done. Then buy a bull and several cows. And some pigs. And, most important of all, some good horses, including at least a half-dozen broodmares worthy of our Feldteufel. I will expect you back in three or four days, ready to start running a fine farm for me. A horse-breeding farm which will give Schloss Varn stables some competition to worry about." She suddenly laughed, her eyes sparkled and her face glowed with anticipation. "We can do it, Prytzie! Why not,

when we already have their best stallion and their famous stablemaster? A good start!"

Master Prytz was staring at the draft, which he had unfolded with trembling hands. His head began to shake.

"Well, what's the matter now? Isn't there enough money
there?" Tessa asked in alarm. She had never in her life disbursed
more than a few thalers and only had the vaguest concept of
monetary values.

"Of course. It's a small fortune," he answered. "But I am
sure your father did not intend you to spend it on Glaumhalle."

"You forget I am a Falkenhorst of Glaumhalle now," she
said. "And so are you, by your own choice."

"What will your husband think about it?"

"I'll face that problem when *and if* he comes back here,"
she answered with a shrug. Her eyes had been caught by the
Breslauer Zeitung brought by the postman that morning
which lay on the table. Bold headlines proclaimed: "**PRUS-
SIAN CAVALRY SPEARHEADS DEEP INTO FRANCE, SEEKING
DECISIVE BATTLE.**" Master Prytz noticed her glance and picking up the newspaper, he handed it to her and silently pointed
out a short notice printed in a box at the bottom of the front
page. While he carefully folded the bank draft, put it in his
wallet, and then started to pack for his journey to Breslau, Tessa
read about her father:

> It has been announced at Royal Headquarters, August 10, 1870, that
> His Majesty has been graciously pleased to appoint Colonel Count Frederick
> Paul von Beckhaus und Varn to the post of Inspector General of Military
> Railway Transport. According to General Staff Order XXXVI, all railway
> traffic operating in the Kingdom of Prussia, Confederation of North German
> States, and Occupied Enemy Territories, will be under the direct control of
> His Excellency Colonel Count von Beckhaus und Varn.

Tessa gave a wry smile to the still-dazed Master Prytz and
dryly observed: "How nice for dear Papa! Now he has all the
railroads to himself. Everybody is enjoying this war except you
and me, Prytzie. And the poor horses."

At that moment, Colonel Count Frederick Paul von Beck-haus und Varn was feeling things to be anything but nice for him. He was traveling through occupied enemy territory, not on a captured French railroad of which he would be executive director in His Majesty's name, nor aboard one of his own model Prussian trains, but in a horse-drawn open landau heading into Pont-à-Mousson. The creaking conveyance was not even drawn by a team of his splendid Schloss Varn pacers, but by a pair of plodding plough horses. They had been requisitioned all the way back at Saint-Avoid where it had become obvious that the French rail system was snarled beyond immediate redemption, even if not deliberately sabotaged. "I can assure Your Excellency," he had told General von Moltke, the first Commander in Chief ever to base his primary strategy on rail transport, "that the condition of the enemy's rail communications will allow us many mistakes in the field without jeopardizing ultimate victory." Of course, Count Frederick was intelligent enough to realize the terrible glut of misdirected freight cars and stalled locomotives would also obstruct the German advance until his technicians could put some order into the confusion—a formidable task! This fact made his temper edgier than it normally would be under these abominable field conditions. The French roads were as badly maintained as their rails, besides being churned up by huge marching armies, their artillery and transports, in whose destructive wakes the Count was forced to travel. And since he had to keep up with Royal Headquarters, his progress was constantly obstructed by a jam of carnival corteges belonging to assorted German princes, potentates, and margraves who had attached themselves to the King of Prussia in anticipation of favors and spoils. The least troublesome of these was the Kurfurst Georg von Blaumar-Keistler who trotted along in a medieval suit of armor with a single embarassed equerry, like a Don Quixote with his Sancho; the most troublesome was the sophisticated Molière character who was King of Bavaria and needed 40 wagons and 120 horses in order to keep up with the war. Both extremes were roundly cursed by Count Frederick.

He was also troubled by the grimmer aspects of a war to which he was still fundamentally opposed. During the last hectic ten days he had passed battlefields littered with German and French corpses being collected in putrid heaps by villagers impressed into grisly gravedigger's work. The progress of his landau was frequently halted to allow the columns of wounded to pass in the opposite direction, and he was sickened by the sight of their bloody bandages and the stench of gangrene which hung over their tortured formations. He forced himself to look at the dead and the maimed as a sort of penance for his noncombatant part in the war, and their memory caused him to turn rudely away in open disgust from the Minister of War, General von Roon, when the latter complained over "being denied any battle of consequence." In spite of his loud grumblings, Count Frederick was not bothered by the actual physical discomfort of keeping up with the war in the old landau, which was so overloaded with his baggage, dispatch cases, and rolls of railway maps that there was barely room for his own diminutive person and the slender frame of his single adjutant—Albrecht von Falkenhorst.

Gustaf's wedding had had one very fortunate result for his younger scholar-brother besides feeding him unusually well for a few days. Instead of being drafted into the Prussian Army as a common soldier, as Gustaf had so direly predicted, Albrecht found himself with the fascinating job of personal secretary to the new Inspector General of Military Railroad Transport. For appearance' sake, and much for the same reason that the Count himself wore a uniform in an essentially civilian capacity (as indeed did Chancellor Bismarck), Albrecht wore that of an Assistant Railroad Inspector. He also carried a sword which he did not know how to use and which got in his way, making him feel conspicuously clumsy. No matter! He knew that Count Frederick had not engaged him as a swordsman; if physical danger threatened, their bored escort of four mounted Landwehr dragoons would be galvanized into effective ferocity. Albrecht had his job because of his quick mind, his command of languages, his fluid pen, and most of all because of a rare flexibility of intellect for a young Prussian nobleman. Family connections had nothing at all to do with it beyond having put him at the right place at the right time. And he had done so well during the brief two weeks of his tenure that the Count was inwardly damning himself for not having married his daughter to Albrecht, rather than Gustaf.

As the landau drew closer to Pont-à-Mousson, the plough horses had to decelerate their listless trot to a fitful stop-and-go walk. The road became clogged with troops compressed into the approaches to the single bridge crossing the Moselle River in this small Lorraine town. The leading units of the Second Army had swept south of Metz and started across the day before, but with the one passable road, few narrow streets, and an even-narrower span squeezing everything together at this point of the advance, there remained two divisions and half the Army's supply train on the right bank. There were also some hundred-odd German princes who, along with their enormous undisciplined baggage convoys, were milling about looking for billets within prestigious proximity to Royal Headquarters, which was to be established here, pending further developments on the other side of the river. Count Frederick knew that the main body of the French Army had already crossed the same river at Metz, only thirty kilometers north, and as his carriage jerked to a halt on a rise just outside of the town, offering an appalling view of the teeming bottleneck, he exclaimed: "If one French general woke up with enough enterprise to turn the right crank, he could put our balls through a wringer here!"

Albrecht, who had developed an effective technique of complementing the Count's profane witticisms, countered: "But, sir, aren't *we* supposed to have the enterprise and the French the balls?"

Count Frederick allowed a flash of a grin before resuming his customary scowl and impatient squirming in the narrow space between valises and dispatch cases. "After you're no longer useful to me, I'll get you a job as jester with some court or other. God knows there are enough of them cluttering up this campaign. In the meanwhile, go to work. Get on La Misère, ride ahead, find the railroad yards, inspect them like a good Assistant Railroad Inspector, then try to report your findings to me without either over- or understatements of the true facts."

"The tracks are on the other side of the bridge," Albrecht breezily reminded the Count.

"I've memorized the wretched maps as well as you have. The point is that there is a bridge and you stand a better chance of squeezing across it on horseback than does this damned cart. Be careful. I don't want anything to happen to my poor Misère."

La Misère was a battered, but blooded, French mare whom they had rescued from a battlefield abattoir where wounded strays were being systematically put out of their misery. The three horrible saber slashes which marred the animal's neck and haunches were not as serious as they looked, and the Count's educated eye for fine horseflesh had perceived something worth saving. He decided to try to nurse her back to health while trailing her behind the landau on a lead rein, and had whimsically named her La Misère because of her great suffering in the lost cause of a now, doubtless, very dead French cavalry officer. To the escorting Landwehr dragoons, who had to accomplish the actual nursing and foddering, she was a confounded nuisance. To Albrecht she was a great convenience when sent on errands such as this one to reconnoiter the railroad yard of Pont-à-Mousson. By hauling in the lead rein and bringing La Misère alongside their carriage, he could simply stand up, put his foot in the stirrup, and swing himself into the saddle with a minimum of effort, then press his way ahead through the glut of troops.

It took Albrecht nearly a half hour to ride through the winding cobbled streets jammed with supply wagons and reach the bridge. There he had to wait for another ten minutes while battery after battery of artillery rumbled across ahead of him. An Uhlan major, acting as provost marshal, eyed his unfamiliar green uniform and cap with suspicion, and haughtily informed him the bridge was closed to all civilian traffic. Albrecht produced credentials which the Count had had the foresight to have stamped with the Great Seal of Royal Headquarters. The major shrugged, made an uncomplimentary remark about railroads, then finally allowed him to trot across between a couple of ammunition wagons. When he reached the modest railway station and freight yard on the opposite bank, Albrecht found that his efforts had been for nothing. The station house and tracks were intact, but for once the French had shown some efficiency and evacuated all rolling stock and locomotives ahead of their invading enemy. A pathetic small group of refugees were slumped among their bundles and suitcases, hopelessly waiting for a train. Albrecht stared at them with amazement, then announced in French: "It will be some time before we can get passenger traffic back on regular schedule. You had better return to your homes."

The men stared at him in sullen silence, but a woman who was nursing a baby through her open blouse replied: "We have no homes anymore, Monsieur," and spat.

"I am terribly sorry," Albrecht said. He turned La Misère and carefully guided her over the tracks to the other side of the yard where a company of sappers was preparing to move out with a rail-trolley loaded with crowbars and pickaxes. He addressed their captain: "Why are no guards posted around the station, Herr Hauptmann?"

The Captain shrugged. "None of my business. My orders are to march north along the tracks for a couple of kilometers and tear them up."

"Tear them up? It's the policy of the Inspector General to preserve and protect all railroad property."

"Very interesting. It's my commanding general's policy to destroy it so the Frenchies can't comfortably ride into battle against us." Several of his nearby sappers laughed.

"I'm countermanding your orders, Herr Hauptmann," Albrecht told him pleasantly.

Now the Captain himself laughed. "Who the hell are you?" he asked, making a face at the rankless green uniform worn by a beardless youth. Yet there was a trace of caution in his manner because the horse with its barely healed saber wounds looked like it might have carried its rider through some heavy action. When Albrecht patiently showed him his impressive credentials, he became confused and undecided. "Well . . . all right, Herr Freiherr von Falkenhorst, so you are a Deputy Inspector of Military Railroads. But does that give you authority over my company of sappers? I doubt it."

"Don't!" Albrecht assured him. "Not as long as you are operating along these tracks. The Inspector General is just arriving at Royal Headquarters and as soon as I report to him, you'll be receiving new orders. If you tear up the rails, you'll only have to relay them again."

"So what am I supposed to do in the meanwhile?" the sapper captain testily inquired. "Don't you know the French are giving us battle to the north? Can't you hear the cannon fire?"

Albrecht cocked his head and listened for a moment, but all he could hear was the steady din of caissons rumbling over the bridge. "I suggest you post sentries and wait, Herr Hauptmann," he advised with a smile. "And if you have any rations to spare, why not share them with those poor people on the platform over there? Then I'm afraid you must ask them to leave. It is also the Inspector General's policy to declare all railroads military zones prohibited to civilians." With a courteous salute, he wheeled La Misère and started making his way back toward the bridge which he would have to cross this time against its teeming one-way traffic.

There was no Uhlan major controlling traffic on this side, and it appeared an almost-hopeless proposition to force one's way against the current. But Albrecht was not alone in this predicament. He noticed a strange horseman waiting next to the bridge abutment, a slight man with a reddish brown beard and a dark blue uniform of completely foreign cut. The tunic was more like a frock coat with a single row of gold buttons, no epaulets, only a pair of stars framed in stitched boxes set crosswise on each shoulder. No breeches, but ordinary trousers of matching material stuffed into short boots. On his head he wore a peculiar wide-brimmed hat which was adorned only with a wreathed insignia and a plain gold cord which ran around its creased crown. He was unarmed, lacking even a saber, and was certainly not dressed like a soldier, yet sat his horse like a seasoned cavalryman as he eyed the formations pouring over the bridge with a cool professional glance. After they had waited close to each other for several minutes, Albrecht nudged La Misère closer and ventured to observe: "At this rate we may be here all day."

The stranger turned his head and his deepset eyes flashed a quick, mildly puzzled appraisal of the youth in the green uniform. "I regret I hardly speak any German," he answered in English with a surprisingly deep voice.

"Oh, you are English?" Albrecht asked, switching to that language.

"American," he answered, then proceded to introduce himself with little formality. "An officer of the Army of the United States, presently attached as neutral observer to the Prussian forces. Philip Sheridan's the name."

"General Sheridan!" Albrecht exclaimed, startled. He had heard this famous American officer was observing the war from the Prussian side, but had never seen him nor imagined him to look like this. "Forgive my clumsiness, Your Excellency. I did not realize who you were."

"No reason why you should," General Sheridan answered with a glint of amusement at the young man's embarrassment. "And don't address me as 'Your Excellency.' American generals are just plain generals. The plainer, the better, some figure it. What's your own rank and unit, sir?"

Albrecht became completely flustered, especially over being addressed as "sir" by the Major General. "Only a Deputy Inspector of Military Railway Transport, nothing more."

"A job with a future if you appreciate its opportunities, Mr. Deputy Inspector . . . you have a name too, don't you?"

"Freiherr Albrecht von Falkenhorst . . . sir."

"A Freiherr, eh!" the American general repeated, still puzzled but trying to act suitably impressed.

"Quite a meaningless title," Albrecht explained, "usually given the youngest son of a noble family after the better ones have been handed out. My older brother, for instance, is a baron."

"The fellow assigned as my escort and interpreter is too," General Sheridan allowed with a shrug. "Very educated sort of baron who speaks almost as good English as you. But he managed to lose me somehow while we were riding about your front lines to the north of here. Reckon he'll show up again soon enough."

"I will be delighted to take over and escort you to Royal

Headquarters on the other side of the bridge, General Sheridan," Albrecht eagerly offered.

The American General eyed the bridge, which now was more jammed than ever with bobbing columns of infantry which filled the span rail to rail from one end to the other. "Very kind of you," he answered with a laugh. "But no hurry. This is as good a place as any to observe your lads marching." He kicked one foot out of its stirrup and raised a leg to hook its knee over the pommel, leaning back in the saddle as if making himself comfortable in a lounging chair. Then he reached for the inside pocket of his tunic and produced a long, thin cigar, which he popped into his mouth at a rakish angle. A match rasped against the sole of his boot, flared brightly into flame. In the next moment his bearded face was wreathed in blue tobacco smoke as he contentedly puffed away: "Care for a Spanish cigar, *Freeherr?*"

Albrecht politely declined, fascinated by this casual behavior. Prussian officers never smoked cigars except in the privacy of their mess, nor would they dream of sitting their horses that way in the presence of troops. He was aware of the curious stares of soldiers marching past them but did not let this bother him any more than it did the American General. "What do you think of our war, sir?" he asked.

"Haven't made up my mind yet," General Sheridan replied without the slightest hesitation. "Don't know if I were fighting it, whether I'd want to be in the Frenchman's position or yours. You've both got yourselves some interesting opportunities right now, especially the Frenchman."

"My superior was saying very much the same thing just this morning," Albrecht told him. "He is the King's Inspector General of Military Railroads."

"Perhaps he should be a fighting general," the American answered in a tone which was half-caustic, half-sincere.

After a silence between them which was filled with the tramp of hundreds of boots, Albrecht asked: "Is this anything like the war you recently fought in America, sir?"

This time General Sheridan thought over his answer for a moment while intently studying the glowing tip of his cigar. "It isn't as yet and I hope it never will be. Ours was a *people's* war, and they are the most difficult, bloodiest kind to fight and win. This one's so far a war between professionals. Professionals like to keep things tidy and run according to the rules."

Albrecht nodded thoughtfully, then noticed that a string of cook-wagons and field ambulances were coming over the bridge on the heels of the last infantry regiment, offering them an opportunity to squeeze past. "I must report to the Inspector

General at Royal Headquarters," he said to the American officer. "I think we can get across now, sir."

General Sheridan resumed a proper cavalryman's posture in the saddle but kept his cigar firmly clenched between his teeth. "All right, *Free*herr! Lead the way!"

Meanwhile, Count Frederick Paul von Beckhaus und Varn's landau had managed to penetrate just far enough inside of Pont-à-Mousson for him to lose all patience and decide to proceed on foot. A young Leutnant, leading his company of grenadiers along the narrow sidewalks in order to bypass the wagons filling the streets noses to tailgates, was startled to find himself joined by a diminutive Colonel carrying his own dispatch case and a roll of maps who asked: "Where can I find the King?"

The Leutnant, a Bavarian who considered *the* King to be Ludwig II of Bavaria, not Wilhelm I of Prussia, stammered: "I believe His Majesty is at Lunéville, sir."

"Nonsense!" Count Frederick snapped. "He's somewhere here in Pont-à-Mousson. I hope you know where the war is." Leaving the befuddled Leutnant, he turned into a side street which he hoped to be a faster detour around the clogged main thoroughfare. He immediately found himself trapped by another infantry unit in the process of breaking billet. Turning again, this time down a narrow lane between shuttered houses, he had a tantalizing glimpse of the main square and, from a roof above it, the Royal Standard waving limply in the still summer air. Royal Headquarters was no more than a couple of hundred meters away, but he found himself approaching it from the rear with his progress obstructed by a labyrinth of small backyards and gardens connected by ever-narrower, winding alleys. When he stood on tiptoe to peer over one of those garden walls, he suddenly spied the King, General von Moltke, Minister of War von Roon, and Chancellor von Bismarck, all standing beneath a ramshackle gazebo, two gardens removed. The four most important men to the future of Prussia and Germany—indeed all Europe—were holding a council of war in that shabby little backyard of Pont-à-Mousson and the Count had come very close to interrupting them with an anguished bellow for directions. However, he was not quite so distraught as to create such a terrible breach of court etiquette, and when he suddenly found himself face to face with a bearded trooper of the Royal Guard du Corps, he somewhat sheepishly announced: "I am Colonel Count von Beckhaus, attached to His Majesty's staff, and I've damned well managed to get myself lost."

The guardsman scrutinized him, his carbine resting lightly in the crook of one arm, his left hand on the hilt of his saber.

"Your Excellency will follow me, please," he finally said, then led the Count out of the labyrinth and into the main square of Pont-à-Mousson. He pointed to the entrance of the Town Hall, which was guarded by several other duplicate giants wearing spiked helmets and gleaming breastplates. "The Guard Officer of the Day will assist Your Excellency from here."

The square itself merely formed a backwash to the mainstream flooding against the bridgehead and was therefore not clogged with a press of military traffic. Troopers of First Uhlan Regiment, dismounted but alert, saw to it that no stray formations blundered in to disturb the relative quiet within His Majesty's immediate proximity. The open, cobbled expanse nevertheless swarmed with couriers and their mounts, parked baggage trains and carriages belonging to high staff personnel, their coachmen and postillions. Among these, the King's coach was the most conspicuous—after his chancellor's landau, whose team of splendid brewery horses had been borrowed from a beer baron of Mainz at the outset of the campaign. The surrounding houses were not shuttered like the rest of those in town, and flags of the North German Confederation and personal standards of nobles hanging from windows and balconies suggested they had been commandeered as billets for the royal entourage. There was not a Frenchman in sight, only a few dogs who had switched allegiance to the better-provisioned invaders.

Count Frederick took in this whole scene at a glance, a fairly familiar one by now, then confidently trotted over to the Town Hall and bounded up the steps to push his way inside. The dingy vestibule was filled with minor princes and staff officers. He was met by the Guards Officer of the Day who called over one of the King's military adjutants who, in turn, asked him to await His Majesty's pleasure until after an important council was over. He then nodded perfunctory greetings to a Westphalian baron and a Saxon general, both of whom he knew slightly but not well enough to permit them any informal cordiality. Royal Headquarters was regrettably infested with sycophants and parvenu officers whose most outstanding talents lay in designing their own uniforms. The Count not only considered them to be bores, but positive hindrances to the prosecution of the war. The real staff work was accomplished by a mere handful of trained professionals personally selected by Moltke and Roon, men like Major von Fritwitz whom the Count spotted making his way out of the building with purposeful strides, sidestepping all the military poseurs. "What is the situation?" Count Frederick asked him, falling in momentarily with his brisk walk.

Major von Fritwitz slowed enough to make a terse, but

courteous, reply: "Uncertain, Your Excellency. We know most of Bazaine's army is retreating across the river. All else is unconfirmed reports and idle rumors. Please excuse me."

Count Frederick started to follow him outside to wait on the front steps of the Town Hall because he was bothered by the company in the vestibule and nauseated by their sickly sweet odor of sweat and toilet water. But then he suddenly noticed a lowly Landwehr captain standing aside against the wall and staring at the floor with weary resignation, his muddy uniform a shabby contrast to the gaudy little paladins chattering around him. The Count's face brightened as he recognized Krindle, Prince Eugene of Hanover's adjutant, and he roughly shoved his way past a Pfalz colonel in order to reach him: "Is the Prince here at Royal Headquarters?" he eagerly inquired.

Captain Krindle gave a start. "Oh . . . Count von Beckhaus! . . . No, Your Excellency, he is not here."

Count Frederick's expression crinkled back into irritation. "Well then, Krindle, where is he? What the devil are you doing here? What is going on?"

"I don't know what's going on," Captain Krindle replied with such a violent shrug that miniature cascades of dust fell from his epaulets. "I left His Highness over three hours' ride from here. Near a place full of Frenchmen . . . I think called Vionville. He sent me back to report to General von Moltke and . . . and *the King!*" His eyes rolled as if he were still overwhelmed by the mission, then shut tight in desperation. "So here I am waiting. The King is busy, of course. And I dare say, that's just as well."

"What do you mean? You dare say that's just as well?" Count Frederick demanded. "If His Highness sent you all the way back with a report to Royal Headquarters, it must be of some importance."

Krindle dropped his voice to a confidential whisper. "Your Excellency should know that the Prince has ordered all our advanced supply trains to dump their loads. Sent a dragoon leutnant riding back down the line, ordering them to dump everything and load the wagons with . . . *infantry!*"

Count Frederick raised his voice to an impatient pitch: "Is that what you are supposed to report here, Krindle?"

"No, not exactly that, Your Excellency," the Captain tried to explain in an even-lower whisper. "There's a lot of confusion over the French at Vionville and General von Redern's brigade and. . . ."

Count Frederick's voice rose so high that it silenced all the chatter in the vestibule: "What is the report, Krindle?"

Krindle shoved himself hard up against the wall, looking as

though he wanted to vanish through it as all eyes suddenly focused upon him. Reaching into the dispatch case slung from one shoulder, he fumbled forth the piece of paper on which Prince Eugene had hastily scribbled in pencil: *Bazaine's army is strung out along the Metz-Verdun road like a migration of gypsies. Eugene v. H.*

Count Frederick snatched it out of his hand, read it, then looked up with a smile. "Even if you don't have the vaguest idea about what you've done, you might just get an Iron Cross for this, Krindle. I'll see what I can do about it." Turning and taking advantage of the shocked silence around them, he bellowed: "Officer of the Day! Front and center!"

The Guards Officer of the Day, a major, came rushing up with a clatter of spurs and cuirasse. "Sh-sh-sh! What is wrong, Your Excellency?"

The Count waved the piece of paper in his face and exclaimed without in the least moderating his tone: "You have been delaying an urgent message to His Majesty about enemy troop movements!"

"I was not properly informed of its importance," the Major said, shooting a furious glance at the quaking Krindle. "I will see to it His Majesty receives it at once."

Count Frederick held the message well outside his reach. "No. You will be so good as to arrange for me to deliver it in person—at once, if you please."

The Guards Officer of the Day hesitated only a second before nodding and motioning him through the crowd, which made way for them with a certain supercilious deference. At the end of the vestibule a royal adjutant barred the way, but after a brief whispered conference with the major, opened a door and took over as escort to the royal presence. A long dark corridor. A gloomy little office which must have belonged to the ousted mayor. Another door opened by one of those magnificent troopers of the Guard du Corps. The weedy little garden and its gazebo which Count Frederick had spied from over the wall. And suddenly there was King Wilhelm I of Prussia, looking up from a clutter of maps spread over a rusty wrought iron table. Only *he* looked up. Minister of War Theodor von Roon, Chancellor Otto von Bismarck, and Chief of the General Staff Helmuth von Moltke continued to busy themselves with the maps. The King took a step away from the table and cordially exclaimed: "My dear Count Frederick, I'm delighted to see you!"

The adjutant drew a sigh of relief and withdrew with a peculiar crablike motion. Count Frederick made a bow which was clumsy because of the dispatch case, roll of maps, and message he was carrying. "At Your Majesty's command!"

"I'd like to command a miracle," the King said with a benign smile. For all his military bearing and bemedaled uniform, he gave more the impression of a kindly bewhiskered Saint Nicholas than the soldierly monarch he was. "A miracle to give us prescience in maneuvering our armies and their supplies. Or just a small miracle improving the situation with the railroads so we could concentrate our forces more quickly."

Count Frederick was aware of the veiled reproach. His railroads which had served the Prussian cause so well during the initial mobilization maneuvers had become more and more snarled as the war progressed. But he made no excuses even though there were plenty of valid ones—most of which the King was aware in any case. "I can report no such improvement," he confessed to his sovereign. "However, I have intercepted a message from the Prince Eugene of Hanover which may interest Your Majesty and his General Staff."

The King accepted the piece of paper, read it, gave a puzzled smile, then read it out loud. Moltke, Bismarck, and Roon all looked up from their maps. "Where is the Prince?" Moltke asked.

"According to his adjutant, he's at Vionville and in sight of the enemy, Your Excellency," Count Frederick informed him. "And, I gather, making urgent efforts to move up reinforcements."

The Prince's message passed around the table from hand to hand, and was carefully scrutinized by each individual, last reaching Chancellor von Bismarck, who snorted and exclaimed with his usual blunt sarcasm: "It seems we are blessed with a witty new field marshal!"

"Hardly a precise intelligence report," von Roon grunted.

Count Frederick, who disliked von Roon and Bismarck about equally, brazenly snapped back: "On the contrary, very precise. It tells us where the enemy is. On the Metz-Verdun road. How far along it? At least as far as Vionville. In what strength? Bazaine's whole army, or roughly 170 thousand strong. In what disposition? One of disorganized route march." Flashing a contemptuous look at Chancellor von Bismarck, he addressed him directly with a matching sarcasm of his own: "Your witty new field marshal has compressed all that information into two lines instead of the two hundred our verbose politicians might be expected to use."

"Ah, I was mistaken," Bismarck retorted. "We have *two* witty new field marshals—both self-appointed."

Unshaken, Count Frederick shrugged off the insult and turned to the King: "Your Majesty, I will personally guarantee the integrity and competence of Prince Eugene of Hanover. He is a very old friend of mine."

"A compromising admission, Count von Beckhaus," Bismarck shot in with a scowl on his bulldog face.

The King became annoyed. "Gentlemen, please! Our nerves are frayed enough, so let's show some courtesy and consideration toward each other." In a milder but very serious tone, he said to Count Frederick: "We have full confidence in the Prince, otherwise would never have commissioned him in our service—service to our Intendantur, not our field forces. As badly as we need information, we hesitate to act upon his message and change complicated plans."

"What plans?" General von Moltke suddenly asked. This tall gaunt Dane with a sensitive, almost melancholy, face had been maintaining a pensive silence. Now he spoke in a low, yet crisp voice which commanded everybody's attention. "I do not want Your Majesty to be under any illusions about plans. Three weeks ago they were entirely based upon defending the Rhine against a massive French invasion. But a string of encouraging little victories upset all our calculations and now we are the invaders. If any plan remains, it is nothing more than a very general one, really only an intention, to somehow maneuver our enemy into a decisive battle. If we can win such a battle, it will be worth losing half our armies. But we can win twenty incidental clashes like Froeshwiller or Borny and still lose this war. No matter how terrible the cost, decisive battle is the only excuse to make war, because it is the only kind of action which will bring it to an end. This must be a professional prerequisite as well as a Christian humanitarian one. For the moment I cannot as Chief of the General Staff offer any better plan for victory."

A tense silence followed within the gazebo which was broken by Chancellor Bismarck's rasping voice: "Does this mean that the Chief of the General Staff proposes to make strategic decisions based on this kind of intelligence?" He crumpled up Prince Eugene's message and threw it down on the maps spread over the table.

There was not a flicker in General von Moltke's sad gaze. "Perhaps," he admitted. "At least it is beginning to suggest a course of action when considered along with other fragments of information we have received." He spread apart his thin bony hands, then curled the long fingers into a cupping motion and brought them together like interlocking talons. Somehow the gesture ended in an almost prayerlike attitude. "God willing, tomorrow we shall know how to deal with the situation."

Both von Roon and Bismarck drew sighs of relief, and the

✠

latter exclaimed: "So, no hasty decision is necessary then!" Suddenly switching from caustic surliness to a gruff joviality with that bewildering and bewitching manner so characteristic of the man, he smiled at the gaunt Chief of the General Staff and gave him a nudge with his elbow. "Helmuth! I do believe you're stealing a march on us politicians and turning into an opportunist!"

General von Moltke's colorless lips raised slightly from their downward curl, almost forming a smile, but the eyes remained ice-cold. "It is *your* war, Otto. How could I conduct it otherwise?"

Chancellor Bismarck's grin froze and his eyes bulged out of their pouches. "Damn you, sir!" he exploded. "Are you implying I connived you into it unprepared?"

Von Moltke's thin smile stretched slightly and his voice dropped to a whisper. "As a personal friend of Louis-Napoleon, you might have perhaps given us a more-accurate appraisal of his capacities as a soldier. But then, as you yourself obliquely point out, you are a politician, not a soldier. And for better or worse, matters now rest solely in the hands of soldiers."

Bismarck's fist crashed down on the table, and his voice echoed around the brick walls enclosing the dismal little garden: "Matters may never rest solely in the hands of soldiers, sir! They neither know when to start a war, nor when to stop it!"

King Wilhelm bristled and lost every trace of affability. "I will not tolerate your debasing yourselves—and *me*—with this kind of petty bickering," he icily told his Chancellor and Chief of General Staff. "I command it cease forthwith!"

Bismarck, always ready to make a humble apology for his quick temper when it suited him, bowed his head and said: "I beseech Your Majesty's pardon!" Tears were streaming down his jowls, but whether out of shame at having offended his King or rage at General von Moltke, there was no outward sign. The Chancellor was known to be a compulsive weeper when under severe stress, while the Chief of the General Staff would only show emotion when unburdened by troubles of any kind—therefore, almost never.

Count Frederick was still holding his load of paraphernalia, an impassive expression hiding his delight over witnessing Bismarck's being goaded out of control by Moltke and both being reprimanded by their sovereign. But General von Roon came up with a timely diversion: "If His Majesty so pleases, it is time for lunch."

"Yes, and we are hungry," the King quickly agreed. "Count Frederick, we would be pleased to have your company at table."

Count Frederick graciously declined. "With Your Majesty's permission, I will forego the honor and make myself available to my staff, who are attempting to make use of whatever scraps of French railroads have fallen into our hands during these past twenty-four hours."

Wilhelm nodded. "Very well, but we insist upon your company at dinner tonight."

As the sovereign and his warlords departed, a pair of staff majors seemed to pop out of the shrubbery surrounding the gazebo. They approached with that self-effacing efficiency of their breed to collect and roll up the maps left on the table. Before they could do so, the Count snatched up Prince Eugene's message, carefully smoothed out the wrinkles, and folded it into a neat square which he slipped into his pocket.

The vestibule was more crowded than ever with minor potentates and their brightly caparisoned military satraps, all waiting in the hope of being invited to take lunch with the King of Prussia and his small, but formidable, staff. As Count Frederick shoved through the throng, he overheard fragments of the rumors which infected this group like a delirium fever:

"Bazaine is just feinting a retreat in order to draw us into a trap!"

"Napoleon is sick. Last stages of syphilis."

"The Crown Prince and Moltke have had a terrible row."

"Von Rheinbaben invested Verdun this morning!"

". . . So don't drink any of the local water. The French dumped tons of arsenic into the Moselle."

"Lots of wounded are coming back over the bridge. There is a big battle on the other side."

Count Frederick reacted to this last fragment and grasped the elbow of the speaker, who turned out to be the Duke of Bamberg. "Where exactly is the battle?" he eagerly asked.

"Outside of Nancy," came the cocksure reply. "My own regiment is engaged in heavy fighting there."

"Between themselves over the loot," the Count shot back with a derogatory snort. "Nancy capitulated two days ago to a handful of Prussians."

Leaving the Duke of Bamberg spluttering with indignation, Count Frederick pushed on through the crowd to the spot where he had left Prince Eugene's adjutant. Captain Krindle had not moved, nor in the least changed his hangdog demeanor. "I delivered the Prince's message to the King, but, I regret to say, without causing any changes in the fortunes of war either to our side in general or yourself in particular, Krindle." The blank, stupid look on the Captain's face stopped him from making a more-detailed explanation. Instead, he gave him patiently precise orders: "Ride back and find the Prince. Tell him I am here at Royal Headquarters and will see to it that any other messages of his will also be brought to His Majesty's attention. Tell him I can do no more than that, but assure him of my personal admiration and confidence—and my deep concern for his safety. Do you understand, Krindle?"

Krindle managed to both shake and nod his head. "Yes, Your Excellency," he sighed. "I will do as you command. That is if I can find His Highness at all by now. If only he were like all these other Highnesses who stay where they belong, close to His Majesty. But the Prince Eugene . . . God knows! . . ."

Prince Eugene had not moved from his vantage point on the hill, which, he came to realize by midmorning, was affording him a sweeping panoramic view which few men would experience in a lifetime: a formal battle involving nearly a quarter-million soldiers. Perhaps Hannibal's battle of Cannae had presented a spectacle like this, perhaps Frederick the Great's Rossbach, which the Prussians had won against the French, or Jena where they had been defeated by an earlier Napoleon, or Borodino where another brilliant Napoleonic victory had eventually turned to ashes. To the victor defeat, to the defeated victory! Thus often was ironic fate dispensed by the gods of war! In mulling this over, the Prince could find little satisfaction in being proved right in his earlier estimate of the situation, because it was becoming more and more obvious to him that the German forces had blundered into a very danger- ous predicament. The only hope was that their French enemy would be so inept as to fail to take advantage of it. General von Rheinbaben's opening cannonade had been nothing but a per- functory intimidation using too few guns and too little ammuni- tion, the compromise of a commander torn between the de- mands of audacity and caution. He had precipitated a critical moment when it appeared as if the enemy cavalry division would charge up the hill, overrunning the few guns and scatter- ing von Redern's brigade. But for some strange reason they had wavered at the climactic moment of their threat and retired instead to the other side of Vionville, slightly mauled by the few shells which had exploded in their camp, yet quite intact as a fighting unit of the French Army. The main effect of the brief bombardment had been to stamp out of the ground a multitude of enemy troops. Two entire corps appeared outside of Rezonville, their infantry formations looking in the distance like bristling reddish blue caterpillars, then changing into swarms of ants as they deployed over the fields facing Prince Eugene's hill. Supporting cavalry and artillery units emerged out of the wooded slopes on the other side of the verdant plain. Beyond the far hills, both north and east, great columns of dust rose up and merged with the cumulus clouds, staining their white convolutions a dirty brown, signaling marching divisions as yet out of sight, but only a few miles away. As this opening act of the drama unfolded before the Prince's eyes, he knew that whatever reinforcements Gustaf von Falkenhorst might bring up in a few supply wagons would be woefully inadequate unless considerably stronger German forces also marched upon the scene. Those could only be Alvensleben's III and Voigt-Rhetz's X Corps, both of which had been reported strung out far to the south and unsupported by the main army.

When the batteries ceased fire to conserve their dwindling ammunition, Generals von Rheinbaben and von Redern had reappeared on the crest of the hill to look over the situation and this time they voiced recriminations against each other which were not couched in polite terms. Von Rheinbaben accused his brigadier of having drawn their division into a trap with his impetuous advance. Von Redern retorted that the division commander had thrown away an opportunity for surprising the enemy by his useless bombardment. Both were quite correct in their appraisals of each other's errors, but to argue over them now was divisive and dangerous. Von Rheinbaben decided it would be wise to fall back on the main army and ordered his artillery limbered up and prepared for withdrawal; von Redern insisted this was premature because the enemy formations in sight were taking up defensive, not attack, positions. Unlike themselves, the French could not *see* what they were up against, so why not let them suspect that considerable German forces were at hand? And infantry reinforcements really were on the way, he announced. Thus, the division commander got wind of the Prince's scheme and demanded the details, flying into a terrible temper when told about them. Spotting the originator sitting on the ground nearby, he spurred his horse over to him and angrily exclaimed: "Your Highness will honor me by not meddling in tactical decisions involving my command!"

Prince Eugene heaved himself to his feet, but not out of respect. He immediately sat down again on a stump, imperiously, as if occupying a throne. "I consider it my duty to offer

Your Excellency's staff whatever advice I am able to contribute," he told the fuming General.

"That should be confined to matters of ammunition and supply," von Rheinbaben rudely retorted, "which I am given to understand are now abandoned helter-skelter along the roads to our rear. If I run out of ammunition, or it otherwise goes bad for my division, Your Highness may have much to answer for."

"I also consider it my duty to assume certain risks," the Prince of Hanover drawled. "As a fellow general, if not a prince, Your Excellency must agree that this is one of the hazards of holding our rank."

Von Rheinbaben took the subtle rebuke like a slap in the face. "I don't need Your Highness to remind me of the responsibilities of my rank," he furiously shouted.

"Assuming responsibility and assuming risks are not quite the same thing, my dear General," Prince Eugene dryly pointed out.

The division commander's jaws flapped open and shut several times without a sound as he tried to think of a suitably devastating riposte against this fat, deposed princeling of a subjugated kingdom. He was saved from stooping to outright barrackroom language by the sudden arrival on the hill crest of General Voigt-Rhetz and his staff and used this as an excuse for his abrupt withdrawal. Prince Eugene overheard him greet the commander of X Corps with an alarmed: "We are facing Bazaine's whole damned army down there!" to which General Voigt-Rhetz exclaimed: "Excellent!" and taking out his telescope, he began to scan the teeming arena between Vionville and Rezonville. What else was said between them became lost in the general chatter of dozens of staff officers who closed in around their commanders.

Prince Eugene remained seated on his stump and motioned to his orderly to approach. Anton timidly emerged from behind a clump of scrubby oaks where he had been hiding with their horses and was informed that his master was feeling pangs of hunger. He rushed back to fetch a saddlebag which contained cold chicken, bread, apples, pears, and a bottle of wine, and nervously proceeded to lay down a formal picnic on a white linen cloth. As the Prince began munching a savory piece of chicken, he heard the first dry rattle of musket fire in the distance beyond their right flank. Good! That had to mean other German forces were arriving to engage the French near Rezonville. He noticed that after Voigt-Rhetz's arrival there were no more signs of withdrawal and that General von Redern went galloping back to his cavalry brigade with a look of grim satisfaction on his face. The cannons of the horse artillery remained unlimbered and ready, their black muzzles gaping at Vionville. Then, while he was finishing his second helping of chicken, the Prince heard the rumble of wagons pounding up the reverse slope and turned to see them disgorge a company of Bavarian infantry who, rapidly recovering from what must have been a wild cross-country ride, deployed in front of the guns within full view of the enemy. Several minutes later another seven wagons arrived with nearly a hundred Prussian grenadiers. The isolated hilltop suddenly seemed to be swarming with friendly troops, and as the Prince poured a tot of wine into a silver cup, he smiled to himself and mused: "Our Gustaf is doing himself proud!" But when he looked back down at Vionville and saw a line of artillery pulling into firing positions alongside massed cavalry formations, he had to fight down an uneasy feeling. Why didn't the French attack? Or start a bombardment of their own? There were at least fifty thousand of them within sight, a fact which even his orderly noticed and found ominous enough to disturb his own very rudimentary tactical concepts:

"His Royal Highness is lunching in a very exposed position," he ventured to hint to his master.

"Yes, a splendid view, isn't it, Anton," the Prince agreed. "Have yourself a piece of chicken. We don't stand on formalities here in the field." He began to peel himself a pear.

The crackling musket fire on the right flank was augmented by the deeper percussion of cannons. A dirty pall of smoke swelled out of a sward below Rezonville and began misting the view in that direction. Suddenly a battery a short distance from where the Prince was seated banged out a single salvo which burst squarely among the red roofs of Vionville. Instantly, the line of French artillery winked and puffed smoke in reply, but their shots fell far short, blowing useless craters into the lower slope of the hill. Cheers rose from the Prussian gunners and they gleefully patted the barrels of their superior Krupp cannons. In the sedate circle of high-ranking officers gathered around the division and corps commanders, the reaction was also pleasurable, even if more restrained: a ripple of nodding silver-spiked and plumed helmets followed by a relaxation of their tense postures. A few even went so far as to make their horses prance about in an arrogant, challenging fashion. One colonel detached himself from the group and rode over to Prince Eugene: "Your Royal Highness should stand up and make himself more visible to the enemy," he cheerfully suggested. "We want them to believe they are facing a dangerous force on this hill."

Prince Eugene recognized Colonel von Caprivi, Chief of Staff to General Voigt-Rhetz and an old friend, one of the few he could still call a friend within the Prussian High Command.

"That's all very well," he replied without making a move but wagging his head with a mischievous laugh. "But if I showed myself too clearly, the French might take to their heels before we can beat them in a fair fight. That would be a pity, considering this remarkably classical setting for a battle. Have some lunch, Georg?"

"Thank you, but I'm told soldiers fight better on empty stomachs," von Caprivi answered, smiling. Nudging his horse closer to the stump, he leaned down and spoke with mock severity: "I hear you've been making yourself unpopular again."

The Prince shrugged his huge body. "I'm interested in victory, not personal popularity. Have a cup of wine? Gives you courage, you know."

"You should have offered some to von Rheinbaben," von Caprivi answered with a demuring gesture. His face suddenly went completely serious. "You will get no thanks for what you are doing here, Your Highness."

Prince Eugene shrugged again and, filling his silver cup, rose ponderously to his feet and offered it to the Colonel. "Well, even if *you* don't need more courage, Georg, why not drink to victory? It's quite a decent wine, you'll see."

Von Caprivi accepted the cup and, holding it high, made a toast: "To victory and to one of its unsung heroes, Prince General Eugene of Hanover!" After draining the wine with one long gulp, he flipped back the cup with a grin, then wheeled his mount and galloped off to rejoin his corps commander. The Prince eased himself back down onto his stump and proceeded to slice wedges out of an apple and pop them into his mouth, his eyes gazing with a phlegmatic look over the battlefield. The young Chief of Staff of X Corps had not exactly explained the situation in detail, but it was becoming plain enough anyway. The French were assembling formidable forces to defend the Metz-Verdun road, which was not only their main artery of supply, but also the withering ganglion of retreat connecting them to the nerve center of Paris. The sound of cannon and musket fire a few kilometers east, now a sustained din, made it clear that other German units had made contact—hopefully, advance units of General von Alvensleben's III Corps and not merely his flank screens. The commander of X Corps had obviously prevailed upon the vacillating von Rheinbaben to stand his ground and by some aggressive posturing keep the enemy off balance and on the defensive. Even as he munched his apple, Prince Eugene watched the redoubtable von Redern lead his entire cavalry brigade out of their concealment and parade them along the crest of the hill to the roaring cheers of the gunners and thin line of infantry. This sight must have been unnerving to the French because they fired off several more salvos which again fell woefully short. There followed a kind of hiatus of inaction, like a tense intermission between acts of a great dramatic spectacle. Then Gustaf von Falkenhorst arrived with thirty wagons loaded with infantry.

The Leutnant immediately spotted Prince Eugene and dashed his lathering horse over to him: "All wagons between here and Thiaucourt accounted for and present with the requested reinforcements, Your Highness," he reported with excited satisfaction in his voice.

"Excellent, my boy!" the Prince exclaimed, eyeing the swarms of grenadiers and jaegers with outward appreciation, while inwardly wondering whether these splendid soldiers were about to be sacrificed to maintain a bluff or would really tip the scales toward victory. "Looks like nearly four hundred rifles. Excellent!"

"Four hundred and ten," Gustaf corrected him. His own eyes swept the vast enemy formations without a flicker of surprise, then eagerly sought out his own Second Dragoon Regiment, riding prominently in the fore of von Redern's brigade as it brazenly maneuvered into attack formation on the north slope of the hill.

"I trust more units are marching this way on their own feet," the Prince said, managing to sound entirely casual about it.

"At least five battalions of infantry from X Corps should be here within the hour, Your Highness," Gustaf replied. "May I now rejoin my own regiment, sir?"

Prince Eugene noticed the breathless eagerness of the request and instantaneously made up his mind to refuse it. If it lay within his power to prevent this brave, foolish boy from sacrificing his life in the carnage which was about to sweep those fertile Lorraine fields rippling below the hill, then he must do so. There were hundreds of young Prussian officers like him who at this moment were within a couple of hours of being killed or maimed and there was nothing he could do for them—but this one, the son-in-law of his best friend, he could save through a perfectly valid excuse which would protect the boy's honor. "I am sorry," he said with the formal tone of a general addressing an impetuous subordinate. "The wagons must fetch all the ammunition and supplies they left behind. You will return with them to the rear and make certain neither our guns nor our men want for anything today."

Gustaf's face turned a mottled white beneath the sweat streaming down from under his helmet; his voice shook with anger as he replied: "I submit, Your Royal Highness, that you are assigning me duty which rightly belongs to a sergeant of the Intendantur."

"How can that be when General von Rheinbaben personally expressed to me his concern for those supplies?" Prince Eugene harshly asked. "No. The mission calls for a leutnant at the very least. You shall go."

For a moment Gustaf completely lost control of himself and shouted: "You've got no damned right to use a dragoon officer for such piddling rear-echelon chores when he is needed in battle!"

Prince Eugene's chin suddenly emerged rock-hard out of its folds of fat. "You are presuming too much on the friendship between our families and are being grossly insubordinate, Herr Leutnant Baron Gustaf von Falkenhorst."

Gustaf spun Kugel around to take a frantic look at von Redern's brigade with its magnificent lines of cavalry facing the battlefield beyond, then completed the agitated, stamping circle to make a last desperate plea: "I beg Your Highness's pardon . . . and beg you reconsider!"

"I regret I cannot."

"May I at least ride down to my squadron to see if all is well with the men?"

"I am sorry, but there is no time for that." The Prince's stern expression wavered. "The best I can offer you is a few minutes to share my food. You must be hungry and I'd enjoy your company." His pudgy hands waved enticingly toward the picnic spread before his stump. But Gustaf glanced down at the chicken and fruit and wine with an expression of contempt. His riding crop whistled and struck Kugel's haunch with the sound of a pistol shot. The exhausted horse squealed, reared and spun, then took off toward the wagons, his hoofs throwing up dirt which splattered Prince Eugene's face and sullied the food on the white cloth. For a brief moment the Prince seemed to sag, his whole rotund body caving in as if all the bones inside it had suddenly turned into rubber and only the straining buttons of his grimy uniform were holding it together. His moist jowls and flatulent pink cheeks trembled and the eyes blinked like those of a child trying to hold back tears. But this collapse was only a matter of seconds, just a fleeting reaction which nobody, least of all Gustaf von Falkenhorst, noticed. When he called out to his orderly, both his voice and body were once again massively firm: "Anton! You may clear away lunch. Then bring me my horse. Sounds like there is action on our right flank and we had better move to the east slope so we can see what's going on."

From the southeastern rim of the plateau of rolling, unbroken farmland, the din of battle swelled with the sound of an approaching storm. The sporadic skirmishing which had begun when General von Alvensleben's cavalry screen probed up the ravine below Rezonville and ran into alert lines of French infantry, quickly flared into a general engagement as Prussian grenadiers and jaegers first trickled, then gushed through the narrow defile. Fluffy white puffballs of rifle fire blossomed all along the perfectly aligned French formations standing rank upon rank in the open according to their centuries old military tradition. But they failed to follow up their devastating volleys with bayonet charges, which could have turned the dangerous German threat against the vital Metz-Verdun road. It was fear for their right flank, so lightly disturbed at Vionville in the early morning, which immobilized them on the defensive; it was ignorance caused by a deplorable lack of reconnaissance which kept the Germans pressing on against vastly superior forces they thought to be nothing but stubborn rear guards of the enemy's retreating army. Stolidly courageous Brandenburgers responded to the shouts of their officers and stood fast where their attack had been stopped among heaps of dead and wounded comrades. The losses were grievous from the one superior French weapon, the chassepot rifle, but their stand enabled their own superior artillery to squeeze out of the ravine behind them and deploy along the crests of low hills to the west; soon fifteen batteries began blowing gaps in the French formations. The frontal assault turned into a flanking movement of the kind which obsessed French fears. The entire southern edge of the huge amphitheater seemed to catch fire while at the same time obscuring itself in palls of smoke through which the sun burned with a dull glow, shedding more heat than light. Too late, some French regiments counterattacked and although they drove back some overbold German artillery and littered the slopes with corpses in Prussian blue, they could not break the ominous pattern of envelopment. The tiny hamlet of Flavigny blazed up and fell to the Germans as Prince Eugene mounted his horse and took up his customary lone position near the staff officers surrounding the generals. Shortly thereafter, he was able to watch the infantry he had been responsible for bringing up join with X Corps units trickling in from the east for an assault on Vionville, resulting in the expulsion of the single regiment of *chasseurs* defending it. The Verdun road was cut. The bluff begun that morning had succeeded—*so far*. But the battle was far from over.

The French High Command, now thoroughly alarmed and completely ignorant of the fact that they were being intimidated by only two enemy corps, called for cavalry attacks, usually the last resort when used against unbroken infantry. They sent in two brigades of guards and cuirassiers who came on as massed squadrons in full glittering panoply, plumes and pennons flying, howling war cries and sounding their trumpets. Their splendid alignments gradually fell apart as they galloped forward, first disrupted by the soft, broken terrain, then decimated by murderous fire from German rifles bristling outside the still brightly burning Flavigny. Not a single Prussian infantryman was skewered by a lance nor put to the sword. Hundreds of horses tumbled into bloody kicking heaps, littering the ground with riders who lay where they fell, or crawled for cover, or got up and ran away if they were able-bodied enough. The few mounted survivors scattered as General von Redern came charging down the hill he had so impatiently occupied since dawn, his three regiments of dragoons and lancers thundering behind him to counterattack an already shattered enemy. Close behind the brigadier, and leading the First Squadron of Second Dragoon Guards, Rittmeister von Manschott hurled himself into battle with a single worried backward glance. It was directed at the Third Squadron led by an untried replacement because Gustaf von Falkenhorst had been detached on special duty with the Royal Pudding. Even though the squadron seemed to be pounding along in good ferocious order, von Manschott made a mental note to protest to Colonel von Hardel the usurping of a valuable officer during a critical action. Then he concentrated all his attention upon the bloody business at hand.

Von Redern's brigade plunged out of the clear air of the hill into the swirling smoke below, swept around the glowing ruins of Flavigny, and galloped past lines of gleefully shouting infantrymen who waved them onward across the fields they had just heaped with French horses and cavalry troopers. The expected shock of clashing head-on with enemy cuirassiers never came; there remained only remnants of the attacking French regiments, dazedly trying to sort themselves out among scores of frantic, riderless horses. The German brigade fanned out and chased them all the way back to their own infantry and artillery lines where the action suddenly broke up into wild individual melees.

In the fuming vortex of this violent, but insignificant, part of the battle, there was a man who had no business being there because he was the Commander in Chief of Napoleon's Army of the Rhine. But while Marshal François Bazaine sadly lacked the qualities of a great army commander, he did amply possess those of a good plodding soldier, who stakes his professional reputation on tactical details and stubborn personal courage. Thus, none of his subordinate generals knew where to find him during a battle, while any Prussian private trooper might do so and sever the head of the French Army with a lucky stroke of his saber.

As it happened, Rittmeister von Manschott spotted him through the smoke, a heavyset swarthy man mounted on a black horse and wearing gold epaulets and a laureled scarlet kepi. He never realized this to be Bazaine himself, especially since he seemed to be puttering around the emplacement of a cannon like a common artillery captain, ignoring the nearby clash of sabers and the whistling of bullets around his head. Von Manschott only recognized the uniform of a French general officer and immediately went for him with but two of his own troopers following him, the rest of his squadron having dispersed in the confusion. For an instant it looked as if the strange enemy general would be an easy kill, but there happened to be nearby another French officer who *knew* who he was. Sub-lieutenant Victor de Bretagne had just managed to collect a handful of his Twelfth Imperial Cuirassiers after the disastrous charge, which left him for the second time that day the regiment's only surviving officer. De Bretagne was crying with rage over their defeat when he was shocked to spot Marshal Bazaine in the thick of the fray and three German dragoons spurring their horses toward him. For a fraction of a second he hesitated over the terrible thought of letting the stupid old soldier find an honorable death in battle, but then he found himself bawling to his cuirassiers: "Save the Marshal!" before hurling himself toward the leading German.

Rittmeister von Manschott had charged to within a few yards of Bazaine and was aiming the point of his saber at the silver starburst medal pinned to the man's left breast when another horse collided violently with his own. He had a surprised glimpse of a Frenchman, a mere boy whose face was twisted into an expression of agonized hatred and whose uniform hung in blackened tatters on his body, his saber flashing in from a full backswing. He tried to parry, but both horses were locked together, stumbling and throwing him off balance. The boy's stroke hit home, cutting cleanly through the steel collar of his breastplate, biting deep into his neck and shattering his collarbone. The stunning force of the blow knocked him out of the saddle and he pitched headfirst to the ground. An iron-shod hoof plunged into his groin and he felt his pelvis crunch like breaking porcelain. Then a horse fell kicking and screaming on top of him, impaling itself on the spike of his helmet and wrenching it off his head as it struggled to its feet. Von Manschott barely managed to roll himself over and away from more flailing, stamping hoofs, but he could only raise his chest off the ground with his arms, the rest of his body dragging numb and inert, as if it had already died. He had a hazy impression of men slashing at each other all around him. A body tumbled heavily, a French cuirassier whose helmet rolled in the grass with its black horsehair plume trailing like the tail of a terrified animal. Suddenly the man he had tried to kill towered above him, still securely seated on his black horse, staring down with a pale, unperturbed, almost uncomprehending look, the medal on his chest glinting like a talisman of invincibility. That boy-soldier flashed by again and his voice pierced the din with a high-pitched, childish temper: "For God's sake, Marshal, get the hell out of here at once!" The Marshal seemed to shrug and calmly trotted off among the fighting cavalrymen. A darkness filmed over von Manschott's eyes as he sank back into the stubble, an almost pleasant lassitude inundating his whole body. He tried to fight against it and force himself to rise up, grab one of the riderless horses, and rally his dragoons. But this last desperate thought of his duty somehow dissolved into an incongruously muddled one involving Freida and Ruprecht. He momentarily had a vivid picture of his infant son suckling his wife's rich, firm breasts. Then all faded away.

By noon the local fighting between Rezonville and Flavigny died down to sporadic shelling and sniping while the main battle shifted eastward along the rim of the plateau and erupted with particular violence around Vionville, where the French unleashed a heavy bombardment in the hope of driving out its German captors. Up on his hill, Prince Eugene saw the III Corps commander, General von Alvensleben, join his colleagues and dampen their exultation over the smashing of the French cavalry charge. Without being pessimistic, he emphasized the seriousness of their situation, which remained one of insecure flanks while facing superior numbers. Tall clouds of dust still rose on the northeast horizon, clearly foretelling the arrival of more enemy troops. If the Metz-Verdun road was to be held, French batteries pulverizing Vionville would have to be driven off and since no infantry reserves were available, that called for a massive cavalry attack, one which might well turn out as disastrous for the Germans as had that of their enemy before Flavigny. General von Redern had not reformed his brigade after its morning chase, so the task had to be assigned to General von Bredow's six squadrons. A less-dashing but more-methodical officer than von Redern, he took plenty of time to organize the attack, which included a stealthy approach toward the French positions screened by the smoke of their own guns.

Neither Alvensleben nor Voigt-Rhetz, nor the ever-gloomy Rheinbaben remained on the hill to observe whether he succeeded; each of these generals galloped off with his staff to take more direct control over his own thinly spread command. Only Prince Eugene remained, seated like a stuffed green sack on his mare, one eye squeezed tightly shut while the other bulged in the eyepiece of his telescope which was aimed toward the fields beyond the pyre of Vionville. Between the shrouds and billows of gunsmoke he was able to view in microcosmic close-ups fragments of the savage battle which took place when von Bredow's squadrons closed unnoticed within eight hundred meters before hurling themselves into the French lines. The Hussars and dragoons did indeed suffer terrible casualties as had their enemy counterparts a few hours earlier, but at least the objective of their attack was made good. Before being driven back, von Bredow overran the French guns, killed most of the gunners, and broke up their supporting infantry. Something less than three battered squadrons made it back, but for the time being Vionville was secure, and its defenders (and terrified peasant population cowering in cellars) found relief from the fearful shelling. Yet, even as the violence abated in this part of the battlefield, it flared up elsewhere, even farther westward as the opposing forces kept maneuvering for each other's flanks. Once again Prince Eugene changed his position on the hill, this time to give himself a better view of the villages of Tronville and Mars-la-Tour around which thick lines of infantry were surging. The thicker lines the Prince spied through his telescope were French, one of the dust columns of the horizon having materialized into a full, fresh corps. The crisis was rapidly approaching and in spite of their reverses in previous engagements, the enemy still held the advantage. The Prince was just apprising himself of this fact when one of von Rheinbaben's staff captains galloped up and announced with acid courtesy: "The General's compliments to His Royal Highness and his urgent request for ammunition and victuals!"

"Inform His Excellency they will be made available shortly," Prince Eugene answered, unruffled.

"The need is immediate," the Captain snapped, his tone suggesting that General von Rheinbaben's compliments had contained much malice.

The Prince unhurriedly pried his watch out of a tunic pocket. It showed a quarter after three; Gustaf von Falkenhorst had been gone for nearly four hours. "Within the hour, whether that is considered immediately or shortly," he informed the Captain, who accepted this with a surly salute and left. After he had gone, Prince Eugene called out to his orderly: "Come, Anton! We've been spectators long enough. Now we must locate our tardy supply trains and drive them into battle." He kicked his mare into a clumsy canter, wincing with the pain the effort rubbed out of his saddlesores.

Leutnant Baron Gustaf von Falkenhorst was shepherding the last of his reloaded supply wagons back toward the battle with sullen efficiency. The bad temper with which he had started the return mission had had its edge dulled by sustained frustration and mounting fatigue. The broiling August sun was stewing his head, chest, and back in sticky body juices trapped inside his uniform. For hours he had been taunted by the sustained rumbling of cannons and the more brittle echoes of rifle fire reaching his ears from distant Vionville; for hours he had watched black clouds of battle boiling up into the sweltering atmosphere far to the north and been stung by the pronouncement of a wounded infantry colonel being carried to the rear: "The glory of one nation or the other is going up in smoke this afternoon!" Damn Prince Eugene—that meddling Royal Pudding—for making him eat the hot dust of supply wagons instead of bloodying his sword in a crucial battle! If the wounded Colonel was right, perhaps the *last* battle of the war. Perhaps the last *war* of his lifetime. There had only been two, after all, during his father's entire thirty-four-year service with the army. No doubt they were getting farther and fewer between, and a man had to be lucky to find a chance to distinguish himself in battle. Gustaf was coming to realize how drudgery and routine could deprive a soldier of the glorious clash and clamor of arms, specifically, the endless crawling supply trains which had to be kept plodding along in the rear of armies. Whatever excitement had at first aroused these lowly Intendantur men and beasts had now faded back to an obstinate minimal effort to accomplish the routine chores of moving shot, powder, bread, and fodder. Neither the threats nor entreaties of a mere dragoon leutnant could hurry them. Even more demoralizing for Gustaf was the plight of his own horse, Kanone Kugel, who had begun to wheeze and stumble by midafternoon. Unlike the common, unblooded breed pulling the wagons, this thoroughbred seemed willing to burst its heart rather than refuse to respond to its rider. But with no remounts available, Gustaf realized that such a supreme sacrifice would leave him trudging on foot with the menial infantry, a most-degrading predicament for a cavalryman. So he allowed his spent horse to match its pace to the lumbering wagons rather than lead them at a speed they would probably not follow. His own spirits sank into a fuming despair when he entered the hamlet of Chambley, occupied early that morning by only four Uhlans, but now glutted with pungently sweating troops of the X Corps being force-marched toward the battle.

Glancing over the bobbing stream of helmets, he was shocked to spot Prince Eugene waiting on his gray mare like an equestrian statue sculpted out of pure suet. It was several minutes before they could press to within speaking distance of each other.

"Good afternoon, Baron Gustaf! Have you all my supplies with you?"

Gustaf gritted his teeth over the "my supplies" and barely managed a respectful salute. "Yes, Highness."

"Splendid, my boy. Well, the situation has changed somewhat. Only a couple of wagons each of ammunition and victuals should go to Vionville, which is now in our hands. The rest of the train will proceed toward Mars-la-Tour, which we may or may not have captured by now. In any case, the brunt of the fighting has shifted to that locality."

"I have no idea where Mars-la-Tour is," Gustaf said with forebearance.

"Never mind. I will take the wagons there myself," the Prince cheerfully told him. "You go to Vionville."

Gustaf realized he had once again been maneuvered out of the center of the fight. "How goes the battle?" he wryly asked.

"So-so," the Prince answered, fluttering a pudgy hand back and forth. "We have plenty to worry about, but so has the Frenchman, and he is more apt to get addle-brained. Our chances are quite good."

"And how goes it for my regiment, Highness?"

"They had some brisk action about noon," the Prince admitted and took the cold, accusing look from the dragoon leutnant without flinching. "Some of your comrades have fallen, but from what I observed, most of them were surviving up to a couple of hours ago."

"And where are they now, Highness? Near Mars-la-Tour?"

"If I knew the exact position of every one of our regiments in this battle, I'd be a field marshal," the Prince retorted and squirmed to relieve the pressure on his saddlesores. He looked like he was about to crash to the ground with a resounding thump, but somehow managed to remain on his horse and also change the subject from that of the Second Dragoon Guards. "You didn't happen to spot my adjutant anywhere along the road?"

"No, sir—wouldn't know him if I had."

"A faithful dog of a man who always manages to sniff his way back to his master long after the chase is over. Answers to the name of Krindle. But never mind about him. How are you holding up? Your horse looks ready to collapse. Perhaps you should switch mounts with my man Anton."

Gustaf threw a disparaging look at the nag ridden by the Prince's orderly. "No thank you, Highness."

"Oh, very well. Stop fidgeting about so and break out four wagons from the train and take them on to Vionville. When you have them within gunshot distance of the village, and if you don't run into a hail of bullets, consider yourself relieved and free to find the kind of excitement you obviously expect out of war. If you are half the man I hope you are, you may come out of it wiser and more human. That may be well worth the risk. Thank you and good luck, Baron Gustaf!" The distraught young Leutnant was further disconcerted to find himself formally saluted by the Prince General, who then pummeled his placid mare into a rocking canter, ploughing her through the columns of marching infantry, and soon vanishing beyond their stifling pall of dust. He melted into the multitude just abreast of a tall oak planted in front of Chambley's schoolhouse and from whose boughs dangled the corpse of a peasant with the sling of his sniper's rifle wrapped around his strangled neck. Gustaf found himself staring at that corpse long after the Prince General Eugene of Hanover was out of sight.

The hill rising south of Vionville, which had been the observation point for such an illustrious group of German generals that morning, was by late afternoon entirely deserted except for a wagonload of dead dragoons who had been collected from the fields beyond Flavigny. Von Rheinbaben's horse artillery had long since pulled out to take up new positions inside the ruins of Vionville, as had the infantrymen who so dashingly rushed up here to intimidate their enemy. Even the commanding view had changed by the time Gustaf von Falkenhorst finally led his four wagons onto the crest. Palls of battle-smoke shrouded the entire plateau, drifting about in obscuring swirls which sporadically flashed, crackled, and boomed with the cacophony of battle. Soldiers could only be clearly seen when moving about in battalion formations, appearing and disappearing in the misty unevenness of the terrain, leaving sprinkled grains of pepper over the green to mark where they had sowed their dead. There was no pinpointing the epicenter of the struggle, nor any way of determining which side was holding its own where. The little villages which had been bastions savagely exchanged could only be spotted by the intensity of smoke they belched up through the dismal haze covering the entire thirty-square-mile arena. The sun, now drifting low on the western horizon like a distorted burning balloon, shot the scene through with shafts of amber light which kindled weird optical illusions out of the atmosphere. Through it all, the Metz-Verdun road meandered uncertainly through the fumes. Gustaf peered at the sight, disoriented. "Where is Vionville?" he shouted at one of the two dismounted dragoons tending the wagon full of corpses.

"Right over there, sir—what's left of it!" the man answered, waving toward a darker swirl boiling up out of the haze below the hill. Gustaf's eyes followed his point, then flicked back to the wagon and grew wide with the shock of recognition. Lying on top of a bloody heap of dead troopers was the body of Rittmeister von Manschott, the features of the face unnaturally flabby and chalk white, the head nearly severed from the body by a terrible saber slash. The sight of him caused such pain to suddenly swell inside Gustaf's chest that he actually lost his breath and could only gasp out: "For God's sake! . . . What's happened here?"

The trooper stared at him in confusion, but his companion, one of the regimental butchers who had been slaughtering wounded horses as well as collecting the bodies of dead cavalrymen, stepped forward, wiped his hands on the gory apron he wore over his uniform, and saluted smartly: "The brigade smashed hell out of the Frenchies, sir! These are all our dead we could clean out of the battlefield afterward. Only twenty-six. There were a few more wounded, of course." Following Gustaf's appalled gaze to von Manschott's body, he somewhat more solicitously inquired: "A friend of yours, Herr Leutnant?"

"Yes . . . but what are you doing with him?"

"He is dead, sir," the regimental butcher patiently replied to the near hysterical question. "It is very hot, so he must be buried with the rest as soon as possible."

"Now? Here?"

"No, sir. We are taking the bodies to the graveyard in Chambley where the brigade chaplain is supposed to await them. Everything will be done in a Christian manner."

"Can't you at least cover him up decently?" Gustaf shouted at the man in a quaking voice.

"With what, sir? We have not been issued shrouds. Only shovels." The officer wheeled his horse and escaped back to the head of his wagon train. Turning to his companion, he said, not unsympathetically: "Another dashing young gentleman with a lot to learn about the seamy side of war."

With the wagons rumbling behind him, Gustaf plunged numbly down the hill into the acrid haze where he saw dead lying scattered over the lower slope. French and German infantrymen, some looking as though they had lain down for a nap in the grass, others horribly mutilated by wounds in which swarms of bluebottle flies were already feeding. But he acted as if he did not even see them, his mind's eye still transfixed by the sight of von Manschott grotesquely sprawled on top of those corpses piled into their improvised hearse. His shock gradually changed into a deep rage, aggravated by an increasing sense of guilt. He was not mourning a close friend—their relationship had not been that, in spite of von Manschott's having acted as best man at his wedding—but rather felt violent resentment that an admired superior officer, a model of Prussia's military aristocracy, could be defeated and butchered, ending up as a shapeless lump on top of other shapeless lumps who had once been the smart troopers of his command. Could this tragic, revolting end have been prevented if he had been fighting at his side instead of safely riding through the rear on the Royal Pudding's errand? Could he have parried the fatal saber stroke? Had von Manschott died because he had had to battle for an absent officer as well as for himself? While these dark, troubled thoughts were searing themselves in Gustaf's mind, some *live* soldiers appeared suddenly in the haze ahead, Prussian grenadiers forming a picket line outside the smoking ruins of Vionville. A mounted leutnant with his hand wrapped in a bloody bandage spurred toward him and bellowed a challenge but then recognized the wagon train.

"I hope you bring ammunition!" the Leutnant exclaimed. "Lots of ammunition!"

Gustaf nodded and asked: "Do we hold Vionville?"

"By the skin of our teeth, but now the chances are better," the other officer replied with a relieved grin. "Get those wagons to the command post at the church. They'll be needed to evacuate wounded on their return trip."

Gustaf was surprised at the hard calmness of his own voice as he answered: "You will have to handle that yourself, Herr Leutnant! My responsibility ends here as long as we safely occupy Vionville. Can you direct me to my regiment, the Second Dragoon Guards?"

"Oh, they rode past here a couple of hours ago, heading west toward Mars-la-Tour," the Leutnant told him. "From the sound of shooting coming from that direction, I'd say you'd be better off staying here. God knows what you'd run into if you ride after them alone."

Gustaf kicked Kugel into a wheezing canter and called back over his shoulder: "I hope some damned Frenchies!"

"No doubt you will!" the Grenadier shouted back, then bawled at the teamsters to drive their wagons into the ruins of the nearby village.

Gustaf guided his horse over a smoke-veiled field littered with the collapsed and torn tents of an abandoned French bivouac. There were corpses of cuirassiers and stiff-legged cadavers of horses killed by the horribly maiming wounds of artillery shells; a cook-wagon was still steaming unattended, its huge black cauldron exuding fumes of burned beans and onions. Kugel almost fell as he blundered into a shredded mess tent where an eviscerated French colonel lay with a bloodstained napkin clutched torchlike in rigor mortis. Beyond the shattered bivouac they plunged into a brownish pink pall which reduced visibility to less than a hundred meters. There were no more corpses, no more collapsed tents. Only the uneven grassy folds of the fields dissolving into nothingness beyond the periphery of vision, empty and lonely, yet filled with ominous rumblings of cannon and rifle fire which seemed to swell and recede without any particular orientation to guide him toward the main battle. He pressed on, edging a little to the right, intending to pick up the Metz-Verdun road which had to run straight through Mars-la-Tour. Suddenly it materialized ahead of him, but even as he saw it, he heard nearby the characteristic high-pitched notes of a French bugle; he did not recognize the call, but it had to mean enemy troops were just beyond the road or even marching along it. Gustaf's rage was not quite suicidal, so he veered Kugel away and spurred him into a gallop toward the protecting shrouds of smoke; after covering several hundred yards, he reined back to conserve his horse's failing strength. Volleys of rifle fire echoed ahead, and he thought he discerned shouting. The ground became rougher, changing from a reaped meadow to broken tussocks interspersed with scrub.

Then the smoke parted and he found himself riding toward some dense woods before which lay, in almost-orderly lines, hundreds of fallen soldiers—Westphalian infantrymen whose skirmish lines had been mowed down as they advanced into the open. They lay so thickly on the ground that Gustaf had to slow Kugel to a walk and carefully guide him past the bodies. They were evidently not all dead because he heard sobbing groans which made him stop and peer at the inert shapes for signs of movement. Seeing almost an entire regiment of his countrymen lying in the glutinous mud of their own blood, he was once again overwhelmed by the terrible sense of unreality he had felt at seeing von Manschott's body.

Suddenly he became aware of startling hornetlike zips followed by splattering sounds in the grass around his horse; a daisy magically popped off its stem and sailed away, a brightly spinning little pinwheel. The shots did not register on his hearing, but as he stared over his shoulder in surprise, he saw the road emerging out of the battle smoke some three hundred meters behind him, its crown lined with rows of strange red blobs. It took several seconds for him to realize he was staring at the red kepis of French infantry lying in a ditch and taking potshots at him as he paused among the Westphalians they had just slaughtered with their deadly chassepots. For another two seconds he savored a wild urge to draw his saber and charge them singlehanded, then the more-sensible instinct for self-preservation jolted him into whipping Kugel into a frantic dash toward the protection of the woods, reaching it just ahead of a hail of bullets. Branches scratched his face and nearly knocked off his helmet. Kugel stumbled time and again as they tore through the dense growth. He heard wounded men calling out for help, but he did not stop as he was sure the Frenchmen were hard on his heels. The woods gradually thinned and he emerged into another open field where he blundered upon a ragged column of surviving Westphalians retreating from their disastrous encounter on the other side of the copse. Many were wounded and there was not a single officer left among them. "What is happening?" Gustaf called to a sergeant. "Where are you going?"

"We're being licked, that's what's happening," the sergeant answered without slowing his plodding retreat. "Back to where we started from, that's where we're going!" He waved an arm toward a village whose broken tile roofs were shimmering in the haze on the other side of the field. As Gustaf drove Kugel toward it, he passed stragglers of other infantry units, Bavarians, Brandenburgers, and Saxons, all streaming away from the din of artillery to the northeast. What made it incomprehensible was that there were no Frenchmen driving them, indeed, no Frenchmen in sight anywhere. Gustaf began shouting at the men as he cantered past them: "Get some order into your ranks! Face the enemy and stand fast!" But it had no effect at all.

The village he was approaching was not Mars-la-Tour, but the smaller Tronville, whose narrow lanes and modest square were so jammed with Prussian troops and caissons, mostly bent upon a hasty evacuation, that it seemed unwise to try forcing an entry through that mob. The confusion was heightened by sporadic salvos of enemy artillery which burst in haphazard patterns among the houses, the flying splinters of brick and tile creating as great a danger as the actual explosions. The church took a direct hit through its steeple, its bells crashing out of the belfry, which turned into a truncated flue belching black smoke. Gustaf hunched low in the saddle and skirted some gardens to reach the opposite, more-sheltered side of the unhappy little community. There he suddenly happened upon his own regiment in the orchard of a burning farm and his heart leaped when he noticed that its squadrons were not only fairly intact, but moving with their customary precision—*toward*, not away from, the enemy! In a pasture beyond the orchard, the rest of von Redern's brigade was following suit, wheeling north with sabers drawn, guidons snapping, helmets gleaming in the evening sun like moving silver walls. No feeling of defeat and retreat here! And there was Colonel von Hardel flanked by his color sergeant and bugler, the spike of his helmet shot crazily askew, but ramrod stiff in the saddle as he rode at the head of his regiment. Only his eyes moved when Gustaf pulled alongside of him and reported himself ready for duty. "Good afternoon, Herr Leutnant Baron! It's high time you rejoined us. What, may I ask, has been delaying you for so long?"

"The Prince refused to release me until the wagons had retrieved all the supplies," Gustaf gasped, finding himself much out of breath. "I had to deliver them back to Vionville."

"Ah, then we still hold Vionville?"

"Yes, sir. But on my way from there, I passed through lots of our infantry who appeared to be breaking before the enemy."

That direly spoken information did not overly disturb Colonel von Hardel. "We are on our way to put that to rights," he said while stolidly posting onward. "Now that you've seen fit to honor us with your company, you might as well make yourself useful. Take command of First Squadron in the place of Rittmeister von Manschott, who has also been absent since this morning's activities."

"He was killed, sir," Gustaf blurted out. "I saw his body being taken to burial just an hour ago."

Swiveling stiffly in the saddle, the Colonel looked directly at Gustaf. "Oh, dear! That is bad news indeed! A very fine young officer. Oh, dear. The old cliché about the best going first must have something to it, unfortunately. But you mustn't say anything about it to his men for the time being, Falkenhorst. Want to keep their morale high, you know. On our way to attack the enemy, we'll be passing through some of that broken infantry you saw. They need bucking up. So keep your squadron looking confident and smart. Right. Get on with it then."

Gustaf considered asking to be excused for a little longer while he found himself a remount to replace his sorely tired Kugel, who had doubtless covered better than forty kilometers, mostly at the gallop, since early morning. But the regimental commander was obviously in a huff over his long absence, and he thought better of offering any further excuses—even legitimate ones. Besides, he had a burning desire to participate in this action and avenge von Manschott. With a smart salute, he left Colonel von Hardel and took his place at the lead of the First Squadron, temporarily commanded by Sergeant Pluskat. That grizzled veteran greeted him without much cordiality and pointedly asked: "Any news of our Herr Rittmeister."

Gustaf hesitated too long before replying, "No, no news of him for the time being." Pluskat immediately knew the truth, but had the good sense to stare grimly ahead between his horse's ears and keep still about it.

In the waning light of the late afternoon, General von Redern's brigade of cavalry, still over seven hundred strong, moved toward the enemy at a brisk trot. They passed through disorderly ranks of German infantry who had been badly mauled by the French and retired beyond the range of those murderous chassepot rifles; some cheered and most of them visibly braced at the sight of these cavalrymen advancing in disciplined columns to fill the critical vacuum created by their retreat. Even the simplest private, whether a mounted trooper or footsore infantryman, sensed that the crucial moment of the day was at hand; the devastating shock of a massed cavalry charge was about to take place and could tip the scales decisively. The French were doubtless fumbling toward such tactics themselves, but now too late. The initiative had passed back to von Redern's brigade, spearheaded by von Hardel's dragoons. The whole attack sparked by the redoubtable General Voigt-Rhetz who prodded into action his vascillating cavalry commander, General von Rheinbaben. Pure luck balanced against inherent ineptitudes would decide the day, but fortune would inevitably favor the bold—and the French had hesitated even when victory was surely within their grasp.

From Marshal Bazaine down to his lowest-ranking brigadier, none of the French generals seemed to have thought of *defeating* the Germans in this battle, though they all would have eagerly gone over to the offensive *if* only the right order had been given at the right time. But from the morning's opening cannonade at Vionville through to the evening's climactic engagements on the extreme western flank of the battlefield, the French strategy had been to protect its line of retreat toward Verdun and Paris, and, failing this, to maintain at all costs that line back to Metz from where the retreat had started the day before. Metz, a fortified enclave on the Moselle River, far too cramped to protect Bazaine's huge misled hordes, had become a fatal illusion fixed in the inflexible mind of the Commander in Chief. His lack of offensive spirit had already infected his subordinate generals, their confusion compounded by a total absence of any clear tactical directives. Yet the failure of these French generals was cruelly sweetened by local successes, especially those won by their common infantrymen's marksmanship with a superior rifle. The corpses of thousands of Prussians fed into the battle as they arrived upon the scene after grueling forced marches from the south, littered these Lorraine fields. Lower-ranking Frenchmen exulted at the sight, and from their myopic view of the fight, thought themselves victorious. Only a few gifted with a broader military sense, like young Sub-lieutenant Victor de Bretagne, suspected their magnificent effort would come to naught. For him, at least, the frustration had become a physical agony such as neither his division commander nor Commander in Chief could feel through their stultifying crust of professionalism.

Victor de Bretagne had ranged through the thick of the fighting from Vionville to Flavigny, back to Vionville, on westward to Tronville Woods and the savage skirmishing between two armies grappling for each other's flanks, ending up after twelve bloody hours on the open slopes north of Mars-la-Tour where broad stubble fields beckoned the cavalry of both sides toward a culminating clash before sundown. Three horses had been shot out from under him during the course of the day. He had taken a bullet through the calf of his left leg, filling the boot with blood; a glancing saber blow had cut his shoulder. His uniform, already torn that morning by the shell which had killed all his regimental officers at breakfast, hung on his body in blackened, gory rags. He had long since become separated from General Forton's division. Of his regiment, only Sergeant Major Rodignolle and nineteen battered cuirassiers still followed him, or clung to him, rather, with a passionate ferocity sustained by a deep newfound admiration, one perhaps best described by the soubriquet with which one of them had baptized him in the heat of fighting: *"notre enfant terrible."* There was something effeminate about this nineteen-year-old boy and his shrill war cries for a decrepit emperor who had long since fled the scene in a landau especially cushioned against the agony of his chronic gallstones. But his effeminacy also had a pure touch of Jeanne d'Arc, which confounded cynical captains and inflamed simple troopers with the mystical spirit of the patron saint of all French soldiers. Perhaps this child-lieutenant would eventually be burned at the stake of some dusty garrison parade ground for having today insolently bearded many superior officers, including Marshal Bazaine himself, but he had in the meantime hurled himself time and again at the enemy so recklessly as to acquire an aura of invincibility bound to stir even the most sluggish heart. Yet, for all the outward manifestations of his fighting spirit, he seemed unable to overcome a deep foreboding of defeat, of anguish over the futility of individual heroism which, in the end, could never make up for vacillating leadership of the army as a whole. The feeling became unbearable when he reached the fields north of Mars-la-Tour and found in a shallow vale a confused mass of French troops amounting to an entire corps; infantry, cavalry, and artillery, most of them milling about and trying to sort out their teeming formations in uncertain anticipation of what the *Germans* would do next. Only two batteries of cannon were firing desultory salvos into distant targets entirely shrouded by the gathering misty gloom. Followed by his ragged little band of cuirassiers, Victor de Bretagne rode up to an agitated cluster of staff officers and brazenly accosted a major: "Why don't we advance over the Verdun road?" he demanded. "It's not a wall, you know, and we might as well cross it before the enemy does."

The Major glared at him through frazzled strands of fur hanging from his shako over his bloodshot eyes, his expression showing first outrage, then sympathetic concern. "You should ride to the rear and find a surgeon, *mon petit sous-lieutenant*," he mildly suggested. "You look like you've done your bit for today and should go lick your wounds."

It was a constant source of irritation to Victor that senior officers invariably tended to address him as *mon petit sous-lieutenant* and he as invariably took delight in sarcastic ripostes delivered with feigned childish innocence. "Thank you, sir," he retorted. "I was just wondering if I should do what everybody else is doing—*nothing!*" Before the Major could splutter out a reply, Victor trotted on over to the Captain of a battalion of grenadiers, whose disordered command seemed mostly concerned with refreshing themselves out of their canteens, the purplish trickle of liquid on their chins betraying the fact that they were fortifying themselves with wine rather than spring water. Some of the ranks had sat down in the grass with their rifles in their laps, while others had broken up into chatty little groups. "When the aperitif hour is over," Victor loudly chided their Captain, "how about getting on with shooting Germans?"

The Captain's mustachioed lip curled with contempt. "Let them come if they dare! We'll be ready, like we were back in the woods an hour ago! We didn't let a damned one get within a hundred meters of us."

"That is perfectly obvious, sir," Victor sneered and, before the insult had sunk in, removed himself beyond range of the Captain's curses. He passed another infantry battalion, dusty and disgruntled from marching, but unbloodied by action, then paused close behind one of the batteries banging away into the haze which made it impossible to observe the fall of their shot. The gunners were serving their brass-barreled muzzle-loaders in a methodical, but unhurried, manner, bantering and joking with each other as they danced by rote the intricate ballet of swabbing, reloading, and resighting between rounds. "What are you shooting at?" he asked one of them.

The sweating gunner looked puzzled for a moment, then asked the same question of his comrades who shrugged and answered: "Mars-la-Tour or Tronville, I think."

"How do you know you are hitting your target?"

"So what does that matter?" the gunner countered, "just as long as the bastards know we are still here!" With great aggressiveness he brandished his eight-foot-long ramrod toward the invisible enemy.

Victor de Bretagne shook his head and cantered toward the right wing of the corps where a regiment of Hussars and two squadrons of *chasseurs* were resting at ease, some of them dismounted and watering their horses. A small group of their senior officers had collected on a knoll which afforded an excellent view of the open terrain to the south and were leisurely discussing its features exactly as they were used to doing on maneuvers. They were startled when the ragged, bloody Sub-lieutenant suddenly rode in among them and boldly asked: "Gentlemen, when do we attack?" He was not in the least abashed to discover that one of the officers was a Brigadier General whose whiskers were carefully modeled after those of Emperor Napoleon and who begged the pertinent question with a vapid one of his own:

"*Mon petit sous-lieutenant,* where is your helmet?"

Victor blinked at him and ran a hand through his dusty black mop of curls as if just discovering that this vital piece of his uniform was missing. "Oh-la! I must have lost it at Vionville . . . or perhaps it was at Flavigny! But please, my general, don't worry too much about it. I promise to go back and look for it the moment the battle is over."

"Who are you and where is your regiment?" the General's adjutant barked at him.

"Sub-lieutenant de Bretagne, at your service," Victor introduced himself, bowing in his saddle rather than saluting since that would have been improper military etiquette without a helmet. He waved behind him toward Sergeant Rodignolle and his pathetic collection of troopers. "There is my regiment, the Twelfth Imperial Cuirassiers, sir."

"Good God!" the General exploded. "Is that all that's left of the Twelfth? What about the rest of Forton's cavalry? Cut to pieces, I suppose. And Grenier's infantry? Pushed back, obviously! Damnation! My left flank must be dangling in thin air like a ripe plum!" As he jumped from one alarming conclusion to another, he worked himself into a nervous lather which was aggravated by his adjutant, who evidently considered it his duty to repeat all his master's words in an even louder voice. The three other officers, a colonel of the Hussars, one of the *chasseurs,* and a major of the artillery, all pressed in with advice, most of which being that the corps commander, General Ladmirault, should be advised of the critical situation before any action was taken—only nobody knew exactly where to find General Ladmirault.

Victor tried to nudge his horse in closer to the excited Brigadier but was blocked by the others surrounding him. He called out three times, loudly but reasonably politely: "If you please, sir!..." but to no avail. He peered back over his shoulder at his little band of cuirassiers who appeared to be slouching in oblivious exhaustion on their equally exhausted horses, but he knew they were really intently watching and listening. Rodignolle actually dared look up, smirk, and make a lewd gesture with his index finger, pointing it directly at the General's broad posterior. Victor grimaced, drew in his breath, then screamed at the top of his shrill and adolescent voice: "General, will you please listen to me!" The sound of it cut through the basso rumble of battle like the sudden scream of a woman caught in a brawl of men. The brigadier swiveled around and, together with his subordinates, stared openmouthed at the source of the disturbance. Victor took advantage of this brief moment of undivided attention to address them with a contrasting calm which would preclude any accusations of hysteria:

"If you please, gentlemen!" he said. "I have within the last three hours been involved in two engagements along your left flank. Vionville is occupied by the enemy and perhaps Mars-la-Tour too. But nowhere else has he been able to hold any position along the Verdun road. I've not run into a single live German on this side of it, only Frenchmen waiting for orders. That is why I ask: When do we attack?"

The adjutant inflated himself for a withering reprimand, but his General cut him off with a slicing gesture and answered himself: "Thank you for that information and accept my compliments for your zeal—if not for your manners, *mon petit sous-lieutenant!* As for the attack, you will have to wait along with the rest of us for matters to develop according to regulations and orders."

"Whose orders and regulations, *mon general?* The Prussians'?" This culminating piece of sarcastic impertinence brought gasps out of these officers, but there was something in his eyes which were no longer looking at them, but at something in the distance, which made them turn about and once more anxiously face the direction of their enemy. Then they all gasped again: Long, dark blue lines of German cavalry, their armor and weaponry sparkling in the setting sun as they emerged out of the thick haze on the far side of the broad fields, were methodically maneuvering their columns off the road to line them up for an attack.

It was the artillery Major who first reacted: "I'm not about to have my pieces overrun by those devils again!" he exclaimed, then dashed off toward his batteries still blithely shooting away far above the enemy's heads. "Cease fire and limber up!" he yelled as he approached them. "Limber up and pull back!"

The brigadier did not try to stop him but turned surprisingly resolute as befitted a French general in the face of the enemy. "Very good, gentlemen!" he snapped at the two remaining colonels. "They have to be stopped. The time has come to sacrifice our brigade for the glory of France!" With that questionably suitable piece of dramatics, all three of them galloped off to arouse their waiting cavalry regiments, leaving Victor de Bretagne alone on his horse on top of the knoll, a bedraggled, somewhat pathetic, yet still-inspiring figure of frustrated defiance.

Sergeant Rodignolle snarled at his troopers to close up around their *enfant terrible,* joining him to contemplate in silence the enemy squadrons massing without interference for the impending attack. There was at least a full brigade opposite them, and even as they watched, more columns materialized from the direction of Mars-la-Tour, seen only as a darkly smoking smudge in the distance. Others kept coming on from Tronville, which could not be seen at all. Cuirassiers identifiable by the glint of their armor; Uhlans and dragoons whose formations bristled with lances, sabers, and guidons of blue and white. The peal of their bugle calls floated across the intervening expanse of grass, pleasantly muted by the distance and mingling with the trills of larks still soaring unperturbed in the evening sky. A few French infantrymen fired shots in the direction of the enemy horsemen, but the better than thousand-meter range was too much even for their splendid chassepots and did not in the least disrupt the Germans' regulation-perfect preparations for the charge.

"*Eh bien, mon sous-lieutenant!*" Rodignolle softly growled at Victor. "What do you want us to do? Fight a bit more?"

"Are you still ready to follow me?" Victor countered.

Regimental Sergeant Major Rodignolle was a hardened old professional soldier who had campaigned in Italy and Africa, but like some hardened old professionals, he had a romantic streak which on rare occasions could be kindled into something absolutely heroic. He managed to look insulted and loudly asked the boy: "Haven't we followed you, our last officer, all day? Why should we stop now . . . even if it means the end of the Twelfth? Who wants to survive a regiment gone down in glory?"

Victor de Bretagne soberly contemplated him and his battered troopers for a moment, then cast a critically inquisitive glance over the corps which had begun to bestir itself in the shallow valley below their knoll. The cannons had fallen silent and were being hurriedly retired into the woods behind the fields; the infantry were likewise falling back to take up defensive positions around the precious guns. Only the cavalry brigade seemed to be organizing its squadrons into something like attack formations, but he noticed that their officers were still conferring, perhaps arguing with each other, their brigadier cantering from one group to the other. With the painful memory of his fiasco of the morning when he had attempted to lead his division against some German artillery, Victor hesitated, not from flagging courage, but from a harshly learned realization that courage can be a horribly wasted commodity in battle. Perhaps these last twenty men of the Twelfth deserved to be spared. Perhaps it was folly to fight a regiment to the very last man. There was such a thing as honorable surrender to overwhelming misfortunes of war. Then he noticed that out of the woods more mounted *chasseurs* followed by Imperial Dragoons debouched onto the field, passed through the retiring artillery and infantry, quickly wheeling in their direction. They would even things up a bit if that brigadier did not procrastinate too long. There really was no choice.

"Bugler!"

A boy even younger than himself spurred his horse forward. "Sir!"

"When I give you the order, I want to hear the loudest, clearest, most beautiful charge you've ever blown. It will likely be your last, so make it your best. Do you understand?"

"Yes, sir."

"Rodignolle! Try and put together something that looks like a squadron of the old Twelfth!"

The troopers roused themselves, grinned, and formed into a precise line of twenty abreast; without awaiting the next command, they drew their sabers. But Victor de Bretagne was not quite ready. He peered at the enemy and then back at the reinforced French brigade he expected to support him—and this time he would make sure of it! He spotted the Brigadier down there, his own bugler close by with his instrument before his lips. The General appeared to be gaping transfixed at the little band of cuirassiers formed up a good hundred yards ahead of his own forces, suddenly remembering that insolent *petit sous-lieutenant* who had so persistently inquired about the attack and who was now ready to rob him of the dramatic order to launch it. They stared at each other during a moment of tense silence when everything seemed in a state of suspended animation. Then the General shrugged and raised his saber. Victor bawled: "Charge!" and his young bugler cut loose a stirring clarion call exactly as expected of him. The clear, high notes raised repeating echoes down the lines of the brigade as other buglers took them up, followed by other, faintly mocking and discordant ones from far across the field as the Prussians simultaneously launched their own attack. The ground began to tremble as well over two thousand horsemen suddenly hurled themselves against each other.

Leutnant Baron Gustaf von Falkenhorst knew that he was about to be ingloriously cheated out of this battle too. Even as he moved out at the head of his squadron to meet the Frenchmen thundering toward him in long ragged lines which seemed to solidify and gain power as they approached, Kugel began to falter. The horse was giving its last full measure of effort, but its breathing came in uneven spurts out of rhythm with its stride and with groans which communicated its agony to the rider. Gustaf felt a brief pang of distress for the valiant animal, yet a stronger one over his own plight and frustration. The danger of finding himself galloping in a head-on collision between two charging brigades on a dying horse did not immediately register upon him, only that the pounding hoofbeats of the front ranks of the squadron he was supposed to be leading were rapidly overtaking him. He had the appalling thought that they might believe *he* was faltering rather than his mount, and that made him mercilessly beat and spur the wretched animal while screaming at his men: "Forward! Forward! Close up and ride forward!"

The ranks had to open to pass him, then closed again, leaving him behind. He was forced to veer out of the way of the following squadron, then the next. They blotted the enemy out of his sight, and for a moment he had an extraordinary view of the charge as seen from the rear, hundreds of bobbing rumps with tails streaming out behind them. Then the opposing brigades smashed into each other with a tremendous swirl of dust rising in the evening sky together with the clashing of steel and screams of men and animals. At that very moment, Kanone Kugel, the champion gelding of Schloss Varn's famous stables, stopped in his tracks and with a surprisingly gentle motion, sagged to the ground, rolled over, and died of a burst heart.

Gustaf easily threw himself clear through the soft grass and sprang back to his feet, cursing, tears streaming down his face as they had not done since he was a small boy. He stood for an instant, flailing at thin air with his saber and yelling at his dead horse until shocked into the full realization of his peril by columns of Uhlans bearing down on him, lances leveled as they charged at the full gallop into the savage melee less than a hundred yards ahead. In the nick of time he dove back for the protection of Kugel's body and one trooper actually hurdled them in a perfect jump. He was pelted by flying clods of sod and choked by dust raised by hundreds of hoofs as they pounded by. When he dared to look up again, he saw a flailing maelstrom of men and horses which gradually shredded itself out into wild individual combat. Animals fell heavily, kicking and screaming, tumbling troopers rolled and dodged, clutching their wounds until knocked senseless by flying ironshod hoofs. A French *chasseur* and a Prussian dragoon swept toward him, stirrup to stirrup as they slashed away at each other, each parrying the other's blows with ringing sabers until the Prussian suddenly drew his pistol and fired it full in the Frenchman's face. The corpse bounced to within a foot of Kugel's head and lay twitching, all scrambled brains and shattered teeth. A Uhlan flew by screaming, dragged from a stirrup as his horse bolted out of a thrashing tangle of troopers. A wild-eyed, helmetless young French cuirassier fought his way clear of the milling throng and attacked a Brandenburg Hussar with a backswing whose power belied his slender build and virtually decapitated his opponent; he did not give his fallen enemy a second glance but looked around for another victim until his eyes locked on Gustaf. Then he spurred his horse forward with the gory point of his saber aimed straight for him.

Gustaf managed to get up on his knees and raise his own saber to parry the coming thrust, but, knowing there would be too much force behind it, he clawed at his holster in a desperate effort to draw his pistol. The Frenchman rode his horse like a maniac, bending low along its neck, peering along his blade for a sure kill while giving out a high-pitched scream. A fraction of a second before the two sabers clanged together, Gustaf pulled the trigger. As the cuirassier fell on top of him, his horse tripped on Kugel and crashed down on both of them. Gustaf felt his ribs cave in, and all the wind squeeze out of him, before a stunning blow on the side of his head blacked out his senses. When he regained consciousness, he thought only a second or two had elapsed and instinctively began thrashing around to defend himself again, only gradually becoming aware that the noisy holocaust of battle had died to an eerie silence, broken only by low sighs and groans. It was almost totally dark, and it took him several dizzy minutes to focus his eyes and realize the fight was over and night had fallen. The low rumbling and muted flashes from the distance were not from cannons, but thunder and lightning of a faraway storm.

For a long while he lay in the dewy grass, propped up on his elbows, feeling a dull pain in his head and a sharper one in his ribs, but his whole being flooding with relief over having survived without being badly hurt. There was a pale half-moon shining through some ragged clouds overhead, casting just enough light to show the field around him strewn with the grotesque shapes of fallen horses and men. Suddenly a groan from very close by made him sit up. There, a few feet away from Kugel's already stiff-legged carcass, lay the young cuirassier who had so nearly killed him. Gustaf crawled closer on his hands and knees. Looking into the Frenchman's face he saw in the pale moonlight that one eye had been shot out of its socket, leaving a gory hole full of coagulated blood; the other eye stared back at him so unblinking that for a moment he was certain the boy was dead. But then a feeble, childish voice suddenly pleaded: *"Tuez-moi, s'il vous plaît!"*

Gustaf had only been schooled in elementary French at his military academy, but he understood his young enemy's pathetic plea to be mercifully killed. He sat down next to him, fumbled inside his tunic, found his handkerchief, and tried to dab the blood gently out of the empty eye socket. "You are wounded," he said, "but not so badly as that. *Pas très mal.*"

Victor de Bretagne did not move, but tears began to roll out of his good eye and for the next five minutes he kept sobbing softly over and over. "I am blind! . . . I am blind!"

Gustaf remained by his side, worrying about how to alleviate the boy's terrible injury, yet more concerned about himself and the possibility that he had fallen inside the French lines and would be taken prisoner, the ultimate degradation, he thought, to end this ill-starred day. When the boy's sobbing stopped, Gustaf leaned down and whispered: "I am sorry, but you are my enemy and I can't stay with you. If I can, I will send help. Good-bye!" Leaving the handkerchief in the eye socket, he staggered to his feet and stumbled away.

At first he was completely disoriented in the gloom of the battlefield, tripping over bodies and, at one point, blundering into a tangle of them and falling into their rigid, sticky embrace. Struggling on, he spotted what looked like distant fires. Deciding they must be from the still-smouldering village of Mars-la-Tour, he turned in their direction. Then, in a clear moonshaft, there stood a live, riderless horse, calmly browsing among the corpses. It raised its head and snorted uneasily as he drew closer. There was no way of telling whether it was a French or German horse, but that did not matter. He spoke softly, soothingly to it, reached out and stroked its inquiring muzzle, then took up the dangling reins. Gustaf was so weak that it took considerable effort for him to hoist himself into the saddle, but the gentle, placid animal patiently waited for him to make it. When he was mounted, they began to tread their way carefully off the battlefield toward those fires. From somewhere in the darkness behind them, a man was crying: "Mama! . . . Mama! . . . Mama!" It was impossible to tell his nationality.

A few minutes later Gustaf stopped with his heart in his throat as different lights suddenly appeared ahead, bobbing lanterns. There were voices too, muffled and low, but as they drew closer he recognized them as German. It was a litter-carrying party collecting the wounded. Only a dozen men to succor the hundreds who must be lying out there. Gustaf called to them and in the next moment the lanterns were shining into his face. "Are you wounded, Herr Leutnant?" a voice asked.

"I can make it. Got myself unhorsed but found this one. Am I safely inside our lines?"

"Certainly so, Herr Leutnant. The Frenchies were driven off this field by our cavalry. Don't you know that?"

"I was knocked out for a while," Gustaf bitterly admitted. For some reason he thought of the boy-cuirassier lying in the grass with his right eye shot out. "I'll find my way now, but there's a Frenchman back there I had to shoot. He's still alive and badly wounded. Find him if you can."

"We'll do our best, Herr Leutnant, but a lot of our own boys need help too."

"Yes, of course. Thank you."

He came up on the road from where his brigade had launched their attack, and from there on he was able to move at an easy trot toward Mars-la-Tour until he was challenged by sentries posted outside the village. In the light of their lanterns he realized he was riding a French horse whose bright red caparison carried the gold Roman numerals XII. After the sentries passed him on, he found that the fires he had seen were not from smouldering buildings, but the campfires of the X Corps. Very few of the soldiers were huddled around them, most of them lying where they had collapsed after a long day of marching and fighting, long sleeping windrows of infantry, artillery, and cavalrymen lying in the streets, in gardens, in doorways of the shattered houses, and among the ruins of those destroyed by shellfire. The silence was oppressive, only broken occasionally by the groan of a wounded man and by the soft snoring of those in exhausted sleep. Nobody paid the slightest heed to Gustaf as he listlessly ambled his French nag past prostrate shapes huddled even in the gutters of the narrow streets. Then he slowly rode into a small square in front of a half-demolished church and there, by the biggest campfire of all, imperiously perched on the tailgate of one of his supply wagons, he found Prince General Eugene of Hanover. His batman was busily feeding him succulent slices from a pig roasting on the embers when Leutnant Baron Gustaf von Falkenhorst suddenly materialized in the red glow before him. The massive jowls, still sweating in the humid heat of the August night, fell motionless, then split into wrinkles of a questioning grin:

"God bless me if it isn't the Baron Gustaf! It *is* you, isn't it?"

Gustaf stared blankly at him and nodded: "Yes, it is."

"Well, well! And you've had your battle?"

Gustaf nodded again, this time in tight-lipped silence.

"And captured yourself an enemy horse, I see! Well, well, well." The Prince waved a piece of pork impaled on his silver picnic fork and became quite exuberant. "Get down and share in my own humble booty, a very delicious French pig! Let's celebrate this glorious day! The French are retreating back toward Metz where we'll surely trap them tomorrow and you've survived your first battle. A glorious day!"

"It has most certainly not been glorious for me, Your Highness," Gustaf tersely blurted out, "so please excuse me if I do not join in your celebration." He wheeled his horse around and vanished into the darkness beyond the Prince's campfire, seeking some corner of solitude in Mars-la-Tour where he could lie down like the common soldiers and let flow the tears he felt unable to restrain any longer.

December 1870

Francs - tireurs

✠　✠

t had been a depressing week for Colonel Count Frederick Paul von Beckhaus und Varn, one during which he had taken leave of the war in order to attend the double funeral of his elder daughter and his grandson, the Princess Esther von Brattelbach and Prince Otto Frederick Karl. The little prince had not even been able to greet life with a protesting wail before it was all over for him, and within two days his mother had died of childbed fever. Her father could not help feeling that the uterine baptismal, performed during the difficult delivery by a priest wielding a syringe full of unsterile water, had something to do with their deaths. The Count was not a religious man, but his Lutheran-Prussian prejudices were nevertheless very strong and sometimes made it difficult for him not to be anti-Catholic. At any rate there had to be a *reason* for the tragedy, and since he was neither fatalistic nor superstitious, the Catholics' insistence upon baptising a dying infant aborning, even at the peril of the mother, was something tangible upon which to vent one's bitterness—the helpless attending physicians had certainly been unable to provide anything better. Thus, his eldest daughter whom he had so devotedly arranged to become a Princess of the Palatinate, and his grandson, who was the first male of direct von Beckhaus descent since his own son had died twenty years earlier, had both been sealed for eternity into their dark crypt beneath Schloss Brattelbach. And

now there was only that intransigent tomboy, Tessa, and whatever unlikely heirs she might produce *if* her husband survived
the war. It was a bleak outlook for the house of von Beckhaus
und Varn.

If nothing else, the melancholy proceedings at Schloss Brattelbach had been relatively brief. Although the actual funeral
ceremony in the castle's chapel and crypt had taken five hours,
the party of mourners had dispersed by midafternoon, led by a
misty-eyed Prince Hektor, who pleaded urgent business with
his regiment on garrison duty at Sedan. Count Frederick Paul
was able to get away quickly since no other von Beckhaus relatives had been able to come, his wife being too prostrate with
grief to make the journey and Tessa too far away in Silesia to
arrive in time. Thus, he traveled alone with his brooding
thoughts, first in a coach provided by Prince Hektor to Kaiserslautern, then without pause for the night, he boarded a train
to return to his post outside of besieged Paris.

He sat up all night in his private compartment, staring into
the blackness beyond the window which gradually became
crusted with fine snow, the first heavy fall of the winter. For a
while he tortured himself with the memory of Esther as he
remembered her best, a strikingly beautiful little girl growing
up to look exactly like her mother when she was the beautiful
Viennese girl he had courted twenty-five years ago. He would
have to write a letter to Antoinette with details about the deaths
and funeral, one which would no doubt cause her more fainting
spells. He would have to write to Tessa also. So far there had
only been time to send brief, blunt telegrams. He was trying to
compose these painful letters in his mind when the train
stopped at Saarbrücken. The stationmaster, who had been fore-
warned that the Inspector General of Military Railroad Transport was aboard, presented himself at one o'clock in the morning to offer his respects, a tray of cold meats, and a bottle of
cognac. Because he had neglected to eat dinner and suddenly
found himself very hungry, the Count had to suffer the pompous man's company while the train waited in the station.

"I am aware of the tragic nature of Your Excellency's journey," he intoned, watching the Count cut himself a slice of
liverwurst and spread it with mustard. "Please accept my most
heartfelt sympathy."

"Yes-yes. Thank you, Herr Stationmaster."

"I have myself lost a beloved girl-child. Scarlet fever, you
know. A terrible disease. So I understand what Your Excellency
is suffering at this moment."

"I am trying to enjoy the food you so kindly have provided," Count Frederick Paul answered with his mouth full.

The stationmaster filled the second glass he had thoughtfully provided for himself and raised it: "To a beautiful deceased lady, the Princess Esther von Brattelbach, née von Beckhaus! May she join the angels with whom she belongs!"

The Count failed to raise his own glass to the toast and instead inquired with sarcastic amazement: "You knew my daughter, Herr Stationmaster?"

The railroad official squirmed and wiped his chin on his sleeve. "The beauty and charm of the Princess Brattelbach was known to all Germany. She will be sorely missed, Your Excellency!"

During the next ten minutes he kept up a steady one-sided chatter of commiseration in which he enumerated all the deaths in his family over the past three generations, mourning, in turn, a grandfather killed at Jena, an uncle who had died at sea while emigrating to America, a father and mother who had expired of old age, and a brother-in-law slain in the war just two months ago. The Count listened patiently enough but was finally moved to ask: "When does this train proceed to France?"

"Not until I announce His Excellency has finished his supper, of course," the stationmaster officiously replied.

Count Frederick Paul virtually threw the depleted tray and bottle at him. "Such nonsense! The schedules of my railroads are not to be held up for anybody, do you hear? There is a war going on, dammit!"

The befuddled official tumbled out of the compartment and scurried down the platform, frantically blowing his whistle at the locomotive engineer. The train jerked into motion, rumbled out of Saarbrücken and plunged into the wintry darkness of Lorraine. Count Frederick Paul found relief in being alone again with his thoughts, but the loneliness also weighed heavily on his spirits. The stationmaster had neglected to trim the wick of the single oil lamp lighting the compartment, and it began smoking badly; he cracked open the window and allowed the cold wind to sweep in, bringing with it snowflakes, which swirled about before melting and scattering their droplets over the red plush seats. When it turned too cold, he closed the window, blew out the lamp, and sat in the dark with his greatcoat wrapped around him, listening to the clickity-clack of the wheels and thinking of Tessa. This difficult child whom he had never been able to understand was his only direct descendant now, and through her the von Beckhaus fortune would eventually make wealthy the impoverished von Falkenhorsts. For the first time since the sixteenth century, Schloss Varn would not be occupied by an owner carrying on the family name. He told himself this would have come to pass even if Esther and her son had lived, in which case his weak, charmingly frivolous, elder daughter would have meekly turned over the family affairs to Prince Hektor, who was neither astute nor thrifty.

It struck him that for all her faults, Tessa might, through her stubborn unfeminine nature, insist upon her interests and guard them better, especially if her soldier husband occupied himself exclusively with his military career. The Count began to reconsider the letter he had composed in his mind to Tessa, now dwelling little on her sister's death, instead planning how to groom her for her future responsibilities. He decided to visit her as soon as King Wilhelm would release him from his duties as Inspector General. Perhaps then father and daughter could yet become close; perhaps as she grew older (she was not yet nineteen after all!) she would come to accept his influence and curb her own impetuousness. The idea struck him that with the King's permission and an agreement with the von Falkenhorsts, the two family names could be combined so that if Tessa had sons, they would still carry on the name: von Falkenhorst-Beck-haus und Varn. The prospect relaxed his uneasy brooding and he finally dozed off. When he awakened, the train was pulling into Metz as a snowy dawn was breaking.

The depot was crammed with military supplies taken from Bazaine's army after it had capitulated two months before, most of it still being sorted out for transport back to Germany. The whole area was heavily guarded by Prussian sentries, and the Commandant's adjutant, a wiry little Major, together with a Deputy Inspector General of Military Railroads, met the train and escorted Colonel Count Frederick Paul into a private office of the stationhouse where breakfast had been spread out for him. The rest of the passengers, all military personnel, had to take their victuals from a canteen. The Count accepted a steaming cup of coffee and stood by the frosted window, peering out disapprovingly at the glut of freight cars in the railroad yard. "This does not look like an efficient operation, gentlemen," he grumbled. "Even if the great battles are over and the French Emperor our prisoner, the war continues. You seem responsible for a bottleneck in the vital supply line necessary to bring it to conclusion."

"It is not really here at Metz where we have troubles, Your Excellency," the Deputy Inspector excused himself. "Rather they happen along the lines outside of the town. It is difficult to dispatch trains when the military responsible for their security can't keep French farmers from tearing up the tracks and taking potshots at our locomotives."

The Major bridled at this but had his own excuse: "Since the main body of the Second Army was transferred to siege duty outside Paris, we have only a small garrison stationed here, Your Excellency. Even so, we catch and hang several *francs-tireurs* a day. Last week we burned down a whole village whose inhabitants had tampered with a railroad bridge."

"Possibly we are provoking the troubles ourselves," the Count suggested. "Those farmers believe they are defending their country against us. If we treated them with reasonable fairness, perhaps they could be convinced to leave the fighting to professionals of both sides and keep this damned war as civilized as possible. At least I have never known farmers anywhere to take up arms unless sorely provoked."

"I don't make policy, Your Excellency," the Deputy Inspector whined. "I only try to keep the trains moving as long as the tracks remain clear."

"And we keep them as clear as is possible with the forces we have been given," the Major alibied.

"All right, all right," the Count said. "I'm on a personal journey, not an official inspection tour. I'll deal with your problems and excuses when I return to Royal Headquarters. In the meantime, tell me when I can expect to reach Versailles."

"Via a roundabout route with many delays expected, Your Excellency," the Deputy Inspector explained. "There is no connection to Châlons-sur-Marne via Verdun, which would be the shortest way. The French laid out their railways in a most illogical fashion."

"Perhaps not from their point of view, since they cause their enemy so much frustration," Count Frederick Paul wryly observed. "Maybe I should proceed by road to Verdun and Chalons. It might be quicker."

"No doubt it would, sir," the Major answered. "The Commandant would be honored to provide Your Excellency with a coach and strong Uhlan escort."

The Count made up his mind quickly. "I'll accept the coach but no large escort, thank you. Why should I draw the attention of *francs-tireurs* and invite them to attack me? Besides, if you have men to spare, use them to patrol my railroads."

The Major protested. "A large escort is better than just a few men, sir. Most of the guerrillas operate in bands of a dozen or less and are intimidated by any show of force."

"Perhaps. But I insist you use your soldiers for the duty they are intended, not my personal safety. I will travel light and fast, and as inconspicuously as possible." He cut off any further argument by concentrating on a platter of half-cold fried pork and potatoes. The Major departed and returned some twenty minutes later with a huge stagecoach under the command of an Uhlan leutnant, driven by a burly sergeant, with five troopers perched on the roof between the driver's bench and the baggage rack. Instead of the normal team of four, it was pulled by six spirited artillery grays. The most simpleminded French peasant would instantly spot this conveyance as transporting somebody of extraordinary importance, but Count Frederick Paul decided not to waste more time making an issue of it. With luck he could make Verdun by early afternoon, then Châlons-sur-Marne late in the evening—*if* there were no delays. After thanking the Commandant's adjutant and urging upon his Deputy Inspector greater diligence, he climbed into the spacious compartment of the coach together with the Uhlan Lieutenant whose fierce taciturnity boded ill as a pleasant traveling companion. As they rolled across the bridge over the Moselle, the young officer opened a window and let in the dank vapors streaming off the river on this chill December morning, informing his august passenger: "The Major warned me not to come back alive if anything happens to Your Excellency!" With that he drew his pistol out of its holster, laid it in his lap, and settled down to an alert watch of the road ahead.

The horses labored up the steep grade of the escarpments of the river's left bank, moving at a snail's pace until they topped the high Lorraine plateau where they broke into a brisk trot which began gobbling up the sixty-five kilometers separating Metz from Verdun. They were traveling along the very road over which there had been such savage fighting last August, its ditches still cluttered with the wreckage of caissons and commissary wagons and passing many clusters of fresh graves standing forlorn in the snow with their frozen bunches of withered flowers. Over twenty thousand Prussians had died on this bleak white plateau, and the autumn storms had eroded many of their shallow graves and exposed their bones to the scavenging rooks who still soared in black flights over the vast battlefield. They had died here, only to make possible the culminating set-piece battle of Sedan and its smashing victory under the very eyes of their King—yet failed to end the war. The coach rumbled through the ruined villages of Gravelotte, Rezonville, and Vionville, none showing any signs of life beyond a few thin wisps of smoke rising out of broken stumps of chimneys. Between them Count Frederick Paul noticed the blackened timbers of burned farms and realized why these peasants were left nothing better to do than engage in guerrilla, really *bandit* activities along the German lines of communication. He made a mental note to suggest to King Wilhelm that these people be given compensation to encourage them to devote their energies to reconstruction and agriculture. That would doubtless be an astute investment, one cheaper and more effective than chasing them as desperate *francs-tireurs* all over the countryside. Besides, the cost of such a program could be added to the indemnities the defeated French government would be forced to pay. His mind busied itself with problems like this rather than dwelling upon his dead daughter and grandson or worrying about Tessa. Orderly, logical thought processes were the Count's greatest strength—as well as his weakness in dealing with more-emotional mortals. As his coach rocked through last summer's bloody battlefields, uppermost in his thoughts were the forthcoming discussions at Royal Headquarters where, even more than usual, von Moltke and Bismarck were at loggerheads with each other while their monarch vacillated between exultation and vexation.

After the splendid victory at Sedan and Bazaine's capitulation at Metz, no cohesive regular French forces remained in the field. There remained only stragglers, National Guards, Guard Mobiles, sailors, and marines, a polyglot host, either sealed up inside the ramparts of Paris or floundering about the Loire countryside under the tenuous discipline of factious leaders. Any sensible government would have made peace, haggling over Bismarck's admittedly exorbitant terms until an accommodation was reached. That is what King Wilhelm had expected, indeed what Bismarck had expected. But after their tentative feelers, the French had not haggled at all. The volatile left-wing politicians of Paris had deposed their prisoner-emperor, proclaimed a republican Government of National Defense (unconfirmed in the provinces), and declared their intention of fighting to the bitter end without ceding "an inch of French soil or a stone of her fortresses!" Via balloons and pigeon-post they sent directives and agents out of their besieged capital to inflame the rest of the country into raising levies of citizen-soldiers, most of them equipped with nothing but patriotism, in order to continue the war. Thus, by December 1870, the German armies had had the glories of their unprecedented six-week summer campaign reduced to that most-dangerous tedium to afflict any invader: a complicated siege operation at the end of overextended lines of communication deep inside a hostile country.

While there was doubt that the rump government under Léon Gambetta could raise an army capable of relieving Paris, foreign governments had begun to show alarming sentimental antipathies at the proposed bombardment of the City of Light with heavy Krupp cannons; they might well start diplomatic interventions which would rob the Prussians of any meaningful victory. Such a high personage as the Crown Prince was showing doubts over the morality of the siege itself, having openly expressed his humanitarian concern for Parisian infants and children deprived of milk because their starving elders had soon butchered and eaten all the cows. Colonel Count Frederick Paul von Beckhaus und Varn, although a powerful man within the realm, was realistic enough to know the limitations of his influence on diplomatic and military policies. This was the price he had to pay for having dedicated his life to building railroads and breeding horses rather than to the civil and military service, as most of his Junker peers were wont to do. Nevertheless, he had the friendship of the King, even if he lacked von Moltke's and Bismarck's, and as he traveled through this devastated countryside whose mantle of snow covered so many French and German dead, he determined that he would din the royal ear with one important axiom: For a peaceful Europe, three of her nations, France, England, and Germany, must never be humiliated to the extent that revenge had to become national policy. He believed King Wilhelm would consider this well, that even the bombastic Bismarck understood its fundamental importance. But it was that peculiar new institution, the Prussian General Staff, represented by Helmuth von Moltke's enigmatic intellect, which acted as an *éminence grise* influencing every political and diplomatic decision, that might well make a just and, therefore, lasting peace impossible. Of the two principals, the austerely taciturn von Moltke and the sybaritic crude genius who was Chancellor of Prussia, Count Frederick Paul really preferred the former, who was far more controlled in his habits and expressions. But he decided this morning on his way to Verdun that he would have to start actively supporting Bismarck's more flexible and opportunistic views over von Moltke's narrow, militaristic ones. Since there was no more question of winning the war, but of winning the peace, it was choosing the lesser of two evils, the *logical* choice. This decision relieved the Count's mind, just as had his realization that Tessa's emergence as his principle heir might be all to the family's good.

At Mars-la-Tour, about halfway to Verdun, there was a small cavalry garrison stationed for the purpose of patroling the vital road, and the coach paused there to change teams. The Commander, a high-strung young Rittmeister, was not pleased to find a high official of Royal Headquarters traveling through his territory, and once again the Count was offered a heavy escort of Uhlans. Again he cheerfully refused. The fresh horses were not as spirited, but the coach still made reasonable speed as they left the Woevre plain and entered the more heavily forested country east of Verdun. By late morning the sun broke through the overcast and set the snow-crusted boughs sparkling along the ridges of the Meuse hills, illuminating the winter landscape with a desolate beauty which further raised Count

Frederick Paul's spirits and moved him to attempt some conversation with his guard. The Leutnant had not spoken a word or budged from his intense watch at the window for the past four hours.

"This is a very pretty land," the Count said to him. "The hunting should be excellent."

The Leutnant peered at the scenery as if noticing it for the first time and answered: "I believe I prefer my East Prussia, Your Excellency. The evergreen forests are prettier and surely the hunting there is of the best."

After a long moment of silence the Count asked with genuine curiosity: "You do not like France?"

The Leutnant gave him a surprised look and replied: "Of course not, sir." Obviously he would have considered any other answer unpatriotic.

Count Frederick Paul suspected that his next question was beyond the intellect of this young officer, but decided to ask it anyway: "What are you expecting us to gain out of this war, Herr Leutnant?"

The Uhlan did not hesitate at all. "To keep what we have won with our blood. To be able to face any nation in Europe without ever having to worry about France again." It was in its simple way a good straightforward answer. But the Count was curious to pursue the matter in greater detail:

"Ah, then you expect more wars?"

"What else, Your Excellency, if we are to become a great nation?" the Leutnant countered.

The Count imagined that this same statement, perhaps more artfully phrased, could have come from General von Moltke, and was mulling over the answer when the first shots were fired at his coach. He actually saw the body of one of the troopers riding on its roof tumble past the window before he heard the shooting, but he instantly knew they were being attacked by *francs-tireurs*. The Uhlan officer cocked his pistol and yelled at him: "Your Excellency will lie down on the floor!" To which he indignantly replied: "I will do no such thing!" In the next instant one of their lead horses was killed in its traces, causing the coach to slew violently sideways across the road and come to a jarring stop. There followed the shattering report of rapid volleys fired by the coachmen and guards, then some distant replies from the crest of a scrubby ridge. Two more troopers tumbled to the ground with piercing screams.

The Leutnant yelled again at the Count: "For God's sake, sir, get down on the floor!" He fired two wild shots out the window with his pistol, then opened the door and started climbing up the side of the coach. He was not able to pull his lower torso out of sight before a bullet drilled through it, splattering the compartment with blood. As his body slipped down, Count Frederick Paul made a lunge to break its fall but missed and was left sprawled along the upholstered bench. Three more bodies rolled off the top of the coach, falling heavily into the frozen ruts before the sounds of the shots reached his ears. After the rattling echoes died away, the Meuse hills fell silent and still in the bright sunshine. He knew he was the only one alive and that as soon as he showed himself, he, too, would be killed by the invisible enemy. So he lay still on the bench and waited for the last minutes of his life to run out.

They emerged out of their ambush concealment, three men and a lad who could not have been more than fourteen years old, sauntering down the slope with their rifles at the ready, chattering excitedly to each other as they advanced. Two of the men wore French infantry kepis, but their coarse clothing clearly marked them all as peasants; the boy wore a green muffler wrapped around his head and carried a musket which was a foot taller than himself. As Count Frederick Paul watched them through the open door, it seemed to take a long time before they reached within fifty paces of the coach; at that point he decided he was not going to wait to be shot like an animal in a trap. Jumping out and straddling the body of the dead Leutnant, he shouted at them in French: "It is madness what you are doing!"

The three *francs-tireurs* and the boy stopped in their tracks, jerking their weapons to firing position. But when the Count raised his hands above his head and shouted that he was unarmed, they began cautiously advancing again. When they stepped onto the road, they surveyed with open satisfaction their prisoner, the seven dead Germans and five surviving horses. "Those are fine-looking animals," the older man, a sinewy, bewhiskered farmer, exclaimed with satisfaction. "Let's liberate them!" Then he gruffly addressed Count Frederick Paul: "You speak French. Are you a traitor or an educated German?"

"I am a Colonel of the Prussian Landwehr," the Count replied. "And I repeat what I just told you: what you are doing is madness. It is not war, just simply murder!"

The bewhiskered one nudged the boy standing next to him. "Did you hear that, my son? Your first German is to be a Colonel, no less. You are in luck!"

One of the other *francs-tireurs* made a cautioning protest. "This isn't supposed to be a business for children. Let one of us execute him."

The bewhiskered one adamantly shook his head. "My boy becomes a man today. You help Jean with the horses." To the

Count he said with a mocking politeness: "We have no means of caring for prisoners, my colonel. I trust you understand."

The other man gave out a sudden urgent whistle and exclaimed: "Look out! There's a patrol coming!"

Count Frederick Paul felt a surge of hope when he saw a full squadron of Uhlans cantering around a curve in the valley below. The Commander of the garrison at Mars-la-Tour had evidently backed up his misgivings shortly after the coach had departed—but too late. The patrol was nearly a kilometer down the road and their appearance merely expedited the inevitable. The man who was trying to unhitch the horses cursed the unfamiliar German harnesses, and the older bewhiskered one shouted at him: "Never mind! Shoot them! We leave nothing alive for the enemy!"

"I can't shoot perfectly good horses! That's barbarous!"

"Nothing is to be left alive!" the leader bawled, then nudged his boy again, pointed at Count Frederick Paul and said: "You've been wanting to kill a German. Now the moment has arrived."

The boy's face framed in the green muffler turned as white as the surrounding snow. "I d-don't know if I can, Father," he stammered, unsteadily raising his musket.

"Aim at the middle of his chest and pull the trigger!" the leader of the *francs-tireurs* commanded him. "Hurry!"

At that moment the other two men started shooting the horses, and it was the crash of their shots which triggered a nervous reaction making the lad fire his musket at the slight, elderly German officer facing him only ten feet away. It was not a clean shot, and the recoil almost knocked him off his feet, but the heavy lead bullet severed Count Frederick Paul's jugular artery as it tore through his neck, slamming him up against the coach and dropping him on top of the dead Uhlan Leutnant. The boy's father dispatched the last kicking horse, then all four of them raced back up the wooded slope, one of them shouting: "Come on! The patrol is bound to stop. Maybe we can pick off a few more of the bastards!"

Colonel Count Frederick Paul von Beckhaus und Varn, Inspector General of His Majesty's Military Railroad Transport, lay in snow turning to red slush as his life's blood drained out of him. Before the Uhlans arrived, he gasped: "Oh, dear God . . . what a stupid way to die!"

ecember 13, 1870, began as one of those rare days when Albrecht von Falkenhorst felt the war might provide some enjoyable experiences for him. In the early morning he took care of Count Frederick Paul's correspondence, spending no more than a couple of hours writing routine replies to routine letters from the dozen Deputy Inspectors strung out between Paris and Strasbourg. He checked through daily reports of train operations, tonnage of supplies delivered to the siege depots, and attacks by guerrillas resulting in significant damage and delays, and perused through written complaints from area commanders of the Intendantur who had not received their quotas. A telegram arrived from Kaiserslautern announcing that Colonel Count von Beckhaus had left there by train the previous evening. Albrecht calculated he could not possibly reach Versailles before tomorrow afternoon because of long detours and delays along the lines. He would undoubtedly arrive in one of his terrible tempers, full of resolve to reorganize, even rebuild, the French railroad system, proceeding to drive his staff into a frenzy of activity. So Albrecht determined to make this day a leisurely and pleasant one which would fortify him for his coming ordeal; it was to culminate with a dinner at the Crown Prince's mess which he had been commanded to attend—not because he had attained any lofty position at Royal Headquarters, but rather because the affair was to be in honor of foreign military observers and His Royal Highness had need to intersperse the seating with linguists. Since their chance meeting at Pont-à-Mousson, Albrecht had on several occasions been detailed to act as escort-interpreter for the American general, Philip Sheridan. He had found himself enjoying the company of foreigners and developing a deep curiosity about the country which had produced such a forthright, democratic general officer as the American observer. It was to be a pleasant day and interesting evening, and as soon as he had accomplished his routine duties, he ordered La Misère saddled and rode off in the bracing cold December morning toward Villacoublay where his brother was stationed with the Second Dragoon Guards.

There was little feeling of war in this suburban countryside, the bulk of the investing troops occupying positions closer to the ring of forts defending Paris. He met a few Intendantur wagons rumbling along the roads and several cavalry patrols which appeared to be merely exercising their horses. La Misère, who had completely recovered from her wounds and fully justified Count Frederick Paul's judgment that she belonged to the nobility of French horseflesh, broke into eager gallops when Albrecht gave her her head across the frozen pastures. When they reached the high knolls near Châtillon, Paris came into view, seen through the tracery of naked poplars and elms, a vast dark sea of roofs, spreading to the horizon and spiked with sharply etched church spires. She lay silent in her Seine basin with little smoke rising out of her starving hearths and ovens to stain the clear blue sky above her, giving no visible or audible sign of defiance against her besiegers. No cannons boomed, nor were there any crackling reports of rifle fire. On this morning both sides were acquiescent, waiting with stubborn patience for the other's next move. Probably on this coming Sunday, as on many in the past, the Paris bourgeoisie would make excursions to view, and be viewed by, the German armies ringing their capital. Each side enjoyed peering at the other through telescopes, engaging only in perfunctory artillery duels which were normally suspended for the Sabbath. Since two disastrous sorties, the city's huge ill-trained garrison had appeared satisfied to remain behind its ramparts, waiting hopefully for a relief army which never came. This morning there was a stillness which gave an illusion of peace. An illusion which infected Albrecht with cheerfulness because, at the age of twenty years, he had already seen enough of war. As he peered at the sprawling city from among the trees of the knoll, he said aloud: "For God's sake, Paris, capitulate so we can get this over with! I want to stroll your boulevards and meet your women!"

He met instead his brother, Leutnant Baron Gustaf von Falkenhorst, outside his billet at Villacoublay and found him as depressed as he had been the week before. He was examining some remounts requisitioned from nearby estates and did not seem in the least pleased to see Albrecht. "Have you nothing better to do in this war than promenade about like a dandy on a bridle path?" was his sour greeting.

"That's precisely what makes this a pleasant day," Albrecht cheerfully agreed. "I wish your father-in-law were absent on a happy, rather than sad, mission. But since he is absent, I am free of my usual work and troubles. Why shouldn't I take advantage of it? How about having a glass of wine with me?"

"I have more important duties," Gustaf snapped, yet, after looking over the last of the horses, he obviously had nothing else to do and rode down to a café in the village where he joined his brother in some wine and sausage. As soon as they sat down inside the stuffy establishment where a dozen other young Prussian officers were eating and drinking, Albrecht regretted not remaining in Versailles where he might have found more interesting company among the motley characters who hung around Royal Headquarters. He might even have been able to escort General Sheridan on an observation tour of the siege-works and enjoyed fascinating conversation about America. He had little affinity, he decided, for the younger military who tended toward the extremes of arrogant bombast and dour Spartanism; ever since the battles in Lorraine his brother had been unusually dour and withdrawn. For a painfully long while, they had nothing to say to each other until Albrecht decided to broach something extremely personal to jolt him out of his bleak silence.

"I don't know whether you have given it any thought, but since Princess Brattelbach and her son died, you and your wife become principal heirs to the von Beckhaus fortune."

Gustaf took a sip of his wine, wiped his mouth, peered at his brother through narrowed eyes and curtly answered: "Yes, I've thought about it. And decided it can't make any difference to a soldier. All I need is my regiment, my horse, and my weapons."

"Besides yourself, there is your family."

"You mean *you?*"

Albrecht turned very red and very angry. "I am not an heir. But I am a von Falkenhorst."

"Then act like one."

Albrecht switched to a different tack, even if one perhaps more sensitive. "What has happened to you since the war, Gustaf? Can't you talk about it?"

"What is there to talk about? We are all in the same war."

"Yes, we are. If you are troubled by it, why hide your feelings? At Sedan I watched men being slaughtered like we would never permit cattle to be slaughtered. It made me sick. Just as it makes me sick to think of fighting our way into the magnificent city lying beyond this village."

Gustaf gave him a cold smile. "The thought of fighting makes *you* sick? *You* who trail behind our armies as a clerk to a glorified stationmaster?"

Albrecht stared at him in shock for a moment but then remembered that while he had ridden in Count Frederick Paul's coach to Sedan and witnessed together with the entire Royal Headquarters staff the French Emperor's final defeat, his brother had lingered in the rear, assigned to light duties because of some painful, if insignificant, injuries received during the cavalry fighting in Lorraine. Obviously this rankled in his mind. "There is a lot of luck which determines whether or not you will get in the way of fighting and, therefore, of bullets," Albrecht told him, suddenly matching his gloomy mood. "As far as I'm concerned, I never want to see another battle."

"Not even from a comfortable carriage perched on a hill?" Gustaf cruelly prodded him.

"Not from any point of view," Albrecht evenly answered. "But if you are looking for more battles, dear brother, I'm sure you'll find them. Mankind being what it is, all you have to do is stay in that uniform and be patient."

Gustaf appeared to think that over for a moment, then started venting his bitterness in a barely controlled tirade: "All the important battles are over now. I had my chance and lost it. This siege is for sappers and artillerists and can only peter out in a capitulation. We are faced with nothing but a rabble, anyway, a rabble we can sometimes hear fighting among themselves. No, there will be no more battles and the war will end any day. I'll be sent back to garrison duty. No fighting. No promotions. Just eventual retirement as a Rittmeister, or Major at best. That's it."

Albrecht peered incredulously at his brother, then acidly comforted him: "Cheer up! There will always be more wars."

"After this one? With whom?"

"Oh, there are lots of candidates. England and Russia, just to mention a couple."

Gustaf snorted: "That's ridiculous! The English Queen is mother-in-law to our Crown Prince. The Romanovs and Hohenzollerns are all aunts and uncles to each other. You might as well predict a war with America! I tell you, there will be no more in our lifetime."

Albrecht sent up a fervent silent prayer that this was so, then persisted with genuine concern: "I ask you again, what happened to you in Lorraine."

"Nothing," Gustaf snapped.

"Well, *something* must have happened."

"Why?" Gustaf belligerently inquired.

"Because I overheard Prince Eugene of Hanover telling Count von Beckhaus he is recommending you for the Iron Cross. I was not going to say anything about it until it became official, but. . . ."

"Nonsense!" Gustaf shouted, his face almost comical with its confused expression of anger and disbelief. "Don't talk to me about that royal ball of suet!" When the officers at the other tables looked toward them in surprise, he dropped his voice and hissed: "It's because of him that I missed fighting with my regiment. So don't talk to me about the Prince Eugene."

"All right, Gustaf. I won't." They sipped their wine and nibbled their food without talking for several minutes, listening to a lewd discourse from a neighboring table about the availability of French women. It finally somehow moved Albrecht to ask his brother: "Have you heard from Tessa lately?"

"No."

"Haven't you written her?"

"I'm about to this evening," Gustaf irritably procrastinated. "To offer my condolences for the death of her sister."

"That's decent of you."

"It's the correct thing to do, isn't it?"

"Yes. Of course."

They had no more to say to each other. Albrecht bitterly told himself he would waste no more precious leisure time visiting with his brother. The war, rather than drawing them closer together, seemed to have widened the gulf between their opposing personalities.

Albrecht rode back toward Versailles via a roundabout route in order to use the time remaining in the afternoon, pausing once again to look at Paris from the Châtillon knolls. It was a sight which never ceased to fascinate him and it briefly restored his spirits after the depressing meeting with Gustaf. He could pick out the dome of the Invalides where rested the remains of the first Napoleon; he could also see the crown of his Arch of Triumph rising above the shimmering mass of rooftops in the far distance, silvery glimpses of the Seine as she looped through the city, and several of her famous bridges. How desperately he wanted to enter Paris, not as a Prussian conqueror, but just as an enthralled visitor. From where he viewed her, it appeared a simple matter, no more than an hour's ride to reach her fabulous boulevards and, for an insane moment, he toyed with the preposterous idea of trying to bluff his way through the lines for a night on the town! There were rumors about daring young Prussian officers successfully attempting such escapades, but those were probably just wild barrackroom stories. There were also rumors about spies being lynched by the wild Paris mobs, more likely true! And as he was sitting on La Misère, wistfully staring at the giant city, so close, yet so far away, he spotted a cluster of white puffs of smoke belching out of the drab ramparts of Fort de Vanves as its guns suddenly initiated an impromptu afternoon duel with Prussian batteries dug in at Châtillon. It was a half-minute before the sound of their firing rolled across to him, but then continued as a sustained din. The war *must* go on! Paris *was* in the grip of a tight, cruel siege. Sadly, he turned La Misère and trotted back toward Versailles.

Albrecht's billet was a modest house on rue de Chesnay with a small stable attached to it, making it most convenient for La Misère. The owners had long since fled to Bordeaux, but their two servants had remained behind, a surly old couple who rarely spoke to their German guests while nevertheless performing their duties with a sluggish efficiency. They had to tend to the needs of a Saxon artillery Major and another young civilian official who was a telegraphist and cryptographer attached to Second Army Communications. The Major, a pompous sort who seemed to consider it beneath him to associate with junior civil servants, had taken over most of the house for his private use, including the master bedchamber, dining room, and salon, where he occasionally entertained colleagues with silent card games. Albrecht and the telegraphist had to make do with what was left over, two attic bedrooms for sleeping and a small parlor off the front entrance where they took their meals. They got along well together, holding each other in a sort of mutual awe, the telegraphist, whose name was plain Adolf Schmidt, being very impressed with a titled university student acting as adjutant to a high official of Royal Headquarters; Albrecht, in turn was impressed by a technician able to control the transmission and reception of coded dispatches over thousands of leagues in a twinkling. Although Adolf Schmidt was fairly discreet, the nature of his duties sometimes made him the source of accurate information—information which Albrecht had, upon occasion, found useful to pass on to Count Frederick Paul. When they met in the parlor in the late afternoon of this day, he found Schmidt in an agitated state, as if he had something of great importance to reveal, yet was hesitant to do so. "Have you heard from His Excellency, the Inspector General?" he nervously inquired.

"Not since yesterday," Albrecht told him. "He left Kaiserslautern last night by train."

"By train?" Schmidt asked. "Are you sure by train?"

"Yes. The telegram must have gone through your own office. Don't you remember it?"

"We process three to four hundred telegrams a day," Schmidt answered apologetically. "It is difficult to remember all of them. One came through this afternoon reporting a Prussian Colonel killed by *francs-tireurs* outside of Verdun. There was no name given and I went off duty before more details came over the wires."

Albrecht felt a momentary pang of uneasiness. But the dead Colonel could not possibly be Count Frederick Paul. "My chief would be routed through Metz and Nancy. There is no connecting railway over Verdun, so how could he find himself there?"

"Yes, this happened on the road, but. . . ."

They were diverted by the appearance of the artillery Major who had come down from his master bedchamber to impart the sort of communication he sometimes condescended to: "The *pissoir* in the garden," he exclaimed, using one of the few French words he had learned during the war, "is in deplorable sanitary condition. I do believe one of you young gentlemen should reprimand the servants about it. While we are in residence here, I expect the household to meet German, not French, standards of hygiene!"

Albrecht, who had twice noticed the Saxon officer emptying his chamber pot out of his window, rather than taking the trouble to use the facility in the garden, smiled and said: "It shall be attended to, Herr Major." However, Adolf Schmidt volunteered for the task, obviously believing it far too menial for a young aristocrat. Albrecht left him, and climbed the steep flights of stairs to his attic bedroom to change into his dress uniform for the Crown Prince's dinner, still feeling in a reasonably good mood in spite of his meeting with his brother and Schmidt's ominous news. As he dressed, he put all unpleasant thoughts out of his mind and considered the questions he wanted to ask General Sheridan about America. He was buttoning up his tunic when Schmidt suddenly appeared breathless at his door.

"Well, what is the matter now, Adolf?" he asked. "Are the servants in revolt against our Germanic mania for cleanliness?"

"There is a messenger from Royal Headquarters waiting for you downstairs," Schmidt told him, his face pale with awe.

"From Royal Headquarters? Oh, dear! Could the Count have somehow returned already?"

"It is a member of His Majesty's personal body guard!"

Albrecht began to feel a gnawing uneasiness which he found difficult to hide. He hurriedly finished dressing and went downstairs where he found a corporal of the Royal Guard du Corps who crisply announced: "His Majesty sends his compliments and commands the Freiherr von Falkenhorst's immediate presence at his apartment in the Palace of Versailles."

"As His Majesty commands, of course," Albrecht replied. "But I am embarrassed by also being commanded to dine with His Royal Highness, the Crown Prince."

"I am to inform the Freiherr von Falkenhorst that His Royal Highness's entertainment for this evening has been canceled," the corporal stiffly informed him.

"Good heavens! What has happened?" Albrecht exclaimed, now completely bewildered.

"I have no details, sir," the corporal somberly answered, "but I believe an important member of Royal Headquarters has been killed."

Albrecht gave a startled look at Schmidt, who had followed him downstairs. "Do you really think? . . ."

"I don't know," Schmidt stammered, ". . . but you can't keep His Majesty waiting. Hurry!"

By the time Albrecht reached the palace, he was fully steeled to receive tragic news. The corporal of the Guard du Corps escorted him to an antechamber of what had once been Louis XVI's private apartment; he was met there by the Military Adjutant of the Day, who asked him to wait while he inquired whether His Majesty was ready to receive him. Less than a minute later he was ushered into a small gold-and-white salon where a gloomily subdued party of high officers surrounded King Wilhelm. There were present the Chief of the General Staff General von Moltke, the Prince General Eugene of Hanover, the Crown Prince Frederick of Prussia, and the American, General Sheridan, wearing his usual peculiar frock coat with its gold buttons. The King himself stepped forward to meet Albrecht and after receiving his respectful bow, spoke to him with an expression which contained both sorrow and anger:

"It grieves me to tell you, Freiherr Albrecht, that your relative and chief, our esteemed friend Count Frederick Paul von Beckhaus is dead. Please accept our deepest sympathy over the several tragedies which have struck the von Beckhaus and von Falkenhorst families during this terrible week." He shook his hand and also gave him a fatherly, comforting pat on the shoulder. Each of the other officers in the room stepped up to offer their condolences, Prince Eugene with the moisture of genuine tears gleaming on his heavy jowls, the American General with a firmly spoken: "I am very sorry. He was a fine man."

After shaking hands with each one, Albrecht asked the King: "How could this have happened, Your Majesty?"

"He was murdered by *francs-tireurs*," King Wilhelm answered in a shaking voice, then, looking straight at von Moltke, said: "This war is taking a barbaric turn not acceptable to our Christian standards. Why could we not have ended the matter with the military decision at Sedan?" He shook both his fists in the air, more a gesture of helplessness than defiance.

"The final decision can only come when we take Paris, Your Majesty," von Moltke softly replied.

"And we had better be careful how we go about that," the Crown Prince interjected darkly, "or the results may be even less fruitful than our other great victories."

"The siege of Paris is a perfectly legitimate military operation against a fortified city," von Moltke said with a subtle rise in tone. "Guerrilla actions are not."

"They are criminal," the King seethed.

"But unfortunately quite effective," the American general suddenly exclaimed, "unless met by a ruthless policy of reprisals. Believe me, gentlemen, I learned this to my sorrow during my campaigns through our South. We could not prevail until we executed captured guerrillas and starved their families by devastating their lands."

The Crown Prince, who spoke excellent English, shook his head: "We have no wish to fight such a war."

"Neither did we, Your Highness," General Sheridan told him.

Albrecht thought that the gathering was about to break into a general discussion about the war when the door to the antechamber opened and the same adjutant ushered in his brother. Gustaf was wearing his field uniform and had evidently ridden hurriedly over from Villacoublay without any inkling of the reason for the royal command. When the King informed him of his father-in-law's death, he looked confused and shocked. Then his face hardened as he solemnly, silently accepted brief comforting words from the others; Prince Eugene attempted to show him his personal sorrow, but Gustaf drew away from him with cold politeness. Then King Wilhelm addressed both brothers:

"We wish we could attend Count Frederick Paul's funeral and personally do him the honors he deserves. But because of our duties here, that becomes impossible. We would send our son, but he must remain in command of his army at this critical time. We have temporarily appointed the Prince General Eugene to Count Frederick Paul's post, so he is also unable to go. It is our wish that you travel immediately to Verdun, escort the remains home to Schloss Varn, attend the funeral in our name, and extend our personal sympathy to the Count's widow and daughter."

Albrecht bowed in obediance to the King's wishes, but to his surprise, Gustaf blurted out an objection:

"Your Majesty, rather than bury my father-in-law, I prefer to avenge him."

"There will be time for that too," the King sadly told him.

But Gustaf persisted. "I feel time is running out, Your Majesty. I beg of you to allow me to remain with my regiment to hunt down these *francs-tireurs*. My brother was closer to the Count than I, and will represent me at the funeral."

The King gave him a searching, somewhat puzzled look,

then reluctantly agreed: "Very well, Baron Gustaf. Do as you feel you must." He stepped over to an escritoire and picked up a small black case which he handed to Albrecht. "Here is the Iron Cross we are posthumously awarding Count Frederick Paul because we know he died bravely as a soldier and those abominable *francs-tireurs* can in no way detract from his honor. It will be placed on his casket during the funeral ceremony, then turned over to his widow, together with our citation. Now you must hasten to Verdun. Our adjutant will give you your formal orders in writing. Go with our blessing, Freiherr Albrecht."

In the vast cobbled expanse of the darkened palace court-yard, the von Falkenhorst brothers had a last bitter exchange before they parted:

"I think it was improper of you to refuse His Majesty's request that you escort the body to Schloss Varn," Albrecht reproached Gustaf.

"I did not refuse. I asked his permission to remain with my regiment for good reasons which you, as a clerk, cannot under-stand, but the King, as a soldier, does."

"I believe he had in mind that you comfort your wife and mother-in-law with your presence, rather than just serve some official function at the funeral. You should have taken that un-der consideration yourself."

"With me, the war gets first consideration," Gustaf snapped.

"Damn the war! You've used it right along as an excuse for your boorish heroics. You were given leave from it to be with your new bride, but left her on her wedding night. You were just given leave again to comfort her in her bereavement, and again you desert her. You are less human than any of your commanding officers, from the King on down to that stiff-necked von Manschott who got himself killed."

For a moment Gustaf completely lost his temper and shouted: "Your kind doesn't understand how a soldier feels about his duty!" His voice echoed against the walls of the vast Palace of Versailles and the reverberations seemed to startle him back to his senses. When he spoke again, it was less in anger than in desperation, and much lower: "I wish you would try to un-derstand, Albrecht, what I can and cannot do. That I can avenge Count Frederick Paul's death, but can't comfort his weeping women. I simply wouldn't know how! But let me find some of those damned *francs-tireurs* and . . ." His voice trailed off into silence.

"All right, Gustaf," his brother sighed. "All right. As His Majesty told you, do what you feel you must. Good-bye."

Gustaf curtly answered good-bye and trotted off with a

metallic clatter against the cobbled yard, vanishing into the night beyond the tall gates.

It took Albrecht von Falkenhorst nearly two days to reach Verdun, and there in a barren little room of the old Vauban citadel, which had been captured by the Germans only a month and a half earlier, he found Count Frederick Paul in a plain oak coffin put together by a local carpenter; during the prolonged siege of the town, the undertakers had run out of respectable caskets. They had also run out of embalming supplies, and only the intense cold which penetrated the unheated room had kept the body from badly decomposing. When, to his intense dismay, the Commandant required him to view the remains for purposes of positive identification, Albrecht was nauseated by the faint odor of putrification which the boughs of hemlock tucked around the cadaver could not overcome. For a terrible moment he even hesitated over the identification. After four days of death, this was only a grisly caricature of the face it had been in life. Yet, there was no doubt it was Count Frederick Paul von Beckhaus und Varn.

The Count would have to start his last journey over the same road upon which he had met his death, heading back to the railroad depot at Metz, thence by train to Wolin, and, finally, by cortege to Schloss Varn. But before the journey could begin, the Commandant of Verdun drew up his entire occupying garrison on parade because King Wilhelm had personally ordered full military honors for the deceased. It was a bitterly cold morning with low snow clouds scudding over the Meuse hills and as the troops doffed their helmets and sang the solemn strains of *"Wie Wohle ist Mir, O Freund der Seelen,"* their breaths wreathed their bare heads with vapor. The plain coffin acquired dignity as it stood draped by the Prussian flag on a pair of trestles serving as a catafalque, flanked by four Landwehr Dragoons with their sabers drawn, points down. The chaplain's voice rang across the bailey of the old fortress as he read the Lutheran service in a high tremulous baritone. Then the ranks intoned in unison The Lord's Prayer, and four dragoons lifted the coffin onto an artillery caisson where it was strapped and covered with a tarpaulin for the sixty-five kilometer ride to Metz. Freezing cold and unbearably depressed, Albrecht shook hands with the Commandant and chaplain and climbed into the same big stagecoach which the Uhlans had retrieved after arriving too late to save its occupants; the Count's baggage was still strapped to its rear. As they pulled out of the citadel to start rolling through a broodingly silent Verdun, the troops dipped their colors and a pair of cannons boomed out a parting salute. This time, the Count's escort consisted of the four dragoons and a complete squadron of Uhlans commanded by a senior leutnant.

Albrecht rode alone in the coach with his dark thoughts, brooding over the futile waste of a war which Count Frederick Paul himself had assured him could not, *must* not, result in the total crushing of France. Then why fight it? Why suffer this carnage? Nobody ever mentioned anymore the dead issue of the Spanish succession which had started the fighting—yet it went on. There were strong rumors around Royal Headquarters that the unification of all Germany under the Prussian crown was about to result from the war with France, but what kind of Germany? What kind of Prussia? Would she gain power but lose all her friends? Could either France or Germany come out of this war with clear consciences and the respect of Europe? Albrecht also thought of having to face the surviving von Beckhaus women who had had to bear a triple tragedy within the last two weeks. How was he going to explain the Count's death to them so they could feel there was the slightest justification for it? He found himself thinking particularly about Tessa and what he should tell her. That her father had died in Lorraine so this part of France could be annexed by a greater Germany? As he stared out the window at those bleak snowy hills, he suddenly felt himself hating this Lorraine which had cost so many Prussian lives and exclaimed aloud: "It is not worth it! Not worth it at all!" He did not think about the *francs-tireurs* who might be lurking in those hills.

But they were lurking there and struck within a kilometer of where they had ambushed the same stagecoach four days earlier. The attack came as suddenly, but this time their shooting was not as accurate. None of the horses was hit, and only one bullet found its mark, smashing through the coach's window and grazing Albrecht's shoulder before burying itself in the upholstery. For an instant the compartment seemed full of flying glass, a sliver of which slashed his cheek. Before he could recover from the shock, he heard the Uhlan Oberleutnant yelling at the drivers: "At the gallop! Move out at the gallop!" Then with a detachment of his troopers following him, he veered off the road and went churning through the underbrush up the slope of the forested ridge from where the shots were fired. Albrecht clutched his wounded shoulder with one hand, desperately hanging on with the other as the coach began bouncing and rocking wildly, its team whipped into a flat-out gallop down the winding, rutted road.

A Uhlan sergeant pulled alongside of the racing stagecoach without in the least slowing his own horse and shouted at Albrecht in passing: "Are you badly hurt, Herr Freiherr?"

✠

Albrecht's face was bleeding as well as his shoulder, but he felt neither pain nor fear for himself. But as the cortege hurtled around a curve with half its remaining escort, he glimpsed the caisson bucking over the ruts with its wheels literally flying through the air. "I'm all right!" he shouted back. "But for God's sake be careful with that coffin!"

The Uhlan sergeant raced to the head of the column and took over its lead, but did not give orders to slow down until they broke into the more-open country of the Woevre plain, and then only enough so as not to drive the horses to death. When they finally reached Mars-la-Tour and stopped at the encampment of its small garrison, Albrecht was covered with blood, badly shaken up, and beginning to feel the pain of his wounds. The sergeant returned to the coach with the ever-harassed garrison commander, but Albrecht would not allow himself to be taken to a doctor before making certain the coffin had not been damaged.

The doctor was not a Prussian medical officer, but a gaunt bearded Frenchman who lived in a shell-scarred house, one of the few left in the ruined village. His face was both hard and sad as he examined Albrecht's wounds, but there was a glimmer of satisfaction in his eyes as he took a pair of scissors and cut off the sleeve of the German uniform, ruining it completely. His hands were professionally competent, but far from gentle, as he swabbed the bloody furough clean with a compress soaked in stinging alcohol and applied a tight bandage. He cleaned the facial cut with equally efficient roughness. There was not a whimper out of his patient, but the sergeant who had followed them into the dispensary out of concern for his important charge, snarled at him in broken French: "Take it easy! Do you think you are treating a dog?"

That brought a flicker of a smile to the village doctor's lips, but he did not answer.

The sergeant tried to reassure Albrecht, saying, "If we are not delayed here and can reach Metz before dark, I can promise the Freiherr will not be bothered again. We cleaned out the country ahead of all Frenchies last August. There's hardly a house left standing."

"I will be ready to proceed when you are," Albrecht told him, then peered thoughtfully into the Frenchman's face and said in French: "It is a terrible war, but your people are making it worse."

"Speak to me of that if Frenchmen ever invade your country, monsieur," the doctor evenly answered.

"You have, you know. Many times."

The Frenchman shrugged. "It appears then that yesterday's

barbarities must hopelessly compromise today's civilization. There! You are as well bandaged as I can do it with what you Germans have left me of my dispensary." With a final rough tap, he tamped down a plaster over Albrecht's facial cut, finally making him wince with pain. "You will go home with some slight scars of the flesh, but I imagine none of the soul."

The Uhlan sergeant could not follow the doctor's rapid French, yet he understood the inflection, caught Albrecht's miserable expression, and angrily exclaimed: "You had better not be insolent, Monsieur Doctor! Remember you are a conquered people."

The doctor shook his head. "No sergeant. *You* are. By a new madness of arms such as the world has never seen before."

There was a loud clatter of hoofs from outside and when Albrecht stepped into the village street, he saw that the Oberleutnant of his escort had caught up with the cortege and was reporting to the garrison commander. He had lost three men, but two of their horses were being brought in on lead reins and in their saddles were a big bearded peasant wearing a French kepi and a young lad with a green muffler wound around his head; their hands were bound behind their backs. The Rittmeister was asking the Oberleutnant, "Are these the ones who attacked you?"

"Two of them at least. There are their weapons. An old musket and a modern French chassepot."

The Uhlan troopers yanked the *francs-tireurs* to the ground and then booted them back up on their feet. The man in the kepi spat at them but kept silent. The boy began to sob but also cried out between sobs: *"Vive la France! La mort aux Allemands!"*

"Hang them," the Rittmeister ordered his men. "Immediately."

Albrecht moved closer and saw that the man in the kepi was well over fifty while the boy not more than fourteen. He felt an overwhelming revulsion and reaching out for the Rittmeister, took him by the arm and pulled him aside. "Please let them go."

The Uhlan officer stared at him in surprise. "That is impossible, Herr Freiherr."

"Somewhere, somehow, all this killing must come to an end," Albrecht pleaded with him. His voice rose now so that all the surrounding troops could hear him: "Please let them go!"

The Rittmeister's expression went from alarm to a hard contempt as he looked up and down Albrecht's ruined railroad official's uniform. "This is a military matter, Herr Freiherr von Falkenhorst," he coldly informed him. "You must leave it to us. And you must proceed on your journey at once. Your horses are changed and escort ready." He snapped a salute, turned his back, and as he passed the troopers holding the prisoners, growled again, "Hang them!"

As the caisson, stagecoach, and escort pulled out of Mars-la-Tour, the last searing impression Albrecht had of the melancholy village was of the two *francs-tireurs* being hanged from a splintered tree off the square. The old man hardly struggled at all, going limp almost at once, his kepi falling off his head. But the boy wriggled and choked like a hooked fish at the end of a line. The coach turned a corner, blotting out the horrible sight; Albrecht leaned out of the window and vomited in the path of the Uhlans trotting behind him.

The road connecting Glaumhalle with the highway to Breslau had been made virtually impassable by a heavy snowfall, followed by a sudden thaw, then intense freezing weather, which presaged one of the worst winters to hit Europe in living memory. It was a miracle that the postman had been able to deliver the telegram announcing the death of Tessa's sister in childbirth, then barely a week later, another reporting that her father had "fallen on the field of honor." The first one did not really bring Tessa grief, only a feeling of guilt at having never been close enough to Esther during her lifetime to genuinely mourn her death. After a brief discussion with Master Prytz, they jointly decided she could not possibly travel to the Palatinate in time for the funeral, and besides, there was too much vital work being done on the restoration of Glaumhalle which, if she left, the Dowager Baroness von Falkenhorst would do her best to disrupt. But to the second telegram she reacted differently. It had been delayed for two days, and when it finally arrived, came as a great shock. While in this case, too, she could not feel profound grief born out of mutual affection, her sense of guilt over this fact turned unbearably sorrowful. She threw herself weeping into Prytz's arms. The old man cried too, with that tremor of his chin caused by great emotional stress and silent tears streaming down his cheeks, trickling through his drooping moustache. After she had collected herself somewhat, Tessa told him: "This time I must go."

"Yes, you must. I will take you back to Schloss Varn, my

poor Tessa. At once, so that we will be in time for the funeral."

When she went into the dark, musty little salon to announce to the Dowager Baroness von Falkenhorst the reason for her immediate departure, her mother-in-law screeched, "God is punishing you for what you are doing here, virgin-strumpet!" Then, in the next wheezing breath, she wailed, "My own beautiful husband was killed, you know, by those pig-suckling Austrians!" She was more senile than ever, continually switching from senseless maudlin self-pity to screaming cruel insults at her daughter-in-law. Tessa, who now only endured her company when absolutely necessary, fled upstairs and hastily packed a few necessities.

Before leaving, she and Prytz gave careful instructions to the most intelligent of the four newly engaged farm laborers, appointing the German-Silesian man as foreman over the three Poles who were repairing and cleaning up *der Feste*, which now housed seven new horses, four cows and a bull, three sows, and a boar pig. "You will take no orders from the old Baroness," Tessa bluntly told the foreman. "She is very ill and doesn't know what she's saying. Do you understand that?" He said he did, but looked very apprehensive at the prospect of clashing with the dowager chatelaine of Glaumhalle.

Because the decrepit Falkenhorst coach would never be able to negotiate the terrible road conditions, they mounted horses to ride the thirty kilometers to the nearest railroad station, leading a third as pack animal to carry their baggage. The wind raced in wild squalls out of the frozen wastes of the Polish plains, hurling daggers of cold and sweeping up drifts of snow which sometimes reached to the horses' withers; it was the hardest, most brutally freezing ride Tessa had ever experienced and it took them nearly seven hours to reach Ols. By then it was after dark and since no train was expected until the middle of the next morning, they had to put up in a simple little inn for the night.

As soon as the shops opened, Tessa purchased a black veil and mourning dress. Then they caught a train which rumbled through the wintry countryside, reaching Breslau two hours later, where there was another long wait for a connection to Wolin via Frankfurt an der Oder. Here they became more aware that there was a war going on, the isolation of Glaumhalle having made it seem remote and unreal except for the telegram about Count von Beckhaus's death. There were not many military among the crowds waiting in the station for trains whose schedules were disrupted by the war, but the civilians passed the time belligerently discussing the newspaper headlines which urged the bombardment of Paris by Krupp siege guns as a special Christmas present to its stubborn citizens. Tessa realized that the approaching holiday season, too, had been far from her mind at Glaumhalle; with a pang of nostalgia she recalled how Christmas had always been anticipated weeks ahead at Schloss Varn and thought what a sad one it would be this year. In the vestibule of the Breslau station there was already a Christmas tree attended by a one-legged soldier taking a collection "to provide traditional roasted geese for our wounded heroes," and she was moved to contribute a thaler. This action was observed by a wealthy looking traveler wearing a thick astrakhan fur collar and beaver hat; folding up his newspaper, he approached, bowed, and inquired with a courtesy containing something less than pure gallantry: "May I offer my protection to the bereaved young lady on her journey?"

Tessa felt like lifting her veil and showing him the plain freckled face which went with her lithe figure, but Master Prytz intervened with his impressive bulk and stern visage: "Thank you, sir, but *I* am escorting the Baroness to meet her husband, an officer of the Second Dragoon Guards, at the graveside of her father, a Colonel Count of Royal Headquarters who fell in battle against the French."

The traveler bowed again, this time so low that he almost fell on his face, then backed away in awe, retiring to the restaurant to recover himself with a schnapps. Tessa would almost have preferred to join him rather than remain seated on the hard bench of the vestibule. But then, unconsciously, she had temporarily surrendered to a new father image, just as Master Prytz had officially assumed it, and meekly obeyed his wishes.

When the train finally arrived, they pressed into a crowded compartment, which was unbearably stuffy despite a freezing chill. They had to sit in it, rocking in a dazed half-sleep, until early the next morning when they pulled into Frankfurt after innumerable intermediate stops, there to seat themselves on another hard vestibule bench to await the final connection to Wolin. However, Prytz was able to find an empty compartment and these last hundred kilometers of their tedious journey took them through familiar country, the Baltic lowlands of Pomerania with fens interspersed by dells of pinewoods, which remained a rich green even in the gray-whiteness of this severe winter. Cross-timbered farmhouses rolled by with their high-peaked roofs, solid stone barns, composts faintly steaming in the cold December air, windmills frozen to stillness with motionless, icicled wings. They had distant glimpses of the sea shimmering with that peculiar glint of ice flocs bobbing on the swells, jet-black rooks soared over the pure white fields slumbering beneath their mantles of snow, and foxtails, pale russet in color and weaving on slender stalks, poked through the silver ice covering the ponds. And above all, the salty fragrance of marsh and shore which somehow overwhelmed the railroad coach's sticky smell of sweat, steam, and smoke. In spite of the melancholy reason for her return home, Tessa suddenly felt a great joy at seeing this land again, and with an exhuberance which was a kind of reverence she pressed her face against the frosted windowglass and exclaimed: "Oh, Prytzie, Prytzie! Do you think we could ride over it just once more?"

The old stablemaster nodded solemnly. "Yes, I think so. You and I may be able to sneak away for a ride over the dunes, like we used to in the happy old days. I am sure His Excellency would not begrudge us that."

When at last they reached Wolin they were met by the stationmaster, who, of course, knew them both very well. After a confusion of greetings, condolences, and Christmas felicitations, the flustered official blurted out the fact that Count Frederick Paul's remains had passed through his station thirty hours earlier and that the funeral had taken place that very morning. They were too late! With a deep sigh of bitter disappointment, Master Prytz rushed off to hire a coach for the last leg of their long trip while Tessa warmed herself in the stationmaster's cluttered little office. It was past nine o'clock in the evening when they rolled through the gates of Schloss Varn and up the familiar crunching gravel driveway, which tonight was soft and silent beneath its cushion of snow. The great double doors of the castle's front entrance were draped with heavy black and purple crepe, and as Tessa got out of the coach and climbed the steps, she steeled herself to meet her weeping mother and stoically controlled husband. Knabel let her in, and he looked exactly as she had expected, a mourning rosette tied to his left sleeve, his lantern jaw set so rigidly it made his face longer than usual. But to her surprise, she was met in the foyer only by Albrecht von Falkenhorst, haggard and slightly disheveled looking in an ill-fitting green uniform, his left arm in a sling and an ugly plaster on his face, yet with a smile which illuminated his whole being as he exclaimed: "Tessa! Thank God you've come!" Her emotions had built up to such an extent during the past days that she threw her arms around him and passionately hugged this young man she scarcely knew at all.

When they drew apart, there was a fleeting moment of embarrassment between them, then Tessa said: "The funeral is over, isn't it?"

Albrecht nodded. "We buried him this afternoon. The whole district came to pay their respects. Bishop Putzkammer conducted an . . . er, impressive service."

She gave a nervous little laugh. "I can imagine! Poor Papa

would probably have coughed his head off to cut it short." Her hand flew to her mouth, and she muttered through it: "God forgive me! I shouldn't have said that."

Albrecht smiled and put his free arm around her shoulder. "You are perfectly right, Tessa. It was difficult to tell whether he was commending Count Frederick Paul's soul to God, or the entire French nation to the devil. But the many of us who loved your father had only thoughts for him. Even the King would have come if the war had not prevented him."

"But where is your brother?" Tessa asked, then clumsily corrected herself: ". . . I mean, my husband."

"The war prevented him, too, from coming," he managed to tell her with only a slight hardening of tone. Then he lied outright: "Gustaf asked me to convey to you his deepest sympathy and affection."

Tessa found herself suppressing a sigh of relief before saying, "And I suppose poor Mama is in a state of collapse?"

"She bore up quite well, but went to bed when the last guest departed a couple of hours ago," he told her. "Only the Reverend Bishop is still here. Perhaps we had better let him know you have arrived."

Tessa glanced toward the main staircase, much preferring to climb it and go to her own room and the bed she had missed for so long, but she allowed Albrecht to escort her toward the library. She had a glimpse through open doors of the Great Hall where footmen and maids were still silently removing the remains of the funeral supper for more guests than had attended her own wedding breakfast. In the library she found the Bishop seated by the fire in her father's favorite chair, on the table nearby a decanter of cognac and a glass. When she entered, he rose ponderously to his feet and, spreading his arms in a gesture which was somehow a corpulent travesty of the Crucifixion, intoned with sonorous emotion: "Come, bring your grief to me, dear child. Let your Uncle Augustus become your father as well as your spiritual shepherd."

Tessa almost recoiled from him but could not avoid being smothered in an embrace reeking of cognac. After disengaging herself, she said: "I am sorry I came too late for the funeral, Reverend Bishop. We left as soon as the telegram came, but it had been delayed."

"This hard winter and terrible war make travel difficult," the Bishop rumbled. "But your father in heaven as well as your Heavenly one know you did your best and bless you for it."

Tessa had always held the imposing-looking Bishop Putzkammer in a certain childish awe, but now she understood for the first time why her father had been barely able to tolerate this

'sanctimonious churchman whose interminable sermons dribbled platitudes. It suddenly became difficult for her to remain
polite. "My brother-in-law tells me you conducted a beautiful
service, Reverend Bishop," she said to him.

"I always tried to do my best for cousin Frederick Paul,
God rest him. But now, dear child, in private you must call me
Uncle Augustus."

Tessa found herself freezing up completely. "Papa told me
you are not a real uncle and to call you Reverend Bishop," she
tersely informed him. "You must excuse me if I leave now. I will
see my mother, then go to bed. I am very tired."

Bishop Putzkammer's archly benign expression turned into
that of a bloated, petulent cherub. "You know I can only stay
another day," he huffily exclaimed, "because I have been called
to deliver the Christmas sermon in the cathedral of Frankfurt.
With so little time, we should retire together to the chapel
where I will help you pray for your father's salvation."

Albrecht caught the desperate look on Tessa's face and
firmly interceded for her: "The Baroness has had a long, trying
journey from Silesia," he told the prelate. "I believe that tonight
she would prefer to be alone with her prayers."

"Yes, I would prefer that," she agreed, giving him a grateful
glance.

The Bishop sank back into Count Frederick Paul's chair
and reached for the glass of cognac. "Oh, very well then, " he
conceded without the slightest grace, "I will see you tomorrow.
Good night."

After they had left the room, he angrily muttered to himself: "She is just as rude as her father. Just like him!"

Albrecht silently escorted Tessa up the staircase and along
the dimly lit halls to her mother's apartment in the east wing
of the castle, leaving her at the door. A single lamp was burning
in the little sitting room cluttered with baroque furniture and
porcelain figurines; a maid was slumped fast asleep in a chair,
her embroidered cap slightly askew on her head. She did not
awaken as Tessa softly crossed to the open bedroom door, half
expecting to hear sobs muffled by pillows. But the bedroom was
dark and silent. As her eyes adjusted to the faint light reflected
through the doorway, she made out a voluminous black dress
and tangle of veils carelessly thrown over a chair, an open,
half-empty box of bonbons balanced on top of the Bible on the
night table, and the huge bed with a shapeless lump breaking the
billows of its comforter. Only a few curls of the Countess An-
tionette von Beckhaus's head could be seen in the middle of the
untidy pile of silk and lace pillows. Tessa's nostrils became filled
with the familiar scent of her mother's perfume, which per-

meated the stuffy warmth of her bedroom, and she heard a thin, small sound breaking the stillness, the delicate, rhythmic snoring of peaceful sleep. She advanced to the foot of the bed and stood holding her own breath for a moment before turning and tiptoeing quietly out, past the slumbering maid. She stepped into the hall where she found Albrecht waiting as if he had known she would be back almost at once. "Mother is asleep. I did not awaken her."

"Yes, I thought she would be. I will take you to your rooms now. They have been waiting for you since the day before yesterday."

As they quietly moved down another flight of stairs and dim hall, Tessa became aware that Albrecht had been wounded and that she had not yet asked him about it. "What happened to you?" she whispered. "Were you in a battle?"

"No. It's nothing at all serious," he answered, not wanting to tell her of his brush with the *francs-tireurs* or of how they had killed her father. "I only had sort of an accident, really."

"You brought Papa home, didn't you?" she asked.

"Yes. From Verdun where he was killed. The King personally asked me to bring him home." He opened the door to her apartment for her and stopped on the threshold. "Try to sleep well. Tomorrow I will take you to his grave. Early in the morning, if you like. Before our Reverend Bishop gets out of bed."

Tessa nodded. "Yes, that will be best. And I would like to bring Master Prytz with us. He loved Papa very much and has also come a long way." Suddenly she reached out and took his hand in hers. "You have been very kind and considerate to me, Albrecht."

He tightened his grip on her hand and drawing her closer still, gently brushed his lips against her cheek, just as he had done on her wedding day. "Good night, Tessa."

In the freezing dawn of December 22, Leutnant Baron Gustaf von Falkenhorst was leading his squadron of Second Dragoon Guards out of Villacoublay for a routine patrol when he spotted the balloon rising out of the mist shrouding a silent, besieged Paris. While it did not gain much altitude, it grew in size, suggesting that it was drifting directly toward him, wafted along by a light north wind which contained a smattering of snowflakes. Gustaf halted his column of troopers and began to watch it intently so as to gauge its exact course, and when he realized it was bound to pass almost directly overhead at no more than two hundred meters' height, felt a surge of excitement. These balloons had caused the German forces investing the city endless frustrations. Over fifty of them had ascended and blithely soared above their lines to escape with important dispatches, passengers, and the carrier pigeons which kept Paris in touch with the outside world. That fanatical, erratic patriot, Léon Gambetta, had himself flown off in one like a bird of ill omen to rouse the rest of France to contend against her inevitable defeat. Prussian infantry occupying their siege-works ringing the city were never able to hit the fragile targets with volleys of rifle fire, the artillery were even less effective despite their special high-angle, antiballoon cannons; the cavalry, who chased them far and wide across the countryside, had only been on hand to capture two upon landing. Gustaf knew that if he were to get the third, it would be worth a deserved Iron Cross; it looked as if this one were about to present him with such an opportunity. So he promptly ordered his squadron to draw their carbines, cock them, take careful aim as the balloon drew nearer, and await his order to fire. One out of the twenty-five shots must surely puncture that fat gasbag, and one small hole would suffice to bring it down near enough for him to capture the occupants.

"If we shoot down that balloon," he shouted to his troopers, "I will personally supply the squadron with extra Christmas rations of good German schnapps!"

The balloon closed at a slow hovering drift which augured well for the expected pursuit, yet building the tension to an agonizing degree with its very slowness. "Steady now, boys," Gustaf exhorted his men as the target grew into a huge silken yellow bullseye against the gray sky. "We won't shoot till it's right over us. Steady now!" Suddenly he realized that he should have dismounted them for better aim, but there was no time now. He silently cursed himself. The balloon was so close that he could clearly see the three passengers leaning over the waist-high rim of the basket, which was festooned with sacks of sand ballast and crates of carrier pigeons. The dragoons squinted along the barrels of their carbines, most of these simple Prussian lads in awe of the fantastic aerial conveyance floating into their sights.

Just before they passed overhead, one of the balloonists shouted down tauntingly, "*Au revoir, salauds!*"

Gustaf yelled: "Fire!"

Twenty-five carbines crashed through the stillness of the dawn, followed by the snorting clatter of startled horses, then a metallic rattling as the troopers feverishly reloaded. From the intense concentration of the volley, Gustaf fully expected to see the gasbag collapse and start a fatal plunge toward the snow-covered ground. Yet it miraculously maintained its perfectly symmetrical inverted pear-shape and, as the pilot hastily dropped ballast, began to rise, rather than fall. Mingled with the trailing plumes of sand was a pearly glitter of liquid. One of the balloonists was leaning out of the basket and urinating down upon the heads of his German enemy as he sailed high above them.

"Keep shooting!" Gustaf bawled in rage. "Fire at will!"

Another, far more ragged volley crackled after the infuriating balloon, but it kept rising majestically higher and drifted on totally unperturbed, finally passing safely out of range. The troopers cursed and a few of them snapped off a few more useless shots before giving up. But Gustaf was determined to get that balloon even if he and his squadron had to chase it clear across France or until the last horse dropped of exhaustion. "After it! At the gallop!" he shouted, spurring his horse over the roadside ditch and galloping across a wide field whose furrows were frozen rock-hard. An old French farm woman dressed in patched rags, her back bent by a load of fagots, stamped her feet and gleefully cackled after the dragoons the same insult she had heard the balloonists throw down to them: *"Au revoir, salauds!"*

The chase did not have to be kept up at a gallop because a fast trot sufficed to match the speed of the balloon drifting along on the gentle currents of a light wind. However, its course was free and unhindered through the wintry skies of France, while the earthbound pursuers had to negotiate the natural barriers of her terrain, adding leagues as they traversed her undulating snow-covered topography, losing time when obstructed by dells through which they had to thrash in single file behind their eager Leutnant. Thus, the initially easy pace turned out an illusion and gradually began telling on the men and horses. They rode through a village whose streets were deserted and houses shuttered, but with a feeling that their passage was being observed and quietly jeered at by the invisible inhabitants. They had to force their way through a small forest whose naked boughs obscured the yellow ball in the sky, and when they broke out in the clear again, it was a mere distant speck hanging over the gray horizon. A half-hour's gallop had them nearly caught up again until they had to ford a stream in whose freezing water half the troopers floundered before they could drive their horses over the irregular bottom and up the ice-encrusted opposite bank. Two men fell off and nearly drowned. By the time the squadron had collected itself, they were caught in a heavy snowfall which reduced the visibility to a small periphery of gray white emptiness. Yet Gustaf pressed on for the better part of an hour after their quarry had vanished in the murk, his squadron doggedly following behind him with greatly dampened enthusiasm. Finally Johan Kluge, who had been promoted to sergeant since Vionville, drew his horse alongside and dared suggest: "Herr Leutnant Baron, we are at least thirty kilometers beyond Villacoublay, and several of the men are frozen stiff in their saddles."

Gustaf snapped: "I am wet and frozen too. What of it?"

"I have a feeling, Herr Leutnant Baron, that besides having lost that balloon, we have ridden far beyond the support of our own troops."

Gustaf reined in his horse, halting the column and impatiently yanking a map out of his saddlebag. He examined it, trying to match its features with what could be seen of the country, which was nothing more than some misty wooded ridges and empty white fields separated by the broomlike lines of naked poplars. He hated to give up the chase, but sober consideration of the situation made him realize that the mission was a failure and the time had come to turn back. "We will cut across these fields until we run into a road," he told Kluge. "Then find a village where we can rest and dry out for a half hour before returning."

They found the road and then a village, as silent and deserted as the one they had passed through earlier. But it had a small inn with a plume of blue smoke rising out of its chimney, and Gustaf dismounted his squadron in its yard. After two troopers were posted to guard the horses, the weary, frozen dragoons pressed inside the simple establishment and crowded around an open hearth whose glowing embers radiated the warmth they so desperately needed. Nobody answered their shouts for service, and when Gustaf and Sergeant Kluge began exploring the premises, they found a kettle of soup simmering on the kitchen stove, giving forth a tantalizing aroma of chicken and onions; on a table were two loaves of sourdough bread and a large chunk of cheese. The rear door leading to the garden was wide open, and the tracks in the fresh snow clearly told of the precipitous escape of a man and woman.

"A very rude way to receive customers," Gustaf remarked to Kluge, "but at least they were considerate enough to leave us some hot soup. Ration it out so each man gets at least a couple of spoonsful. And there's enough bread and cheese to go around if you make the slices thin."

When he returned to the dining room, Gustaf ordered the two troopers who had been totally immersed in the stream to strip off their uniforms and dry them out before the fire. On a shelf behind the serving counter he found three bottles of red wine and one of cheap cognac. Warmed both internally and externally, the squadron's spirits began to revive, and there was even some hilarity over the two men crouching stark naked in front of the fire. Gustaf stoically refused his share of the soup so that the sentries outside would be assured a portion, accepting instead a double ration of cognac, which he sipped while seated apart with his map spread over a table, trying to locate this nameless village. He would not admit to being lost, but unless they could rout out a local inhabitant to guide them, finding their way back to Villacoublay before nightfall would be a matter of luck. Guessing his predicament, Sergeant Kluge tactfully suggested: "Maybe we should search a few houses and take some hostages."

"Hostages for what, Kluge?"

"Our safe return, Herr Leutnant Baron."

Gustaf mulled over the idea for a moment, then decided against it. "That would make us look ridiculous. I have a pocket compass. If we ride northwest for two or three hours, we are bound to reach our lines somewhere near Versailles." He drew a notebook out of his pocket and began writing as he spoke: "Three liters of soup, two loaves of bread, one kilogram of cheese, two bottles of wine, one bottle of cognac—fifteen francs seems a fair price." He counted out the money and handed it to the Sergeant. "Put it where the innkeeper will find it, Kluge. Then relieve the sentries outside so they can eat and warm themselves. We leave in fifteen minutes."

Kluge took the coins and hefted them in his hand, hesitating. "I was just thinking, Herr Leutnant Baron," he said, "about this empty inn with all that soup waiting on the stove. Some customers were obviously expected."

Gustaf peered at him, roused himself out of his lethargy of cold and disappointment, and wondered at the sly cunning of good Pomeranian peasants. "Yes, Kluge. But judging from the amount in the kettle, less than half our number. Right?"

"Right, Herr Leutnant Baron," the Sergeant answered, satisfied that his commander was now alert to potential dangers. He put the money in a dish on the service counter, called out the names of two men to relieve the sentries, then went out through the front door to check that all was well with the horses outside. As soon as he stepped out of the cheery warmth of the inn into the silent chill of this drab December afternoon, Kluge was struck by an uneasy feeling. It was snowing so hard that he could not see the end of the street in either direction. The houses opposite the inn appeared as deserted as before, yet he noticed some windows with their shutters open and was certain they had been closed when the squadron had first arrived. As he stood in the yard thinking this over, his ears caught a faint brittle sound, like breaking glass. Several of the horses snorted and stirred uneasily. In the next instant the stillness of the village exploded in a violent fusillade of shots, at least twenty riflemen revealing their hidden positions in windows, behind walls, and even from rooftops, as their rifles belched forth powdersmoke among the snowflakes.

Kluge yelled at the sentries to take cover but saw them both fall before they were even able to raise their carbines. Whirling around, he made a dash back to the door, but as he reached it, a bullet hit him in the back, pitching him across the threshold and into the arms of a pair of startled troopers. As he was dragged inside, numb with shock, the fire from the concealed enemy poured in, ricocheting around the dining room with shrill whines. Most of the dragoons threw themselves to the floor, knocking over tables and chairs. As one of them rushed up to the door, slamming it shut, two bullets drilled through it, and the man fell with a scream, clutching his stomach.

Gustaf had reacted instantly to the shooting; jumping to his feet, he bounded over to a window and broke the glass with his pistol. As he did so, several more bullets shattered the rest of the panes, forcing him to duck down on his knees. When he cautiously peered over the edge of the sill, he had a glimpse of men running in among the horses, shouting and waving their rifles to stampede the animals. He managed to fire two badly aimed shots before a bullet grazed his helmet, knocking it off his head and momentarily stunning him. There followed the sound of whinnying and the receding clatter of hoofs as the horses bolted down the street. A couple of troopers smashed the remaining window and blindly fired their carbines at the houses opposite the inn but were quickly driven back by an accurate volley. Then, for a moment, all shooting stopped and one of the men cried in anguish: "My God, we are trapped without arms! We can't defend ourselves!"

To his horror, Gustaf realized that over half his men had left their carbines in the scabbards attached to the saddles of their horses. Besides their sabers, useless in this predicament, only nine out of the twenty-two troopers had firearms, his own pistol making the tenth. Two men lay dead outside and two more were writhing on the floor, seriously wounded. The rest appeared close to panic and for a moment he, too, had to fight down a wave of self-recrimination and fear. But he managed to steady both himself and his men. He shouted orders for the defense of the inn, assigning three troopers to the windows of the dining room, three more upstairs, and the remaining three to follow him to the kitchen and cover the rear of the building. He hoped they could escape as the innkeeper and his wife had, over the garden wall, and then fight their way out of the village into the snowy mist of open country. But as soon as he cracked open the back door, bullets slammed into it, showering him with splinters. The inn was obviously completely surrounded by a strong force of *francs-tireurs*.

Gustaf slammed the back door, helped his troopers barricade it with the kitchen table and chairs, then broke the one window and emptied his pistol at the garden wall. As he reloaded, his troopers fired another blind fusillade, ignoring the bullets whistling back through the window and shattering the crockery lining the shelves on the opposite walls. Then one of the men fell, shot through the head. Gustaf pulled the other two away, shouting: "Keep down! Save your ammunition! Don't shoot unless you see them." Picking up the dead trooper's carbine, he ran back to the dining room and passed the same order to the rest of the defenders. The shooting stopped and an uneasy silence fell over the inn until disturbed by a French voice shouting from outside: "Surrender, Prussians! Or we'll burn you alive!" All understood but nobody answered. The eleven unarmed dragoons crouching on the floor around their wounded comrades stared at their Leutnant with helpless, frightened looks.

Gustaf swallowed hard against a pressing nausea, then reassured them: "Never mind, men! To set fire to this place, they'll have to show themselves, and then we'll be able to pick them off." He handed the carbine to a trooper and sent him to replace the one killed in the kitchen. "If a man is hit, another must pick up his weapon and replace him," he ordered. He next commanded the front door and windows to be barricaded with tables and chairs, distributed reserves to the kitchen and upstairs, then took the time to kneel down and examine his two wounded men. The one who had been shot in the stomach was clutching a jagged wound, caused as much by oak splinters as by the bullet, his eyes already filming over with the veil of death. Sergeant Kluge was lying on his side with a small round hole drilled through the back of his tunic. He was perfectly conscious even though his spine was shattered and he was paralyzed from the waist down. He only moved his eyes as he looked into Gustaf's face and said: "I think there are more customers out there than the innkeeper cooked soup for, Herr Leutnant Baron."

Gustaf felt himself flushing, and in his embarrassment sounded harsh as he answered, "Don't worry yourself about that, Kluge. How do you feel?"

"I don't feel anything, Herr Leutnant Baron. Damn this country with its civilians who play soldiers with live ammunition."

"We'll teach them to stick to their shops and turnip patches," Gustaf answered with far more assurance than he felt. Turning to another trooper, he ordered, "Find some towels and sheets. Make bandages to dress the wounds of these men." Then he hurried to one of the windows, pulling aside its defender, and peered out into the blank opaqueness of the snowfall.

Because the inn was set back from the street to form a sidewalk café area for summer use, the adjacent buildings blocked Gustaf's view up and down the street. He could only see three two-story houses directly opposite and knew that sharpshooters were likely occupying each of their windows, ready to fire either between the louvers of the shutters or through broken panes. The falling snow misted the intervening fifty meters and combined with the early dusk of the December afternoon to reduce visibility, a condition affecting the besiegers as much as the besieged. He could see the bodies of the two dead dragoons already turning into shapeless white lumps as they became covered by snow, but otherwise there was no human being in sight nor any sound of activity. Yet, he sensed the enemy was all around them and probably far from inactive. As Gustaf watched and waited, he subverted his gnawing sense of failure and apprehension by trying to devise an escape plan. Nothing in his military training had equipped him to cope with a situation like this; everything taught at the military academy and on maneuvers had been oriented toward classical cavalry warfare involving either the shock tactics of massed formations or reconnaissance screens operating in support of troops. There had, of course, lately been discussions about counterguerrilla measures, but even these only concerned tactics against saboteurs and individual hit-and-run snipers. It crossed Gustaf's mind to shout out of the window for a parley on the terms of surrender. It was not incompatible with his code to surrender honorably in the field after losing a brave fight—to an *honorable* foe. But it was unthinkable for a professional Prussian officer to surrender to a *franc-tireur*!

Thus, he concluded that his only hope remained a fighting sortie out of the inn, escaping from the rear after dark, and breaking out of the village. More of his men would certainly be shot down, but it was the only chance of saving any part of his squadron. He heard the clock in the steeple of the village church chime four strokes and knew that darkness was less than an hour away. While there was still some light, he had better climb to the second floor and try to reconnoiter an escape route beyond the garden wall, but before he could do so, he heard a sudden rumbling from the street. As he was straining his eyes and ears to locate and identify the sound, smoke puffed from the windows opposite with the crackling report of hidden rifles. A dragoon fell with a groan, but this time Gustaf did not duck behind the sill. He kept his exposed position and watched with a peculiar detached fascination as a large, two-wheeled farm cart swung around the corner of a flanking house, propelled by six burly French peasants shoving on its shafts. It was piled high with straw and fagots which had evidently been soaked with oil, because even before smashing into the side of the inn, it burst into bright, searing flames. The troopers defending the dining room windows fired uselessly into the burning mass shielding the enemy, but Gustaf waited until they !et go of the shafts and scattered for cover, taking careful aim and dropping two with his pistol before the rest vanished. He saw them skid and fall in a spray of snow near the dead dragoons before he and his men were driven from the windows by sustained covering fire from across the street. In the meantime the cart had dumped its pyre squarely against the wall of the inn, sending fire and smoke toward the wooden overhang of the eaves. From the second floor there came terrified screams: "We are burning! We are burning!"

Three kilometers south of the village of Pernas Lieutenant Victor de Bretagne was awakened by the sound of distant shooting. His sleep had been a deep one after four consecutive nights of riding through country patroled by Uhlans and made almost equally dangerous by trigger-happy *francs-tireurs*. For a moment his memory stalled and he could not recognize his refuge, which was the ice-cold loft in the Le Brun farm's stable. His good eye had trouble adjusting to the dim light filtering through dusty panes of the one small window, his blind one throbbed with the familiar hurt which never seemed to leave the empty socket, and his bones ached as he lay shivering beneath his greatcoat on a bed of sacks of grain; they had seemed blessedly soft when he had lain down on them seven hours earlier, but had turned cruelly hard in the meantime. It took a conscious effort to force his mind to overcome pain and confusion and begin to function intelligently. Then he rolled off the sacks and crawled over the rough floorboards to the window to peer through its dirty glass. Beyond a screen of dancing snowflakes, the main farmhouse loomed as a blur against a gray void. He wondered if he had possibly only dreamed about shooting, but then he heard it again, a series of sharp pops rising and falling in intensity before fading back to silence. It came from far away but was the sound of a full-fledged skirmish between large numbers of riflemen, not just a few snipers. Crawling back to the sacks, Victor fumbled among their coarse lumps until he found the black patch he wore over his blind eye and adjusted its band around his head. Next he buckled on his belt with its pistol and saber. He was squirming into the black civilian greatcoat, which was a thin disguise over his uniform, when his ears caught a faint creaking sound, freezing him into immobility.

"*Psst! Mon lieutenant!*" a voice hissed out of the darkness of the stairwell. "Are you awake?"

Victor let out his breath with relief as he recognized his wheezing host, the farmer Le Brun. "Yes. What's the shooting about?"

Le Brun materialized, tiptoeing toward him in a tense, crouched position. "Germans!" he whispered. "We've trapped a whole regiment of them in the village."

Victor put on the plain woolen cap to which he had not been able to resist affixing the brass insignia of his regiment, the Roman numeral *XII*. "A whole regiment of them, eh?" he repeated with mocking delight. "Are you sure your information isn't wrong and it's the *village* which is trapped?"

"N-no—our boys have them cooped up in the inn," Le Brun excitedly assured him, still whispering as if the Germans might overhear him. "Parvus has come to fetch you to take charge. They don't trust the Italian to bring it off without botching everything."

"All right, let's go," Victor said, squeezing past him between the stacked rows of sacks. He carefully descended the steep wooden steps leading from the loft to the stables below, and walked past empty stalls to the one where his horse was waiting, saddled and ready, but not entirely recovered from last night's long ride. He unhitched the animal and led it out into the yard. There a man was waiting, seated bareback on a plump cart horse, the snow swirling around them and dusting them with white powder—all except the rider's nose, which seemed to glow like a wilted strawberry between his upturned collar flaps. "Are you Parvus?" Victor asked him.

"Yes, *mon lieutenant*. Parvus, the courier for the First Brigade of *Francs-tireurs* of Seine and Oise."

"A brigade yet! And you've trapped a regiment of Germans, I'm told."

"Well, a half a regiment or so," Parvus hedged. "You had better come quick."

Victor did not hurry. He adjusted his cinch strap and stirrups and said: "Ah, only a half-regiment. Still, quite a force. As a former prisoner of war who is violating his parole, the Germans will shoot me if I'm recaptured."

"Don't worry, *mon lieutenant*," Parvus exclaimed with a reassuring laugh. "We have this bunch in the bag. When they went inside the Vert Gallant, we surrounded it, stampeded all their horses, then pinned them down with our musketry. Now we're about to set fire to the place and burn them out. Hurry, or you'll miss the fun."

Le Brun, who had followed Victor outside, and held his horse as he swung himself into the saddle, spoke with his rasping whisper: "Yes, hurry. We don't want the Italians to get credit for this coup. The big battles should be conducted by our own people, after all. *Vive la France!*"

Victor ignored his outburst of patriotism and listened intensely for a moment to the brittle rustling of the snowflakes and the wind rattling the icicled branches of a barren chestnut tree growing next to the stables. There was no sound of sustained volleys coming from Pernas now, only the muffled cracks of sporadic shots interspersed with long periods of silence. "How many of our people are engaged in this battle?" he asked Parvus.

"The whole brigade should be there by now. Thirty-five or forty men, at least." Parvus suddenly turned sarcastic as he added: "You should be quite safe, *mon lieutenant*."

"Good!" Victor exclaimed with a dry irony in his voice. "Since losing one eye, I have tended to become a little cautious. But because I don't believe you've trapped a whole half-regiment of Germans, I'll take a chance and go with you." He dug his spurs into his horse and headed the animal out of the yard at a brisk trot.

Parvus looked down at Le Brun and said with a shrug: "That one is supposed to lead our *francs-tireurs*? They'll eat him alive."

They rode down a narrow lane bordered with thickets

which had turned into solid white walls. Victor's extinguished
eye burned with a dull black pain and his head began to throb
with the headache which always set in a few minutes after
awakening from sleep and would continue for all his waking
hours until sleep would again provide its merciful anesthesia.
His good eye watered and smarted as the snowflakes drove into
it, obscuring his vision and aggravating his fear of losing the
sight of that one too. The very whiteness of the lane, the bushes,
the fields, the cold air itself against which all shapes and con-
tours were like faintly penciled lines, heightened his terrible
feeling of approaching blindness. It would have been easier for
him to let Parvus lead the way so he could follow the broad black
rump of his cart horse, but Parvus was keeping well behind,
grunting in time with the snorting of his lumbering mount.
Then, as they rounded a bend, he called out, "Look ahead, *mon
lieutenant!* They must have already set fire to the Vert Gallant!"

Victor peered ahead but could see only the filmy outline of
the lane vanishing into the whiteness. But the firing sounded
much closer than before, so close he could distinguish the crack
of Prussian carbines from the deeper reports of chassepots and
tabatiers. He spurred his horse into a gallop and although Parvus kicked and cursed his nag to keep apace, the noise of his
efforts began rapidly fading behind.

The lane widened into something more like a road and
became lined with frosted poplars instead of thickets. Suddenly
Victor was able to see an orange glow with a dark smudge of
smoke rising and spreading in the gray whiteness of the sky; if
it stopped snowing, the pyre of the Vert Gallant would be seen
for miles around. The shapes of houses loomed out of the mist
to his left as the road ran obliquely into Pernas, then skirted
some walls enclosing gardens. The shooting again subsided but
he could hear excited shouts. He ran into a handful of men who
had rounded up the riderless German horses, and when Victor
reined in for a quick look, he spotted the regimental crest of
Second Royal Prussian Dragoon Guards—the same regiment he
had twice clashed with in the battles of Vionville and Mars-la-
Tour.

"Get those horses out of sight and hide all the equipment
and saddles!" he ordered the men before hurrying on toward the
inn, which was now throwing flames high into the air and
sending brightly glowing cinders swirling over the rooftops of
the village.

A minute later Victor reached the scene of the battle in time
to see the entire roof of the inn collapse, sending an explosion
of sparks skyward out of the brightly glowing shell. A large
crowd of excited men, all armed with rifles and muskets, surged

back from the searing heat, which was beginning to incinerate the bodies of Prussian dragoons piled outside the doorway and beneath the windows; they had dragged clear three of their own dead. Everybody was shouting and cheering, and an especially noisy group had collected around two prisoners, both wounded and burned, one so badly that he was lying at the mercy of the kicks of the mob of *francs-tireurs*. Victor spurred his horse right in among them and shouted in a voice which still had its adolescent shrill: "Let's get some order here! Put out that fire at once! Bury the dead and remove every trace of what has happened! At once!"

"Who the hell are you?" a tall, black-whiskered man shouted back. Victor instantly knew him to be the Italian, Gerucci, by his accent and his eccentric dress. He wore a sheepskin jacket, a slouch hat adorned with cock feathers, a red sash around his waist in which were tucked a pistol and a dagger, and black jackboots reaching almost to the crotch of his brown corduroy breeches. Victor had been warned about Gerucci, a member of Garibaldi's professional revolutionary fighters who had volunteered their services to the French Government of National Defense. Together with their flamboyant leader, most of them had been assigned to the quieter southern sectors where they terrorized the local population more than the few Prussians there. But this Gerucci had somehow worked himself into the Seine and Oise Sector and established himself in command of its *franc-tireur* bands. He looked the ruthless, cruel egotist he was reputed to be.

Victor dismounted and quickly introduced himself: "I am Lieutenant de Bretagne, assigned by the commanding general of the Army of the Loire to coordinate guerrilla activities in this district with the official strategic plan."

"The official strategic plan!" Gerucci scoffed. "But there are a dozen a week. All conflicting. None worth a damn." When Victor started moving toward the prisoners, he grabbed him by the arm and roughly spun him around: "You claim to be taking command here? So where are your orders to that effect?"

Victor yanked his arm free. "There is no time to exchange credentials or go into formalities right now," he snapped, but unbuttoned his greatcoat so that everybody could see the uniform it had covered. His face was still very much that of a boy, but the harsh red glow in his one eye, reflecting less the light of the burning inn than a cold inner fire of its own, made Gerucci hesitate, and Victor took advantage of that hesitation by turning his back on him and addressing himself to the Frenchmen: "How many Germans were here? Please don't waste my time with exaggerations."

"Besides these two prisoners, nine of their dead are roasting over there," one man answered with relish.

"Eight were killed trying to escape out of the back," another said, brandishing his musket. "We heard a couple more screaming inside as they burned."

Yet another, a rawboned farmer with bright eyes but a sluggish drawl, said: "I counted twenty-five of the bastards when I spotted them this morning. They were chasing one of the Paris balloons."

"A Paris balloon!" Victor exclaimed. "What happened to it?"

The rawboned one shrugged. "Just flew on and vanished. I thought it more important to watch the Prussians."

"Are you sure none of them has escaped?" Victor asked after making a quick mental calculation and deciding the whole action could not have involved more than a squadron of enemy cavalry.

"None!" a number of voices chorused.

"And now we shall execute the two survivors!" Gerucci announced.

"We will proceed in a legitimate, military manner," Victor countered.

"But certainly, sir!" Gerucci jeered. "Now that we are honored with the presence of a genuine regular officer, we shall form a proper firing squad, prop the prisoners against a wall, and shoot them according to nicest military etiquette."

"Stand back!" Victor firmly commanded. He shoved his way through to the prisoners and saw that the one lying in the trampled snow was a sergeant who had lost consciousness from a bullet wound in the back and had burns on his face and neck; he would not live long. The other was still on his feet, his arms pinioned by a pair of *francs-tireurs*, the blond strands of his bared head blackened by fire, and blood trickling out of his scorched, torn greatcoat. A silver epaulet dangling from a broken shoulder marked him as an officer. "Was this man in command of the enemy troops?" Victor asked.

"I suppose so," the rawboned farmer drawled. "We shot him down when he first came out of a window. Then he crawled back in and dragged out that one on the ground. That's when we took 'm both."

Victor resorted to the crude German he had learned during his six weeks as their prisoner before being exchanged for other wounded. "*Zind sie der befehlshaber?*" he asked the dazed Prussian officer.

Leutnant Baron Gustaf von Falkenhorst tried to focus on the one-eyed Frenchman, muttered a weak "*Ja,*" then peered down at the dying Sergeant Kluge lying at his feet in the blood-splattered snow.

"Form up the firing squad!" Gerucci bellowed. "Six men, at least. Got to make it impressive and official."

Victor spun around on him and shouted back: "You shut your mouth, Italian! This is our war, not yours. You will obey our general orders or go back where you came from. Those orders are to take all the prisoners we can. They are not to be uselessly killed as long as they may be a source of information or used as hostages for our own people. Understand? Very well, then—now you will form a bucket brigade and put out that fire."

"Another brilliant order!" Gerucci snorted with a fearful scowl on his swarthy face. "Rush to save what's already done for!"

Victor turned from him in exasperation and explained to the surrounding crowd of *francs-tireurs:* "Other patrols must have chased that balloon. As it gets dark, this fire can be seen for miles, leading them right to us. Besides, they will soon start searching for their missing comrades. They must find nothing and be made to believe this was an accidental fire."

There was a sobered murmur of approval. Three men picked up Kluge and carried him into a house where he was laid on the floor just inside the door. Gustaf von Falkenhorst was made to sit down next to his inert shape and an armed guard left to watch over both of them. Victor de Bretagne remained outside and began to feel pleasantly warmed for the first time in a week as he stood next to the glowing mass of the Vert Gallant, watching the *francs-tireurs* form a chain from the watering trough and throw bucket after bucket into the embers. They worked cheerfully, noisily, still stimulated by the great excitement of having ambushed and obliterated an entire squadron of Prussian cavalry. But Gerucci had lost interest now that the killing was over and stood sullenly aside, glaring at the young French officer who had suddenly appeared to usurp his leadership. At first the fight against the fire seemed completely ineffectual, but the snowfall was changing to a thick sleet which, combined with the buckets of water, slowly subdued the pyre and turned it into black, steaming wreckage. The innkeeper and his wife poked cautiously about to salvage a scorched utensil here, a cracked plate there, then accosted Victor with demands for restitution from the Government of National Defense.

The cheerfulness subsided to a grim silence when it came time to collect the bodies, pile them in a cart, and transport them to some hidden burial ground outside the village where the backbreaking toil of digging graves in the frozen soil would reach far into the night. Victor made Gerucci responsible for seeing that the job was properly done and, to balm his feelings told him: "I am not relieving you of command of these *francs-tireurs*. I have to concern myself with several other companies in the district as well as yours. My duty is to make sure you engage in military operations against the enemy, not simple brigandage. You may expect me to check on your activities frequently and to control them in the interest of our people and country."

Gerucci spat and insolently answered: "Yes, General."

"Lieutenant," Victor corrected him. "I am a lieutenant of the Twelfth Imperial Cuirassiers."

"Ah, yes," Gerucci snorted. "One of the Imperial Napoleon's own!"

"One of France's own," Victor again corrected him, then watched him skulk off after the gravediggers before entering the house where the two prisoners were being held. It was the dark, cluttered abode of Pernas's apothecary, a thin wisp of a man who had just come out of hiding and was still in a terribly nervous state after having his home and pharmacy used, first, as a redoubt from where the *francs-tireurs* poured their fire into the inn, then as a jail for their prisoners. He was kneeling over Sergeant Kluge, and when Victor entered, whined at him: "This man is dead. You can't leave his body in my house. I'm a patriot, but you can't embarass me with a dead German."

Victor merely glanced at the body, then turned his attention to the wounded Prussian officer slumped against the wall; blood was still seeping out of his wounds. He motioned to the guard to help raise him to his feet and half-drag him into the room which served as the apothecary's laboratory and dispensary. There was a pungent odor of medicine and gunpowder; the floor was littered with empty cartridge hulls and broken glass from the window. They propped Gustaf on a chair, and Victor removed his greatcoat, letting it fall to the floor. Then he opened the bloody tunic and peeled back the gory undershirt.

"Is there a doctor available?" he asked the apothecary.

"He left us to join the Army of the Loire. I am a patriot, you understand, but I simply can't handle a situation like this."

"You have no choice, monsieur. You must have medicaments and bandages. Dress his wound as best you can." He turned to the guard, a scowling villager wearing a blacksmith's leather apron and carrying a still-cocked musket. "I am removing this prisoner as far from here as possible tonight. We will need a horse and cart. Please fetch one immediately."

"My own was used to set fire to the Vert Gallant," the man grumbled. "It is completely ruined. But perhaps I can find another." Somewhat reluctantly he uncocked his weapon, slung it over his shoulder, and marched off on his errand.

The apothecary rummaged about the drawers and cabinets, picking out bottles and bandages while whimpering like a frightened dog. But once he began treating his patient, he did so with a certain clumsy enthusiasm, like a man who considers himself to possess unrecognized talents for medicine. He reacted with chagrin and apologized when Gustaf could not restrain a groan of pain.

Victor leaned down and examined the wound; a heavy musket ball had ploughed through the shoulder near the base of the neck, breaking the collar bone and laying it bare in a deep furrow. The Prussian's singed head and badly burned hands looked equally painful, but he decided that none of his injuries would be fatal provided gangrene could be prevented.

"It is not so bad," Victor said to him, giving him an encouraging pat. *"Nicht so schwer."*

The two young officers looked into each other's faces and each suddenly had a fleeting feeling that he had seen the other before. But, because they were both overwhelmed by more urgent problems, neither probed into the origin of his strange feeling.

Only the weather was properly traditional at Schloss Varn on Christmas Day 1870. It dawned and continued throughout crystal clear with a crisp cold which was only slightly warmed by a brilliant sunshine. The snow dazzled the eye with its sparkling beauty and crunched with a metallic sound under boots and runners. The fens gave off soft sighing sounds as the faint Baltic tides stirred beneath the ice covering the sloughs. The dells of birches and pines, left in rare peace by the stilled gales, stood motionless and silent, as if afraid to break the fragile strings of diamonds with which the hoarfrost had sprinkled their boughs. Red-breasted bullfinches, their bodies puffed round by the cold like animated Christmas balls, flitted about the thickets, making melodious pipings of delight when their foraging was rewarded by a frostbitten berry. The castle itself acquired a magic fairy-tale quality, the severe symmetry of its steep roofs and sharp towers softened by woolly caps of snow, its craggy stone facade ablaze with the glitter of hundreds of luminescent icicles. Even its older ramparts and ruined stump of a keep, ancient foundations built upon a long-forgotten Swedish dream of empire, were pleasantly blended into the present by the white brush strokes of winter. Black windows, like clear sheets of ice covering dark waters, were illuminated by plume-shaped designs of frost, delightful, yet unable to counter entirely the gloom of mourning within. The somber crepe draperies had been removed from the front doors, but instead of holiday wreaths of braided green fir and scarlet alder berries, black ribbons had been tied to the massive iron knockers; they would, according to custom, be left there for six weeks after Count Frederick Paul von Beckhaus's funeral.

At sunrise, which in December comes a few minutes before nine o'clock on this Baltic coast of Prussia, Master Prytz drove up from the stables in a sleigh pulled by a pair of excited Varn pacers, making the castle walls echo with the merry sound of the bells adorning their harnesses in silvery strings. He had hesitated over the propriety of such a Christmas frivolity when the purpose of the trip was to be a visit to Count Frederick Paul's fresh grave in the cemetery of Varnmunde, but then had decided the young people deserved some merry sounds to break the melancholy silence of the castle. He was certain that the widowed Countess von Beckhaus would not participate in the pilgrimage; rumors of her absolute seclusion had reached the stables from the pantry. And he became satisfied that his judgement in the matter had been correct when only Tessa and her brother-in-law Albrecht von Falkenhorst came down the steps to climb into the sleigh. They lost their tense pallor and flushed with pleasure as he tucked them in beneath the luxurious fur of Russian lynx. "May the spirit of Christ's birth comfort my Baroness and Freiherr!" he exclaimed, tactfully refraining under the circumstances from using the customary greeting of "Merry Christmas." Just the same, they both smilingly used that greeting to him.

The old stablemaster became flustered, clumsily kissed his mistress's hand, then climbed onto the box, looking like a big brown circus bear in his fur coat and cap. A smart crack of his whip released all the latent energies of the horses in an eager forward lunge. The jubilant major-key chords of their bells made intricate rhythmic patterns as they were reined back from an initial bursting gallop to a prancing canter, then settled into a fast-pacing gait with their chestnut tails streaming behind them like flaming torches. The sleigh moved swiftly, more like a boat coursing over a magic white stream than any landbound conveyance bumping along a man-made road. Powdered snow hissed in twin bow waves from the runners and smoked back in a swirling wake. Tessa remembered that along with galloping over the fens on Kugel, this had been the greatest excitement of her girlhood, first experienced nestled in her father's lap. Esther and her mother had been terrified by the speed, but Tessa had shouted in delight, causing her father to exclaim with a certain biting wistfulness: "My Tessa should have been a boy! She fears nothing, the silly girl!" That had been another, happier Christmas of ten years ago. She tried now to recapture some fragment of its delights by shouting at Prytz: "Faster, Prytzie! Faster! Make them fly!"

Master Prytz did not pull up at the front of the church where crowds of worshippers were tethering their steaming horses but stopped by the gate of the small cemetery where ten generations of the von Beckhaus family lay buried. The plain granite mausoleum built in 1682 had become filled with the bones of Tessa's ancestors already a hundred years ago, so her father had been interred outside of it, next to her grandfather, grandmother, and a brother who had died in infancy before she was born. The grave had no headstone as yet, and was marked only by a fresh mound of black frozen earth starkly contrasting with the surrounding snow; it was crowned by a great heap of wreathes decorated with ribbons of the Prussian national colors, flowers being unobtainable in Pomerania this time of the year. Albrecht followed behind Tessa as she walked up to the grave for her second visit since returning home. He removed his cap and bowed his head, believing himself to be joining her in a silent prayer, but after a short moment of silence, she suddenly said: "Why, Albrecht, will you not tell me how Papa died?"

He had, indeed, deliberately avoided this subject to spare her the sordid details; yet, because he feared the question, he was prepared for it. "He and his escort ran into an ambush. Nobody survived the attack," he gently told her.

"I have overheard our servants say he was murdered," Tessa said, looking him straight in the eyes. "Tell me the truth, Albrecht. I do not have to be coddled like Mama."

"He was shot by French guerrillas," Albrecht answered, then gave in to the hard questioning look remaining on her face and confirmed the full truth: "Yes, it was murder. The Uhlans, who arrived too late to save him, reported he must have been shot down at close range after the others were killed in the fighting. Yes, it was murder." He put a comforting arm around her shoulder to stem the expected shocked outburst of grief, but she merely nodded her head and said: "I thought so."

The church bells began to ring, and Albrecht felt a strange

restless uneasiness welling up very strong inside of him, and with it a desire to return to Schloss Varn as quickly as possible. She did turn from the grave after spending less than two minutes at its side, but took his arm and quietly announced: "Now, I would like to attend the Christmas service."

Varnmunde's church was filled to capacity and warmed by several charcoal braziers and clusters of candles whose bright, still flames gave the altar a festive look. The opening hymn had already started when Tessa and Albrecht entered, and although the congregation's strong voices never faltered as they sang "Oh Bright Star of Bethlehem," they could feel all eyes glancing up from the hymnals as they were escorted down the aisle by the sexton to the front pew reserved for the inhabitants of the castle. Albrecht had hoped to slip into one of the rear ones, but his discomfort at being the focus of attention was quickly diverted by his surprise at hearing Tessa's beautiful contralto singing voice. Pastor Hess conducted the traditional Lutheran Christmas service, adding to his prayers of thanksgiving for the birth of the Saviour a fervent plea for peace. This he phrased in the form of a supplication to the Almighty that He intercede with the French, commanding them to capitulate in accordance with His will and that of His Majesty King Wilhelm I of Prussia. It was a jarring piece of religious sophistry no doubt inspired, perhaps even composed, by Bishop Putzkammer during his recent visit; it received from the worshippers a nearly thunderous "Amen!" At one point during his sermon, Pastor Hess peered down from his pulpit directly at Tessa von Falkenhorst and said: "It is part of the miracle of Christmas that its spirit of joy must lighten the burden of those bowed by personal sorrow. Being a Divine spirit, it is not one to be denied!" Those words were certainly his own.

When the service was over, none of the congregation budged, except for a few restless tots, until Pastor Hess had conducted Tessa and Albrecht out of the church. As they emerged into the bright winter sunlight, he took her hand and gave it a firm squeeze, saying: "I am delighted you came, my dear." To Albrecht he spoke a quick, somewhat guarded aside: "Thank you for bringing her, Freiherr von Falkenhorst. I am sure your absent brother will also thank you."

Albrecht was reminded of his brother's seeming indifference to Tessa's trials, but answered graciously: "I am grateful to be of some comfort to my sister-in-law."

The Pastor hovered around the sleigh as Master Prytz tucked them back into it and smiled when Tessa complimented him on his sermon, but when he asked whether he could call on her mother that afternoon, his smile wavered as she somewhat abruptly told him: "We are not receiving guests as usual this Christmas." She began to formulate a reasonable explanation for her mother's peculiar seclusion, but at that moment the church bells began pealing in the steeple above their heads, their din making unseemly shouting necessary. The worshippers were now piling out of the sanctuary, the children yelping in delight, the attention of the adults inevitably drawn to the slender young woman in black and the young man wearing a civil service uniform with its mourning armband. Instead of making her explanation to Pastor Hess, Tessa found herself making it to Albrecht after their sleigh had pulled away and was jangling across Varnmunde's square. "Mama is being very difficult," she said. "She refuses to see anybody or even leave her rooms."

Albrecht thought about his own mother's chronic, unnatural grieving for a husband she had never given a moment's peace in their home, but managed to sound optimistic as he answered: "She will recover. Remember it has only been three days since the funeral."

"You have not seen her since then," Tessa told him. "You would be surprised if you had."

"By her tears? I don't think so."

Tessa looked into his face and shook her head. "She sheds no tears now. She used to often when she was married to Papa, and she probably did at his funeral because she was nervous and frightened. But now she has stopped, and I don't think she'll weep anymore." When she noticed his expression of consternation, she reacted with a flash of temper: "You want us to keep hiding the truth from each other, Albrecht?"

She asked the question with such intensity that he could not help retorting: "Of course not!" but with painful emotions ranging from embarrassed dismay to tender pity, he could say no more, only mutely realize that she, too, had grown up with parents who had lived together in misery. His hands fumbled for hers beneath the fur rug.

Tessa glanced up at the back of Master Prytz, making sure that the music of the bells and the thick cap pulled down over his ears would prevent him from hearing them. Then she flatly stated: "I, too, have a loveless marriage." When his grip merely tightened without any other response, she turned to him and drove the point home with a bluntness, which was all the more painful for its complete lack of passion: "Gustaf left me on our wedding night on this very road. I have since had exactly two short letters from him, the first telling me how much he enjoyed my favorite horse he took from me, the second announcing its death in battle. I suppose we were at least aware of our mutual affection for poor Kugel—sort of. But otherwise there is nothing between us except being caught in the same trap sprung by our families. One wanted to catch a name, the other money. Papa himself put it this way to me: It was the best possible arrangement he could make for me. So be it! Since he was such a clever and powerful man, he was, no doubt, right in his way. But it is a loveless marriage just the same. And obviously that must not matter. Not for our kind." Her own hands suddenly tightened around his, turning his grip into an uncertain, trembling one. "Now, Albrecht, tell me again that Gustaf asked you to give me his love along with his sympathy. Remember. The truth between us. Always!"

Albrecht tried to calm himself by taking several deep breaths of the ice-cold slipstream flowing over the speeding sleigh. His voice sounded choked and unconvincing as he answered, "Neither of you has had a chance yet. The war came between you."

"I think the war gave us both a reprieve," Tessa said.

A moment later she burst out laughing. Albrecht was shocked until he realized that she had abruptly dismissed the whole subject from her mind. "It is a very beautiful Christmas Day," she exclaimed. "One of the few I can remember when it was not either snowing or sleeting. There's only you and I to celebrate it together, so let's try to enjoy it a little. Even Pastor Hess hinted that would not be a sin." Her voice rose to a merry shout. "Faster, Prytzie! Make them fly! Faster!"

Tessa's determination to pay some tribute to the Nativity became even more evident after they returned to Schloss Varn. As they were warming themselves before the fire in the library, she surprised Albrecht by handing him a small package wrapped in white paper and red ribbons. His surprise turned into flustered embarrassment when he found it to contain a pocket watch with the von Beckhaus crest beautifully engraved on the solid gold case.

"It belonged to Papa," she explained. "I know he would approve of your receiving it as a Christmas gift and a remembrance of your service with him." She turned aside his initial protests, and when she noticed that the gift had moved him to the brink of tears abruptly excused herself on the grounds that she must call upon her mother upstairs. Albrecht was left alone by the fire, unsteadily sipping a glass of hot spiced wine served by the ever-solemn Knabel, feeling miserable because he had nothing to give Tessa in return. She had not even received a letter of condolence from Gustaf, no Christmas greeting—nothing. Damn him!

Countess Antoinette von Beckhaus was propped up in her bed against a rampart of pink silk pillows, wearing an embroidered violet bedjacket with matching nightbonnet, snacking with listless gluttony from a silver tray of small cakes nestled on her lap. When Tessa startled her by suddenly appearing on the threshold, she snatched a handkerchief and began to dab at her eyes. But she let it drop as her daughter greeted her with a "Merry Christmas, Mama!" in a somewhat ironic tone.

"Merry Christmas, my poor fatherless darling," the Countess replied with her tremulous voice. "I suppose it is proper that we wish it to each other in the privacy of my bedroom."

"Yes, of course, Mama," Tessa said. She had an immediate urge to go over to the steaming windows and throw them open to cleanse with fresh winter air the stifling, perfumed heat generated by the huge tile oven. But she perched herself on the edge of the bed and gave her mother a dutiful kiss on the cheek. Some cake crumbs stuck to her mouth, and she quickly brushed them off.

"Did you go to church, dearest?" the Countess asked.

"Yes—Albrecht took me. We had a glorious sleigh ride just like in the old days. Almost."

"Did you pray for your poor Papa?"

"We visited his grave."

"That was sweet of you. Albrecht is such a dear, understanding boy."

"Yes. Very." Tessa looked around the bedroom and noticed that the black mourning dress and veil which had been left draped over a chair for the past three days was gone; the maid had only laid out a white dressing gown. She also noticed a trunk standing open in a corner, still dusty from its long storage in the castle's vast attic; in it were a few neatly folded corsets and bodices. "Are you not coming downstairs for Christmas dinner?" she asked.

"I could not bear it, Tessa dearest. I have no appetite and would only spoil things for you and Albrecht." The Countess began to pop another cake into her mouth but caught herself and put it back on the tray.

"But I see you are planning a trip," Tessa said, her eyes on the trunk.

The Countess flushed and began her old nervous wigwagging with the handkerchief. "Well, no . . . I mean, yes. Only to visit my family in Vienna. Your Uncle Franz and Aunt Clara. But not right away, of course. That would not be fitting. And I wouldn't dream of leaving while you are still here, Tessa dearest!"

Tessa knew from her mother's flustered defensive tone that she intended to leave Schloss Varn as soon as possible and to stay away as long as possible. She recalled how her father had avoided visiting his Austrian in-laws, whom he had described as "boring dilettantes living in the decadent capital of a decaying empire." It had been six years since her mother had been permitted to visit her beloved Vienna, six years of continuous residence in this castle she hated, with only a couple of excursions to the pompously grim court in Berlin. Realizing that her mother was asking her a question, Tessa reassured her. "Don't worry, Mama, I am leaving tomorrow afternoon. But what about all our servants and farm people?"

"Oh, our steward and Papa's solicitor will see to them."

"I mean what about them *today*, Christmas Day. Remember Papa's custom of inviting them to gather in the Hall to sing carols and receive gifts."

"Oh, dear! I forgot about that!" the Countess exclaimed in dismay. "I believe he did leave instructions the custom was to be carried out in case he was absent for Christmas. Oh dear!"

"Well, he is absent, Mama."

"But, Tessa, he's *dead*!" She fluttered the handkerchief in the air, scattering more cake crumbs. "Surely you aren't proposing singing and dancing as usual."

Tessa began to lose her patience. "We have no Christmas tree to dance around this year. But I see nothing wrong with singing a few carols or drinking a glass of ale or eating some cake." She glanced meaningfully at the tray in her mother's lap, then added, "And certainly our people should receive their usual gifts of silver thalers."

The Countess became more agitated. "Well, I suppose they should. I forgot all about it. Everything's been so upsetting these last few weeks with my darling Esther passing on and Papa's terrible funeral and everything. Anyway, I never handle money matters. The steward is supposed to pay everybody."

"Only their wages. Papa always personally handed out their Christmas gifts and now you should do it." When her mother looked horrified and showed signs of pulling the bed-clothes over her head, Tessa quickly said, "Very well, Mama! Then *I* shall do it."

"Oh, thank you, dearest!" the Countess exclaimed with relief. "I'll give you the key to Papa's cashbox. He left it with me when he went to war and . . . oh dear! What did I do with it?" She threw off the comforter, upsetting the tray of cakes, and, jumping out of the huge baroque bed, skipped over to the cluttered dresser and began to rummage frantically through its drawers. Hatpins, hairpins, combs, little silver boxes of rouge, vials of perfume, gold rings and diamond brooches, and wispy tangles of lace handkerchiefs in pink, violet, and white, all erupted from the frantic groping of her chubby fingers. Suddenly she burst out in a loud wail: "I've made a mess of everything! I simply forgot all about Christmas presents. I have nothing for anybody. Not even for you, dearest Tessa!" Then, just as suddenly, she shouted in delight, "But of course I have! How stupid of me! Here you are, my sweet girl! Merry Christmas!" She removed a small black leather case from one of the drawers and eagerly thrust it into her daughter's hands.

Tessa turned the case over hesitantly. When she opened it, she found herself staring down at the Order of the Iron Cross lying on its cushion of Prussian blue satin, the black-and-white ribbon of its neckstrap neatly folded beneath it. She felt the color drain out of her face, leaving her freckles burning as glaring, white-hot blotches.

"The King gave it to Papa," her mother shrilled. "To your own dear Papa for dying like a brave Prussian soldier. You must treasure it always."

Tessa felt like screaming that her father had not died like a soldier but had been *murdered*, and that was all this trinket would remind her of. She snapped the case shut and after swallowing hard several times managed to suppress her voice into a hoarse whisper. "Thank you, Mama. Now we need the key."

"Oh, yes. The key. What did I do with it?" The Countess Antoinette looked up at the chandelier as if expecting to see it dangling up there among the sooty clusters of crystal teardrops. Then she gave up with a helpless shrug and confessed, "I must have lost it."

"Never mind, Mama. We will manage somehow."

Her mother promptly scampered back to the silken refuge of her bed and snuggled down beneath the quilted billows of the comforter. "I'm sure the servants will understand," she chirped. "This year it simply isn't practical to celebrate a proper Christmas."

Tessa left her mother's apartment, walked down the long halls to the opposite wing of the castle, and entered her father's private study. She had not been in it since he had summoned her to announce the final details of her betrothal to Gustaf—almost a year ago. The room still had that particular smell she associated with him, a pleasant faint aroma of leather, tobacco, and sealing wax. Except for the chill of the empty fireplace, everything was as he must have left it on the day he departed for the war. Leatherbound books, hundreds of them, lined the shelves in orderly ranks from floor to ceiling, only parting to make room for a window with a magnificent view, a hearth, and, above it, an equestrian portrait of Great-grandfather von Beckhaus glaring down from his painted rocking-horse charger as he rode into the battle of Rossbach. On the mantlepiece there were a model locomotive and a bronze bust of Frederick the Great—"*der Grosse* Fritz" as he used to call him. His big desk looked like a sarcophagus with its carved Teutonic knights bowed under the weight of its black marble top, leaning on their broadswords as if mourning their dead overlord. A pair of silver candlesticks flanked a bronze inkwell whose lids were fashioned into the heads of Varn stallions. A cabinet fitted into its left side artfully concealed his massive iron cashbox. As Tessa had expected, it was locked and too heavy for her to pull out. She yanked on the bell cord hanging next to the hearth and, while waiting for Knabel to respond, sat herself down at the desk, opened its center drawer and took out the big ledger book in which were penned, in her father's bold perpendicular script, all the names and vital statistics of Schloss Varn's servants, laborers, and tenant farmers. By the time Knabel appeared, she had refreshed her memory of these people, most of whom she had known all her life, and was ready to give him terse, exact orders. "Go and fetch Master Prytz. Tell him to bring a heavy hammer and chisel. Then notify everybody that the Christmas gathering will take place as usual in the Great Hall. I expect everybody to attend cheerfully and be served coffee, cake, and ale."

On her way down to dinner, Tessa passed two maids on the stairs carrying up an elaborate Christmas meal on covered trays to her mother's apartment. The grieving widow was, after all, not entirely reduced to nibbling on small cakes, she mused to herself as she hurried on to rejoin Albrecht, whom she found still waiting in the library, rubbing the stiffness of his wounded shoulder and staring absently into the fireplace. She apologized for having left him alone for so long and tried to comfort him by saying, "One thing Mama has not neglected this Christmas is the traditional feast."

"How very thoughtful of her," Albrecht answered, brightening at the prospect of a good meal. "How is the Countess feeling?"

"Hungry!" Tessa wryly told him, and, taking his good arm, began leading him toward the Little Dining Room. "Let's go see if there's anything left for us!"

The Little Dining Room of Schloss Varn had a table of such dimensions that they found themselves separated by a fifteen-foot expanse of white damask and obscured from each other by a pair of huge, five-armed candlesticks. Tessa immediately objected to this seating arrangement, and they remained standing while Knabel and a footman reset one place next to the other at the head of the table. Then Tessa refused to sit in her father's old place, insisting that Albrecht take it instead. "As stand-in for my husband, that's where you belong," she pronounced.

Albrecht sat down in Count Frederick Paul's seat, its stiff-backed discomfort adding to his unease and embarrassment at not providing entertaining chatter. It seemed it had all been exhausted and nothing remained but serious, sensitive subjects which he felt obliged to avoid. The war, because he felt it would make more painful the memory of her father; Gustaf, because the mere mention of his name made her tense; Glaumhalle, because he knew her life there had been far from happy. But during this Christmas dinner, a sumptuous meal with roast stuffed goose as the main course which was served by two liveried servants in the contrived intimacy of a corner of the huge table, it was Tessa herself who led the conversation into these very subjects. She asked about the war in France, particularly about the *francs-tireurs* who had killed her father. She asked about Gustaf, not really as would a wife about an absent husband, but rather impersonal questions about his life as a soldier. Then she described her experiences at Glaumhalle, speaking in a cheerful, matter-of-fact tone of being rejected and abused by her mother-in-law, then telling of her plan to restore the estate and convert it into a productive stud farm. "What worries me very much," she said, slicing into the rich, brown goose meat, "is whether we will be breeding fine horses just to be slaughtered in future wars. I can't forget what happened to Kugel."

Albrecht did not doubt for a moment that what really worried her was his mother, of whose aberrations he was well aware. More than anything else, it was Tessa's account of her life at Glaumhalle which disturbed his normally healthy appetite, making him pick at his food in a distracted manner while floundering over excuses for his mother's behavior and protesting Tessa's generosity toward a home which had turned out so inhospitable. This only made her smile, shrug, and change the subject to the ceremony about to take place in the Great Hall of the castle. She laughed as she told how she and Master Prytz had to force her father's cashbox because her mother had lost the key. "It took a lot of hammering and prying, let me tell you!" she exclaimed with her green eyes sparkling. "All the while I wondered if it might turn out empty. But not much chance of that, of course. Papa always kept a lot of silver money. He used to say that the paper kind burned too easily, or the banks printing it might get caught on the wrong side of a war."

"That was wise," Albrecht agreed, but he was pondering this girl's own fascinating mixture of shrewdness and consideration.

The silver thalers burglarized from Count Frederick Paul's cashbox were stacked in fifty-three shining columns on the center of the Great Hall's long table, most of them containing five coins for those who had served the von Beckhaus family for over ten years, some with only three for those with less service, some teetering twenty-high for retainers and tenant farmers who had worked on the estate for over twenty years. On each side of the piled coins were arranged rows of platters filled with cakes and sweetmeats. There was a roaring fire in the enormous hearth, its heat wafting turbulent currents up to the vast vaulted ceiling and animating the slack folds of faded regimental banners served under or captured by long-departed chatelains. Suits of armor hanging on the walls like skeleton-shells of slain knights shimmered faintly in the warm glow of fire- and candlelight. There were also fifty-three living people pressed together near the pantry entrance, waiting shoulder to shoulder in a dumb, motionless silence. But when they entered, the entire assembly bowed and curtseyed with a rustling of starched linen and pressed broadcloth. In years past they had shouted a rousing Merry Christmas to their lord, but it came now as a confused, uncertain whisper, more a collective sigh than a greeting. The sound of it startled Tessa, making her catch her breath and pause for a moment. Her eyes flicked over the room and narrowed as they focused on the spot behind the table where a tall, sparkling Christmas tree usually stood. She had not expected it to be there, of course, yet neither had she expected in its place the ornately carved oak throne from which the founding Graf von Beckhaus had held court in this cavernous chamber some three and a half centuries ago. Her father would have occupied it now had he been alive, but the empty seat held a black-ribboned laurel wreath propped up as a stark remembrance. This doleful touch, unmistakably Knabel's, was entirely correct according to the strict Prussian-Lutheran customs of mourning but completely destroyed the spirit Tessa had intended for the occasion. Her initial impulse was to march up to the chair and cast aside the wreath, but she sensed that the silence of the crowd was largely out of reverence for that symbol of death, and that these simple servant folk would consider such an action a desecration. So she compromised by striding up and blocking it from their view, then providentially recalled Pastor Hess's sermon and paraphrased his words in a clear ringing voice: "Let us enjoy Christmas for a while. Being a Divine spirit, even here it must not be denied!"

Albrecht could not help gasping aloud in admiration at her mastery of a difficult situation, the sound disturbing her as she was by no means as composed as she seemed. It was Master Prytz who came more positively to her support by stepping out from the grave assembly, a sternly patriarchal figure with his bristly moustache and mane of silver hair, his deep voice reverberating around the walls of the Great Hall as he shouted: "God rest His Excellency and bless his gracious daughter! Three cheers for the Baroness von Falkenhorst!"

The first cheer came more as a desultory muttering, the second louder and livelier, the third bursting into a full-throated roar which must have rolled through the whole castle and reached the ears of the widowed Countess in her bed high up in the west wing. Then she as surely must have heard the strains of the new Bavarian carol *"Stille Nacht, Heilige Nacht"* and paused in her compulsive snacking, listening and thinking without a trace of envy how well her daughter had taken over the tedious duties of chatelaine.

During the singing of the carol, Tessa tried to recall the words of the benediction her father used to pronounce before the distribution of gifts and partaking of refreshments. But her mind short-circuited on disconnected snatches of the prayer and again it was Master Prytz who caught a flicker of desperation in her eyes and came to her rescue.

"May the Lord God accept our thanks for the bounty He has bestowed upon this house," he boomed into the silence which fell after the singing. "The Lord giveth, the Lord taketh away! Blessed be the name of the Lord!" They were the exact words used by Count Frederick Paul in times past and were followed by a rumbling "Amen!" from the gathering, who then shuffled forward and began forming into a long line before the center of the table and the silver stacks of coin. Each maid and footman, scullery girl and stable boy, groom and cook, tenant farmer and crofter's wife, arranged themselves in order of seniority behind Master Prytz and Knabel. To each one Tessa handed the allotted gift of money together with a gracious smile and a greeting by name, receiving from each a stiffly formal, yet heartfelt, thanks.

Albrecht von Falkenhorst stood several feet away from his sister-in-law. He felt a stranger, apart from the ceremony she was conducting, but at the same time deeply moved by it. He watched her performance with both a curious detachment and an intense personal response. He saw her severe plainness accentuated by the copper strands of her hair drawn into a wire-tight braid around her head, by the freckled reddish pallor of her face in the flickering candlelight, by the unadorned blackness of the satin encasing her angular, reed-thin body; but he also saw a beauty which was so subtle in her delicate, yet strong, features, so full of latent vitality in her still-girlish, yet mature, poise, that he felt nobody but *he* could possibly perceive and appreciate it. His efforts to sort out and bring under control his conflicting reactions only resulted in a sequence of terribly disturbing thoughts. That his brother Gustaf was not worthy of Tessa and would never be able to cope with her unconventional character and independent spirit, that their marriage could only bring out and harden the worst traits in each of them, that *there really was no marriage at all!* It was a sham, a mockery; as a covenant before God, a blasphemy; as a civil one, a crass dynastic convenience in the most blatant Byzantine tradition. He would not as yet admit to himself that he was falling in love with his sister-in-law and feeling for the first time in his life a searing jealousy of his brother. But neither would he dismiss the idea that he must intervene in the situation far beyond the degree tacitly agreed to by Gustaf. His frustration and excitement caused an internal physical pressure to build within his whole being, and it suddenly made the wound in his shoulder throb with pain. And that triggered the realization that he was not at all ready to return to the war in France—and he had a perfectly valid excuse not to do so. As he stood watching Tessa hand out the silver coins, he resolved to accompany her back to Glaumhalle. She would need him there more than here, certainly far more than he was needed at Royal Headquarters in Versailles where the business of the Inspector General of Military Railroad Transport had degenerated into routine bureaucratic drudgery. The Prince General Eugene of Hanover, who had taken over after Count Frederick Paul's death, must surely have received a report from Verdun about his wounds and a simple telegram requesting extended sick-leave would suffice to cover his absence from duty. And where better to recover from his hurts than at home in Glaumhalle—where he could continue to be near Tessa and protect her from the neurotic machinations of his mother?

As Albrecht thought over his plan and justified it in his mind, his bearing stiffened and his face flushed in anticipation, the half-healed scar on his cheek hardening his look of determination as he kept his eyes on Tessa. Only one person among the crowd in Schloss Varn's Great Hall took notice of the peculiar intensity of his expression and, in a sudden disconcerting flash, realized the nature of the emotions behind it. Master Prytz momentarily faltered, scowling, as he nudged on the recipients of gifts from the hands of his beloved mistress.

At Glaumhalle, three days after Christmas when a spell of sunny cold weather was broken by a gathering gray overcast presaging another blizzard, the postman from Ols prodded his weary horse up the deep rippling drifts of the hillside and dismounted in the clearing shoveled out of the immediate vicinity of the manor's kitchen entrance. He was a stubborn man with a cynical touch to his absolute devotion to duty, an alert observer with keen eyes for any signs of activity along his long, lonely mail route, whether they be animal or human. He was quick to notice and interpret, for instance, some tracks in the snow which ran from the back of the keep and down the hill, crossing the frozen river at its base, then continuing in a thin disappearing line into the silent white waste beyond the frontier. "Ah, I see your three Polish serfs celebrated Christmas by running away," he exclaimed to Hult, the Silesian foreman who came out on the kitchen stoop to meet him.

"Yes," Hult glumly confirmed. "They preferred to face the Cossacks than what's in there." He thumbed over his shoulder at the manor.

"Well, that's what happens when you give too many rights to the serfs," the postman wryly shrugged, tying a feedbag of oats to his horse's head. The Polish laborers were not serfs at all, of course, serfdom having been abolished in Prussia over fifty years before. But he habitually referred to common farmworkers as such, especially Poles. With the innate conservatism of a petty civil servant, he firmly believed that rights should be granted according to rank, of which he considered himself to enjoy a significant smattering by virtue of employment in His Majesty's Royal Postal and Telegraph Service. He was also opposed to such innovations as universal compulsory education, but for the selfish reason that if every stablehand and crofter along his route learned to read and write, his lightly loaded mailbag would soon become an intolerable burden. It was tedious enough to serve the half-dozen manor farms strung out over a thirty-kilometer trek along the frontier, especially with the forbidding, inhospitable Glaumhalle as the terminal point. Matters there had improved somewhat since the young Baroness von Falkenhorst had moved in last summer, and she had on several occasions lodged him overnight in the stables before sending him rested and well fed on the return trip to Ols; but he knew that both she and her doughty stablemaster were away over Christmas, leaving the estate once again under the snarling tyranny of the crippled Dowager Hildebrun. He would have to ride back for ten kilometers in falling darkness and temperature to find haven at the neighboring von Birkenheim estate. However, Hult did at least invite him to come inside and warm himself in the dark cavernous kitchen where, as of old, there were no inviting kettles percolating on the stove. He dumped his mailsack on the table, pulled off his mittens, and began fumbling inside it. "I bring a telegram from France," he announced. "Telegrams are the devil's invention. They are conveyed by means of electricity, but where the wires come to an end, an old-fashioned flesh and blood postman must carry them on to their destination. Usually as an extra, unscheduled trip. And then they never seem to bring joy to the recipient after all the trouble involved."

The postman spoke his last sentence with an ominous inflection, suggesting he already knew the message contained in the sealed envelope. He had, in fact, looked over the shoulder of the Ols postmaster as he penned it out in his laboriously perfect scrawl. Hult, who dreaded having to deliver it to the Baroness Hildebrun and so place himself within range of her abuse, wondered where Anna, the cook, and Nina, the scullery girl, were hiding. Then he noticed the address. "But this is for the Baroness *Theresa* von Falkenhorst," he exclaimed with relief. "She is away. Won't be back for several days."

"You think I was born yesterday and don't know what's going on in my district?" the postman asked, opening up his shapeless coat of frazzled wolverine fur to expose his uniform to the meager heat radiating from the banked fires of the stove. "Do you know the von Birkenheims always have a pot of soup on the fire? Turnip and cabbage cooked in good strong stock. The week before Christmas they offered me a schnapps too. They don't have much, the von Birkenheims, but they share."

"We have had two deaths in this family during the last month," Hult said, holding up the telegram against the gray light of the window. "Would this be telling of a third?"

"Perhaps so," the postman darkly hinted.

"Yes, and perhaps this family is cursed," Hult muttered, shaking his head. "At least those Poles thought so."

"Poles are superstitious clods," the postman snorted. "The

von Birkenheims had a roast goose for Christmas. It was a thin, tough bird, but they gave me a slice. Hauptmann von Birkenheim is away at war, you know."

"I wish I could find it in me to desert my job like those Poles," Hult sighed.

"Ah, but you are German," the postman told him with sardonic severity, turning around and lifting the skirt of his coat to expose the seat of his breeches to the stove. As he did so, the Dowager Baroness Hildebrun von Falkenhorst suddenly shuffled into sight on the threshold of the pantry, her right hand leaning on the crook of a cane, her left clutching the shoulder of a cowering Lena with a taloned grip. A black shawl was draped over the untidy strands of yellow white hair, hooding her face so that only the cold glitter of her eyes and the bitter lines around her mouth stood out clearly. She presented a startling picture of a black witch supported by her hexed chattel; the postman's reaction to the sight seemed as contrived as his cheery greeting: "Merry Christmas, Your Ladyship."

"Christmas is over," the Baroness Hildebrun rasped back, thumping her cane against the floor, "so don't come expecting to get fed."

"I am merely begging warmth for my body, not to feed it," the postman answered, accentuating his sarcastic tone with exaggerated diffidence. "I am delighted to see that the blessings of Christmas have included restoring Your Ladyship to her feet—praise God!"

Baroness Hildebrun had in fact staggered to her feet and begun to hobble about her musty manor with the help of her cane and the scullery girl on the very day Tessa and Master Prytz had departed. But she acted now as if she had only just accomplished the feat at great pain. "An abandoned widow must be ready to defend her property, regardless of illness," she said to the postman. Throwing her full weight on Lena and at the same time shoving her toward the kitchen table, she raised her cane and slammed it down on the mailsack with a resounding crack. "What have you brought me?" she demanded.

"A telegram, Your Ladyship," the postman told her.

"Well, where is it?"

Hult timidly showed it to her and mumbled: "It is not addressed to Your Ladyship. It is for the young Baroness Theresa."

"How dare you lay your filthy hands on our mail!" Baroness Hildebrun screeched at him, flourishing her cane like a saber. "Give it to me and get out of my sight! Go to hell together with that Polish trash I sent packing. The devil feed you, because I'll certainly be damned if I will!"

Hult dropped the telegram onto the table as if it had suddenly burned his fingers, spun around, and fled into the yard, slamming the door behind him so that the icicles broke loose and clattered on the stoop in brittle showers. The postman maintained a defiant, but slightly ridiculous, position by the stove, still holding up the rear of his shabby fur coat. The scullery girl whimpered and cringed under the claws digging into her shoulder as her mistress reversed the cane and used its crook to reach across the table and pull the envelope toward her. She tore it open with her sharp fingernails and squinted at the message, twisting it this way and that in the dim lighting of the kitchen. "Where are my glasses?" she demanded.

"You broke the last pair yesterday, Madame Baroness," Lena squeaked.

"Then you read it to me, stupid wench!"

"But I can't read, Madame Baroness," Lena squeaked again, looking ready to collapse on the spot and, without her support, the Baroness Hildebrun on top of her.

The postman thought, "Ah, there is a proper serf!" then advancing to the table, said aloud: "If Your Ladyship will permit me, I would be pleased to oblige."

"So you can pry into my business, eh?" she snarled.

"Forgive my presumption," the postman retorted, withdrawing a step, then slyly adding: "Since it is addressed to the young Baroness Theresa, it is of course no business of either of us."

"I am mistress here!" the Baroness Hildebrun yelled and, flinging the telegram at him, commanded: "Read it to me!"

Because he had already memorized the contents, the postman was able to comply with a virtually rehearsed dramatic impact which included adjusting of spectacles and much noisy throat clearing: *Headquarters, Second Royal Dragoon Guards, Villacoublay, France, December 25, 1870.—To Her Ladyship, the Baroness Marie Theresa von Falkenhorst, Glaumballe, District of Ols, Silesia.* . . .

"Yes-yes! I know where we live, dammit! Get on with what it says!"

I regret to inform you, the postman read on, *that your husband, Leutnant Baron Gustaf von Falkenhorst, is reported missing after leading a patrol deep inside enemy territory on December 22. No reliable details are presently available, but from the few confirmed facts gathered, it appears that his squadron was ambushed by superior numbers of guerrillas and it seems unlikely that the Leutnant Baron would survive an action in which his entire command perished. Any information to the contrary will be transmitted to you as soon as possible. In the meanwhile, please accept the respect and deep sympathy of all his regimental comrades as well as my own very personal distress over this sad event. Signed: Kurt von Hardel, Colonel Commanding Second Royal Dragoon Guards.*

The postman expectantly awaited the reaction to his clearly enunciated, funereal delivery but found himself met by such a silence, the scullery girl so dumbly glassy-eyed and the Baroness Hildebrun so blankly scowling, that he decided neither had understood a word. He was about to repeat his performance with considerably shaken aplomb when the crippled dowager suddenly burst out in a wheezing cackle of mirth and shrilled: "God be praised! Now that virgin-strumpet will know what it means to be a soldier's widow! God be praised!"

Lena would have broken free but for the relentless grip on her shoulder. "But Madame Baroness, it is about your own son!" she squealed, her voice fading into terrified mouselike peeps as her mistress shook her into silence.

"Be quiet! What do you know about my son, you baggage. I forbid you to speak his name, do you hear?" The Baroness Hildebrun kept shaking the wretched girl with such violence that the postman wondered whether he should physically intervene. But then she regained a tenuous control of herself and said to him with haughty assurance: "You have made a mistake. My sons are away at school. It is my husband who is at war. The war against the Austrians, may God curse their black souls to hell and damnation for all eternity!"

The postman became aware of the glitter of outright madness in her bloodshot eyes and began to lose his supercilious detachment. "But Your Ladyship," he stammered, "the war with Austria has been over for more than four years! We are at war with France now. Your son Gustaf is fighting the French!"

"Good! They are a dirty, lecherous people too," she railed. "And after my Gustaf gives them a sound thrashing, he'll send his Austrian wife packing as soon as I tell him what she's been up to around here. Bringing in Poles! Damn her! Damn the Austrians! Damn the French! Damn all of you!" She resumed shaking Lena by the neck. "And damn *you* for letting strangers into my house!"

This time the scullery girl's instinct of self-preservation overcame her slavish submissiveness, and she tore herself loose with a scream which contained rage as well as fear. Jumping back to dodge a slash of the cane, she spun away and ran for the cellar door, tore it open, and hurled herself through it, her hysterical sobs fading as she vanished into the darkness below. The Baroness Hildebrun stood swaying unsteadily with a look of surprise on her gaunt face, then half-fell across the table, barely managing to catch herself and collapse into a chair. A torrent of profanity erupted from her and continued unabated for a full minute until her voice wore itself down to a rasping, incoherent splutter of blasphemies. Her eyes kept glaring at the open cellar door; when she managed to regain her breath, she turned to the transfixed postman and with a bewildering switch of tone wheezed at him: "Be so good as to close the bolt and lock her down there, please."

The postman, who had never heard such an outburst of swearing, not even in barracks during his stint with the Land-wehr, shook his head, partly in disbelief, partly in refusal. With a wary eye on the cane, he reached out and yanked his mailsack off the table, where he then dropped the telegram. "I am very sorry," he exclaimed with a voice reduced to an awestruck whisper. "Very sorry for the Leutnant Baron Gustaf, and for his wife, the Baroness Tessa . . . and for you, Your Ladyship, but. . . ." He had to jump backwards to avoid the whistling swoop of the cane as it came crashing down on top of the piece of paper. He remained paralyzed for another instant, watching her tear it to shreds, scattering the bits all around her; then he, too, fled, bringing the remaining icicles clattering down as he burst through the door onto the kitchen stoop.

Hult was waiting outside, standing next to the horse with his hands in his pockets, staring at the gray white expanse stetching toward the eastern horizon, his eyes following with envy the thin tortuous tracks of the escaped Polish laborers. He barely reacted to the postman's precipitous exit from the manor. The two men stood next to each other in silence for a long moment. Steaming vapors wreathed the postman's face as he cleansed his lungs with deep gulps of cold, fresh air, taking his time to regain his composure before exclaiming: "Your old Baroness is even crazier than I imagined! Completely mad, obviously."

"Just another privilege of our nobility," Hult grunted. "If it were you or me, we'd get ourselves locked up in the asylum."

"Maybe you. Not me!" The postman was in a great hurry to leave Glaumhalle and began to remove the feedbag from his horse's head. "I may talk to the ravens that fly over my route and to the hares and foxes that run across it. But I'm a perfectly sane functionary of the Royal Post and Telegraph Service just the same. There's nothing in the King's regulations which requires me to deal with mad patrons. This is absolutely the last time I ever set foot inside this house."

Hult gloomily watched him attach the feedbag to the saddle and tighten up the cinch straps. "The witch never bothers us in the stables," he said. "Couldn't possibly make it over there through the snow with her bad leg. Can't even hear her screaming from the kitchen door. And now that the Poles have gone, we'd have the place all to ourselves. The forge is hot, and I've stashed away some oatmeal and sausage we could cook on it. Besides, it looks like a hard snow coming up."

The postman reacted only to the last sentence and, squinting toward the Polish plains beyond Glaumhalle's hill, took notice of the dark, angry-looking clouds welling up above the undulating white sea of snowdrifts. They made him think of his father, who had also carried the mail along this route and who had been found together with his horse, both upright and headed along their prescribed rounds, frozen to death in the terrible blizzard of 1859. It had been the elder Major Baron Gustaf von Falkenhorst who had dug them out of the huge drift, which had entrapped and congealed them; afterward bringing the postman's body back to Glaumhalle to store it board-stiff in the snow piled outside the stables until the next thaw cleared the road sufficiently for it to be taken by sleigh into Ols for burial.

"I pity you your loneliness in this place," he said to Hult, looking back with a shudder, "but not enough to share it with you. So forgive me if I leave right away. I must make the von Birkenheims' before the storm breaks. They always have soup on the stove, you know. Turnip and cabbage cooked in good strong stock. . . ."

"Yes-yes, and they even gave you a schnapps for Christmas," Hult interjected bitterly. "I do believe, Herr Royal Post and Telegraph Functionary, that stuffing yourself with good meals barely comes next in importance to delivering the mail."

The postman swung himself into the saddle and replied with his old cheerful cynicism: "What else do you expect? That I act as doctor and domini on my salary? Each to his own and in his own place, I always say! And let the Devil take him who does not know it. Season's greetings and a good evening to you, friend!"

Hult watched the postman ride back through his own tracks down the hillside, a starkly shaggy brown figure gradually receding into an insignificant dot in the whiteness of the vast snowscape. As the first tentative flakes of the gathering blizzard began wafting around Glaumhalle's grim, ice-crusted walls, he turned and trudged back to the silent, safe solitude of his crib inside its old keep.

January–February 1871

The Armistice

✠　✠

ew Year's Day 1871, was spent by Tessa, Albrecht, and Master Prytz in a drab little coal-mining community called Grunberg, located about two-thirds of the way along the railroad line connecting Frankfurt an der Oder with Breslau. It had taken them a full three days to travel that far on their return journey from Schloss Varn to Glaumhalle. There seemed to be twice the normal number of travelers vying for half the usually available space on trains whose schedules had been cut to a third. Harassed conductors and stationmasters explained that the disruption of traffic was caused by extraordinary military requisitions in support of the impending bombardment of Paris. Albrecht von Falkenhorst, who was traveling in his Deputy Inspector's uniform and still carrying credentials with the impressive stamp of Royal Headquarters, was able to determine that the excuse was at least partially valid, but even though he was respectfully treated by local railroad officials, his influence proved insufficient to produce nonexistent trains or to reduce the tedious waiting for those few running.

He was even more helpless to do anything about the abominable weather which, in fact, had contributed far more than the war to the breakdown of schedules. It had begun to snow on December 28, initially a steady fall of wispy light flakes which by the afternoon of the twenty-ninth had developed into a full blizzard storming through New Year's Eve with unabated fury. The train which finally took them out of Frankfurt would not have made it to Grunberg if its conductor had not drafted all the able-bodied male passengers in third class to help dig the locomotive out of a huge drift blocking the tracks. Then it could barely wheeze into the half-buried station of the small town—where it burst its boiler in a final steaming convulsion. Master Prytz had then proved far more effective than the lightly built Albrecht in keeping Tessa ahead of the horde of passengers laboriously stampeding through hip-deep snow toward the Furstenhof Hotel, a very modest establishment despite its regal name. When Tessa refused to abandon her companions to share the last available bed with a distraught nursing mother and her squalling infant, all of them had settled for the night on a sofa in the hotel's crowded vestibule, fidgeting in vain search of rest against its hard lumps and scratchy leaks of horsehair stuffing. Tessa had accepted all these hardships in better spirits than either Albrecht or Master Prytz and kept joking about them until, overcome by drowsiness, she dropped her head against her brother-in-law's shoulder and fell asleep, leaving the two men sitting bolt upright and ignoring each other while staring with red-rimmed eyes at their fellow travelers who had slumped into every chair and sprawled over every bit of floor space. Thus they spent the long New Year's night.

In the morning, they had to wait over an hour to use one of the hotel's two bathrooms, another hour before being admitted into the small dining room for a breakfast of cold hard-boiled eggs, thin gristly ham, and weak tea. Outside, the blizzard was still lashing the town with undiminished fury and huge drifts had built up to block the first-floor windows (which at least cut off the icy drafts leaking through the sills). At midmorning, the train conductor made a brief appearance, blowing into the vestibule with a squall of snowy wind, and, after brushing the icicles out of his whiskers, he made the depressing announcement that the locomotive could not be repaired and no replacement was expected before the next day. He officiously parried a torrent of complaints (especially bitter from holders of first-class tickets), then brusquely turned his back on his distraught passengers and thrashed his way back through the storm to the superior comforts of the stationmaster's house. At noon there was a noisy crisis in the Furstenhof's kitchen, which was running out of food; henceforth, strict rationing would have to be enforced. Lunch consisted of a watery bowl of lentil soup without sausage and slices of rye bread without butter. Morale sank to a low ebb when the supplies of beer and schnapps also began to run low. Children, who had at first taken the whole disruption as an exciting adventure, became fretful; adults turned grumpy and quarrelsome. As nerves became frayed, several people angrily blamed the French for their predicament even as the North German blizzard kept whistling and pounding around their crowded prison.

In the early afternoon, already as dark as night, Master Prytz could no longer stand the oppressive, cramped inactivity of the vestibule and, rousing himself off the sofa, began putting on his greatcoat. With a reproachful look at Albrecht, he announced that *something* had to be done before the three of them were trapped into another miserable night like the last one, that *somewhere* in this blighted mining town there had to be better food and lodging available, and that he, indeed, had an idea about where they could be found. Over Tessa's objections he clamped his fur cap down over his ears and marched out into the storm with dour determination. Forty minutes later he returned frozen and crusted with snow, but smugly triumphant.

"I tracked down that stationmaster who's more used to handling transport of coal than people. I convinced him he had best accommodate a high-ranking Prussian lady and her escorting railway official, or it would go ill for his future. He conveys his apologies and offers the hospitality of his house. It is not much, but less crowded than here, and his wife is cooking a roast of pork—if my nose did not play me tricks."

"Prytzie! You should not have bullied the poor man into putting himself out for us," Tessa scolded him, but not too severely.

Albrecht gave him a backhanded compliment for his initiative by exclaiming: "By God, Master Prytz, you show all the instincts of an Uhlan sergeant!"

Prytz eyed him coldly with a mocking bow. "When I was your age, Freiherr von Falkenhorst, I *was* an Uhlan sergeant." He then busied himself with helping Tessa into her coat and gathering up their suitcases. As soon as they evacuated the lumpy sofa and started to leave the Furstenhof Hotel, a quarrel promptly erupted among six other stranded passengers over the vacated space.

The stationmaster's modest brick house was located hard by the station and only a few hundred meters down the street from the Furstenhof, but it took the three of them ten minutes to struggle their way there against the blowing snow and deep drifts. They were freezing when they finally reached it, yet the suffering turned out to be worthwhile once they were inside the snug, warm little home, whose owners appeared eager to do justice to the visit of high Prussian nobility—even if that visit were the result of intimidation. Besides the stationmaster's wife and four children, there were present the locomotive engineer and his fireman, and the conductor (whose attitude was one of strained politeness, having been evicted from the spare bed), so the conditions were nearly as crowded as at the Furstenhof Hotel. But after an initial embarrassed silence, conversation flowed freely. After the subject of the terrible winter had been exhausted and by the time they were squeezing around the dinner table, the discussion had inevitably turned to the war. The engineer asked Albrecht about railroading in the war zones of France, and the two older children asked about battles fought. Albrecht rose to the occasion with some eloquent descriptions of his experiences, more to entertain than to boast, and when he finally admitted that, because of his service with Tessa's father, he had met King Wilhelm during the course of the campaign, their hosts and fellow guests were enormously impressed. The stationmaster turned belligerently patriotic and, pounding the table, shouted, "We Prussians must teach those French a lesson and shoot Paris to bits with our cannons!" The conductor roused himself out of his ill humor and agreed. "Yes, it's a sinful city which God commands us to destroy like Babylon!"

When Albrecht shook his head and said, "It would be a pity to have to do that," they all looked surprised, including Tessa, who had been listening to him as raptly as the others. But it was Master Prytz who said: "We must remember that the Freiherr von Falkenhorst is not a soldier and cannot take a soldier's hard viewpoint on war. As a Heidelberg student, he rather favors soft humanitarian ideals."

Albrecht felt the barbs in the inflection but nodded his head and replied: "Our Crown Prince Frederick is a soldier who is also a humanitarian. He is in charge of the siege of Paris, but, like any civilized man, shrinks from a war which means killing or starving women and children."

"So let the garrison of Paris consider their women and children and surrender," Prytz growled but checked himself from launching a diatribe against the brutality of the *francs-tireurs* out of consideration for Tessa's feelings. The strained moment at the dinner table passed when the stationmaster's oldest boy asked about the famous Paris balloons and wondered why the Prussians did not make some of their own, chase after the enemy, and engage them in aerial battles. The youngster's imagination thus ended the meal on a note of condescending laughter and shortly after, Tessa excused herself to retire. She and Albrecht had a moment alone at the foot of the steep, ladder-like stairs leading to her nook beneath the eaves of the roof and she took the opportunity to ask a question which had evidently been troubling her since his exchange with Master Prytz at dinner. "Do you really believe we should show mercy to the French?" she asked him. "Even after what they did to my father?"

Albrecht was taken aback but remembered that she expected blunt straightforward answers from him even if they were unpleasant. "Tens of thousands of fathers have been killed on both sides, Tessa," he said. "If each one had to be avenged, there would be no end to the war—or war to the end of everybody. Surely we can't allow any such thing to happen."

She frowned and shook her head. "Of course not. That would be impossible. Good night, Albrecht." She leaned towards him, presenting her cheek to his lips, but drew back before they could touch when the Frau Stationmaster appeared with a candle and freshly laundered pillow and started up the steps with another of her cheerfully delivered excuses:

"Our simple little bed in the attic will not be up to the Baroness's standards of comfort, but at least she will have privacy and be warm next to the chimney. I've already changed the bottom sheet, so everything's clean, too! Follow me, please, Baroness . . . and mind the third step. It's a bit loose."

Tessa took off only her shoes and dress before lying down on the cot next to the hot bricks of the chimney, wrapping a blanket around her which still retained a lingering odor of sweat and locomotive smoke from its previous user. In spite of her great fatigue she could not immediately fall asleep and after blowing out the candle lay staring into the absolute darkness, listening to the wind as it whipped the snow on the roof a few feet above her head. She found herself thinking about Albrecht again and how very different he was from Gustaf, then scolded herself for comparing them when she really did not know Gustaf at all. Well, they certainly did not look alike, she thought, Gustaf being the handsomer, stronger, and taller of the two. Yet, when she tried to picture the two of them together, Gustaf's image remained a total blank in her mind; she had forgotten his features beyond recall. But his voice somehow came back to her, and she could clearly hear him saying: "You will be my prize and my booty . . ." and it sent a cold shiver through her body even though she had begun to feel uncomfortably warm beneath the blanket. Its heat and smell suddenly stifled her. She squirmed and tossed, then threw it off and lay on the creaking cot in her petticoat and bodice, detecting in the sound of the wind a wailing note which reminded her of the sounds of Glaumhalle on a stormy night. The vision of the Dowager Baroness von Falkenhorst materialized out of the blackness, her eyes blazing with hate as she advanced, brandishing her cane and cackling her favorite epithet: "Virgin-strumpet!" as she hobbled up to the foot of the cot and raised her weapon for a slashing blow which Tessa found herself incapable of dodging, her muscles paralyzed by a hypnotic inertia. Then Albrecht burst out of the darkness, leaping in front of the snarling Baroness and waving a lighted candle in her face whose glare magically dissolved her whole threatening being into nothingness. Tessa sat up with a scream of terror and threw herself into her brother-in-law's arms.

"Tessa! Tessa! Everything is all right, dearest! You must have had a bad dream."

"She wants to kill me!" Tessa whimpered. "How could I dream it when I haven't fallen asleep yet?"

"But you must have," Albrecht reassured her, holding her tight and tenderly stroking her bare shoulders. "It is five o'clock in the morning. The storm is over and a train has made it into the station. We must get on it in the next twenty minutes. The stationmaster has arranged seats for us. You have to dress and hurry downstairs so we won't miss it. Come on, Tessa darling."

Tessa awakened to the fact that he really was there and that she was clinging to him in her revealing underclothes. Yanking away from him and grabbing the blanket to cover herself, she shrieked in mortification: "What are you doing here?"

"I came to awaken you, of course," he answered, and, noticing her embarrassment, began blushing too. He hastily lit her candle from the one he was carrying, then scrambled back down the steps with an urgent admonition for her to get dressed at once. Tessa almost succumbed to an overwhelming desire to cuddle up in the blanket and go back to sleep. But then she became aware of a chuffing clatter from the nearby railroad tracks as a locomotive shunted through the station sidings, and forced herself to get up and put on her dress and shoes.

The train was a mixed freight out of Frankfurt which had spent most of New Year's Day stuck in the snow some fifteen miles up the line, then made it in to Grunberg when the wind, rather than shovels, swept the tracks clear. The crew were frozen and exhausted, their locomotive festooned with bizarre ice sculptures fashioned by the clash of scalding steam and bitter cold. Their passengers were in a numb state of shock, most of them preferring to accept the indifferent hospitality of the Furstenhof to the perils of further winter travel with the Prussian State Railways. Their most valuable freight, seven prize Frisian heifers, had perished along the way. But in spite of all calamities, the doughty Prussian railroad men were determined to do what they could to salvage the demolished schedule. Besides the urgent necessity of getting the frozen cattle to a Breslau slaughterhouse before a sudden thaw rendered them totally worthless, it was agreed by the stationmaster and respective conductors that the glut of rolling stock and stranded passengers had to be relieved. The one available locomotive would swap crews with the disabled one, and three freight cars would be disconnected and substituted with two passenger coaches; a single train made up of the two must then proceed to Breslau. A considerable number of passengers would be left behind because traction power had to be reserved to plough through drifts, but because of their newly won influence with the local railroad officials, Tessa, Albrecht, and Master Prytz were among the lucky ones. They were even installed in one of the few first-class compartments. Tessa need not have hurried so much to leave her cosy nook in the stationmaster's attic. A pale blue dawn, its vacuumlike stillness emphasized by the crackling cold, broke over the little town before the harried crews could water and refuel their locomotive, make up the train, fend off those passengers excluded, sort out those chosen, and keep them together with their baggage, thaw out frozen switches, then finally start rolling with noisily clanging jerks, proceeding at a snail's pace into the desolate wintry Silesian countryside.

The trip to Ols, over Breslau and Posen, uncomfortable and interrupted frequently when the crew had to climb down and dig the locomotive out of snowdrifts, passed without further incident. They reached Ols late in the evening, and the innkeeper was delighted to see them; the recent blizzard had isolated the little Silesian town and business was terrible. He gave them each a room and a bed, into which Tessa, Albrecht, and Prytzie immediately collapsed, too exhausted even to eat. That day, January 3, 1871, was Tessa von Falkenhorst's nineteenth birthday, but it had passed without any celebration because she decided not to mention an occasion of which Albrecht was ignorant and which had been forgotten by Prytz during the hardship of the journey.

At a quarter past nine the next morning, Master Prytz brought three riding horses and one pack animal from the livery stable next door. Before allowing Tessa to mount, he peered into the pale blue sky and sniffed the frigid air like a sailor gauging the weather which might make perilous their departure into a white sea. But it was Albrecht who made the decision with unusual firmness: "You know Pomerania, Master Prytz, but I know Silesia where I was born. There will be sunshine today with cold, which will put a good strong crust on the snow for riding. Let's get started so we reach Glaumhalle before dark."

Prytz muttered some doubts under his steaming breath about Albrecht's reliability as a weather prophet, but when he saw how easily he swung himself into the saddle despite his cumbersome, and somewhat ridiculous-looking, fur coat, he decided Albrecht might be a competent horseman. After rechecking Tessa's horse and helping her mount, and making some final adjustments to the straps securing their baggage to the pack animal, he got on his rented stallion which was obviously one of those small, but tough, Russian Cossack brutes Polish brigands sold across the nearby border. The innkeeper handed him the lead rein and waved a hasty farewell before escaping out of the blistering cold; the small party departed, moving down the deserted, snowbound main road of Ols.

At first, the only signs of life were a few barking dogs and thin wisps of smoke curling from the chimneys of silent houses —evidently the little town was still hibernating. But when they turned a corner and came abreast of the post office stables, they suddenly ran into a solemn group of men gathered around a horse-drawn lumber sled. There was that unmistakable air of tragedy about the scene which made them rein in, and Albrecht quickly recognized the postmaster in spite of his bedraggled, overstuffed appearance in a bulky ankle-length overcoat and a gray muffler tied over his uniform cap to protect his ears.

"What is the matter here?" Albrecht asked without any preliminary greetings.

The postmaster looked first at Albrecht and then at Tessa. His expression changed from weary melancholy to surprise, then confusion. "Freiherr von Falkenhorst! Baroness!" he stammered. "I am sorry! What a terrible homecoming for you." The four men with him, three local peasants and the fourth a constable, stepped away from the sled, faced them and respectfully took off their caps. As they did so, a sixth man came into view. He was lying on the rough boards of the sled in a strangely huddled position, looking peacefully asleep, but with his face as pale as the snow and ice sealing his closed eyelids, mouth, and nostrils. It was their postman, still wearing his mailsack strapped over one shoulder. He was frozen to death.

Tessa had never seen a human corpse before and, after staring down at it in fascinated disbelief for several seconds, let out a shocked gasp of horror.

Albrecht, who had seen much death during the past five months, could not help exclaiming: "Dear God! Poor Bruno. Died just like his father before him."

The postmaster nodded in a distracted daze. "Yes, just like his father, he was caught in a blizzard between Glaumhalle and the von Birkenheims'. We found him yesterday and have just managed to bring him back." He peered up at Tessa, his unshaven face blotched by chilblains and crinkled with pain. "I beg your pardon, Frau Baroness, for exposing you to this when you have so many sorrows of your own. We should have covered him up, but . . . well, he's dead and the horse needed the blanket. My post office has already lost three horses in this terrible winter."

Tessa finally managed to tear her eyes away from the dead man. "I understand, Herr Postmaster," she said in a low voice. "Please convey my deepest sympathy to Bruno's family."

"That is most nobly gracious of Your Ladyship," the postmaster mumbled with a stiff, clumsy bow. "Specially under Your Ladyship's own circumstances of grief . . . for which please accept the condolences of all the officials and citizens of Ols. We did not know your honored father or Her Highness, your late sister. But, of course, your husband grew up among us and was known to us all, and. . . ." He stuttered to a stop, hesitated while rubbing his bloodshot eyes.

Tessa and Albrecht both felt a stab of guilt because the postman had perished while delivering mail to their isolated home, but before either of them could find suitable words or truly comprehend what the postmaster had said, Master Prytz spoke up with his own brand of tribute:

"He died doing his duty, God rest his soul!"

Then there was nothing more to be said or done and they rode on toward the open country shimmering with a cold sparkling beauty beyond the end of the roadway.

On January 18, 1871, an event took place at Versailles which marked the official accession of Germany to the status of a world power, and ironically concomitant with the occasion, the relegation to the realm of remote improbability all of Prince Eugene's hopes for recognition of his hereditary claims upon the ancient German kingdom of Hanover. On that date, King Wilhelm I of Prussia was proclaimed in the great Hall of Mirrors of the Bourbon palace to be German Emperor, *Kaiser* Wilhelm I—a title derived through tortuous linguistic genealogy from the Roman one of *Caesar*. This momentous event, meticulously planned and manipulated by Chancellor Otto von Bismarck, did not come off very well in spite of unseasonably mild weather, splendid military parades, and all the pretentious pomp provided by the presence of some two hundred princes and other nobility. There had been too much bickering, too many reservations and doubts afflicting the principals for them to participate without an uneasy feeling that each had been coerced into conceding too much or gaining too little. The actual ceremony turned out an unforgivable insult to the French people, consummated as it was in a shrine "dedicated to France and all her glories," while a few kilometers away the new Kaiser's artillery was bombarding her besieged capital. The few French citizens remaining in Versailles closed their shutters and turned their backs on the smart columns of German troops parading to the strident din of their bands. In the Hall of Mirrors, the assembled princes suffered inward trepidations over the prospects of their petty sovereignties under Prussian overlordship, while the generals argued among themselves over the way to secure a still-elusive victory. The Kaiser himself failed to appear before them as a confident and triumphant emperor, looking pale and weary as he accepted the bellowed *hochs* led by the Grand Duke of Baden. He had, in fact, hesitated over accepting the promotion from King to Kaiser, fearing that the new title and position could compromise, and even endanger, his more-solidly historic one of King of Prussia. However, he had been subjected to Bismarck's persuasive arguments, and once persuaded, bitterly resented the idea of being proclaimed "German Emperor" rather than "Emperor of Germany"—the small semantic difference being considered vital to the sensitivities of his vassal princes. Wilhelm was possessed of that peculiar Hohenzollern trait of combining great personal simplicity with a rapatious ambition for his royal prerogatives. Being the absolute King of Prussia, he wanted to be absolute Emperor of All Germans if he were to be emperor at all. But he had to yield to Bismarck on this point as well; thus, the glittering affair in the Hall of Mirrors produced a disappointment he was to nurture for the rest of his long life. For the Prince General of Hanover, it was equally disappointing and certainly devoid of compensating benefits.

Eugene was not invited to the coronation ceremony as a Prince of Germany because Hanover had already been annexed by Prussia in a previous war and most of her royal family had long since followed their king into exile in England. The fact that Queen Victoria was herself related to the House of Hanover had not moved Bismarck to treat Eugene on an equal footing with other German princes; after all, the formidable little English monarch's own daughter would one day become Queen of Prussia and German Empress, so she was not likely to make trouble over minor dynastic iniquities, involving distant kin. In any case, Prince Eugene had taken his chances by remaining behind as a pretender trying to fit himself into the new Prussian order of things, to support his family's claims by service to the cause of a united Prussian Germany rather than contending ineffectually from the safety of foreign exile.

Eugene had, of course, been invited (or commanded, rather) to attend the festivities in the Hall of Mirrors, but as a German general—not as a prince. Even as a general he found himself considerably outranked as one of the lowly, glamourless Intendantur, and a railwayman at that, and relegated to a rear position from where he could barely glimpse the proceedings between hedgerows of Prussian blue backs and golden epaulets.

During Bismarck's long-winded and remarkably spiritless reading of the Imperial Proclamation, he permitted himself several deep yawns which did not exactly reflect the nature of the thoughts coursing through his always-active mind. He was thinking that if the Empire became as strong as Bismarck intended, these princes were approving their own abdications and it was only a matter of time before they found themselves in his predicament. There may have been a tinge of smug malice in this prophetic notion, but being a man without self-delusions it only led him to consider that his personal situation had deteriorated much out of proportion with theirs. Even his purely military position had become insecure since taking over from Count von Beckhaus as Inspector General, largely because the bombardment of Paris had enormously strained the tenuous supply lines with Germany. For all his facile intelligence, Prince Eugene did not possess Count Frederick Paul's administrative ability or his brash personality, which had goaded superiors and subordinates alike into productive action; more important, he had none of his basic knowledge of railroad operations. Since taking over the post, Eugene had become exactly what he had set out to avoid at the beginning of the war, a figurehead general, a comically fat one right out of one of Offenbach's *opéras bouffes*, and this at a time when his department was being critically eyed by the generals in charge of the investment of Paris. As his colleagues were huzzahing their new Kaiser, he guessed that he would soon be removed from their midst, either to be put on the inactive list or relegated to some insignificant assignment far from the center of things. In his forty-ninth year, his military career would be over too! But even before leaving the glittering, yet strained tumult, in the great hall he had begun to scheme against the seeming inevitability of his fate.

The stubborn and ever-pugnacious Parisians celebrated the self-elevation of their German enemy to the rank of empire in a characteristic manner. They assaulted him with a fighting sortie which, more by chance than deliberate planning, was aimed at Versailles, the scene of the insolent event. On the second day of his reign as Emperor, Kaiser Wilhelm I's already-frayed nerves were stretched to the breaking point by being awakened with the news that the French had breached his lines at Plateau la Bergerie, less than six kilometers from his imperial bedstead! By midmorning the Hall of Mirrors had been converted into a vast hospital ward resounding with the groans of wounded Germans rather than their cheers. All the underlying doubts and unbridled tempers of the German High Command came to the surface when at least 100 thousand men of Paris' conglomerate garrison took the offensive. The humiliating necessity of ordering preparations for the evacuation of Versailles had to be faced and were actually being implemented when, at noon, Prince General Eugene of Hanover lumbered up to Third Army Headquarters on his white mare and dismounted. In a corridor, teeming with clerks and orderlies carrying out files of vital records, he met the harried Army Commander, Crown Prince Frederick. "Good morning, Your Imperial Highness," he greeted him, using his new one-day-old title and adding with phlegmatic certainty: "I believe that as of today, the end is at last in sight. Paris must capitulate within ten days at the most."

The Crown Prince, who had just come from a pessimistic conference with his Imperial father and General von Moltke, had intended to brush past Prince General Eugene with no more than a courteous recognition. But he found himself stopping short with a startled look on his handsome face and asking: "How do you know that?"

"Because, Your Imperial Highness, I have just spent two hours watching the fighting and clearly saw that what may at first have appeared to be determination on the part of our enemy, will turn out to be nothing more than desperation ending in the resignation of defeat." Eugene did not bother with details which he knew the Crown Prince had no time to listen to. But he had, while out riding that morning, been attracted by the nearby din of battle and reverted to his old habit of finding a strategic observation point from where he could make his own evaluation of the action. He had indeed seen the Prussian lines severely buckled by the leading wave of attacking Zouaves, but also spied through his telescope the sure signs of demoralization and inept leadership among the French troops. A battalion of the Paris National Guard failed to respond to the beat of their drummers and shouts of their officers urging them to advance in support of the Zouaves, their ragged ranks firm only in refusing to expose themselves to Prussian fire. Another unit advancing out of the morning mist clinging to the banks of the Seine had become alarmed by the noise of musketry and discharged a panicked volley into the flanks of their neighboring regiment, mowing down scores of their own comrades. Eugene had seen, and could have told, his army commander about other incidents which led him to the conclusion that this sortie would turn out to be as abortive as the others made by General Trochu's armed mobs during the past two months. But his only additional comment was: "All we have to do now is stand fast, then await the end."

Crown Prince Frederick received glances from his two aides-de-camp which suggested both doubt over this judgment and a deprecation of its source. However, he bowed with his unfailing graciousness and said: "I sincerely trust Your Excellency's confidence is fully justified!" then hurried on.

Eugene did not fail to notice that the heir to the new German empire had addressed him as "Your Excellency," not "Your Royal Highness," but this did not overly disturb him. He had committed himself to an optimistic forecast of the outcome at a time of crisis, perhaps with little effect upon the stresses of the moment, but he knew his prediction would be remembered by the future ruler *after* it had been vindicated. So he proceeded toward his offices with some satisfaction and a far more serene demeanor than that displayed by his fellow officers. When he reached those offices, he responded to the disruptive excitement there with a massive calm which only seemed to annoy his Chief of Staff, First Deputy Inspector General of Military Railroad Transport, Leutnant Colonel Julius Wrinkleman. The Colonel excused the chattering dither of clerks, who should have been scratching away busily with their pens, by saying: "We are considering carrying out our files for evacuation!"

"Good heavens! Why?"

"Doesn't His Highness know that the French are reported breaking through our lines near Versailles?" Wrinkleman exclaimed. He was a reserve officer drawn from the higher bureaucracy of the Prussian State Railway, a very efficient and dedicated man in a single-minded way, but one who allowed his somewhat justified low regard of Eugene's grasp of railroading to fatally prejudice him regarding his chief's overall worth. "Does His Highness not realize what would happen if all the department records fell into enemy hands?" he asked as if reproving a doltish child.

"Certainly I do. It would considerably add to their confusion since they couldn't possibly make head or tail out of them," Eugene replied. Wrinkleman failed to perceive that Prince Eugene was attempting to calm him by pulling his leg and merely pouted in irritation. So the Prince became more explicit: "Our lines may have buckled a bit here and there, but they will hold. The siege will continue. The files will stay where they are. Our work will proceed." He sat down at his desk, causing the Louis XIV chair to squeak alarmingly under his ponderous weight, glanced through the morning traffic reports and affixed his signature to the few documents needing it, then left as soon as he was sure that his Chief of Staff had reestablished normal routine in the department. As always, his perfect sense of timing told him when his presence was necessary and when it was superfluous, and somehow he managed his duties without disrupting his personal habits, such as eating, sleeping, and horseback excursions to interesting points of the siege. Accordingly, he returned on time for his lunch at his villa where he found his billet-mate, the Kurfurst Waldemar, just rising from his bed with an extremely sore head, suffered while excessively toasting the new Empire during yesterday's celebrations. To him the Prince General gave a graphic account of the morning's developments, entirely omitting any reassuring evaluations of his own. The Kurfurst listened with an appalled look on his bloated face, then rushed off, shouting for his orderly to fetch his armor and broadsword, leaving Eugene to enjoy a dish of veal kidneys sauteed in a rich wine and mushroom sauce, immaculately served by his faithful Anton.

By that afternoon, the breach in the investing lines was effectively sealed and by evening, the fighting sortie had turned into a disorderly retreat back into Paris leaving behind in the muddy slush of thawed grounds between Saint-Cloud and Buzenval some five thousand dead and wounded. As Bismarck had refused a truce to collect them, their cries and stench unnerved both sides until all was stilled by a return of freezing weather. A carrier pigeon flew into the city bearing the belated news that the Army of the Loire had been decisively beaten by Prussians at Le Mans, further reducing any chances of relief for the starving Parisians; even rats were getting scarce and the poor, particularly, were suffering from cold and malnutrition. Capitulation was in the air, yet ironically those very poor, the volatile proletarians of the slums of Belleville, resisted, while segments of the bourgeoisie, who could still afford food at black market prices, clamored for an end to their privations. On January 23, Prussian pickets could hear the rattle of musketry coming from far inside the city as groups of contentious Parisians clashed in the streets. At Imperial Headquarters in Versailles the tension and bickering continued, no longer over strategy but over the terms of peace to be imposed upon the French. The General Staff led by von Moltke wanted to destroy totally France's capacity to make war and, therefore, to maintain herself as a great power; the diplomats and politicians headed by Chancellor Bismarck wanted some of the same results, but modified by considerations for the future peace of Europe as affected by a balance of power. As usual, the sorely tried old man, Kaiser Wilhelm I, found himself caught between the two factions and was forced to issue an edict that military matters were to be handled by the military, diplomatic matters by the diplomats, and that henceforth the two should stay out of each other's business; under the circumstances this was a piece of casuistry which satisfied no one.

In the late evening of January 23 (when shooting could still be heard from inside Paris), Jules Favre, a white-haired old man in a shabby top hat and frayed frock coat, Foreign Minister of the Government of National Defense, rowed across the Seine in a leaky boat, was passed through the Prussian lines and conducted to Bismarck's residence, where his first decent meal in six weeks was ruined by the armistice terms courteously, but adamantly, stated by his host. The negotiations were kept secret, especially from the seething Paris proletariat, but Bismarck emerged from them whistling an old hunting call: "The Chase is Over!" Poor old Favre made several more round trips in his leaky boat to haggle over details, once accompanied by a military aide, a General Hautpoule, who was so mortified over his part in the proceedings that he got himself maudlin drunk. But by January 27, the armistice was signed and the war was, for all practical purposes, over. All German siege artillery punctiliously ceased fire on the stroke of midnight and in the following oppressive silence of a dark winter night, one could almost hear the sobs of a crushed Paris.

For Prince General Eugene of Hanover there was little satisfaction in this turn of events which he had so accurately predicted. He knew with equal certainty that his own defeat was at hand and, therefore, what to expect when summoned for a meeting with Chancellor Bismarck on January 28. What he did not know was that the chancellor had already been at least partially thwarted in his plans for him. His suggestion to officers of the General Staff and Army Headquarters that the Prince General be removed from his post and retired on a minimal pension had been deemed another example of his constant meddling in military affairs and no action was taken, less out of esteem for the Prince General than out of cliquish resentment. Bismarck had not pressed the matter because of the Emperor's edict and the necessity of trading more important military concessions during the peace negotiations, but as any royal pretender within his new Empire was clearly a political matter, he proceeded to deal with that phase of the problem himself. Privately he had a grudging admiration for this portly Prince of Hanover—whom he knew to have given valuable service in the war and to be possessed of more intelligence and initiative than most of his breed—but this, of course, only made him so much more of a threat. And then there was the matter of the vast Hanoverian fortune confiscated by Prussia, a fortune Bismarck freely used as a convenient fund for bribes, for which he did not have to make any public accounting. Europe was full of poor, harmless pretenders who sponged about ineffectually in any court which would tolerate them, but a resourceful pretender in the new Germany with a legitimate claim upon a great deal of money was quite another matter. As Chancellor, Bismarck could not afford to be lenient or influenced by personal sympathies, nor was it in his ruthless nature to be so. He intended, in fact, to be specially severe since he suspected the Kaiser, who had shown the Prince favors because of their mutual friendship with Count von Beckhaus, would find means of mitigating any blows against him. His Imperial Majesty was known to show sentimental streaks in such cases. Thus, when the Prince General Eugene of Hanover obeyed the summons to the Chancellor's residence on rue Provence, Bismarck received him without trying in the least to control his bad humor over the wearisome armistice negotiations and the neuralgia and varicose conditions which the tensions had aggravated; nor did he bother with any formalities due his visitor's alleged rank. He met with him in midmorning when no libations were expected to be offered, in a cluttered study in the large villa which he maintained as his personal bachelor's quarters; he was unshaven and wearing a rather garish brocade dressing gown. After a minimum of grumpy preliminaries, he gazed at Eugene's impressive waistline which surpassed his own considerable one and said: "I see Your Excellency has lost no weight during the course of this war!"

Eugene again noted the omission of his royal title but he was steeled for any eventuality. "A siege operation doesn't give a soldier the exercise he needs," he answered. "And I seem to share with Your Own Excellency a great appetite for good French food and wine."

Bismarck, who was actually very proud of his enormous capacity for rich victuals, maintained his truculent demeanor. "I am not concerned with your activities as a soldier. That is not my business. But I hear you continue to permit yourself to be addressed as a Royal Highness. That *is* my business."

"I am so addressed by some old friends and associates out of habit," Eugene replied with a shrug. "I do not in practice demand or accept royal prerogatives under my present circumstances."

"Good. Those circumstances will not change," Bismarck stated, coming to the point with brutal frankness. "I have asked you here to sign an official document formally renouncing any royal pretensions." He flicked the prepared document on his desk toward his visitor.

Eugene did not lower his eyes from Bismarck's face. "I have neither legal or moral right to do such a thing without the approval of the head of my house, King George IV of Hanover. As Your Excellency is aware, he is absent in England."

Bismarck was not about to engage in a debate over legal or moral points, nor make the obvious suggestion that this pretender travel to England for a conference with his uncle, the deposed King, an excursion bound to result in the spreading of firsthand information about dissensions and weaknesses within the newborn Empire, and certain to reach Queen Victoria's ears. "It is not as if you held the claims of an erstwhile Crown Prince," he scoffed. "Aren't you fifth or sixth or seventh down a long list of succession? A personal renunciation on your part could hardly be of much importance to your family."

Even in the face of this affront, Eugene kept his dignity. "I am only sixth in succession," he blandly admitted. "But the numerical order or my position in the House of Hanover has no relationship to my duty toward it. Surely, Your Excellency being himself a servant of a royal house must understand this."

"I understand the interests of the Hohenzollerns and the Hanovers have nothing whatever in common," Bismarck said, his voice turning high-pitched with anger. "If Your Excellency won't sign this renunciation, then I will, as Imperial Chancellor, make it an instrument of revocation. It will have the same effect."

"Not upon our other German princes of the blood," Eugene shot back. "It will make them even more fearful of their own future."

"And therefore more cautious. But in any case you are again overestimating your own importance."

"My rank stems from the divine right of kings. A principle dear to the hearts of your Hohenzollerns, I believe."

"A principle reduced to pure twaddle in the light of practical politics," Bismarck retorted. "Rights have a direct relationship with power, nothing else. They are upheld by a powerful sword or a powerful pen, as the case might be." To show his contempt and prove his point, he picked up a pen and scrawled his signature on the document lying between them on the desk, folded it and slipped it into a drawer. Then he said: "I suggest you henceforth call yourself simply General von Hanover, or better yet, use one of your more-obscure family names. Thank you for coming. Good day, Herr General!"

Eugene, who had not even been asked to sit down, had to see himself out after being so rudely dismissed. He rode back to his offices at Headquarters where he found his Chief of Staff, Colonel Wrinkleman, contentedly and efficiently adjusting the department to the reduced schedule of the armistice. The Inspector General took his usual ten minutes to peruse the daily reports, then ten more to write out a request to be relieved of his post, addressing it to Commander, Third Army, His Imperial Highness, Crown Prince Frederick, dispatched it by special messenger, then returned home to eat a leisurely lunch and await developments.

That evening, the Kaiser became aware of what must have transpired between his chancellor and Eugene when he found the instrument of revocation buried in the batch of documents sent up to the palace for his signature. In spite of his improved disposition over the armistice, this quite insignificant item irritated his latent temper and made him exclaim to his Chief of Civil Cabinet: "How can Bismarck involve me in this sort of thing at a time like this? It's intolerable! One would think he himself had more important matters to bother over." The venerable Chief of Civil Cabinet, who knew the broader aspects of the case and the Kaiser's probable reaction to it, agreed that the Chancellor had a remarkable talent for "simultaneously driving horses, donkeys and goats." His Majesty was not amused by the homily and protested: "How can I ever face Prince Eugene if as a reward for his service in this war I strip him of his birthright? That would in a way be denying our own."

"Perish such a thought, Your Majesty! But as to having to face him, he will most likely join his family in exile."

The Kaiser shook his head. "Not according to what I know of the man. Nor would I wish him to, this long after our troubles over Hanover. It would make us appear vindictive and damage our good reputation."

The Chief of Civil Cabinet, who wanted to get on with more important matters (including dinner), made the inspired suggestion that His Majesty, instead of countersigning the offensive document as Bismarck had intended, merely write "duly noted" on its margin in his own hand. The Kaiser grumbled: "As always, I find myself sitting between two uncomfortable chairs!" but he dipped his pen and wrote what had been suggested. Then he had an idea of his own which rekindled his good humor: "The Hanovers were originally barons and counts before they were annointed to the purple way back in the Dark Ages. Very well! Let us reconfirm that and leave this poor deposed prince at least a German count. It will make me feel much better about the whole thing—and possibly he will too!"

"Shall I summon him for an official knighting?" the Chief of Civil Cabinet inquired with a touch of irony.

The Kaiser stroked his luxurious side-whiskers as he thought for a moment longer about the problem of Eugene of Hanover. He was at heart a very decent man who knew that he should personally attend to softening the blow against fellow royalty and a comrade at arms, but was also human enough to shrink from a confrontation which was bound to turn into another painful trial. And in the back of his troubled mind lurked the fear of another clash with his insufferable, indispensable Chancellor, this one over a minor issue when momentous ones were hanging in the balance. "No," he answered. "Let my son, the Crown Prince, his immediate military superior, handle it. Remind me to mention the matter to him. Anything else of importance?"

The Chief of Civil Cabinet shuffled through the remaining papers on the desk and said: "Only a memorandum proposing we seek an immediate exchange of wounded prisoners during the armistice, Your Majesty. Really routine."

"Ah, but vital to some of our unluckier lads," the Kaiser exclaimed. "It is our wish everything be done to end their suffering as soon as possible. Again, an excellent project for my kind-hearted son. And now dinner?"

"Yes, dinner, Your Majesty!"

"And just *en famille* for a change, I hope?"

The Chief of Civil Cabinet sympathetically shook his head and produced a list out of his pocket. "There are fourteen guests invited to join Your Majesty, including the Grand Duke of Baden."

The Kaiser took the list with a deep sigh of resignation and studied the names. "This means five rich courses and six different wines, I suppose."

The Chief of Civil Cabinet gave his monarch an encouraging smile. "No—it's Your Majesty's favorite tonight. Stewed chicken and dumpling!"

"Ah, excellent! At least I won't have to go to bed with indigestion and have my sleep disturbed by nightmares." Rising from the desk with his good humor still reasonably intact, he left the study and proceeded through the Bourbon palace's labyrinth of corridors to accomplish his final duties of the day.

n additional two days passed before Eugene of Hanover's case came up on Crown Prince Frederick's crowded agenda. Celebrations over the armistice and apparent victory had been strangely restrained at Versailles, almost as if the coming dire results of the conflict were already casting their shadows upon victors and vanquished alike. There was much more to do than accepting congratulations, making toasts and gloating over the anticipated spoils. For instance, there was the matter of taking the surrender of twenty-odd Paris forts and redoubts and occupying them with German troops, the immediate repairing of destroyed roads and bridges, and the repositioning of investing lines and artillery against the unlikely possibility of hostilities being resumed. The armistice was to last for three weeks in order to allow the French time to elect a new National Assembly, which would then join the refugee Government of National Defense in Bordeaux, and presumably approve continued negotiations toward a permanent peace; considering that the French electorate was not only divided between those who wanted to continue fighting and those who wanted to surrender, but also between Republicans and Royalists, the outcome was by no means foregone. Crown Prince Frederick had to make certain that Paris with its still-powerful garrison would never again become a threat. But he was also deeply troubled by the plight of its civilian populace. When he discovered that the city's officials had greatly overestimated the remaining food supplies and he had personally witnessed Parisians approaching the picket lines to beg food for their children, he prevailed upon the Kaiser to order 6 million Prussian army rations donated to the people of Paris. It was not until he had taken care of these matters that he was able to turn his attention to the problem of Eugene of Hanover, allotting him very little time, but, unlike his father, meeting the unpleasant duty head-on without equivocation, and, unlike Bismarck, with an informality meant to be a compliment rather than an insult. He invited Eugene for a glass of brandy in his private salon in the Bourbon palace.

"I was sorry to receive your resignation as Inspector General," he tactfully began after dismissing his aides to spare his guest the embarrassment of their presence. "If this is your decision, I will accept it, but with deep regret. I can't help remembering that two weeks ago you gave me considerable encouragement when things looked very bad for us. Encouragement which did not turn out to be the empty words a commander is supposed to like hearing."

"I have never doubted the outcome of this war, Your Imperial Highness," Eugene answered. "The only question has been how long it would last, and how much it would cost us?"

The Crown Prince puffed on his meerschaum pipe and peered with genuine interest at Eugene through clouds of tobacco smoke. "I am curious to know your feelings about the war. Your personal ones, if I may presume. Why did you choose to join us on active service when the rest of your family preferred to leave Germany?"

Eugene decided to be completely candid. "I feel it has been a justifiable war for Germany in spite of Chancellor Bismarck's manipulation of the *casus belli*. Therefore, I could take part in good conscience . . . and in spite of ulterior motives."

"Meaning restoration of your princely rights?" the Crown Prince asked sharply. "You must know that is impossible."

"I know it now," Eugene admitted after taking an appreciative sip from his glass. "So it only remains for me to serve Germany as a German soldier. But after my meeting with Chancellor Bismarck, I have come to wonder whether, even in that capacity, I am an embarrassment to His Majesty and Your Imperial Highness. That is why I beg you to relieve me of my present duties."

The Crown Prince sprang out of his chair and began pacing the room with characteristic agitation. In accordance with strict court etiquette, Eugene also rose to his feet and kept turning to face him as he passed back and forth. "I am very unhappy over this whole affair," the Prince exclaimed, his pipe weaving wisps of blue as he gesticulated with it. "My father and I owe you an apology for ourselves as well as for our Chancellor."

Eugene tried to soothe him with a smile and shrug, saying: "Please, Your Highness! Do not let it upset you so! I was really very badly suited as Inspector General. Since we lost Count von Beckhaus, the job should obviously be filled by a professional railroad expert. You don't even need a general. Leutnant Colonel Wrinkleman would do very well, especially since he has actually been running the department for over a month with little supervision from me."

"Yes-yes! But I was referring to the business of revoking your title as Prince of Hanover," the Crown Prince replied. "I want you to know—strictly *entre nous*, of course—that while His Majesty is unable to alter the Chancellor's decision, he has refused to countersign the official document. It is no more than a gesture of sympathy and we know that you deserve better from us. But we can do nothing else, except . . ." He stopped his pacing in front of Eugene, looking him straight in the face as if forcing himself to make an offer he knew to be almost degradingly inadequate: ". . . except confirm your rights to one of your lesser hereditary titles and the lands that go with it. We would be very pleased if you chose to remain in Germany as the Count von Kleisenberg."

Eugene hid his surprise with as deep a bow as his girth would allow, but when he straightened himself, he qualified his gratitude by saying: "The Kleisenberg estate has been in our family for over four hundred years and cost us money for as long. Would any of the Hanover funds be forthcoming to allow me to support this honor, Your Imperial Highness?"

The Crown Prince resumed his agitated pacing. "The granting of funds does not lie within my power. As you must know, Bismarck has got his hands on all the Hanoverian fortune. But he can't remain Chancellor forever and, God willing, I shall live to choose another."

"I hope I will never be so selfish as to advise Your Imperial Highness to take such a step," Eugene quickly retorted, stopping him in his tracks.

"You can still say that to me after what he has done to you?" the Crown Prince asked with startled admiration.

"Certainly I can," Eugene answered, then with a sly twinkle in the small eyes, sunken deep behind the damp round cheeks, he added: "At least until I see what kind of peace he obtains and how well he knits together this new empire of ours. I will not expect him to do anything for me, but everything for Germany. I hope I will not be disappointed."

Crown Prince Frederick shook his head in wonder. "You are a very unusual, generous man. One we cannot afford to lose. I think I would be foolish to accept your resignation from your present post."

"It would be best for both of us if you did," Eugene insisted.

"Are you telling me you wish to leave our service altogether?" the Crown Prince protested from the other end of the salon.

"Of course not, Highness! But a change is in order, most especially to keep Chancellor Bismarck in the best frame of mind possible during the coming weeks. I thought he looked very poorly the other day and don't want to contribute to his bad health in the least way. That notwithstanding, I shall always be at Your Imperial Highness' service."

Crown Prince Frederick thought for a moment while furiously puffing on his pipe, and suddenly his bearded face lit up with inspiration. He veered from his pacing and throwing open a door, called for one of his aides to bring him his dispatch case. When it was opened on a table, Eugene recognized among the papers it contained, the one which Bismarck had tried to make him sign two days earlier. But the Crown Prince shuffled it out of sight and produced a thick folder which he thrust into his hands: "That is a list of our people being held prisoner by the irregular French forces—those damned *francs-tireurs*," he eagerly explained. "Most of them are undoubtedly wounded and have probably suffered all sorts of cruelties at the hands of those freebooters. There are some 350 men, including 70 officers and 5 of our civil servants. Will you please act as my personal representative in negotiating their exchange during the armistice?" Eugene bowed in acceptance, but the Crown Prince still gave him an opportunity to refuse the assignment: "It will mean contacting the most unsavory enemy characters. Outright bandits, most likely, and far beneath you in rank. And as this sort of thing does not strictly fall within the terms of the armistice agreement, we cannot give you much official support. But both His Majesty and I are very anxious for the safety of these men and would be most grateful for anything you could accomplish toward their release. Will you try?" When Eugene bowed again in complete agreement, he turned to his aide-de-camp and issued him a direct order: "The General Count Eugene von Kleisenberg must be given every possible assistance in his mission. Please see to it. And he is relieved as Inspector General of Military Railroad Transport and replaced by . . . by . . ."

"By Leutnant Colonel Julius Wrinkleman," Eugene prompted him.

"Yes, Leutnant Colonel von Wrinkleman! And perhaps he should be promoted to full colonel."

"Not necessarily as yet, Highness," Eugene interjected. "He is just *plain* Julius Wrinkleman, a very excellent railroad administrator."

"Oh, I see. Well, yes then not necessarily yet. Will you have another glass of brandy, my dear Eugene?"

"No thank you, Highness," Eugene demurred, feeling he had gained everything possible from the interview. "I intend to get an early start in the morning to seek contact with those terrible *francs-tireurs*. So with Your Imperial Highness' gracious permission, I beg to be excused."

The Crown Prince Frederick was so pleased over the pleasant outcome of what he had expected to be a painful session that he decided to escort the new Count von Kleisenberg downstairs to his horse personally—and so made him the inadvertent participant in an embarrassing domestic disturbance within the Imperial household. Young Prince Wilhelm, Frederick's oldest son and heir, had been brought from Berlin to Versailles for the double purpose of witnessing his grandfather's elevation to Emperor and to celebrate his own twelfth birthday. In accordance with the strict Hohenzollern concepts of rearing royal children, the boy had been dressed in the uniform of a leutnant of the Pomeranian Grenadier Guards on a few official occasions, but was otherwise kept out of the public eye and confined to the care of his family's personal staff. This was quite normal procedure for any child-prince, yet a certain aura of mystery seemed to surround this one. He was specially shielded (it was rumored) because the birth defect of a withered arm could make him lose his balance and topple over at the most inopportune moments; he had a totally unpredictable temperament which typically expressed itself in a famous incident (according to gossip) when at a luncheon given by his grandmother, Queen Victoria, he crawled under the table and removed all of his clothes. The General Count Eugene von Kleisenberg (und Hanover), who as a life-long bachelor detested children, had paid scant attention to these tales, and thus was very startled when walking down a corridor of the Bourbon palace in the company of the Crown Prince and his aides, they suddenly came upon this strutting miniature leutnant harrying a rigidly mortified sentry of the Royal Household Guard, shrilling at him in childish outrage: "I saw you move! Move, do you hear! I was watching you from around the corner and you moved when you thought nobody was looking. Consider yourself on report!"

Crown Prince Frederick stopped, made the universal gesture of the all-suffering father, then took his son by surprise with a peremptory: "Willy! Come here!"

Prince Wilhelm turned with a start, a flash of fear crossing his face before he advanced, saluted, and came to attention like a proper Prussian leutnant. "Yes, Your Imperial Highness. At your command!"

The Crown Prince impatiently played along with the game, returning his salute, but then deflated the arrogant child by telling him: "You are exceeding your authority, Herr Leutnant! It is time you reported to bed."

"Somebody has to check these guards, sir," Prince Wilhelm protested. "The Emperor is surrounded by enemies."

His father gave him an amused but irritated smile. "Willy!

Say good night to the General Count von Kleisenberg, then go to bed. At once!"

Prince Willy gave up his play-acting and at the same time every vestige of politeness which had been part of it. As his bearing sagged from one of a make-believe soldier to that of an insecure, thwarted child, he used his good hand to lift the crippled one from the hilt of his toy sword and hide it in his tunic pocket. His eyes shifted from his father to Eugene, taking in his obese figure with a petulant glance of contempt, then chirping: "You are too fat to be a real Prussian general!"

Eugene felt a prickly sensation in the back of his neck and barely restrained himself from slapping the Imperial brat's face. "Your little Highness is very observant," he heard himself say. "I am a Hanoverian." Almost simultaneously, the Crown Prince struck a lower blow than his own hands had been itching for, connecting with a resounding smack against the posterior of his son's Prussian blue breeches. Prince Willy dissolved into a sniveling boy being chastised by an angry father and was forced forthwith to apologize.

"Escort His Royal Highness to his bed, please!" the Crown Prince commanded the junior of his two aides. "By the scruff of the neck, if necessary!"

After Prince Wilhelm had been dragged off with very unroyal screams of protest, his father escorted Eugene down the stairs to the front vestibule and apologized again for the incident: "With the coronation, his birthday, the armistice, and all the excitement of recent events, things have gone to Willy's head."

Eugene answered with a tinge of irony: "As they may well go to the heads of many young Germans."

The Crown Prince gave him a thoughtful look, "Yes, that is a worry," he agreed; then wishing Eugene luck on his new assignment, he said good-bye with a gracious cordiality.

Despite his considerably reduced rank and the disconcerting brush with a future sovereign of the Empire, General Count von Kleisenberg rode back to his billet through the silent dark streets of Versailles with the pleasant feeling of having opened up new opportunities for himself. He had established a personal relationship with Crown Prince Frederick who was bound to succeed his seventy-four-year-old father before too long and, as he was a vigorous man in his early forties, little Prince Willy would have some twenty-five to thirty years to improve his deportment before ascending the throne. What made the prospects seem even brighter was the fact that Eugene found he genuinely liked Frederick, which was good for his self-respect since it made his determination to cultivate him seem less venal.

It was, in any case, useless to dwell further on the lost cause of his royal claims and title; as Bismarck had so crudely put it, they were "reduced to pure twaddle in the light of practical politics!" What had to be done now, was to make the name of Kleisenberg one to be reckoned with. Having been freed from the onus of a deposed Hanover, with a powerful friend and a powerful enemy (important in establishing one's own importance), he considered his chances good. Only money remained a discouraging problem. German generals were expected to support themselves mostly by the income of their estates, and his resources were meager. But even as Eugene rode up to his billet and turned over his horse to a sleepy groom, he had arrived at a solution: because he no longer had to consider dynastic consequences, he could *marry* money! The field of eligible heiresses was, of course, a much wider one than that of eligible princesses. The very idea of marriage was distasteful to him, yet it could become a tolerable sacrifice if the price were right and it helped to consolidate his new position with an aura of respectability! But in the meantime he had to concentrate on the mission he had been given by the future Emperor of Germany.

Upon entering the villa, General-Count von Kleisenberg roused his faithful orderly, Anton, and commanded him to start packing their field kits for an early morning departure into the hinterlands of what still had to be considered hostile *franc-tireur* country. The Kurfurst Waldemar was absent, carousing with a more important blueblood, so Eugene penned him a brief note of farewell, informing him he would henceforth have to assume the total expenses of their establishment. Then he lay down for the last time in his comfortable bed and, before blowing out the ornate brass lamp on the night table, leafed through the lists of prisoners the Crown Prince expected him to rescue. His eye was caught by the twenty-sixth down in the column of officers: *G. von Falkenhorst, Leutnant Baron, Second Dragoon Guards.* He stared at the name, feeling a tingle of excitement coursing through his huge body. Von Falkenhorst made him think of von Beckhaus, and von Beckhaus made him think of his late friend's widow. The Countess Antoinette was past her prime, probably a year or two older than himself, a superficial woman of limited intellect, true, but of impeccable background, conveniently conditioned to a subservient wifely role after twenty-five years of marriage to Count Frederick Paul—and, of course, *very rich!* As he blew out the lamp and settled down beneath the warm covers, Eugene decided he now had additional incentive to throw himself into his new assignment.

There were many blanks in Gustaf von Falkenhorst's memory of the period between his capture and his incarceration three weeks later in something approaching an official prisoner-of-war camp. Those blanks mercifully obliterated the memory of his worst sufferings while being shunted on makeshift litters or farm carts in winter nights from one secret *franc-tireur* lair to the next, ending up in cold cellars or lofts of isolated farms. After Lieutenant de Bretagne left him on Christmas Day, his captors made certain only that he would neither be rescued nor escape, otherwise seeming to care little whether he lived or died. Certainly escape was out of the question. His burns quickly became infected, the bullet wound in his neck and shoulder turned into a suppurating gash of agony, and he contracted pneumonia from continuous exposure and malnutrition. For six days he was delirious, but only once did a doctor attend him, a very old man terrified of involvement with the *francs-tireurs* who could do no more than swab his wounds with hot water and pour some foul-tasting syrup down his throat. He vaguely recollected as a hazy nightmare his next transfer, lying bound and gagged in a cart beneath a load of hay through which seeped a freezing rain as they jolted him along a backroad for seven hours. He never remained in the custody of the same *francs-tireurs* for more than two days, each group as callous as the next, but some showing more imagination in their cruelties than others. One sadistic jailor offered him a dead rat for dinner which he had taken the trouble to parboil into a revolting glutinous stew of entrails, fur and tail, gleefully justifying his brutal joke by exclaiming: "That's what you Prussians are making our people eat in Paris! See how you like it—*bon appétit!*" Another guard in an old mill situated above the rapids of a frozen stream, dragged him off the floor and propped him up before a window to watch an Uhlan patrol trot past on the road of the opposite bank. "Thought you'd like to wave to your comrades, Prussian!" the man teased him. "They searched this place yesterday, which is why we brought you here today." That time Gustaf lost control of himself and tried to break the window and scream after the vanishing troop of Uhlans. He had a violent battle with his guard before being hurled back to the floor, but it was doubtful that, even if he had succeeded, his wheezing would have carried to the road.

All of this took place in territory ostensibly occupied by the Germans, but, in fact, teeming with the undisciplined, loosely organized bands of *francs-tireurs* who were far too preoccupied with their deadly hit-and-run games to bother over the humane treatment of prisoners. Gustaf was indeed very fortunate, because most German prisoners were summarily shot or hanged, their bodies left as demoralizing examples to the occupation troops, but, in practice, triggering savage reprisals which, in turn, inspired more-brutal guerrilla tactics, setting a standard of warfare which had not been experienced in Europe since Genghis Khan and Wallenstein. He could have been executed at any moment during his three-week ordeal and was saved, not so much by Lieutenant de Bretagne's orders to keep him alive, as by the expectation that he was about to die of his own accord. Thus, on the night of January 17, he was passed through the nebulous lines into a district still entirely controlled by the French and delivered to a prisoner's hospital located in a half-ruined abbey near Pontarlier and the Swiss frontier. His agonized trek had taken him nearly three hundred kilometers from the burning inn.

The Abbey Saint-Luze had not been occupied by monks since being sacked by revolutionary troops in 1791 and although some efforts were made by intervening royalist regimes to restore it as a splendid example of thirteenth-century Gothic architecture, it remained in deplorable condition and quite unfit for human habitation—yet, the local French military authorities decided, good enough for wounded German prisoners. The desecrated chapel, whose once-magnificent stained glass windows were shored up with odd planks and crocus sacking, served as an unheated communal prison ward for over threescore enlisted Uhlan, dragoon and Hussar troopers, few of them able to drag themselves out of their vermin-ridden sickbeds which consisted of nothing more than a filthy blanket laid over a sodden pile of straw. Four German officers and a civilian inspector of the Royal Prussian Post and Telegraph were lodged in the privacy of cells which once had been the austere living quarters of the monks and were now bitterly cold, stone iceboxes of solitary confinement where they were dying as surely as their lowlier comrades, but in a terrible loneliness. Into one of these cells Gustaf was deposited on a cot and left shivering in the dark, his body racked by the clash of high fever and cold chills, his mind befuddled by delirium. The terrible pain of his inflamed wounds and the unrelenting fight to keep breathing through the phlegm clogging his lungs had brought him to the brink of a final, fatal lassitude. But two things shocked him into recoiling from that brink. He suddenly heard from somewhere out of the darkness the sound of German voices, the first since his capture three weeks ago. They were by no means reassuring as one of them was cursing and praying in an extremity of pain which must have at least matched his own. Then he made out others, a feebly croaking chorus trying to sing the old Lutheran hymn "A Mighty Fortress Is Our God." The realization that he was no longer totally alone, that comrades, no matter how desperate their plight, were close by, had an immediate resuscitating effect on his spirits (he was never to know he owed this vital tonic to a dying Uhlan lance corporal who every evening led his fellow prisoners, lying on the chapel floor, in an impromptu vesper service). Gustaf's second inspiration to keep fighting for his life came when the darkness of his cell was dispelled by the soft glow of a lantern and in its light there appeared a young woman of such startling beauty that the mere vision of her seemed to magically exorcise all pain and fear. When she knelt by his side and put her hand on his icy damp brow, warmth and life itself were transmitted through her gentle touch. Most startling of all was that she spoke to him in quietly soothing German: "Try to sleep so that tomorrow you will wake up rested and stronger."

Gustaf's racking tremors were stilled by the mere touch of her fingers, but he found himself whimpering like a sick child and unable to stem a flow of tears: "Oh God, please help me," he begged her through rasping sobs. "I am so cold. So hungry, I hurt so much. If you are German, for God's sake have mercy. . . ."

She took a handkerchief, wiped away the tears and then the cold sweat frosting the infected burns on his head and face. For a moment the serene beauty of her face was marred by a twinge of pain as if the healing current flowing through her hands had been reversed and shocked her with the suffering of this wounded man. Then she smiled and said: "We will do everything we can to help you get well. You must feel safe here."

Gustaf detected the strange accent of her speech and asked: "You are not German?"

She shook her head but her smile remained. "No. I am French. From Alsace."

"Then you will soon become German," Gustaf whispered.

There was the faintest flicker of resentment in her blue eyes, but none in her gentle voice: "We are what we are and cannot be changed," she said as she tucked the shredded thin blanket around him. "Please try to sleep. Tomorrow we will dress your wounds and give you medicine for your fever. We have a good doctor here, you will see. Now good night."

When she left Gustaf drifted into his first sleep in weeks which was not disturbed by nightmares about his screaming troopers trapped in flames laced with flying bullets.

Louise Hunsecker hoped that by morning there would be medical supplies available to succor this very sick young German officer, that Dr. Polignac would find time to visit him, and that a better blanket could be found to ward off the terrible cold of his stone cell. Yet she feared that these necessities for his survival would fail to materialize, except the blanket, which could probably be obtained from any one of several prisoners expected to die within the next twenty-four hours. Medical supplies were needed by the ragtag levies of General Bourbaki driven into this bleak mountain province of the Jura, and Dr. Polignac, one of that army's few professional medical officers, had hundreds of cases of wounds, frostbite, and pulmonary infections among his own hard-pressed soldiers; he could give little time to the German prisoners in the abbey. Louise Hunsecker herself did not nurse these prisoners out of particular sympathy for Germans. If anything, she had cause for a grievance against them since they had most likely killed her husband who had been missing since the battle of Vionville last summer. She did it because as a Calvinist, her religion commanded her to be charitable toward all those in need, even if they had committed injuries against her; she had also been asked by her superiors to assume the task because, although not a formally trained nurse, she spoke fluent German (for which talent some of them held her in suspicion). She was also a woman possessed of very fundamental female instincts, making it impossible for her not to respond to the suffering of a wounded man, regardless of his nationality. Hatred did not lie in her nature; love and, even, passion did. Therefore, she was constantly pleading with the Commandant of Abbey Saint-Luze to relieve the terrible conditions of the prisoners in his charge. After leaving Gustaf, she told the Commandant: "We have received another German boy who will die unless we can give him better food, medicine, and warmth. It is a miracle he got here alive."

Commandant George St. Pol occupied the only livable quarters of the abbey; they had belonged to the abbot and contained a fireplace. In fact, Commandant St. Pol looked somewhat like an abbot himself with his pear-shaped figure, his vacantly beatific expression, and his habit of clasping his hands together in a prayerlike attitude. Besides years of routine garrison duty, he had served with plodding distinction in the Crimean War and come out of retirement to do his part in this one, wearing a uniform twenty years out of date and utterly unable to adjust himself to the gratuitous brutalities of the present conflict. He reacted to his predicament by alternating between aloof callousness and ineffectual protests over the degeneration of warfare from a strictly regulated sport for professionals to disorganized mob savagery. He was a patriotic Frenchman, but this quality was closely tied to his dignity as a soldier—which had of late been severely compromised. He both pitied and despised his prisoners, both reviled and defended the slovenly company of guards under his command. The beautiful Alsatian nurse who came up from the village each day to administer to his charges he treated with a pompous chivalry although she annoyed him intensely, partly because she was such a pretty girl, possessing a charm to which he was too old to react without feeling ridiculously self-conscious, partly because she was constantly nettling his conscience as warden of this prison, a job he heartily detested. Being in one of his callous moods this evening, he said to her: "My dear Mme Hunsecker, it would be better for you to think of the new prisoner as just another Prussian, an enemy who has invaded and devastated our beloved France. Why tear your heart out over notions of Christian charity which are impossible to implement? May I offer you a glass of wine?"

Louise Hunsecker had argued with him so often that she knew exactly which points to press and which to pass over. "I'd like some wine," she said, "but I will take what is left in your bottle, *mon commandant.* I don't feel it proper that I drink here."

"You are incorrigible, Madame!" he exclaimed with an unhappy laugh. "I know perfectly well you don't want the wine for yourself. You intend to dribble it into your new patient. Why? He will probably die anyway." However, he gave her the bottle.

Louise put it inside her empty first-aid sack, thanked him graciously, then asked with that gentle persistence which always upset him: "Will Dr. Polignac come tomorrow?"

"I don't know. I will send my sergeant to remind him. But you must remember he is responsible for a lot of our own soldiers."

"Of course. But we are responsible for these prisoners who are also human beings."

"Yes, when they are sick," St. Pol shrugged. "Otherwise they are devils. And if we cure them, they'll become devils again. May I have the honor of escorting you back to the village, Madame?"

✠

"Please do not trouble yourself, *mon commandant.*"

"It is a dark night and the roads no longer safe," he ominously warned her, buckling on his sword.

"But I hear the Germans are still miles away," she protested.

"I am unfortunately not referring to them," St. Pol sighed. "It's our rabble packs prowling the countryside in the guise of soldiers which makes it dangerous. There have been many ugly incidents lately."

"Since when may a respectable woman not walk the countryside of France for fear of Frenchmen?" Louise asked, shaking her head.

"Since our regular army was defeated, our Emperor imprisoned, and the Republicans permitted to conduct the war as a form of tribal brigandage," he bitterly answered. "They have sullied the honorable profession of arms and brought about horrors no respectable woman could stand."

"But I am standing them," Louise told him with her beautiful smile. "I have been standing them every day for two months."

"Don't think I'm not filled with admiration and gratitude, Mme Hunsecker," he said with an inflection clearly revealing deep reservations. He shouted for his orderly to fetch his cape and old-fashioned shako, its scarlet plume somewhat frazzled. When the man appeared, his patched uniform covered by a dirty apron, his face unshaven and sullen with indifference, St. Pol vented his ire by rumbling at him: "You are a disgrace to the French Army!" Then he gallantly offered his arm to Louise Hunsecker, led her down the musty weeping halls of the abbey and out into the blustery darkness of the winter night. The walk to her lodgings in the village took twenty minutes each way, time enough for him to freeze his nose and ears, and he despaired of being invited into the rooms of this strange, beautiful young widow. It had become hard to maintain the standards of an officer and gentleman, but the more degrading the war, the more desperately George St. Pol clung to his superficial codes of chilvalry. In this way, he clung to his last shreds of dignity as a worn-out and defeated old soldier. At least he got to kiss Louise's hand before being sent trudging back up the hill to the last, most-inglorious post of his forty years' service. As he returned through the crumbling Gothic portals and the sentry failed as usual to properly present arms or even bother to step out of his shelter to take notice of him, he shouted his standard reprimand: "You are a disgrace to the French Army!" *"Et toi, mon commandant?"* the sentry hissed back, spitting at his tracks in the slush, *"Tu as bien baisé ce soir?"* The contempt existing

2 3 8

between the Commandant of the prison-hospital of Abbey Saint-Luze and his garrison of guards was entirely mutual.

The morning after Gustaf von Falkenhorst was delivered to the abbey, he was, if anything, in a weaker condition than the night before. But Louise Hunsecker came back on duty before dawn and from what passed as a kitchen, snatched a double ration of hot porridge (boiled from a mixture of oats, barley, and potatoes) which she took the time to spoon-feed through his chapped lips, washing it down with a few sips of the wine she had wheedled out of the Commandant. Later in the morning she brought him a blanket taken from a Hussar trooper who had finally expired from the septic infection spreading out of a small bullet hole in his thigh. She also salvaged two meters of putrescent bandage from the dead man's body, laundered it in the big iron kettle she kept boiling on the guardroom brazier, ironed it dry inch by soggy inch, exchanging it with the pus-saturated rags covering Gustaf's neck wound. As the medical supplies had failed to arrive, there were no antiseptics, no medicines with which to fight his infections. She dared not even swab his grimy body clean with warm water because there were no towels with which to dry him, no fresh clothing to replace his filthy singed uniform. The best she could do was to make him drink the last drops of the wine she had been hoarding and after he painfully choked them down, the cloudy look in his eyes cleared as he focused on her face, taking in its every detail with an intense look. "You are golden!" he whispered. "A golden angel! Nobody like you can exist."

"Of course I exist," she answered and let him hold her hand to prove it. His grip was strong enough to give her hope that he still had a chance. She let him keep hold of her hand even after his eyelids dropped sleepily over still-clear blue eyes and found herself gazing down on him, thinking that beneath the grimy yellow stubble, scabby burns, and deep lines of pain there must be a very handsome young face. What kind of man—or boy, rather? What kind of women waited for him at home? A mother most likely, but a wife too? Whom did he love? Had he ever loved? Or been beloved? Could her own Emile be in the same terrible condition in some German prison . . . *if* he were alive? If so, he would look just like this one, because they must have looked alike when they rode off to war as dashing young cavalry lieutenants. The thought of her lost husband made her draw her hand away from Gustaf's, pick up her bag and lantern, and quietly leave his cell.

She returned to the abbey's central purgatory of collective human despair, the chapel which once had resounded with the voices of monks chanting Te Deums and Magnificats, but was now filled with sighs, moans, and sporadic outbursts of agonized profanities. Among the sixty-two wounded prisoners there, was a coarsely misanthropic old sergeant with a broken hip whom Louise Hunsecker had to force herself to touch because he not only reeked of urine and excrement; he always greeted her with lewd vulgarities in spite of his absolute helplessness. As a penance for having shown favoritism to one who had aroused sentimental emotions within her, she now devoted herself to caring for this most-miserable and repulsive of her patients, giving him her undivided attentions until, in the sleeting twilight of the late afternoon, Dr. Polignac drove up to Abbey Saint-Luze in a donkey cart.

The doctor arrived in time to witness a pathetic travesty of the military ceremony of Retreat which Commandant St. Pol insisted be observed daily by his slovenly company of guards. As the tricolor was hauled down from the spire of the belfry, a bugler blew some off-key notes while the ragged ranks, bundled against the cold in layers of mixed civilian and military clothing, presented their mismatched arms. Polignac did not even bother to salute. An old army surgeon who, like the Commandant, had been called out of retirement to resume active duty, he was a hard-bitten cynic whose impatient temper had risen in proportion to France's misfortunes of war. When St. Pol apologized to him for the sloppy parade with his usual "These men are a disgrace to the French Army!" he snapped back: "Then why make them pretend to be something they are not and have no intention of being? You only make our situation look even more preposterous than it is—which takes some doing!" Climbing out of his donkey cart into the dirty snow of the abbey yard, he ignored the angrily flushing Commandant and marched over to Louise Hunsecker who was waiting for him at the chapel door. "Well, Madame? Did the medical supplies arrive at last?" When she shook her head, he wheeled furiously on St. Pol who had trailed behind him. "Then why did you send your sergeant to summon me? I am not a faith healer. I can't do a thing without medicines, disinfectants, and fresh bandages. And I can't waste my time commiserating with you over appalling conditions obvious to anybody. You should have left me to more useful work."

Commandant St. Pol shot an accusing glance at Louise before folding his hands over his stomach and answering: "It is true I sent my sergeant to remind you of your duties here. I also instructed him to go to the cantonment depot with a new requisition for the supplies. He has not returned as yet."

Dr. Polignac snorted: "As typical of orders we issue in this war, it was given backwards. He should have been sent to the depot *first,* then I would not have had to make a useless trip. My poor donkey is worn out." He stepped over the threshold of the chapel and peered into its gloomy interior, sniffing the fetid odor of human waste and gangrene, studying the rows of huddled shapes lying on the stone floor in their straw bedding, listening to their groans and asthmatic breathing. "How many are left?" he asked Louise.

"One died this morning," she quietly answered, "but it still leaves us sixty-six. A young dragoon officer was brought in by *francs-tireurs* last night. He has lung fever, burns, and blood poisoning."

"He is the last prisoner I'll accept here," Commandant St. Pol grumbled. "Why should I take on more responsibilities which will only result in besmirching my reputation?"

Dr. Polignac gave him a withering look of contempt before opening his medical kit and showing its meager contents to Louise: "Look! This is what I have to treat your sixty-six patients, Madame. Hardly enough for one case. But perhaps I could at least do that one some good. I suggest you choose who that one shall be."

Louise found herself making an instant subconscious choice, yet recoiled from it and gasped: "I can't do that, Doctor!"

The Commandant threw in a shocked supporting protest: "No, Polignac! You can't place such a burden on Mme Hunsecker!"

The Doctor gave them each a wry smile and agreed: "Very well! Let me make the choice. Who better than I knows the hypocrisy of the Hippocratic oath, after all?" Moving back outside the chapel to use the fading twilight for a quick inventory of his supplies, he rooted about the loose clutter of stained instruments, frayed rolls of laundered bandages, and a collection of nearly empty bottles of tinctures, pills, and purgatives. His attention was caught by a small jar of black salve which he opened, and smelled. "This is good for burns, so I'll choose your new patient, the dragoon officer you mentioned, Madame. If he's the healthy young animal most of them are, nature may help me not waste my efforts on him. Lead the way, please."

Louise was hardly able to suppress a sigh of relief as she picked up her lantern and started off towards the wing of the abbey containing the monk's cells. Commandant St. Pol did not follow, but called after them: "Do join me in a glass of wine later!" before retreating toward the warm hearth of his abbot's quarters, muttering invocations under his breath for God's intervention in this degrading war.

Dr. Polignac showed his proficiency at his trade in the way he treated Gustaf—and it was to him a trade rather than a profession. Under fire at Sebastopol, Solferino, Gravelotte, and an endless string of intermediate garrison assignments between those battles, he had learned to treat every soldiers' affliction from bunions to amputations, typhus to Crusader's Crotch. Although he had little formal medical education and only a rudimentary grasp of such modern techniques as Lister's antisepsis, he was endowed with a natural healer's instinct backed by thirty years of experience. His approach to a patient was as ruthlessly efficient as it was devoid of mystical sham. Thus, his first order to Louise was to help him strip off every stitch of the filthy uniform and underclothing Gutaf had been wearing for weeks and to swab his whole body clean with hot water. When she objected that he might freeze to death from the icy cold and the lack of fresh clothes, he gruffly told her that would be a more merciful death than one caused by lying wounded in one's own filth. After wetting his scalpel in the few drops of carbolic acid left in his supplies, he proceeded to debride the gangrenous parts of Gustaf's neck wound, working by the light of the lantern Louise held above his head. Fortunately for the patient, the first slice of the knife severed him from the realm of consciousness and allowed his writhing, shivering body to fall limply still. After dressing the wound with his salvaged bandages, Polignac smeared salve on the burns covering head, face, and hands, then put his ear against Gustaf's chest and listened for a moment to the bubbling wheeze of his breathing. "His lungs are infected, but still quite strong," he pronounced. "Even if we had medicine, there are none that would do as much good as warmth and nourishment. But we can't provide those either—which is more St. Pol's fault than mine. I've done what I can."

Louise covered Gustaf's body with the two thin shredded blankets and repeated: "He will freeze to death like this. I could launder his clothes, but never dry them in time."

"If this is the man you choose to save, you had better try, Madame," Polignac brusquely told her, closing up his now-empty bag. His craggy, pockmarked face suddenly broke into the only kind of smile it could show, more a cynical leer. "As a last resort, remember that nothing can warm a man as much as having a beautiful woman lie in bed with him." When a deep flush spread across her face, he added somewhat more gently: "I am sorry, Mme Hunsecker. We live in dire times when all the old genteel standards have turned into useless pretenses. Perhaps it will teach us how little they really mattered. Please do not expect me here again unless your Commandant obtains some supplies with which I can do some good. Good night!" With that he left her, hurrying back to his donkey cart, whipping the wretched animal into a last effort for the day as he went rattling through the abbey gates, vanishing into the darkness beyond.

For the first time since being assigned to Abbey Saint-Luze, Louise Hunsecker did not return to her lodgings in the village that night. After leaving her lantern in Gustaf's cell, more for its feeble warmth than light, she took his bundle of dirty clothing down to the guardroom and boiled it in the big kettle on the brazier, ignoring the soldier's protests at the rancid-smelling steam. The cook violently objected when she tried to dry the laundry in his kitchen, the only really warm room in the abbey besides that occupied by the commandant; she had to drape Gustaf's underwear, shirt, and uniform over an empty stall of the deserted stables. Then she tried to attend her other patients who appeared to be in for another very bad night. The wind had been rising all afternoon and was now whistling through the crumbling structure in chilling noisy squalls, which drowned out the weaker moaning of the inmates.

In the chapel only a few weak voices joined in the hymn and prayers of the evening service led by the Uhlan lance corporal; most were too sick, the rest too dispirited. In the end, the service was ruined by the old sergeant who suddenly went out of his mind and started dragging himself over the floor in spite of his broken hip, rolling and flailing about him with an imaginary saber while yelling curses and threats at the top of his voice. It took two guards and a fellow prisoner to subdue him and even after they left him trussed up in his foul bedding, he kept up his torrent of profanities until his voice wore down to a venomous croaking. Louise could not bring herself to go near him this evening; in fact, was warned against it by his own comrades, so that she turned her attention instead to two of the weakest prisoners who were no longer able to feed themselves, spooning their watery soup into them a few drops at a time. She comforted several others, sensing from their gratitude that even if she could offer nothing else, some kind words spoken in their own language helped raise their spirits, and, in turn, helped raise her own.

They were Germans—enemies—yet all of them reduced to such suffering that only their humanity mattered, most of them so young that in spite of the dirty fuzz on their sunken faces, they looked like waifs crying for their mothers. She was particularly drawn to the Uhlan lance corporal whose minor saber slash was almost healed, but whom Dr. Polignac had pronounced to be suffering from a terminal case of consumption. He sometimes summoned enough strength to help her feed and clean some of the patients and always conducted his little vesper service, but otherwise would lie wasting in the nest of straw he had piled where the chapel's altar had once stood. On this evening he confided to her with a voice racked by coughs that upon returning home to Magdeburg, he intended to study for a pastorate; his eyes glittered in wonder over the prospect, but more so over the expectation of death. Louise tucked his blanket around him to ward off the icy drafts rattling through the loose boarding of the chapel's glassless windows, then returned to the monk's cells and five lonely officer-prisoners. There was the captain with an amputated leg, another with peritonitis from a bullet wound in the stomach, the lieutenant who hardly had a whole bone in his body after being brutally beaten by his *franctireur* captors, and the middle-aged Prussian civil service officer with no visible wounds but whose mind had rejected survival and reason, reducing him to a rotting vegetable. For each one of these men she could do very little, appearing out the cold darkness in a momentary glow of warmth before vanishing again.

She reached Gustaf's cell last and found him still unconscious, his body racked by such tremors that she became convinced he was going through the final convulsions of death. She thought of rushing to fetch his clothes and put them on him even if still wet, but knew they would be frozen board-stiff in the exposed stables. Then she remembered Dr. Polignac's recommendation for a last resort and only hesitated long enough to realize he had known that last resort *must* come tonight and had cynically reveled in the test it would put her to. Here and now, a man's last slender chance to survive rested entirely with her! The warmth of her own body, as cold as it felt to her, could make the difference between living and dying. And in truth, this was the one *she* had chosen to save—more so than Polignac. Thus, it was only a matter of seconds before she made the decision and raising the thin blankets off his naked body, squeezed herself onto the creaking cot and wrapped herself, her cape and skirt around him.

The violent tremors continued, transmitting themselves through to her own body until she tried to smother them by clasping him with all her strength; then they began to subside and she could gradually relax her grip. He passed from unconsciousness to sleep, stirring a little without awakening, lying still for long periods, so still that she put her hand on his chest to make sure his heart was still beating. When he mumbled some anguished words about "burning up" and his hands clutched at her, she knew his strength had risen enough to support the effort of a nightmare. It lasted only a minute or two before he became still again, his breathing full of thin little wheezings, but steady. She must have drifted off into sleep herself after seemingly staring for hours at the wall with its droplets of moisture gleaming in the uneasy light of the lantern left burning on the floor.

Commandant St. Pol's voice took her completely by surprise as it gasped in shocked indignation: "This is disgraceful! A disgrace to the French Army!"

The commandant of Abbey Saint-Luze had evidently roused himself from his comfortable hearth to make a rare midnight inspection tour of the prison. He stared at the couple huddled on the cot, his eyes popping in disbelief. Behind him, his Corporal of the Guard stole a quick look and gave off a lewd noise. Louise froze feigning sleep, but braced herself in the expectation that the outraged St. Pol would step inside and furiously yank her off the cot. But that would have been entirely out of character for him; for all of his years as an army officer, he was a man who naturally shrank from violence, his only natural talents for his profession confined to its ceremonial aspects. He cut short a vulgar remark by the corporal, then merely repeated "A disgrace!" several times over with such pomposity that when the following silence indicated he had fled the offensive scene, Louise could not help smiling a little. Would he henceforth cease his awkward advances to her, or make them more direct, she wondered? No matter. She would give him no more opportunities for either kind.

Two hours before dawn, Louise gently disengaged herself from Gustaf, slipped out from under the blankets and wrapped them back around him. He stirred but did not awaken. Picking up the lantern, she walked down the hall past the guard who was seated in his chair, fast asleep, snoring in his tattered greatcoat; his own lantern had gone out. Before the crotchety cook arrived on duty to start the morning rations, she fetched Gustaf's clothes from the stables and dried them over the stove, risking a severe reprimand for wasting precious fuel by stoking it up to full heat. When she returned to the patient's cell with a crumpled but warmly dry bundle under her arm, she found him awakening from a renewed attack of tremors. But she knew he was feeling much better because he sat up, flushing with embarrassment and wrapped the blankets around his nakedness as she approached. "Thank you, Fräulein! I will dress myself without help, please!" he told her dazedly, but with determination. Fingering the bandages on his shoulder and neck, he asked: "Has the doctor gone?"

"Yes, he left last night. It is almost morning." She gave him his clothes, then stepped outside of the cell and listened to him struggle into them and finally crawl back into his cot. "Goodbye and good luck!" she softly called, and without looking in on the other prisoners, whom she could hear stirring and groaning as they awakened to another hopeless day of pain, hunger, and cold, walked out of the building. Louise Hunsecker had at last reached the point where she could take no more of the Abbey Saint-Luze. After resting in her lodgings for a few hours, she would go to the cantonment dispensary and ask Dr. Polignac for another assignment, and, if he refused, she intended to pack up her few belongings and begin the final portion of that long trek which had started last August from her home in Alsace.

She had done all she could, and no matter what might be insinuated by that old stodgy military relic, St. Pol, her conscience was clear even if her once staunch Calvinist faith was fatally damaged. "Good-bye and good luck!" she called out again, this time as she wrapped her cloak around her and walked out the gate, startling the sentry out of his frozen half-sleep because she spoke the words in German. He watched with a perplexed frown as her figure receded down the icy ruts of the road to the village and was slowly swallowed up by the pink gray mist of the wintry dawn. Then he shrugged, stamped his feet, and shook some circulation into his arms before sagging back on his rusty musket.

During the next week Gustaf von Falkenhorst struggled both to keep alive and to avoid certain aberrations of the mind which he came to fear might border on insanity. There were still blanks in his memory, but also memories which seemed more like hallucinations and revolved around a beautiful young blond woman who had brought him his clothes, clean and dry, that morning when he woke up naked beneath his ragged thin blankets. That was the only reasonably clear recollection he had of her, and he might not have been certain of her existence if he did not also have fragmented, unreal dreamlike recollections of her spending much more time with him and speaking in German. When she did not return, he asked the surly guard who brought him his food about her, but the man only spoke an unintelligible French dialect and besides had no interest in talking to him. The doctor showed up twice, dressing his now-healing wounds with a rough efficiency but refusing to speak beyond muttering to himself about the lack of medicine. An elderly officer wearing a heavy cape and plumed shako, which looked like they had seen service in the First Napoleonic Wars, visited him once, giving him to understand he was the commandant of the prison, but otherwise only peering at him with an expression of truculent distaste; he was obviously making a required tedious inspection tour and neither wished to, nor was he able to, converse with his German prisoners. Once a bearded priest looked in on him, asked if he was Catholic and, upon receiving a negative headshake, immediately vanished. His days were lonely, filled with pain and the unrelenting damp cold, constant pangs of hunger, and a gnawing uncertainty as to both his past and future. The nights were worse than the days; he was either unable to sleep on that hard cot made of three planks supported by trestles, or plagued by nightmares in which he rode into the battle of Mars-la-Tour on a dying horse, or found himself again trapped in the burning inn. In these dreams, the beautiful mysterious girl would appear, approaching him with outstretched hands, but then suddenly vanish just before touching him. He would then awaken, finding himself calling desperately after her to come back.

Another bleak day would seep in through the cracked glass of the tiny window located too high for him to see out of it, but allowing him to hear the sounds of the guards standing morning muster in the yard and their Retreat at dusk. With no other indication of the nature of his prison, he assumed it to be some sort of old fortress and longed for the company of the other prisoners whose groans and curses sometimes reached him. (Their prayers and hymn singing had ceased when the Uhlan lance corporal finally succumbed to his tuberculosis and the terrible privations of the chapel.)

Yet, for all his suffering and lonely isolation, Gustaf gradually regained his strength, the burns beneath Polignac's sticky black salve stopped stinging and turned into itching scabs, the wound on his neck no longer soiled its bandage with pus and its stiff soreness decreased as he tried to exercise it by flexing his shoulder and twisting his head. Then he became strong enough to get out of his cot and push his pail of foul-smelling slops to the far corner of his ten-foot cell and, finally, the day came when he found to his surprise that his door was not locked and he was able to step out into the hall. He had imagined guards to be posted close by, but there was only one man stationed at the far end of the rows of cells and when he saw Gustaf emerge, left his musket propped up against his chair and ambled up to him without any concern. "Ah, I see you're well enough to get about on your own feet!" he growled. "Congratulations! You may be

☩

our first real cure in this rotten hospital. Good! That means you can clean out your own dirt! March!"

Gustaf only understood him when, indicating the pail of slops and motioning for him to pick it up, he escorted him to the end of the long hall where the monks had installed a rudimentary sanitary system. It was merely an opening in the wall, a sort of chute which in warm weather must have given off terrible odors. From then on, Gustaf made it a practice to walk out of his cell and dump his pail every time he had to relieve himself. It was exercise, a break in the stultifying monotony, and a slight improvement in the appalling hygienic conditions.

In doing this chore, Gustaf soon came to realize that the guard at the end of the hall did not really care if he stepped out of his cell, that he little feared any of his charges would escape for the simple reason that they were too weak to try. He did not even object when Gustaf started exploring the long row of monk's cubicles and so came to discover his two remaining fellow prisoners in the block (the amputee and the peritonitis patient had both died). He was at first overjoyed at the prospect of companionship, but when he saw the vacant glassy stare of the civil service officer, mutely and ceaselessly rocking back and forth on his cot, the Hussar leutnant lying on his with two ill-mended broken legs, a chestful of fractured ribs, and a smashed mouth through which he was unable to speak, he knew they would be no comfort at all. Instead of joy, Gustaf felt an impotent rage welling up inside of him at his own helplessness to relieve their suffering and even more at the barbarous neglect of their French captors. When the Commandant made one of his sporadic inspection tours of the monk's quarters that afternoon, Gustaf all but flew at him shouting: "You butcher! You are deliberately letting my comrades die!"

Commandant St. Pol drew his stooped shoulders erect and knitted his gloved fingers over his stomach. "I do not speak German, Monsieur."

Beside himself with frustration, Gustaf yelled at him in an odd mixture of French and German words: "Medicine! . . . Food! . . . Doctor! . . . Clothes! . . . Heat! You must give them to us or we will die!" The Commandant nodded his head and shrugged. The guard, attracted by the shouting, showed up behind him carrying his musket with a fixed bayonet, an uncertain scowl on his unshaven face. Gustaf regained control of himself and lowering his voice, spoke more slowly, pronouncing each word as clearly as he could: "Bring the lady who speaks German. I must make you understand. The lady who speaks German—please!"

A ripple of understanding passed over St. Pol's flaccid expression, then quickly turned into one of malice: "Ah, the lady who speaks German! Oh-ho! You want her again, do you? My boy, you should really try to control your romantic notions. This is a prison-hospital, not a whorehouse." When the guard leered and broke into a raucous guffaw, the Commandant squelched him with a haughty glance, then untwined his fingers and poked one of them into Gustaf's chest: "You will not defile a French woman again—not even *her* kind! As long as you are feeling so frisky, you can work off your excess energy by cleaning up your comrades and their cells. They are a disgrace even to *your* army!"

Recoiling from the Commandant's breath which reeked of wine and garlic, and confused by the accusing inflection of words he could not understand, Gustaf stepped back just in time to have the door slammed in his face.

The next morning, the guard made Gustaf empty the slop buckets of the other two prisoners and, giving him a broom, indicated he was to sweep out their cells. He objected at first, but the soldier made threatening gestures with his musket and looked perfectly willing to use it at the slightest provocation. Besides, as menial as it was, this labor would be of some benefit to his more-wretched countrymen as well as an activity to relieve his own terrible boredom and loneliness. So he went about the work with a will, sweeping the floors and even asking for a pail of hot water which, when grudgingly delivered, he used first to wash their grimy faces, then to scrub out the filth saturating the stone flooring around their cots. Nothing he did for the old civil service officer received the slightest recognition, nor did more than slow down his compulsive rocking; this lack of reaction was unnerving, especially as the guard would look in and find it cause for sneering laughter. But the Hussar Leutnant's eyes followed his every move and when Gustaf came close enough, he would reach out to clutch his arm with a feeble grip, making gurgling, clacking sounds through his fractured, toothless jaw which Gustaf finally interpreted as meaning: "Thank you! . . . Thank you! . . ." Although the man was incapable of intelligible speech, Gustaf could tell by his eyes that he understood and desperately wanted to be talked to, and so kept up a one-sided conversation just to let him hear his mother tongue and speak it himself:

"We will get out of this yet, my friend!" he reassured him before leaving. "When I was taken prisoner a few weeks ago, we were about ready to start bombarding Paris where we've got a million of these French bastards sealed up and eating rats. You've never seen such cannons as we're bringing up. Barrels as big around as factory chimneys! My colonel, who is a very educated man, says that when Paris falls, France falls; it has been so throughout history. So keep up your courage, because if Paris hasn't fallen already, it's just a matter of a day or so."

The Hussar made his pathetic clacking sounds with feeble nods of his head, but there was a hopeless, disbelieving look in his eyes. By the next morning, when Gustaf came to take away his slops, he found his pail empty, his last night's supper uneaten, and the man dead. The guard sent for the Commandant who barely glanced at the corpse, then sniffed the cell and said to Gustaf: "You have done an excellent job of cleaning up in here, my boy. It smells much better."

"Murderer!" Gustaf yelled, turning on him so violently that the old neck wound shot a painful stab through his whole body.

The German word was close enough to the French equivalent that Commandant St. Pol understood him and a look of perfect innocence came over his face. "I have done all I could for him!" he protested. "You must realize our own people are suffering terrible deprivations. If you would offer us an honorable peace, but. . . ."

"Murderer!" Gustaf repeated without having understood a word of his excuse.

Commandant St. Pol closed his eyes and shook his head so that the plume of his shako twirled like a frayed red halo. "No, no, not at all, God be my witness! I am as much a victim of circumstances as you are." He gave the dead Hussar another look and this time honored him by crossing himself, then started backing out of the cell, saying to Gustaf: "I am very sorry. My condolences. You may, of course, attend the funeral of your fellow officer if you feel well enough. No matter what you think of us, we French observe civilized codes . . . insofar as possible in this disgraceful war."

The Hussar Leutnant's funeral filled Gustaf with a mixture of despair and hope. It was both a climax and turning point in his experience at Abbey Saint-Luze. For the first time since his arrival he was allowed outside the monk's quarters and discovered he was not imprisoned in a fortress, but a dilapidated abbey situated on an open slope of rugged, snowbound hill country. He also came to meet, at last, some of the prisoners of the chapel ward. Four of the less-sickly ones were assigned as pallbearers and grave-diggers. They were gaunt, bearded scarecrows in their ragged uniforms, barely strong enough to perform their melancholy duty, but Gustaf noticed that the small detachment of guards headed by Commandant St. Pol did not look much better. As no coffin was available, nor lumber to make one, the dead officer was wrapped in a shroud made of fodder sacks and carried on a stretcher through the deep snow to a corner of what must have once been the abbey's vegetable garden. It had been turned into a cemetery and Gustaf counted with a sickening feeling thirty-four crude crosses poking out of the drifts without any alignment or order; only a few had names carved into them. The four German soldiers gently lifted the body off the stretcher and eased it into the shallow grave it had taken them all morning to hew out of the frozen ground. Then they stepped back, formed a line and, with their eyes on Gustaf, braced their emaciated bodies at a semblance of attention. The French guards merely leaned casually on their muskets. Their expressions indicated they had gone through this often enough to make it routine; but Commandant St. Pol took off his plumed shako and said apologetically to Gustaf: "I regret we cannot spare the powder to fire the customary salute and our bugler has . . . er, taken leave. But if you care to say a prayer. . . ." Only then did it dawn upon Gustaf that he was expected to conduct the funeral service.

At first, all that would come to mind was the Lord's Prayer and, after reciting it, he remembered snatches of others he had heard at the few funeral ceremonies he had attended: "Lord God, receive the soul of our fallen comrade at arms! . . . The Lord is my shepherd, I shall not want. . . . Bless, oh God, the sword of the righteous and reward their good fight with Your eternal peace! . . ." Then he found himself addressing directly the four freezing, bedraggled cavalry troopers and, as he did so, suddenly became far more eloquent: "I do not even know the name of our fallen comrade, but I ask you to join me in the determination not to let him have died in vain. We must remember him always, even if we did not know him personally. Let him be a symbol of our sacrifices and whenever we meet Frenchmen, in peace or war, let us think of him here—of all our dead here. I am sure God will forgive us the hatred we will feel because He is himself punishing this evil people. Amen."

"Amen!" Commandant St. Pol echoed, crossing himself, and putting his shako back on his bald head, spoke a quick aside to his corporal: "And thank God he made it short!" He then ordered all but two of the guards dismissed and marched off with them, leaving Gustaf to witness the final act of interment accomplished by the four German troopers. They were so weak that it took them considerable time to shovel the icy clods of dirt over the human shape in the grubby sacking and to fill the grave. He watched them until he felt that his emotions might get away from him so he turned away and stared at the misty white panorama of the Jura hills framed by a crumbled breach in the wall surrounding the abbey's garden. It was then that he noticed something which raised him out of his despair.

There was a valley winding between the hills, tumbling down from a horizon diffused by the shredded veils of snow flurries. A large village nestled at its far end where opposing slopes almost touched each other, but were separated by a stream gleaming with ice and a road churned into a thin brown serpentine by hundreds of turning wheels and thousands of plodding feet. It was that road which riveted Gustaf's attention, because it looped to within a kilometer below the abbey and he could clearly make out long ragged formations of infantry, their supply wagons and artillery crawling along it. The tenuous column stretched over the full length of the valley and, as it moved, kept shedding small fragments which had to be soldiers dropping with exhaustion, and larger chunks which had to be wagons or caissons being toppled into the ditches as their teams collapsed. When a cold sunshaft broke through the scudding clouds, he could even see flashes of red-white-and-blue, the tricolor banners still holding together the retreating remnants of an army. Gustaf caught his breath and called out to the men filling the grave: "Look down there, boys! Just look at that!"

They paused in their work and followed his pointing finger with dull, weary eyes. "Oh, those!" one of them answered. "They have been marching past all morning. French troops, Herr Leutnant."

"Of course they are French!" Gustaf exulted. "Have you ever seen *our* soldiers marching like crippled beggars? Don't you know a beaten army when you see one? Look, boys! Look!"

The German troopers stared hard and as the details of the wretched parade silently winding past their high prison rampart registered, their faces brightened first with amazement, then delight. "By God, the Leutnant is right!" one of them shouted. "Look at those bastards crawl! They've had the hell beaten out of them, all right!"

The object of their sudden excitement also drew the attention of their two guards and one of them had enough pride left to react with anger: "That's nothing for you to laugh at in your situation, Prussians! Get on with burying your friend. Be quick about it."

A low cloud swept over the wooded crest above the abbey, dragging a curtain of fine snow over the scene and blotting out the valley. Gustaf returned his attention to the grave with more hope than he had a few minutes ago. He suddenly felt a moral superiority over the sullen guards and meant to transmit this to his fellow prisoners. "How many of you are left?" he asked with a casual voice.

"Fifty-one left, sir," one of the men answered.

"An even fifty," another corrected him. "Wirtz died an hour ago."

"How many could stand muster?" Gustaf asked.

"Five, sir. Us and one more."

Some of Gustaf's fresh confidence drained out of him, but he managed not to show it. "Pass the word to everybody that a beaten French Army is retreating within our sight. Tell them our own forces must be close behind the enemy and our deliverance near at hand. Every man able to act must be prepared to do so when the time comes."

"How, sir?"

"The security is pretty sloppy around here and. . . ."

"Silence!" a guard ordered, but with so little severity that when they were trudging back to the abbey after driving the unmarked wooden cross into the fresh mound, they dared to talk again. "The bastards can afford to be sloppy by keeping us in the condition they do," a trooper bitterly told Gustaf. "Those of us who aren't dying of festered wounds are starving and freezing to death."

"I intend to protest about it to the Commandant," Gustaf said, as if it were a pretty simple matter. "I'll let him know he better watch how he treats us, now that our own army is obviously closing in on this place. But I need an interpreter to make him understand. Does anyone speak French?"

"Not since Wolfschmidt died last week, sir."

"What about that woman?" Gustaf asked with a rise in inflection. "The blond one who came around to nurse some of us? Didn't she speak German?" When he noticed the troopers exchanging peculiar glances he had a sudden panicky feeling she had been a hallucination after all and that he had betrayed a mental quirk to these men. It made him shout in an almost frightened, high-pitched voice, "Well, damn it, you know who I mean . . . don't you?"

"Yes, sir—you mean Frau Hunsecker, sir," one of them answered and became so flustered that he stumbled and had to be retrieved out of a snowdrift by his comrades.

"Silence! Shut up! Keep moving!" the guards urged, but

kept their muskets slung over their shoulders and their hands deep in their overcoat pockets.

"Ah, Frau Hunsecker!" Gustaf repeated with a tremendous surge of relief which he then camouflaged by tersely asking: "That must be the one. Where is she? And why are you all so nervous at the sound of her name?"

The men again exchanged mysterious glances as they ploughed through the deep snow toward the abbey, then the oldest of the four stiffly twisted his shaggy head and spoke over his shoulder to Gustaf: "No secret, Herr Leutnant. She's gone, but our felicitations just the same, Herr Leutnant."

"What are you talking about?" Gustaf asked, wondering if perhaps these men might not be out of their heads.

"Wolfschmidt overheard the guards before he died, sir," the man rasped back through the side of his mouth. "He told us they were all gossiping about her getting kicked out of here by the Commandant because she slept with a Prussian dragoon officer. We miss her. But felicitations just the same, Herr Leutnant!"

"What!" Gustaf gasped, coming to a dead stop in the snow. "Halt! Tell me that again!"

The guards had by now been aroused by the strange behavior of the prisoners. One of them roughly prodded Gustaf in the back with the butt of his musket while the other shouted: "March! Silence!" in a voice which indicated he finally meant business. When they reached the cleared part of the abbey yard and entrance to the chapel, Gustaf made a move to follow the cavalry troopers inside to see the conditions there for himself, but he was firmly turned away and shoved toward the monks' quarters. He heard the older shaggy-maned trooper shout after him in a voice which was almost cheerful: "It's done us good to meet you, Herr Leutnant. We didn't believe a story too good to be true in this goddamned place, but now we know it is. We'll tell all the boys—about everything! A damn good funeral! We'll show these bastards yet!"

hen Gustaf returned to his cell, he began pacing with a seething impatience, confusion, and excitement. The matter of the beautiful blond young woman had been clarified only to leave a perplexing mystery, but he cast it aside for the more-important consideration of approaching rescue. He felt quite certain he had good reason to be hopeful and had been right in raising the hopes of his fellow prisoners, yet doubts still lingered. It was maddening not to know what was happening in the outside world. Taking apart his cot, he leaned one of its planks against the wall beneath the tiny window, forming a precarious ramp which enabled him to raise himself high enough to look out. Snow plastered against the cracked glass obstructed much of the view, but he could see part of the yard below, the belfry with a frayed French flag snapping in the snowy wind, a corner of the chapel, and beyond it, a distant misty piece of the valley. The road was out of sight, preventing another reassuring glimpse of the retreating troops. But as he looked, a group of guards gathered in the yard and appeared to engage in an agitated discussion. One of the men kept gesticulating toward the valley with a demoralizing effect on his comrades. Suddenly they all dispersed. Commandant St. Pol appeared, hesitated, and stared after them uneasily. Suddenly the plank was kicked out from under him, dropping him to the floor with a resounding crash. "If you're thinking of squeezing yourself out that window, be prepared to die!" he was roughly told. All three planks of his cot were taken away and he now had to sleep on the hard stone floor.

That evening Gustaf did not hear the usual Retreat ceremony take place and his supper was not brought to him by a private soldier, but by the corporal of the guard whose surly behavior was marked by a distinct nervousness. For the first time, he was locked in his cell for the night. Unable to sleep on the hard stones or relax enough to rest more than a few minutes at a time, he paced back and forth in the freezing blackness. When the shimmer of a clear dawn illuminated his window, the silence continued. There was no muster of the guards in the yard below and the hour passed when his breakfast of boiled gruel should have been brought to him. He began to suspect that the garrison might have evacuated the abbey, abandoning all their sick prisoners and leaving him locked up to die of cold and starvation. Uhlan patrols could pass for days through the valley before bothering to check the ruins far up the hillside. His fear increased when there was no response to his angry pounding on the bolted door. After another hour of restless pacing he considered picking up his slop bucket and hurling it through the window to attract attention when he heard the bolt draw back and the door opened. To his amazement, one of the scarecrow prisoners who had helped dig the grave yesterday was standing on the threshold. "I have been sent by the Commandant to fetch the Herr Leutnant."

"What in God's name is going on?" Gustaf asked.

"I believe most of the garrison deserted during the night," the trooper answered, a wry grin spreading over his gaunt face. "As far as we know, there's only one man left besides the Commandant, sir."

All of Gustaf's excitement returned in a flash. "That means we can break out of here!" he exclaimed.

"I believe the Herr Leutnant should look over the situation before deciding that," the trooper answered. "Please follow me."

Before leaving the monks' quarters, Gustaf glanced in at the mad civil service officer and found him still rocking on his cot, with a vacant stare; there was no point in taking him along. Then they walked past the abandoned guardpost, descended the stairs, crossed the empty yard unchallenged, and entered the chapel. Gustaf had trouble adjusting his eyes to its dark gloom after the brilliant sunlight reflecting off the snow, but the stench prepared him somewhat for the sight he was to see. Of the fifty men confined in this musty Gothic cavern, only three were on their feet and were able to come to attention when he entered; a dozen others managed to sit up or raise themselves on their elbows out of their moulding straw bedding, a few of them making hoarse rasping sounds which were supposed to be cheers. All the rest lay inert, only their labored breathing indicating they were not dead. Gustaf stared, speechless with horror and fury. The trooper who had brought him whispered in his ear: "Now the Herr Leutnant can see why there is little question of breaking out. A handful of us might make it, but the rest of these men would be left to die. None of them have had any food or care since yesterday noon. Two were dead this morning."

"Where is the beast who calls himself the Commandant?" Gustaf seethed.

"In his quarters. I wanted you to see this before seeing him, sir."

"Take me to him!"

All that was left of Commandant St. Pol's garrison of guards was his own personal orderly who was serving his master lunch at a table set before the fireplace in the abbot's apartment, a sight which further enraged Gustaf. "What about my sick, starving men, you swine?" he shouted at the French officer.

St. Pol rose from his table with an almost courtly show of politeness when he saw Gustaf and the trooper. "Ah, our love-sick young lieutenant! I'm surprised to see you looking so well. But then you've had special treatment, after all. Since you are so favored, I suppose I should offer you a glass of wine."

Gustaf smashed the proffered glass to the floor. "I do not drink with your kind. I demand medicine and hot food for my men!" He noticed with a sinking feeling that except for the bottle of wine, the Commandant's meal was little better than what he had been served in his cell. But he persisted in his rage: "*Food! Medicine!* At once, do you hear!"

St. Pol sank back into his chair with a deep, disappointed sigh. "Very well! Act like a Teuton bore, if you like. If you had any intelligence, you'd see that we are both equally humiliated and beaten. But go ahead and make a scene if you like. Me, I am going to try and live out the last hours of my miserable last command with some semblance of order." He sipped a spoonful of soup, following it with a swallow of wine, the small finger of his right hand arched as he held the glass. There was a look of placid indifference on his face which fooled Gustaf into making a lunge toward the platter of stale gray bread and mouldy sausage before him. With unexpected quickness, the Commandant whipped forth a pistol, which had evidently been concealed under his napkin, deftly cocking the hammer as it appeared over the edge of the table, the muzzle pointed at Gustaf's shrunken belly. "Stop! There is still a limit to what I'll stand from you!"

His orderly gave a squeal of fear and jumped back. "Please, *mon commandant!*" he whined. "No more killing at this stage, please!"

The German trooper reached out and tugged on Gustaf's sleeve. "Humor him, Herr Leutnant. Let's not get ourselves killed so near the end."

Gustaf backed away from the table, but only one step. St. Pol gave him a tremulous smile as he put his pistol down next to his bowl of soup. "That is better, my boy. Now listen to me and try to understand. There are rumors that Paris has surrendered and an armistice signed a whole week ago. Still there was fighting near here yesterday, so who knows what is going on?

✠

In any case, I find myself in the position where I have no choice but to ask you to take charge of your own men here. Mine have all run away, you see. Do you understand at all?"

"Food! Medicine! For my people!" Gustaf stubbornly hissed at him.

"He does not understand," Commandant St. Pol exclaimed with a despairing shrug, "and here French is supposed to be the universal language of diplomacy and the military." He spooned another mouthful of soup, thoughtfully, dabbed himself with the napkin, then appearing to have reached an important decision commanded his orderly: "Jules! Please give me my sword." When it was handed to him, he rose from the table and resting the hilt on his left forearm, extended it toward Gustaf: "Please accept my surrender as Commandant of the Prison Hospital of Abbey Saint-Luze, Monsieur, under the civilized rules of war which our nations are obliged to respect!" He pronounced the words in a sonorous voice, as if reading a liturgy. The formal effect was promptly destroyed when his orderly burst into tears. "Jules," he reprimanded him, "Must you disgrace the army to the bitter end?"

Gustaf was stunned into silence. Then he snatched the sword from the Commandant and exclaimed to the equally amazed trooper: "Damnation! I believe he is surrendering to us!" His eyes lowered to the pistol lying on the table, but when he made a tentative move toward it, St. Pol quickly grabbed it beyond reach and tucked it into his own belt. "Ah, no! This is only supposed to be a symbolic surrender," he said, obviously piqued that Gustaf had even accepted his sword. "Force of circumstance. Consideration of humanity. Concession to practical realities. Nothing more. I still expect the honors of war due a French officer." He abruptly sat down again and there followed an awkward silence broken only by the orderly's barely suppressed sobs. It was to him that Commandant St. Pol addressed the words which closed this painful, pathetic and quite-insignificant episode in the Abbey St.-Luze's six hundred year history: "For heaven's sake stop sniveling, Jules! It's all over. The whole disgraceful war and everything. Take this Prussian officer and show him what supplies we have left. Maybe then he will understand why we have been able to do so little for our prisoners."

The next three days turned out in many respects to be the most trying Gustaf von Falkenhorst had spent in captivity. Although no longer a prisoner in the strictest sense, he was imprisoned within the grim cold walls of the abbey as surely as if the deserted garrison were still guarding him. What prevented him from simply walking through the gates and striking out on his own in search of the German army was the fact that he now had on his hands forty-seven men too sick and debilitated to care for themselves. And most infuriating was his inability to help them. The dispensary had nothing but a collection of empty bottles on the shelves and a few rusty instruments in the cabinets; the commissary stocks had enough food for four days if severely rationed; the main staples, consisting of three mixed sacks of potatoes and onions, were mostly rotten. Even fuel was in short supply and, as the temperature remained at ten degrees below freezing, the cold which permeated the entire complex of crumbling, unheated buildings presented the most dreadful hardship. Gustaf partially solved this problem in the chapel by using the Commandant's sword (which he now conspicuously wore on his own belt) to chop up a confessional booth and some carved paneling, and building a roaring fire on the floor of the chancel. Until he also knocked out some boards covering the altar windows and created a proper flue, the sick men almost choked to death in the smoke, but those who could crawled close to the flames and those who could not were dragged there by Gustaf and the four soldiers who had the strength to help. Commandant St. Pol looked in and when he saw the bodies packed around the fire and what was burning in it, he raised his hands in horror and muttered something about destroying one of France's architectural treasures. But, although armed with his pistol, he made no attempt to interfere and soon fled back to his quarters.

Gustaf pressed the Commandant's orderly into service as camp cook and, after making certain every prisoner received his ration of half a boiled potato and crust of bread, he left the chapel and trudged through the snow to the cemetery, taking up a position by the broken wall and intently watching the now-empty road winding through the valley below. He hoped to spot the cavalry screens of the German army he felt sure was near, but except for flights of rooks spiraling on black wings down on some dead horses left by the retreating French, he saw no signs of life. Even the village nestled between the silent hills lay smokeless and deserted. The sun dropped low in the west, dipping its misty disc into clouds which blazed blood red for a moment, staining the vast snowscape a delicate glittering pink before gradually fading into a gloomy blue twilight. The Jura hills turned deep purple, then became stark black silhouettes against the afterglow. Gustaf could feel the temperature start plunging toward the low it would reach during the coming night, cutting through his tattered uniform, numbing his face and hands. With a depressed feeling, he started back to the abbey.

When he reached the yard, Gustaf noticed Commandant St.

Pol standing in position for the Retreat, staring blankly at the empty space where his garrison should have been on parade. His eyes moved to the belfry and the limp flag hanging from its spire, then he shuffled over to where the lines had been tied to the trunk of some dormant ivy. His fingers fumbled with a frozen knot which refused to come undone. Gustaf came up behind him, drew his sword, said, "Please allow me to help haul down your colors," and parted the line with a swift slash of the blade. Commandant St. Pol gave a cry of anguish and almost fell as he skidded about the icy crust in a clumsy dance, trying to catch the sacred rag as it came fluttering down from the belfry. He succeeded, but ended up with a tangle of line and frayed red-white-and-blue folds draped over himself in such a ludicrous fashion that Gustaf had his first laugh in over a month.

"You are a son-of-a-bitch, sir!" the Commandant pronounced.

"You are quite welcome!" Gustaf answered with a mocking salute. Returning the sword to its scabbard, he stalked off. His moment of levity was quickly over when he reentered the grim chapel. He spent the night with the men huddled around the fire, which they kept going by periodically chopping up a door and feeding pieces into the smoking flames. Even the Commandant's orderly joined them, unable to stand the eerie loneliness of the deserted barracks, and did his share of work in spite of taunts and insults, eventually earning a grudging respect. The mad civil service officer, whom Gustaf had ordered brought down from his isolation in the monks' block, rocked back and forth, crouched in his pile of straw, his staring unseeing eyes reflecting the dull embers of the fire. Toward dawn he suddenly rolled over with a deep sigh, as if at last finding rest, and it was not until later in the morning that they discovered he was dead. There were also four cases of severe frostbite among the rows of men farthest from the fire.

Even before accepting his breakfast ration, Gustaf went to his observation post and scanned the valley for any sign of rescue. Yesterday's clear weather was over and had given way to a dull gray overcast full of fine snowflakes. He could barely see the road and village, which were as deserted and forlorn as ever; even the rooks were gone. When he returned to the chapel and told the four able-bodied but weakening soldiers the discouraging news, one of them suggested they go to the village and beg for help. Gustaf had considered this, but after his experiences with the *francs-tireurs*, he did not have the slightest trust in the French civilian population; they were unlikely to help any unarmed German soldiers and might even murder them. He explained that they were safer at the abbey—at least for another day. However, he went to the abbot's quarters intending to convince Commandant St. Pol that *he* should go to the village for supplies and aid and was even prepared to give him back his sword if he would show some cooperation. He found his quarters almost as cold as the chapel, its hearth burned out, its occupant lying in bed fully clothed and covered by three blankets and his flag; two empty wine bottles stood close by on the floor.

St. Pol sat up when Gustaf entered the room and drawing his pistol from under his pillow, ordered him to leave at once. Argument was useless, especially through the language barrier. So Gustaf quickly left him and sought out instead his orderly, Jules. With the help of one of the German troopers, he was able to make the man vaguely understand what they expected of him, and after supplying him with a pair of German boots which were better than his own, they escorted him to the gate and gave him a shove down the road to the distant village. "Bring food . . . medicine . . . a doctor! Hurry!" they called after him, but Jules shuffled off quite unwillingly, shaking his head.

Gustaf and the four troopers spent the rest of the day feeding and caring for the sick as best they could and ransacking the abbey for firewood. As a last reserve they kept in mind the Commandant's bed, table, and chairs. They did not waste their failing energies burying the dead civil service officer, but moved his body to an improvised morgue where two other corpses were preserved by the intense cold. A watch was kept on the road and valley until the fine snowfall thickened to a near blizzard which blotted out everything from sight. Commandant St. Pol did not come out of his quarters, but Gustaf saw him peering out of his window, watching him hack limbs off an apple tree with his sword. The orderly had failed to return by evening and there was nothing to do but settle down for another terrible long night around the fire on the chancel floor. Gustaf tried to bolster the spirits of his men by leading them in prayers, but only a few could pronounce the words through their shivers and he feared that several more of them would be dead by morning. The wind whistled and wailed through the abbey, the freezing drafts whipping bitter smoke into their faces and often blowing live sparks into their bedding. By morning snowdrifts had piled up eight feet deep against the walls.

Miraculously all but one survived through to the next day and were able to eat a further-reduced ration of breakfast, but Gustaf knew they were close to the end. One of the troopers who had been able to stand on his feet yesterday, could not get up this morning. His own strength which had grown for a while after he recovered from his infected wounds and pneumonia, was now ebbing from constant exposure and starvation. Yet he was the strongest one left and realized that, regardless of the risks, he would have to go in search of help. Unless he found it, most of these men would die by tomorrow. After helping to feed the weakest, he handed his captured sword to the strongest trooper and appointed him in command. Then he took the dead man's blanket, wrapped it over his head and shredded uniform, and shoved his way outside through the drift blocking the chapel door. He was immediately engulfed in a white pall of flying snow and it took tremendous effort just to push himself to the gate, but he did not stop to rest at the deserted guardpost. "I have failed again," he bitterly told himself as he ploughed onto the road which could only be dimly traced by the trees bordering it. "I should have gone yesterday when the weather was not as terrible as this."

With each labored step he sank up to his knees and it was a desperate effort to take the next one; the wind pierced his blanket, the cold closing on his body like a steel vise. He realized it would take him two hours to cover the five kilometers to the village and he doubted he could survive that long. But to pause now would mean certain death. His feet turned into heavy lumps of pain, then began to grow numb as they froze, but he kept pumping his leg muscles and leaning into the wind. The abbey vanished behind him in the flying spume, and ahead he had tantalizing glimpses of the village in the valley when the squalls parted in their wild chase. He reached a roadside shrine to Saint Augustine, the eroded stone figure rising out of the snow with two icicled fingers pointing back to the abbey, as if warning him to return. He leaned against it for a moment, staring up at the carved face with its rock-hard expression of saintliness and shouted, half-praying, half-cursing: "God! Give me strength to go on!" But he took only a dozen more steps before stopping again and brushing the sharp needles of flakes out of his eyes with his frozen hands, staring in disbelief at a sight materializing out of the gloom.

At first they were nebulous, floating shadows diffused by the swirling sheets of snow, but gradually solidifying; the leading shape suddenly turning into a cart pulled by a laboring donkey followed by other shapes which became horsemen plodding in its tracks. As the procession drew nearer, step by slow step, Gustaf recognized the two bundled figures in the cart as Jules, the orderly, and the French doctor who had attended him several times during the past weeks. The horsemen were unmistakably Uhlans in spite of the heavy hooded capes they wore over their characteristic helmets and the white flag of truce snapping from the color-sergeant's lance. But it was the leading rider of their column who riveted Gustaf's attention with a shock of disbelief which choked his cry of geeting. He was enormously fat and heavily encased in extra layers of clothing, including several yards of woolen muffler wound around his head and neck. Yet this man was so indelibly impressed on Gustaf's memory that he knew him at once, even if doubting the very sight of him. Lunging forward and staggering past the donkey cart, he threw himself against the snorting white mare on which the fat rider appeared to be fast asleep as she struggled to carry him up the hill. "Your Highness!" Gustaf croaked at him, "Prince General Eugene! For pity's sake hurry! Our men are dying!"

General Count Eugene von Kleisenberg had been half dozing in the saddle, trying to shut out the misery of the long climb up a blizzard-lashed slope on what would probably turn out another abortive attempt to locate lost German prisoners. He had been riding for five days through this inhospitable, snowbound Jura country which was such a bleak contrast to everything one expected of *la belle France*, thwarted by the flight of all military authorities who preferred internment in Switzerland to capitulation, and by the civilian population, who either deliberately lied or knew absolutely nothing about anything beyond the confines of their villages. The scarecrow deserter and surly doctor who were leading him on this particular expedition would probably turn out as unreliable as all the rest and Eugene was having difficulty in keeping himself from sinking into a pessimistic lethargy over his assignment. Thus, it came as an unexpected shock when his horse shied him awake and he found himself staring down at a horrifying apparition of a human being who was clawing at his stirrups. His first reaction was to raise his crop and beat off the beggar, but he noticed the torn shapeless remains of a Prussian uniform beneath the filthy blanket wrapped round the apparition and, most startling, he was gasping at him in German and using his old princely title! Then he too felt a flash of incredulous recognition and exclaimed: "God help me! Is that *you*, Baron Gustaf?"

"Yes . . . Leutnant Baron von Falkenhorst reporting for duty, Your Highness," Gustaf gasped and sank down in the snow in a sitting position from which he was unable to rise. Tears streamed down his sunken cheeks and congealed into rivulets of ice as they trickled through the matted strands of his yellow beard, his body racked by sobs of relief and shame.

General Eugene von Kleisenberg swung his ponderous bulk out of the saddle and squatted in the snow next to Gustaf. It was Dr. Polignac who made the first useful move by climbing out of his donkey cart, producing a canteen of brandy and forcing some of its contents through the collapsed man's frozen lips. "He may live if we can get him to shelter and warmed up," he told Eugene. "Compared to the rest at the abbey, he's one of the strong ones."

"If he's an example of your care of prisoners of war, you may have a lot to answer for," Eugene replied with a threatening scowl.

Dr. Polignac signaled to the leading Uhlan troopers to dismount and help lift Gustaf into the cart. Then he peered into Eugene's chilblained jowls, framed by swathes of brown woolen muffler and sneeringly inquired: "Who is most to blame, *monsieur le général?* The one who drives another to extremes of brutality, or the one who allows himself to be driven to them?"

The Commandant George St. Pol had watched from his window as Gustaf von Falkenhorst staggered out through the abbey gates and vanished in a swirl of blowing snow. He considered himself to have taken enough from that young Prussian, whose arrogance seemed as durable as his amazing physical stamina, but guessing the mission he had set for himself, asked in advance that God receive his heretic Lutheran soul. The Commandant knew that even if he managed to struggle all the way down to the village, he would be unlikely to find any help for his dying comrades. The small army cantonment had broken camp and followed in the wake of General Bourbaki's retreating army as it chose internment in Switzerland rather than surrender. The remaining civilians would certainly not yield up any of their carefully hoarded supplies to a distressed German; those hard-bitten independent shepherds and vineyarders had lately even turned their backs on their own starving soldiers! So the young Prussian officer's mission was hopeless, he was bound to perish on the long uphill return trip. Good riddance! Yet St. Pol felt an irritating twinge of conscience which stemmed from the uneasiness of his subverted Catholic faith and deeply compromised sense of chivalry, and this drove him to collect the last four bottles of wine he had been hoarding in the secret cache (doubtless used for the same purpose by the last truly anointed Abbot of Saint-Luze), carrying all but one to the chapel where he personally fed a bracing tot into each of the forty-five men pressed around the fire. The men neither refused the libation nor thanked him for it, nor did they understand him when he exclaimed: "You are brave soldiers and I hope that some of you will at least remember me as a kind one." Then he rambled on as he poured the wine into a tin mug for each in turn: "I know a lot of you are angry with me and I don't blame you. But then something went terribly wrong for all of us in this disgraceful war. *Prosit!* Here's hoping the next one will be better. At least not so long. And not fought all through such an awful winter as this. No. And that it will be kept where it belongs, just between us soldiers. Yes. *Prosit!* Otherwise it will be the end of us all. Absolutely."

After retreating from their cold, suffering silence, George St. Pol returned to his lonely vigil at the window of his abbot's quarters, watching the snowdrifts smoke and surge across the abbey's yard like sluggish white combers, sipping out of his tin mug the last of an excellent 1866 Bordeaux he had saved from his act of penance. He became quietly drunk during the next hour, and when Dr. Polignac drove his donkey cart through the gate at the head of a column of German cavalry, he had no hesitation at all in lying down on his bed, wrapping the flag around his body, and blowing his brains out with the pistol he had taken care not to surrender to the last surviving Prussian officer among the prisoners of Abbey Saint-Luze.

March 1871

Delusions of Peace

With postal deliveries restored by a younger and some-what less-punctually dedicated carrier than the late Bruno, Glaumhalle received its biweekly mail on March 2—one day late. The previous delivery had been missed altogether, as had two others during the month of February, and all but one during January. On this date the postman came riding through the slush of thawing snowdrifts to bring only two letters and four outdated copies of the *Breslauer Zeitung*.

One of the letters was addressed to Albrecht and bore the new stamp of Imperial Headquarters at Versailles. It conveyed in terse official language a refusal to extend his sick leave and orders to report back for duty at Versailles by March 10 or forthwith resign his appointment with the Military Railroad Transport Authority; the order was signed by one Colonel Wrinkleman, an officer whom Albrecht vaguely remembered as holding an administrative post under Count von Beckhaus, but who obviously had considerably improved his station as he now used the title of Inspector General. What had happened, Albrecht wondered, to Prince Eugene of Hanover who had, as newly appointed head of the authority, telegraphed approval of his first request for extension of leave little more than a month ago? But more important, what was he to do? Remain in a service where he had already attained more rank than normal for his age, or resign from it and devote himself entirely to family problems—specifically the tangled, sensitive relationship between himself and Tessa.

Tessa was taking advantage of the thawing weather and melting snow to exercise her beloved horses together with Master Prytz and so was not in the manor when the mail was delivered. The other letter was addressed to her in her mother's erratically slanted hand, its Austrian stamp canceled a full three weeks ago. Albrecht had to resist all temptation to open it. Suppressing an anxious feeling that it would not contain good news, he diverted his impatience by opening up the bundles of newspapers.

A few minutes of glancing at the headlines gave him a belated, capsulized impression of the course of events in France and Germany during the past two weeks:

CRUEL ATROCITIES BY FRENCH AGAINST PRISONERS OF WAR—
BERLINERS DEMAND RETRIBUTIONS

FRENCH REPUBLIC SHAKEN
AS BOTH LOUIS NAPOLEON
AND RADICAL PARTIES ARE DEFEATED IN ELECTIONS—
PARIS MOBS RIOT

BAVARIAN COUNCIL OF MINISTERS DEMAND HEAVY INDEMNITIES

FORMER EMPEROR NAPOLEON RELEASED—
JOINS EMPRESS EUGÉNIE IN BRITISH EXILE

CHANCELLOR BISMARCK THREATENS
TO END ARMISTICE
UNLESS HAGGLING OVER PEACE TERMS CEASES

Albrecht barely skimmed through the articles that followed these headlines in order to absorb the essentials until he came upon the latest issue, dated February 28, 1871, proclaiming an event which might profoundly affect his own situation:

PEACE TREATY SIGNED!
ALSACE AND MOST OF LORRAINE
BECOME GERMAN!
FIVE MILLIARDS INDEMNITY TO BE PAID!

As the complete terms of the treaty had not been released in this early dispatch from Versailles, Albrecht could glean no more than its main provisions, which included the permanent surrender of the fortress-cities of Metz and Strasbourg, the triumphal entry into Paris by Kaiser Wilhelm and his army, and the occupation of strategic areas of France by German military forces until the astronomical indemnity was paid in full. The *Breslauer Zeitung's* correspondent rounded out his skimpy report by gleefully assuring all his "patriotic readers" that France had

had her proud nose rubbed in the dirt of her own soil and "will henceforth exist only as a second-rate power in Europe at the pleasure of our new German Empire!" Reading these words, Albrecht had a brief twinge, remembering Count von Beckhaus's warning that such harsh peace terms would surely bring on more bitter wars between the two countries; but he was too preoccupied with the implications for his and Tessa's lives to give any prolonged thought to international politics. The war was over! Peace had been declared! How this would come to influence their relationship and future was all that mattered to him now, and he began pacing the barren little study trying to sort out his troubled thoughts.

When he and Tessa had finally reached Glaumhalle on January 5, after their arduous journey from Schloss Varn, they found conditions there far worse than either of them had anticipated. To Albrecht, who was returning after an absence of almost two years, it came as a greater shock. The Dowager Baroness Hildebrun had barricaded herself inside her gloomy manor, having terrorized her two servant girls into taking refuge with Hult and the livestock in *der Feste* (where they settled under circumstances of want, squalor, and dubious propriety). For five days the demented, crippled woman had rattled around in frigid isolation, completely unable to keep adequate fires burning in the stove and hearths to provide her body with warmth and nourishment, yet screeching noisy threats against anyone (real or imagined) approaching her dismal sanctuary. It had been only with great difficulty that Albrecht was able to cajole her into unbolting the door. It was some time before she recognized him as one of her sons and when she did, she continuously mixed him up with his older brother or her dead husband, in each case heaping them all with violent accusations or whining reproaches. However, she had instantly recognized Tessa, and greeted her with all the old insults. She even attempted to beat and shove her back out into the snow.

While Albrecht had no memory of his mother's being anything but an unloving selfish tyrant, he was stunned by the awful deterioration which had taken place since he had last seen her—and overwhelmed with pity for Tessa because of what she must have gone through. Within an hour of returning home, he came to the agonizing conclusion that his mother had gone mad and there was no alternative but to deal with her strictly before she did more harm to herself and others. With the help of a grimly mortified Prytz, they carried her bodily, struggling and snarling, up the stairs she had been unable to climb alone, and deposited her under a smother of blankets and comforters in her bed. Tessa vehemently objected to locking her in her bedroom, so Albrecht compromised by confiscating his mother's cane, without which she was unable to hobble more than a few feet on her ill-mended hip. He had thus confined her ever since, visiting her every day to make sure she was warm and nourished and as clean as possible under the circumstances, but resisting her stratagems to break out of her room.

Once the problem of restraining and caring for the Dowager Baroness Hildebrun had been taken care of in a practical, if somewhat ruthless, manner, Albrecht and Tessa threw themselves into the urgent business of improving living conditions for themselves and their servants at Glaumhalle. Since the great New Year's blizzard there had been no severe storms, only a few prolonged squalls which had added centimeters of snow to the already two-meter-deep covering over the entire countryside; but in between snowfalls, the temperature plunged to twenty degrees below freezing in spite of the sun burning through a misty gray blue overcast, and the searing cold was made so much more biting by a wind that whipped frosted spume off the moving drifts. *Der Feste* became uninhabitable because there was no way of adequately heating it or keeping the winds from penetrating its many open ports and embrasures. The water troughs froze solid inside it and even the deep well had a crust of ice which had to be broken by repeated poundings before a usable liquid slush could be drawn from it. Tessa made sure that the smithy's forge and several braziers were kept constantly burning in order to alleviate the suffering of her precious Schloss Varn stallion, Feldteufel, his newly aquired brood mares, and the cattle and pigs she had purchased. But the *people* had to be moved into the manor and lodged in those few rooms they could keep warm by supplementing the dwindling supply of coal with daily choppings of firewood. Hult, the foreman, and the two servant girls, Lena and Anna, not only resisted the move, but were obviously looking for a way to follow in the obliterated footsteps of the Polish laborers. It took much cajoling on the part of Tessa and Albrecht, and some less-subtle threats by Master Prytz to convince them to stay. Thus, an expedient way of living through these hard times had been arranged, recalling those days when progenitor Falkenhorst Junkers had been forced to share Glaumhalle's meager comforts in democratic intimacy with their humblest servitors and yeomen. Only the mad Dowager Baroness Hildebrun had privacy, all the others being thrown together in the kitchen and dining room during the day and allotted sleeping space at night, dormitory fashion, according to sex, in the two other rooms they were able to keep heated. This arrangement of enforced communal living left everybody's nerves in a constantly edgy state, yet they tried as best they could to be considerate of each other. Tessa, Lena, and Anna overcame their reserve to cooperate effectively in those housekeeping chores of cooking, mending, and cleaning; Albrecht, Prytz, and Hult shared equally in the heavier work, such as carrying coal, cutting firewood, caring for the livestock and, when the meat supply began to give out, grimly accomplishing an amateurish bloody butchery of one of the pigs. Their isolation from the outside world became complete, broken only by the postman's sporadic visits. Through him, Albrecht had sent a message to the doctor at Ols, asking him to come out to treat his sick mother, receiving a reply over a week later to the effect that impossible travel conditions and the pressing needs of other patients prevented him from answering the call at once, and advising in the meanwhile to "keep the Baroness Hildebrun warm, calm, and well fed with rich broths in her bed." That had been the most difficult chore of all, one which Albrecht and Tessa had to take on without much help from the others.

For the first time in two decades, there were packs of wolves prowling the district, driven by starvation out of the northern forests and emboldened by the scent of the animals sheltered inside *der Feste;* their eerie, threatening howls were unnerving at night, especially when Baroness Hildebrun awakened and answered them with inhuman cries of her own.

But for Tessa and Albrecht, the worst problem had been precipitated soon after their return when they discovered evidence which made them suspect, then quickly become convinced, that Gustaf von Falkenhorst was *dead*!

They had their first inkling of this when Prytz was furiously chastising Foreman Hult for letting the Polish laborers desert, for leaving the crippled Baroness Hildebrun to shift for herself alone in the manor during a five-day blizzard, and for allowing the postman to ride off to his death in the same storm. Hult sulkily excused himself on all counts. The Poles had sneaked away early one evening and were across the border before they were missed the next morning. The Dowager Baroness was at the time vigorous enough to lash out at everybody with tongue and cane, and after driving them all out of the house, had effectively discouraged any reentry. As for Bruno, he had refused to remain a minute longer at Glaumhalle than it took him to deliver that telegram from France.

"A telegram from France? For whom? About what?"

"For the young Baroness Tessa . . . about something happening to her husband, Baron Gustaf."

"Where is it, for God's sake?"

"I don't know," Hult shrugged. "I didn't stay while Baroness Hildebrun read it. But I think Anna did."

When pressed for information, all the befuddled and nervous Anna could recollect hearing was that Baron Gustaf and his entire troop had been wiped out in a fight with the French . . . that they were quite sure he was dead and were very sorry about it . . . but that Baroness Hildebrun had made such a commotion that she had not understood the details. After giving up on the sobbing Anna, Albrecht and Tessa next spent a painfully frustrating hour with the Dowager Baroness, trying to wheedle out of her the contents of the telegram and what she had done with it. At first it was impossible to penetrate her clouded mind with even the most carefully worded and patiently repeated questions. An angry blank stare coupled with muttered irrelevancies, complaints, and accusations was followed by vehement denials of ever having received a telegram or that the postman had visited Glaumhalle since before Christmas. Then she suddenly switched her story and with a horrifying addled mixture of glee and grief, admitted throwing him out of the house after "he sneaked in on me to steal my food and devil me about how my poor Gustaf was killed in the war by those rotten, pig-suckling Austrians!" When Albrecht reminded her with gently firm persistence that his father, the elder Gustaf von Falkenhorst, had been dead for over five years, she momentarily broke through her shadowed confusions and exclaimed with chilling indifference: "Oh well, then he must have been talking about Gustaf, my son . . . not Gustaf, my husband." In the next breath she again denied any knowledge of the matter and the desperate questions regarding what had happened to the telegram only brought on more senseless, disconnected protestations which threatened to escalate into a wild tantrum.

The next step had been to make a thorough search through every closet, drawer, and nook where Baroness Hildebrun might have hidden or lost the now-vital telegram. For the better part of a day they hunted through the dark musty rooms and halls, upstairs and down, carefully going over every place she could conceivably have reached on her game leg, then, when about to give up, suddenly finding it, or what was left of it. A torn scrap of the original sheet of yellow paper had fallen into a wide crack between the stove and wall of the kitchen. It read: *. . .nd deep sympathy of all his regimental comrades as well as my own very personal distress over this sad event. Kurt von Hardel, Colonel Com . . .*

As they read and reread it in stunned silence, it suddenly struck them both that it explained the strange behavior and words of the Ols postmaster when they had come upon him and his companions bringing back Bruno's frozen remains. The postmaster had known, obviously, the tragic news contained in the telegram. They did not even bother to search for more scraps since the demented Dowager Hildebrun had certainly torn it up and thrown the pieces into the stove.

From that moment on, Tessa and Albrecht had accepted the fact that Gustaf was dead.

"Well, it seems that I, too, have become a widow," Tessa had exclaimed in a dull, listless tone containing more resignation than grief. Allowing Albrecht to embrace her in a gesture meant to be comforting, she ruefully sighed: "Nothing came of our marriage together . . . nothing at all. I never even came to know him."

Albrecht was unable to fully express his own conflicting emotions. "Neither did I," he answered in a low, choked voice. "We were brothers, only three years apart. But it is almost as if a little-known stranger has died."

Tessa disengaged herself from him and stared into his face with sad, searching, but completely dry eyes. "Are you saying he has died unloved?" she asked.

"No!" he protested with a restrained anguish. "No. He and my father were very close. They loved each other, were proud of each other. And my mother loved him well as long as there was some reason left in her. And I loved him as best I could . . . at least well enough to try to understand him. I tried from our childhood until the last time I saw him in Versailles, only three weeks ago. But . . . ." He fell silent, shaking his head.

"But his *wife* did not love him, that's what you are leaving unsaid," Tessa bluntly prompted him.

"How could she be expected to?" he countered with intensity and again opening his arms to her. "You had no real courtship, no intimacy of married life, not even a honeymoon together . . . only an arrangement between families which circumstances robbed of any chance to turn into love."

She rested her head against his shoulder for a moment longer and sighed: "All that may be true . . . but my father once told me that there are other loves besides the storybook kind. I find them very difficult to discover and understand."

"They are. But the one kind does not exclude the other."

Although Gustaf had continued to trouble their innermost thoughts throughout the following weeks, they barely mentioned him. For one thing, they rarely found the necessary privacy; for another, they sensed each other's reticence toward the subject. While each was aware of the strictly practical aspects of the situation as it affected the von Falkenhorst and von Beckhaus estates, they were far too emotionally involved to give these more than cursory consideration. Albrecht immediately wrote two letters, one to Colonel Kurt Hardel of the Second

✠

Dragoon Guards Regiment at their last address in Villacoublay, and one to Prince General Eugene of Hanover, their last influential contact at Royal Headquarters in Versailles, asking for confirmation and details.

When five weeks had gone by without any answers, they became even more convinced that Gustaf was dead. Even so, there were none of the usual melancholy and morbid memories of a bereaved family. With all the hard work necessary to keep the household alive and functioning there was little time for brooding, only an occasional surreptitious caress or an understanding handclasp.

Now February had slipped into March, bringing a sudden and welcome thaw, but no change as yet in their isolation, dismal routine, and strain of unspoken, suppressed feelings. The manor no longer moaned under the constant thrusts of wild north winds; instead it had become filled with the small sounds of trickling, dripping water as the heavy snowcap on the roof and clusters of thick icicles hanging from the chimneys and eaves slowly, steadily melted away. That biting dry cold had been replaced by a raw dampness which was no easier to bear since it permeated every room except the kitchen, moisture filming the walls and adding to the dank, sour smell of clothing which could never be completely dried out. Fuel was still in very short supply. But a ray of bright warm sunshine poured through the window of the study, making it tolerable for Albrecht to sit there alone, his thoughts undisturbed by the inane chatter of the two servant girls. He moved the chair away from the desk in its cold, shadowed corner and sat by the window, bathing in the delicious warmth of the sunray while pensively staring down the slope of the hill which was showing widening patches of dull green between the glistening brightness of receeding snowdrifts. Gnarled apple trees were raising their naked branches toward the luminous sky, inviting the sun to kindle life into strings of pale emerald buds. Spring was on its way, and with spring would come new life and *peace*. With this prospect so clearly in evidence, decisions would have to be made to cast off the old, to break with the sorrows and trials of the past winter's war. But a new life, he decided, would be impossible for him without Tessa.

This thought took firm root as he brooded about her, reviewing their relationship through all the difficult trials of the past three months and finally admitting to himself without any equivocating reservations or rationalizations that he was deeply in love with his brother's widow. It must be resolved regardless of, and perhaps against, all the inflexible Lutheran-Prussian conventions imposed upon their class. He felt certain those conventions did not really apply in their case since her marriage could not have been consummated. Even the Pope of Rome had been known to declare such marriages annulled. But, of course, it might be much more difficult to make their narrowly puritanical society and fundamentalist church adopt anything approaching such a liberal attitude. Albrecht could not help grimacing as he visualized Bishop Putzkammer's reaction. Well, to hell with Bishop Putzkammer and all his ilk! The situation had to be faced and something had to be done about it at once . . . or Tessa and every chance of happiness for both of them would surely slip away for ever!

But when he heard the jingling of her spurs as she approached the study, his determination to declare his love suddenly wavered. What if she did not love him? If she were merely grateful for his help and company? If such a declaration would turn out a horrible embarrassment for both of them? If she laughed? . . . Then she was suddenly on the threshold, looking in on him with a face that was joyfully flushed from her exhilarating gallop through the brisk spring morning. Her boots and dress were splattered with mud, bronze strands of hair fell in disarray from beneath a white shawl, her freckles were startling flecks of gold on her glowing cheeks. To him she appeared as a revelation of girlish loveliness.

"What a wonderful ride we had!" she breathlessly exclaimed. "You should have come with us, Albrecht. The snow is really melting now and one can feel the breath of spring in the air. Absolutely feel the land shaking off winter. Our horses felt it too and Feldteufel was as frisky as a young colt. He's going to be a father, you know. Two of his mares are with foal! Oh, you should have come, Albrecht!"

"I see it's done you a lot of good to ride your horse again," he told her. "I would have liked to go with you, but I had some things to attend to, some important things to think over alone. You see, the postman came while you were gone."

Her cheerfulness was instantly marred by old tensions. "He did? Well, what sort of news did he bring us?"

"This, for one," he said and showed her the newspaper with the headlines proclaiming the peace treaty with France.

She glanced at it and observed rather stiffly: "So it's over! About time! It seems to me this war has dragged on far longer than necessary. What else?"

"Here is a letter for you, I think from your mother." He handed her the envelope which she turned over in her hands several times before slowly, reluctantly prying it open. Taking it to the sunlit window, she leaned lightly against his shoulder and unfolded the letter so he could easily follow the slanted writing as she read it aloud:

My Poor Darling: I am crushed by the news about your dear Gustaf and feel so, so desperately sorry for you. Sweet Prince Eugene wrote me about it from Versailles such a dear kind letter. He wants to do everything he can for me and you too and will find out and arrange everything to help. My heart bleeds for you all alone in that dreadful Silesia so far away from me and everything. Do take care of yourself and be brave. Don't worry about me as I am being so beautifully comforted in your Uncle Franz's house in lovely Vienna. The Piednichs have absolutely taken me back into the family and everywhere to all the receptions and balls although I'm still in mourning for poor Papa of course. Such music and dancing and lovely dresses and uniforms you can't imagine! I was even presented to Emperor Franz-Joseph. A very dear gracious Majesty he is, so very regal. You must think of joining me here soon or at least go back to Schloss Varn when the weather gets better. I worry so about you and beg you don't punish and be hard on yourself like poor Papa. You are too young for all this sorrow. Your everloving and devoted Mama.

When Tessa finished reading the letter, she could not help exclaiming with a melancholy smile: "Well, Mama hasn't changed a bit. She's just as confused and confusing as always."

Albrecht thought that for all its clumsy attempt to show concern and sympathy, the letter revealed a stupidly callous superficiality; but he did not comment upon that, stating instead with some irritation: "You'd think that Prince Eugene would have written *you* about Gustaf, not just your mother. That he'd at least have answered *my* letter by now."

"He's been very busy with the war and, as Mama writes, we are very far away from everything. She makes it quite clear what he did write her: that Gustaf was killed. We have already come to accept that." Tessa folded up the letter and put it back in its envelope, then asked in a matter-of-fact tone: "What else did the postman bring us?"

Albrecht fumbled among the pile of newspapers, found the

letter containing his orders from the Military Railroad Transport Authority, and handed it to her. "This one came for me and gives us very little time to decide what we must do."

As she read and reread it, all her self-control seemed to slip away from her. She was suddenly clinging to him, trembling with emotion, her voice rising in anguish: "But the war is over! Why should they order you back now? What need is there? . . . Unless you *want* to go. Do you?"

"Of course I don't want to go!" he exclaimed with choked intensity, slipping his arm around her waist and drawing her closer still. "The last thing in this world I want is to leave you now, my darling Tessa!"

"Then you will resign your appointment?" she pleaded. "Then you will stay?"

"If you wish it, my dearest," he managed to whisper. He was losing control over his own emotions and, in spite of his effort to check himself, tears were suddenly brimming out of his eyes as he pressed his cheek against hers.

"If I wish it?" she echoed in a quavering protest. "But what would I do without you? Don't you know how much I need you?" Then she felt his tears and became even more upset. "Oh, Albrecht! I'm making you cry! I'm being awfully selfish and callous. I should have understood that mother's letter would make you even sadder about your brother. I'm sad about him too, but . . ." She stifled some dry little sobs by pressing her face against his neck.

It took Albrecht a long moment before he could speak again, and when he did it was to say: "No, no, Tessa. I'm crying for *you*. For *us*. You see . . . it happens that I have fallen in love with you. Very, very much in love with you and . . . and I don't quite know what to do about it."

For an instant he felt her body tense against his and he responded by tightening his grip around her waist. But then she gave a loud gasp and yanked herself away from him with such an abrupt action that it froze him with fear of having offended her. Through tears which he could not stem, he glimpsed her face distorted in anguish, her eyes wide with surprise but staring past him toward the door. Twisting around in the chair to follow her gaze, he felt a twinge of humiliation as he saw Master Prytz's massive figure standing on the threshold, his bristly eyebrows drawn down in a coldly disapproving scowl.

"Excuse me!" the stablemaster rumbled with more irony than contrition. "I did not mean to intrude upon such a very private moment between you two. I hope it's not brought about by more bad news?"

Albrecht could not help testily retorting: "Well, you could

have announced yourself with a knock, Prytz!" A silly thing to say, he instantly realized, since the door to the hall was wide open. He covered up his embarrassment by pulling out a hand-kerchief and vigorously blowing his nose while at the same time mopping away his tears.

Tessa was quicker to recover her composure. She hastily picked up the *Breslauer Zeitung* and flashed its front page at the stablemaster. "The war is over, for one thing, Prytzie," she told him in carefully measured words. "For another, we have re-ceived condolences from my mother over Baron Gustaf's death. She had been informed about it by Prince Eugene himself."

"And is there official word addressed directly to you from the military authorities?" Prytz asked her, his eyes moving from the newspaper and spotting the envelope with the distinctive Imperial Headquarters seal.

As Albrecht was still blowing his nose and mopping his face, Tessa informed him: "No, the other letter contains orders from Versailles for Freiherr von Falkenhorst."

"Ah, then he will be returning to duty," Prytz exclaimed with evident satisfaction.

"No, he will not," Tessa firmly replied.

Prytz's scowl returned, deeper and darker. "He will not?"

Albrecht collected himself sufficiently to speak, although not with an entirely steady voice. "I don't really see why you should concern yourself so over my business, Master Prytz," he huffily scolded the stablemaster.

Prytz met his red-eyed anger with an unflinching, ice-cold stare. "I concern myself over the honor of two houses," he retorted. "The house of von Beckhaus und Varn, *and* that of von Falkenhorst since my lady now carries its name as her own."

Tessa gave a gasp of surprise. "Really, Prytzie! What is the matter with you?"

For a moment Albrecht was rendered speechless by the man's insolence. A certain coolness had developed between them over the past two months, but one which up to now had not been marked by outright insults. "You are overstepping your bounds, Master Prytz," he rasped at him. "I'll try to excuse it on the grounds of overzealousness . . . even a touch of winter madness from being snowed in too long here. But don't ever speak like that to us again. Do you understand me?" The answer was a stony silence, but Albrecht managed to ignore it and abruptly dismissed the subject by asking: "Was there something you wanted, Prytz?"

The stablemaster shifted his stare from Albrecht to the portrait of the elder Baron Gustaf hanging above the desk. His expression did not change except for a slight tremor of his chin which caused his moustache to twitch as he spoke through clenched teeth: "I came to advise the Freiherr that the thaw will soon make the snow too soft for sleds and the ground too muddy for wagons. If we are to bring in the firewood we need for next week, we should drive into the forest and cut it this afternoon."

Albrecht nodded. "A good idea. You and Hult hitch up a sled. I will join you in a few minutes. Thank you."

When Prytz had vanished down the dark tunnel of the hall, Tessa shook her head after him in perplexity and exclaimed: "I simply don't know what made him act so rudely."

"He heard what I said to you and it shocked him," Albrecht replied with a disconsolate shrug. "His kind would never understand. Nor would many others of our kind, for that matter. That's what I meant when I said I don't quite know what to do about the love I feel for you, my Tessa."

She was suddenly smiling again and looked into his unhappy face with an excited glitter in her eyes. Her hands reached out and shyly touched his cheeks with a tentative caress. "It is enough for me to know you love me, dear Albrecht, and that you will not leave me. That is all that matters. The rest we shall deal with as we must."

Albrecht's heart leaped in his chest, but he resisted the impulse to passionately embrace and kiss her. Instead he gently, tenderly kissed only her hands and the insides of her wrists, causing her to give a strange low cry of pleasure. Then she pulled away from him and exclaimed with a warm coy humor he had never known in her before: "How did we ever get into this situation, you and I? Really quite scandalous. But then, I suppose . . . we just couldn't help it."

Spring thaws started earlier in the Jura district of Eastern France than in Prussian Silesia, but here it was an even slower process of melting away the mantle of an exceptionally hard winter. By the first days of March, the north slopes of the hills were still covered by residual layers of slushy snow and in the deep valleys, swollen streams roared and rattled with broken ice floes butting their way through rocky rapids. The small farming and vineyard communities scattered over this rugged country seemed to be prolonging their hibernation, waiting as it were for better, safer times before venturing forth to till their soil and pasture their scrawny flocks of sheep and goats. Besides the unsettled weather, changing one day to the next, from balmy sunshine to blustery cold snaps laced with snowflurries, there were Uhlan patrols marauding along lanes and roads made impassable to anything but their sturdy, sure-footed horses. It had been reliably reported that these German cavalrymen did not hesitate to requisition livestock, seed grain, even precious cuttings from the vineyards, not to mention kegs of immature wine which they guzzled as indiscriminately as any aged vintage they happened upon. So it was best to lie low behind closed shutters and not draw attention to oneself by starting early planting or grafting new vines—especially if one had daughters in the house between the ages of thirteen and thirty, or a young wife who had not already become pregnant during the winter.

The number of Uhlans infesting the district was considerably exaggerated in the reports passed from village to village, partially because of the natural inclination to inflate one's own importance by inflating the power of one's enemy, partially because of the Uhlans' ability to cover a great deal of territory swiftly and methodically. However, there were, in fact, only three squadrons of them based at Pontarlier, some seven kilometers from the Swiss frontier. Including a few service troops and administrative personnel, this meant a force of somewhat less than five hundred men charged with the security of three hundred square miles of still-hostile countryside.

A little over a month ago the Jura had been the scene of the last large-scale military operations of the war, when a German army under General von Manteuffel and a much larger French force commanded by General Bourbaki attempted to maneuver each other into a decisive battle. Both sides were nearly paralyzed by deep snows and temperatures dropping to twenty degrees below freezing, both hampered by delayed, unrealistic, and conflicting orders from their respective distant Headquarters, both trying to cope with shattered morale as their troops floundered under the most appalling conditions from one untenable position to the next, neither able to come seriously to grips with the other. Only fierce little skirmishes where the blood literally froze as it flowed (with one gruesome exception occurring when French and German combatants were roasted to death as they fought hand to hand through the halls of a burning castle), but no decisive battle. After this final campaign, eighty thousand surviving French soldiers had streamed through Pontarlier on February 1, a frozen, starving, disorderly mob trudging toward the Swiss frontier post where they dumped their arms and were interned by their neutral neighbor. They dragged with them their General Bourbaki, dazed and half-blind from a severe head wound which he had inflicted upon himself while trying to expiate his honor by suicide. His opposite number, General von Manteuffel, although physically unscathed except for frostbitten ears and nose, had also passed through Pontarlier in a state of acute depression and injured professional pride. As his superior General Helmuth von Moltke had caustically hinted in dispatches from his palatial office in Versailles, he had failed to gain a signal victory for German arms and the marshal's baton he coveted would likely never be his as the war had fizzled out in an uneasy armistice. But von Manteuffel, one of the most intelligent and sophisticated of Prussian generals, did not nurture his humiliation by remaining in the area with his suffering troops. Having correctly assessed that Bourbaki's army had neither the will nor the power to break out of internment to resume operations in an area where the local population was sick of both armies, he departed northward to regroup his forces between Belfort and Strasbourg to cover von Moltke's overextended supply and communication lines to Germany, leaving behind only a skimpy force of Uhlans to occupy the Jura.

Major Kraft Brandeis, a tough, pragmatic cavalryman from the East Prussian town of Elbing, had been made commandant and chief tactical officer in the modest German headquarters of Pontarlier. He exercised his duties with efficient self-confidence, sending out daily forage and security patrols which he often led in person, and keeping a sharp surveillance over the Swiss border, behind which he knew the eighty thousand inadequately guarded French soldiers were seething in internment, and otherwise managing by simple draconian measures to keep the sullen population intimidated and under control. Brandeis was a born leader who enjoyed wielding authority but who lacked the imagination to worry about the consequences of finding oneself heavily outnumbered and isolated deep in enemy territory. Pontarlier reminded him of his own Elbing with its medieval structures, narrow winding streets, and nearby dominating fortress-castle of Château la Cluse; the surrounding terrain and severe winter weather were only slightly more rugged than what he had known in East Prussia. He felt quite at home in these forbidding surroundings, entirely competent in his difficult assignment, and completely undaunted by its threatening aspects of danger. The only thing that bothered him since General von Manteuffel had left him in charge was the sudden unannounced arrival of another German general who rode into the town without troops or respectable staff and escort, a strange corpulent individual seeming as ill suited as he was ill equipped to be an officer of such exalted rank. As a matter of fact, Major Brandeis had initially refused to believe that he was a general at all. But he was forced to change his mind after scrutinizing his orders to accept him as the senior officer present and provide him and his ragtag retinue with the most comfortable billets available in Pontarlier. Those orders, while somewhat vague, identified the bearer as Leutnant General Count Eugene von Kleisenberg. They were signed by Crown Prince Frederick William himself. That this mysterious general was actually the deposed Prince Eugene of Hanover he did not find out until three weeks later.

General von Kleisenberg did nothing to interfere with Major Brandeis's conduct of his duties, but neither did he consult or enlighten him regarding his mission to locate and obtain the release of German prisoners of war still being held by the French in spite of the armistice. He had arrived with two wagons and a donkey cart transporting twelve German and seven French soldiers, all in too deplorable a condition to be able to shift for themselves, a French Army surgeon whom he had somehow captured and impressed into his service, his own batman, and a disheveled, frostbitten troop of eight assorted dragoons and Uhlans who had joined him along the way after becoming lost or separated from their units. In Pontarlier he immediately requisitioned a schoolhouse and enough beds to create a small hospital for the care of his charges; his own headquarters and billet he established in the large villa Brandeis had chosen for him, occupying only three of its ten rooms, but those with a splendid view of Château la Cluse and the distant, snow-capped mountains of Switzerland. He visited the patients in his hospital every day, making firm demands for their care and comfort, regardless of whether they were German or French. But he spent most of his time ranging out over the surrounding countryside looking for more, riding along with his wagons and small escort under flags of truce and the Red Cross, probing into the hills far beyond areas normally patrolled by Major Brandeis's Uhlans. He rode out in fair weather or foul, was usually gone for ten or twelve hours at a stretch, sometimes overnight, and seemed quite pleased when all this trouble resulted in bringing in a total of seven more sick and wounded Frenchmen and just two half-dead Germans. Brandeis was irritated at his independent ways and uneasy lest the General get himself killed in the area under his jurisdiction. "Your Excellency should be aware," he warned, "that I do not have enough troopers to cover more than the main roads and villages of the district. Beyond them the country is still infested with *francs-tireurs*, bandits who disregard the armistice or haven't even heard of it."

"But, my dear fellow, they are precisely the people I am here to deal with," Eugene told him with a deprecating gesture of pudgy hands. "By the way, my hospital needs more coal. The weather is still quite chilly, you know. See to it, will you please?"

During the last week of February it had become known in Pontarlier that General Bourbaki's army had taken with them into Switzerland a number of German prisoners—over two hundred, it was rumored—some as willing to get out of the war as were their captors, others taken against their will. General von Kleisenberg immediately acted upon this information. Taking off the quasi-military garb he had been wearing on his expeditions deep into *franc-tireur* territory (sheepskin coat covering his tunic, woolen muffler wound around his cap and collar), he put on his best field uniform, that of a Hussar general. And riding up to the frontier post, he there demanded a conference with the highest Swiss official available. This turned out to be a slightly nervous, but stubborn, Colonel who refused to discuss the matter without consulting his government. But when Eugene showed the Colonel his orders signed by the Crown Prince of the victorious new Empire of Germany, the Colonel's nervousness increased and his intransigence lessened to the point where he agreed to talk "in principle." They talked in principle all that night, Eugene pressing the doubtful legality of Switzerland's interning German prisoners who had been forced across the border, and the inhumane aspects of so treating wounded and sick men. The Colonel refused to admit to any legal errors in his position, but around four o'clock in the morning gave in on the humanistic point, agreeing to return the sickest German internees at once. By the following noon, a weary, but triumphant, General von Kleisenberg rode back into Pontarlier at the head of a hastily assembled ambulance train which delivered eighty-two more patients to his makeshift hospital.

Major Brandeis was impressed, but not particularly pleased, with General von Kleisenberg's accomplishment. For one thing it required him to aggravate the barely pacified town population by requisitioning eighty-two more beds and bedding from their households; for another, there was the matter of finding rations and medication for eighty-two additional sick and starving bodies. The General then made the situation more difficult by backing up his insolent French surgeon's request that nursing help be forcibly recruited—nuns, midwives, harlots, housewives, any able-bodied women between fifteen and seventy able to make themselves useful in the now overcrowded wards of the schoolhouse. Uhlan troopers had to be pulled off vital patrols covering the precarious lines of communication in order to make a house-to-house search, ferreting out unoccupied beds, hoarded foodstuffs, and women whose presence was not vital to the survival of young children or elderly parents. Enough beds were collected to take care of not only the present glut of patients but also those which the energetic General Kleisenberg might produce during the next few days. (He had warned Brandeis that he expected to negotiate successfully the release of *all* 207 remaining internees in Switzerland before March 1.) The unearthing of hidden comestibles had been less rewarding: 300 kilograms of flour, 150 of assorted hams, sausages, and tinned beef, 96 jars of preserved fruits, and 1842 bottles of wine and liqueurs. More disappointing was the resentful collection of women which the Uhlan press-gang had routed out of the cellars and garrets of Pontarlier's shuttered houses. They were herded into the school playground for General Kleisenberg's and Dr. Polignac's inspection, most of them either decrepit old crones, with hate in their eyes, or girl-children too terrified to be of use. Among the few mature, able-bodied ones were two nuns of a contemplative order who volunteered their prayers and whatever menial tasks they could perform in the hospital. But then Dr. Polignac spotted among them one he knew to be an experienced nurse and called upon her by name:

"Ah, Mme Hunsecker! What a pleasant surprise to find you here. We can again rely on your excellent talents."

Louise Hunsecker lowered the shawl with which she had been trying to hide her face, but she made no move to step forward as a volunteer. "I am trying to travel home to Alsace," she answered him. "I am only here because I was delayed by the war and weather. I do not wish to become associated with you in another disgraceful business like Abbey Saint-Luze, Dr. Polignac."

Eugene von Kleisenberg stepped closer, looking at her with sharp interest. "Madame, what do you know about Abbey Saint-Luze?" he politely inquired.

"Enough to turn my stomach every time I remember it," she answered lowering her head and frowning at the slush in which she was standing.

"Mme Hunsecker did her best to act as my nurse there," Polignac explained shortly.

"And you lost most of your patients," Eugene said with an accusing inflection in his perfect French, but without addressing either one in particular.

When Louise Hunsecker maintained a guilty silence, Polignac stated flatly on her behalf: "Madame is not to blame for what happened at Saint-Luze. You were there and saw for yourself the conditions she faced. Which we *all* faced. And I remind you, General, that Saint-Luze was not officially a hospital. It was a prison."

"A charnel house for which all among you disclaim responsibility," Eugene retorted with a flash of angry disgust. "But we shall see. Since we now have two prime suspects in the crime as well as several surviving victims to bear witness . . . we shall see who is responsible and who is not." He let the unmistakable threat sink in during a tense silence, broken only by frantic whispered prayers from the two nuns. Then he said to Louise with reassuring courtesy: "There will be no Abbey Saint-Luze here, Madame. If you are a good nurse, you will be given every opportunity to prove it. And, by the way, will be paid one franc a day for your work. Dr. Polignac will show you what must be done."

"In other words, I have no choice," Louise said.

"I regret that you have not. But if you need a balm for your patriotism, then know that we are also caring for some sick Frenchmen here. We are Christian soldiers, not barbarians."

Along with the two nuns and two other women chosen for their hefty physiques, Louise was taken into the schoolhouse whose halls and five classrooms were packed with almost one hundred bed patients. She was recognized at once by the survivors of the infamous abbey, and Eugene was relieved at the friendly, even enthusiastic, greetings she received. There were none who did not remember her and she remembered *them*, many by name. Inquiring in fluent German about their particular ills, she became genuinely distressed when she realized how few had survived. "I shall try to make up for your suffering," she told them and without further reluctance, put herself and the other women to work.

Eugene watched her efforts with mounting satisfaction. "Well, it seems that you've at least got yourself an effective chief nurse," he told Dr. Polignac. "Maybe between the two of you, you'll be able to relieve some of the misery here!"

"We are not barbarians either," Polignac snapped back. "Nor are we miracle-working saints, my General. So don't expect anything superhuman."

"I'll try to adjust my expectations to your limited capacity," Eugene replied and lumbered off to resume his hunt for more patients.

One survivor from Abbey Saint-Luze whom Louise did not find in the schoolhouse-hospital was Leutnant Baron Gustaf von Falkenhorst. After only four days as a patient there, Dr. Polignac had pronounced him recovered enough to vacate valuable bed space and convalesce in General von Kleisenberg's requisitioned villa. Eugene's regular adjutant, Captain Kringle, had fallen ill at the very outset of their rigorous mission and had been sent back to Versailles, so he appointed Gustaf as temporary replacement without any intention of making heavy demands upon his weakened energies. It was a convenient sinecure, a kindly gesture, but at the same time not entirely an unselfish one. As soon as he had arrived in Pontarlier, Eugene wrote a letter to Antoinette von Beckhaus, informing her that he had found and rescued her son-in-law and that, under his care, he was recovering from wounds and a prolonged ordeal as a prisoner of the infamous *francs-tireurs*. The letter was, of course, intended to maintain a solid contact with her by playing upon her oversensitive emotions. *It is gratifying to me*, he had written, *that in all the miseries of this campaign, I have been given this opportunity to relieve a part of the suffering and anxiety you bear, to give some expression of my great affection for the von Beckhaus family and for you, my dear Countess!*

However, Gustaf failed to take more than a perfunctory interest in his very light duties (on the Doctor's advice he was for the time being confined indoors). Nor did he respond to frequent attempts by Eugene to establish something closer than a purely formal relationship. During their meals together, he made easy conversation difficult by sitting stiffly at table, speaking and answering questions with a minimum of words, frequently falling into long, gloomy silences. During the day when he had nothing to do (which was most of the time) he would sit alone in his room, sometimes trying to write letters to Tessa which he burned unfinished; more often, staring for hours on end out the window at the bleak ramparts of Château la Cluse; at night he restlessly paced the floor, or, if he slept, tossed and turned in his bed, jabbering his anguish with far greater eloquence than he would allow himself when awake. Although his body was healing, his spirits were not, and Eugene soon diagnosed his troubles as acute mental depression over what he considered his failures as a model Prussian officer. This was confirmed to him when he overheard Gustaf muttering absently to himself: "How can I explain to my family, to my regiment, what happened to me? . . ."

Eugene startled him by answering in a firm, fatherly way: "That will be easy enough once you accept the fact that your childish notions about the glories of war have been stripped from you. It is a matter of facing realities, my boy! One being that there are other admirable forms of bravery besides that of charging into battle and cleaving heads to the blare of trumpets. Another is that the glories are an illusion, a false glitter on the surface of a deeply demeaning and brutal business which tries the souls of all but beasts among men. You and I should thank God we have survived it all with body, spirit, and honor reasonably intact."

Gustaf's face became animated by a rare sardonic smile as he replied: "Perhaps an acceptable rationale for generals, Excellency, but hardly for leutnants." He then instantly reverted back to his dull introspective brooding.

"Stop punishing yourself!" Eugene admonished him with mounting impatience. "And let me balm your pride with this: I thought well enough of your performance to recommend you for the Iron Cross." He hoped this announcement would snap Gustaf out of his depression.

"*You* are recommending me for the Iron Cross, Excellency?" he asked with a vacantly incredulous stare. "Why? For what? And to whom? Surely not my Regimental Commander who lost a whole squadron because of me?"

Eugene had actually already written and sent off the citation to Crown Prince Frederick's Headquarters along with the reports he had conscientiously dispatched by courier every other day since installing himself at Pontarlier. There had been no return communications from Versailles, but he attributed this to the very tenuous, overextended courier service and the Prince's preoccupation with more important affairs of state. He still counted upon an eventual favorable response and confidently assured Gustaf: "My dear fellow, your Colonel von Hardel lost over half his regiment in one way or another during this damned war. So don't worry about him. As it happened, you performed your exploits when fate twice removed you from his control and more or less into mine. At Vionville and later at Abbey Saint-Luze, remember? Very well! So, yes, *I* made the recommendation directly to His Imperial Highness in Versailles. Quite properly so, I may add."

Gustaf dazedly shook his head and muttered: "I am not worthy, I'd rather not accept. . . ."

"Not accept?" Eugene exploded. "For heaven's sake, why not, man? Remember that your father-in-law was awarded the Iron Cross just for getting himself murdered by the *francs-tireurs*. So why shouldn't you get it for saving yourself and eleven men after falling into their clutches, and for performing a vital, though tedious, duty in a crucial battle? No! If His Imperial Highness agrees with my recommendation, there will be no question of your not accepting. If you feel unworthy, then adjust and make yourself so. Stop moping around and feeling sorry for yourself."

Gustaf swallowed hard, managed a wry, barely courteous

response: "Yes, I shall try, Excellency. Thank you. I am sure you mean well." With that he excused himself and retired to his room, bitterly recalling the promise he had made to Tessa when they had parted last July. How horribly different everything had turned out from his expectations. Even if he could return to her with an Iron Cross, what would it be worth? *Really* worth?

Two more dreary, dull days passed, during which Eugene bundled himself into his sheepskin coat and woolen muffler to continue his search for German survivors in the Jura, but without success. On February 28 he rode back to the frontier post to resume negotiations with the local Swiss commandant, who this time received him with greater cordiality. By a quirk of wartime communication the senior Swiss officer was better informed about current events in Versailles than was his opposite number across the border in Pontarlier; he seemed delighted to announce that a provisional peace treaty had been signed between Germany and France two days earlier, confirming the accuracy of this report by his own eagerness to be rid of his German internees as quickly as possible. All the formalities were concluded by the morning of March 1, and, making good his somewhat rash prediction, Eugene marched into Pontarlier that afternoon in a freezing rain, leading a small army of wasted, ragged, but exuberant soldiers of various Germanic states—the first and last army he was to command in this, or any other, war. He also brought with him the latest editions of Swiss newspapers from Berne and Neuchâtel whose front pages he plastered on the walls of the Kommandantur where all could read about the final triumph of Germany and the humiliation of France. By evening, the only sober Germans in Pontarlier were those too sick to celebrate, Major Brandeis (who refused to consider the war ended without official notification from higher authority), and Gustaf von Falkenhorst. Neither of these officers could enter into the spirit of the victory party which General von Kleisenberg laid on in his villa and which continued far into the night. Both excused themselves from the revelries as soon as possible, the one to ponder the problems of evacuating his small force and over two hundred assorted casuals and casualties, the other to brood over the shambles of his career.

But with the dawning of the following drizzly day, Gustaf was finally forced to rouse himself out of his melancholy torpor. When he reported to Eugene that morning, he was surprised to find him lying, a mountain of suffering, beneath the quilted layers of his bedding. Besides having overly fortified himself with cognac during last night's celebration, he had caught a severe chill while riding back from Switzerland through yesterday's sleeting weather. "Now that the war is over, I'm allowing myself to become a casualty," he feebly croaked at his adjutant. "You will have to overcome your own ailments enough to help me do what remains to be done here." After clearing his throat with some painful coughs, he gasped a series of orders to be accomplished before noon: The billets of the released internees were to be inspected for adequacy of shelter and their rations made as generous as possible; their earliest evacuation to Strasbourg should be expedited through Major Brandeis and their names, ranks, units, along with physical condition of each man tabulated and forwarded to General von Manteuffel's headquarters by courier; and, most important, the now-swamped facilities of the makeshift hospital had to be made as bearable as conditions would allow. It was the mention of this last item that moved Gustaf to suggest: "It seems to me, Excellency, that you yourself are in need of medical attention. Dr. Polignac should be summoned to attend you."

Eugene snorted a disparaging laugh. "That cantankerous quack? He's probably drowned his sorrows in the same brew with which we celebrated our victory. But very well! Send him to me after he's taken care of our more-seriously sick. First things first!" He became convulsed by a series of violent sneezes, making the bed shake and creak as if it were about to collapse under his heaving weight, weakly waving Gustaf on his way as Anton, his orderly, rushed into the room with a cold compress for his aching head and a heated warming pan for his shivering body.

Gustaf left Eugene with his spirits suddenly revitalized by a strange combination of sympathy, contempt, and relief over at last being called upon to make himself useful to a man whom he fundamentally despised, yet to whom he owed his very life. It was also his first opportunity to break away from the confines of this oppressively gloomy villa. Therefore, he lost no time in setting forth upon his assignment in spite of having to wear a uniform assembled from the garrison's Intendantur Sergeant's salvaged garments, armed with a pistol and saber retrieved from the French weaponry littering the road to Switzerland, and riding a scrawny French cavalry horse from the stable of remounts captured by Major Brandeis's Uhlans. He was escorted by another scarecrow, a Hussar trooper, who had become separated from his unit during the last days of the Jura campaign and had fortunately been able to join General von Kleisenberg's peculiar roster of orphans.

As they rode through the narrow streets of Pontarlier, Gustaf felt invigorated by the raw cold air in spite of the depressing atmosphere of street after deserted street. Those inhabitants who had not fled across the border with General Bourbaki's army remained out of sight behind closed shutters, occasional wisps of smoke betraying occupants huddled close to their hearths. The silence was only broken by the clatter of their horses' hoofs and the pervading drip and trickle of thawing icicles and snowcaps still clinging to the roofs. He first visited the Kommandantur, located in the town hall on the half-flooded main square, where Major Brandeis responded to General von Kleisenberg's orders with his usual harassed irritability. Yet, he insisted everything be run on a war footing and acidly observed: "I can't take a chance on either the enemy or my General von Manteuffel not having read the Swiss newspapers!" Gustaf next rode down to the railroad station where the more able-bodied among the released internees were billeted, 170 of them crowded into the small stationhouse and an adjacent, unheated freight shed. Most of them had lost the initial euphoria which followed their deliverance and had adopted a stoic forbearance, only a few complaining that conditions had been much better in their Swiss internment camp. Although looting and "midnight requisitions" were strictly forbidden, a lot of wine, some sacks of potatoes, and supplementary firewood (looking suspiciously like chopped-up furniture) had been obtained by enterprising forage parties. In the interest of morale, Gustaf only mildly reproached these sorely tried men and encouraged them to think about their eventual repatriation. The last stop of his tour of inspection, a distasteful one as he had developed a sickening aversion to makeshift hospitals, was Pontarlier's elementary school.

The schoolyard was a quagmire of mud churned up by the many ambulances and supply wagons which had made deliveries there during the past weeks. Two field kitchens were steaming near the entrance to the brick building, tended by army cooks busily preparing the next meal for the patients inside. Tattered urchins were standing hopefully nearby in a drift of wet snow, likely evicted students of the school whose parents had lacked the means of escaping the occupation and, judging from the pinched hungry look of their children, were unable to feed them adequately. Gustaf averted his eyes from them as he rode through the mud toward the schoolhouse, staring instead at a conveyance which he recognized: Dr. Polignac's donkey cart. The same scrawny, but incredibly tough, little beast who had hauled its irascible master up the steep road to Abbey Saint-Luze many times through the worst of last winter was still hitched up, waiting to haul him still farther with all its stubborn, asinine faithfulness. The Uhlan trooper escorting Gustaf thoughtfully spurred ahead, leaned down over the donkey, picked up its reins and dragged it and the cart away from the steps so that Gustaf could dismount without muddying his boots. As he started for the door, Dr. Polignac emerged, carrying his medical field kit, haversack, a rolled blanket, fully dressed for travel in his red kepi and faded blue greatcoat with its many missing buttons. The grizzled French Army surgeon and young Prussian cavalry officer, who looked hardly less shabby, contemplated each other in silence for a moment before launching into an exchange that quickly became acrimonious in tone despite their inability to fully understand each other's language:

"Where are you going, Doctor, and on whose authority?"

"*Das Krieg ist fini, Monsieur Leutnant.* You won. We lost. Now peace has been declared—*Friede, ferstehen Sie!* So I'm no longer your prisoner and am leaving to lick my own wounds and those of my countrymen. *Adieu!*"

"*Non,* Doctor!" Gustaf firmly objected, blocking his way to the donkey cart. "The war is not officially over—*pas fini encore.*"

"*Mais oui c'est fini!* You got our gold and Alsace and Lorraine, but not all France and Frenchmen. Certainly not me. Get out of my way. *Raus'mit!*"

Gustaf refused to budge. "*Non!* You have no right as a prisoner to leave when you please, no right as a doctor to abandon your patients. Besides, the General von Kleisenberg has sent for you. *Le général von Kleisenberg vous demande.*"

"*Le général von Kleisenberg?* Bah! He can demand no more of me. Tell him thank you for his considerations, but now we are done with each other. *Viele danke aber nicht mehr . . . Auf Wiedersehen!*" He sprang sideways with surprising agility, sidestepping out of Gustaf's reach, and made a dash for his cart.

"Halt!" Gustaf shouted, moving his right hand toward the holster on his belt.

"I will not halt!" Polignac shouted back with obdurate defiance. But the steps were slick with mud and he slipped, lost his balance, and pitched headlong into the brown ooze between his donkey's legs. The animal merely turned its head and looked down at him with a sad, reproachful look and a flick of its drooping ears. The cooks working the field kitchens burst into mocking laughter, as did all the urchins except one, a girl older than her companions, who gave a cry of rage and ran forward to help the fallen French medical officer. But before she could reach him, he had picked himself and his soiled baggage up, and though covered from head to boots in mud, managed to preserve a certain pathetic dignity. Without bothering to clean himself off, he quickly threw his things into the cart, scrambled aboard, grabbed the reins and urged his donkey forward with a sharp command: *"Uh-ho, cocotte! En avant!"*

The little urchin-girl encouraged him on with shrill yells of: *"Allez! Allez! Décampez!"* and then turned her full wrath on Gustaf with an outburst of insults which would have done credit to a prostitute from the Paris slums. The cooks became absolutely convulsed over her performance and faces of ambulatory patients, attracted by the commotion, appeared grinning in the windows of the schoolhouse.

Gustaf stopped his motion to draw his pistol. The Doctor, now energetically driving his donkey cart toward the open gate of the schoolyard, could not be allowed to flout his authority so openly. Ignoring both the laughter of the cooks and abuse from the ragamuffin, he called out to his escorting Hussar trooper with as much control as he could muster: "Take Dr. Polignac to General von Kleisenberg's billet on rue de l'Est. Deliver him in person to His Excellency and stand by there for further orders. Use whatever force necessary to do this."

The trooper, who had been watching the scene with a mixture of amazement and suppressed mirth, came alive and spurred his horse after the cart; he pulled alongside it and leaned over to take the reins away from Polignac. There was a brief struggle in which the Hussar received a smart crack against his helmet from the whip, but he yanked the reins out of the doctor's grip, then moved ahead with them so that he had full control over the donkey and cart, pulling them on behind him. At this, Polignac gave up and allowed himself to be led away, but sat erect on his seat with head high and arms crossed over his chest. An erratic barrage of dirty snowballs flew after him, hurled by the urchins who were at last inspired by the brave, noisy protests of their female companion to demonstrate their own resentment. While they were aiming at the Hussar, most of their missiles hit the wrong target or none at all.

Gustaf swore and muttered to himself: "Disgraceful! One damned disgraceful situation after the other!" But worse awaited him. When he turned around to enter the schoolhouse, he found himself facing a woman who had occupied his thoughts far more than Tessa—indeed haunted him for all the past painful weeks. The sight of her startled him into gasping: "My God! Is it you? Really you?"

"After the way you treated our doctor, I can't imagine we are acquaintances," Louise Hunsecker coldly replied in German. She did not recognize Gustaf. When she cared for him at Abbey Saint-Luze he had been a scarred, burned, wasted scarecrow—one of many who all looked alike in their misery—his features obscured by an unkempt growth of beard.

Gustaf blinked and stared at her, trying to connect fading memories with the shock of this moment. He felt a resurgence of old agonies, but also a peculiar throbbing excitement. "You are the Alsatian lady . . . Mme Hunsecker . . . aren't you. You must be she!"

"Yes. I am Louise Hunsecker." She gave him a hard puzzled look, now probing her own memories for a clue to his identity. "But who are you?"

He blurted out his name and when it failed to register, stepped closer and reminded her with flustered eagerness: "But I am the Prussian leutnant you nursed last January at the abbey. The one with burns, and a wounded neck and shoulder, lung fever, and half-dead from cold and starvation. Remember? The *francs-tireurs* had ambushed and taken me prisoner near Versailles. They dragged me halfway across France without medical treatment or food or shelter from the cold. Then they delivered me to that brute of a major in charge of your prison where I almost died. Remember? You were there and you were kind, comforting me with German words and treating my sickness and . . . I only vaguely remember this . . . you even tried to keep me from freezing with the warmth of your own body. And. . . ."

"Oh!" she gasped, her hand flying to her mouth. "Oh! You are *that* one!"

He felt himself turning scarlet and became even more flustered. "Yes . . . but . . . well, you see, I really was very sick at the time," he clumsily tried to reassure her. "Really too sick to take advantage of you, Madame. But . . ."

She recovered from her surprise and was suddenly laughing at him, not cruelly, but with genuine amusement. "Don't worry about it, Leutnant von Falkenhorst! Neither of us was compromised. Now that you've recalled the incident for me, I remember it more clearly than you. Don't think for an instant that it was anything but a desperate act to keep you alive." Her laughter faded, but not the beauty of her face which became sadly reproachful, rather than angry, as she jabbed an accusing finger at him. "You *are* alive, by the way, not so much because of me as because of the French doctor you just humiliated with such rudeness. He scraped up the last of his medicines to heal your wounds and fever. And it was actually *he* who suggested the method I used to keep you from freezing to death. You can be sure I'd never have thought of it myself."

Gustaf felt his blush turn into a steady burn. The ragamuffin at the foot of the steps had fallen silent only to contort her face into brazen mimicry; the cooks by the field kitchens were no longer laughing, but watching with sly grins. With a gesture meant to be casual, he took her by the arm and led her inside. "Why me?" he asked as soon as they were out of sight from the eyes in the yard.

"As I remember it, you seemed most likely to respond to what little help we could give," Louise grimly recollected. "So many others were too far gone. In your case there was enough hope to make the effort worthwhile. That's why *you*, Herr Leutnant. But perhaps we were wrong."

"I hope not," Gustaf lamely said, letting go of her arm. They stopped inside the long, dark corridor running the full length of the schoolhouse, which was clogged with occupied beds lined head to foot along the walls. There was a sickening tinge of gangrene in the fetid air which revived his memories of the Abbey Saint-Luze. But Louise smelled more strongly of soap and carbolic acid—clean and almost pleasant by comparison. "For all I may owe you and the doctor, I still have my duty to perform," he tried to explain to her. "You as a woman might find this difficult to understand. But Polignac as a soldier should accept the rules of war, not to mention those of his profession. From the way he is acting, it seems to me he considers himself above both those obligations. So how can you expect me to treat him with polite respect?"

"He has his faults as a doctor and soldier, but if he were a man who shirked his obligations, you would be quite dead today," she softly retorted. "And if you had taken the trouble to question him about it, you would know he had good unselfish reasons for leaving here."

"Whatever they are, this is where he is most urgently needed."

Louise gave a despairing shrug. "I have long since learned the uselessness of arguing against inflexible Prussian opinions. Like the pennants on your Uhlan lances, everything is black and white to you. No colors or nuances, no subtle shades accepted. So all I will tell you is that Doctor Polignac did not leave without giving me very precise instructions about the care of each patient during his absence."

Everything she said to him seemed to contain barbs which hurt. So he was driven against his will to fall back on the protection of a more impersonal, official tone. "As adjutant to General von Kleisenberg, I am here to make certain those patients are being decently treated. Are they?"

"As far as it is possible, considering that there is still a shortage of medical supplies and wholesome food. Visit them and see for yourself, Herr Leutnant." She moved ahead to the door of the nearest ward and beckoned him to enter it. Before he could reach the threshold, she alerted the occupants by calling inside with a forced cheerfulness: "Your attention, boys! Here's a nice Prussian officer paying a call on you."

An odd assortment of twenty-five beds were jammed into a room designed to hold no more than that number of children's desks. Of eight men able to shuffle around on their own, four were seated in the sunlight of the windowsills, four huddled around the heat of a pear-shaped black stove, all with blankets thrown over their emaciated shapes. Seven others were propped up in their beds, looking like living, bearded cadavers; however, their sunken eyes glittered with curiosity as they focused upon the door. The remaining ten were no more than inert shapes in their bedding, too sick to take notice of their surroundings. A nun was hunched in silent vigil next to one of these whose blanket flattened out even with the mattress where his feet should have been; her head covered by its gull-winged hat bobbed faintly as she mopped the man's pain-racked face with one hand and fingered the beads of her rosary with the other. The smell of gangrene was strong and the flush of Gustaf's face began rapidly fading into the pallor of nausea. "Good morning, men!" he huskily greeted them. "Any complaints here?"

"Good morning, Herr Leutnant," the conscious patients chorused back at him with varying degrees of enthusiasm. There was a negative muttering in answer to the question about complaints. One man sitting on the edge of his bed caustically exclaimed: "It's the best hotel we've found so far this year!" Another waved his bandaged, frostbitten hands at Louise and shouted in an unmistakable Berlin accent: "We've found at least one angel in France!" But one of the men by the stove expressed the sentiments of all his comrades by asking: "Has peace really been declared? If so, when do we go home, Herr Leutnant?"

All the weary, suffering, sunken eyes concentrated upon Gustaf, pleading for an encouraging answer. After a long hesitation he was able to collect himself enough to give it to them: "There have been some credible reports in Swiss newspapers that the war is really over. But we must await official word from our own Headquarters which can be expected at any hour. Then we'll see about getting you out of here as quickly as possible." To Louise, standing behind him, he said in a lower voice: "Some of them don't look well at all."

"It was necessary to amputate in several cases of frostbite or wounds turned septic," she told him. "Others are sick with secondary infections of the lungs and intestines because of prolonged hunger and exposure. But we are not losing as many as at Abbey Saint-Luze."

"Keep up your good spirits, men," Gustaf called out to the patients and quickly retreated from the ward. Crossing the hall, he peered inside the one on the opposite side, saw the same sight, gave and received the same greetings, answered the same question, and left even more hurriedly. He felt his nausea rapidly mounting.

"The worse cases are in the other end of the building," Louise told him, pointedly adding: "Mostly French soldiers."

But Gustaf turned in the opposite direction. She followed him out on the steps where he had to take several deep breaths of the fresh air before he could speak: "I'll trust you to do the best you can, Mme Hunsecker. I'll report to General von Kleisenberg that you are."

"Thank you," she answered, looking into his face with a perception which was not without sympathy. "I'm glad that you have recovered yourself, Leutnant von Falkenhorst and that you survived your ordeal with some human sensitivity left in you."

The sickly pallor she had noticed quickly changed back to a healthy, embarrassed blush. He gave her a stiff little bow together with a rather clumsy salute, turned and waded through the ankle-deep mud of the yard to his horse, feeling very annoyed with himself. Why this attack of squeamishness after all he had experienced during the past seven months? Why this surge of emotion and almost-adolescent ineptness in handling the unexpected meeting with Louise Hunsecker? Even as he rode away from her loathsome hospital he found himself wanting to return. As a strange perverse reaction, he thought of Tessa and, for the first time since his recovery, considered what *she* must have suffered during the long silence of their separation. He must write her at once, at least a few words, no matter how difficult. It would never do, he decided, to have his wife hear the news of his reappearance through some other source. But while he tried to compose a letter in his mind Louise Hunsecker kept intruding upon his thoughts. It struck him that he had actually spent more time, more intimate moments, with the beautiful Alsatian nurse than he had with his wife. He found himself having difficulty even recalling what Tessa looked like.

Eugene von Kleisenberg seemed more ill and tired than three hours earlier, but he had propped himself up in his bed and was feverishly scribbling reports on sheets of paper spread on a tray balanced on the curve of his belly. He paused to listen to Gustaf's account of his morning tour of inspection, drily, crisply, accurately delivered, then worriedly commented: "We must lose no time in sending dispatches about our situation to von Manteuffel. He must send us relief and the means of evacuating our sick at once. Otherwise, regardless of victory and peace, there will be disaster for a lot of our people here!"

"What about the doctor, Excellency?" Gustaf asked. "Did he not report to you as I ordered?"

"Yes, but you sent him to me under armed guard and in such a state of mind that he was more inclined to maim than to heal. Under the circumstances I felt it safer to rely on my own recuperative powers. So I dismissed his guard and let him go on his way to Switzerland."

"To Switzerland, Your Excellency?" Gustaf exclaimed incredulously. "But he is needed here by you, by a lot of sick soldiers."

"Not as badly as he is needed by several thousand of his sick and wounded countrymen languishing in internment camps across the border," Eugene explained with a painful wheeze. "I could not find it in me to prevent him from obeying the commands of his conscience. Besides, he has left behind a very competent nurse. I suspect more competent than himself."

Gustaf's frown deepened. He suddenly understood why Louise Hunsecker had reacted with such anger over the way he had treated Dr. Polignac. But he also wondered how much the General knew about her connection with *him*. "Is your Excellency aware that this nursing sister also worked at Abbey Saint-Luze?" he cautiously inquired.

"I am," Eugene answered, giving him a searching look through his red, swollen eyes. "You obviously know her. Is she not to be trusted? Was she in any way responsible for what happened to you and the other prisoners at the abbey?" When he received a vigorous, tight-lipped headshake, he exclaimed with relief: "Good! None of your fellow survivors have faulted her either. I am glad of it because I detected in Mme Hunsecker qualities of character and good breeding to match her beauty. Did you not do the same, Gustaf?"

"Yes, Excellency," Gustaf found himself eagerly blurting out and seizing the opportunity to suggest: "And it might be wise to have her call on you here. I mean . . . to help you quickly recover from your bad cold." He felt himself blushing once more.

Eugene gave a rasping laugh and his fevered eyes momentarily sparkled with amused understanding. "A very good idea! A visit from a beautiful lady should do us both some good. But . . . ." He had to interrupt himself to let pass a fit of sneezing and coughing. "But that pleasure will have to wait. First, these reports must be written and dispatched by courier no later than one hour after noon. They have to get at least as far as Besançon by this evening if they are to do us any good. First things first!" He settled his bulk back against the triple tier of pillows and resumed his writing, a difficult feat as a continual tremor of suppressed coughs kept jiggling the tray holding his paper and inkwell.

Gustaf backed out of the door and retreated to his small room at the end of the hall. He spent no more than five minutes staring out the window at the bleak view of Château la Cluse and the misty gray vista of thawing hillsides beyond it. Then, remembering his resolve, he picked up pen and paper and wrote with a grim, intense concentration:

Dearest Theresa: I am afraid that you may have worried much about me because of my long silence but, you must understand, it has been impossible for me to write letters for several months. Shortly before Christmas I went on patrol with my squadron and was wounded in an ambush by cowardly guerrillas who killed all my men and took me prisoner. I spent many hard weeks in their hands and was among the few rescued alive. Things are better with me now and my wounds quite well healed. Although the war is supposed to be over, I am stuck in this wretched little outpost-town of Pontarlier, over one hundred kilometers away from our main forces who seem to have forgotten us here. There are only one thousand or so Germans with me, half of them released prisoners in very poor condition. We have won, but the end of the war, actually no part of the war, leaves me with any feeling of triumph. Quite the opposite. I failed in many respects and regret that I could not avenge the death of your father. At this point in his letter, he almost succumbed to a resurgent pang of his former depression and came near to tearing it up. But he forced himself to continue: *I hope all goes well for you at Glaumhalle. I shall write you again after getting out of here and rejoining my regiment. That may take some weeks yet, so please be patient. Please convey my affectionate greetings to my mother. Your Devoted Gustaf v. F.*

After quickly sealing and addressing the letter, he returned to Eugene's sickroom and asked permission to have it posted, together with the afternoon's urgent dispatches. Eugene eyed him with a baleful, almost accusing stare.

"It's about time you let your wife know you are alive."

he evacuation order reached Major Brandeis's Kommandantur in Pontarlier when suddenly the single telegraph
line crackled to life after a five-week silence. The first
message gave official confirmation of the provisional peace
treaty and announced the German march into Paris. It was
immediately followed by a second, ordering all German forces
occupying the Jura, Doubs, and Belfort districts to forthwith
withdraw to Strasbourg—now a *German* city! Both messages
originated from General von Manteuffel's headquarters and
were accepted by the cautious Major Brandeis as authentic. The
next pleasant surprise came an hour later, at sunset, when the
first locomotive to reach Pontarlier since Bourbaki's rear guard
had torn up long sections of tracks came puffing into the station,
pulling a work-train whose crew of mixed French and German
railwaymen had repaired the line all the way from the junction
at Besançon. They brought with them few of the badly needed
rations, but several very welcome sacks of delayed mail and
dispatches. With communications restored and the assurance of
an early return home, the Uhlans and their wards of rescued
prisoners showed a great improvement in morale. It mattered
little that the work-train had too few cars to transport everybody because word quickly spread that Major Brandeis had
prevailed upon General von Kleisenberg to add the weight of
his rank to a telegraphic request for a special train. The encouraging reply came back before midnight, promising the ar
rival of another locomotive and six passenger cars within the
next thirty-eight hours. Even the dourly moody Gustaf von
Falkenhorst was roused into something approaching good humor as he joined Brandeis and his leutnants in an all-night
celebration, getting himself slightly, very slightly, drunk in the
process.

Eugene von Kleisenberg was still bedridden, yet he too
enjoyed a considerable improvement of morale, as the mail
delivered by the work-train had included a long, and anxiously
awaited, acknowledgment of his many reports to Crown Prince
Frederick. He read and reread with great satisfaction the note
penned in the Prince's own hand which commended him for the

success of his mission and concluded with the flattering accolade: *His Majesty joins with me in congratulating you, my dear Eugene, for accomplishing so much in a humane cause under what must have been very trying circumstances. You may rest assured that your selfless and devoted service will be remembered by our soldiers as well as Ourselves!* . . . There was no hint of a promotion (which he had not dared hope for) or of a decoration such as the Order of the Black Eagle, (which he wanted and thought he deserved), but the Crown Prince had shown perceptive consideration for Eugene's most-urgent practical needs: In a separate enclosure there was a draft on the Royal Privy Account made out in his favor for the amount of five hundred thalers, indeed a princely gift which would provide financial security for the immediate future. He took great satisfaction in this and the obvious fact that he had further strengthened his position with the future sovereign of the Empire. That there was no letter for him from Vienna was a little disappointing, and he wondered whether Countess Antoinette was still there or had returned to Schloss Varn. Well, if he had to pursue her to dull Pomerania instead of the far more enjoyable cosmopolitan capital of Austria, so be it; those were the fortunes of war!

The last item in the mailpouch from Versailles gave Eugene additional satisfaction in that it proved his influence with Royal Headquarters. His recommendation that the Iron Cross First Class be awarded Gustaf von Falkenhorst had been approved without question; both the medal and certificate of commendation were on hand. However, Eugene decided not to tell Gustaf yet. There was no guessing what his reaction would be, and now, while he was still confined to his bed, he needed Gustaf's help. He also worried about whether he would be well enough to participate in the planned evacuation to Strasbourg the next day. Yet, though his health showed little improvement in spite of Anton's potions of hot cognac laced with milk, honey, and a dash of wine vinegar, Eugene determined he would make it in the style expected of a former Prince of Hanover. "When the time comes for us to evacuate Pontarlier," he told Gustaf, "it will be done by formal parade by all the able-bodied men we can muster. We shall march from the town square to the railroad station with flags flying and a general—*me*—at their head. It's been a rotten war. But neither the lowliest of our soldiers nor Pontarlier citizens will be left with any doubts about who won it. Be sure that von Brandeis is informed." He deliberately did not tell Gustaf that the parade would provide the occasion for the awarding of his Iron Cross.

Gustaf's inspection tours of billets, Kommandantur, and hospital became a daily routine; he also led one last sweep over the countryside to search for any straggling German prisoners who might have been missed. The capricious weather turned almost balmy, with a clear, bright sun and a mild southerly breeze filling the air with the scents of approaching spring, making the ride a pleasantly invigorating one for Gustaf. However, despite covering better than fifteen kilometers at a brisk trot and visiting several isolated farms and villages, the patrol found no more countrymen to rescue. They met a few farmers along the way who, having heard rumors about the peace, were trudging towards Pontarlier in the hope of purchasing supplies for their critically depleted larders. Gustaf confirmed the rumors of peace for them after receiving their assurances that they knew of no Germans still being held by the *francs-tireurs*.

It was dusk when Gustaf arrived back at the villa. He found the General being tended by Louise with gentle professional efficiency. She had prepared a hot vapor bath of pungent camphor and dried mint leaves, which she directed Eugene to breathe deeply as he bent over the steaming bowl held in his lap, a towel thrown over his head, forming a tent to concentrate the pungent medication. While he obeyed with much coughing and snorting, she directed Anton in the preparation of a mustard plaster to be applied later to his inflamed chest. The whole room reeked of camphor, mint, and mustard, and when Gustaf stepped over the threshold, he announced himself with a series of violent sneezes.

Louise looked up from the muddy compresses of mustard with a concerned smile and exclaimed: "Ah, Leutnant von Falkenhorst! I hope you haven't got yourself a relapse by riding about the countryside in the dampness of the spring thaws. After what you've been through, you should be more careful about your health. With everything else, I can't treat more than one bad cold at a time."

Eugene raised the towel off the bowl, draping it over his head so that he suddenly took on the appearance of an obese Arab sheik sprawled among his pillows sniffing incense. "Yes, Gustaf, you must take care not to overexert yourself," he rasped, peering at him through eyes irritated to tears by the fumes. "Mme Hunsecker should not have to bother so much over you and me when there are so many other more seriously sick to be cared for—Anton! Give the Herr Leutnant Baron a tot of cognac to brace him up a bit."

Anton stopped stirring the pot of hot mustard paste long enough to pour the drink and hand it to Gustaf, who drained the glass with a series of restrained sips while accounting for his activities of the afternoon. He finished both the cognac and his report by drily stating: "It is unlikely any more of our people are left alive outside Pontarlier. So there is no point in wasting time on anything besides getting out with those we have saved. I hope Your Excellency will agree and be able to leave when the relief train arrives."

"We'll have him ready to travel by tomorrow," Louise cheerfully predicted. "I doubt if your soldiers would depart without taking along their most popular general." When Eugene made a disparaging gesture with a pudgy hand, she said to him: "Oh, yes! I hear a lot of their talk. They know to what lengths you went to find, rescue, and help them, and are very grateful. I've even heard many Frenchmen express their gratitude."

"Well, naturally your French patients will be evacuated along with our own," Eugene told her. "They must be taken to Besançon where there is a real hospital with several doctors. And you, Madame, will, of course, accompany and care for everybody on the journey. I imagine you are as anxious to leave as the rest of us."

Louise looked agreeably surprised, almost delighted, but then on second thought, doubtful: "Yes, I'd like to leave, but I don't know if it would be right. I did promise Dr. Polignac that I would stay here."

"Meaning to stay with your patients," Eugene quickly pointed out. "And so you would be, since we are leaving none behind."

For once Gustaf eagerly supported the General; the prospect of having the lovely Louise's company on the train, of prolonging their relationship for a few more hours, perhaps another whole day, made him exclaim: "His Excellency is absolutely right, Mme Hunsecker! You must come. For the sake of all of us who need you. For your *own* sake. I mean . . . whatever reason would you have to remain in this God-forsaken place?"

It was now Eugene's turn to look surprised. He had never before heard Gustaf react with such emotion. But in the next instant, the reason for it flashed clear and he had to cover up his amusement with a feigned fit of coughing. "I believe he means, Madame," he managed to splutter, "that we would be much obliged. . . ."

"Yes, certainly . . ." Gustaf stammered, ". . . much obliged!"

"We have run out of mustard," Anton suddenly chimed in. "All but a few grains I've saved for tonight's sausage."

They all laughed at the General's orderly and his suddenly embarrassed expression, but then Louise gave in with a shrug and flattered smile: "Oh, very well, then! If there is room and need for me on your train, I'll join you as far as Besançon. And . . . thank you for your confidence as well as your consideration for my sick compatriots." She let her smile linger a moment longer, her beauty and gracious charm completely captivating the ailing Eugene and his flustered young adjutant. "Yes, very well!" she repeated and, reverting to a briskly professional manner, began repacking her small supply of medicines into a tattered satchel. "Much remains to be done before we will be ready to leave. I must hurry back to my hospital. In the meantime, apply the mustard plasters to your General's chest and keep him warm through the night. Another vapor bath, perhaps, to relieve the congestion. But a good night's sleep will do more than anything else to build up his strength."

"I'm already feeling much stronger than before you came," Eugene wheezed. "You must remain a while longer, Mme Hunsecker. At least long enough to have dinner with us. You too must build up your strength."

"You are *not* getting up for dinner, Excellency," she firmly ordered him. "And please put the towel back over your head. You are wasting the vapors by useless talk. I have no more herbs and oils to spare."

"You will have dinner with Leutnant von Falkenhorst," Eugene answered with equal firmness, but complying with her to the point of dropping the towel-tent back down over the still-steaming bowl held in his broad lap. His voice came through, muffled by the damp folds: "Anton! Stop fiddling with that mustard concoction and turn out the best meal you can from the kitchen. Then serve it properly to Mme Hunsecker and Leutnant von Falkenhorst in the dining room downstairs. I'll call you if I need any help with those messy plasters. Ugh! So go! Hurry! None of us can afford to waste any time." The bed shook and creaked as he waved everybody out of the room, keeping his face draped behind the towel.

When Louise hesitated, Gustaf whispered to her: "You cannot refuse him. And I would be most unhappy if you refused *me!* Please stay for a while longer. Then let me escort you back to your hospital."

"Yes . . . very well . . . I'll dine with you if it does not take too long," she softly agreed, the prospects of a good, hot meal decently served overcoming her conflicts of conscience. "But first, I really should make myself a little more presentable."

Gustaf thought this funny, coming from the most beautiful woman he had ever known, beautiful even in these dingy surroundings and in her drab, much-mended nurse's garb of a plain black dress and white apron from which no amount of laundering had removed all the stains of the blood which had splattered it. "You look lovely as you are," he exclaimed with a nervous laugh, "but if you feel you need it, we have several empty rooms here where you can have privacy. Let me show you to one and send Anton up with some soap and hot water."

"That would be wonderful!" she agreed and, shedding for the time being all her professional reserve, she gave him a coquettish little smile and made an entirely female confession: "I have in my bag a few drops of special medicine I've been saving just for myself all winter long. Quite scandalous of me, but now, at long last, I feel like using them up. A few drops of *perfume!*"

"Ah! Perfume! A very powerful medicine, I've been told," Gustaf said and let her into a vacant room. After lighting the lamp for her, he went to his own in order to wash and brush the mud off his boots and makeshift uniform.

ustaf hurried to the dining room where he found the table set for two with clean napkins and cloth; there was an appetizing smell rising from two covered tureens. But Louise was taking her time and he had to wait alone for five minutes, pacing impatiently back and forth in front of the fireplace, in whose hearth glowed their last lumps of coal. Candles were also in short supply, so there were only four half-burned ones lighting the room, two on the table and two on the mantelpiece, their flames too feeble to cheer up the atmosphere of seedy pretentiousness of this *petit bourgeois* abode. But the room seemed to brighten considerably when Louise finally entered.

"I am sorry I took so long," she apologized. "I looked in on your General once more to make sure he's not cheating on his vapor treatment."

Gustaf's nostrils flared as they picked up the scent of the precious perfume. "I am sure another visit from you did him more good," he said, unable to suppress a tone of jealousy. "He is quite taken by you, you know."

Louise flashed him an incredulous, amused smile, then glanced around the room and at the table, her blue eyes sparkling and her freshly combed hair a silken gold in the candlelight. "Ah, this is very cozy," she exclaimed, "and the food smells delicious. It really makes me feel guilty to be offered such luxury."

"You must not expect too much," Gustaf warned her, gulping his words. "There is a scarcity of good food in this house as everywhere else."

As he spoke, Anton came through the pantry door carrying a bottle of wine, the one product of France which never seemed to run out. He had obviously heard what Gustaf had said, because he murmured with testy deference: "I made the best sausage I could from what scraps of pork and veal I could scrape together." He lifted the lid of the larger tureen, letting escape a whiff of deliciously aromatic steam and allowing a glimpse of five fat sausages swimming in a thick broth. The other one he cracked open less confidently to reveal its soggy green and yellow contents. "Turnips and turnip greens," he apologized, "but at least simmered in wine." Then he flourished the bottle he had brought and proved he was accustomed to serving a princely palate by reverently identifying it: "A *grand cru*, Clos Vougeot, of 1862."

Anton was quicker to pull out her chair than Gustaf who had never seen her more beautiful, not even when she had appeared as a saving angel to dispel his nightmares of Abbey Saint-Luze. Her smell of salve and carbolic was replaced by a delicate one of perfume. She had rolled down the sleeves of her plain gray dress and taken off her apron with its high front and embroidered red cross. The top three buttons beneath her collar were undone, revealing a delicate gold chain encircling her neck and the rising curve of her breasts. There was a tiny tan-colored mole just above the closure of the fourth button and it began to exercise an almost hypnotic attraction upon Gustaf as he sat opposite her. "Well . . . shall we eat then!" he urged hoarsely and rather ungraciously.

"I thought that you devout Prussians always spoke grace before your meals," she softly chided him with a trace of irony.

Gustaf stared open mouthed at her for a second, then clenched his hands together over his plate. "Dear God . . . bless this earthly sustenance provided by Thy bounty . . . and shine Thy merciful grace upon us who partake of it. Amen. Anton! We shall serve ourselves."

Anton gave a belated, sonorous amen and started for the pantry door. As he reached it, Louise called after him, as if to countermand his order, but she only said:

"Anton! The General asked that you bring him a hot milk and cognac, please, as soon as you are through here."

The General's orderly turned, bowed and answered, "Certainly, Madame," and backed out the door and closed it.

As soon as he was gone, Gustaf said with a gesture toward the ceiling: "He's never too sick to quaff his cognac and milk, and Anton knows it."

"You don't approve of him, I can tell," she said. "I find him unusual, but certainly a decent kind man at heart. Won't you grant him that?"

"He certainly is unusual," Gustaf conceded shortly. He briskly removed the lids from the tureens and pushed them toward her. While she helped herself to generous portions of sausage and vegetables, he filled her glass, then his own, brimful of wine. With his eyes drawn irresistibly to the mole above her breast, he offered a toast: "*Prosit!* To my one piece of good luck in this miserable war, that of having met you, Madame!"

"Why, thank you, Herr Leutnant Baron!" she exclaimed with a beguiling smile. "May I add, to peace and healing of wounds . . . at least our individual ones?"

She took a small sip from her glass. Nervously, he took a large one from his. She pushed the tureens back within his reach and politely waited for him to serve himself. Then they began to eat.

After an uncomfortably long silence Louise asked, "Will you tell me something about your home and family?"

Gustaf washed down a mouthful of sausage with wine before answering: "We live in eastern Silesia, not far from Breslau and right on the Russian frontier. My father was a soldier who was killed in our war against Austria, five years ago. My mother is alive but not well since she broke her leg in an accident last year. I have a younger brother who was until recently studying at Heidelberg University. Last I heard of him, he was working as some kind of civil servant with our Military Railroad Authority." He made a wry face, then excused his brother's lowly status by hastily adding: "Albrecht is still very young and hasn't quite found himself. Not yet twenty, as a matter of fact."

Louise waited for a moment. "Is that all you have to tell me about what surely must be an old and illustrious family?"

"Yes, we are quite old. Grandfather Manfred used to amuse himself by tracing us back to the Dark Ages. Facts and legends were all mixed up in his mind beyond two hundred years. But, yes, that's at least how old we are. The family, I mean."

After another long pause Louise softly asked: "What is your wife's name? How long have you been married?"

The questions took him completely by surprise and for a horrifying moment he could *not* remember his wife's first name. He tried to hide his confusion by taking a long, deep draught of wine. "Theresa . . . yes, her name is Theresa von Beckhaus. Well . . . now von Falkenhorst, of course. They call . . . I mean *I* call her Tessa." In his desperation he threw his knife and fork down on his plate and, tearing his eyes away from that hypnotizing little mole, stared directly into her eyes, only to become even more disconcerted by the change in them. They had gone from a glinting sapphire blue, to a gentle, sympathetic blue gray. "You see, Louise," he tried to explain, suddenly addressing her without hesitation by her Christian name, "we were married only last July on the day the war was declared. That very evening I reported back for duty with my regiment."

"That very evening? . . . "

"Yes, that very evening." He took another gulp of wine, this time draining his glass. "It was my duty as an officer in my father's . . . my grandfather's . . . old regiment." He gave an involuntary shudder, as if his subconscious had reacted to a half-truth.

"You speak of it like a brush between strangers," Louise said in a near whisper. "Surely you knew each other better than that. Surely you had met before, with time to fall in love . . . ?"

Gustaf reached for the bottle of Clos Vougeot and refilled his glass, then realizing his gaffe, splashed wine in hers back to the level of the brim, spilling quite a bit in the process. "Yes, of course. Tessa and I had met several times in Berlin before we were married. Naturally, our families were acquainted. . . . Would you like some more sausage?"

Louise glanced down at her plate which was still quite full, gave him a helpless smile and said: "I have no more room for so much food. I'm . . . not used to it." Even though he had not finished his own portion, and what little appetite he had was gone, he picked up his fork and speared another sausage just to give his hands something to do while he hid their trembling. She, too, resumed eating. One of the candles on the mantelpiece spluttered and expired in its last puddle of tallow which had dribbled messily down the fluted column of the pewter candlestick. The increased darkness seemed far out of proportion to the failure of that feeble flame.

Gustaf was able to collect himself a little during the ensuing silence, concentrating on his food and wine. Finally he spoke up with brittle cheer:

"Well . . . so you've got me to talk about myself! But what about you? You must have an interesting story to tell of your own."

"It's not unlike yours," she answered with a wistful sigh. "My maiden name was de Pelisier, also an old family with a grandfather who doted over our ancestry as far as the original Huguenot branch. . . ."

"Ah! You are Protestant!" Gustaf interrupted with a pleased exclamation.

"Of the Calvinist denomination," Louise briefly elaborated. She took a sip of wine and dabbed her mouth with her napkin.

✠

"My husband's family was of similar background. We owned some properties, bore good names, but were far from rich. . . ."

"Neither are we, I assure you!" Gustaf interrupted again with a terse little laugh.

"We lived only some twenty kilometers apart," she continued evenly, "the de Pelisiers in Sarrebourg, the Hunseckers near Saverne. But Roland and I were brought together by our families less than two years ago. *We* were married last June. *He* went to war three weeks later, and three weeks after that, he fell in a battle over Vionville. By strange coincidence, he, too, was a lieutenant of cavalry."

Gustaf stared at her in surprise, suddenly recalling the young French cuirassier officer whom he had shot through the eye in the midst of the wild, bloody battle near Vionville. Could he have been her husband? As he pondered the improbable idea, he suddenly connected that incident with a later one, in which a youthful French lieutenant wearing a patch over one eye had appeared in time to save him from execution by the *francs-tireurs*. The idea was impossible! Yet he tensely asked, "Are you quite certain your husband is dead?"

"Yes. A comrade who saw him killed wrote me about it. He lies buried somewhere on that battlefield, only God knows where, among thousands of other graves."

Gustaf drew a deep sigh of relief and sympathy. "I am sorry. Very sorry." He could eat no more, only uneasily drink his wine while waiting for her to finish her food. He tried to dispel the sad silence between them by telling her: "You are still young and very beautiful, Louise. Soon you will be home and able to begin your life over again. You will find another husband, I'm sure. Our train will be going to Strasbourg, you know, which is very near where you live."

"You forget it is now German territory," she answered, stating the fact without rancor.

"What difference will that make? You will be welcome and allowed to live in peace with us."

She shook her head. "No. I have decided to go to Paris as soon as I'm no longer needed by the wounded." She put down her knife and fork on her empty plate, and finished her wine. When she saw how glumly he was looking at her, she smiled and said teasingly: "That's not so bad, you know. They say that Paris is just the place for a young widow. And I believe that far more young men are left there than in the provinces."

"Paris is a wicked city," Gustaf archly told her. "It would be safer for you to come home with us."

"But I am a Frenchwoman and Paris is the capital of my

country, wicked or not." Her eyes were again sparkling like sapphires with a taunting amusement. "Are you worried about my virtue? How flattering! How chivalrous of you!"

Her laughter cut deeply, making him exclaim with adolescent misery: "You don't like us. . . . You don't like *me*."

"You are very sweet, after all!" she protested and reaching across the table, put her hands on his as they clenched his glass. "I am glad you did not die in that horrible abbey, because I do like you very much. Not as a German, but for *you*. And if it will make you worry less about me, I have an uncle in Paris who is a very respectable man. A professor at the Sorbonne, no less. A member of our Académie Française. So, you see, Gustaf, I shall be quite safe and well cared for."

Her touch went through him with a gentle, yet painful tingling sensation. She did not pull her hands away as he grasped them. He could not bear looking into her face, but the mole was exercising its hypnotic effect. "Louise . . . I wish . . . I wish," he stammered, then abruptly stopped and let go of her as the pantry door suddenly opened and Anton appeared on the threshold.

The General's orderly did not show a flicker of surprise at catching them holding hands. "For dessert there are some apples which are half-spoiled, I regret," he announced. "But I can offer you an excellent Roquefort cheese. And a passable cognac. Rémy Martin, 1850."

For some reason, Louise found his intrusion more comical than inopportune. "Stop your pampering, Anton! It was all too delicious, but I can manage not another mouthful, not another drop."

"That will be all, Anton," Gustaf snapped with unnecessary sharpness to hide his embarrassment. "You may leave."

Anton took his time to obey. "His Royal Highn . . . I mean, General von Kleisenberg . . . asked me to convey his compliments to Mme Hunsecker and his pleasure in anticipating Madame's company during tomorrow's journey." Not until he had clearly enunciated this message did he remove himself.

Louise rose from her chair. "This has been quite a day for me," she said. "I've treated a sick Prince. And . . . I've had supper with you, Gustaf." She emphasized the last, and the twinkle in her eyes softened as she spoke. Then, almost regretfully, she sighed: "Now I must get back to the hospital. I have a lot to do before tomorrow morning."

Gustaf was struck by a faint dizziness as he got up. "May I escort you?" he asked.

"But of course! You promised to, didn't you, Gustaf?"

The temperature had rapidly fallen after dark and the night turned misty, dimming the glow of the few lighted windows in the black mass of the town. As they walked along the deserted streets, frequently having to slow their steps to grope their way through especially dark sections, Louise slipped her arm into Gustaf's and pressed close to him. They hardly spoke at all, except when she drew his attention to a constellation of stars whose jeweled string of lights shone through the mist directly overhead. He told her it was also seen in Silesia where they called it the Little Bear. "Ah, we share the same stars at least!" she said, giving his arm a squeeze. "Yes, that's something!" he agreed, squeezing hers back.

The windows of the schoolhouse-hospital showed very dim lights, as if each ward were lit by no more than one candle; but the lantern above the entrance burned with a harsh brightness, the mist creating a wavering yellow halo around it. Two ambulatory patients were sitting on the steps beneath it, sharing a single pipeful of precious tobacco which they silently passed back and forth. Gustaf and Louise came through the gates and entered the still-muddy schoolyard, hesitating as they approached the hazy circle of light, then stopping short of it.

"If you like, I'll wait for you until you are through for the night and ready to return to your lodgings," he said.

There came that maddening little laugh of hers. "That would not be appropriate at all, Gustaf," she whispered. "My lodging is the school's attic where I sleep with the sisters between stacks of old books."

"Oh, well, I'd rather not get mixed up with the sisters," he said, trying to treat her refusal casually. He twisted around to face her as she lowered the black woolen shawl she had wrapped around her head and shoulders. Even in the dim light, her hair reflected a lovely pale gold, her eyes a deep cobalt blue. "So tomorrow on the train, then. I will still try to convince you to travel all the way to Strasbourg with us." He pulled her hand from out of his arm and raising it to his lips, gave it an ardent, clumsy kiss.

Turning her hand around in his, she brought its palm against his cheek with a gently lingering caress, then with a tender impulse, returned his kiss, her lips brushing lightly against the corner of his mouth. He tried to hold her for a moment longer, but she broke away with a softly spoken "Good night!" and hurried toward the steps of the entrance. As she reached them she scolded the two ambulatory patients perched there for exposing themselves to the raw night air just to smoke. They made some laughing excuses, but were quick to follow her inside.

As he walked back to the villa, he guiltily tried to put her out of his mind by thinking about Tessa, but he found himself unable to picture her clearly in his mind. He remembered freckles, copper red hair drawn into a symmetrically braided crown, and bony shoulders, that was all. No coherent features, not the slightest lingering of a personality. Were her eyes green or light brown? He could not even remember that! But he knew they were not blue, not the lovely, mysteriously shifting blue of Louise's eyes. Such eyes haunted forever, would never allow themselves to be forgotten. But he *had* to forget them . . . or would do so after tomorrow . . . or the day after . . . or whenever the final parting came.

Just before he reached the villa, he was diverted out of his brooding by a muffled rumbling sound in the otherwise silent night, rising and falling in the misty darkness with sonorous rhythmic overtones. He stopped to listen, puzzled. It seemed to be drawing closer, adding metallic rattlings to the strange echoes reverberating down the narrow streets. Then he heard a high-pitched whistling shriek, a frightening angry scream: the train! The promised evacuation train was pulling into Pontarlier much earlier than expected. The troops billeted at the railroad station must have heard it too, because distant voices of men swelled into a faraway, but distinct, cheer.

"Well, tomorrow all this madness will be over," Gustaf told himself, "It's good-bye forever to this wretched place." But as he let himself into the house, he felt a restless sadness, almost as if he were disappointed that the train had come.

y the following dawn the mist had thickened into a heavy
fog, draping Pontarlier in a sodden opaque veil of dismal
gray. It settled in sheets of moisture on the horses and
uniforms of Brandeis's Uhlans as they maneuvered through the
town square to form up for the parade. It chilled and dampened
even more the mixed company of infantrymen made up of
released internees, who had been marched up from the station
for the formal march back to it. There was some confusion and
grumbling, curses and bad-tempered commands from noncommissioned officers trying to sort things out in the square. But by
the time Gustaf von Falkenhorst rode into it, leading the odd
assortment of troopers that General von Kleisenberg had picked
up as his personal guard, there was order in the formations of
men and horses, giving an illusion of military smartness in the
drizzly gloom.

Gustaf rode up to the entrance of the Kommandantur
where Major Brandeis was waiting with his four leutnants and
three internee officers. He looked even more irritated than
usual. "His Excellency will be delayed ten minutes," Gustaf
informed him after dismounting. "The inclement weather
convinced him not to risk appearing in his only dress uniform.
He is changing into something more practical."

"We can wait. We have nothing else to do of importance,
after all," Brandeis sarcastically exclaimed. He then bawled out
at the dim lines of his troops waiting at attention: "Parade!
... Stand at ease!"

Ten minutes went by ... fifteen ... then twenty of waiting
in the raw dampness. Some children brazenly trotted down the
front ranks of the Uhlans, like inspecting officers, one of them
mimicking a goose step strut to perfection, causing ripples of
laughter among the shivering, sodden soldiery. An officer
barked for silence in the ranks, then chased the children away.
They ran off shrieking with laughter, stopping somewhere inside the misty pall shielding the far side of the square to chant
a childish vulgar rhyme:

Un, deux, trois,
Je merde sur toi!
Quatre, cinq, six,
Allemand plein de piss!

Five minutes later, General von Kleisenberg made his belated entrance onto the square, materializing out of the fog on his plodding white mare, Anton trailing behind him on a much less sturdy mount loaded down with saddlebags and field kits. The General had put on his field uniform, the now-familiar, shapeless sheepskin coat and the mottled muffler spiraling three times around his neck to protect both his chin and earlobes. No insignia of rank. No weapons. Yet, somehow, a massively impressive figure and one so eagerly awaited that the sight of him raised a ragged, good-natured cheer from the troops.

Eugene acknowledged this spontaneous, unmilitary ovation with a broad grin and friendly wave of a gloved hand. Then it was cut off by Major Brandeis's stentorian bellow as he ordered the ranks to attention, then to present arms. The General stopped waving and smiling, but touched the short visor of his ridiculously small and battered garrison cap, turning this odd salute to the rigid collection of officers when he reached them at the Kommandantur entrance. "Good morning, gentlemen!" he greeted them. "A rotten day for traveling. But travel we shall. And because most of us are going home, it will be a good day just the same." He ponderously heaved himself out of the saddle.

Brandeis stamped forward three steps closer to him, his right arm and hand still firmly fixed in the saluting position, as were those of all the other officers. "As Your Excellency ordered, this occupation detachment of Seventh Elbing Light Cavalry Regiment is all present and accounted for, ready for field march inspection. Likewise a force of temporarily attached casuals numbering 192 men. A fatigue detail is assigned the movement of the 134 wounded to the railroad station. We await Your Excellency's orders."

"Thank you, Major Brandeis. Very good. Very good. At ease, gentlemen, and you may bring the troops to parade rest. We have a special little ceremony to perform which will take only a few minutes."

As Gustaf dropped his hand from the salute and relaxed, he could not help smiling to himself. Kleisenberg and Brandeis were playing their parts to the hilt.

The General turned, and, motioning to Anton to follow him, waddled out to a point halfway between the officers and first rank of mounted Uhlans. There he stopped, mopped the drizzle running down his cheeks like sweat with the tassled end of his muffler, then adjusted its folds around his chin so that he could address the parade: "Well, men, our mission here is completed," he told them with a shout which echoed through the fog-shrouded square. "It has been a difficult one without much glamour or glory. We've been wet, cold, sick and weary . . . our lot right to the end, it seems. But you've conducted yourselves well, and faithfully done your duty. Even those of you who had the misfortune to be captured and had to be rescued from the enemy . . . or a forced sejour with our Swiss friends . . . have conducted yourselves with credit under bitter circumstances. Circumstances which offer little opportunity for heroics, only grit and forbearance. Yet, there is at least one among us whose courage and fortitude has been such that it attracted notice at Imperial Headquarters. It is with pleasure that I obey their command to honor this man here and now. You can all take pride in him, and through him, in yourselves." Turning slowly to face the officers, he allowed a dramatic pause before calling out: "Leutnant Baron Gustaf von Falkenhorst! Front and center!"

Gustaf felt a hot wave of embarrassment flush his face. For a moment he was absolutely unable to move. Major Brandeis, who was standing next to him, snarled in sarcastic whisper: "So this whole thing is for *your* benefit, eh, hero? Well, what are you waiting for? Get out there and perform for us." A hard prod in the ribs started him forward, and he moved toward the General with an odd, stiff-legged gait.

Eugene's damp jowly face split into a wide grin, his small eyes sparkling with sly good humor. He now held in his hands a flat black box and the Order of Commendation, which Anton had produced on cue out of his dispatch case. Gustaf went rigid again, forgetting to salute and clamping his arms to his sides as if trying to hold himself upright. "Attention to orders!" Eugene shouted, then launched into a reading of the Commendation, his voice as loud as ever as he attempted to make it heard all over the square, but the cadence quickly degenerated from clear enunciation to a hasty running together of the flowery sentences. The document had turned soggy in his hands and, because Versailles had yet to embrace the use of waterproof ink in communicating with their forces in the rainy provinces, the fine penmanship was dissolving into illegible runs and smears. But Eugene knew most of it by heart and, when he did not, had little difficulty ad-libbing. At least he made it fairly clear to all but those in the rearmost ranks of the farthest formations, that Gustaf had accomplished some remarkable feats. According to the official version he had not only contributed to the victory at

Vionville by bringing up reinforcements at a critical point of the battle, but later forced the surrender of an enemy prison fortress and released a number of fellow prisoners of war. No mention was made, of course, of his disastrous chase after the balloon which resulted in the loss of his entire squadron. He was to be awarded the Iron Cross, and the Commendation Order was signed by Crown Prince Frederick himself—a fact which Eugene shouted loudest of all.

When he finished reading he handed the document back to Anton, telling him to put it back in the case before it became completely ruined. Then came the actual awarding of the medal which he almost botched because he had great difficulty in opening the box with his gloved hands. While he fumbled with it, Gustaf heard, as if in a bad dream, the hollow bellow of Brandeis's voice ordering the parade back to present arms, managing to inject a sour, sarcastic note into the command. The General finally got the box open, but had more trouble unraveling the long black-and-silver loop of a ribbon attached to the medal. It was not until he was ready to place it around Gustaf's neck that he noticed the recipient's peculiar expression. "Please bend over a bit so I can hang this thing around your neck," he said, still smiling broadly. "And don't look so glum, my boy. This little ceremony is supposed to inspire the troops as well as yourself."

"I . . . was not prepared for this, Your Excellency," Gustaf stammered with a barely audible voice. "I do not deserve. . . ."

"Nonsense! The Crown Prince and I decided you do deserve it," Eugene snapped, without a tremor in his smile. In a brisk motion he caught Gustaf's head in the loop of the ribbon, almost knocking off his cap as he yanked it down like a noose around his neck. "There! My felicitations, my boy! You are now officially marked the very model of a young Prussian officer."

"Thank you, Excellency . . . but I don't feel it."

"Act it, anyway," Eugene said and grabbing him by the right hand, gave it two short pumps, then: "Very well. That's all. Let's get these men loaded onto the train."

Gustaf managed something approaching a proper salute, croaking: "Yes, Excellency. For the good of these men and our army." Then, still moving as if in a trance, he marched back to the group of officers waiting and watching on the steps of the Kommandantur.

As Eugene had assured Major Brandeis, the ceremony had taken no more than five minutes, but five of the longest, most-trying minutes Gustaf could remember having ever lived through, including the wedding ritual at Schloss Varn. Now the coveted Iron Cross hung like a stone from his neck, which suddenly began to ache. He wanted to tear the thing off and cast it into the gutter, or at least to slip it off and into a pocket, but he could not, as he was surrounded by all the other officers eager to congratulate him—all except Major Brandeis who pointedly ignored him.

The station bustled with activity as the sick and wounded on litters were loaded into the cars. The relief and work-trains had been combined to form one long train pulled by two locomotives coupled together. A flatcar and covered freight car which the French had left derailed on a siding, had been jacked back on the tracks, repaired, and coupled to the others. But even so, it was already obvious that traveling conditions were going to be miserably crowded. As Major Brandeis had suspected, he and his Uhlan troopers were going to have to ride horseback the full forty kilometers to Besançon, following the muddy road which paralleled the railroad tracks for most of the distance. But at least they could travel lightly, carrying only their weapons and hardtack rations in haversacks; all their baggage was stowed aboard the train. The two field kitchens were rolled onto the flatcar where the cooks kept them in operation to provide hot soup for the sick during their journey. Only one horse could be transported: General von Kleisenberg's gray mare from whom he refused to be parted was installed in an enclosed freight car under Anton's care; the privileged animal had to share this accommodation with twenty ambulatory patients. The General himself had a compartment in one of the six third-class passenger cars, which he had to share only with Gustaf and a released internee captain.

Eugene gallantly offered Louise Hunsecker a seat in his comparatively comfortable and uncrowded compartment. She had been too busy supervising the entraining of her patients to take notice of his arrival at the station, and when he pressed his attention upon her, she hastily explained that she must travel together with her most serious cases. But she took time to greet Gustaf with a warm smile and when her eye was caught by the shiny new Iron Cross, she exclaimed in surprise: "What is this? A brand-new decoration, isn't it, Gustaf?"

"It's nothing," he dourly replied, taking the opportunity to remove it from around his neck.

"There you go wallowing in false modesty again," Eugene chided him, then began telling her: "It's for his exploits in the battle of Vionville and . . ."

"Vionville!" she interrupted with a gasp, her eyes darting an anguished accusing look at Gustaf. "You fought at Vionville?"

"Yes, but, you see . . . I wasn't really in the actual fighting," he miserably tried to explain to her. But she did not stay to listen. Turning away from him without another word, she hurried off toward the last of the litter patients who were being put aboard the train, vanishing among the multitude of soldiers waiting their turn on the exposed platform. After she was gone, Gustaf glared at the puzzled General von Kleisenberg and said: "It was cruel of Your Excellency to remind her of the battle where she lost her husband!"

Eugene showed surprise, then genuine distress. "I did not know," he mumbled. "Poor girl! How clumsy of me! She told me her husband fell in the war, but not where."

The fog was as thick as ever and the drizzle had turned into a cold penetrating rain as Gustaf helped Eugene into his car. The litter cases became wet before they were racked in tiers inside the train, the ambulatory wounded and casuals soaked by the time they were compressed on wooden benches, twelve men to a compartment. Worse off yet were the unfortunates for whom there was no room *inside* the train; they had to perch in exposed positions on the locomotives' coal tenders and on the roofs of the passenger cars. Unlike the riding Uhlans who wore heavy capes over their uniforms, these men had no such clothing to protect them from the elements. Yet, the little grumbling they gave vent to was tempered by a fatalistic humor. Nobody wanted to be left behind. Everybody waited impatiently for the train to start—which it did not do even after the last passenger had hauled himself aboard.

Instead, the two engineers climbed out of their cabs and held a conference which they would not hurry despite urgent shouts and catcalls from the sorely tried troops. When they finished talking, they did not climb back into their locomotives, but marched back down the length of the train, impervious to the insults thrown at them, until they were met by Major Brandeis who was very angry over the delayed departure, principally because it was delaying his own. "What the devil is the matter," he shouted in exasperation. "Why don't you get going?"

"We do not have enough coal to get us to Besançon," one of the sooty-faced fire-eaters growled. "We must find more. At least a half-ton."

"Imbecile!" Brandeis yelled, finally losing his temper. "Why didn't you take care of that before?" His wrath was echoed by the men huddled on the roof of the nearest car, but he rejected their support with a bellowed order for silence.

"We did not anticipate a load like this," the engineer protested vehemently. "We must have more coal. At least half a ton, Herr Major." His French colleague held up a correcting finger and injected:

"*Un tonne, pour être sûr!*"

✠

"One ton! You're crazy! You won't find ten lumps of coal left in this whole town."

"We must have it, or you'll walk the last fifteen kilometers to Besançon."

"*Plutôt vingt kilomètres,*" the Frenchman corrected, flashing all ten fingers twice in Brandeis's face.

The argument raged for another ten minutes on the platform, the engineers reinforced by their equally pessimistic firemen and Major Brandeis by one of his leutnants and two harassed NCO's. The men on the car roofs and hanging out the windows listened in tight-lipped misery. Finally, the matter was settled. Since there was no coal available in Pontarlier, the locomotives would have to burn wood which would be chopped out of forests along the way. The locomotive crews warned that burning wood ruined the boiler tubes of the locomotives, to which Brandeis replied that he didn't give a damn what happened to the locomotives *after* they got to Besançon.

After another five minutes' delay to find axes, the two locomotives lunged into motion with a roaring whoosh of steam and clanging of skidding drivers. The exterior passengers had to hang on for their lives as the train went through a series of violent jerks before traction was gained and it began rattling along the tracks more smoothly; then they let out a hoarse cheer that was quickly smothered by a suffocating cloud of sooty smoke. The engineers allowed only one short blast of their whistles to conserve steam and were soon throttling back to their most-economical speed—about fourteen kilometers per hour. Major Brandeis and his Uhlans were easily able to keep pace by settling down to a steady fast trot.

Behind the train and its cavalry escort, Pontarlier remained silent in its sodden gray shroud for several minutes. But then, as the clang and clatter of wheels and hooves began to fade in the distance, the bells in the church steeple, which had been silent for two months, burst into a wildly joyous clarion of thanksgiving. They continued pealing until the bell-ringers fell from their ropes in sheer, happy exhaution.

April 1871

The Lovers

⌘ ⌘

If we cleared away some of the rocks and those dells of useless birches, this would make a fine pasture," Tessa enthusiastically told Albrecht with a sweeping gesture. They had dismounted and were standing on a knoll overlooking a wild meadow whose thick yellow grass was showing the first signs of turning to a lush green. They had ridden over a kilometer north of Glaumhalle manor, which loomed in the distance like a cliff above its hilltop. The wind was chilly as it swept in from the Polish plains, but there was a tingling warmth in the sunrays when they broke through the ragged white clouds moving swiftly across a pale blue sky.

"I'm afraid that land does not belong to us," Albrecht told her. "We are standing almost exactly on our property line. Anyway, what do we need it for?"

"For more horses, of course," she answered and eagerly continued: "I have been thinking of sending Prytzie back to Schloss Varn for some really good stock. Mama never cared about horses, you know. So I'm sure she will let us have what we need. Part of my inheritance from Papa. As for the land, let's buy it from whomever owns it. Obviously they are not making any use of it."

The idea of sending the obstreperous old Master Prytz away for a while appealed to Albrecht, but he felt he could not take advantage of his sister-in-law's generosity. Putting his arm around her shoulder, he shook his head and exclaimed: "Oh Tessa, Tessa! I can't allow you to waste more of your inheritance on Glaumhalle. For over ten generations it has been able to support only a handful of poor soldiers. If Gustaf were alive, it would be different, perhaps. Besides . . . the land you are looking at belongs to the Crown."

"So much the better!" Tessa answered, snuggling happily inside his grip. "Papa was quite friendly with King Wilhelm. His Majesty always rides horses from Schloss Varn. I'm sure we could convince him to sell us a little piece of his land so that we could breed more of the same strain for him and his officers." She gave a pleased little laugh at her idea.

Albrecht shook his head again, as much over her imaginative enterprise as his doubts of its practicality. "I have no doubt that you could charm the King out of that piece of wilderness," he gently told her. "It would be a bargain for him at any price. But for you, a costly generosity toward the von Falkenhorsts. I'm afraid you'd get little in return for it."

"I'm surprised you can't visualize what could be done here," Tessa scolded him with good-natured obstinacy. Breaking away from him, she impetuously sat down on a tussock of matted dry grass and began to run her fingers possessively through its blades to the cold moist soil underneath. Her eyes were on her horse, the magnificent Feldteufel, browsing a few feet away next to the fine mare whose glossy chestnut sides were beginning to bulge with his progeny. "We could breed the finest horses here. As fine as Schloss Varn's. There are good pastures for them. Fields can be cleared for winter fodder. We can bring in enough oats and hay every autumn to support a stable of over a hundred. And cattle and swine too. It's only a matter of acquiring and cultivating all the land we need to breed and feed the animals." Completely carried away with her vision of fat herds of Glaumhalle livestock, she pointed beyond the wild meadow to a farther one nestled in a bend of the shallow stream which was swollen enough by the spring thaws to warrant its name of Orla River. "There is the best piece of all! Look how green it already is. Good bottom loam with plenty of water. Foals and calves will grow fast and strong down there, believe me. We must buy it too!"

Albrecht could not help laughing. He crouched down behind her and put his hands on her shoulders. "Then you'll have to charm the Russian Czar in addition to our own King Wilhelm. You see, everything on the other side of the Orla is part of his Grand Duchy of Poland."

Tessa looked disappointed and annoyed. "Of course it is! I should have remembered that because I've seen his Cossacks ride by out there. It's difficult for me to get used to living within a few minutes' walk of a foreign country. I keep thinking of all this as . . . well, as *ours*."

"That is natural," he said, giving her shoulders a tender squeeze. "Only we who are born and reared on this frontier are aware of it. Poles and Cossacks are constantly fighting each other over there but neither shrinks from occasional cattle and horse-thieving expeditions into Silesia. A state of affairs which should discourage your ambitious plans, my dear Tessa. They would soon spot your lovely fat horses and cows, then—poof—one morning after a dark night, you'd find them all gone."

Tessa swiveled her head, bringing her nose within an inch of his, her amber green eyes flashing belligerently: "That is outrageous! If they try it, we must shoot them!"

"We have shot several in the past," Albrecht confessed rather sadly. "But generally they leave us alone in this district. Because we are almost as poor as they are, I suppose." He shrugged, then smiled and nudged her chin. "But never mind, Tessa. I know where there is better land, lots more land, much more peaceful and free land than this."

"Where?" she asked with excitement. "Let's get on our horses and go look at it."

"It would be a long ride, then a longer swim," he laughed. "It is in America."

"America!" she repeated in astonishment. "You are teasing me, Albrecht. Making fun of me when I'm trying to be serious."

"I am being entirely serious too, my dearest."

"And maybe a little mad? America! What on earth do you know about America?" She laughed derisively now, trying to tease him back.

"I met an American officer during the war who told me about it," he soberly explained. "And what he told me was very exciting. About *one* country stretching over six thousand kilometers from the Atlantic to the Pacific oceans, can you imagine. About millions of hectares of virgin land awaiting the plough, all there for the taking by those who will claim and work it."

"Ah, I thought so!" she scoffed. "Wild soldiers' tales which become wilder as they fill up on wine. There's a bit of von Münchausen in all of them."

"This American is one of their most famous generals," Albrecht persisted. "He rode with our army as a neutral observer all the way from the Rhine to Paris. He is a friend of our General von Moltke and of *your* friend, King Wilhelm. As a matter of fact, he talked to your father several times. His name is General Philip Sheridan."

Tessa was no longer laughing at him, but stared in puzzled

wonder: "I've never heard of him. But even if he is a famous foreigner, I don't understand why you would want to leave Prussia and go to his country just to buy land. We have plenty here. There really must be some other reason, Albrecht."

"There is. They are developing a social system very different from ours. One in which circumstances of birth, family, marriage, and tradition are not all-important." When he saw the mounting incomprehension, even alarm in her expression, he became flustered but could not help blurting out: "What I mean is . . . there, in America . . . we could be *married!* Married without objections from our families, without whispered gossip behind our backs. There nobody would know us or our past. We could make a new life together."

This was the first time he had made definite mention of marriage, and because her expression did not change, he had a panicky feeling that she was about to reject him. But instead she said: "But your family has lived here at Glaumhalle for more than three hundred years. Are you telling me you'd give it up to marry *me?*"

"Yes, my darling," he ardently told her, grasping her hands. "Glaumhalle is nothing. A ruin, crumbling in a fallow wasteland. What worries me much more is what *you* would have to give up: Schloss Varn, one of Germany's greatest estates! But I . . . I would give up my life for you, Tessa. Or give *you* up rather than ruin yours," he added miserably.

Her wide-eyed confusion lasted a moment longer while she seemed to consider his passionate declaration. Then she tightened her hands in his: "You are proposing to me, my dearest," she whispered. "But how silly to do it while in the same breath you mention giving me up . . . giving up your own life. Why? What good would our love then be? For you? For me? Why not just ask me to marry you with the full intention of doing so, no matter what happens? Why not?"

He was overwhelmed by feelings both of ecstasy and despair. When she pressed hard against him, his muscles went limp and they both collapsed flat in the grass, bodies close, arms entwined. "Oh, God! . . . I do love you so much, my Tessa," he gasped. "So much that I'm afraid. . . ."

She put two fingers against his lips in a tender, silencing touch. "Don't be afraid, dearest. I'm not. All that matters is that you love me, that you proposed to me . . . that I accept!"

He gently, but firmly, brushed her fingers aside: "No matter what or how?" When she eagerly nodded, he pulled her face closer to his, his lips seeking hers, then meeting and joining in a long, very long, kiss. Her whole body went limp for an instant then began to tremble when their tongues touched; then she

326

disengaged herself from him with a little gasp. It made Feldteufel raise his head from his browsing, perk up his ears and, after
staring at them for a second, give off a soft, lusty whinny. That
made them both sit up and laugh.

"If we do go to America, we must take Feldteufel with us,"
Albrecht exclaimed. "He obviously approves of our love."

Tessa's laughter faded into a worried smile. "You still insist
that we must go there?"

"I only insist we love each other—forever and wherever!"
He pulled her back down into the grass. She yielded to him for
a moment longer, but her kisses playfully evaded his mouth
with a series of tantalizing pecks around it, the last one squarely
on the tip of his nose. Then she rolled away from him and
sprang to her feet. Very shakily, very happily, yet quite reluctantly, he also got up off the ground.

"We have lots of time to decide about America," she said,
picking up Feldteufel's reins and swinging herself with lithe
grace into the saddle. "I want to hear a lot more about it. Maybe
tonight, Albrecht. In the meantime, let's enjoy what we have.
Let's not cheat Feldteufel and his mare out of a good gallop."

Tessa led the way down the gentle slope of the meadow she
coveted, keeping the energetically snorting Feldteufel down to
a restrained canter out of consideration for the pregnant mare
Albrecht was riding. When they reached the flooded banks of
the Orla, she turned northward to follow the bulging loop of its
curve, splashing through the water coursing around the trunks
of alders and willows growing on the banks. She reached out
and broke off a twig in passing, looked at its fuzzy clusters of
bursting buds, then waved it happily at Albrecht. "The pussy
willows will be out in a day or two! Lilies of the valley won't
be far behind!" "Yes, the worse the winter, the better the
spring!" he called back. When they reached the apex of the
curve, she reined in to a stop. There was a small rapid at this
point where the muddy brown waters tumbled over rocks and
floating dead branches and rushes; beyond, on the opposite bank
of the Orla, another wild meadow preened itself in the soft light
of sundance and cloud shadows. "How beautiful!" she exclaimed ecstatically. "Beautiful enough to try and steal it from
the Muscovite Czar!"

Albrecht laughed. "That would be fair enough. It is here
that his brigands often ford the river to steal from us!"

For a moment she seemed to brace herself to spur Feldteufel across the rushing water on a retaliatory marauding expedition of her own. But then she was diverted by a sudden rustling
in a nearby thicket. A big brown hare burst out of cover within
a few feet of their horses and took off with long, erratically

zigzagging bounds over the open field. Tessa launched a hot pursuit in which Albrecht joined, but soon fell behind on his slower, clumsier horse. The hare laid its long ears back, twisting and turning, even running a complete circle which forced Feld-teufel to lean into a dangerously tight turn as he pounded along hard on the furry heels; then the fleet little animal streaked across the meadow at top speed and, an instant before being run down, made a high, flying leap into the safety of a brambled outcropping of rocks. Any rider less skilled than Tessa would have crashed after it in a painful fall, but she swerved and stopped just short of that.

When Albrecht caught up with her, a little shaken by her reckless riding, she shrugged off his concern and exuberantly exclaimed: "How exciting! How beautiful! What fun!—You can't tell me, Albrecht, there is anything better than this in America!"

He shook his head, sadly resigned. "If this is what you want, then this is what you'll have. We will work things out somehow. Above all else, I want you to be happy, my darling."

Their lathering horses touched flanks and she reached out to touch him. "I've never been as happy as I am now," she assured him. "No matter what troubles come, we'll face them together. *Here* at Glaumhalle . . . which reminds me, your mother will be needing our attention."

The mention of his mother sent a cold, angry shiver down his spine. And as they turned their horses and began an easy trot back toward the manor, a dark cloud passed over its hilltop, casting an ominous shadow over the harsh square outlines of its structure and shrouding it in the mist of a passing shower of rain. They could not avoid the chilling downpour before reaching shelter of *der Feste*.

That evening the entire Glaumhalle household, except the encarcerated Dowager Baroness, took dinner together as they had throughout the past two months of cold and want, sharing the same table and frugal meal of pig knuckles and boiled potatoes. It was the last such meal they would eat together.

"Tomorrow we will go back to our old ways of living at Glaumhalle!" Tessa suddenly exclaimed, startling both Albrecht and Master Prytz. "After all, the hard winter, the cruel war, the sorrows and troubles are past. There is no need for us to suffer and sacrifice any longer. With God's help we can start living for better times, start making them come about! And let's start by regaining a little privacy for ourselves. There is plenty of room here, so as of tomorrow, let's use it." She shot a kindly but uncompromising smile at Lena and Anna: "You can return to your rooms in the attic without fear of freezing to death. And you, Hult," she said, transferring her glance to the foreman, "had better return to *der Feste* where you can be close to the animals. Soon our mares will be foaling and our cows dropping calves and our sows piglets." Her amber eyes flashed from him to Master Prytz, intense, mischievous: "As for you, Prytzie! It's time you returned to Schloss Varn!"

"Back to Schloss Varn?" the stablemaster repeated uneasily. "You no longer have a need for me here then?"

"Of course we do," she assured him. "After a nice visit with your old friends, you will return to us. You will bring with you some good horses and cattle. I shall send Mama a letter about it so you will have no trouble picking out the best they can spare. By this summer we shall have a proper farm operating here and by next year . . . the finest in Silesia."

Albrecht raised his eyebrows and wagged a finger at her. "But, Tessa, I already told you today that we cannot accept this. You can't strip Schloss Varn of its best stock and bring them here. . . ."

"Nonsense!" she interrupted, playfully slapping down his finger. "They have more than they need while we do not have nearly enough. Anyway, it's all for the good of the family." Having firmly turned aside Albrecht's objection, she returned her attention to Master Prytz: "You should have no trouble driving a wagon through to Ols now. Take Hult with you and send him back here with supplies we need. Perhaps you can find some farm workers too. We could use at least two strong hands, maybe three. Don't forget to buy seed. At least two hundredweight of rye. I've picked out a couple of fields we must plant as soon as possible. And, yes, we'll need a team of plow horses. And a new plow! The one we have has rusted to pieces. Come to think of it, let's get *two* plows and *two* teams. Then, after you've taken care of that, take a train to Schloss Varn. We'll expect you back in May with some fine animals and we'll be ready for them. All right, Prytzie?"

Master Prytz looked more worried than pleased: "I shall do your bidding as always, my lady. But is it wise for me to leave

✠

you alone here under the circumstances?" he asked, emphasizing the word *alone* while staring directly into Albrecht's suddenly frowning face. There was a distinct edge to his voice as he answered:

"You may be certain I'll let no harm come to her. She is more dear to me than even to you, Master Prytz."

Tessa gave him an adoring glance and touched his hand for a moment before exclaiming with delighted assurance: "Then it's all settled!"

Hult fidgeted nervously and grumbled through a mouthful of potatoes about the unlikelihood of recruiting any reliable laborers before demobilization had been completed. "All we'll find are more renegade Poles and rejects from the army," he direly predicted. "Even those are likely to have already been snapped up by farms closer to Ols and Breslau." Prytz nodded in agreement and Albrecht pessimistically conceded: "Glaumhalle has always had a way of resisting ambitious plans. When times are hard elsewhere, they are hardest here. When they are good elsewhere, we are the last to enjoy it. No, no matter what you spend, or how much work you give it, Glaumhalle will never become a Schloss Varn. Not even a shadow of it."

Tessa gave him a sidelong glance and, her exuberant good humor undaunted, chided him: "I hope you are not about to start talking about America again, Albrecht." Speaking to the rest of the table, she exclaimed: "Can any of you imagine giving up this land to emigrate to America? Tell me, honestly! Would any of you do that?"

Lena and Anna stopped eating to exchange perplexed glances, then gave a mutely noncommittal shrug. Master Prytz spat out an obdurate: "Certainly not!" Only Foreman Hult seemed to give her question serious consideration and finally admitted cautiously: "I was once tempted to go there. A cousin of mine was very keen on it and asked me to join him in emigrating. I almost did. Just as well I thought better of it, because I never heard from him again after he sailed out of Hamburg. My aunt, his mother, is sure he was killed by Indians . . . or perhaps in the Civil War they had a few years ago."

"Ah, you see!" Tessa said to Albrecht, again gently touching his hand. "America has wars too! And like we have Cossacks lurking around our home, so they have Indians. What could be gained from such an exchange?"

"Perhaps some hope for you and me," he whispered back to her barely audibly. While Lena and Anna had returned their attention to cleaning off their plates, Master Prytz and Foreman Hult had caught the undercurrent of emotion he was trying to hide and were watching him intently. Somewhat foolishly he tried to cover up by tritely exclaiming: "There is a big, wide world stretching far beyond our ken in Silesia . . . even Schloss Varn's Pomerania . . . even all Prussia!"

"Come to think of it," Master Prytz said with a sly hard look at him, the Freiherr von Falkenhorst might well find better opportunities in America. I understand he already has an American friend."

Before Albrecht could answer him, Tessa exclaimed with a touch of impatience: "That is out of the question! We shall make our lives here in Germany where we belong, of course. We shall work the land that is ours. We shall keep it and our families together. Nothing else will do."

"Spoken like your good father, Count Frederick Paul," Master Prytz sighed with an approving smile. Albrecht also heard an echo of her dead father in her manner and words, but was too troubled to comment; he desperately wanted this conversation to end.

But the following silence was short. Tessa leaned forward and addressed the servants across the table from her in an excited confidential tone: "You have all been wonderfully loyal and shared very hard times with us last winter. That is why we share our plans with you for the future and, when we bring it about, will share its happiness and plenty too. For the same reasons, we want you to know something about Freiherr Albrecht and myself." She leaned closer to Albrecht and put her hand on his arm before continuing: "We have become very close to each other. So close that we have fallen in love. And so we will marry when the time comes after our period of mourning for Baron Gustaf is over. So you see, the fortunes of our families will still be as one."

Lena and Anna stared at her, openmouthed, then gave off shrill little squeals of surprise. Foreman Hult was also speechless for a moment; then he muttered an almost unintelligible, but plainly embarrassed, congratulation. Master Prytz turned pale and rigid, his eyes misting as they stared at her in utter disbelief, the tip of his chin and moustache twitching fitfully. Albrecht flushed scarlet, shocked by her unabashed announcement of what he considered a most-intimate secret between them; it was only with the greatest difficulty that he could bring himself to put his arm around her and stammer out: "Yes . . . well, we do love each other, but . . . there are complications . . . difficulties. We must be patient and . . . very discreet."

"I can well understand that," Prytz rasped.

"O-o-oh! Are we going to have a wedding soon?" Lena shrilled, clapping her hands together. Anna began chuckling in anticipation.

"It will have to be a very small, private wedding when and where it takes place," Albrecht said, adding miserably: "Probably not even in a church."

"I can well understand that," Prytz rasped again, this time so intensely that he was startled by his own harsh tone and attempted to correct it by adding: "But, of course . . . my fondest wish is always for my lady's happiness."

Tessa became aware of the effect her announcement had had on the two men she loved most in her life and looked perplexed by it. Her freckles burned in the dim lamplight of the cheerless dining room, her body trembled slightly as she leaned into the stiff embrace of Albrecht's arm, but her eyes smouldered at Master Prytz with a reproachful pleading: "Do you remember, Prytzie, our last ride together on the beach of Schloss Varn?" she asked him. "Do you remember what we talked about alone on that rainy morning?" When he nodded in tight-lipped silence she softly admonished him: "Then you must be able to understand what has happened."

Prytz gave no indication that he did. Albrecht rose from his chair and pulled Tessa with him. "If you will excuse the Baroness and me," he said, "We do have some plans to talk over in private. Good night and thank you, one and all."

When they had gone, Lena and Anna began cleaning off the table, chattering in eager whispers, and breaking into loud giggles as they carried out the dishes. Foreman Hult and Master Prytz remained seated for a while longer, nursing the last precious drops of Glaumhalle's homebrewed beer. Neither of them spoke until Hult suddenly gave a grunting laugh and said: "I can't wait to pass this news on to the postman. It will be worth several drinks to him on his route through the district."

"You say a word to him about it and I'll wring your scrawny neck," Prytz snarled with fury. "And you'd better make those stupid girls keep their mouths shut too, you understand?"

Hult put on a surly surprise: "If the Baroness herself chose to speak openly of it, who the hell are you to hush it up, Herr Stallmeister Prytz?"

"She is only nineteen years old," Prytz burst out in a barely suppressed sob. "An orphan girl and a widow at nineteen!" He slammed his fist down on the table with a resounding crash which made the remaining plates and glasses jump and clatter. Even Hult jumped slightly and spilled some of his beer. Then he quickly drained the rest and got up, saying with a strained control:

"I for one hope I never become as emotionally involved with my employers as you. It does no good for either party."

"All your emotions are in the crotch of your pants, Hult," Master Prytz raged, rising and towering threateningly over the foreman.

"That's where most of us carry it, if the truth be faced. Commoners and nobility alike!"

Prytz aimed a hard clap into Hult's grinning face, but missed because his eyes were full of tears and merely scuffed him over the top of his head. At least it had the effect of making the foreman take flight through the kitchen toward *der Feste*. "You have your orders for tomorrow!" Prytz bellowed after him. "Be ready to leave at dawn!" Then with his massive shoulders bowed and his face contorted in sorrow, he stamped past the cringing maids in the kitchen to go to the stables and make sure the wagon and harnesses would be ready for the trip to Ols.

Albrecht and Tessa had retired to the study on the opposite side of the house from the dining room. They could only hear the altercation between Master Prytz and Hult as a distant thumping of garbled voices, indistinct but unpleasant. Tessa's cheerful confidence had given way to uneasy doubt, increased by Albrecht's agitated solicitude. He was pouring some schnapps out of a decanter he kept on a shelf above the desk and she noticed that his hand shook as he filled two small glasses. His smile and voice were tense as he offered her one of them: "Well, my dearest . . . since this turned out a strange betrothal party, let's at least drink to it—to us, the troubled lovers of Glaumhalle! *Prosit!*"

Because her own hand was trembling and spilling the overfilled glass, she quickly took a drink. The taste of schnapps always reminded her of the first one she had ever had, when Frau Hess, the pastor's wife, made her drink some to give her courage to go through with her wedding to Gustaf. It was as unpleasant this time, yet after the burning sensation passed, as strangely fortifying. "I'm afraid I displeased you tonight," she said in a softly challenging tone of voice. "You think I was too blunt, too forthright in explaining our situation."

"Quite aside from the generosity you insist on heaping on this house, and which I find difficult to accept, you spoke the truth about our love." He clinked his glass against hers, then added with a frown: "But, as you could tell, you shocked our servants, and to some extent *me!* I thought you understood our very delicate situation and would keep it entirely between us for the time being. You must have noticed Prytz's reaction."

"Yes, I did!" she instantly agreed. "I wanted to find out how he felt. Hult and those two scullery maids don't matter a whip. But Prytzie is quite different. You can count on him to react exactly as would our noble friends and relations. Do you know it was *he*, even more than Papa, who made sure I kept my appointment with your brother at Varn church last July? If it had not been for him, I would have ridden my poor Kugel a hundred kilometers away from there . . . or out into the surf of our beach and drowned us both. . . . Oh, my poor Kugel! That might have been better for both of us!"

"Don't talk such nonsense, Tessa!" Albrecht told her with sharp alarm. He tried to put his arm around her, but she pulled away. The memory of her favorite horse had choked her with emotion. After impulsively draining her glass with a grimace as the fiery liquid seared her throat, she took a grip on herself and hoarsely said:

"Since you expect so much trouble over our marriage, I wanted to test Prytzie and get an inkling of what to expect. To forearm myself. I am sorry if it made you angry."

"I'm not angry with you, Tessa," he reassured her soothingly and tenderly caressed her cheek. This time she did not pull away. "I could never be angry with you. I love you too much."

"Are you sure, Albrecht? I wonder if we're not bad luck for each other, the Falkenhorsts and the Beckhauses?" She looked questioningly into his eyes, almost fearfully. "I don't want to bring you bad luck, Albrecht!"

"I feel myself the luckiest man in the world," he answered, drawing her closer. "We have shared tragedies, but now, if we have faith in our love, we can share great happiness. Of that I am very sure, my Tessa." He kissed her lips, gently at first, then with a mounting intensity of desire, whispering while still touching: "Kiss me again like we did this afternoon, my love! Open your mouth to me."

She did for a passionate instant before breaking away, breathless, but smiling: "That is enough for now! What if Prytzie caught us again kissing in here like that? The poor old man would have a fit. My goodness! I believe that drink you gave me must have gone to my head."

Albrecht laughed and with a deliberate motion reached out to push the door to the hall completely shut: "Let your devoted stablemaster confine his interests to our horses. At least make him knock before intruding on us." He deftly splashed another finger of schnapps into her glass before she could pull it away. "A little lightheadedness will do us both good. Indeed we deserve it. So . . . *prosit!*"

They entwined arms to drink, but this time Tessa took only a token sip, then teasingly told him: "You mustn't be hard on Prytzie. I love him very much, you see . . . as I suppose a daughter should love a father. Anyway, I think he'll give in to us soon enough. I think he knows now we'll only take his advice about horses." She resisted his move to sit down and pull her into his lap. "No, Albrecht! I'd love to kiss you some more . . . but it must only be good night, my sweet."

"I'm not going to bed in that dormitory tonight," he said, making a wry face. "Hult smells like a billy goat and your Prytzie snorts and snores through the night like an old boar in rut. I'll take my pillow and blankets back to my own room and bed, thank you."

She nodded and laughed. "As a matter of fact, that's exactly my idea. Lena talks in her sleep—quite indecently about shocking subjects! And Anna grinds her teeth when she's not thrashing through a nightmare. Come! Let's move back upstairs!"

"I'll take my good night kiss when we've made our beds," Albrecht exclaimed, reopening the door and motioning her out of the study with an exaggerated flourish.

Tessa gave him a playful slap and said, "Sh-sh-sh! We must be very quiet and careful. Remember, your mother is upstairs."

"Ah, yes! So she is," Albrecht answered, his ardor considerably dampened by the reminder.

aster Prytz and Foreman Hult left Glaumhalle early next day, which dawned blustery but clear, with a capricious chilly wind veering between north and east. All the snow had melted off the manor, *der Feste*, and the craggy slopes of their hill, but during the night, thin crusts of ice had formed over the puddles and turned frostily brittle the ridges of mud crisscrossing the yard. The wagon crunched down the deep ruts of the road, pulled by a team of two sturdy horses and followed by two spares trailing behind on lead reins. That left only one draught animal at Glaumhalle besides Feldteufel, a two-year-old stallion, and four mares in foal; likewise, it left only one man, Albrecht, in charge of the four women. Master Prytz started out on the thirty-kilometer journey to Ols with misgivings in spite of Albrecht's assurances of being able to watch over the women, and Tessa's confident manner as she sent him on his way with precise instructions and a heavy purse.

As the creaking wagon slithered and squished down the steep slope of Glaumhalle's hill, a flight of wild geese suddenly swooped up from the flooded Orla and cut a tight circle above the manor and the jagged tower of *der Feste*. With their swift, graceful passage through the pale sunrise, they gave out a series of deep haunting calls. Tessa pointed at them as they flashed overhead, clutched Albrecht's arm and exuberantly cried: "Look! Wild geese! The best good luck sign of all! Wild geese in March, then storks in April. That means an early spring and a long fine summer!"

Master Prytz also looked up at the great birds as they completed their circle and called back somewhat less impressed: "Yes, good luck, let's hope! But take care, my lady!" Foreman Hult, rocking uncomfortably on the bench alongside him, barely gave the geese a glance, yet one appraising enough to mutter under his breath: "What a meal flying away from our pot!"

As soon as Prytz and Hult had vanished, Tessa launched a determined spring-cleaning program to alleviate the dark, musty winter grime still permeating the manor. Her cheerful enthusiasm combined with the continuing clear weather to stir some energy even out of the lethargic Anna and Lena, and moved Albrecht into participating in what would normally be entirely women's work around the house. Windows and shutters were pried open to allow in fresh air and sunshine. Tessa decreed that firewood no longer had to be burned stick by precious stick but was to be lavished on heating all the water necessary for scrubbing and laundering. By noon, the barren little orchard on the south slope became festooned with gaily flapping sheets, pillow cases, shirts, skirts, underwear, petticoats, blankets, and comforters, all strung out like bunting on lines which Albrecht had rigged between the apple and cherry trees. He also took over the duties of farmhand and turned their small herd of cattle out to pasture for the first time since the previous December. The cows and their bull broke out of their long, gloomy confinement inside *der Feste* with exuberant lowings of delight.

A much less enjoyable chore, which Tessa insisted upon doing herself in spite of Albrecht's misgivings, was that of cleaning out and airing the gloomy, smelly bedroom where the Dowager Baroness had been secluded in self-imposed squalor for the past nine weeks. She met her daughter-in-law's efforts with her usual snapping and snarling. But Tessa gritted her teeth and proceded to pull aside the heavy drapes and throw open the window, letting in a bright shaft of sunlight and cleansing whiff of March breeze. The Dowager Hildebrun screeched protests and tried to bury herself beneath the soiled linens of her bed, but Tessa rolled up her sleeves and reaching into the tangle, yanked her clear of it and, with a measured force, pulled her out of bed, propping her into a chair next to the open window. "Stop your mean sniveling, Madam!" she roughly ordered and twisted her around to face outside. "If you take a deep breath and a good look, you'll notice a fine spring day! Maybe it will make you feel better." The Dowager Baroness was so shocked by this treatment that she meekly settled into the chair without further resistance, sniffing and staring at the splendid view of her lands as if it had been revealed to her for the first time. "See how beautiful it is!" Tessa encouraged her, throwing a blanket over her trembling shoulders before going about the distasteful business of stripping the rest of her bedding down to the stained mattress.

"Yes . . . it is a fine day, deary!" the Dowager Hildebrun agreed in an almost-normal tone of voice. She virtually leaned back and relaxed, basking in the sunray illuminating her desiccated face.

Albrecht, who had tensely watched the performance from the threshold, gave a long admiring sigh: "Thank God for you, Tessa! You've made her human again, even if only for a moment."

Tessa pushed past him with her arms full of bedding. "Sit with her while I have these laundered. Perhaps the company of a son will do her even more good."

Albrecht did remain with his mother for a while, attempting to engage her attention with casual conversation. But it was like trying to talk with and amuse a retarded child, and he soon lapsed into a sad silence as she ignored him and prattled incoherently to herself while staring out the window. He took small comfort from the fact that for once her prattling seemed childishly inoffensive. Then she began nodding and dozed off with her head lolled back, the harsh lines of her face turning almost serene in the warm caress of the sunlight. After gently tucking the blanket closer around her body, he left her to attend more important matters.

Feeling pleasantly weary and satisfied with a good day's work, Albrecht and Tessa had dinner together alone in the dining room, served by a clumsily solicitous Anna. It was pork and potatoes again, but it was a mutual relief for them to be able to enjoy each other's company at table without the inhibiting presence of their retainers. He had brought up a bottle of wine from the cellar for the occasion and she produced four candles out of the dwindling supply to augment the smoky coal-oil lamp with some festive light. Upstairs, the Dowager Hildebrun was tucked back into a clean bed after having been fed a rich mash of potatoes, gravy, and lean scraps of pig knuckles; her rare mood had continued throughout the day to their great relief.

Albrecht unstintingly praised Tessa for these improvements. She answered that there was a lot more to be done and suggested that as soon as Master Prytz returned with new horses and cattle, the two of them should travel on a shopping expedition to Breslau: "We could make it a very pleasant, useful trip!" she enthusiastically exclaimed. "We could buy the sort of things that old Prytzie could never pick out for us. New bright-colored drapes and curtains. Two or three really comfortable chairs. Maybe a new sofa for the drawing room. And some rugs. And some new china. Almost all our china is cracked and chipped, you know. And I really think we should buy *you* some good clothes. That moth-eaten old Railroad Inspector's uniform of yours is not only unfashionable but badly worn out!" She gave him a teasing laugh and an affectionate pat on the hand.

"How about some pretty new dresses for you, my dearest?" he asked with a sly glance at her plain, faded gray dress.

"Oh, so you find me dingy looking!"

They both laughed uproariously because as they looked each other over, it was obvious that neither one came close to representing any degree of the elegance expected from the nobility of the new German Empire. He assured her that she was the most beautiful girl he had ever known, even if she were dressed in rags. She gave him a similar compliment, but insisted that he would be even more handsome if draped in the latest cut of new cloth. "Well, we may make a trip soon to Breslau and buy a few things we need. Perhaps that's where we should think about eventually getting quietly married. There is an old lawyer friend of the family there who might arrange things for us."

"Let's drink to that, my darling! *Prosit!*"

They happily clinked glasses. "Shall we take coffee in the salon?" Tessa impishly invited. There was, of course, no coffee left in the house and the salon was still in a disarray of rolled-up carpets and stacked furniture. But they went in just the same, arm in arm, and happily shared a make-believe cup which turned the bleakly disordered room into one of comfortable elegance. An imaginary fire glowed in the cold black maw of the stone hearth. The sooty lightless lamps came aglow. She led him to the window whose drapes had been taken down to have the dust beaten out of them. There they leaned close together, looking out on the very real beauty of the wild orchard and distant plains, now delicately illuminated by the pale pink afterglow of a clear sunset. "It is lovely," she whispered. "It is just waiting for spring and us to work it. Then it will be lovelier yet, you'll see!"

"With your magic touch, I'm sure even Glaumhalle will bloom, my dearest," he answered. He started to take her in his arms to kiss her, but suddenly tensed and instead put his face closer to the glass and stared hard through it.

His eyes had been caught by a movement beyond the swollen stream of the Orla, but obscured in the deepening shadows of its bordering clumps of willow trees. For a moment he thought that distance, the gathering darkness, and the breeze stirring branches and reeds had tricked him into seeing men and horses. Then they appeared quite clearly: six or seven horsemen trailed by four or five men on foot, stealthily probing along the flooded east bank as if looking for a suitable ford for crossing over to the west. Even in the fading light of the sunset he could instantly tell that they were *not* part of a Cossack border patrol; Cossack uniforms were easily recognizable and, besides, they hardly ever moved up to the very edge of the Russo-Prussian frontier. A band of Polish refugees looking for asylum, perhaps? Not likely at this time of year, nor did they usually invite pursuit by escaping in groups of more than three or four people; rarer yet could they afford horses. Cattle thieves then! Authorized travelers always approached the frontier at the custom stations located either at Racwicz, twenty-five kilometers northwest, or Krotoczyn, located nearly twice that far to the southeast. So they had to be cattle thieves on the prowl—or worse, casual bandits desperate enough to kill for just a few chickens and household goods!

Albrecht assessed the situation in a matter of seconds, then came to the chilling realization that he was facing this threat *alone* with four women on his hands. For another instant he wrestled with the urge to rush Tessa and himself toward *der Feste*, saddle up their horses and take flight toward the interior. But he knew she would never go.

A quick glance at her face told him that she had not seen the men. Her eyes were looking upward, focusing in wonder at the first glittering of the evening star. "I think I had better go and make sure all is well with our animals in *der Feste*," he told her with a forced casual tone. "Remember, neither Hult nor Master Prytz is here to care for them."

"Good. I'll go with you," she said, turning from the window. "Just let me fetch my shawl."

"No!" he answered more sharply than he had intended. "No—you light some of our lamps in here and upstairs. As many as you can."

She looked surprised. "Why?"

"To make the place look . . . well, more *lived* in," he somewhat irrationally explained. "Like it already is the bright, bustling home we shall make it. I'd like to see it tonight the way it will be then." Realizing how eccentric he sounded, he covered with a lame laugh and odd joke: "It's a sentimental old saying: 'keep a candle burning in the window for me' . . . well, for *me*, Tessa, I expect one from you in every window!"

"Sometimes you have quite mad ideas, Albrecht!" she laughed and gave him a kiss on the cheek, then keeping her mouth close to his, inviting a kiss in return. But the one she received was hasty and less ardent than she had come to expect. After the briefest parting embrace, he hurried out of the room, calling back over his shoulder: "Don't worry if I'm not back for a while, dearest! If you get tired, go to bed. I'll put out the lights when I come back."

On his way out through a side door, Albrecht stopped by the gun cabinet located in a back hall of the manor and picked out the heaviest-gauge shotgun, his father's old dragoon pistol, powder horn, and bag of shot. The pistol was kept loaded, but he had neglected to check it since his return to Glaumhalle and feared the loads would misfire after lying in the chambers for better than a year. The shotgun was useless until filled with a charge of powder, paper bags of shot rammed down its barrels, and percussion caps inserted under the hammers, a procedure which would take better than a minute even when he was in practice—which he was not.

Hurrying outside with the pistol stuck in his belt, he shouldered the shotgun and, crossing the wide yard separating the manor and *der Feste*, deliberately slowed his step, hoping there was enough of the twilight left for the marauders to spot an armed man on guard. He was desperately hoping that Tessa would humor his whimsical request for lights in the windows, which he hoped would give the impression that Glaumhalle was far better populated than it actually was. As he slowly crossed the yard, stopping in the middle of it for a full minute, only the kitchen and one hall window glowed feebly out of the gloomy mass of the manor. *Der Feste* loomed a totally dark silhouette against the fading shimmer of the sunset.

Feldteufel snorted and pawed the floor of his stall when Albrecht entered the stable, but he paid no attention to him. Groping through the darkness he found a lantern hanging on its customary hook and lit it; by its light he found two others and lit them also. Then he loaded the shotgun and hurriedly checked the pistol before leaving *der Feste* with lights showing through its open door and several lower embrasures. Now moving quickly and keeping in the shadows, he circled around the back of the building and its compost heap, ran in short, cautious dashes wide of the manor, through the orchard and down the hill toward the Orla.

On reaching the foot of the hill, he stopped to peer toward

the stream, crouching behind the trunk of a gnarled white oak. The darkness was much deeper than ten minutes ago and he could distinguish no men or horses through the gloom of reeds and willows growing in thick clumps along both banks; nor could he hear anything besides the steady rush of water and the soft, mournful cry of an owl. Yet he felt certain that the strangers were somewhere close by. Looking back toward the manor, he noticed with disappointment that Tessa still had not placed those candles in the windows; but at least *der Feste* showed three feeble, but constant, glows.

Halfway between the oak and the stream he could distinguish a cluster of young alders. After looking and listening for another minute, he made a rush for them at a crouching run, almost falling as the ground became soft and full of tangling mats of dead grass. From this position he again carefully peered and listened for the marauders. The sound of many swift little rapids was stronger and an owl, who had been perched in one of the alders, took off with an angry screech which set his nerves even more on edge, and brought him to within a fraction of firing the shotgun blindly after it. His own hard breathing and the heavy thumping of his heart seemed to him noisier than any of the natural night sounds he could hear. He cursed himself for having allowed Hult and Master Prytz to leave that day—which he knew to be a foolish self-reproach since the same situation could have arisen tomorrow night, the night after, or any time in this isolated frontier district. It was a risk he had been brought up with and even as a child learned to take for granted. He remembered that when he was ten years old his father had driven off Polish cattle thieves, shooting down two of them as they tried to cross the Orla; and three years later, Gustaf had shot dead two bandits in the very act of breaking into the stables. They had had dogs then who gave plenty of warning when strangers were prowling about. But the last of their hounds had died last year.

The owl he had disturbed did not fly far away and he could hear it hooting from a tree closer to the stream to his left. Then it suddenly screeched again and Albrecht knew for certain that the marauders were lurking close by. His knees began to shake, but without hesitation he moved out from the alders and began walking toward the bank. When he reached a point where muddy water began sucking at the soles of his boots, he cocked both hammers of the shotgun, stopped, took a deep breath and called out into the rustling darkness of the Orla: "Who are you? What do you want here?"

Except for the sound of tumbling water and faint rustling of reeds, the answer was silence. The owl was hooting again, but now much farther upstream. He was about to turn around and start a slow retreat back to the alders when he caught a barely audible creaking and clinking of tack and saddle-leather, then the soft nervous snort of a horse, followed by the urgent calming whisper of its rider. Raising the shotgun to his shoulder and aiming it in the general direction of the faint noise, he repeated his challenge. And this time there was a reply: "We come in peace!" a voice boomed back, speaking in German with a thick Polish accent. "We are not armed. We have traveled far and just wish to camp here for the night."

Albrecht strained his eyes, trying to make out the speaker, wondering whether he had already crossed over to the west bank and how many companions he had. "Why are you hiding in the dark?" he asked. "If you are camping, why don't you light a fire and show yourselves?"

"We were just about to do that," the deep voice answered. "We had considered asking for shelter in your fine big house. But if we are unwelcome we will camp on this side of the frontier."

"That is best for you!" Albrecht belligerently shouted back. "If you trespass on Falkenhorst land . . . German land, we're ready to shoot you!"

He realized with a shudder how empty was this threat: he had six shots in the pistol, of which one or all might misfire, and just two in the shotgun which he was not proficient enough to reload quickly in the dark. There was no answer, but he could plainly hear a burst of low, excited Polish chatter above the sounds of the stream. Then a bright small light suddenly flared among the trees of the opposite bank, flickered, almost went out, then spread into dancing flames which turned into a crackling campfire. It cast a smoky yellow glow, in which the figures of several men could be dimly seen moving around, and a pool of reflected light in the swirling waters, revealing two mounted men who had waded their horses nearly halfway across the Orla. It had been one of these two who had spoken to him. "Go back!" he shakily ordered them. "Go back at once!"

The two horsemen did not come any closer, but neither did they turn back. "Would you at least sell us some flour and fresh eggs," one of them asked. "We can pay with a silver rouble."

"No! We have too many of our own people to feed here to spare any food," Albrecht replied, hoping his answer would suggest a large force available to defend Glaumhalle.

"Listen, friend!" the one with the deep voice persisted. "We are close to starving. Just a couple of scoops of flour and a few eggs will help us complete our journey. In God's mercy don't deny us that." He began to edge his horse forward. Then a combination of the current flowing around the animal's flanks and the rough rocky bottom caused it to lose its footing and lunge to regain its balance.

Albrecht could only vaguely distinguish the violent motion and interpreted it as a deliberate charge. He cried out a last warning, but his muscles tensed in a movement which was transmitted through to the fingers curled around the double triggers. The shotgun rent the night with the roar of a small cannon as both barrels fired their charges simultaneously, slamming him backward. Stunned, he sat in the mud for a moment, dazedly glimpsing the two mounted marauders as they fought their rearing horses, then wheeled them around and churned in wild retreat back to the Russian side of the Orla; one of them fell off as he tried to drive his mount up the bank, then scrambled after his bolting animal on all fours, wet but unhurt. Other horses were heard breaking their tethers and, with terrified whinnies, thrashing off through the marshy growths. The men by the campfires screamed loud Polish curses and threw themselves flat on the ground, covering their heads from a rain of branches and twigs which the double charge of heavy pellets scythed out of the tree tops. One of them yelled in a furious, high-pitched, fractured German:

"Rotten German swine! You're no better than those heathen Cossacks! Satan take you all!"

Albrecht struggled to his feet and ran back to the protection of the stand of alders through the darkness, slipping and staggering. He fumbled frantically through the procedure of reloading the shotgun, spilling a lot of powder and shot before finally succeeding. Then he sank down on his haunches in the cold damp loam, trying to catch his breath while listening and watching through the darkness of the Orla. The campfire burned, making shadows dance among the surrounding trees and the waters sparkle with reflections of its flames, but now there were no silhouettes of men and horses within its circle of light. He could barely hear voices calling to each other through the swampy underbrush, then fading as the horses stampeded by his shot drew farther and farther away. His heart leaped when he glanced back up the hill and saw that several windows of the manor were now showing lights—then as he watched two more came ablaze.

Albrecht remained where he was, crouching among the alders, for another half hour. By then the night had become silent and completely black beneath its glittering vault of stars; the marauder's abandoned campfire turned into a dying red flicker. But behind him, Glaumhalle crowned its hill like a festively illuminated castle. Rising up from his defensive position, he shouldered the shotgun and walked, almost strutted, back up the slope toward it. Upon reaching the seldom-used front entrance of the manor, he was amused to find that the massive wrought iron lanterns flanking it had been lit, probably for the first time in ten years. But he had to pound the iron knocker several times before the bolts rattled and the heavy oak door creaked open just enough for a gun barrel to poke out. "Is that you, Albrecht?" Tessa's voice challenged.

"Well, who else, dearest?" he asked with an entirely false bravado.

The gun barrel pulled back and the door was opened wide enough to let him slip inside. There was Tessa, greeting him with a grim mixture of relief and anger, her freckles in stark contrast to the pallor of her cheeks. She had undressed for bed shortly after he had left the house and was wearing a quilted robe over her nightgown. She had unbraided her hair and it now hung in a disordered tumble of copper waves around her shoulders and back. Behind her, Anna and Lena were cringing against each other in mutual fear, trying to keep a shaky hold on a pair of dribbling, flickering candles. "Who were you shooting at out there?" Tessa asked, carefully uncocking the hammers of the household's only other shotgun.

"Oh, you heard that shot?" Albrecht casually inquired. He noticed that although Tessa seemed to have a good hold of herself, Anna and Lena were on the brink of hysterics, and so without hesitation proceded to lie about the situation. "I didn't mean to frighten you. Dusk is a good time to stalk waterfowl along the sloughs of the Orla. I was trying to shoot us a good goose dinner. I'm sorry, but I missed and the flock has flown away—*far away!*" Pointing at the weapon Tessa was clutching, he asked: "Were you going hunting too, my dear?"

Tessa stamped her foot, an ineffectual gesture since she was wearing neither slippers nor stockings. But her eyes told Albrecht that he had not fooled her in the least, though she firmly told the two servant girls: "You can go upstairs to bed now. There is nothing to worry about. The Freiherr and I will put out the lights."

After they had scurried off toward their cubbyholes in the attic, squeaking like frightened mice, Albrecht said to Tessa: "Let's leave the lamps burning a little longer. You have no idea how cheerful the house looks from outside." Avoiding her accusing glare, he hooked his arm into hers and led her down the hall to the staircase, where he stopped and asked: "By the way, is that shotgun loaded?"

"Do you think me a child?" she snapped back.

"No. I gather then that you know how to load and shoot a

gun." He retracted a move to take her weapon away from her.

"Yes. Prytzie taught me that before I was twelve years old. I have shot partridge and ducks and geese and hares, and would have shot a stag if Papa hadn't interfered." Her voice suddenly rose in shrill anger: "You could have trusted me, Albrecht! You could have told me the real reason why you wanted all these lamps and candles lit. You could have told me you had noticed intruders trying to cross the river. You didn't have to face them alone!"

"Next time I will tell you, now that I know how brave you are," he told her and started leading her up the stairs. "Was Mama frightened by the shot?"

"It did not even awaken her. But it gave *me* quite a jolt and terrified poor Lena and Anna out of their wits. Really very inconsiderate of you, Albrecht!" Her voice switched to a lower, breathless tone as she asked: "Who were they? Did you have to kill any of them?"

He could not help suppressing a laugh. "I was too frightened to shoot straight, thank God. I'm not really made of heroic stuff, like poor Gustaf. But neither were those strangers, and thank God for that too. They ran away and I haven't seen or heard them for over a half hour."

"Were they robbers like those you told me about yesterday?" Tessa asked.

He waited until they had tiptoed past the Dowager Brunhilde's closed door before answering: "Maybe, maybe not. Perhaps they were just another band of lost refugees from Poland. The trouble is, we must always treat strangers approaching us from the east as hostile. Especially after dark." They entered his small bedroom at the end of the hall which faced the Orla. She had lit his lamp and moved it to the windowsill, but he now moved it back to the bedside table, then stared intently through the window. He could faintly make out the almost extinguished glow of the campfire. "I think it best I keep watch for a while," he said. "From here and some of the windows on the other side of the house. We must guard against their circling around us. But you can go to bed now, dearest."

"No, I will stay up with you. And before you do anything else, get out of those wet, muddy clothes. I'll go take a look from my room."

Albrecht took off his jacket, pulled off his boots and quickly changed into a pair of dry trousers, then padded down the hall and looked into the several empty rooms where Tessa had placed lighted candles in the windows; some of them were already down to within a few minutes of burning out, and he knew there were very few spares left in the house. Yet they would have to spend at least one more night like this, perhaps two, before Master Prytz would complete his errand in Ols and send Hult back to Glaumhalle—hopefully with two or three reliable farmhands. With this in mind, he extinguished all but one, which he carried to light his way down the darkened hall to Tessa's room—formerly Gustaf's room. He found her with her face pressed against the dark glass, tensely on watch and still clutching her fowling piece. "One of the lamps you lit in *der Feste* just went out," she told him. "But I think it went out by itself for lack of oil. We have less than one liter left."

He peered out at the massive black shape of *der Feste* with its single pinprick of light, and put a comforting arm around her shoulder. "Perhaps it would be best if I take you and the maids to Ols tomorrow morning. We could put them and Mama in the cart and . . ."

"No!" she firmly interrupted him. "We'll never abandon Glaumhalle because of a few cowardly cattle thieves. Never!"

He gave her cheek a quick, admiring kiss. "Very well. We'll stay. With your courage we'll manage until Hult returns with some men. But I wish now that you hadn't sent Prytz back to Schloss Varn."

She gave a short, taunting laugh. "I thought you were glad to be rid of him. Anyway, we must learn to depend on ourselves. Or had you intended to take him to America with us and protect us against wild Indians?"

"Such impudence! You know perfectly well that I want you all to myself. And so I have at long last! Wait here for me while I make rounds of the house and turn out more lights. Just two or three will do to show that we are on guard."

He went downstairs and made sure that all the doors were locked. He stoked the fire in the kitchen stove and left a full lamp burning there, then blew out those in the dining room, sitting room and study to conserve fuel. Then he bounded back up the stairs, taking two steps at a time, and moving so fast that his candle almost went out. Returning to his room with the intention of extinguishing the lamp there and taking a long, careful look from its commanding view to the East, he was surprised to find it already in darkness and Tessa waiting for him by the window. Outside, a wan quarter-moon had risen to add its pewter sheen to the starlight, still not bright enough to reveal details in the orchard or the river bottom below it. The campfire had gone out, but its smoke still hung in the windless night above the willows, a faintly luminescent pall drifting through the moonbeams. "I can see nothing down there," she softly reported.

"On a still night like this, it is better to listen than to try to see," Albrecht said and quietly unlatching the window, opened it wide. The result was a chilling waft of cold air and absolute silence.

Tessa gave a shudder and retreating from the window, sat down on the edge of the bed. "We must buy some dogs as soon as possible. At Schloss Varn we had two bull mastiffs and four Swedish elkhounds. No stranger could get near us without their barking an alarm."

Albrecht half-closed the window to keep out some of the cold air, yet still let in any unusual sound from outside; then he sat down next to her. "I was thinking exactly the same thing," he said. "We used to have several dogs here. A big Great Dane called Wotan who was my father's special pet and who bit everybody else at some time or other before he died of the colic three years ago. A really mean beast! Then there were Pupschen, a staghound, and Gabelschwanz, a noisy terrier who'd take on a badger twice his size, and Kunstig, a big mongrel who was half-wolf, half-shepherd. Kunstig was my favorite. When I was a little boy, Kunstig played with me when Gustaf wouldn't. I would throw a stick as far as I could and Kunstig would chase after it and bring it back. We used to hide together in the hayloft, and run together, far away on the other side of the Orla. And sometimes we both got beaten for running away too far...." After a long silence, he sighed deeply and said: "Kunstig was the last of our dogs to die, and he's the one I miss the most."

Tessa gave him a light, sympathetic pat on the knee and said: "We'll buy another good dog like Kunstig."

He put his hand on hers and gently held it against his leg. "It's a funny thing," he answered in a low whisper, "but one cannot buy mongrels like Kunstig. Mastiffs, elkhounds and terriers, yes. But mongrels like Kunstig are one of a kind and will never happen again."

She was silent for a long moment before replying: "Any living being dear to one is hard to lose. But then one must find others to love."

There was a long silence before he asked: "Have you found another, Tessa?"

"Well, if you are talking about animals, no!" she teasingly answered.

"That is a cruel thing to say," he murmured in a hurt tone. "You know perfectly well I'm not talking about animals."

"Oh, I thought you were," she said with a brittle laugh. As she spoke, a sudden cold breeze wafted in through the half-open window, blowing out the candle he had placed next to the bed. It left them in complete darkness except for the faintly luminous square filled with winking stars. When he made a fumbling move to find a match, she stopped him by saying: "I think you should understand that all I've known in my short life is the love of animals. So don't be ashamed to speak about yours for a dog. In my case it was a horse."

"Don't you know how much *I* love you, Tessa?" Albrecht whispered with passionate dismay, clasping her with such violence that he pushed her down into the pillows. Her body tensed as she whispered: "I'm afraid! Terribly afraid!"

"Of those prowlers? Don't be! I won't let them harm you. . . ."

"No, not of them. . . ."

"Then what, my darling?"

"I have never had a man make love to me. I don't know anything about it. That's why I'm afraid, and because . . . well, Mama told me it is hard and painful, but . . . but that we must submit." The last words came out in a barely audible resentful whisper.

"That was an awful thing for her to tell you, Tessa," he said with shock in his voice. "If there is pain in making love, it is a delightful pain. It is not hard, but gentle. It is the one natural ecstasy with which God has blessed man and woman."

"Poor Mama does not think so," she sighed. "But perhaps she never experienced it. Not as you must have, Albrecht?" She paused for an answer.

"Enough to be sure of how wonderful it could be between us. Enough to want you so much, it has become real suffering for *me.*" He abruptly sat up and started to get off the bed. "But if you are not ready, if you are still afraid of our love, then let's wait. I'll go take a look at *der Feste.* . . ."

Tessa reached out and pulled him back down to her. "No! Don't leave me. What must be between us, let it be now. Lie with me and take me for yourself."

"You want that, even though you are afraid of it?"

"Yes."

His hands groped passionately for her trembling body, his mouth found her lips and joined with them in a kiss which lasted until all else was obliterated from their minds except an intense desire to close in the most intimate embrace.

Gustaf von Falkenhorst got off the train at Ols in the middle of market day. The little town was full of farmers ready to trade and shop. He was wearing a new Dragoon Guard uniform already somewhat rumpled from traveling continuously for five days and four nights since leaving Strasbourg. Although very tired, he managed to keep a properly aloof military bearing as he started to march across the crowded marketplace, followed by many curious and admiring glances. Two small boys ran up alongside him and begged the privilege of carrying his knapsack; he refused their offer with a stiff smile meant to be friendly. Then a town constable recognized him, hurriedly intercepted him, and with a smart salute offered himself as escort and porter. "What a joyous miracle," the man happily exclaimed. "You were reported killed, Herr Leutnant Baron. But now you are back, praise God, and as a hero of the Iron Cross, I see."

"I'm alive and quite fit, thank you, Constable," Gustaf confirmed with some amusement. "How are things going here?"

"Oh, they are getting better now," the constable answered, "but we had the worst winter any living soul can recall. Besides the six men who gave their lives to the war, we lost four more in the deep snow and frost. God knows how much livestock!" He used his sheathed saber to prod a group of farmers haggling over some very emaciated-looking cattle out of their way. Gustaf took notice of their poor condition and the general paucity of fowl, meats, and produce. Only the tinkers had ample stocks of pots and pans, and the clothiers their usual bolts of textiles; neither seemed to be doing much business. Most of the farmers and their wives were clustered in quietly gossiping coveys, rather than roving about in search of sales or purchases. The marketplace hardly gave the impression, Gustaf thought, of a victorious prosperous nation. He had seen better in defeated France.

The constable strutted along with him, swelled with self-importance, while at the same time announcing the names of the six sons of Ols killed in the war and delivering an eulogy for each one in a lugubrious voice. Before he could get around to the less-glorious demise of civilian victims of the past brutal winter, Gustaf got rid of him by asking that he deliver his knapsack at the inn and arrange for his overnight accommodations there. He himself proceeded to the livery stables where he intended to purchase a horse to ride to Glaumhalle the next day. He would present it to Tessa as a replacement for her lost Kanone Kugel.

The livery stables were located on a side street off the marketplace and next to Ols' largest building and business establishment, Graustark und Sohn Geschaft, which, in fact, owned the stables, rented and sold horses, dealt in cattle, hogs, fowl, seed, grain, food staples, hardware, sundries, and (most prestigiously) acted as local agent for Silesia's largest bank, the Breslauer Kredit Anstalt. Augustus Graustark sometimes tried to put on the airs of an important city banker, but he never compromised his sure touch as a small town's most wealthy and influential businessman. Today he was worried by an unusual volume of credit transactions with his hard-pressed customers, all of them pleading inability to pay old bills, or make cash deposits against new purchases. Fortunately, however, he had just made one very profitable cash transaction—740 thalers, no less!—with the heretofore very penurious Falkenhorst account. He was perfectly aware, of course, that the von Falkenhorst family had recently become related by marriage to the von Beckhaus und Varns, reputed to be one of Prussia's wealthiest families; an official of the Breslauer Kredit Anstalt had dropped him a note about it last August. Since then he knew a number of tragic events had befallen both the von Falkenhorst and von Beckhaus families, yet apparently not of the kind to affect the wealth of the latter. So Herr Augustus Graustark was just congratulating himself for having concluded such a profitable piece of business with Glaumhalle when he happened to glance out the window of his cluttered little office and saw a young Dragoon Guard officer whom he immediately recognized as Gustaf von Falkenhorst. "God in heaven!" he exclaimed, slamming closed his ledger book. "That man is supposed to be dead! The postmaster told me he was dead! Glaumhalle's stablemaster told me he was dead! Idiots!"

Gustaf strode into the muddy rectangle of the yard separating the livery stable from Graustark's emporium without the slightest inkling of the surprise awaiting him there. A pair of stableboys were pitching hay into a corral which contained a half-dozen work horses. Two carts were parked while their owners shopped inside. A large wagon alongside the warehouse entrance was being loaded with considerable cargo by three men while two others were engaged in a heated argument. Gustaf was not paying any attention, but then one of them raised his voice to a near shout, angrily exclaiming:

"I can't handle this load and pigs and cows and horses too! Not with three new, inexperienced hands over a barely passable road. I quit! To hell with Glaumhalle!"

Gustaf stopped in his tracks and spun around, staring at the two quarreling men. He had never seen Foreman Hult before, nor, of course, the three laborers who were struggling to lift a heavy packing case into the wagon. The fifth one had his back to him, but he vaguely recognized his voice as he bellowed at Hult: "I'll have your hide, you blackhearted swine! If you fail me now, I'll see to it you'll never get another job in Prussia. I'll break your goddamned . . ." he stopped in midsentence and stared in complete shock at the Dragoon Guard Leutnant who suddenly stepped between them and asked in a steely voice:

"What was that about Glaumhalle?" Then, as he recognized Master Prytz, he added: "You are Stablemaster Prytz of Schloss Varn, aren't you?"

Prytz's jaw went slack for an instant before flapping open and shut as he stammered in horrified surprise: "My G-god, no! L-Leutnant B-baron v-von Falkenhorst! . . . B-but you were reported dead! Oh, my poor wretched Tessa!" He looked on the verge of toppling over in a rigid faint.

"I'm not in the least dead," Gustaf snapped. "And what do you mean: *your* poor wretched Tessa? Is there something wrong with my wife?"

"N-no, Herr Leutnant Baron. She is quite well, except . . . except. . . ." His voice trailed off into an unintelligible whimper.

"Except what, Prytz?" Gustaf demanded.

Master Prytz was given a moment's reprieve by Herr Graustark, who came rushing out of his emporium to greet Gustaf with slavishly effusive enthusiasm: "Welcome home, my dear Baron! God be praised for your safe return. Such a marvelous, blessed surprise after so much bad news—entirely false, thank God. What would victory be to this district if we had lost the head of the house of von Falkenhorst? Empty indeed! Empty indeed!"

Foreman Hult, whose outburst of temper had been dampened by the confusion, suddenly realized the significance of this handsome young officer's presence. He took three steps backwards, rolled his eyes heavenward and muttered: "Jesus! It's *him!* I would not miss what will happen next for the Devil himself!" Fortunately, Gustaf did not hear him because of Herr Graustark's louder outpouring of emotions:

"You have no idea, Herr Leutnant Baron, how we have all

✠

worried over you and your dear family. That poor sick mother of yours. That lovely wife who's suffered so much in her young life. How they will rejoice over your return and clasp you to their bosoms. . . ."

"Yes-yes, Herr Graustark, I'm glad to be back," Gustaf said, trying to fend him off. "I just got off the train, so pardon me if I don't quite understand what is going on here? Have we gone into the freight business at Glaumhalle? Surely all these goods are not on our account?"

"Every bit of it!" Herr Graustark jubilantly exclaimed. "Seven hundred and forty thalers' worth paid by check drawn upon the great Rothschild bank of Frankfurt. The purchase includes, besides what you see here, two fine dray horses, one two-year-old saddlebroken stallion, five milch cows and a yearling bull, one boar and a shoat with piglets, and. . . ." He was brought up short by the expression on Gustaf's face and worriedly suggested: "With the Herr Baron's fortuitous arrival, perhaps he will wish to personally inspect all items and livestock concerned. Perhaps. . . ."

Gustaf turned his back on him and started a slow turn around the wagon to examine its many crates, boxes, and sacks. Master Prytz, who had finally recovered from a state of near collapse to one of grim resignation, followed behind him, hoarsely identifying the contents as he tapped them with his riding crop. He admitted that the team of horses hitched between the shafts were not of the best, yet pronounced them as good as available in the area, better, he said, than what was currently available for plowing and dray work at Glaumhalle. As Gustaf dourly completed his round of inspection and rejoined the now distinctly nervous Herr Graustark, Prytz tried to explain: "All of these goods, all the stock, have been purchased upon instruction by Her Ladyship, the Baroness, Herr Leutnant Baron."

"And paid for in full," Herr Graustark injected.

Gustaf deliberately ignored Ols' one and only influential merchant-banker, fixing his icy blue gaze instead upon the painfully strained lines converging over the bridge of Master Prytz's nose. "Unless my wife has taken leave of her senses, which I doubt, *you* have grossly failed in the duty you agreed to perform for me during my absence, Herr Stallmeister. How else can I account for this . . . this senseless extravagance? No! No excuses, if you please! Unload everything, return all animals to Graustark und Sohn Geschaft for refund. Everything goes back except necessary rations and fodder. Understood?"

"I believe it is the Herr Leutnant Baron who does not understand," Prytz protested in anguish. "The Baroness has been under some strain, but I assure you she is healthy and of sound mind and is doing her best to improve conditions at Glaumhalle. Furthermore, your brother, Freiherr Albrecht, is helping her and. . . ."

"Albrecht!" Gustaf repeated in loud surprise. "Is Albrecht at Glaumhalle now? And since when, may I ask?"

"Since last January 5, Herr Leutnant Baron," Prytz reluctantly told him.

Gustaf appeared to flinch slightly, his gaze flitting from Prytz to the gaping laborers who had frozen motionless on top of the loaded wagon, to Foreman Hult who had been intently listening with a barely concealed smirk on his fleshy lips, and to Herr Graustark who was wringing his hands. "That explains some of this nonsense, I suppose. Yes, obviously. Albrecht is behind much of it. . . . Well, we shall see about that!" Then he turned to Herr Graustark and forcefully ordered him: "Have your men unload my wagon of all this claptrap at once!" He made a sweeping motion towards Hult and the three laborers.

"They are *your* men, Herr Leutnant Baron," Herr Graustark huffily corrected him. "*Those* three as of this morning. *That* one, I believe, employed by your Lady Baroness as foreman as far back as last August."

Foreman Hult straightened up and introduced himself with an exaggerated flourish as he swept off his shapeless cap. "Martin Hult is my name, sir. And it is true that I have been working at Glaumhalle all through the past terrible winter."

Gustaf did not acknowledge the introduction. "As of this moment, Herr Stallmeister," he curtly told Prytz, "you will take your orders from *me* in all matters regarding Glaumhalle. Those are that we shall return there tomorrow morning with no more goods than we reasonably need for the next month, and no more labor than we used to get through last winter. No extravagances of any kind will be tolerated. Nothing more is to be purchased than what can be paid for with *this* money." He reached inside his greatcoat pocket and produced a wallet from which he extracted a single hundred-thaler note and handed it to the dazed stablemaster. "I will expect any change left over," he admonished him. "And, of course, an accounting of credits due us with Graustark und Sohn Geschaft. I will expect you to report to me at the inn, where I am staying the night, but no later than six o'clock. I am very tired and going to bed early." With that, he abruptly turned and marched back to the marketplace toward the Ols Gasthaus.

Prytz remained transfixed for another minute, his only motion a faint shaking of his head and twitching of his moustache. Then one of the laborers blurted out a pertinent question about a day's wages and he growled an assurance that it would be paid in full; next, Foreman Hult slyly asked him whether he were still going to take the evening train to Breslau, thence travel on to Pomerania and Schloss Varn? To which he answered with great vehemence: "I'm not a coward who runs from trouble like some around here. Nor do I blindly obey orders, regardless of circumstances." Suddenly breaking the bounds of his pent-up rage, he yelled at Hult: "I'll not hesitate to kill you if you make trouble for my Lady Tessa. Now get that damned wagon unloaded!"

Gustaf walked back to the inn where his room had been reserved for him by the complaisant constable. Removing his tunic and boots, he stretched out on the bed, the first time he had been able to comfortably lie down since leaving Strasbourg last week. It had been a tiresome journey, slow, with frequent delays and long waits in crowded stations for connecting trains that were invariably late. But as he progressed towards Silesia by fits and starts, his depressed mood, the lingering pain over parting with Louise Hunsecker, had gradually passed. It hurt him deeply that after she had learned of his part in the battle of Vionville, she had avoided him; her final farewell in the teeming railroad station of Besançon had been a polite, firm "Good-bye, good luck!" spoken with a sadly reproachful smile. No kiss. Not even a touch of hands. For days he had fretted over her and not until his train carried him far inside Germany did his emotions abate enough for him to force Louise out of his mind and think instead of Glaumhalle and Tessa. As each turn of the clattering iron wheels brought him closer to reunion with his wife, he became more determined that it had to be a happy one, that all the suffering and sadness of the past months had to be put irrevocably behind him. By the time he reached Breslau he had convinced himself to look forward to his return home, four weeks of leave, and the honeymoon he and Tessa had missed. When he got off the train at Ols, he was genuinely eager, even excited.

But when he had run into Master Prytz's extravagant shopping expedition, he found out that his brother Albrecht was in residence with his wife at Glaumhalle. No more than a slightly annoying development, really, yet one which left him strangely uneasy so that it became difficult for him to keep up his hard-won optimistic spirits. "By God, Albrecht will have to clear out while I'm home on leave," he told himself. "Tessa and I must be left alone together!" With that thought firmly set in mind, he relaxed and fell asleep.

The next morning dawned a rainy gray, promising a wet, muddy trip to Glaumhalle. The departure was delayed a half-hour because Gustaf had relented enough to haggle with Herr Graustark over the young stallion which Master Prytz had chosen and then been forced to return the previous afternoon. In the end it was bought for the same price, but with saddle and bridle thrown in so that Gustaf could ride it home. He refused to pay for the horse with his wife's funds, and Herr Graustark reluctantly agreed to another credit transaction against a mere ten-thaler deposit. With this business completed, a tarpaulin was tied down over the wagon's modest cargo of two sacks of flour, a keg of coal oil, and a half-dozen boxes of assorted food staples—less than a quarter of yesterday's load. It was pulled out of Graustark's by the same team of horses with which it had arrived two days earlier and, trailing on lead reins, the same two spares. "Since we can switch teams halfway," Gustaf instructed the grimly silent Master Prytz, "you will drive at a brisk trot. I expect to reach Glaumhalle in less than five hours." He moved some thirty paces ahead of the wagon to ride alone.

Hult wryly exclaimed, "Imagine, clods like us having the escort of a Royal Guards officer. Makes one feel very important."

"Well, you're not, so shut up about it," Prytz growled, cracking the reins over the horses' rumps. He had spent a restless night, agonizing over how to soften the blow about to befall Tessa. He had considered hiring a horse and galloping back to Glaumhalle to warn her but he dared not leave Hult alone with Gustaf. He had then considered sending Hult ahead with a letter, but he doubted the foreman's ability as a horseman to accomplish the long ride at night. Then he had thought of tactfully explaining the situation to Gustaf, appealing to him to use reason and understanding in handling a shocking confrontation. But he decided he lacked the eloquence to plead such a delicate, personal case with a young nobleman whom he scarcely knew beyond a suspicion that he was not easily swayed by either understanding or reason. So in the end, Prytz had tossed through the night, tormented by his own helplessness to protect Tessa and by nightmarish visions of the terrible scenes in which she was soon likely to become embroiled.

Even now, as he drove the wagon out of Ols into the cheerless Silesian hinterlands, his spirits were oppressed by a terrible sense of foreboding. He was still groping in his mind for a way to avert disaster, but all he could think of was to snarl another threat at Hult: "Remember! If you betray any confidence you've overheard at Glaumhalle, repeat a word of malicious backstairs gossip, or as much as make a hint of scandal within hearing of Baron von Falkenhorst, then I'll kill you. Silence and work is what I expect of you. That better be all you produce. And I'll hold you responsible for the tongues of the two wenches as well."

A heavy rain shower passed over them and within a minute, their already damp coats were soaked through. Hult began to emit the peculiarly pungent stink of a wet billy goat. "Let me know when you want me to relieve you," he said to Master Prytz, then tucked his collar around his dripping ears and wedged himself into a corner to doze off in spite of the downpour and jarring discomforts of the creaking wagon.

They reached the halfway mark between Ols and Glaumhalle shortly before noon, a tributary stream to the Orla with a tiny hamlet clustered around its crude wooden bridge, which had a habit of collapsing during the spring floods. Beyond it, the rutted road (really no more than an occasionally traveled wagon track) wound its way through thick woodlands interspersed by stretches of wild meadows which eventually blended into the open plains of Poland. From this point on, there were only a few modest farms besides the isolated, run-down estates of the Frankenheim and Falkenhorst families. It was in fact the poorest, wildest slice of Silesia, its people eking just enough sustenance out of the soil to subsist, relying heavily on hunting and trapping to supplement their basic diet of turnips, potatoes, and pork. Gustaf rode up to the foot of the bridge and stopped, raising his hand over his head, cavalry-fashion, to stop the wagon behind him.

As Prytz and Hult started switching teams, a lone horseman appeared trotting toward them along the puddled ruts of the Ols trail. From his green cap and greatcoat, and the leather sack slung over the pommel of his saddle, they recognized the rural postman. He, too, stopped by the bridge to rest himself and his horse. "It is rumored that the Poles have started revolts against the Czar earlier than usual this spring," he told them with somber earnestness. "That means all sorts of unscrupulous and desperate characters spilling over the frontier, thieving and hiding among us. It's safest to travel in groups through these parts."

Gustaf did better than offer him protection; he made it unnecessary for him to ride any farther by relieving him on the spot of the mail addressed to Glaumhalle and assuring him that Prytz would deliver that of the Frankenheims, the only other family along the way. The postman hesitated only a moment before agreeing to an arrangement which seemed sensible and convenient, even if not entirely according to regulations. Besides a bundle of Breslau newspapers, Gustaf was given three letters. One made him shake his head with a surprised smile; it was the one he had written to Tessa from Pontarlier nearly five weeks ago. Another, bearing the seal of the Military Railway Transport Authority, was addressed to his brother Albrecht. The third was addressed to Tessa and evoked his immediate curiosity as it was postmarked at Frankfurt am Main and bore an impressive seal which he did not recognize. Stepping away from the wagon and turning his back to the drizzly wind, he opened it and found it to contain a statement from the Rothschild bank to the effect that in accordance with the Count Paul von Beckhaus und Varn's will, the sum of 25 thousand thalers had been transferred to the private account of Baroness Maria Theresa von Falkenhorst from his estate; another, larger sum could be expected within the near future when the settlement of the estate was completed; it was signed by Edmond Rothschild himself. Gustaf read quickly through this twice, then put the letter away in his greatcoat pocket together with the other two, feeling no particular emotion over the confirmation of his wife's independent wealth.

"I shall ride ahead," he called out to Prytz, mounting his horse. "You will ford the stream below the bridge. I will expect you at Glaumhalle no more than one hour behind me." He spurred the young stallion into a clattering canter across its loose boards, breaking into full gallop as soon as he reached the other side.

"He's going to ruin a perfectly good two-year-old," Prytz angrily growled after him.

"Among a lot of other things," Hult sarcastically added.

essa had spent the third consecutive night in Albrecht's bed and they had made love more times than she could count. They fell asleep making love and seemed to wake up making love; during the day they kissed and caressed and embraced whenever the maidservants were out of sight. It was difficult for them to be together without touching each other. Albrecht wistfully expressed a hope that Hult would be unable to drive through from Ols with his unwieldy caravan, giving them another blissful day alone, another night in each other's arms; but he started keeping as careful watch on the road to Ols as he did on the frontier across the Orla. There was still a lingering fear of marauders, although less than before because they had spotted several Cossack patrols during the past two days and knew they were, after their peculiar Russian fashion, as dedicated to preventing people from escaping their country as entering it. There was very little food left, no candles, and only a quarter-liter of oil for the lamps. But in their blissful isolation, none of this mattered. "You've really involved me in a most scandalous situation," she lovingly teased him, her arms around his waist as he peered out the window.

"That's because you're such a lovable, irresistible hussy," he teased her back.

They laughed and kissed. Yet Tessa felt a certain uneasiness and guilt beneath her happiness. She was the product of a strict Lutheran upbringing which proscribed that a woman could only give up her virginity with the blessing of the church, that adultery was a mortal sin specified in the Ten Commandments, especially sinful if committed with a husband's brother. There remained, after all her rationalizing, a deep-down uncertainty over whether she really was a widow, whether Gustaf might possibly be alive? Her deepening love for Albrecht made the uneasiness and guilt seem insignificant and she totally suppressed it most of the time. But it was there nevertheless. And this morning something had happened which startled and rekindled her guilt.

The Dowager Hildebrun had continued over the past four

days in an unusually patient and uncomplaining mood. She had not thrown a single tantrum, cursed or yelled, or thrown at Tessa her favorite insult of virgin-strumpet. On this morning when her daughter-in-law came into her room to feed and clean her, she seemed again in a compliant, almost pleasant humor. Tessa was so delighted that she complimented her on the improvement and promised that if it continued, she would be allowed downstairs and perhaps out in the orchard on the next sunny spring day.

"That would be nice, deary," Dowager Hildebrun sighed in a frustrated, but normally modulated, voice. "But you know Albrecht locked me in here. I don't think he ever intends to let me out. He always was a very difficult boy with strange ideas. Haven't you noticed how strangely he can act, deary?"

Coming from her, the question struck Tessa as very amusing and she could not help laughing. "Albrecht is quite all right," she reassured her. "It is you who have been so ill that we had to confine you to your room for a while. But now you are looking and acting so much better."

Suddenly the Dowager Hildebrun's tightly pursed lips cracked open a toothy, mirthless smile. "The name 'virgin-strumpet' doesn't really suit you any more, does it, deary? No, I think not! I'll have to think of another."

Tessa was barely able to hold back a shocked gasp and had to turn away from the bed and pretend to adjust the window drapes in order to hide the sudden red flush of her face. How could the crippled Dowager Hildebrun *know* about her relationship with Albrecht? She could not have seen or heard anything from her room. Had she betrayed herself with a careless word? Or was there a mysteriously perceptive spark of intuition in that addled head? Or—hopefully—had it been an entirely innocent remark which accidentally hit a sensitive spot? Tessa decided to ask Albrecht, but when she joined him for breakfast, she could not bring herself to mention it.

A few hours later, after he had pleasantly tarried with Tessa over some chores in *der Feste*, Albrecht was carrying an armful of dry firewood back to the manor's kitchen when he spotted the shape of a lone horseman coming around the bend of the Ols road at a fast pace and heading up the hill. For a moment he thought it might be the postman but then he remembered that the postman *never* galloped and wore a green, not blue, uniform. This was a soldier, a *cavalry* soldier! Then, even before the rider drew close enough to distinguish his features, he recognized the figure in the saddle, dropped his load of firewood and raced back to the stable entrance to yell through the open doors:

"It's Gustaf! Gustaf is back!"

His frantic voice so startled Feldteufel that he whinnied and reared in his stall.

"Do you hear me, Tessa?" he bawled again. "It's *him!* Gustaf is alive and here, right now!" He waited a few seconds for an answer which did not come out of the dark interior, then, warned by the rapidly approaching hoofbeats, turned around and with a tremendous effort to control his reeling emotions, strode through the puddles to meet his brother as he burst into the yard through a splatter of muddy spray.

Gustaf was the first to speak. "Good day, Albrecht! What a surprise to find you at home," he greeted him in a flat voice as he dismounted. "The war must have ended sooner for you than the rest of us. How are things at Glaumhalle?"

Albrecht swallowed hard and coughed to clear his constricted throat. "Oh, we managed to get by somehow," he answered with strained affability. "I'm home on sick leave. That is . . . I've actually resigned from the Railroad Authority since the war is over. I'm also surprised to see you, Gustaf. You were reported dead, you see, and . . . well, welcome back, anyway."

Gustaf gave a short, cynical laugh. "Thank you, dear brother. But don't feel badly about it. My return seems to have come as a shock to you. How is mother?"

"She has been quite sick. You must be prepared to find her more difficult than ever."

"I more or less expected that. And how is my wife?"

"Very well considering the hard times she's been through."

"Yes? Well, things should improve all around, now that I'm back for a while," Gustaf said and started leading his lathering, mud-splattered horse toward the open stable doors. As he turned toward them he found himself suddenly facing Tessa. She was staring at him with a stunned, horrified expression, and not looking at all like his rather hazy memory of her. Her hair was not neatly braided around her head, but tumbled in loose coppery cascades over her shoulders. She was wearing a coarse black skirt hitched up above the tops of a pair of muddy boots, revealing bare, bony knees, and a loose-fitting yellow blouse with sleeves rolled up above her elbows and unbuttoned to the cleavage of her breasts; dust and chaff clung to her clothing which was badly wrinkled and showed every sign of having been very hastily, carelessly put on. Only the freckles burning bright against the creamy white skin of her face and the amber green glitter of her eyes with their lost, tense look, were as he seemed to remember them from their wedding day. The sight of her made him stop short so that the horse bumped against his back and slavered a white foam of saliva over his shoulder. Her appearance shook him out of his casual nonchalance, making him exclaim with surprise and uncertainty: "Tessa? What's the matter with you, for God's sake? What's happened to you? Don't you know your own husband?"

She began to brush the straw off her skirt with one hand and button up her blouse with the other. Her expression of stricken surprise hardened into one of resentment, then outright anger. "Yes, I know you, Gustaf. You look very fit. Obviously you suffered no mortal wounds, as we'd been led to believe here. Why did you not write me, at least let me know somehow that I am not a widow?"

"Yes, that was damned inconsiderate of you, Gustaf," Albrecht vehemently interjected.

Gustaf ignored his brother. "Ah, yes, the letter!" he exclaimed. He produced it out of his greatcoat pocket, taking care not to reveal the other two, and offered it to her. "Here you are. Written between five and six weeks ago, you'll notice. Before that I was somewhat incapacitated, you see. And I could do nothing about the delayed mails. Only relieve the postman of it when I met him along the way and deliver it an hour or two sooner. As a husband returning from the dead, do I not deserve a kiss from my wife?"

Tessa accepted the letter with trembling hands and as she gave him a reluctant, almost distasteful peck on the cheek, noticed the scars on his neck and jaw. "You really were wounded. I'm sorry."

"Nothing very serious," he assured her. "By the way, I bought this horse as a present for you, Tessa. He's not as fine as the gelding I borrowed from you, but . . . the best I could find in Ols." He handed her the reins of the young stallion who was soaked with rain and sweat and trembling and panting from fatigue. "He is yours and your privilege to name, of course."

"You've ridden him too hard," she said, accepting the reins and stroking the horse's pulsating muzzle. Her thank you came belatedly and was tensely spoken.

"Under your expert care he'll quickly recover," Gustaf told her. "Since Kanone Kugel the Second is hardly appropriate, maybe you should consider naming him Ricochet?" When this piece of humor failed to cause her or Albrecht to smile, he shrugged and said: "Well, since you both seem to be acting as stablehands around here, will you rub him down and walk him a bit before putting him in his stall. I'll go into the house and greet Mama. Maybe she'll give me a more loving welcome than I've received from my wife and brother." With that he turned away from them and tramped across the yard toward the manor.

"Mama may not even recognize you," Albrecht called after

him. "Remember, she's been very sick and not only suffering from a broken hip."

Gustaf gave no reaction, nor slowed his steps in the slightest.

Tessa leaned against the exhausted horse as if she were herself on the verge of collapse. "Oh, my God, what shall we do, Albrecht?" she pleaded in a low anguished voice. "Tell me what we can do?"

Albrecht stared at her in helpless misery. "Nothing, my darling. There is nothing we can do. Not even forget what has happened between us."

"He is alive. He is back. I am his wife. And that is that." Tessa spoke with her eyes tightly shut, then opened them as if awakening out of a dream. "Well, now!" she exclaimed, speaking to the horse. "Let's take good care of you, young fellow! Let's make you welcome at Glaumhalle. . . . God help you, poor animal!" She yanked on his bridle and led him inside the dark cavern of *der Feste*.

Gustaf scraped some of the mud off his boots against the scraper on the kitchen stoop, then burst in on Anna and Lena who were cleaning pots and pans. They both gave out terrified shrieks upon seeing him, Lena staring at him transfixed, and Anna crumbling to the floor in a faint. The effects of his entrance amused him. "No, I'm not a ghost," he announced. "Your Baron Gustaf is alive and back home." He stepped over the prostrate servant girl and went to the front hall where he took off his wet greatcoat, unbuckled his saber and pistol, and hung them on a hook. After glancing into the empty drawing room, he ran up the stairs but did not go directly to his mother's bedroom. Taking a turn through the upper hall, he looked into his own room which he found in its usual spartan neatness, the bed made and without a wrinkle in its green counterpane, only Tessa's two heavy leather trunks added to the simple furnishings. He glanced into the four other bedrooms which, as had been the case for the past ten years, were empty, unoccupied cubicles with only bare mattresses on their beds. Albrecht's room was somewhat disordered, as he remembered it always to be, clothing carelessly thrown over the chair, some stockings and rather dirty shoes scattered over the floor, the bed unmade and looking as if it had been so for days. He stood on the threshold staring in with a disapproving frown at this evidence of his brother's casual way of living, then retraced his steps down the hall to his mother's closed door and softly knocked on it. When there came no invitation to enter, he knocked harder and called out:

"Mama! It is Gustaf. Can I come in?"

He heard a hoarse, cawing cry, like that of a startled crow. Taking a deep breath, he turned the doorknob, half expecting to find it locked. But it was not.

The Dowager Hildebrun had crawled deep beneath her bedding and even pulled a pillow over her head, trying to hide herself. Now she was peering out from beneath it. "What do you want" she screeched. "Who did you say you are?"

"Gustaf, Mother," he repeated. Walking up to the bed, he sat down on its edge and tried to pull the pillow gently off her head, making a motion to embrace her.

"Gustaf is dead," she yelled, keeping a clawing grip on the pillow and bedding. She started to burrow deeper under the covers, but when she felt his hands groping for her, she suddenly recoiled and pushed herself up into a sitting position hard against the headboard. "Keep away from me! Don't touch me! I don't want you in here, whoever you are."

Gustaf withdrew his hands and stood up, his face ashen as he stared at her. "But I am your son, Mother!" he exclaimed in anguish. "You know I wouldn't hurt you. I've just returned from the war and am back to take care of you."

The Dowager Hildebrun did not relax her rigid body, but her emaciated face crinkled into a confused grimace as her eyes darted all over him. "Gustaf? Are you really my Gustaf?" she croaked.

He forced an encouraging smile. "Of course I am, Mama. I just returned to Glaumhalle a few minutes ago. The war is over. We won it."

"Ah, you beat those pig-suckling Austrians," she exclaimed with a sudden glee. "You weren't at all beaten and killed by them. So I was lied to. I knew it!"

"We were fighting the French, Mama," Gustaf corrected her. He turned away from her bed to stare out of the window at the orchard below, hiding from her the tears that were suddenly brimming out of control. "What a homecoming for a soldier!" he sighed, more to himself than to her. "My wife and brother receive me like an unwanted stranger. A servant faints at the sight of me. My own mother does not recognize me. What a homecoming!"

"Well, there have been disgraceful goings on here, let me tell you," his mother angrily told him.

"What do you mean by that?" he asked.

"They've kept me locked up in my room for a year!" she screeched.

Gustaf wiped his eyes with his knuckles, sighed deeply, and

turned to face her. "Mother, Tessa only arrived here last July and I saw Albrecht in Paris just before Christmas. Your door was not locked. I walked in without using a key."

"They took away my cane, which amounts to the same thing. You know that I can't move without my cane. Will you please fetch me my cane, Gustaf?" Her rasping voice changed from outrage to wheedling.

He looked around the room for the cane, but could not find it. "Perhaps they thought it better you stay in bed and not try to move around on your bad leg, Mother. Perhaps it is Dr. Priller's orders."

"Dr. Priller!" she shrilled. "That charlatan almost killed me. I won't let him in the house. To hell with him. To hell with all of you. Fetch me my cane and I'll take care of myself."

Gustaf leaned over her and as she pressed away from him against the headboard, he saw the madness in her eyes. "Very well, Mother," he sadly soothed her. "I'll find it for you soon. I'm sure that Tessa or Albrecht or one of the maids has it handy somewhere."

"Lies! More lies!" she hissed at him. "You are trying to keep me locked up in here until I die. You want everything for yourselves, you and your Albrecht and that bitch . . . that God-damned Austrian bitch! They killed my Gustaf, but they'll never get me! Fetch me my cane and I'll break her spineless back! Fetch it, do you hear!" She lashed out with a hand whose fingers were curved into sharp talons, barely missing his face as he jumped away from her.

"I'll come back later, Mother, when you have calmed down a little," he gasped, backing towards the door. "I'm sorry . . . I suppose the shock of my return was too much for you. . . . I'm sorry!"

"You should let me tell you what's been going on here, Gustaf," she yelled after him, then, when he reached the door and started through it, switched to a pathetic pleading: "Gustaf . . . oh, Gustaf . . . come back. Don't leave me alone with *them*. Don't let them lock me in here again. My cane . . . oh, please, my cane. . . ."

Gustaf did not close the door, but he could not return to her bedside. Thoroughly shaken, he fled down the stairs and took refuge in the study where he managed to collect his senses by the time his wife and brother joined him.

uring that rainy afternoon the three of them sat in the cheerless study, Tessa and Albrecht recounting in flat, listless voices all the events which had involved them at both Schloss Varn and Glaumhalle during the nine months of Gustaf's absence. They spoke in deliberately measured tones and carefully chose their words to conceal their deep involvement with each other. Gustaf sat motionless in his chair, listening with few comments, his eyes sometimes staring searchingly into their faces, but usually fixed absently on the rain-streaked window. He did not begin to relate any of his own adventures in the war until they sat down to supper, and then he recounted them in a dry, matter-of-fact way, as if giving an official report. Having removed the Iron Cross from around his collar before arriving, he did not mention it; nor, of course, did he speak of Louise Hunsecker. He showed some feeling only when speaking about his dealings with Count-General Eugene von Kleisenberg, mentioning his loss of princely rank and describing his activities at Pontarlier. He made it perfectly clear that he held the Count-General in very low esteem, which made his brother acidly observe:

"It strikes me that you owe that man a debt of gratitude if not your very life, Gustaf."

"Yes, unfortunately so," he admitted with a frown, then explained with a sidelong glance at Tessa: "Besides rescuing me and my comrades from prison, there was his close friendship with the von Beckhaus family. He never let an opportunity go by without reminding me of it, a very embarrassing relationship between a junior and his senior general officer."

"At least he was considerate enough to write to a member of the family about you," Tessa injected.

"Yes, but as usual doing more harm than good," Gustaf said.

"I imagine that was more Mama's fault than his," Tessa answered with a bitter whisper.

"Undoubtedly he will be seeing your mother in a short time," Gustaf informed her. "Through his connections at court, he managed to get himself appointed a military attaché to our

✠   365

embassy in Vienna. When we parted at Strasbourg, he was happily packing for Austria and a sinecure which should suit him to perfection."

The forced conversation lagged as Lena entered the dining room to serve dessert. She was still upset by Gustaf's return, trembling in his presence so that the dishes and platters on her tray rattled. After she left, he abruptly asked Albrecht: "What are your plans, brother?"

"I don't know," Albrecht glumly replied. "I thought it my duty to stay here and help Tessa through a very trying period for her. But now, I don't know."

"I thank you for helping my wife," Gustaf drily said. "But it seems to me you were taking advantage of her wealth and generosity. Fortunately I arrived at Ols in time to prevent more foolish extravagances."

It had been rankling Tessa that Prytz and Hult had returned to Glaumhalle with only a meager portion of what she had ordered them to purchase and now she exploded: "That is a very unfair and mean remark. Albrecht even protested against what I was spending. But it is *my* money and it needed to be spent. I could see no reason why we should live here in want and discomfort. That, to me, is foolish."

Gustaf's face reddened, but his voice remained even. "You must understand, Tessa, that as your husband, I am responsible for your money and how it is spent. There can be no question about that at all. I am sorry if you have suffered want and discomfort here, but I—and *only* I—will determine what can be done to improve things if they need improving. Albrecht has nothing to do with it." He gave his brother a hard look, then opened his tunic, produced the letter from the Military Railroad Authority and flipped it across the table to him. "The postman had this for you today. Perhaps it will help you decide about your future. Since you refused to become a soldier even when we were at war, you might consider taking advantage of a fair start in the civil service."

During the following strained silence, Albrecht opened the envelope with trembling fingers, glanced through the two sheets of official papers it contained, then dully announced, "It is a confirmation of my resignation and a voucher for my back-pay. One hundred ninety-two thalers."

"Not bad money considering you spent half the war absent on leave," Gustaf observed. "More than I received for risking my neck, getting myself wounded, and winding up a prisoner of the French for nearly two months."

"Albrecht was also wounded," Tessa shouted at him, her rage and despair beyond control. "He took leave to help my family, to help *me* when we all thought you were dead . . . but when you were actually quite alive and too busy playing the hero to give us a thought, let alone write." Her voice rose in outrage: "One letter! One single letter since last August, Gustaf! That's all I ever heard from you. Seven months ago! Now you suddenly show up here without warning and criticize us and everything we have done to keep body and soul together. And you presume as head of this run-down ruin of a household to tell me how to spend *my* money on it? Well, I won't stand for that! I won't stand for such rudeness. I won't stand for this stupidity. If that's going to be your attitude, I'm leaving here tomorrow morning. I'll have Prytzie take me back to Schloss Varn." She finished her tirade by violently pushing away her plate of untouched dessert and rising from the table.

Albrecht reached out in a shaky gesture to restrain and calm her, spluttering helplessly: "Tessa . . . oh, my poor sweet Tessa . . . please don't be so upset. . . ."

Gustaf stared at her, speechless for a moment, then archly scolded her: "Please try and control yourself, Theresa. There is no need for such outbursts of temper. Sit down and finish your supper." But she was already half-way to the door and now hurried through it, making him angrily shout after her: "Your place is here, by my side! You are my wife, Theresa! Remember that!" He almost got up to chase after her, but sank back into his chair and scowled miserably at his plate.

After a long painful silence, Albrecht said: "You really haven't learned a thing about handling women, have you Gustaf."

Gustaf looked up with a start, glaring across the table at his brother, but finding himself thinking of Louise Hunsecker, of her beautiful, sad face when they were parting in the crowded, dismal railroad station of Besançon. The scene had been witnessed by General von Kleisenberg from the window of his railroad compartment and he had commented on Gustaf's performance with exactly the same words Albrecht had just thrown at him: "You really haven't learned a thing about handling women, have you Gustaf."

"I suggest you stay out of our business from now on," he warned his brother.

"And I suggest you use some tact and discretion with Tessa," Albrecht persisted with intense seriousness. "Try to be just a little gentle with her. Don't harp so blatantly on your husbandly rights. Especially not tonight, for God's sake!"

Gustaf slammed his fist against the table: "I said, stay out of our business! Shut up!" With difficulty he lowered his voice: "As a matter of fact, get out, Albrecht. You have enough money to get by for a while. And you have connections at court to help you find something that suits you. Later on, when you've settled down to some kind of life of your own, you'll be welcomed back for a visit. But in the meanwhile, get out of ours."

Albrecht slowly folded up his napkin, then rolled it carefully to fit through the somewhat dented silver napkin ring with his name engraved on it in Gothic letters. "I shall go pack my things. I'll leave as soon as there is daylight. Could I presume on your hospitality to lend me a horse as far as Ols?"

"Of course. Leave it at Graustark's where we'll pick it up next week."

Albrecht rose stiffly from his chair and moved toward the door, faltering to a stop when he drew alongside of his brother. They stared into each other's faces, neither flinching from the other's guilty, accusing glance, neither able to penetrate through the other's troubled soul. Finally Albrecht said in a melancholy, rather than angry, tone: "Fate has been unkind to the Falkenhorsts, Gustaf. Our only salvation is patience and understanding. Principally understanding."

Gustaf recovered himself enough to reply: "Oh, I don't know if we made out that badly. Many people are far worse off. Like the 100-odd thousand who lost their lives in the war. Sometimes slowly, cruelly, painfully."

"As Tessa's father lost his, don't forget," Albrecht reminded him, then bitterly added: "A simpler, more straightforward calamity to cope with than the one you have wrought by returning from the dead."

"An unusual situation, perhaps, but you must forgive me for coping with it as best I can. I *am* alive, dammit, and hardly see that I owe you an apology for that."

Albrecht shook his head in desperation. It was on the tip of his tongue to blurt out that he and Tessa had fallen in love and that their love had been repeatedly consummated during the past several days. But something warned him that in spite of Gustaf's anger, he did not suspect things had gone so far between them, that bringing it up would only aggravate an already intolerable situation. A hopeless situation. The best he dared to do was to plead: "Please allow me to speak to Tessa before I leave. Perhaps I can make things easier for her . . . for both of you. Please let me decently say good-bye to her."

"Theresa is obviously overwrought. It is my duty to calm her, not yours. A matter between husband and wife in which a brother-in-law should not enter. No—it would be best that you do not talk to each other. If she is up when you leave tomorrow morning, you may say good-bye, properly but briefly. Otherwise, I'll convey your excuses on the grounds of urgent business.

Which, I dare say, is the case, brother. So please be ready to ride away from Glaumhalle at first light tomorrow morning."

Albrecht reluctantly turned toward the door.

"By the way," Gustaf called over his shoulder, "Before you leave, Albrecht, please return Mama's cane which I understand you've hidden from her. I'm going to let her out of her room tomorrow and she'll need it to get around."

Albrecht paused on the threshold long enough to say: "It's in the upstairs closet next to your room. Before you give it back to her, you had better be aware she is quite likely to whack Tessa, or the maids, or even you over the head with it. You will be arming her with a dangerous weapon."

"As usual, you exaggerate, Albrecht," Gustaf answered and added with a dry, disparaging laugh: "You and I, everybody at Glaumhalle have survived some whacks of Mama's sticks. So don't worry about it. The exercise will do her good."

Albrecht muttered: "Jesus Christ!" then stumbled toward the stairs and up to his room. He flung himself on the bed where he had made love to Tessa that morning, buried his face in the pillow which still carried a tantalizing scent of her, and wept as he had not wept since his father's death.

Gustaf remained seated at the table, his facial muscles gradually softening from hard anger to an aggrieved pout, his icy blue eyes misting as he stared unhappily into the flame of the nearest candle. He had not wanted to take this leave when General von Kleisenberg first offered it to him, he recollected, pleading that he instead be returned to his regiment which was still stationed outside Paris. His reasons, which he could not reveal to the General, had been to collect himself and get over Louise before facing his domestic problems; his spoken excuse was that he was certain his regiment needed him, that he could not leave his commanding officer with the impression that he was completely shirking his duties. But the fat, meddling General had opposed such a patently contrived idea and even stung him by suggesting: "This could not have something to do with a desire to chase after our fair Louise all the way back to Paris, could it?" When faced with a vehement denial he had cut off any further discussion by declaring: "Enough good Germans have been wasted in France. It is time we save a few and send them home as healthy husbands. Besides, I consider myself accountable in this matter to your mother-in-law, the Countess Antoinette. I intend to see her next week in Vienna and my long friendship with the von Beckhaus family requires me to report that you have safely rejoined her daughter. So off you go, my boy! Give my fondest regards to your lovely Baroness Tessa!"

Tessa perplexed him completely. There was a marked

change in her bearing, but she was no longer the shy, awkward girl he remembered. Of course, their courtship had provided few opportunities to get to know each other. But either his first impression of her had been entirely wrong or she had changed considerably since last July. Even as he puzzled over Tessa's behavior, even as he remained haunted by visions of Louise, he found himself desiring this strangely defiant girl-woman who was his wife. If he were ever really to fall in love with her, if she were to fall in love with him, they would have to consummate their marriage. The time had come—now, tonight. Still he hesitated, not entirely sure of himself, dallying at the table for another ten minutes before rising and starting upstairs.

Tessa was seated on the edge of the bed, her elbows on her knees, her chin cupped in her hands and her eyes staring half-closed through the dark glass of the window. She did not move when she heard the click and clink of Gustaf's cavalry boots approaching down the hall, nor when the door slowly creaked open and his reflection appeared on the black glass. She had been expecting him.

"Tessa, may I come in?" he asked, entering and moving into her line of vision by the window.

"It's your room," she dully answered.

"It's *our* room," he corrected her. "Although not really adequate for the two of us, I know. We belong in the master bedroom. Mama will have to move out of it tomorrow and we shall move in."

She gave him an incredulous look, but made no comment.

"I want you to be comfortable, Tessa," he assured her. "I want you to be mistress of my house. I even agree there are a lot of things we should buy to improve the house and the farm. But I must have a hand in it. We must sensibly plan everything together. Is that unreasonable?"

"It is your house," she said with a shrug.

"It is *our* house. I am the responsible head of it," he replied as if explaining a particularly subtle point of difference. He was trying very hard to keep an even, pleasant tone, but his nervousness caused fine cold beads of perspiration to break out over his forehead. He tried to think of something gentle, something light to say which would dispel the tension between them, but the best he could come up with was a sort of lame commiseration: "Much bad luck has befallen us since we parted on the Wolin road last July. As if fate has been against us. Yet, here we are in spite of everything. Remember the vow I made to you before leaving you that evening? . . ."

"I won't hold you to it, Gustaf," she answered rather too quickly, still staring out the black window. Then something small but heavy and hard fell into her lap, making her jump in surprise. It was his Iron Cross, loosely wrapped inside its silk neck ribbon.

"I did not earn that as well as I hoped to," he said, "but at least it should prove to you that I tried. That I'm not altogether unworthy."

Tessa could not suppress a bitter little laugh. "It's exactly like the one they gave Papa, except after he was quite dead," she said, gingerly picking up the medal and twirling it before flipping it aside on the bed. She got up and squeezed past him to the armoire, opening it and taking a nightgown off a hanger. "Yes, all the soldiers in our family have been recognized as brave and true. So now I must prove myself a good, dutiful wife. I too must be true to my vows as best I can—right?" She began to undress quickly as she spoke.

Gustaf blinked at her, swallowing hard, his face reddening with embarrassment as she peeled off her blouse, revealing her broad, bony shoulders, lean, sinewy arms like a boy's, and above the flat curve of her shapeless white bodice, a smooth, hard expanse of chest dappled by a golden patina of freckles. There was no suggestive cleavage of satiny white skin, no fascinating mole to hypnotize his eye, no alluring curves promising generous breasts. Her action was entirely devoid of sensuality. Yet, no woman had ever before undressed before him as she was doing now, nor had he ever imagined in his adolescent, erotic dreams that it would happen this way. Despite his puritanical mortification, he had a wild urge to grab her and violently rip off her clothes, rather than stand there, transfixed, watching her deliberately, unemotionally strip herself, button by button, hook by hook, strap by strap. But he could only gulp: "I'll disrobe next door! Call me after you've turned out the lamp! He beat a flustered retreat just as she flopped onto the bed and wiggled her lean, muscular thighs and calves clear of the folds of the petticoat. Her thighs, he noticed in a flash, were as smooth and white as marble.

Tessa pulled her nightgown down over her head, blew out the lamp and stretched out on the bed without bothering to call out through the half-open door that she was ready. She could hear Gustaf stirring about in the adjoining room, the thump of his boots as he pulled them off, the scrape of a chair almost knocked over, the rattle of drawers being opened and shut. He would come in within a minute or two, she was certain, whether she called him or not. In the meanwhile she lay there in the darkness, waiting for him, her body tense but numb, her heart aching for Albrecht, going over and over her insoluble dilemma. "You are an adultress!" she told herself. "And nothing will ever

 ✠

371

change that." Another thought struck her with bitter irony; if she were to find herself pregnant, how would she know *which* Falkenhorst was the father—Albrecht or Gustaf? Not until after the child was born and had time to grow into the likeness of one or the other of the very unalike brothers would she really know for sure. Three or four years from now at the earliest! But maybe Gustaf already suspected that she had been unfaithful, or might become convinced of it tonight? It was a frightening possibility, yet one which she found herself rejecting. She would not resist him, but neither would he find her easy to make love to. The constriction she felt in her lower abdomen and thighs was a painful assurance of that.

With these thoughts racing through her brain, Tessa waited and waited. The minutes dragged out interminably, long after the sounds next door had ceased. Had he decided not to come to her, after all? To leave her waiting in this unbearable tension? Still she refused to call him as he had asked; instead she gave out a series of impatient, dry little coughs. Almost immediately the door whined plaintively on its hinges and she heard him groping toward the bed in the dark, breathing hard and fast as if he had already gone through a great emotional exertion. The mattress creaked and sagged as he lowered himself onto it. For a moment he lay motionless and silent. Then he said:

"I wish I could have courted you properly, the way a bride should be courted by her husband and lover. But . . . it did not work out that way for us. And soon I must leave you again. So even now there's so little time for us to . . . to become husband and wife, you see. . . ."

"Yes, yes, Gustaf. I understand," she sighed.

His hand fumbled through the dark and came down heavily on her thigh, tightening momentarily in a fitfully hard grip, then changing into a nervously gentle one. To her amazement Tessa felt her cramps suddenly dissolve into a tingling, yielding lassitude.

From the window of his room Albrecht watched the first pale streaks of dawn breaking over the horizon of the Polish plains beyond the Orla. The stars continued to sparkle and only gradually winked out as a luminous pearly twilight washed out the night. Delicate wraiths of mist rose and drifted off the river where he heard the sound of wild ducks chortling and flapping their wings as they took a morning bath. In the orchard a nightingale rendered its softly fluting repertoire of songs, a sure harbinger of spring. From the compost heap behind *der Feste*, a rooster roused his hens with a series of cocky, raucous calls. As Albrecht broodingly watched and listened to the sounds and sights of daybreak over Glaumhalle, it struck him that this would be for him the last time, that he would never be present for another.

It was a melancholy thought with a painful sting to it, but a fleeting one. His mind was still grappling with the tragedy which had struck him and Tessa just as their devotion seemed to be flowering into the most passionate love. During the last two hours of darkness he had been sitting at the small table by the window, trying to compose a tender farewell note to her, one that would lay bare the agony in his own heart while at the same time comfort her. But after two hours of agonizing, he had been unable to unravel his tangled emotions enough even to put down a single word on the blank sheet of paper before him. He had long since stopped weeping, even before he had heard his brother's boots tramping up the staircase and receding down the hall toward the room where, he knew, Tessa was trapped into awaiting his pleasure. Now he also gave up agonizing over the composition of this final love letter, over the whole, hopelessly tangled skein of their love affair, and forced himself into urgent practical thoughts and action.

"It will be America after all," he told himself. "For me alone."

It took him only minutes to pack his few belongings into his battered canvas gladstone bag, one suit which had become too small but still had some good material in it, four shirts, some underwear, and two pairs of shoes. The Heidelberg fraternal uniform he left hanging in the armoire; it would be useless in America. He decided that his Railroad Inspector's uniform would be appropriate for travel at least as far as Hamburg, or Bremen, or wherever he took ship for the New World, so he put it on. In a few more minutes he sorted out his identification papers and credentials, then counted up his financial resources which amounted to 78 thalers in cash, plus the voucher from the Railroad Authority for 192, a total wealth of 270 thalers. Not very much money for the long voyage and establishing of a new life, but he remembered General Sheridan having said that immigrants, rich or poor, were welcomed to America if they were willing to work. The main thing was to get away from *here*, to get *there!* He hurriedly slipped the documents and money into his leather wallet which he stuffed into the inside pocket of his greatcoat, his only imposing garment because it was the newest, purchased in a fit of vain extravagance during the halcyon days at Versailles. Then he was ready to leave.

But that blank piece of paper still beckoned on the table and he took another few moments to sit down again, this time staring at it only a few seconds before picking up the pen, dipping it in the inkwell, and boldly writing: *No matter how long the silence or how far the distance, remember that I love you forever. Albrecht.*

He stared at the words with something like shock while waiting for the ink to dry. The letters were a stark blue black against the white paper, which was now reflecting a reddish tint from the dawn seeping through the window. How to deliver this message to Tessa? Certainly it must not fall into Gustaf's hands. Could he trust Master Prytz to handle it tactfully? Maybe —maybe not. Without any definite course in mind, he folded up the sheet of paper four times over and put it in his pocket. Then he picked up his bag and walked out into the still-dark hall. He paused and hesitated for a moment upon reaching the door to his mother's bedroom, listening to the faint rhythmic wheezing of her sleep. Remembering her stick, he fetched it from a nearby closet and left it leaning against the door. "Good-bye, my poor unhappy Mama," he softly whispered before continuing to the head of the stairs. He paused there too, staring towards the darkness at the end of the hall where Tessa was lying with Gustaf in his room; he whispered again: "Good-bye, my darling!"

As he passed through the small vestibule, his eye was caught by Tessa's riding gloves lying on the shelf above the coatrack. He carefully stuffed the note inside one of the gloves and put it back with its mate. Then, intending to leave the house through the scullery entrance, he passed through the dining room, pantry, and kitchen. There he was surprised to find Master Prytz already up and seated at the table, drinking a cup of coffee. The two regarded each other with mutual surprise before the stablemaster gruffly exclaimed: "Well, good morning Freiherr von Falkenhorst. You are leaving us, I see."

"Yes, Prytz," Albrecht answered him. "There is no need for me to stay any longer. My brother said I could borrow a horse which I will leave at the livery stable in Ols. I want to catch the afternoon train to Breslau."

"You shouldn't ride away on an empty stomach," Prytz said. "Have a sweet bun and a cup of coffee. Coffee is a luxury we haven't enjoyed for a while." Prytz poured a cupful out of the kettle on the stove and picked a bun out of the brass breadbin on the counter, then put them down on the table. Albrecht dropped his bag, sat down and began to eat in silence. Prytz watched him with a glint of sympathy in his eyes, but he, too, ate his breakfast in silence. After a couple of minutes the back stairs of the pantry creaked and they both thought that one of the maids was coming down from her attic lair. To their surprise it was Gustaf who suddenly appeared, wearing his nightshirt stuffed inside his breeches, his feet bare. His blond hair hung in tousled disorder around his head, his face was puffy and his eyes red, but the expression on his face was one of dazed, almost smug well-being.

"Good heavens, Albrecht!" he exclaimed with sleepy cheerfulness. "I didn't really expect you to sneak away without saying good-bye to me."

"I was under the impression we said good-bye last night," Albrecht drily replied. Somehow, his brother's expression filled him with suppressed fury.

Gustaf went to the stove and helped himself to a cup of coffee, then said to the dour Prytz: "The Freiherr Albrecht is in a great hurry to get back to his interrupted career. Saddle up our fastest horse for him. That big black stallion. I don't remember its name, but you know the one I mean."

Prytz looked horrified. "Feldteufel? But that is the Lady Baroness' favorite. Surely she'd object to his being ridden to Ols and left among the nags of Graustark's stable, Herr Leutnant Baron."

"Any saddle horse that will get me to Ols will do," Albrecht shrugged.

"No, only the best for my little brother," Gustaf ordered. "Give him Feldteufel. Run along, Prytz, and saddle him up at once. You can finish your breakfast later."

Master Prytz stamped out of the kitchen, shaking his

head as he left the two brothers facing each other across the table.

"Is Tessa awake?" Albrecht asked. He both wished and dreaded a farewell meeting with her—mostly dreaded it.

"I left her still dozing, half-awake, half-asleep. She had a rather restless night of it, you understand." Gustaf gave a little cough, then added: "But it will become better as time goes along. Quite pleasant even."

Albrecht's fury increased, but he also could not help a cold feeling of relief. At least Gustaf was not challenging Tessa's virginity which would have made for one more horrible, possibly violent, scene between them. He hurried to finish his meager breakfast.

"Where are you going?" Gustaf pleasantly inquired.

"To Breslau."

"And from there?"

"Hamburg, I think."

"Hamburg, why Hamburg?"

Albrecht stuffed the last of the bun into his mouth, washed it down with the dregs of the coffee, then defiantly blurted out: "Because I am leaving for America by the first available ship out of whatever port it sails from. There is nothing left for me here, so I'm emigrating."

Gustaf's sleepy eyes opened wide. "Emigrating?" he exclaimed incredulously, and burst into derisive laughter. "You always had idiotic notions, but this one goes too far. People of our class do not emigrate. That's for adventurers and laborers who can't make a go of it at home. But not people of our class."

"I'm not taking my class with me. You can have it and all that goes with it," Albrecht said and getting up from the table, put on his cap and picked up his bag.

Gustaf got up too and followed him to the door. "I can't believe you'd do anything so silly," he scoffed. "Take my advice and go back to the civil service. If you don't like the railroad business but want to travel, try to get an appointment with our foreign ministry. Uncle Herman is a state councilor, you know, and would certainly give you a recommendation."

Albrecht appeared not to be listening to him. He opened the door and stepped out onto the stoop. "Well, good-bye, Gustaf," he coldly said to his brother, extending his hand. "Try to be decent to Tessa. Give her my best wishes and affectionate farewell."

Gustaf took his hand and held on to it. "Don't worry about my wife and me. It is we who will be worrying about *you*. Please don't do anything to disgrace us. Be sensible, for God's sake."

Albrecht pulled his hand away and with a last curt, "Good-bye!" started across the yard toward *der Feste* whose grim old battlements were glowing in the softening pink light of the sunrise. He never looked back. Gustaf retreated from the chill of the dawn, and watched with a perplexed frown through the small window of the kitchen door.

Master Prytz brought the eager Feldteufel out of the stable, helped Albrecht to strap his bag securely behind the saddle, then gave him a leg up. "Ride him carefully and tell that rascal Graustark to take good care of him until we pick him up," he admonished, his scowl tinged with genuine misery. "I wish you well."

Albrecht nodded and leaning down, put his hand on Prytz's shoulder. "You and I never really hit it off," he told the grizzled stablemaster, "but I want you to know that I respect and trust you, Master Prytz. I now ask you to promise me you will watch over our Baroness Tessa. As you well know, she is as dear to me as she is to you."

The old man's chin and moustache quivered with emotion. "I reaffirm the same promise to you, Freiherr Albrecht, which I made last year to the blessed Count Paul von Beckhaus," he gruffly answered, then said again: "I wish you well!"

Albrecht touched his spurs to Feldteufel's flanks and the horse left the yard at a fast, determined trot just as a blood red sundisk rose above the rim of the Polish plains.

essa had not been sleeping at all when Gustaf had left her side, only pretending to. It was not until he had slipped quietly out of the room that she suddenly became very drowsy. But then she heard the clatter of hooves in the yard below and became fully awake again. Reacting to a sudden premonition, she bounced out of bed and dashed to the window. Her eyes were caught first by Prytz standing in his shirtsleeves near the stable entrance of *der Feste*, then, following the direction of his stolid gaze, by the familiar figure of Albrecht riding Feldteufel down the hill toward the Ols road. With a gasp of anguish she threw open the window and yelled after him: "Albrecht! Albrecht! Where are you going? Come back!" Prytz gave a start at the sound of her voice and stared up at her with a helpless, commiserating shrug. But Albrecht was already half-way down the hill and if he heard her cry, his reaction was to spur Feldteufel into a canter which stretched into a fast gallop as soon as he reached level ground.

Without taking time to put on either a robe or slippers, Tessa tore away from the window, burst out of the room, ran through the dark hall and down the back staircase where she virtually collided with Gustaf who was starting back up to dress.

"Where is Albrecht going at this hour of the morning," she shouted at him. "What is going on?"

"Nothing is going on except that my brother has left to resume his own life and business," Gustaf answered her in a tone meant to be reassuring. "Since my return from the dead, he is no longer needed around here."

"You drove him out?" she shrilly accused.

"We agreed that his leaving would be the best thing for all of us," Gustaf answered. "My brother must make his own life, as we must make ours. My dear, you are rather scantily clad. The servants will be up and about any minute. Let's go back to our room." He tried to turn her around on the staircase, but she violently fended him off.

"He didn't even say good-bye to me," she railed. "Did you keep him from saying good-bye to me?"

Gustaf tried to mollify her. "No, dearest. I told him you were asleep. So he asked me to convey to you his respects and affectionate regards. No doubt we'll hear from him soon."

Tessa managed to subdue her anguished rage and, after a moment of tight-lipped silence, bewildered him by switching both the subject and her tone of voice:

"Let me make one thing clear right now and forever, Gustaf," she said in a quiet but determined voice. "I am your wife and will submit to what is required of me as your wife. I already started doing that last night. I'll be your Baroness von Falken-horst and keep house for you at Glaumhalle. But I'm also Theresa von Beckhaus und Varn and the daughter of a Count, a Countess in my own right. I'll resist and stop you from inter-fering with or trying to take over any of my property and monies, because my father left those to me, and me *alone!* Do you understand that, Gustaf?"

Gustaf's face had turned ashen and it was several seconds before he could weakly protest: "What has come over you, Tessa? I only ask that you consult me over decisions involving the family. I understand there are many things you want to change, but. . . ."

"But you have the outlook of a cavalry leutnant," she inter-rupted him, pronouncing his rank with utter contempt. "That does not qualify you to dispose over monies and estates. Nor, as far as I've seen, over people. Not even over your own family, including your only brother. You don't have the slightest idea of the pain you've caused him . . . and *me!* But never mind, Gustaf. You go ahead and be a cavalry leutnant. Maybe soon there'll be another war and you'll be promoted to Hauptmann . . . Rittmeister . . . major, maybe even eventually to general. Fine! But don't interfere with me or what belongs to me."

Gustaf was speechless at this tirade from his nineteen-year-old wife. He tried to collect his wits for an outraged reply, but before he could do so, there came a strident series of imperious screeches from the hall above them. Tessa cocked an ear toward the unpleasant noise of her mother-in-law. "I must tend to your mother," she exclaimed with angry resignation and started back up the stairs toward his mother's room. But before entering it, she faltered and leaned against the wall with her hands covering her face to suppress a convulsive sob.

"Albrecht! Albrecht!" she softly gasped. "Why have you forsaken me? Why did you have so much love and so little strength?"

May–July 1871

Victory

⚔ ⚔

lbrecht von Falkenhorst did not tarry in Breslau, a town which he found depressingly provincial for all its quaint mixture of medieval and Bohemian-baroque architecture; it was far too close to Ols and Glaumhalle, and inhabited or frequently visited by people who knew his family. Upon arriving at the station, crowded as usual with both military and civilian travelers, he immediately got in line at the booth selling tickets to Berlin. To his great relief, the harassed clerk took one look at his uniform and without asking for any further identification, issued the Herr Inspector a free first-class pass on the next express—which took almost eleven hours to reach the old Prussian and new imperial capital.

Albrecht got off the train at Berlin's Schlesischer Bahnhof feeling tremendously tired from the long railroad journey and emotionally wrung out from the abrupt severance of his relationship with Tessa, indeed, from his whole family. His nerves were further strained by the press of the huge crowd milling about the station and competing for an entirely inadequate number of livery-coaches and horsedrawn omnibuses. He had visited Berlin several times before, but never had he seen such a crowd of excited people in the station. The reason for the invasion was proclaimed by the banners hanging from the sooty iron trusses of the station's roof: "**WE HAIL OUR VICTORIOUS TROOPS!**" or "**HAIL KAISER WILHELM OF A UNITED GERMAN**

EMPIRE!" or a more blatantly nationalistic "ALL GLORY TO PRUSSIAN VICTORY." The city was in the throes of a momentous binge, celebrating not only the victory over France, but the meteoric rise of Prussia and its capital to the dominant position within the newborn German Empire. It seemed as if representative units of every regiment which had fought in France—Prussian as well as those of the new satellite states—had been brought into Berlin for formal parades and informal strutting along its boulevards, and that every citizen with the means to do so had traveled from far or near to join in the festivities and pay boisterous homage to the troops and their Kaiser.

With mounting irritation Albrecht waited for the better part of an hour among the mob fighting for transportation at the entrance of Schlesischer Bahnhof, unable even to get near a coach or omnibus. He finally picked up his heavy bag and trudged four blocks to an intersection where he managed to flag down an empty coach. He had the coachman drive him to the only two hotels he knew by name, only to find both filled to capacity. In desperation he asked the coachman (who was half-drunk but reasonably sympathetic) for a suggestion, and so wound up at an unimpressive hostelry named Krone und Kessel located in the bustling, but very unfashionable, Kreuzberg sector. It was by then six o'clock in the evening and he had no energy left to protest either the coachman's outrageous fare or the innkeeper's equally inflated rates for a tiny attic room facing the back yard of a noisy neighboring tavern. He paid out the money from his meager funds, climbed the four flights of creaking stairs, then dropped into the bed after removing only his greatcoat, too weary to seek solace for a gnawing hunger, yet unable to fall immediately into the sleep which his exhausted mind and body required. The tiny dormer window had no curtains to obscure the long twilight or muffle the discordant singing of beer-swilling customers in the *bierstube* below. It was after midnight before he at last fell into an uneasy sleep, one disturbed by nightmares of Tessa crying out to him as she fought against the embrace of Gustaf; he thrashed and tossed and moaned as he tried to go to her aid—but could not. Her cries faded as Gustaf carried her off, leaving him far behind as he crawled sluggishly on hands and knees down the dark halls of Glaumhalle.

Albrecht was awakened early next morning by the din of bells; a church close by the Krone and Kessel was summoning its parishioners to a thanksgiving service. When he had dressed and gone downstairs to the dingy little restaurant for breakfast, the waiter informed him that a big victory parade was scheduled down Unter den Linden that noon which everybody in town would attend. All government offices and most shops would be closed, of course. This meant he would be unable to go the Railroad Authority Headquarters and collect the money owed him; he had also decided to invest in one good suit of clothes for his voyage to America so that he would not arrive looking like an indigent immigrant, but it seemed unlikely he would find a tailor willing to work today. However, also on his agenda was a call on the residence of the American Minister to Prussia where he expected to obtain the necessary immigration permit and visa. Surely the Ministry would not be closed for a purely Prussian celebration, so still wearing his uniform, he set out on foot in search for it.

As he approached the center of the city and the area near Brandenburg Tor, the crowds grew thick and the carriage traffic heavy. The waiter had been right, everybody in town was gathering to witness the parade. It seemed as if every other male was wearing either a military or civil service uniform; the women were dressed in Sunday finery even though it was a Tuesday morning. On the lamp posts of major thoroughfares hung banners and garlands. Troops were lining up and blocking streets leading into Unter den Linden, and every few blocks bands were blaring brassy marching tunes interspersed with repeated renditions of *"Preussen Glorias."* The Berliners' passion for flowers was everywhere in evidence, in pots and vases placed in the windows of their houses, in bright bouquets carried by the women. Infantrymen had even stuck flowers in the muzzles of their rifles, artillerymen had wound wreaths of them around their gun barrels, and cavalrymen had attached corsages to their horses. The excitement of the occasion was increased by the exhilaration of a beautiful, sunny May morning whose bright warmth dispelled all memories of the bitter winter. Everybody was happy and exuberantly optimistic. Except for Albrecht who pushed his way through the multitudes with a grim smile, trying not to appear out of sympathy with the joyous celebration. Even so, the policeman from whom he asked directions to the American Legation regarded him with some suspicion before providing the requested information.

When Albrecht reached the Legation, a rather unimposing house off the Kurfurstendamm, he found it open as he had hoped, but occupied only by a very junior-looking clerk who became quite flustered when the unexpected visitor stated his business: "Oh, dear!" he exclaimed in very bad German and eyeing Albrecht's uniform with confusion. "Usually all applications for immigration to the United States of America are processed by the Assistant Secretary of our Legation who happens to be attending a court function with our Minister today. I suppose I could have you fill out the necessary application, but ... but, aren't you a member of the Prussian Armed Forces, sir? In which case we could not accept your application without written permission from your commanding officer, sir."

"I have just resigned my appointment in the Prussian Civil Service," Albrecht explained in his precisely enunciated university English and produced the official document from the Railroad Authority to prove his statement. He also handed over his confirmation certificate from the Ols Lutheran Church and a somewhat dog-eared paper certifying him as a bona fide undergraduate of Heidelberg University. "I hope we can handle the formalities today," he told the clerk. "You see, I want to leave for America as soon as possible. No later than next week, I am hoping."

The clerk was very impressed by his papers. "Oh, dear!" he exclaimed, insisting upon speaking in his bad German. "You are a railroading expert, an Inspector of Railroads! And a student from Heidelberg! And, oh dear, you are of the *nobility* . . . a Freiherr! Our Legation Secretary Mr. Baldwin will be very interested in you."

"Yes, well, in the meanwhile may I fill out the application you spoke of," Albrecht impatiently asked him.

The clerk opened a drawer and pulled a very simple questionnaire out of a folder: Full name, date of birth, place of birth, nationality, marital status, number of children, and occupation. Albrecht answered these questions very quickly, using the pen and inkwell the clerk put before him. He took a little longer answering the last two questions, which were: *Are you bringing German money with you to the United States of America and, if so, how much?* and *Do you have relations or friends in the United States of America you intend to contact there and, if so, state their names and places of residence.* In the former case, he wrote down after some hesitation: *Approximately four hundred thalers,* in the latter: *General Philip Sheridan of American Army, an acquaintance.* Then he handed the paper back to the clerk who blotted it and began to read through it with eager interest. His first comment was: "Oh dear, why did you not put down your noble title?"

Albrecht bristled and haughtily answered: "I thought such things did not matter in your country."

The clerk gave an embarrassed cough. "Well, not really. But on the other hand we are not against better-class candidates for citizenship. We recognize no nobility as such, you understand, Freiherr von Falkenhorst, but neither are we trying to establish a society of common, uneducated people." He coughed again and without asking Albrecht's leave, dipped his pen in the inkwell and scrawled "Freiherr" above his name. Reading on, he likewise added "Inspector" to where Albrecht had modestly categorized himself as a "railroad administrator." When the clerk read the answer to the final question he was incredulous: "Do you mean to say you are actually a friend of General Sheridan's? That he knows you personally?"

"I believe I stated he is merely an acquaintance," Albrecht coldly corrected him. "We met during the course of the campaign in France when he was attached to our army as neutral observer and I was an aide to the Inspector General of Military Railroad Transport. We also met a few times subsequently at Royal Headquarters in Versailles." He inwardly prayed that if this clerk had a way of directly checking on this, General Sheridan would remember and confirm his statement.

But the clerk seemed too flustered to ask any more questions. He thrust a pen at Albrecht and asked him to sign the questionnaire, then told him to return to the Legation at three o'clock the following afternoon when "our Mr. Baldwin will surely be available to give this matter his personal attention!" Then he came out from behind his polished mahogany counter, escorted him to the vestibule, bowing him out of the building with un-American servility.

Albrecht walked slowly back toward the Kurfurstendamm feeling vaguely uneasy and considerably let down by his initial visit to the American Legation. The whole idea of immigrating to this strange country suddenly seemed preposterous to him; perhaps Tessa and Gustaf were right. Yet there remained that painfully gnawing urge in him to get away—far away—and where besides Africa (populated by cannibals and slave-traders), or Australia (colonized by deported English convicts), could a man build himself a decent new life? No, there was really only America! Feeling thoroughly despondent and lonely, he strolled into a sidewalk café which was surprisingly half-empty, sat down at a table in the back of the establishment and ordered a stein of beer and a plate of sausage and cucumber. It became evident to him why the crowds had thinned out as he heard the distant crash and blare of military bands mingled with sustained cheers and rhythmic huzzas coming from the nearby Unter den Linden where the great victory parade was in progress. The nearest customer in the cafe was a rather shabbily dressed elderly gentleman with a reddish white spade beard, reading a newspaper while sipping a glass of wine; he suddenly became very angry over something he read and almost tore up the newspaper as he threw it down on the floor. Then his piercing eyes caught sight of Albrecht and he loudly addressed him across the three intervening empty tables: "Why aren't you out there braying praise at Bismarck together with the rest of the donkeys, young man? Isn't your blood running hot with the rampant fever of patriotism?" When Albrecht merely stared at him in surprise, the old man sarcastically inquired, without lowering his voice: "What is the matter with you? Why are you looking so glum? Is it that you have an intelligent conscience? Or maybe you're just mooning over some wench who broke your brittle heart?"

Albrecht felt a numbing stab of pain as the chance barbs cut deeply into his most sensitive feelings. He barely managed a civil rebuff: "Sir, I am here to relax for a moment from pressing business which has nothing to do with today's events in general, nor you in particular. Please excuse me." He tried to return his attention to his beer and sausage which he suddenly found himself in a great hurry to finish but could not afford to waste the food by abruptly leaving.

"Do you know that revolution has broken out in Paris, young man?" the cranky stranger shouted as if he were announcing the advent of doomsday. He was momentarily diverted by the waiter who rushed up to his table and nervously asked him to stop annoying the customers, an interruption which he dealt with by administering a shove that sent the man reeling back into the interior of the café. Once rid of him, he approached Albrecht through a series of quick leapfrog advances from table to table, all the while barking out a series of questions which he answered himself: "Who do you think is responsible for the revolution in Paris? *Bismarck!* Will the Paris revolution spread to Germany? *Yes, sooner or later if not immediately!* Can Bismarck's new German Empire prevail against the Paris revolution? *Not without resorting to methods which will bring ruin to the German peoples!* What will be the end results of the victory we are celebrating today? *Wars and more wars, spreading, ever-spreading revolutions, anarchy, and eventually, Armageddon!*" With that dire prophesy he had bounced into the vacant chair at Albrecht's table and with an intensity which reeked of wine and sauerkraut, bellowed into his face: "Can you evade responsibility for today's events by turning your back on them and sitting here apart from it all, swilling beer and stuffing yourself with sausage? *No! Every German must share at least one thirty-millionth part of that responsibility, a tiny fraction of the whole for each individual, but heavy enough to break our collective backs . . . yours, mine, Bismarck's, von Moltke's, the Kaiser's, everybody's!!*"

The other customers in the cafe were by now upset by the disturbance, one couple getting up and quickly leaving, two others crying out loud protests of "Shame!" and "Treason." Albrecht leaned away from his tormentor's foul breath, embarrassed, yet staring with troubled amazement into his desiccated face with its dirty, untidy beard and burning, fanatical eyes. By mustering all the control he could over his emotions, he quietly asked him: "Why are you heaping your misgivings on me, sir? What do you expect me to do?"

The old man's hairy mouth opened into a lopsided leer. "I could see at a glance that you're not an ordinary German donkey, young man. From that, I reasonably deduced that you'd be unlikely to act like one." He suddenly dropped his voice to a conspiratorial whisper, reached out and closed his long bony fingers over Albrecht's sleeve, saying: "That you might have the intelligence to heed the lessons of past history and enough sensitivity to realize. . . ." He got no further as a huge pair of hands clamped down around the collar of his coat and yanked him out of the chair and away from the table.

The waiter had alerted the café owner, who had come storming out of the kitchen, a huge man whose corpulent chest and belly had the firmness and shape of a battering ram spiked with brass buttons, and whose ham fists picked up the offending customer by the scruff of the neck and tossed him out on the Kurfurstendamm pavement as easily as he would have tossed out a stray cat.

But the old man had the resilience of a tough old alley cat and, although he found himself sprawling in the gutter, quickly sprang back to his feet, snarling defiance as he picked up his battered hat, then shouting a string of profane insults which ended with a pronouncement which he spat out like a venomous curse: "All Germans have gone mad! As God is my witness, a madness which will afflict the next five generations! One hundred years of madness to come! That's what we deserve! That's what we'll get! *Pruessen Inglorias! Preussen Ignominius!*"

"Get away from my place, you crazy old fool!" the café owner shouted, hunching his thick neck into his massive shoulders and stamping his feet like a bull preparing to charge. The waiter, the customers—everybody except the stunned Albrecht —jeered and threatened the blaspheming old man. A policeman patroling the opposite side of the street heard the fracas, turned from his beat and, without hurrying, crossed the road, causing several carriages to swerve and come to abrupt stops to make way for him. But before he could reach the scene of the disturbance, the old man chose discretion over noisy valor and scampered off at a far greater speed than would have been dignified for the policeman to match against such a pathetic miscreant. As he vanished into the nearest side street, he threw a parting invective over his shoulder, *"Leichengangers! Heldendrecker!"*

The owner of the café loudly urged the policeman into a more determined pursuit without obtaining any perceptible results, then turned his attention to Albrecht and made a peculiar squatting motion which was the closest thing his enormous girth would allow by way of a bow. "A thousand pardons, Herr Inspector, for the inconvenience," he pleaded in a suddenly ingratiating tone. "The festivities in honor of our heroes has also attracted its share of riffraff and crackpots. All that notwithstanding, *Hoch der Kaiser!* This is a great day for Prussia. Allow me to restore it fully in your favor, Herr Inspector, by offering you all the hospitality my humble establishment can provide to your complete satisfaction."

Albrecht frowned at him. "You were unnecessarily rough with the old gentleman, Herr Kelnmeister," he reprimanded him. "It is not a great day, but a sad one for Prussia when an aged, dissenting eccentric is pummeled and thrown in the gutter. I can find no satisfaction in that."

The owner of the café scowled and lost most of his amiable contrition over a rebuke which he did not fully comprehend. "What I am trying to convey to the Herr Inspector," he grumbled, "is that by way of restitution . . . although I cannot assume responsibility for any senile idiot the authorities leave loose in Berlin . . . I will charge nothing for the Herr Inspector's order of beer and sausage."

Albrecht feigned a sigh of relief. "Well, thank you very much, Herr Kelnmeister. In that case I can well afford to leave it and go elsewhere. Good day!" He got up from his table and, without the slightest hesitation or backward glance, stalked off the premises, leaving the café owner, the waiter, and remaining customers staring after him in dismay.

As Albrecht walked east along the Kurfurstendamm, he could still hear the distant cheers and brassy reverberations from the great victory parade along Unter den Linden. When he crossed Fasanenstrasse, the windows of the surrounding buildings rattled and the lovely blue May sky above their roofs was rent by deep, thundering repercussions of concentrated cannon fire, an unpleasant reminder of his three bloody days around the Sedan, but this time, of course, merely the salute by artillery batteries drawn up at the Brandenburg Tor. As soon as their booming ceased, all the churches in Berlin began to ring their bells in a prolonged, unified clarion call of joy; before their sound faded, the citizens who had massed along the parade route began dispersing down the nearby streets in search of refreshments among the hundreds of restaurants and cafés whose staffs were braced for a profitable business.

By making a wide detour and sticking to side streets and back alleys, (which caused him to become lost several times), Albrecht finally reached the Krone und Kessel in midafternoon, after an arduous long walk. He climbed the steep flight of stairs to his tiny room, and there settled down to write a long letter to Tessa, each sentence an agony of compromise between unbridled emotion and casually prosaic prose. Most frustrating was the fact that he had no idea how to mail it to her without running the risk that it might fall into Gustaf's hands. In the end, he gave up after five pages and left it unfinished to drop exhausted on his bed, staring wide-eyed at the cracked yellow ceiling where a large black spider was slowly, methodically sewing up a captured cockroach in its web.

Outside the dormer window, the *bierstube* throbbed and bawled with great exuberance late into the night. For Albrecht, sleep again came uneasily.

After a breakfast of boiled eggs and very gristly pork hocks, Albrecht walked the thirty-odd city blocks to the Railroad Authority Headquarters where he presented his discharge papers and terminal pay voucher to the Paymaster's Office. He had no difficulty in collecting what was owed him and, to his surprise, found out that he was entitled to a special "Victory Stipend" of twenty-five thalers, a sum which the Assistant Paymaster gleefully informed him was his share of the huge indemnity being squeezed out of the defeated French. Feeling almost wealthy due to this unexpected windfall, he next scouted along the peripheral streets of Berlin's most-fashionable shopping district, looking for a better-class tailor than he had originally intended to patronize. The one he chose offered to sew him a suit of good quality, gray blue broadcloth for ten thalers and, for an additional charge of one thaler, guaranteed its delivery by seven o'clock the following evening. After selecting the material and allowing his proportions to be measured by the tailor, he walked back to the Kurfurstendamm where he entered an expensive restaurant and ordered the cheapest dish and most modest bottle of wine featured on its menu—it turned out the best meal he had enjoyed since leaving Versailles last December. So good that he could not resist topping it off with the extravagance of a tiny tumbler of genuine French cognac. He thus found himself in a rather recklessly confident mood when he promptly presented himself in the vestibule of the American Legation at three o'clock.

The young clerk who had attended him on his first visit greeted him with enthusiastic familiarity and immediately ushered him into the office of Mr. Legation Secretary Eustace M. Baldwin. The office was depressingly modest, its single window affording a view of the closely abutting brick wall of a much larger neighboring house, its furnishings consisting of three chairs and a huge rolltop desk, its only decorations a pair of portraits of American presidents, one a near caricature likeness of the current president, Ulysses S. Grant, staring out of his gilt frame with a kind of dissolute, vacant ferocity, the other of the late, martyred Abraham Lincoln on whom the artist had bestowed the melancholy look of a disillusioned prophet. The only cheerful thing about the dismal little room was Mr. Legation Secretary Baldwin, a cherubic fellow who jovially rose from behind the oak ramparts of his desk and greeted Albrecht in a disconcerting Oxford English accent:

"Do come in and sit down, sir. I have been looking forward to talking to you since our Mr. Potter reported your visit yesterday. My regrets that I was not here to receive you in person, but, as you must be aware, there were some special state functions the Minister and I were required to attend. By the way, my hearty congratulations on your country's magnificent victory over its enemy, sir!"

Albrecht sat down in the hard wooden chair next to Mr. Baldwin's desk after shaking his extended hand and drily said: "Thank you. But I am surprised that you Americans are really pleased over France's defeat by Prussia. If my memory of history is not faulty, I recall that America has maintained friendly relations with France ever since its inception as an independent republic."

Mr. Baldwin's crinkly green eyes gave Albrecht a hard appraising glance. "It is our policy to maintain official neutrality in European affairs," he pleasantly explained, "without necessarily keeping so aloof from them that we cannot offer congratulations or condolences according to the fortunes of friendly foreign powers. It is a matter of form, you must understand. We do expect, of course, that foreign citizens and embassies visiting or accredited to our republic show the same attitude and courtesies. A polite accommodation of *quid pro quo*, we might call it." He dismissed that subject with a chopping motion of his right hand, then opened up a folder. On top Albrecht recognized the form he had filled out the day before. To his curious surprise, there were three or four more beneath it, filled with finely penned writing, giving the impression that a whole dossier had been compiled on him within a little more than twenty-four hours. Mr. Baldwin adjusted a pair of square-cut spectacles on his stubby nose and eagerly, quickly perused the contents. "Let me see now . . . Freiherr Albrecht Gerd von Falkenhorst, born in Silesia, October 7, 1851. Student at Heidelberg, 1869 to 1870. No military service. Appointed Deputy Inspector of Prussian Military Railroads and assigned as secretary and special assistant to the late Colonel-Count Paul von Beckhaus und Varn, the

Inspector General of Prussian Military Railroad Transport. Is that all correct, sir?" He peered myopically over the rim of his spectacles at Albrecht.

Albrecht was taken by surprise. He had not included this last piece of information about his past in the original questionnaire. He nodded and guardedly answered: "Yes, I served Count Paul from July to December of 1870, when he was killed."

"There was also a family relationship, was there not?" Mr. Baldwin shot back at him.

"Yes," Albrecht admitted. "His daughter is married to my older brother, Baron Gustaf von Falkenhorst. What of it?"

"It could or could not be of some importance," Mr. Baldwin answered him in a suddenly clipped, businesslike manner. "It could mean that family connections were used to employ you in a position you were by no means qualified for. On the other hand, Colonel-Count Paul von Beckhaus und Varn was well known for his contributions to railroading, and it is unlikely that he would have appointed anybody as his personal assistant, relative or otherwise, unless he had great confidence in his abilities. I suppose that it was through him that you met our General Sheridan?"

"Actually quite the other way around," Albrecht answered. "I happened to run into General Sheridan in a small Lorraine town—Pont-à-Mousson, as I recall—when he was trying to keep up with one of our earlier actions against the French. It was *I* who eventually introduced him to Count von Beckhaus."

"Indeed! Well, possibly so," Mr. Baldwin exclaimed. He quickly shuffled through the papers in the folder, and after checking certain paragraphs, looked up at Albrecht with a glint of humor. "General Sheridan was quite notorious for riding hither and yon, all by himself, in and out of your battles. Suffice it to be said that he mentioned you by name in his dispatches!" He checked the papers again, then added significantly: "Not of meeting you at the town of Pont-à-whatever, but at your Crown Prince's private apartment in the Royal Headquarters of Versailles. Is that correct, sir?"

"Yes. Only because Count von Beckhaus was attached to Royal Headquarters and *I* was attached to him. I don't see what bearing this has on our business, sir."

"Well, it's not often that we have such a well-bred, highly connected young man applying for an immigration visa," Mr. Baldwin explained with a smile. "And one who obviously has at least one highly placed friend in the United States. General Sheridan, you know, is slated to command our Army. Are you planning to call on him in Washington?"

"I had not considered it," Albrecht answered with a shrug, then asked with some impatience: "Will my visa be granted, sir?"

"What do you plan to do in America?" Mr. Baldwin countered in a chatty tone. "Perhaps complete your education in one of our universities. We have several quite good ones in the North. I personally studied at Harvard and highly recommend it."

"I must go to work almost as soon as I arrive in America," Albrecht told him. "I hope this will be possible."

"With your background and connections it will be easy," Mr. Baldwin assured him, again shuffling through the papers on his desk. "I can virtually guarantee you employment right here and now, Freiherr von Falkenhorst. It so happens that a prominent German steelmaker is looking for qualified young men to sell his products in the United States through his newly established agency in Philadelphia. Philadelphia is a very pleasant little town. Solid citizenry. Quite historic. Herr Friedrich Krupp has requested our Legation to recommend likely prospects among immigration applicants. Have you heard of Philadelphia? Have you heard of Herr Friedrich Krupp of Essen?"

"Philadelphia is the city where your Declaration of Independence was signed almost a hundred years ago," Albrecht replied like a student well drilled in his history lessons, then added with a sarcastic petulance: "Friedrich Krupp manufactures and sells cannons. I know absolutely nothing about cannons, except having heard the noise they make and seen the destruction they cause."

Mr. Baldwin laughed and rubbed his hands together in delight, exclaiming: "Very good, sir! You are well informed. Only you're being somewhat unfair to Herr Krupp. He does not sell cannons to the United States, but steel tracks and wheels for our own railroads which will soon span the entire American continent. A splendidly profitable, peaceful business which I recommend only next to attending the University of Harvard. Indeed, it may actually be a better proposition for you since you already have some practical experience in railroading. Don't you agree?"

Albrecht was beginning to find Mr. Baldwin very trying. "Yes, very well, then," he answered shortly. "I'll accept the railroad business as well as any other honest work, sir. Just so that you grant me the necessary documents without binding commitments I might not be able to fulfill."

Mr. Baldwin's cherubic face showed a flash of protesting dismay. "There is no question of binding commitments, sir. Nor of not issuing you your visa. I was merely trying to give you some advice which might make it easier for you to settle yourself comfortably in a country which, for a Prussian nobleman, might turn out very strange and distant from what he is used to. You do understand that there will be some considerable differences between here and there, don't you?"

"Yes. I am even looking forward to them."

"Good!" Mr. Baldwin exclaimed and dipped his pen in the inkwell. Even from the upside-down view, Albrecht could make out what he wrote out on the last page of his dossier in a fluid, clear handwriting: *Overall excellent impression. Modest but much self-assurance. Determined and enterprising. Will do.* After blotting the ink, he closed the folder and returning to an official business-like tone, stated: "Usually our consul in Hamburg processes immigration visas. We shall make an exception in your case and handle everything from this Legation. I will also include a letter of introduction to a Herr von Bohlen who represents Herr Friedrich Krupp's American business interests in Philadelphia. You may use that at your own discretion upon your arrival in the United States. By the way, may I ask if you have purchased passage on a ship?" When Albrecht shook his head, he produced and consulted a small black leather-bound calendar. "Ah, you are in luck! A very fine ship, the *Herzogin Amalie* of the Han-seatischer Rederie will sail from Hamburg to Baltimore on May 14. You can even make your arrangements at once here in Berlin by contacting their agents at 402 Potsdamerstrasse. By all means, mention my name. Then come back here tomorrow af-ternoon with your ticket. You must have your ticket before we can issue you your visa. Just a matter of form, you understand." He indicated that the interview was over by bobbing out of his chair and extending his hand.

Albrecht left the American Legation with mixed feelings and asked directions to Potsdamerstrasse. He did not have to make detours around any parades, but the streets were still abnormally crowded, primarily by troops and officers who had been given leave to enjoy the sights and relaxations of the capital —all ranks seemingly well fortified or debilitated by excessive quaffing of beer and wine. The great victory celebration in Berlin had degenerated from a disciplined display of military might to something just short of a general orgy. Every café and *bierstube* was jammed with customers. Carriages filled with noisy commissioned and noncommissioned officers, rattled along the streets in search of excitement. Private soldiers and their *Gefreiters* wandered about in disordered platoons on the same errands, many hanging onto each others' shoulders, or a handy lamp post. Albrecht managed to sidestep them all, but had one near miss when a thoroughly intoxicated cuirassier

✠   *3 9 5* leutnant ran his horse up on the sidewalk and fell off it with a clang and clatter like pots and pans falling out of a kitchen cupboard. At that moment, Albrecht spotted, and found refuge inside the offices of Fracht und Reise Agentur at 402 Potsdamerstrasse.

He found himself facing another very junior-looking clerk whose condescending, almost-bored attitude improved slightly when he asked for accommodations on the *Herzogin Amalie*, suddenly becoming even more attentive when Albrecht mentioned that he had been recommended by Herr Baldwin of the American Legation. The clerk unlocked a cabinet, pulled out a file and, after perusing it with some care, regretfully announced: "There are no first-class cabins left on *Herzogin Amalie* for her next sailing to America. Only two second-class remain vacant as of this moment. Those, the Herr Inspector should be aware of, must be shared with five other passengers."

Albrecht gave a deep sigh, partly to pretend disappointment, partly in genuine suspense over the answer to his next question which he managed to ask without betraying his anxiety: "All right, no first class! Then how much will you charge me for a second?"

"Ninety-five thalers," the clerk apologetically informed him, then leaned across the counter and added in a conspiratorial whisper: "For an extra twenty-five, I could arrange for you to take you meals at the Captain's table. Except for having to sleep with five other passengers, that will make your ticket as good as a first at 140 thalers. A bargain, if you take everything into consideration."

Albrecht pretended to think the bargain over while actually making some rapid calculations to determine how much money he would have left after arriving in Baltimore. He finally shook his head, and firmly declared: "I'm not accustomed to paying for the privilege of dining with unknown captains. As long as I must travel second class, I'll adjust myself to the conditions."

"That means taking your meals at the Third Officer's table," the clerk informed him. Albrecht counted out the money and waited patiently for the ticket to be written out. "If you are traveling with household goods or heavy trunks, they will be carried in the cargo hold and charged at the rate of two pfennigs per kilogram," he was told.

"I am taking no more than I can carry myself," Albrecht informed the clerk. He then received his ticket and left.

rriving back in his room by early evening, Albrecht sat down at the rickety table by the window and tried to complete his letter to Tessa. The ache in his heart, which had abated somewhat during this busy day, came back more painfully than ever, inhibiting the flow of words from his pen to a slow trickle and soon drying them up altogether. Disturbed by the noise of revelry rising up from the *bierstube*, his mind clouded by a yearning self-pity, he read over all six pages of the letter and, suddenly appalled by its mixture of stilted platitudes and awkward sentimentalities, angrily tore it to shreds. Despairing of any peace of mind, let alone sleep, he put on his cap and coat and left the room. If that *bierstube* crowd would allow him no rest, then he might as well join the revelers and try to find some distraction that way.

He found the place by walking around the corner of the hotel and a few steps down a dark side street hardly wider than an alley. It was grossly misnamed Die Rosenknospe—"the Rosebud"—and was much smaller than he had expected, considering the tremendous amount of noise it generated. The customers, mostly working-class people with a smattering of soldiers, had to shout to be heard above the singing accompanied by an out-of-tune accordionist. Two buxom waitresses added to the uproar by yelling their orders over a combination bar-grill while banging their metal trays to get the attention of a pair of harassed cook-barkeeps. Customers were expected to share tables which ran in a double line from the entrance, through the smoky tunnellike interior, and on out into a small enclave of a brick backyard where no *rosenknospe* would ever have a chance to bloom. But it was out there that Albrecht found the only vacant chair at a table already occupied by two couples drinking steins of beer. When he politely asked permission to sit down, one of the men stared in mock surprise at his uniform and inquired in joking alarm: "Good heavens! What are you? A general?"

"Civil Service. Railroads," Albrecht answered with a forced smile.

"Well, thank God for that!" the man exclaimed. "I'm just demobilized myself and wouldn't want to have to salute any more damned generals." This brought shrill laughter from the two women and a guffaw from his male companion, who raised his stein and bellowed a toast: "God damn the generals who marched us to war, and bless the railroads who brought us home. *Prosit!*" All four of them quaffed down their beer, then started shouting at the waitress for another order. To Albrecht's relief, they paid no further attention to him, although he remained conscious of curious glances from other tables. When the waitress came charging up with four more steins, splattering him with foam and her own sweat, he ordered a glass of schnapps *and* a beer. It took her nearly ten minutes to serve him, and when she did, he promptly ordered a repeat. The man who had made the toast overheard him and slurred in admiration: "By God, Herr Civil Railroad Servant, you drink like a damned general!" More shrill laughter from the two couples at the table. Like a number of others in the noisy crowd, they soon began to kiss and fondle each other unabashedly. Albrecht tried to ignore them by staring into his beer, but when one couple suddenly got up and left arm in arm, a lone girl of perhaps twenty years quickly slipped into the vacated chair next to him and, snuggling up close, exclaimed with a husky voice:

"You are not enjoying yourself! Our Kaiser has proclaimed this a week of rejoicing. Buy me a drink and I'll help you obey his command."

Albrecht could not help laughing at this glib approach. She was almost pretty, with flaxen blond hair which was not too neatly combed, a round face whose cheeks were emphasized by too much rouge, a pair of gray eyes which were strangely expressionless in spite of her seductive smile. She was wearing a cheap dress of shiny green material which revealed every curve of her figure. "I was not aware of presenting such a sad appearance," he answered her. "That must be corrected. So, yes, I'll be honored to buy you a drink, Fraulein."

She nudged her chair closer. "I've been watching you from over there," she said, indicating a table where three tipsy soldiers were singing along with the accordionist in loud disharmony. "I could tell that this isn't the sort of place, or people, you're used to. I can tell you are a *gentleman*. Maybe one looking to lose himself among us here. Well, what the hell, I said to myself. I'd like to help him do it. So here I am. So let's drink together for a while."

"Very kind of you," Albrecht said, forcing himself to laugh again. He managed to get the waitress's attention and impulsively ordered a bottle of wine rather than beer, startling both her and his new companion. "A bottle of wine is seventy-five pfennigs," the waitress warned him. She rushed off, banging her tray, and was back in a minute this time with the order, collecting for it on the spot.

"Oh dear!" the girl in the green dress sighed as he filled her glass. "I suppose you are really used to entertaining beautiful women with champagne in fashionable restaurants."

"Believe me, Fraulein, I have never in my life entertained such a pretty lady as you in a fashionable restaurant or plain *bierstube*," he gallantly told her. They both smiled over the white lie and clinked glasses. She thirstily drained hers and held it out for a refill.

"I have always wanted to find me a real gentleman who would take me to a classy restaurant on the Kurfurstendamm," she said somewhat wistfully. "If I am good to you, would you do that for me?" She put her hand on top of his. It felt ice-cold in spite of the warm humid evening.

"That would be nice," he said. "But, alas, I am leaving Berlin tomorrow."

She momentarily showed a petulant look of disappointment, like a frustrated little girl, but quickly covered it up with the gamin expression of a woman of the street. "Oh, well! That's my luck. So how about one night of love? All you want for five thalers?" When he hesitated with his smile frozen, she reduced her price to three, then two thalers. Finally she exclaimed with a flash of anger: "What do you take me for? A cheap trollop you can pick up for a few pfennigs?"

Albrecht was again staring miserably into his glass. He had only twice before in his life gone with prostitutes. The first time when he was made to sacrifice his virginity as an initiation requirement of his fraternal order at Heidelberg; the second when he won a raffle in the civil service mess at Versailles which entitled him to one hour in a famous and notoriously expensive bordello featuring Algerian whores. Neither occasion had been entirely pleasurable, although the Algerian whore had given him an inkling of more-sophisticated techniques of sex than he had imagined. The only truly ecstatic experience he had ever had was making love to Tessa. It suddenly occurred to him that he might break that awful spell of loss and yearning, which Tessa still cast over him, by going to bed with this girl. It probably would not make him forget, but at least, he reasoned, he would by this faithless carnal act, irretrievably place himself beyond worthiness of a love which seemed in any case utterly hopeless. "Yes . . . all right, Fraulein," he muttered, "I can hardly afford you . . . but I need you tonight."

His words were lost in an uproar of hilarity when the accordionist toppled off his perch with a resounding dissonant crash. Two or three equally drunken customers propped him

✠   *399*

back up and his audience cheered as he resumed squeezing a waltz out of his battered instrument. The girl in the green dress had not heard him, nor did he catch what she said next until she repeated it by shouting into his ear: "Just one thaler if you'll take me to a decent room and bed!"

Albrecht pointed over his shoulder toward the upper floor of the hotel's rear, looming dingy and dark above Die Rosenknospe's raucous yard. "I'm lodged there," he said. "Just around the corner but a stiff climb to the top floor."

"You're in the Krone?" she disdainfully exclaimed. "Just my luck! I was hoping you'd be staying in a classy place on the other side of town and you'd ride me over there in a carriage. You're not quite the fine gentleman I thought. But, oh well . . . at least you seem clean and nicely behaved." She laughed, squeezed his arm and kissed his ear, tickling it with the tip of her tongue. "My name is Carla," she whispered, "and Carla is feeling romantic tonight. I'll give you all the love you want for a thaler."

"My name is Albert Falk," he introduced himself. *Albert Falk!* Not a bad name, he thought, with a good Anglo-Saxon ring to it. A better one than Albrecht von Falkenhorst to use in America. A new name for a new life in a new country!

"Here's to you, Albert Falk! *Prosit,*" she toasted him and again drained her glass.

"And to you, Fraulein Carla!" he said. "And to a change of luck for both of us!" He also drank up, then broke the glass against the brick wall behind them.

A waitress rushed up, yelling: "You'll be charged ten pfennigs for breaking a glass!"

He laughed, threw several coins on the table, then rose unsteadily off his chair, pulling the giggling prostitute along with him as they shoved their way through the crowd toward the exit. But after only a few steps he turned around and bowed ceremoniously toward his vacated chair, touching the bill of his cap, calling back to an invisible person: "Good night and good-bye, Freiherr Albrecht Gerd von Falkenhorst!" Then he weaved out of Die Rosenknospe, dragging along the somewhat confused, yet entirely willing, Carla behind him.

Nobody else among the noisy revelers paid the slightest heed to the demise and departure of Albrecht von Falkenhorst.

Six days had passed since Gustaf's brother had ridden away from Glaumhalle and left him alone with his bride. Tessa's stoic and taciturn compliance, her way of speaking only when spoken to and then in as few words as possible, was getting on his nerves. All his attempts to show affection, to be pleasant and good-humored, she coolly, politely rebuffed. They slept in the same bed at night, but only once more since his return had she yielded to his aroused passions, and then apathetically, without the slightest physical reciprocity, a stream of silent tears dampening his ardor and slashing his ego far more cruelly than could any violent resistance to his advances.

He had made good his promise and turned his crippled mother out of the master bedroom. The Dowager Hildebrun made quite a scene over this, but quickly quieted down when Gustaf converted the small library downstairs into her private quarters, gave her back her cane, and allowed her to hobble out into the orchard which was bursting with glorious pink-and-white blooms. While his mother cackled happy senilities, his wife helped with the work of moving her without a smile or comment.

Thinking that Tessa was still angry with him for having thwarted her ambitious rehabilitation program for the estate, he had sent Prytz and Hult to Ols with orders, not only to bring back Feldteufel, but also to complete Tessa's original shopping list and hire a farm laborer. He hoped she would be surprised and pleased, but her reaction was a terse: "It's about time you understood something of what is needed around here."

The days were blessed by unusually mild and sunny spring weather, and he invited her to ride with him over a countryside which was miraculously shedding the bleakness of winter and blooming in a fragrant profusion of delicately budding leaves and fresh meadow grass laced with wild flowers. Tessa firmly declined these invitations on the grounds that there were many things needing her attention around Glaumhalle: cleaning and washing, mending of rugs and drapes, tending the livestock and the Dowager Hildebrun, hundreds of little chores which the servants could take care of, yet which she insisted on supervising. Refusing to plead with her, Gustaf had glumly ridden out alone each day with his shotgun slung over his shoulder. He was an excellent shot and skillful hunter, and late every afternoon he returned with wild geese, ducks, hazel hens, hares, and woodcocks. The fare at Glaumhalle's table, which had been so bland and meager during the past half-year, became rich, delicious, and nourishing. But it was served to the Baron and Baroness in the manor's dining room in a silence broken only by a few painfully awkward exchanges, or the Dowager's senseless prattle. When they retired to the large double bed of the master bedroom, Tessa turned her back on him, leaving as wide a space as possible between them. When he attempted to embrace her, she pushed him away with the contrived, curt excuse: "Not tonight, Gustaf. I'm at a time when I can't give myself to you. Good night." He rolled away from her and lay on his side, staring into the darkness, desiring her, yet grimly restraining himself while vividly remembering and longing for Louise Hunsecker. He remembered how sweet had been her smile, how tender her touch, even when given in complete innocence and in spite of everything keeping them apart. He fell asleep dreaming about her and awakened reaching for a fading vision of her smiling at him as she seductively unbuttoned her blouse beyond that tantalizing little mole between her beautiful breasts. He jerked himself into a sitting position, called out her name, then foolishly, embarrassed, stared at Tessa's side of the bed. It was dawn and she had already quietly gotten up, dressed, and left the room.

On the sixth day—the seventh since his return to Glaumhalle—he finally began to suspect that his brother had something to do with Tessa's frigid attitude. The possibility of outright adultery did not enter his mind, but he began to believe that Albrecht had somehow captured her affections. They had, after all, been together continuously since last December and he was aware that although his brother was not as handsome and strong, he had always been more at ease, more charming with women than he was. The weather had turned gray and rainy with sullen dark clouds sweeping over Glaumhalle's hill; as he could not ride out hunting, he sat alone in the study in an equally sullen, dark mood. His suspicions intensified when the postman came sloshing up the hill to make his delivery and Tessa rushed to meet him and showed great disappointment at receiving only a letter from her mother. Gustaf had been a moment ahead of her and already accepted the meager delivery of two outdated newspapers and a single letter, and when she recognized her mother's handwriting on the envelope he handed her, she asked with an unmistakably accusing inflection: "Are you sure there is nothing from Albrecht? Nothing at all?"

"Why should there be?" he countered. "Surely you should know by now that we Falkenhorsts are not exactly enthusiastic correspondents."

"Well, I've found you all quite unalike," she cut back at him with an angry glint in her amber green eyes, then turned and ran back upstairs to read her mother's letter in privacy. But they were soon together again, summoned to the midday meal by Lena's tinkling of the silver dinner bell and joined by the Dowager Baroness Hildebrun who hobbled into the spotlessly drab dining room with gluttonous cackles and sat herself between them. When she muffled those noises by stuffing her mouth with food, Gustaf broke the silence between him and his wife by picking up the thread of his suspicion:

"Tessa, I'm still curious about your concern over Albrecht," he said. "I did not realize you had become so attached to him during my absence."

The Dowager Hildbrun nodded and exclaimed through a mouthful of stewed hare: "I told you so! I told you so! They even took away my cane."

Tessa fought down a pang of guilt and heartbreak and, ignoring her mother-in-law, answered her husband with a steely control: "Yes, Albrecht and I became very close. Between my father's death and your disappearance, he gave me support and affection and made it possible for me to carry on. He stood by me through some very hard times, believe me. And for that I loved him, still love him, and will love him always." She gave Gustaf a defiant glance, then turned to the Dowager Hildebrun who was dribbling a trickle of sauce from the point of her sharp chin and down the already-soiled front of her blouse. "Please, Frau Mama Baroness, use your napkin!"

The Dowager Hildebrun wiped her whole face with her napkin, spat out a piece of lead shot which ricocheted off her plate and bounced across the table onto the floor, then wagged her head at her son with a vacant leer. "I'm not used to being treated this way. I am the daughter of a Colonel of the Guards, the same regiment of which my husband was captain until he was killed by those rotten, pig-suckling Austrians. If you don't believe me, ask my Gustaf. We had a clock with chimes that rang every half-hour, cling-clang . . . ding-dong . . . cling-ding-dang . . . dong!"

"For heaven's sake, Mother, stop being silly and eat your food," Gustaf somewhat cautiously reprimanded her. He shut his eyes for a moment and when he reopened them, they were looking unhappily at Tessa. "I quite understand that you had to lean on Albrecht," he said to her with a shaking voice. "But why brood about past troubles? Why not look to the future? He must make his own life. We must make ours. It's as simple as that."

There followed another of those long silences which characterized their meals together, one broken by the Dowager Baroness after she obliviously chewed through another mouthful of stew and exclaimed in her piercing voice:

"It was the most beautiful clock which had a face like the sun and a body of carved elves and trolls. It stood on brass feet and was *this* high!" She demonstrated its dimensions by unhooking her cane from the back of the chair and raising its tip to the ceiling. "This high, mind you! And every half-hour it would sing to me: cling-clang . . . ding-dong . . . cling-ding-dang . . . dong." She flourished the cane above her head in time with the chimes she was trying to imitate, but wielding it more like a saber than the baton of an orchestra conductor.

"Put that down at once, Mother!" Gustaf cried out in alarm.

"Cling-ding-dang . . . DONG!" she shouted exuberantly at him, making him duck as the cane whistled a few inches above his head.

It also came within inches of Tessa's head, but she barely flinched. "Very well, Frau Mama Baroness, that's enough!" she said with a very loud, yet very calm, voice. "I know now exactly what kind of clock you mean. As a matter of fact, I know where we can get you one just like it. If you will be good to yourself and get well, I'll buy it for you. A present from me to you. A very beautiful, big chiming clock that will sing to you every half-hour. All right?"

The Dowager Baroness gave a start of surprise, lowered her cane and stared at Tessa with a childishly eager expectation. "Will you really get me one like that? Do you promise?"

"Yes, I promise, but only if you are very good and take care of yourself," Tessa told her. She rang the little silver bell and Lena cautiously came through the pantry door, as nervous as always, her tray with bowls of custard rattling in her trembling grip, her eyes darting with open fear at the Dowager Baroness. Somehow she managed to clear off the main course and serve dessert, without spilling or dropping anything. The Falkenhorsts ate the custard in a silence complemented by a suddenly very careful, even ladylike exhibition of table manners by the Dowager Baroness. When she had finished, she again wiped her whole face, her hands, then very daintily folded and rolled up her napkin and neatly inserted it in its napkin ring. Picking up her cane, she rose with a pathetic dignity and excused herself, saying: "I shall now retire to take my afternoon nap, thank you. I'd like to awake hearing it go cling-ding-dang . . . dong!"

After she left, there was only the sound of rain splattering against the dining room window. As Tessa finished eating and was starting to leave the table, Gustaf roused himself out of his brooding unhappiness and tried to compliment her by saying: "You really handle poor Mama quite well. I know she is very difficult for you." She merely shrugged. "About that clock," he finally blurted out. "It is true that we once had one like it. I remember it well, and when my father had to sell it along with several other of our valuable heirlooms. He needed the money so he could maintain his position in the Dragoon Guards, you see, and send me to Royal Cadet School. It is such memories that make me careful about money, even a bit stingy with it. I have known what it means to be poor." He looked at her with a partly defensive, partly ashamed expression, waiting for her to say something. She blinked unhappily, shook her head, but said nothing. "Such a clock would be very expensive," he went on. "Probably about one hundred thalers."

"We can afford to buy your mother the clock she wants," Tessa said, and rising from her chair, started toward the pantry door. "Excuse me, Gustaf. There are several things I must attend to."

"Such as what?" he demanded in a peremptory tone. "What is there you must do that our servants can't do? What are we paying them for."

She stopped by the door. "My mother mentioned in her letter that our bank in Frankfurt has received money—*lots of money*—for my account from Papa's estate," she sharply explained. "I must write them about it and ask for an accounting so I know where we stand. That is what I must do which the servants can't, Gustaf."

Gustaf flinched slightly and felt himself turning very red. He had never given her the letter from the Rothschild's bank which he had intercepted from the postman seven days ago; it was still in his pocket. "That can wait," he snapped. "The postman won't be back for three or four days. I want to talk to you, about . . . well, about what else your mother wrote in her letter."

Tessa took several steps back toward the table, but did not sit down: "She mentioned that General von Kleisenberg arrived in Vienna," she said with a wry little smile curling her lips. "He has called on her several times. It seems that he had much nicer things to say about you than you did about him. He sends you his regards through her. And she is so happy for me to have my husband back." Gustaf's face turned even redder and now she noticed it, but without understanding the reason for his strange demeanor. "Well, that's about all Mama wrote. At least *she* sounds happy. Now I'm going to write to the bank. I'm not waiting for that unreliable postman. I'll send Prytz to Ols with it tomorrow if the weather improves." She started to leave again.

"Wait!" Gustaf shouted at her. "That won't be necessary." He fumbled through the inside pocket of his jacket and producing the wrinkled letter from the Rothschild's bank, held it out to her. "Here. This came for you last week."

Tessa snatched it from him, read through it, then exclaimed with eyes blazing: "What else have you been holding back from me? Something from Albrecht?"

"No, nothing." He squirmed with anger at both her and himself. "Nothing from Albrecht. I forgot the letter from the bank in the excitement of seeing you again, Theresa, and incidentally, *that's* what I want to talk about."

"Well, I do not!" she furiously retorted, "Except to say that your being married to me does not entitle you to open or hide my mail." With that, she stormed out of the dining room and this time he did not call her back. He sat fuming in bitter frustration, listening to her steps as she ran up the stairs to the floor above and violently slammed a door—not theirs, judging from the sound, but Albrecht's.

Gustaf withdrew to the study where he paced back and forth until his temper receded. He noticed the half-empty decanter of schnapps which his brother had left on top of the desk and helped himself to a drink, then another. For the better part of an hour he sat in the chair, staring out through the rain-streaked window, trying to think rationally about the miserable state of his life and marriage. He glanced up at the portrait of his father and remembered the endless suffering silences between him and his mother, occasionally interrupted by acrimonious reproaches and accusations. "My God! Is this what I'm in for too?" he asked aloud. A silence beyond the sound of weeping rain seemed to be the affirmative answer. Then there was the memory, the constantly recurring one of Louise Hunsecker, changing his mood to melancholy until he forcibly drove her out of his mind as another lost cause, another scar on his ego, another failure. He downed one more schnapps and exclaimed between clenched teeth: "Damn all these women!" Then, to divert himself from the torment they were causing him, he picked up the newspapers which had arrived that morning and began to read.

At first nothing registered of the news he was distractedly scanning as his mind remained short-circuited a while longer on his own troubles. But suddenly a headline caught his full attention.

CHANCELOR BISMARCK THREATENS INTERVENTION AGAINST PARIS REVOLUTIONARIES. GERMAN ARMY ALERTED FOR ACTION

Gustaf had been aware of a revolt in the city of Paris even as he left France, but had paid little attention to it then, nor followed the scanty reports in the outdated copies of the *Breslauer Zeitung* which had subsequently been delivered to Glaumhalle. However, he now read this one, which was only three days old, with a startled surprise. Strong insurgent elements in Paris had driven the national government of President Thiers out of the city and formed a rival Commune government under the leadership of the radicals and terrorists. The defeated remnants of the professional French Army had so far been unable to muster enough strength to regain control of the capital, which was once again under siege, defended by some 250 thousand well-armed national guardsmen drawn from the city's rebellious lower classes. The Communard revolution was precariously contained within the walls of Paris, but President Thiers's weak and divided government (which had fled to Versailles) was on the brink of collapse, thus endangering the peace treaty with Germany which the leaders of the revolt were vowing to reject along with its 5-milliard francs bill of indemnity. Chancellor Bismarck had been keeping his eye on a rapidly deteriorating situation and was now sufficiently alarmed to threaten armed intervention by German occupation forces stationed in northeastern France, including those in the perimeter of seething Paris. Such a move might well start the war all over again, but he considered that worth the risk. For Germany to hold on to the great material gains of her crushing victory, it was rapidly becoming urgent to reassert control over French internal affairs by intimidating threats and force of arms if it came to that. To this end, Bismarck had ordered German occupation troops reinforced, with the clear implication that he was prepared to unleash them to fight their way over Communard barricades into Paris. The seriousness of the situation was emphasized by a prominently printed notice in the newspaper's section devoted to public announcements:

LEAVES ARE HEREWITH CANCELLED FOR ALL MILITARY PERSONNEL ON ACTIVE SERVICE AND THEY ARE DIRECTED TO REPORT SOONEST FOR DUTY WITH THEIR RESPECTIVE REGIMENTAL UNITS. BY ORDER OF HELMUTH VON MOLTKE, FIELD MARSHAL.

Gustaf read about these developments with an intense interest which had little to do with the perils they suggested for

Germans and Frenchmen alike. It crossed his mind that if war broke out again, as the newspaper predicted, he would have an unexpected opportunity to redeem his ill-starred efforts in the previous campaigns. He also reasoned that here was a perfect excuse to extricate himself from the oppressive, frustrating atmosphere of Glaumhalle and to postpone indefinitely the threatening showdown between himself and Tessa. Yet the prospects of escape were not as sweet as he might have expected. Not even when he considered that, by rejoining his regiment outside of Paris, his chances of seeking out and meeting Louise Hunsecker again would be removed from wistful fantasy into at least the realm of possibility. But, to his consternation, he found that Tessa was suddenly exerting as strong an influence upon him as Louise. Louise remained a romantic chimera, would he really meet her again if fighting broke out? Tessa was here, in his life now, and probably, forever. She was his wife. She was the only woman with whom he had ever physically made love. It seemed a cruel twist of fortune that another parting must come before they had a chance of building some kind of foundation for a good marriage. Yet, that parting was inevitable now. It never occurred to him not to heed the call printed in the newspaper and wait instead for the postman to deliver direct orders cancelling his leave and recalling him to his regiment, orders which could not possibly arrive before the next scheduled delivery three days hence, maybe four. He only brooded a while longer over how he could break the news to Tessa without further embittering her as his father had embittered his mother and eventually left her a hopelessly scarred cripple.

He noticed that rain no longer splattered against the window and slanting rays of the afternoon sun were breaking through a shredding overcast. The weather was improving; the night would be clear enough for the ride to Ols. Before leaving the study, Gustaf finished the last of the schnapps, raising his glass to his father's portrait and exclaiming to it: "It's a legacy of damnation you left me, father! But here's to you . . . and the regiment! *Prosit!*" Then, with a kind of melancholy determination, he hurried upstairs to change into his field uniform and pack his kit. Not until he had done this did he walk down the hall and knock on the closed door to Albrecht's room.

Tessa was seated at the table writing a letter which had already run to several pages of her fine, clear script; she had finished another which was sealed and addressed in its envelope. When he entered the room she showed a brief flash of surprise over seeing him wearing his uniform again, then frowned and sharply asked: "What do you want, Gustaf?"

"To inform you of a change in plans," he briskly answered

her and came straight to the point: "Things are happening in France that make it quite certain fighting will break out again soon. Maybe it already has. Under the circumstances my place is with my regiment. I must cut short my leave and return to France at once."

He had brought the latest *Breslauer Zeitung* with him and folding it to show the notice and article precipitating his decision, handed it to her and waited while she glanced over it. It was only a matter of a minute before she somewhat impatiently threw the paper on the bed and drily observed: "So the French are fighting among themselves. Is that a reason for us to go to war against them again? For you to go galloping off again?" Her expression turned almost sad and she shook her head. "It is a lot of nonsense, really."

"Is that your way of telling me you will miss me, my dear?" Gustaf asked. When she shrugged without answering, he told her: "I shall leave tonight to catch the first train out of Ols tomorrow morning."

Her sad look turned to one of irritation. "Are you in such a hurry that you must risk yourself and one of our horses in a long night's ride?"

"I'm touched by your concern, Tessa," he said, then added: "But don't worry. Remember I am a cavalryman and know every bit of the country between Glaumhalle and Ols. I could ride there blindfolded. I shall leave right after supper. In the meanwhile, I want to talk to you about . . . about what's been going wrong between us." He looked around Albrecht's room with distaste and added: "But not in here. In our own bedroom if you please."

"I will not discuss Albrecht with you," Tessa said without making a move to get up off the chair. "That subject is closed."

"Very well. It is closed," he agreed. "Just so you understand that he will never come back here to you when I am absent. As a matter of fact, the last thing he told me before leaving, was that he intended to emigrate to America. I hope he is not that foolish, but Albrecht was always impetuous and romantic. We may not hear from him for a very long time. So that is that."

Tessa seemed to sag and the sadness returned to her face, more pronounced than before. To try to cover it, she announced: "I intend to move your mother back to her room after you leave."

"You will only have to move her back downstairs when I return," he said, seating himself on the edge of Albrecht's bed. "And I shall return as soon as things are settled in France. For my regular yearly leave, if nothing else. Then we must live as man and wife and do our duty toward our family. Toward each

✠

other. *That* is what I want to talk to you about. In here, if you wish."

She had swiveled around in the chair to stare out the window at a wet countryside glistening in the pale shimmer of dusk. She did not want him to see the tears in her eyes.

"We have not experienced much love, you and I, but we have both been brought up to do our duty," he said. "It is expected of us. We must demand and expect it of ourselves."

"And exactly what is it you expect of me, Gustaf?" she asked.

"To be my wife," he answered her simply, and after a long silence elaborated the point: "To bear my children and continue our family with honor. I had hoped for love, but will settle for loyalty—but nothing less."

"As you said a moment ago," she replied with irony, "neither of us have much experience in love. I will try to meet your expectations, Gustaf, as long as you respect mine." One of her tears fell on the letter she had been writing (to her mother) and she fumbled for the blotter to clean the inky smear.

From the dining room downstairs came the faint discordant tinkling of the supper bell.

Gustaf got up and stepping close to her, gently put his hands on her shoulders. "When I come back to you, we will have more time together. Things will be more pleasant. We will become closer, friends perhaps . . . and then, maybe even lovers. That would help our duties a little, wouldn't it, Tessa?"

She gave a little laugh. "Yes, Gustaf, I suppose it would," she answered, then nervously exclaimed: "My goodness! Did I just hear the supper bell? Is it that late? Well, we must feed you properly before sending you off to war." She stood still trying to keep her tear-streaked face averted.

Gustaf kept his hands on her, moving them to the soft feel of her neck and cheeks. All his anger and resentment against her had gone and was suddenly replaced by desire. "I am not hungry," he said, ". . . except for you, Tessa. I would rather spend this last hour in bed with you. How else can we have the sons our family needs." He felt her give a start and go tense, twisting away from him with a suppressed gasp which made him quickly withdraw his suggestion with a resigned sigh: "Very well, never mind, dearest. Next time, then. I'm not so naïve about these things that I do not understand why we can't lie together right now. You already made that clear to me."

"Yes, Gustaf . . . next time. Whenever you come back on leave from your regiment, I'll try to be ready for you, to please you, to . . . to be your wife. What else can either of us do than what we must?"

410

"Now you are speaking like a true soldier's wife and a real Falkenhorst," Gustaf said with relieved admiration, then ran a finger lightly over her cheek and asked with a puzzled frown: "But you are crying, Tessa! Are those tears for me?"

"They are for you, for me . . . for *all* of us," she whispered with an almost desperate sorrow of which she only allowed him the briefest glimpse before forcibly shaking it off, breaking away from him and exclaiming: "Oh, there goes Lena ringing the supper bell again. Your mother is probably waiting at table for us. We must go."

But the Dowager Baroness Brunhilde did not show up at the supper table; the damp weather seemed to have aggravated the pain in her crippled leg and she demanded that her evening meal be served her in bed on a tray which Tessa personally brought her before sitting down alone with Gustaf in the dining room. She was feeling unbearably depressed because of the conflicting emotions aroused by her husband's imminent departure. Like him, she was trying to deal with a confused mixture of feelings of relief, guilt, uncertainty, all made more difficult by their inability to open their hearts to each other. Her agony over Albrecht was there, unmentionable, of course, but turning into a resentment against him for having abandoned her to an intolerable situation. She felt cheated and degraded, but was aware that Gustaf might feel the same, while trying as desperately to hide it. He was attempting to keep up a pathetically eager, if not very lucid, monologue about the events in France and why they required his immediate presence there, starting almost every sentence with: "As a woman you may not understand this, but, you see. . . ."

Tessa listened to him more attentively than usual, but nothing he said gave any opening for an easy exchange of feelings and opinions. She found herself ardently wishing that he would understand *her* enough to talk to her as a *woman*, as a deeply troubled *wife*. When he finally paused to catch his breath and chew his food, she gave an anguished sigh and said: "Why? I still don't see why you leave and rush off to France like this? Or for what?"

Gustaf looked startled, almost pleased over her little outburst. It had to mean that she *cared!* "Yes, it is difficult for you to understand as a woman," he gently explained again, then admitted: "It's even hard for me to rationalize as a man and a soldier. But like it or not, war is a risk soldiers must accept. And so must our wives and families."

Tessa shook her head and sighed again. "Papa used to say that war is the collapse of reason. If he were alive today, he would say it again."

Gustaf frowned and paused a moment before answering with a smile: "My dear, your Papa was a very wise man in his way. But not really a soldier. Only a Landwehr officer. A pity, really. Otherwise he would not have played at war, blundered into a trap and gotten himself so uselessly killed."

"Oh?" she exclaimed shortly, then as quickly as she could, changed the subject: "I want to follow through my plans to improve and develop Glaumhalle while you are gone, Gustaf. I consider that part of our agreement."

He seemed about to protest, but gave in with a shrug. "Very well, Tessa. But for heaven's sake do it sensibly. A step at a time. Don't try to change everything at once. As a woman. . . ." He stopped short on seeing the flash of anger in her eyes.

They finished supper in some hurry and then Tessa waited in the vestibule while Gustaf went to say good-bye to his mother. Because the evening was cool and damp after the rain, and she intended to go outside to see her husband off like a dutiful wife, she put on her riding jacket over her dress and drew on her gloves. It was then that she felt the folded piece of paper inside the right glove and instinctively knew what it was. But before she could pull it out, unfold and read it, Gustaf came marching back from a very brief and apparently unpleasant parting with the Dowager Baroness Hildebrun; she barely managed to hide the message again before he was next to her, reaching for his coat and saying: "Mama is really quite impossible. Sometimes I don't think she knows what is going on or what she is doing. I must say I worry about you having to take care of her, Tessa." He buckled on his belt with its saber and holstered pistol, then adjusted his cap on his head. "Imagine!" he exclaimed with indignation. "Her farewell to me, her oldest son, was a shockingly rude word and a whack with her cane."

Tessa barely managed to suppress a wry smile, but said very seriously: "It is my intention to engage a nurse for her. As you know, she terrifies the servants and I can't—*won't*—always be at her beck and call. So I'm going to find some strong, hefty older woman to take care of her."

Gustaf looked unhappy about this solution, yet would not quarrel over it. He nodded and merely warned: "Don't pay her too much," then opened the front door for Tessa and followed her outside.

Master Prytz had been told about Gustaf's departure and had saddled the new colt and brought him over from *der Feste*. He was waiting in the yard with the horse, staring gloomily at the last shreds of pink-tinged rain clouds overhead. When Gustaf and Tessa came out of the front door, he straightened up his hunched shoulders, gave a creaky military salute and announced with his gruff voice: "Your mount is ready, Herr Leutnant Baron."

"Thank you, Master Prytz," Gustaf answered affably. He took over the reins and gave the animal an encouraging pat on the neck. "Well, Ricochet, we're going to have a long night's ride, you and I. Then you'll have a nice rest in old Graustark's stables until you're fetched back to Glaumhalle. Right, Master Prytz?"

"Right, Herr Leutnant Baron."

Gustaf checked the bridle, stirrups, saddle and his bulging knapsack strapped behind it, finding everything to his satisfaction. "You do your work well, Master Prytz," he complimented the old stablemaster. "All your horses and their tack are beautifully taken care of. One can tell you are an old cavalryman. And now I must ask you again to take good care of my Baroness Tessa while I'm on duty with my regiment. Can I count on that?"

In the twilight and shadow of the vizor of his cap, the bleak look in Prytz's eyes was well hidden. "As I promised you the last time, Herr Leutnant Baron," he answered with a touch of irony. There followed a moment of confusion between them as he tried another stiffly formal salute while Gustaf groped for his right hand, found it, and briskly pulled it down for a hearty handshake, followed by a slap on the shoulder and a fervently expressed: "Good man! I trust you implicitly, Master Prytz!" Then he turned from him and reached out for Tessa.

She had been watching with a sort of impassive sadness as though she were now wishing this scene to be over as quickly as possible. There were many things she wanted to say, both of a penitent and accusing nature, but there was no point in dragging out a parting which she knew in her heart to be painful for both of them. When he grasped her hands, she thought she was about to receive the same as Master Prytz, an emotional, but manly, handshake. He surprised her by pulling her close, and kissing her very hard on the mouth. Then he quickly whispered in her ear:

"I very much want to love you, my Tessa! Wait patiently!"

When he let go of her and sprang into the saddle, he twirled Ricochet around in a tight prancing circle, which made Prytz jump out of the way, and cheerfully called out to Tessa: "I will write you very soon, my dearest. Many letters. You'll see!"

Tessa could not help throwing back a half-sarcastic, half-desperate: "Ha! Like last time?"

"You'll see!" he confidently shouted over his shoulder as he made a speedy exit out of Glaumhalle's puddled yard and splashed through the rivulets still streaming through the deep ruts of the hillside road.

✠   413

Tessa and Prytz remained standing in the yard, watching the horse and rider turn fuzzy, then finally vanish in the thick mist swirling up from the Orla and shrouding the base of the hill.

Master Prytz broke the silence by softly growling: "It reminds me of the last time he left you. Same sort of wet evening, same sort of to-hell-with-it suddenness leaving you and me to shift for ourselves."

"It's not at all the same, Prytzie," Tessa replied with a quiet intensity. She could feel the folded square of paper inside her right-hand glove, almost burning her sweating palm. She casually began pulling the glove off while repeating: "It's not at all the same, Prytzie. Nothing will ever be the same."

"Well, what are we to do, my lady?" Prytz asked with a break in his voice. "Everything seems to have gone wrong. Freiherr Albrecht left us. Baron Gustaf no sooner came back from the dead than he leaves us too. All these gentlemen, including your revered father, Count Paul, have all charged me with your safety and well-being, but . . . but, I don't understand anything of what is going on around here . . . except that whatever it is, is making you unhappy, my Lady Tessa. It makes me feel like a useless, confused old man. So how can I protect you?" He gave a snort which was mostly a sob. "What are we to do, for God's sake?"

Tessa was shocked out of her own misery by Prytz's anguished lament, the strong, sensible stablemaster of Schloss Varn upon whom she had relied more than her own father. "Well, you know perfectly well that things started to go wrong for us nearly a year ago," she reminded him with deliberate severity. "But we knew it then and will carry through the plans we made. Nothing has changed in that respect, Prytzie. We shall make this the finest breeding farm for horses in Silesia . . . all Prussia . . . in this whole new German Empire the newspapers and my husband talk about. That is all you have to worry about. The rest is my own trouble which I will have to work out for myself alone. You stay out of it. I'll only tell you this: I have promised my loyalty to my husband. I am and shall act as his Baroness von Falkenhorst of Glaumhalle."

Master Prytz sagged momentarily before straightening up and asking with his gravelly voice: "Very well. So what are the Lady Baroness's orders?"

"I'll give them to you tomorrow," she told him in a softer voice, staring down at the folded piece of paper she had pried out of her glove. "We both need a good night's sleep. In the morning we'll get on with what must be done around here."

Master Prytz gave her a salute like the kind he used to give her father at Schloss Varn. "Yes, my lady. Good night," he said and wheeling away from her, marched back somewhat unsteadily toward *der Feste.*

"Good night, Prytzie!" she called after him. She had unfolded the note from Albrecht, but it was too dark for her to read the two lines scrawled across the page. She could not read them even when she turned the paper toward the pale light of a moon breaking through the filmy clouds drifting above the eastern horizon. She started to move toward the lights glowing from the manor's kitchen windows, but it suddenly struck her that it might be better, less painful, *not* to read Albrecht's parting message, to pretend she had never received it. What could it do but create more pain or false hopes. Better, then, the sharp, clean cut of their parting. As she walked back to the manor, heading for the scullery entrance, she began tearing the sheet of paper into smaller and smaller pieces, then crumbling all the little bits together in the palm of her gloved hands, making a small brittle ball, like a handful of last autumn's dead leaves. As she passed through the kitchen, she asked Lena to lift the stovelid for her so that she could throw it on the glowing embers.

Lena stared at her with her usual nervous confusion, flapped her hands to disperse the whiff of smoke from the burning paper, then let the stovelid drop back in place with a clatter as she curtsied and exclaimed with timid politeness: "At your service, Frau Baroness von Falkenhorst . . . and goodnight."

wo days after Gustaf's hasty departure for France, Tessa and Master Prytz drove by wagon into Ols where they spent two days shopping for supplies, livestock, and retainers to reimplement their interrupted plans for Glaumhalle's future. This time there was no intervention, and Herr Graustark was delighted with the six hundred thalers' worth of cash business that came his way. Three farm laborers were engaged, *three* instead of two because they were middle-aged; most strong young men had been called up because of the partial mobilization declared with the uprising of the Communards in Paris. Another new member of the household staff was engaged, one Frau Emma Jodle, a robust fifty-year-old widow who had assisted the local doctor as midwife and practical nurse for the past ten years, but whom Tessa lured into her employ (over the doctor's churlish objections) by the simple expedient of offering her double her current wages and the title of head housekeeper. It was made clear, however, that her principal duty at the baronial manor would be the nursing of its addled and ailing Dowager Baroness. Frau Jodle proved her mettle at the very outset of her new career by perching herself on top of the heavily loaded wagon and riding it without complaint for the wrenching ten hours of the return journey. Upon seeing Glaumhalle for the first time, its stark structures looming ghostly in a misty moonlight, she exclaimed with undaunted good humor: "It looks soundly built of rock. The Rock of Ages!"

During the following week, Tessa worked hard with Master Prytz to break in the new help and make Glaumhalle into a respectable Junker estate. Fields for growing fodder were to be cleared out of long-fallow land. The small vegetable garden was to be tripled in size and planted with enough potatoes, beans, onions, and turnips to insure against another winter of near starvation. In anticipation of an enlarged breeding stock of horses and cattle, *der Feste's* murky cavern had to be cleaned out, refurbished with new stalls, and its warren of wasted spaces converted to practical use. "We shall eventually have to build an entirely new, efficient barn," Tessa told Prytz. "This medieval monument to the Falkenhorst's military traditions simply won't do for the fine animals I intend to raise."

Prytz looked slightly shocked but could not help agreeing with her.

Tessa kept herself very busy and gave the outward impression of being entirely absorbed by her various projects; but actually Albrecht and Gustaf were never out of her mind. She particularly brooded about them during the long, lonely nights which she tried to shorten by retiring very late and rising very early. She reproached herself for having torn up and burned Albrecht's last note without reading it, sometimes hoping that the postman would bring some further communication from him, some word of comfort and explanation to relieve her lingering sorrow. But the postman brought nothing except statements from the Rothschild bank (her balance was increasing in spite of her large withdrawals) and the *Breslauer Zeitung* with its stale news about the deteriorating situation in France (which, as she read about it, might easily have since progressed into another full-scale war). Tessa had never bothered to more than casually scan newspapers, believing that their contents had little practical bearing on her daily life; however, she now found herself devouring every word printed in them. Because of Gustaf. Because she found herself thinking more about him as his brother faded into a resentful, and increasingly unreal, memory. There were no letters from Gustaf either, but she believed his promise to write her and felt certain he would do so when the pressures of travel, rejoining his regiment and going on active duty permitted. Although he was now far away after their brief painful ten days together, he remained a very real presence in her life. Poor Gustaf! She had, she decided, been harsh and unfair with him in her despair. And so, driven by a troubled conscience and a genuine feeling of contrition, she took the initiative of writing the first letter. After a short account of the activities at Glaumhalle and of her intention to travel to Schloss Varn to obtain stallions and broodmares, she wrote with an emotion she had never shown before:

It is not quite two weeks since you left me, yet it already seems so much longer. Almost as if you had never come back at all. But you did come back and I find myself thinking more about you than any of the difficulties and complications I had thought so important to me. How I regret having made our short time together so unpleasant for you. I was selfish and preoccupied with my own troubles and had little understanding for yours in a situation where you were no less a victim of unkind fortune. It seems to me that we need a better chance at making a good life together, for our own sakes as well as those of the Falkenhorst and Beckhaus families. I am still selfish enough to wish it for our own sakes —yours and mine! So take good care of yourself, Gustaf, and return to me as soon as you can so we may try again. This is my way of telling you that I miss you, that you are the man I need in my life. Your loyal wife, Tessa.

By the end of that week, things were well in hand at Glaumhalle with a suddenly conscientious Foreman Hult keeping the new farm laborers hard at work and Frau Head Housekeeper Jodle taking over the household operations with a cheerful efficiency. The dowager Baroness Hildebrun threw only a few fits of resentment before submitting to the care of her new nurse. Two Polish youths had waded across the river one morning to ask for asylum and employment; as they were sturdy fair-haired lads with clear blue eyes, and passed Master Prytz's careful scrutiny and interrogation, they were hired for their keep and five pennies a day. The Falkenhorst manor had not been so well staffed and the prospects for its future had not been so bright in fifty years. So, feeling it was safe for them to leave, Tessa and Master Prytz took their departure for Schloss Varn on May 25.

They broke their journey for one hectic day in Breslau where Tessa rushed from one shop to the next, buying new furnishings, textiles for bedding, drapes and curtains, kitchen utensils, china, and a melodiously chiming clock standing two-meters high and weighing over one hundred kilograms with its complicated works and elaborately hand-carved ironwood case. This last item cost her 220 thalers, a price which she paid without flinching over the muted protests of Prytz who claimed that three fine horses could be had for the same amount of money. "It will give my mother-in-law pleasure and improve her disposition. She is crazy about chiming clocks," Tessa somewhat wryly explained and ordered the extravagant timepiece freighted back to Glaumhalle together with all her other purchases.

In Breslau she caught up with current events in the outside world, reading the newspaper headlines with mounting uneasiness: **HEAVY CASUALTIES AS FRENCH GOVERNMENT TROOPS ASSAULT COMMUNARD BASTION OF PARIS . . . REVOLUTION-ARIES BURN CITY. TUILERIES PALACE AND LOUVRE IN FLAMES . . . BOTH SIDES ENGAGE IN CAMPAIGN OF TERROR . . . 10,000 GERMAN TROOPS DEPLOYED OUTSIDE PARIS RAMPARTS.** Having had no letter from Gustaf as yet, Tessa worried about him, wondering whether his indifferent luck as a soldier would see him through the danger, or fail him completely in this bloody and, to her, senseless upheaval in a foreign country. But she realized there was no use in allowing her worry to interrupt her journey and, on the morning of May 27, she boarded the Frankfurt an der Oder express together with her grimly watchful escort.

The train passed through Grunewald, a town of bittersweet memories for Tessa, but now as she watched it pass by the compartment window, it was somehow exposed as a depressingly grimy little place stripped of the deep white drifts and mantles of last winter's great blizzard. She was relieved when they rolled through the sooty station without stopping and the next curve in the tracks put the place beyond her sight. They reached Frankfurt on time at two o'clock and took their midday meal there while waiting for the connecting train to Wolin. Shortly before it pulled into the station, the local newspaper put out a special edition which was avidly bought up by the travelers crowding the vestibule and platforms; the banner headline covering most of the single-page sheet read: **LAST OF COMMU-NARDS CRUSHED IN PARIS SLUMS . . . REVOLUTION ENDS IN BLOODBATH . . . THREAT OF WAR PASSES!**

The skimpily detailed communiqué, telegraphed that morning from the Headquarters of the German Occupation Forces outside of Paris, caused more cautious wonder than jubilation, especially for Tessa who asked Prytz: "Do you think it's over at last, I mean *really* over? That our Baron Gustaf did not become involved and will safely return to us in peace?"

"Let us pray so, my lady!" he answered with an uncomforting murmur. "As for peace, we'll only find it at Schloss Varn. Here comes our train. Let's go!"

Schloss Varn was not only a peaceful refuge on the Baltic coast, but more beautiful than Tessa had ever remembered it. Many things she had taken for granted as a growing girl now became precious as they impressed themselves upon her consciousness. The castle's graceful facades of stone were solidly covered by tapestries of lush ivy and blooming vines of honeysuckle, some reaching close to the tops of its twin spires, one of which was crowned with a wagon wheel providing the platform for a pair of nesting storks.

The ancient fortifications and earthworks facing the sea, originally built as protection against marauding Vikings, were overgrown with thickets of raspberries, primrose, blackberries, and phlox. In the turgid waters of the moat, water lilies rose out of the black bottom mulch to break through the sundance surface with heart-shaped leaves and fat buds ready to burst into floating stars of delicate pink and ivory; each pad seemed to support an exuberantly noisy frog, glistening emerald green flecked with gold. In the surrounding gardens, flower beds laid out with Prussian precision and tended with Nordic passion for horticulture, formed intricate patterns of red, white, blue, and yellow squares, circles, and connecting lines both straight and curved. Beyond the immediate surroundings of the castle and its satellite stables and barns, the land spread out in a startling variety of the wild and cultivated. Silvery bright dells of birch trees. Placid, fat cattle and herds of healthy, frisky horses browsed in broad meadows splattered with golden buttercups and sparkling white daisies. Shaggy stands of velvet blue green pines whispered in the sea breeze. Ploughed fields of dark brown showed the delicate tracery of sprouting oats and rye. Flights of wild ducks, plovers and avocets, wheeled over the moist fens, skimming the shimmering ponds and sloughs, swooping in and out of pastel labyrinths of foxtails and bullrushes. Neat crofter's cottages of white stucco, black-tarred crossbeams, and thatched roofs basked in the verdant pools of their vegetable gardens, and toward the edge of the sea, the rippled sand dunes rose like congealed white waves out of the shelving beach and gently glittering Baltic. All this beauty accentuated by the stimulating fragrance of salt, seaweed, rich earth and its blend of myriad scents of a flowering spring.

Both Tessa and Master Prytz were well acquainted with the best bloodlines of the famous Schloss Varn stables and quickly made up their minds about which horses they would select. However, as neither wanted to leave Schloss Varn so soon after arriving, each pretended to the other (and to the anxious new stablemaster) that more time was needed. There were some promising foals whose development should be watched for a week or two, some yearlings they wished to break to the saddle personally, and some fine adult mares and stallions which had to be brought to peak condition before facing the rigors of a long trail and railroad journey to Silesia. Bolstered by these excuses, Tessa spent her days in glorious summer weather doing what she loved best, riding horseback over the delightfully varied lands of the great estate, pampering the animals, while at the same time bending them to her will. She was herself pampered by the servants and relished the security and well-ordered comforts of the domain over which she reigned for a while as a carefree chatelaine. Her mother was still absent on her protracted stay in Austria, but had written instructions to the chief steward that her daughter's every whim was to be accommodated.

To make things even better, three reassuring letters arrived during the second week of June. One was a barely literate, but forthright, note from Frau Jodle that assured her all was well at Glaumhalle. Another, forwarded from there, was from Gustaf, originally mailed from Metz and telling of his arrival at that conquered city on May 19, and his intention of riding on to the German Headquarters outside of Paris with a detatchment of replacement cavalry; it was written in haste and in his usual brief style, devoid of emotion and any expressions of affection beyond the salutations of *"Dearest Wife"* and *"Your Devoted Husband, Gustaf v. F."*—But his second letter was both longer and quite different in tone. It had been mailed May 29, from outside Paris (a suburban village called Le Bourget) and addressed directly to her at Schloss Varn; his words strongly suggested that war and fighting had lost some of its appeal for him since leaving Metz:

> . . . *I have witnessed the ruin of a great city and the degradation of a nation gone mad. From my post just beyond the fortifications of Paris, I saw it all happen in one terrible week, wild street fighting from*

house to house, entire blocks aflame, hovels and palaces going up in smoke, the gutters running with blood, the very air I breathed filled with the stench of fire and death. The principal carnage ended Sunday morning with a final slaughter inside a graveyard (less than two hundred meters from the hill upon which I was standing). But even now, with the revolutionaries mostly killed along with their women and children, I can hear the frequent volleys of the execution squads as they exterminate the few survivors. What has happened in Paris and to her people has filled me with pity and horror, no less so because Frenchmen are killing Frenchmen and I am only watching from across their walls. I dread having to remember for the rest of my life what I have seen here. Only your sweet letter has comforted me, although I now much regret having so hastily left you for no better purpose than to be a bystander in events bound to stain the souls of all men here present. Thank God you are safe on peaceful family lands so dear to us all. I pray He will soon grant your wish, and mine, that we have a better chance together as husband and wife. With my deepest affection, Your Gustaf v. F.

Although it was not exactly a love letter, Tessa was deeply moved by it. She had already read about the awful fighting inside burning Paris in the Wolin newspaper (delivered daily to the castle) and in far greater detail; she knew that Bismarck and von Moltke had pronounced: "the extermination of all French Revolutionaries guarantees the fruits of our victory." But Gustaf's letter caused her a more personal relief as he had, in his own way and for the first time, opened his heart to her; uncertainty over their future seemed replaced with hope for it. She immediately penned him a cheerful reply, also signing it "With my deepest affection," sending it off without delay, and then proceeded to enjoy her stay at Schloss Varn even more. Casting aside all that had caused grief, trouble, and apprehensions, Tessa became radiant with vitality and enthusiasm. Time slipped delightfully past midsummer and on through the first week of a balmy July, but then that wonderful carefree part of her visit came to an abrupt end.

While riding along the beach one morning with Master Prytz and two stable boys, exercising a herd of frisky yearlings along the sun-dappled Baltic surf, Tessa suddenly fell off her horse. For no apparent reason, she swayed dizzily, slumped forward over its neck, weakly tried to check herself by grabbing the mane, then fell heavily into the sand. At first Prytz laughingly mocked her, but became alarmed when he noticed she could not pick herself up. Hurriedly dismounting, he rushed to her side and bending over her, anxiously asked: "What is the matter with you, for God's sake? Are you ill?"

"I . . . I don't quite know," she mumbled in disoriented

confusion. "Everything started spinning around . . . going dark and fuzzy. . . . Yes, I think I'm going to be ill." As a shocked Prytz held her head, she threw up the breakfast she had eaten an hour earlier. A moment later, she began recovering herself and protesting: "No, never mind! It's nothing. I'll be able to ride on. . . . Oh dear, what a mess. . . ."

Prytz kept a strong grip on her shoulders, gathered his wits enough to bellow at the astounded stable boys to let the herd of yearlings scatter over the dunes and, instead, to gallop into Varnmunde to fetch Dr. Schmund and bring him back to Schloss Varn as quickly as possible. Then he tenderly picked up Tessa in his arms and, in spite of her weak protestations, propped her back into the saddle. He took the reins from her fumbling hands and led her horse on foot all the way back to Schloss Varn—just as ten years ago, he had led her home after she had charged into a jump far too great for a nine-year-old and landed in a stunned heap.

When Dr. Schmund arrived and entered her room he discovered Tessa had not allowed the maids to undress her, only to pull off her boots and lay her fully clothed on top of her bed where she fumed over the fuss she had caused, insisting that she was perfectly all right, or would be presently. Dr. Schmund knew her well, having served the von Beckhaus family as personal physician for nearly twenty-five years, delivering all three of their children into this world, of which only this one remained. He was an old man now, with a stern, wrinkled face scarred by various poxes he had caught and survived while tending patients who often had not. Along with her late father, and sometimes Master Prytz, he was among the few men who could intimidate Tessa into obedience, and proceeded to do so by gruffly saying: "You shall disrobe and bed yourself at once, Baroness Theresa, so we may proceed with a proper examination!"

The physical part of the examination was brief and deftly if decorously conducted with sheets intervening between the patient and the Doctor's probing hands. This was followed by a few earthily direct questions about Tessa's functions as a young woman and wife. The whole procedure took no more than five minutes and resulted in an unhesitating diagnosis.

"You are with child, God bless it! You have received warning to curtail any strenuous activities during the next six or seven months. In your case, Baroness Theresa, it is necessary for me to specifically forbid riding about on horseback. Because you have already done so within the time when sensible confinement should have been observed, you must now remain very quietly in bed for the next three or four days. Eat well. Put your mind and body at ease. Above all, do not fear the miracle of giving birth. That is the lot assigned woman by God and therefore her natural fulfillment in this life. I shall return to your bedside tomorrow, dear Baroness Theresa. Good day!"

He gave her shoulder a parting tap, a gesture meant to be both admonishing and reassuring, then left her in a state of subdued agitation in the charge of the castle's very excited senior housekeeper (who, for the sake of propriety, had been present throughout the examination). As Dr. Schmund descended the stairs and passed through the main foyer, where Master Prytz, Head Butler Knabel and three breathless maidservants anxiously waited, he repeated loudly enough for all to hear, exactly what he had told his patient. This triggered gasps of relieved delight and from Master Prytz an exultant: "Praise the Lord! An heir is on the way!"

"Yes, so it seems," the Doctor confirmed, but added with a direct, meaningful stare at Prytz: "*If* you prevail on your Baroness to sensibly abide with my orders and the Lord's will." Whereupon he strode out through the open front doors, stiffly climbed into his brightly varnished two-wheeler pulled by a sturdy gelding pacer (a gift from the late Count Frederick Paul), and vanished at a brisk trot down the graveled driveway.

Within the hour, all retainers, sharecroppers, and crofters attached to the castle and its far-flung estates, knew what had caused their young Baroness Theresa's fall that morning. They rejoiced freely as they had a direct interest in an orderly, uncontested line of succession to the lands which provided their security and livelihood.

But Tessa was not rejoicing in her bedroom. The revelation of her condition had not come entirely as a surprise, but it was a shock nevertheless, one which left her brooding and uneasy. She remembered how often she and Albrecht had made love in contrast to the two dutiful intimacies with Gustaf during their even briefer cohabitation as husband and wife. Who was the father of this child? "Well, you are a *Falkenhorst*, that at least is certain!" she muttered between clenched teeth and kneaded her fists into her still-flat stomach, as if trying to prod a response out of the new life germinating there. Yes, of course it was a Falkenhorst and, she told herself, Gustaf's child. It *had* to be so. Any doubts, justified or not, must be cast aside—even if it mean living the rest of her life with a secret lie. Her marriage depended on it. There was really no use in brooding about it, so she successfully diverted her deep misgivings with a more-superficial irritation, her anger over the prospects of her increasingly restricted activities during the next seven months. Seven months without riding a horse! Perhaps days, weeks in

✠

423

bed! She remembered that her sister had spent virtually her *entire* pregnancy in bed—then died in childbirth. Tessa did not dwell on fears of death, but having to lie in bed for only a few hours had already become an intolerable bore and the doctor had ordered her to stay there for three or four days. Impossible! Reaching for the bellcord, she rang for her maid and transmitted, through her, orders to Master Prytz: Preparations were to be made for departing for Glaumhalle with all the chosen livestock, "no later than the morning of the day after tomorrow."

Tessa had to be satisfied with the equivocating reply "Everything will be ready, but the actual departure must be subject to Dr. Schmund's approval." Far from satisfied, she settled into a drudging, fidgety rest.

On the following morning, Tessa awakened feeling well and full of her usual energy. She was eager to dress, eat a robust breakfast, and take off on an envigorating ride over the fens and along the beach. Although resigned to her pregnancy, she felt no need yet to submit to any overcautious regimen. However, she realized there was little use in defying Dr. Schmund's orders which Master Prytz obviously was ready to support with all his faithful obstinacy. So, fighting down her frustration, she remained in her room, not in bed, but seated by the open window where she could bask in the warm morning sun, breathe the fresh, salty breeze, and longingly scan the meadows beyond the castle gardens where many horses browsed. She dispatched her maids with more orders for Prytz: Dr. Schmund must come as soon as possible to see for himself that she was a perfectly healthy expectant mother; preparations for a speedy departure must go forward. While impatiently waiting, she began composing in her mind a letter to Gustaf, a letter that must strengthen the tenuous bonds of their marriage. A difficult letter requiring careful thought. But in the end, it took her only five minutes to write it: *Dear Gustaf: I am planning to leave Schloss Varn for Glaumhalle tomorrow. The trip will be slow as we shall bring along three stallions and six mares, two each yearling colts and fillies, and a young blooded bull because I believe we should breed fine cattle as well as horses. I had a very slight bilious seizure yesterday while out riding, worrisome at first, but which Doctor Schmund has assured me was nothing but the normal effects of carrying a child. I am praying God to please you with a healthy firstborn son to lead the next generation of Falkenhorsts. But we shall have to be patient until . . .* (she had to pause and again carefully count the months ahead on her fingers before writing) *early January. A special Happy New Years' gift then! I hope this news will make you careful of your safety, as careful as a good soldier can be, and that you will rejoin me at Glaumhalle before another winter and my time comes. With affectionate greetings, Your wife, Tessa.*

The letter was already in the hands of the postman by the time she knew the immediate plans she had outlined in it were to be thwarted. When Dr. Schmund finally visited her in the early afternoon, he insisted that she remain in her room for at least another two days; then he categorically forbade her to travel with what he termed "the company of stablehands and a caravan of livestock." He archly informed her that when he pronounced her fit to return to Silesia, she would do so attended by two female servants old and experienced enough to serve her in her delicate circumstances. Otherwise he would decline all responsibility and so inform the Leutnant Baron von Falken-horst by letter. It was this threat that silenced Tessa's heated protestations and left her in a helpless, seething temper after he took his leave.

But there was worse to come. When she sent for Master Prytz, she was informed that he had ridden off to Wolin during the forenoon to make arrangements with the railroad for trans-porting their horses and bull; he was not expected back until evening. Prytz did in fact not return until the long summer twilight had almost faded into night—past ten o'clock—but Tessa was still waiting up for him. When he presented himself, dusty and tired from his long ride, he was still cheerful as he handed her a telegram which he had found waiting at the de-pot's telegraph office. It had been sent that morning from Vienna by her mother, announcing her impending arrival next afternoon by train together with Aunt Lizel Piednich, General von Kleisenberg, two maids, and the General's valet. *"We rush to join you in glorious delights of Schloss Varn summer days,"* was the closing sentence, one which triggered anything but delight out of Tessa's already exasperated feelings. She was stunned, read-ing and rereading the message, puzzling for a moment over who General von Kleisenberg could be until she recalled Gustaf mentioning him as the deposed Prince Eugene of Hanover, then reacting very much like her late father would have when sur-prised by such an inconvenient development: "Damnation!" she exclaimed in a very unladylike outburst. "Mother and a com-pany of guests will be here tomorrow. Damnation!"

Prytz looked shocked. "But surely this is a time when you need the care and comfort of your mother, my lady," he said.

"You know perfectly well what to expect from poor Mama," Tessa snapped. "She will probably take to her bed and it will more likely be me who will have to comfort and care for *her*. Damnation! Everything is going wrong!"

"It appears to me things have never been so right for us,"

Prytz contradicted her. "All we have to do is to postpone our travel plans for a while. I will notify the railroad officials accordingly."

"You will do nothing of the sort, Prytzie!" Tessa ordered him. "You will leave in two days with the horses for Glaumhalle. Take whatever help you need. I shall follow you a few days later, three at the most, in the charge of a couple of nurses, like a sickly child. Damn!"

Prytz could not help smiling. "A sensible arrangement. I will be awaiting my lady at Ols. Indeed this is turning out a beautiful, fortunate summer for all of us! It has brought us both victory and peace. You are about to have your first child. Germany and your family are blessed with a bright future, praise God!"

"Do not forget to reckon the cost of it all," she testily replied, then, checking her temper and a little ashamed of it, conceded in a milder tone: "Well, I suppose things could be worse and there is still much to be grateful for. All right, Prytzie! Go to bed and have a good night's rest. There will be much to do tomorrow. Good night." As he bowed out of the door and closed it behind him, she wondered aloud to herself: "Why on earth is Mama bringing General von Kleisenberg along? Is the trip too much for her without a man to lean on? . . . Yes, that must be it! She'll be a nervous wreck and she'll take to her bed and leave me to entertain him and Tante Lizel. Damn!"

During late afternoon of the following day, the party from Vienna rolled through Schloss Varn's main gate, a liveried postillion riding ahead of its largest, most luxurious coach which was followed by another, slightly smaller one carrying the travelers' servants and an enormous load of baggage. Gardeners and stable personnel lined the driveway, doffing their caps, bowing and shouting genuinely hearty welcomes. All of the castle's butlers, footmen, maids, and kitchen staff were lined up according to rank and best military precision under the porte cochere and inside the front hall. On the threshold of the open double doors stood Tessa, a little pale, tense, but immaculate in a summer dress of starched green linen and in complete control of herself although she anticipated an embarrassingly emotional reunion complete with shrieks, tears, frantic wet kisses, fitful embraces, flapping and dabbing of damp lace handkerchiefs, and probably culminating in one of her mother's notoriously dramatic fainting spells. For all this she had steeled herself with an outward cool equanimity.

The first to step out of the coach was General Eugene von Kleisenberg and his appearance startled Tessa. She remembered him as the obese Prince of Hanover who had attended her wedding last year, bulging in a gaudy scarlet Hussar uniform spangled with braid and decorations, looking like a comic opera soldier. Now he was still heavy of build, yet at least twenty kilograms lighter, much firmer of posture, and instead of wearing that grotesque panoply of war, was elegantly tailored in a conservative beige suit with a matching silk hat. He looked, Tessa thought, like an imposing Prince, now that he no longer was one. But if he surprised her, her mother surprised her even more. In fact, *her* appearance as the General helped her out of the coach came somewhat as a shock.

The Countess Antoinette had during the past five years neglected her natural beauty and surrendered to dowdy middle-age. Her clothes as well as her personality had vascillated unpredictably between the eccentric and the dull. But today she wore a fashionable dress of white silk, expertly cut to modestly show off her amazingly restored figure, and only sparingly trimmed with black ribbons and hem as a concession to her recent widowhood (this in itself a daring departure in a society where widows traditionally wore *all* black for at least one full year). Her hair, which used to be a casual tangle of mouse-gray curls, was beautifully coiffured according to the latest Vienna style and crowned by a pertly cocked little hat decorated with a delicate plume of egret feathers. Her cheeks were firm and glowing with health, her eyes no longer puffy and nervously darting, but clearly alert and smiling. Indeed, she looked absolutely beautiful and her manner was completely confident in spite of an evident excitement which, a bare seven months ago, would have reduced her to a trembling, unnerved incoherence: "You are a naughty girl!" she exclaimed at Tessa, wagging a gloved finger at her as she sprang, almost soared up the steps in a flurry of billowing silks. "But you are also a brave darling to disobey our fearsome Dr. Schmund just to greet your poor old Mama. Bless you!" She gave her daughter a loving embrace which exuded the scent of exotic perfume.

"Welcome home, Mama," Tessa gasped, completely taken aback by the amazing change in her. "You look . . . wonderful! And, oh dear . . . you've heard about me already?"

"Certainly!" Countess Antoinette laughed with a measured concern. "The steward informed us the minute we got off the train. Do you think you can keep such wonderful news from me? From the castle? From the whole country?" She diverted Tessa's reproachful glance at the steward by eagerly calling over her shoulder to General von Kleisenberg: "Eugene, dear! Doesn't my Tessa look wonderfully lovely?"

Eugene let go of Tante Lizel, the only member of their party who seemed badly travel-worn and distracted to the point of abdicating her role as chaperone, passing her on to the support of Knabel who passed her on, rumpled, perspiring and quite unsteady, into the care of two maids. Then the General bounded up the steps alongside Countess Antoinette and with a gesture of regal familiarity, first formally kissed Tessa's hand before bussing her flushing cheeks: "Yes, my dearest Theresa!" he happily boomed. "You look wonderfully lovely. But the point is, how do you *feel?* Are you really all right, my dear?"

"Yes, Excellency, quite so," Tessa managed to reply before having to accept a moist, limply clinging embrace thrown at her by Tante Lizel as she passed through the front doors and before allowing herself to be half-dragged to her room by the maids.

"You must go straight to bed, Tante Lizel!" Countess Antoinette called after her with a teasing but sympathetic laugh. "Poor Aunty! Modern travel that gobbles up space and time is simply not for her. Railroads with their smoke and steam, the rush to meet schedules, mobs of people who suddenly have the means and a madness to rush hither and yon all over the country, the rudeness, the hustling, the awful food they throw at you in the station restaurants . . . all these things have quite demolished dear Aunty Lizel."

Eugene gave a sardonic chuckle. "Yes, I must agree that the advent of mass steam transportation bodes ill for the once-privileged art of travel. Not to mention the quality of meals one may expect along the way. *Pfui!* But on the other hand, one must measure the good alongside the bad which comes with all progress. We are in time for supper, I trust?"

"It will be served in one hour, Your Excellency," Tessa informed him a little sharply. She was still concentrating her wondering gaze on her mother, recalling her own several difficult railroad trips during the past year and marveling that she had survived this one in such good spirits and with hardly a hair out of place, every fold of dress neat and spotless. Such unruffled insouciance was totally unlike her. "Surely you are tired and need rest yourself, Mama," she somewhat lamely urged. "Your room is ready and you can have supper served you in bed as you used to like. . . ."

"Oh no!" Countess Antoinette instantly countered. "The Prince-General and I shall sup in the Little Dining Room at the time you've arranged it. And you may join us, of course, if you feel up to it." She spun around as a flaxen-haired little girl, the daughter of one of the castle's gardeners, stepped up and presented her with a beautiful bouquet and squeaked *"Herzlich Wilkommen, Frau Gräfin,"* then almost fell over with her deep curtsy. The Countess accepted the flowers while at the same time steadying the child and giving her a warm kiss on the forehead.

"Oh, my goodness, how beautiful," she ecstatically exclaimed. "Thank you, my dearest! Thank you all for such a lovely welcome home. Everything is so very, very beautiful!" She closed her eyes and breathed deeply before adding: ". . . So very, very wonderfully different!"—She swayed slightly on her feet and it was at this emotional climax of her arrival that Tessa would have expected her to dissolve into tears or fall into a faint. Instead she happily flourished her flowers and linking arms with Eugene von Kleisenberg, led him over the threshold: "Come along, my dear Eugene. I know you need refreshments and promise you'll have to wait no longer for them!"

Tessa would have been left sheepishly behind if he had not reached out, grabbed her by the hand, and pulled her inside with them.

They had dinner in the Little Dining Room, just the three of them at the beautifully set, but far from intimate, table; the Countess Antoinette seated at one end insisting the General sit at the other in the chair once exclusively Count Frederick Paul's, and Tessa marooned in the middle with great expanses of polished mahogany between her and them. The tall French windows to the scrubbed sandstone terrace were left wide open, and beyond the balustrade the sea shone like a mirror reflecting the pink evening sky. The air wafting in was laced with lilac and so gentle that it barely ruffled the clusters of candles. The meal was served by two maids in starched white and supervised by Knabel wearing white gloves and velvet breeches. A broth with caraway dumplings, jellied cold trout garnished with medallions of liverwurst, cucumber and potato salad, rhubarb and raspberry ices—a light summer supper by Junker standards and one which evoked appreciative praise from both the Countess and General as they consumed it with relish.

Tessa, on the other hand, could only show a token appetite and participated with strained cordiality in the conversation which was of the typical catch-up kind between family members after a long, eventful separation. Her mother chatted about her stay with the Piednich family in Vienna, evidently consisting of a string of glittering social events among high Austrian society, who had remained untouched by the war and tragedy beyond their own borders. The General spoke amusingly of his assignment as Military Attacheé at the Imperial German Embassy to the Court of Emperor Franz Joseph, giving the impression that his duties had largely consisted of escorting a merry widow to party after party. Of course, they both asked Tessa about Gustaf and Glaumhalle, and she answered in the most cheerfully optimistic vein she could muster, careful to avoid details which might lead to more revealing probings. She was accutely aware that Eugene was intently watching her while more casually indulging her mother's spirited chatter; she found herself increasingly puzzled by not only his presence at Schloss Varn, but also his avuncular attitude toward her. When supper was finished and he smilingly suggested a stroll on the terrace to enjoy the sea air and lingering sunset filled with the fluting song of nightingales, she declined with the partially valid excuse that Doctor Schmund had strongly advised her against staying up so late.

This gave her mother the cue to inquire coyly: "Exactly when may we expect the joyful event, dearest?" This brought a hesitating silence from her daughter, an embarrassed glance toward the General, a sudden glow of freckles against flushing cheeks. "Oh, come now, Tessa!" Countess Antoinette exclaimed. "Don't be silly about my Prince-General. He's as good as a member of the family. An old dear friend of your departed Papa's. Even close to your own Gustaf. Why . . . my goodness! Without him you wouldn't be . . . well, where you are today!"

Eugene von Kleisenberg began looking uncomfortable and concerned over Tessa's reaction. "I think your mother is teasing you a bit. You must expect that," he said with an affectionately reassuring tone, then addressing himself to Countess Antoinette, mildly admonished her: "Really, Antoinette. You know perfectly well when I was able to send Gustaf back to Glaumhalle last spring. From that you can easily estimate the child's birthday, more or less, without asking pointed questions."

"January!" Tessa flatly announced, rising from the table. "Not before early January."

"January!" her mother shrieked in delight as she sprang out of her chair and clapped her hands. "Oh, my dears! What a wonderful month next January will be for our family. The beautiful things that will happen to us then. There will be Tessa's baby and. . . ."

"Antoinette!" Eugene cut her off with a suddenly steely voice which he only slightly softened as he urgently continued:

"Antoinette, I do believe Tessa has had enough excitement for today. Remember her condition. Let her retire."

Countess Antoinette froze momentarily at the sharp tone and Tessa thought she noticed a shadow of her old submissive reactions to well-remembered barks and roars and barbs that once came from the same chair in which General von Kleisenberg was sitting. She bit her lip, then lamely blurted out: "Oh, I'm sorry Eugene, dear. Yes, Tessa must go to bed, of course."

But Tessa could no longer contain her puzzlement and curiosity and took her turn to ask a blunt question of them: "Isn't there something which you have not told me?"

Her mother gave a nervous giggle and a pleading look at the General who gave a capitulating shrug, nodded his head and took it upon himself to answer. "Yes, we also have important news," he said, rising with a smile on his broad face. "As you know, your mother and I have known each other for many years. But during the last two months we became very close. I have asked her to marry me. She has done me the honor, given my heart great joy by accepting. The wedding, of course, will not take place until her year of mourning for Count Frederick Paul is over. January, as a matter of fact."

"Isn't that wonderful news, darling?" Countess Antoinette exclaimed excitedly as she swept around the table, grabbing her daughter by the shoulders. "Isn't that wonderful news?" she pleaded.

"It's . . . it's amazing, Mama," Tessa mumbled with dazed disbelief.

"I am so happy . . . happier than I've been for a long, long time. Can't you tell that, dearest?"

"Yes. Yes, I've seen the great change in you, Mama," Tessa numbly agreed. But then she suddenly found herself bursting into laughter and exclaiming over and over again: "It is amazing . . . amazing . . . amazing!"

"You approve then, my darling?" her mother breathlessly asked.

Tessa answered by giving her a quick kiss and turning to the General while still laughing, said to him: "My felicitations, Excellency. Forgive my reaction, but I'm quite overwhelmed."

The General bowed to her, somewhat stiffly, but graciously and still smiling: "Thank you, Theresa. I understand that this comes as a great surprise. I had hoped to apprise you of it more gradually, but. . . ." he hesitated a moment before continuing: "But who can resist your mother's impetuously exuberant charms?"

"Or yours, Excellency," Tessa shot back, giving him an exaggerated curtsy. "Again, my felicitations, sir! And all happi-

✠   431

ness to you, Mama." She gave her mother another kiss and a hard, fitful hug, then ran out of the dining room—or fled from it, rather, although still laughing.

The next morning dawned gray and rainy, the first steady rain in several weeks. Tessa awakened to the sounds of its liquid patter and the soft moaning of the tall pine swaying in the damp breeze outside her open window. She lay in bed for a few minutes, remembering last night, but now with a feeling of detachment, an almost melancholy indifference, as if her mother and General von Kleisenberg's betrothal was some kind of amusing charade between strangers who did not deeply affect her. Gustaf and Glaumhalle, and the child she was carrying—these were the things, the only things that mattered now. She suddenly felt out of place at Schloss Varn and was glad the weather had turned bad; that would make it easier to depart if it would only keep up for another couple of days. Then she would leave, no matter what Dr. Schmund said.

Having made up her mind, Tessa jumped out of bed, splashed cold water over her face, hurriedly dressed in English riding habit, pulled on her boots, strode out of her room, passing down the long corridors and stairs of the still sleeping castle, then on out into a weeping daybreak. The air smelled strongly of salt and wet loam. The sea rumbled softly against the beach, the waves stirred by a brisk northeaster. Shore birds cried their plaintive calls as they swooped over the tumbling foam.

At the stables, everybody had been up and working for an hour, gathering the horses to be driven or ridden down the Wolin road to the railroad depot, and loading the recalcitrant young bull into the wagon which was to haul him there. Master Prytz was in a bad temper because of the rain that would make the first leg of their long journey to Glaumhalle a muddy, uncomfortable one; when he spotted Tessa approaching through the drizzle wearing her riding clothes, his face darkened even more. He barely managed a respectful salute before launching into protest:

"I trust my lady is not entertaining an idea of riding with us today. That would be unthinkable."

Tessa eyed the wagon in which the bull was bellowing unhappily and slamming its half-grown horns against the wooden slats. "Of course not, since Dr. Schmund has forbidden me horseback riding," she slyly agreed. "But I don't recall him saying anything about riding in a cattle cart."

Prytz looked horrified and his chin and moustache began to twitch. "A long ride in that thing would be even worse for you," he exclaimed in anguish. "Besides, there is no room for you, what with the beast, the drover and baggage for four men. For God's sake, be reasonable, my lady!"

Tessa feigned a disappointed pout, then gave him a teasing poke with her riding crop. "Well, all right! You are really turning into an old fussbudget, Prytzie. I only hope you will let me see you off, at least as far as the main gate. Will you do that without fussing at me?"

"Even so, you'll get wet and likely catch a chill," he grumbled. But he was reassured and led her inside the tackroom where they drank a cup of coffee together while watching through the rain-streaked windows as the grooms he had chosen to accompany him stowed their grips beneath the drover's seat of the wagon. They next packed several bales of fodder around the bull who fell into a quiescent bovine resignation over his fate. Two strong dray horses were hitched to the wagon. Then the animals they had chosen to ride were brought out of their stalls and saddled. The men worked briskly, efficiently, and with a cheerfulness that betrayed their excitement over the long trip ahead; none of them had ever traveled more than fifty kilometers away from Schloss Varn. But Prytz, the seasoned veteran, showed a certain distraction even as he watched them with a critical eye and finally spoke in an almost apologetic whisper about what was troubling him: "Is is true, my lady, what I heard rumored last night? Can it really be that your mother, the Countess, is intending to remarry?"

Tessa gave a surprised start followed by a tense laugh. "My goodness! This old castle certainly has big, sharp ears," she exclaimed; then, after a moment of serious silence, she confirmed it to him: "Yes, that is true. Mama intends to marry Eugene von Kleisenberg, the former Prince of Hanover. I suppose that will make her a sort of once-but-not-quite princess. Yes, it's strange but true."

Prytz gazed into her green eyes and sensed much of the confusion and tension she was trying so hard not to show. He sighed heavily before smiling and softly advising her: "You must try to accept it with pleasure for your mama. She has many good years ahead of her and is entitled to find happiness. She has done her duty as a von Beckhaus as best she could, so now let her become a von Kleisenberg if that is her heart's desire. What does it matter as long as only *you* will provide the next heir to these lands? You and your Gustaf, God bless you! That is a comforting thought, isn't it?" Without awaiting her answer, he abruptly switched to an urgent: "Well, it is time for me to leave. I must be at the Wolin depot with the animals before evening."

Tessa had to give in to a sudden overwhelming wave of

emotion and, throwing her arms around his neck, kissed his leathery cheeks with a desperate tenderness. "You are so very dear to me, my Prytzie," she cried out. "You must be with me always! Promise me! Always!"

The old man held her tightly for a moment, but shook his head as he repeated: "Always? As long as always can be." Then he gently broke away and put on his raincape and strode out into the stable yard to mount his horse. Stable boys threw open the paddock gates and chased out the small skittish herd of horses which the mounted grooms then maneuvered with whoops and whistles behind the wagon as it lurched forward with a disconsolate, farewell lowing from its four-legged passenger. More cheerful sounds came from those stablehands being left behind and a few gardeners who had stopped on their way to work to witness the departure.

Tessa kept apace with Master Prytz, marching alongside his horse while holding on to his stirrup leather. The rain was falling much harder now, and when they reached the huge wrought iron gates gaping open on the streaming country beyond, he reined in and said: "This is far enough for you, my Lady Tessa. Go back. Get into dry clothes and have yourself a good hot breakfast." He bent down and touched the dewy copper-gold braids of her hair with his lips and moustache, then spurred his mount into a canter and, without looking back, moved to catch up with his Silesian caravan.

She did not immediately obey his order to return to the castle, but remained standing in the lee of one of the gateposts, peering after the shapes of wagon, men, and horses as they receded and blurred, and then vanished behind the veils of rain sweeping over fens and meadows. "Take good care of my horses, you hear!" she called out once, receiving no answer. The sound of splashing hoofs, the crunch and grind of wheels and clink of harness faded into a silence broken only by the rustling of the wind in the surrounding birches, the raindrops dappling the puddles. Only then did she start to turn back, but stopped as she caught a hazy shape materializing down the road, drawing closer and solidifying into a man on horseback approaching at a brisk splashing trot. She wondered if it could be Prytzie or one of his men rushing back for some forgotten item. But as the rider drew close she recognized him as Bucholz, the postman of Varnmunde.

When Tessa stepped out into the middle of the gateway, the postman violently reined in his soaked, lathering horse and stared in surprise at the girl wearing a riding habit as wet as his own uniform.

"Good morning, Herr Bucholz!" she brightly greeted him. "Aren't you a bit early this morning?"

434

"Baroness von Falkenhorst!" the man gasped. "What on earth are you doing out here in this weather? Did you fall off your horse?"

Tessa laughed. "I haven't fallen off my horse since . . . well, not since the day before yesterday. What do you bring us? Letters? Newspapers?"

"Those I deliver on my regular schedule, Frau Baroness," he informed her. "This is a special trip made only for telegrams." Fumbling inside his mail pouch, he produced the familiar yellow envelope of the Royal Mail and Telegraph Service and handed it down to her.

Tessa recoiled, then accepted it with a stab of apprehension, yet tearing it open to read it then and there in spite of the rain. The postman solicitously removed his dripping cap and held it out in an attempt to shield the precious piece of paper while her eyes darted over its writing. "I do hope it is not bad news," he said with the polite curiosity common to his breed when delivering an obviously important communication. It made her look up at him, wipe the rain out of her eyes and ask:

"What is the exact date today, Herr Bucholz?"

His reaction was a little puzzled, a little reproachful. "Surely the Frau Baroness knows it is sixteenth of July. The first anniversary of our victorious war against France. There is to be a memorial service for our heroic dead in the Varnmunde church, twelve o'clock sharp. Followed, of course, by a parade and other organized festivities. We are naturally hoping the castle will honor us by attending."

Tessa blinked at him. "You may count on us, to be sure . . . certainly on *me!*" she answered with a merry laugh that disconcerted him even more. "Go on with you, Herr Bucholz! There's a warm stove and hot coffee in the stables. Start your celebration by being our guest." She gave his horse a playful tap on the haunches with her crop, sending it through the gates with a buck that ruined the postman's confused salute.

Tessa followed him at a more leisurely pace, reading the limp telegram again, her face glowing with pink health, flecks of gold, and a smile. She read it aloud to herself even as the neatly penned words of the message began to dissolve under the steady patter of raindrops:

Please accept my most affectionate greetings on the occasion of our first wedding anniversary. May there be many happier future ones because we will celebrate them together instead of far apart. May we close what separates us and become as one. With all my love—Gustaf.